SIX GLORIOUS EPOCHS OF INDIAN HISTORY

VEER SAVARKAR was:

- First political leader who lighted a bonfire of foreign clothes (on 7th July, 1905).
- First India citizen to face a trial in International Court of Justice, Hague.
- First scholar whose title of barrister was withheld for refusing to take oath of allegiance.
- First political prisoner to get two life sentences.
- First writer who despite being deprived of pen and paper, created many literary pieces on walls of Andaman prison with spikes, thorns and even his nails and preserved them for posterity by getting them memorised by his fellow inmates.
- First Indian author to face seizure of his books by two governments, even before they were printed and published.

Tributes Paid to Veer Savarkar by Eminent Persons

"Veer Savarkar led a stormy life of a relentless freedom fighter. He lived an extraordinary life of incessant tireless activity in various fields of national uplift."

—M.S. Golwalkar 'Shriguruji'

"Savarkar means glow, Savarkar means sacrifice, Savarkar means perseverance, Savarkar means element, Savarkar means reason, Savarkar means adolescency, Savarkar means arrow, Savarkar means sword, Savarkar means daze, Savarkar means endurance, Savarkar means bitterness—how many shades his personality had! Poetry and revolution together! The creator in Savarkar flew higher and higher. Savarkar had both highs and lows. His contribution is unforgettable. He will continue to inspire us Indians."

—Atal Bihari Vajpayee

"Veer Savarkar was an exemplary freedom fighter and a great son of India who bore brutalities and atrocities at the hand of Britishers but never gave up. His inspiring life will continue to guide generations to come."

—Lal Krishna Advani

"Veer Savarkar's undying love for India made him fight injustice against our Motherland. He inspired many others to join freedom struggle. His emphasis on social reform and his writing and poetry will continue to ignite the spark of patriotism among people."

—Narendra Modi

"Savarkar ji was a strong votary of an undivided India. His mantra was one nation, one cultural value and nationalism... He was a great patriot, unparalleled freedom fighter and social reformer, great writer, pioneering visionary and strong proponent of Hindu culture."

—Amit Shah

"Mr. Savarkar was one of the earliest revolutionaries who had resorted to remarkable ways of escape. A steady and sturdy worker for the independence of our country, his career was for many a youngster, a legendary one."

—Dr. S. Radhakrishnan

"...if the untouchable class is to be an indispensable part of the Hindu society, then the eradication of mere untouchability will not suffice; but the entire four varnasystem should be uprooted. Very few people have agreed upon the necessity of this. And I'm happy to say, that you are one of them."

—Dr. Babasaheb Ambedkar

"Mr. Savarkar was one of the greatest freedom fighters."

—Dr. Ram Manohar Lohia

SIX GLORIOUS EPOCHS OF INDIAN HISTORY

VEER SAVARKAR

PRABHAT PRAKASHAN

Published by
PRABHAT PRAKASHAN PVT. LTD.
4/19 Asaf Ali Road,
New Delhi-110 002 (INDIA)
e-mail: prabhatbooks@gmail.com

ISBN 978-93-5322-766-1
SIX GLORIOUS EPOCHS OF INDIAN HISTORY
by VEER SAVARKAR

Edition
2024

Price
₹ 900.00 (Rupees Nine Hundred only)

Printed at
Narula Printers, Delhi

A Word in Confidence

It is with great pleasure and satisfaction that I present to the readers this translation of the original book in Marathi. I consider it a piece of good luck to have had an opportunity of translating such an important book by the late Swantantrya-Veer V.D. Savarkar, which cropped up in my casual talk with Shree Balarao Savarkar, the devoted private secretary of that Prince of Patriots. After it was translated, every chapter went to the illustrious author who honoured me by going through it very carefully and when I had the good fortune to meet him personally on the completion of the undertaking, he obliged me by saying that he was satisfied with the translation and appreciated the hard labour it entailed. Would that Swa. Veer Savarkar had been alive today to see this English translation of his book in print!

Veer Savarkar's book "भारतीय इतिहासतील सहा सोनेरी पाने" is a commentary, not a history in its academic sense—on the significant events and periods in our national life, taking a broad survey of the growth and survival of our Hindu race. In a way, this attempt of Savarkar has been singular, barring a few honourable exceptions.

The general trend of the histories, written, read and taught in schools and colleges, has been one of eulogizing the foreigners and deprecating the Hindu race, relying wholly on the biased records of the foreign historians and travellers. Attempts are, happily, being made to reconstruct and restate the history of India from the national point of view, using to the utmost, all available native records of coins and inscriptions and covert allusions in the otherwise non-historical works, slender though they may be, but they are still sporadic and isolated, relating to this or that particular phase of Indian History. This volume presents 'Six Glorious Epochs of Indian History' since the beginning of our recorded history, i.e. from the days of Chandragupta Maurya to the end of the British dominance over India. Hence, like its predecessor,

'The War of Indian Independence of 1857', which galvanized the public opinion and changed the world outlook on the phase of our national life, this book too is very likely to start re-orientation of our historical concepts and the accepted historical theories. A need for an English translation of this book was, therefore, surely felt with a view to introducing it to the people who are unable to read or understand Marathi.

A book of this type had to be substantiated with proofs, especially when it was replete with thought-provoking even at times shocking—statements and conclusions. Basic references were, therefore, an unavoidable necessity, but the author, who had already crossed the bar of eighty years, and whose physical ailments had already created insurmountable difficulties in the very writing of this book, could not be expected to stand the rigour of pinpointing his references, voluminous as they were. I, therefore, had to shoulder that responsibility. The appendage of the basic references to this volume is, thus, my humble contribution. They will clearly show to the reader that the facts mentioned in this volume are fully backed by evidence. The interpretation of these facts and the conclusions drawn from them, however, are the author's special privileges, if only, they obey the laws of logical reasoning. The chapters are numbered serially from one to twenty-three. Each paragraph is serially numbered at the beginning.

My thanks are due to my son, Shri P.S. Godbole for going through the typewritten sheets. I am thankful to Shri B.D. Velankar, the Asiatic Society of Bombay and the University of Bombay for library facilities. I am also thankful to the publishers who have brought out this book.

—S.T. Godbole

Contents

1st Glorious Epoch

1
Chandragupta—Chanakya

1. According to modern historical research, the first phase of the dawn of our national life dates back almost to five to ten thousand years ago. Like that of China, Babylon, Greece and other ancient nations, our ancient history, too, is clothed in the poetical garb of mythology. It is replete with anecdotes, folklore, and deification of national heroes and heroines, and resorts to supernatural and symbolic description. Yet these ancient mythologies (Puranas) of ours are the pillars supporting the edifice of our ancient history. Just as these extensive Puranic texts of ours are a magnificent treasure of our ancient literature, our knowledge, our glorious deeds and our grandeur and wealth, in a similar way, they are a vast storehouse of the accounts of our past, desultory, chaotic, even at times, ambiguous though it may be.

2. Our Puranas, however, are not 'history' pure and unadulterated.

3. Hence, I propose to set aside the consideration of the 'Pauranic times' in the present context. For the 'Glorious Epochs' I am going to refer to, and dilate upon, belong not so much to the Pauranic times as to the historic periods of our national life.

The Beginning of Indian History

4. The main criterion of history is that the dates and places and descriptions of events referred to therein must necessarily bear the stamp of authenticity, and that they should be corroborated, as far as possible, by foreign as well as indigenous evidence.

5. The account of our past which fairly stands this test begins approximately from the time of Lord Buddha. Hence, many Indian and Western Orientalists have accepted the Buddhist period as the beginning of Indian history. The incessant and indefatigable labours of these Orientalists may, in future, include some of the so-called 'Pauranic

period' into the historical one, if some new evidence were to come to light. Till then, at least, we have to regard the Buddhistic period as the starting point of our history.

6. Again, in respect of establishing the authentic history of any nation beyond doubt, the convincing references in the contemporary literature of other nations are really invaluable. The ancient period of our history which can be supported by the now available, unimpeachable evidence in the historical records of countries other than India is the one that begins round about the times of Emperor Chandragupta Maurya. For, since the date of Alexander's so-called invasion of India, numerous references to events in India are to be found in the historical accounts of the Greek writers and the description of their travels by the Chinese travellers.

7. What should be the criterion for determining the Glorious Epochs I am going to discuss here? For that matter, there are hundreds of glorious epochs in the history of our nation that stand the tests of poetic exuberance, music, prowess, affluence, the height of philosophy and depth of theology and many other criteria. But by the 'Glorious Epoch', I mean the one from the history of that warlike generation and the brave leaders and successful warriors, who inspire and lead it on to a war of liberation, in order to free their nation from the shackles of foreign domination, whenever it has the misfortune to fall a prey to such powerful fatal aggression and to grovel abjectly under it, and who ultimately drive away the enemy making it an absolutely free and sovereign nation. Every nation extols such epochs of the wars of independence which inflict crushing defeats on the enemy. Take, for instance, the American War of Independence. The day on which America wrenched her independence from England, vanquishing her completely on the battlefield, is a red-letter day in the history of America and is celebtrated like a festival all over the country. The moment recording this successful struggle for freedom is acknowledged as a glorious epoch in the history of America.

Great Nations and the calamity of Foreign Domination

8. Moreover, the birth of the United States of America is only of a recent date. In the very short span of her history, it is not unnatural that only one such terrible calamity befell her and, consequently, gave her

only one glorious occasion to overcome it. But the nations like China, Babylon, Persia, Egypt, ancient Peru, ancient Mexico, Greece, Rome and many others, which can boast of a history of thousands of years, naturally had many occasions of having been overcome and oppressed by mightier foreign aggressors. From these monstrous calamities, some of these nations freed themselves again and again with exceptional valour, and humbled and routed the enemy. These nations, with a long tradition of thousands of years, are naturally proud of many such glorious moments recording their signal victories over their enemies. The history of India, as compared to that of other nations, has a consistent and unbroken record. Most of the nations that nourished side by side with her in the past, are now extinct and are remembered only by their names. China stands today as an old witness of the greatness of India.

9. Both China and India are vast countries and have maintained their independence and power right from the ancient days. No wonder they had to face many more mortal dangers of foreign domination than the other shortlived nations. The unerring wheel of fortune affected them too. Just as India was attacked by the Sakas, the Huns, the Mughals and others, so was China too a victim of the invasions of these and other alien nations. She had to build the world-famous China Wall all around her territory as a bulwark against the Hunnish inroads. Nevertheless, the enemies did conquer China, sometimes by circumventing the great wall or at times, crossing it. Mostly only in parts, but sometimes at least, wholly, China had to writhe and squirm under the yoke of foreign domination. Yet, every time, she could revive her strength and overthrow the foreign aggression and regain her independence, and even today, she is an independent and powerful nation. This in itself is a marvel of history. An appraisal of Indian history demands the same criterion to be adopted. But specially when our country was smarting under the British sway, many English writers had so much perverted the Indian history and obliged two or three generations of Indian students in their schools and colleges to learn it in such a way, that not only the rest of the world, but even our own people were misled. Absurd and malicious statements implying that India as a nation has always been under some foreign rule or the other or that Indian history is an unbroken chain of defeat after defeat of the Hindus, have been used like currency and are accepted by our people without affront or remonstrance or even a formal protest. To refute these statements is essential not only from the point of view of

the honour of the nation, but also for the sake of historical truth. Efforts being made by other historians in this direction have to be supported, as far as possible, by propaganda. That in itself is a national duty. That is why, I have decided here to describe the historical achievements of those generations and of their representative leaders who vanquished the aggressors from time-to-time and liberated their country.

Alexander's Aggression

10. Alexander's attack on India is the first well-known foreign invasion during the ancient period of Indian history. It took place in 326 B.C., a period of human history when the modern European nations like England, France, Germany and others were not even born. The Roman Empire had not as yet any foundation laid for it. It was only the Greeks, who were resounding the European stage. Small Greek city-states ruled themselves independently. Of these, Sparta and Athens were the most progressive. But when these small separate city-states were invaded by the ruler of a vast, well-organised, unitary and very powerful Persian empire, they were unable to face him successfully. Those small Greek republics did their best to fight the enemy back, but all their efforts proved fruitless before the vast ocean-like Persian armies. Naturally, the Greeks earnestly thought of effecting a fusion of all their separated small city-states into a powerful Greek Kingdom and forming a united front. So, Philip, King of Macedonia, who was fired with the same ambition, conquered all those small Greek republics, but he died before he could develop them into a mighty nation. However, his son, who succeeded him to the throne, was much more ambitious, more eager to gain power than his father, whom he surpassed in valour. It was Alexander. He inspired the whole Greek community with a sense of solidarity and militant nationalism. He organised an invincible army, and marched on the Persian Emperor, Darius, himself, who had been the arch-enemy of the Greeks. This well-organised Greek army simply routed the vast but ill-organised Persian army. At the battle field of Arbela, (331 B.C.) the whole of Persian administration virtually collapsed. With his victorious army, Alexander marched straight on to the Persian capital and after conquering, it he proclaimed himself the emperor of that country. This unprecedented success whetted his lust for conquests. With the Greek and the Persian empires at his feet, the sky seemed to him well within his limit. He was intoxicated with the wild ambition to conquer the

whole world and, therefore, he planned to invade India, of which the Greeks had been hearing so much for generations together. He thought he would run over India as easily as he had crushed the Persian as well as the ancient Babylonian empire. In order to execute this daring plan, he formed a new powerful army with the pick of his Greek soldiers, full of youthful enthusiasm and equipped with glittering weapons. This army consisted of one-hundred-and-twenty thousand foot-soldiers and cavalry fifteen thousand strong. These brave soldiers, mad with victory after victory, had been so much impressed by the unbroken chain of Alexander's conquests, that they looked upon this great General and Emperor as a divine being. Alexander himself began to pose as the son of the Greek God, Zeus.

Geographical Dimensions of India

11. In those days, some two-thousand-and-five hundred years ago, the Indian community and Indian kingdoms had spread far beyond the Indus, right up to the boundary of Persia. The mountain range known today as the Hindukush was at that time called Paropnisus by the Greeks. The modern Afghanistan was called Gandhar, known in Indian tradition by the name Afghanistan, while the river Kabul has been called Kubha in our ancient literature. Throughout the whole region up to the Hindukush mountain, ruled peacefully various states, some small, others large. Right from these Indian states, all along the banks of the Indus, straight up to the place where it leaps into the sea, was a long and unbroken chain of Indian states, which strictly followed the Vedic religion. Most of them were republics and were then called 'Ganas' or 'Ganarajyas'. Their constitution was essentially democratic. There were only two or three monarchies worth the name, one of which, the biggest and strongest, was ruled by a Pourav King, whom the Greeks called Porus.

Dr. Jayaswal's 'Hindu Polity'

12. Dr. Jayaswal, one of the prominent members of the revolutionary party, 'Abhinava Bharat', during the critical years of 1907-1910, and later on a world-famous Orientalist, has given, after a critical research, a very detailed account of the different 'Bharateeya Ganas', spread along both the banks of the Indus right up to its confluence with the sea.

13. According to Greek mythologies, they seem to have believed that their ancestors had migrated as a separate branch of the original

Aryan stock from Gandhar and other regions beyond the Indus. When Alexander's forces entered the precincts of India, they accidentally came across a small community of people who called themselves the original Greeks. They had been completely merged with the Indians, but as soon as they saw this Greek army, they avowed that they were the ancient brethren of those Greeks. Alexander, too, was led to believe that India must be the original abode of his ancestors. He and his whole army were so much delighted at the sight of this, their antique fatherland, that they stopped fighting for some days and celebrated a great festival. The Greeks performed a sacrifice and offered oblations to propitiate their Greek deities.

14. The Greek Gods resembled the Vedic ones very closely. Their names had undergone changes in pronunciation by corruption in course of time. The Greeks too performed sacrifices as the Indo-Aryans did, and offered oblations through the fire to their various deities. They were also called Ionians.

'Lonian' and 'Yavan'

15. It is likely that these Greeks were the descendants of Anu, the son of Yayati! One wonders if Anwayan was later on corrupted to Ionian. This bit of a guess must, however, be left to the research scholars. The fact remains that the Indians called these Greeks 'Yavanas' from the very beginning, as is seen from the Sanskrit literature. It is from the Greek word 'Ionians', that they came to be called 'Yavans' or 'Yons' in India.

Buddha not heard of from Gandhar—Panchanad to Sindh

16. One more fact deserves mention here. The contemporary Greek writers have given in their books detailed descriptions of the varied life of the people from those parts of India where Alexander moved—from Gandhar to Panchanad (the Punjab) and, thence along both the banks of the Indus, to the very place where it flows into the sea. But throughout all these descriptions, not a single reference to either Lord Buddha or the Buddhistic cult or sect can be found, whereas there are numerous references to the Vedic Hindus. From this and, of course, from other contemporary references, it is quite clear that, at least, till that time the Buddhist sect was quite unknown beyond the Shatadru (Sutlej) river. It means that for about two hundred and fifty to three hundred years after the death of the Buddha, the Buddhist cult spread here and there round

Veer Savarkar in a festive mood

Veer Savarkar with Harding bombing heroes Hanumant Sahai and Raja Mahendra Pratap Singh (1957)

Precious moments with near and dear ones

Veer Savarkar with melody queen Lata Mangeshkar

Veer Savarkar with Dr. Munje

Veer Savarkar with Senapati Bapat

about Magadha and not farther off, a fact that deserves special notice for the proper interpretation of subsequent history.

A Greek Means a Yavan!

17. Our contemporary Indian ancestors called these aggressive Greek foreigners, who professed a slightly alien religion, 'Yavans'. But that is not the reason why we should call all foreign aggresssors 'Yavans'. It is obviously a mistake. Especially, when our people began to call the Muslims 'Yavans', they really committed a blunder. Although the Greeks were aggressors and foreigners, they were, comparatively speaking, considered to be particularly devoted to learning and highly cultured and civilized, according to the standards of the time. The Muslim hoarders that invaded India, centuries afterwards, were highly fanatical, diabolic and ruthlessly destructive. It would have been in the fitness of things to call them 'Mussalmans' in view of their demonic nature. To call them 'Yavans' is doubly wrong inasmuch as it unduly flatters them and does a very great injustice to the word 'Yavan' itself. The Mussalmans may be called 'Mlenchhas', not 'Yavans'.

Alexander and stupid Muslims

18. A stupid notion common amongst most of the Muslims is worth a mention here. The name 'Alexander' was corrupted into 'Shikandar' in the Persian language. So long as the Greek empire had Persia under its sway, many of the Persian people highly impressed by the unprecedented valour of Alexander named their new born sons Shikandar. Later on, even after the Persians were converted to Islam, this practice of naming their children after 'Shikandar' persisted. The Muslim converts in India adopted that practice. But ignorant of the historical origin of the word 'Shikandar', thousands of Muslims in India, fondly believe that like Mohammad Ali, Kasim and others, the name Shikandar is a Muslim name, and that valiant Alexander must be some Muslim personality. Nay, he could be so very valiant and a world conqueror simply because he was a Muslim. If any one tries to convince these fanatic, vulgar and vainglorious Muslims that 'Shikandar (Alexander) was not a Muslim, that he could never be one, as Mohammed Paighamber, the founder of the Muslim religion, was himself born not less than a thousand years after the death of Shikandar, these, diehard Muslims, would call that person uninformed.

19. The eastern boundary of Alexander's empire at that time was the Hindukush mountains. After having crossed these mountains, he marched with his vast armies straight to Taxila in India. The King of Taxila, King Ambuj (Ambhi) accepted his overlordship without giving him any battle. Some Greek writers assert that this very King of Taxila had invited Alexander in order to put down his rival, King Porus. If that is so, Ambhi had quit naturally to pay for his treachery by his willing, through abject submission to the Greeks.

University in Taxila and a strange coincidence

20. Taxila was the seat of the most famous Indian University of the time, where students from different countries came to study various sciences and arts. Even the princesses of different states came there, learnt political science and got lessons in the art of governance, warfare and strictly observed the rules of discipline prevalent there.

21. By some strange coincidence, just when Alexander was marching at the head of his army into India, after reducing Taxila, a brilliant youth, who, a little later, was destined to carve a glorious page in the history of India, was learning the sciences of war and politics in the same University of Taxila. He was called Chandragupta. The old teacher who was well-versed in different lores of the time, and was also an astute politician, and was giving lessons in politics and national revolutionary activities to this splendid youth under the portals of the same University, was Chanakya.

22. But in the confusion wrought by this invasion of Alexander, these two exceptionally gifted personalities had not yet attracted public attention in themselves. Both of them had been watching very closely the movements of Alexander's vast forces. Alexander had, as it were, put all the crowns and coronets of kings, and kings of kings and of all the small rav's and kaval's into a metlting pot and forged a single crown to proclaim himself the Emperor of India; while the old sage, Acharya Chanakya, was secretly planning an easy transfer of that covetable crown to his young disciple's head by means of a *coup d'etat*.

War with Porus

23. The king of Taxila, Ambuj or Ambhi had, as already stated, bowed down to the Greek might without fighting a single battle, and, therefore, everybody began to jeer at his treacherous act, as it humiliated

the braver spirits. In order to counteract it, the neighbouring Indian monarchies and republics decided to force a bitter struggle on the Greeks. It is really unfortunate that these various independent Indian states did not think of making it a common cause, or perhaps had no time to do it. As soon as he reached Taxila, Alexander, without any loss of time, sent ultimatum to all the neighbouring Indian states, demanding unconditional surrender, and when Taxila's very next neighbour, King Porus, ignored his ultimatum and took up the challenge, the Greek captain-general marched on him.

24. King Porus mainly depended on his war chariots and elephants, whereas the Greeks relied upon their cavalry brigades. The river Vitasta (Jhelum) separated the two armies. All of a sudden, even before the two armies joined battle, torrential rains overflowing the river with high floods began to assail them all round. Alexander searched high and low and in a few days, found to the north, a place where the river was fordable. With precipitate haste, he crossed the river and with his fine cavalry, dashed against the forces of King Porus. This disturbed the whole plan of Porus. Still, he fought on a fierce battle. But the rains had turned the field muddy, rendering utterly useless Porus's two great instruments of war, namely chariots and elephants. He could not, therefore, successfully check the brisk and energetic attacks of Alexander's horsemen. In the thick of the battle, Porus seated on his elephant and desperately fighting was grievously wounded and fell into the hands of the enemy. Thus, partly because of Porus's misfortune and partly because of Alexander's military skill on the battlefield, the Greeks were crowned with success.

Victory—Shrewd Political Strategy

25. When Porus was taken as a captive before Alexander, the latter asked the Indian King, 'How should I treat you?' Porus promptly replied, 'Like a King'. This apt reply evoked the comment of European as well as our own historians, that impressed by this bold reply, Alexander returned to Porus his territory making him a governor under him, instead of putting him to death. But this interpretation of Alexander's treatment of Porus is wrong, and therefore, such platitudes should be avoided in school textbooks.

26. Obviously, Alexander was not like the artless simple Indian King, Harishchandra, who gave away his kingdom in his wakeful hours

in order to fulfil a promise made in a dream. He knew if he killed Porus or liquidated his kingdom, placing in his place some Greek Satrap, the high-minded people of the state would be aflame with rage and hatred towards the Greeks. Now Alexander wanted to fight his way all along to the chief Capital of India, namely Pataliputra! Could he ever do so with the sole support of his own Greek army? On the other hand, it was far more profitable to win over Porus with apparent magnanimity and kindness, as he had done to King Ambhi of Taxila (Takshashila) and enlist his active support in order to facilitate the accomplishment of his daring plan of the conquest of India. It is, therefore, not for the sake of appreciating the bold rejoinder of Porus but as a clever political strategy, that the arch diplomat Alexander returned to Porus his Kingdom. He even annexed the smaller neighbouring states, which he had conquered immediately before or after his clash with Porus to the latter's Kingdom. He had appointed him his satrap (governor) of this vast Indian Province. Porus too gave his assent to Alexander's proposals simply to wait for his time, for fortune had played foul with him. Porus had done his duty, as a Kshatriya warrior would do of fighting till the end against the enemy of his nation. In fact, तावत कालम् प्रतिक्षेताम् (Bide the time!) is a valuable tenet in political science. Knowing that the submission of King Porus was only time serving, the Indian populace also did not take it amiss. It will be shown later, how at the opportune time, King Porus (now Satrap Porus) turned the tables against Alexander himself.

27. After the end of the war with Porus, Alexander set himself up to the task of stabilising the newly conquered neighbouring states, and began a careful study of the life of the people there and in the yonder regions. Besides, to replenish his army that was depleted in numbers and energy because of the incessant wars from the Hindukush to the Panchanad, Alexander ordered fresh regiments of forces from his Satraps in Babylon and Greece, and sent back those of his fighting forces, who were wounded and rendered invalid and also those who were shirkers.

Inquiry of the Indian Ascetics

28. The scouts, whom Alexander had sent round to survey the local condition of the people in the subjugated as well as non-subjugated provinces, brought, among other reports, detailed descriptions of the penance-groves in the forests, and of the ascetics, anchorites, recluses, freed from all worldly bonds, wandering about all alone in search of

knowledge and also of those sages, who were deeply engrossed in philosophical thought. Alexander himself was fond of learning and philosophical discussions, for he called himself the disciple of the great philosopher, Aristotle. He had already heard much in Greece itself of such ascetics and of austere Brahmins. So, he earnestly desired to see personally at least some of these austere Brahmins in India, who the Greeks called 'Gymnosophists' and have talks with them. So, he sent for some of such hermits from their forest abodes and some he saw in their secluded cells. The Greek writers themselves had given some interesting tales about such occasions. I would like to cite a tale or two from among those in words of the Greek writers themselves, so as to throw some light on the thoughts and feelings of the Greeks and their leader, Alexander.

29. "This philosopher (Kalanos), we are told, showed Alexander a symbol of his empire. He threw down on the ground a dry and shrivelled hide and planted his foot on the edge of it. But when it was trodden down in one place, it started up everywhere else. He then walked all round it and showed that the same thing took place wherever he trod, until at length he stepped into the middle and by doing so made it all lie flat. This symbol was intended to show Alexander that he should control his empire from its centre and not wander away to its distant extremities."

The Canon of Dandamis

30. Alexander keenly felt that he should send for and have a personal talk with one Brahmin, of whom he had heard so much in Taxila (Takshashila). The Greeks called this Brahmin 'Dandamis', but I have not so far succeeded in tracing down his original Sanskrit name. The Brahmin, bent with age and knowledge, was free from all worldly ties and wandered naked everywhere. He did not pay any heed to Alexander's messages. Thereupon, Alexander sent his own officer 'Onesikretos' to this selfless recluse, who told him, "Alexander, the very son of God Zeus (Sansk: Dyus) and a world-conqueror has summoned you to his court. If you still fail to come, you will be beheaded instantaneously." The Brahmin began to laugh vociferously at this threat and replied, "If Alexander is the son of Zeus, in the same manner and for the same reason, I am also the son of that very Zeus (Dyus). As to his boast of being a world-conqueror, it is absolutely vain! He has not as yet seen

the other bank of the river Vyas. If he successfully faces the brave Indian states beyond and, yonder still, the powerful empire of Magadha and still remains alive, we shall have time to consider whether he is a world-conqueror. Alexander offers me land and gold; but go and tell him that ascetics like me spit upon such things. This motherland of mine provides me with everything I want, wilh the loving care of a real mother. If Alexander is going to chop my head off, then my head and body would mix up with this earth of what they are made, but he would never be able to murder my soul. It is invincible, indestructible and immortal. Go and tell him, that he should issue these threats to those, who are slaves of gold and power and are afraid of death. Before us, these threats of a mortal like Alexander fall flat and are powerless. For, a true ascetic Brahmin can never be won over by gold, nor does he ever fear death. I won't come go away."

31. We have quoted only some of the sentences from the reply of Dandamis to Alexander. Greek writers have given the full text of his fearless and direct reply. Plutarch, too, has mentioned these tales. Some writers, astounded by his dauntless and straightforward answer, have remarked, "If, at all, anyone in the world has so successfully defied Alexander, who had conquered so many kingdoms, it was this naked, old Brahmin ascetic of India."

Brahmins hanged for Political Conspiracy

32. In his survey, Alexander came to know that although these world-forsakers, ascetics, recluses and others were wandering all alone, their opinions exerted a powerful influence because of their disinterestedness, fearlessness and their disregard for any consequences whatsoever, upon the governments of Indian republics and also on the monarchies. The tongues of these free and fearless Brahmin ascetics, had sharp edges like the swords of the Indian Kshatriyas and they protested against the unjust Greek aggression very sharply and spread, openly or secretly, great discontent against Alexander amongst the Indian populace. Naturally, his first adoration of these 'Gymnosophists' suddenly gave place to his intense hatred against the Brahmin hermits. Thereupon, he began to seize some such Brahmins and hang them. Before beheading one such Brahmin, when Alexander asked him why he instigated a certain Indian ruler against the Greeks, he fearlessly and firmly replied that it was his most sacred tenet and that, if he were to live, he ought to live

honourably, else he should die honourably." (Plutarch LXIV).

33. After defeating King Porus, Alexander thought his dazzling victory should unnerve the neighbouring states and force them to submit meekly, but his hopes in this respect mostly belied him. As he crossed the Vitasta (Jhelum) and marched onward, the various republics, big or small, on his way began to offer sanguinary battles. Without a decision at the battlefield, they would never accept his overlordship meekly. Although the superior number and might of the Greeks went on overpowering the Indians, the consequent strain of incessant fighting did not fail to make itself felt on the Greeks.

34. Greek writers have described many such battles with various Indian republics, but this is no occasion to mention them, either at some length or briefly. However, some of the chosen incidents have got to be given here at some length, at least as a mark of respect to those brave Indian republics who, though not jointly yet severally, offered the toughest of resistance to that mighty Greek army of a hundred thousand gallant soldiers and their brave, world-famous, captain-general Alexander, who had vowed pompously to trample over the whole of India and conquer the Crown of Magadha for himself, which finally forced him to stirke a retreat homeward, from the very threshold of India.

Republics of Saubhootis and Kathas

35. The constitution of both these republics was democratic. Writes a Greek writer Diodoros "They were governed by laws in the highest degree salutary and their political system was admirable. One special feature of these republics was that with a view to promoting healthy, strong and handsome progeny, the procreation of human species was not left to individual whims and fancies, but was controlled by the state. They were very fond of physical beauty. Hence, marriages were arranged not with an eye on the handsome dowry, but with proper consideration of mutual physical fitness, beauty and health, and the ability of the bride and the bridegroom to bring forth healthy and sturdy children. Even while electing their leaders, who were to guide the nation and bear the yoke of national welfare, sufficient weightage was given to the candidate's build of the body and physical strength. Their laws regarding the proper production of human species were so strict that within three months of their birth, children were medically examined by the state authorities, and if a child were found with some native defect or to be

suffering from some incurable disease or deformed, it was immediately put to death under state orders without any mercy."

35A. Readers of history know well that the Republic of Sparta had similar laws about heredity.

36. Though not so very strict and ruthless as the Saubhootis and the Kathas, there were other Ganas or republics in India, which paid special attention to heredity, and bringing forth of strong and handsome children. The 'Vrishnis' were also very particular, from the ancient times, about the physical beauty and strength of their leaders and state officials. The physical strength and beauty of the world famous leader of these Vrishnis, Lord Shree Krishna, has been immortalized. Lord Shri Krishna's sons, too, have been credited by the Puranas with exceptional beauty.

Republic Subsisting by Arms

37. A good many republics in the Panchanad (the Punjab) and along both the banks of the Indus, right up to its great leap into the sea, were said to be living on weapons. The most remarkable fact about them was that not only the men but the women too in those republics had necessarily to undergo military training so that at the time of war, literally the whole nation could be drafted for military action. Although different from each other in some particular respects, their constitutions, needless to say, were essentially democratic. Whether big or small in size, they were all independent.

The Republic of the Youdheyas

38. The Republic of the Youdheyas, spread far and wide in the fertile lands to the south of the river Vyas in the Panchanad (the Punjab), was the most prominent of them all. It was looked upon with awe and respect by every one because of its valiant youths who always fought for their independence, regardless of their lives. It was truly called, by the foreign historians, 'A nation in arms'. They too had a law necessitating everyone between the ages of 18 and 21 to undergo sound military training, which kept not only their male but even the female population well-equipped with arms.

39. On seeing Alexander march down the Vitasta (Jhelum) and the Chandrabhaga (Chenab) in order to cross the Vyas, after defeating King Porus, the adjoining republics and the hill tribes, the gallant Youdheyas,

who were to the south of the river, spurned Alexander's ultimatum of abject surrender and began all-out preparations for war. Yet the so-called Emperor of Magadha, the cowardly Dhananand, was not roused from his stupor. That lily-livered coward does not seem to have sent any mlitary help to the gallant Youdheyas in order to vanquish Alexander at the very portals of India. Nevertheless, the Youdheyas got ready to face Alexander, relying on nothing but their own strength.

Alexander's Army Struck with Terror

40. When Alexander's army came fighting to the banks of the river Vyas, after crossing the Indus, the Vitasta, and the Chandrabhaga, they came to know that beyond that river, the democratic Youdheyas had taken arms to fight for their independence against the Greeks. Besides, they learnt about their bravery, and also of the fact that beyond the Youdheyas, mightier Indian states along the banks of the Ganges were making ready to fight with them. The Greek soldiers, already spent and disgusted with unceasing warfare with the Indians in the Panchanad, dared not cross the Vyas and join battle with the courageous and daring Indian states like the Youdheyas and others.

41. But the lust for war and conquest of their war-intoxicated, enterprising and exceptionally courageous captain-general and emperor, Alexander was not quenched in the least. He proclaimed, throughout all the divisions of his army, his immutable decision to cross the Vyas, conquer the Youdheyas and march straight off to Magadha. This obstinate declaration of Alexander roused a great furore and rage amongst the already war-weary army, even amongst the veterans! The Greek soldiers secretly began to pass resolutions, group-by-group, to refuse straightaway to go ahead. In spite of the fact that they had been considering Alexander unconquerable and the son of God Zeus, they were extremely disgusted with his lust for power. No sooner did Alexander smell of this dissatisfaction amongst his soldiers, than he delivered an inspiring speech.

Alexander's Speech to His Army

41A. "On seeing that you, O Macedonians and allies, no longer follow me into dangers with your wonted alacrity, I have summoned you to this assembly that I may either persuade you to go farther or to be persuaded by you to turn back if we have driven the Scythians back into their deserts, and if besides the Indus, Hydaspes, Akesines and Hydraotes flow through the territories that are ours, why should you hesitate to pass the Hyphasis also? Are you afraid?

41B. "For my part, I think that to a man of spirit, there is no other aim and end of his labours except the labours themselves.

41C. "But if any one wishes to know the limits of the present warfare, let him understand that the river Ganges and the Eastern sea are now at no great distance off....

41D. "But if we turn back, many warlike nations extending beyond the Hyphasisto Eastern sea and many others lying northwards between these and Hyrkania, to say nothing of their neighbours, the Scythian tribes, will be left behind us unconquered, so that if we turn back, there is cause to fear lest the conquered nations, as yet wavering in their fidelity, may be instigated to revolt by those who are still independent. O Macedonians and allies! glory crowns the deeds of those who expose themselves to toils and dangers.

41E. "Such of you wish to return home I shall send back to your own country, or even myself will lead you back."

41F. According to Smith, "He (Alexander) recited the glories of their wondrous conquests from Hellespont to Hyphasis and promised them the dominion and riches of all Asia. But glowing words fell on unwilling ears and were received with painful silence, which remained unbroken for a long time." (P. 79)

42. But the effect of his inspiring speech was contrary to his expectations. As it was now amply clear from the very lips of Alexander that they would be required to fight more sanguinary wars of attrition, they were scared to the marrow. Dr. Jayswal writes in his *Hindu Polity,* "The Greek army refused to move an inch forward against the nations, whose very name, according to Alexander, struck his soldiers with terror."

43. Alexander was extremely enraged to see that his soldiers disobeyed him by flatly refusing to cross the Vyas in order to save all further trouble, because they were thoroughly exhausted and afraid to fight immediately, without any rest. But Alexander was as cunning as he was brave. Apprehending danger, Alexander refrained from doing any thing rash in a fit of anger, and straightaway walked off into his tent in utter despair. He stopped talking to anybody. He did not show himself outside his tent for three consecutive days. Then he

thoughtfully hatched a new plan in his mind. He, thereafter, gathered the whole of the Greek army and told them that he had given up the plan of crossing the Vyas. He said, "I have now decided to go back to Greece." This statement naturally elated the rank and file of his army. Alexander then asked, "But how are we to go back? If we turn our backs straightaway and go to Greece by the same route as we came along, all this Indian territory we have conquered would rise in revolt, thinking that we are stricken with terror. So instead of turning our back straight off towards the land route to Greece, we should better go a little obliquely to the sea along the banks of the Indus and then return to Persia along the sea-route. Next time when we shall come again to India, we shall conquer the Indian states beyond the Ganges and accomplish our conquest of India."

44. True it is that Alexander said "When once again we shall come to India'—"But O Greek Captain General, once again! Truly! But when? Let alone the kingdoms beyond the Ganges, but if these very states that you have conquered today were to renounce the yoke of your sovereignty and become independent, then? Nay, even before that next time you mentioned, if you yourself were to be no more, then...? Even the race of Zeus can succumb to the ravages of time, may it then belong to Greece."

45. If those Indian Gymnosophists, ascetics and recluses have ridiculed Alexander's threat of coming back again to India in some such manner, it could never have been out of place.

Alexander's Retreat

46. However loudly and pompously Alexander might have swaggered with his mouth, the fact remains that the Greek soldiers took a fright of the Youdheyas and others beyond the Vyas and, hence, Alexander could not dare cross that river! Indian valour had taken the conceit out of the haughty spirit of the advancing Greek army, and so they had to strike a retreat. Alexander did not retire willingly. The Greeks proved to be powerless before the Indians, and, hence, was this ignoble retreat! To hide this simple fact, the Greek and European historians write, "Had he but crossed the Vyas, Alexander would have defeated not only the Youdheyas but the Magadha empire also. The Youdheyas and the Magadhas had never actually defeated the Greek army of Alexander on the open battlefield. These boastful 'ifs' and

'whens' can be answered most aptly on behalf of the valorous Indian Youdheyas in some such way:

का कथा बाण संधाने ज्या शब्देनैव दूरत: ।
हुंकारेणैव धनुष: सहि विघ्नान्यपोहति ॥

—*Kalidas Shakuntalam, Act 3 Shloka 1*

("Why fight with an enemy who flees away at the mere twang of our bow.")

47. Again, this typical itch of the Greek army for fighting in the open field was to be allayed for ever by the Indian military strength a little later! Soon Chandragupta was to make his entry on the military stage of India. Wait a bit, O you, reader!

Alexander builds a powerful Navy

48. Soon after his retreat from the Vyas, Alexander had five to six hundred warships built in order to make his way to the sea along the course of the Indus. Embarking thousands of his well-equipped warriors on these warships, he began to march off to the sea through the river. About the commencement of this voyage of Alexander along the waters of the Indus, arrived the two fresh regiments of forces, ordered from Babylon and Greece. Naturally, the heretofore war-weary and rebellious Greek soldiers of Alexander were cheered up once more.

49. But while Alexander was making his way towards the sea after striking an 'honourable' retreat from the Vyas, a very great political conspiracy began to shape itself most secretly throughout the Greek-trodden Indian territory from the banks of the Vyas right up to Gandhar. But of that conspiracy, we shall have occasion to speak in a more detailed way a little later. Here, it should suffice to say that the Indian republics along both the banks of the Indus, whether big or small—made light of Alexander's threat to come again to conquer India as nothing more than a pompous political stunt, and prepared grimly to oppose his forces, as severely and as stubbornly as possible. But alas! it was a decision taken separately by each particular republic. It was not a well-organized, united effort, under a central authority to destroy the Greeks under Alexander. Hence, the same story of Gandhar and Panchanad was repeated here, and the well-organized army of Alexander, with its superior numbers, could successfully fight each Indian republic and go ahead. Even if these stray battles with various Indian armies did not fail to exhaust and weaken Alexander's forces, they could not crush him completely. There were, of

course, some exceptions to these separatist war efforts. Of them at least two, which even the hostile Greek historians praise wholeheartedly, and which gave such a severe blow to Alexander, deserve a brief mention here.

The Republics of the Malavas and the Shudrakas

50. The two republics led their separate lives along the banks of the Indus. Both were rich, brave democracies with a high sense of honour. Of the two, Malava republic was the more famous from the ancient times and was quite extensive. These two republics had at times been hostile to each other. But when they saw Alexander's powerful navy went on defeating every single Indian state in various battles and kept on forging its way to the sea, the political leaders of both these republics decided to correct the mistake of those several Indian democracies that fought singly with a vastly superior enemy, a mistake that was proving fatal to their wider national interests. So, instead of fighting the Greek army singly, they decided to amalgamate their fighting forces under a unified control. Not only did they unite their men at arms, but they intermarried in order to bring about political and social unity among them. For the intermingling of castes and blood, they had a great collective marriage ceremony, wherein at least a thousand girls from both the 'Ganas' (republics) were inter-married to the youths of the other republic.

51. While this unified army of the Malava-Shudrak republics was fighting tooth and nail with the Greeks, Alexander laid siege to one of their important cities. Although the name of this city cannot be ascertained positively, it must have been some capital city or one of similar importance. As this republican city kept on fighting desperately, the Greek siege had to be prolonged. The haughty Alexander could not bear it. He thought of ordering the ladders to be put up on the ramparts of the enemy stronghold, and commanding his Greek soldiers to climb them up and straightaway storm the city.

52. But the same sort of unrest and disaffection against Alexander began to be seen in his army, as was once experienced at the time of the crossing of the Vyas. The Greek army was avowedly wending its way homeward in order to avoid new wars. But all along the bank of the Indus, they had to fight fresh battles. And they knew that unless Alexander gave up his aggressive designs calculated to pacify his unsatiable lust for conquests, brutal wars were unavoidable. Because of this bitter war with the Malava-Shudrak combined forces, the Greek

discontent reached the climax and there were rebellious whispers openly flouting Alexander's commands.

52A. When the Macedonian soldiers found that they had still on hand a fresh war in which the most war-like nations (गणाऽ) would be their antagonists, they were struck with unexpected terror and began again to upbraid the King in the language of sedition. (Curtius Bk. IX Ch.IV. as quoted in 'Hindu Polity') {*Mc Crindle I.L. by Alexander P. 234*).

53. Still, in the end, Alexander promulgated his command to his soldiers to climb up the ladders and leap straight into the enemy stronghold, which valiantly defied the Greek siege. Seeing that his Greek soldiers hesitated to undertake the daring feat, that exceptionally valiant commander of the Greeks, the mighty Alexander, himself began to climb one of the ladders put up against the ramparts of the stronghold. At this, the whole Macedonian army was suddenly inspired to do the great deed, and all began to climb instantaneously. Once at the top of the ramparts, Alexander straightaway jumped down in the midst of the enemy and there ensued a hand-to-hand fight between the Indian and the Greek forces.

And Suddenly

54. And suddenly an Indian warrior took out an envenomed arrow from his sheath and applied it to his bowstring, and let it fly with an unmistakable aim at the place where Alexander stood edging on his warriors, and shining in his golden helmet.

55. It was not an arrow, it was, in fact, Indian revenge incarnate. To use the lines of poet Moropant (with a slight variation of course) we can say—

तो शर गरधरवरसा पविसा रविसा स्मरारिसायकसा ।
म्लेंच्छ हृदंतरि घुसला वल्मीका माजि नागनायकसा ॥

(with apologies to Moropant आर्याभारत-कर्णपर्व)

Alexander Rolled into a pool of Blood

56. The shaft of the Indian warrior unmistakably pierced the heart of Alexander, and suddenly the emperor rolled down unconscious. A Greek soldier immediately covered him with his shield. There was a sudden hue and cry in the Greek ranks that Alexander had been wounded, that he had fallen unconscious. With exceptional daring, the Greeks lifted him from the pool of blood and carried him safely to his camp.

There, with great difficulty that terrible shaft of the Indian warrior was extricated. The Greeks heaved a sigh of relief when after a long time of patient nursing, Alexander gradually regained consciousness. It took several days for the wound to heal up. During all this time, Alexander was confined to bed.

57. But everywhere in Babylon and Greece the news that was received, reported that Alexander was killed in the war by an Indian arrow. Consequently, there were some uprisings in Gandhar and Persia. But later on, when it was known that Alexander was only severely wounded and was now recovering, the situation came to normalcy.

58. No wonder whatsoever, if the news of Alexander's having fainted by a bowshot was greeted cheerfully throughout the Malava-Shudrak republic. Alexander was so much puffed up with pride when King Pourav (Poros) was wounded in the battle, that he circulated a new coin with a picture showing his fall stamped on it. The coin is still to be seen as a mark of his vanity. That insult inflicted on India was fully avenged by the Indian arrow, which sent the Greek emperor rolling down on the battlefield in pools of blood. The Ionian Emperor, Alexander, who unjustifiably shed Indian blood, was made to atone for it personally by the shedding of his blood.

59. The Malava-Shudrak republic too should have stamped on some golden coin the picture of Alexander, fallen in a pool of blood with an arrow deeply thrust into his chest. Possibly they did.

60. According to his cruel military code, he had been cruelly rushing down the states, which had opposed him. But whenever there appeared any foe, who was equally strong and who retaliated furiously, Alexander had the cunning to dissemble nobility and frankness of heart. When he recovered from his wound, he began to make overtures of peace to the commanders of the Malava-Shudrak army, instead of dictating his usual arrogant terms. For ceasefire talks, a hundred representatives of the joint Malava-Shudrak republic were elected, and for them, Alexander held a grand reception ceremony in his camp. Detailed and very entertaining descriptions of this reception are available in the books of Greek historians. But for want of space, we have to satisfy ourselves with a brief reference to it. The hundred representatives were, even according to the Greek standards, of uncommon height, heavily built, having handsome muscular bodies. They were clad in valuable

embroidered clothes and had worn beautiful ornaments of gold and pearls and precious stones. Everyone of them went to the Greek camp in his well-decorated and well-equipped golden chariot. They had with them elephants, too, with costly and beautiful outfits. The Greeks had always felt a special fascination for the elephants.

61. Although rankling in his mind was the fact that these very representatives of the Malava-Shudrak joint republic had brought upon him, a little while ago, a mortal danger, Alexander showed his magnanimity in that reception ceremony and paraded his own imperial splendour. For every one of those hundred representatives, there was a special golden seat. The banquet given in their honour was attended with costly wines and excellent savoury dishes. The grand banquet was followed by various field games and tournaments, music and dancing. In the end, a treaty was signed by the Malava-Shudrak representatives and Alexander.

62. The divergent accounts given about this treaty by various Greek writers of the time have, at least, this much in common to tell. The Greeks and the Indians had jointly agreed to put a stop to their hostilities and that the Malava-Shudrak republic was not to cause any harassment to the retreating army of Alexander, while it was progressing on its way home along the Indus. Of these, two valiant republics, the Malavas will be referred to later on, when I shall be describing the wars with the Sakas, the Yucchis and other Mlenchha powers. The fact that this Malava republic had been prosperous and strong for many centuries to come, therefore, need not be specially proved.

63. Even the Greek writers could not help recording some more acts of valour during the Indian resistance to the Greek onslaught, although the details of the time and place of their happenings are not available. Two of them are cited here to serve as specimens.

The Treacherous attack of Greeks on Masaga Tribe

64. At Masaga, Alexander captured a small armed community of seven thousand, which included several women. Alexander promised them their lives on condition that they should join his army and fight with his Indian enemies, or else, he threatened them with wholesale man-slaughter, or, as a third alternative he said, he would carry them off as slaves! The leaders of the community agreed to his first proposal, but requested that they should be allowed one night for mutual exchange

of views. Alexander agreed. Thereupon, these seven thousand Indians marched towards a hill, some nine miles ahead of the Greek camp. Writes Vincent Smith, "The Indians being unwilling to aid the foreigners in the subjugation of their countrymen desired to evade the unwelcome obligation." So, they decided to give the slip to the Greeks, but Alexander came to know of their intention. So, while they were sleeping for a little rest, Alexander fell upon them, all of a sudden, with his huge army and began to cut down eveyone. There was a great havoc amongst those Indians. But within a short time, they drew up their swords and other weapons. They made a hollow circular formation, gathering the women and children inside it, and faced the Greek attack most heroically. A good number of women were also found desperately fighting with the foe. Till almost all of them were killed, they kept on fighting for the freedom of their nation.

64A. "The gallant defenders met a glorious death they would have disclaimed to exchange for a life with dishonour." (*Early History of India* by Vincent Smith 1924, p. 59)

The Agrashrenis

65. This little Indian republic of the Agrashrenis too, instead of surrendering, fought to the last with the vast Greek navy of Alexander, as it was making its headway to the sea through the course of the Indus. When the Greeks attacked their very capital, these brave Indian warriors erected blockades and barricades at different intervals, and fought every inch of their ground so tenaciously that Alexander could not enter the city before he had sacrificed many Greek lives. According to Curtius, "When those brave fellows could not further resist the odds, they (the Agrashrenis) set their houses on fire, and their wives and children and all threw themselves into the flames!" That is to say, they 'made johar' (to use a latter day phraseology).

This is the Aame Johar!—Jai Har!!

66. We generally believe that this magnificent and awe-inspiring tradition of 'johar' or self-immolation of large groups of men and women in times of national crisis was originally practised by the Rajputs only. But instances like the one just mentioned, cited by the Greek writers who were astounded to witness them, go to prove that even before the name of the Rajputs was ever heard of, this splendid tradition was

followed by our Indian warriors right from the ancient days. The word 'johar' is comparatively modern. It was perhaps derived from the war cry 'Jai Har'! The Indian God of war and destruction is Har, Har, Mahadev! That is why, the Indians fought desperately, inspired by this deafening war cry! The Marathas too used the same war cry 'Har, Har, Mahadev!' After fighting to the last, when every hope of success was over, or every chance of escape from the enemy was lost, this johar, this martyrdom, this noblest type of self-sacrifice was resorted to by the Hindus as the last unfailing weapon to save their religion, their nation, their own self-respect and to avoid captivity, abject slavery and hateful conversion! As soon as all men of fighting age were slain on the battlefield after taking the greatest toll of the enemy blood, their wives, mothers, daughters, hundreds of them, with babies at their breasts, used to leap into the burning pyres, specially kept ready for the purpose and were reduced to ashes. This was what was known as 'Johar'! It was not an easy job! It was the limit of valour and endurance for the sake of keeping up the prestige of one's self and one's own religion!

67. Whoever had donned this exceptional armour of 'Johar' and its leaping flames were beyond all attempts of an Alexander, an Alla-ud-Din or a Salim-why, even of Satan himself—to pollute them and convert them to his religion! Confronted with this horrible sacrificial fire, the enemy stood aghast, discomfited and crestfallen.

68. The above-mentioned 'Johar'—collective immolation of lives—by the Agrashrenis is one of the many described by the astounded Greek writers, which the Indians preferred to the humiliation of being the captives of the Greeks.

The Janapad Republic of Brahmanakas!

69. At last, when Alexander's naval force reached the mouth of the Indus, fighting incessantly all the way, it met with yet other independent republics. These 'janapadas' or 'Ganas' were like the small Greek city-states, and had none amongst them, which could ably withstand with equal numbers, the mighty and numerous army of Alexander. Still one of them, the 'Brahmanak janapad' made up its mind to cross swords with, rather than submit to Alexander. This was the same 'Brahmanak janapad', that is referred to by Panini, says Dr. Jayaswal. It is already told how, while fighting in the Panchanad (the Punjab) Alexander had wreaked his rancorous revenge against the clan of philosophers,

especially the Brahmins. When Alexander learnt that it was the same clan of Brahmins, this small state belonged to, he decided to whack his malicious stroke upon it with all his might. Plutarch (McCrindle 'Invasion of India by Alexander' p. 306; V.A. Smith E.H.I. p. 106) writes in his 'Life of Alexander', "These philosophers were specially marked down for revenge by Alexander as they gave him no less trouble than the mercenaries. They reviled the princes who declared for Alexander and encouraged free states (in India) to revolt against his authority. On this account, he hanged many of them". (ChLIX)

69A. That little 'Janapad' too fought to the last with these Greeks for the sake of its national honour and independence.

Pattanprastha

70. What now is called by the Muslims, Sindh Hyderabad, was at that time known as Pattanprastha. In Sanskrit language, the cities along the seashore, or at the mouths of rivers, were mostly called 'Pattan'. Pattan is equivalent to the English word 'port'. Perhaps the English word 'port' might have been a corruption of the Sanskrit 'Pattan'. When Alexander neared the sea, this small state of Pattranprastha was confronted with a dilemma: to surrender to the enemy was most hateful to the 'Pattanprasthis', but they knew fully well that they would never be able to fight with the powerful Greek army on equal ground. So they resolved the dilemma by forsaking, collectively their native country, their homes and landed property and motherland with sad hearts.

Alexander's Homeward Voyage

71. That part of the ocean, where the Indus flows into it, should really be called Sindhusagar. Sindhusagar, a name for the sea to the west of India, is a fitting counterpart for the Gangasagar, a traditional name for the eastern sea.

72. On first reaching the sea, Alexander divided his army into two parts. The first batch he sent back to Iran (Persia) by a land route through what now goes by the name of Baluchistan. The whole of Alexander's army had been thoroughly exhausted in this expedition to India. Moreover, Baluchistan at that time, was full of impregnable forests, thoroughly unknown to the Greeks. So, the Greek division, sent this way, somehow reached Persia, after so many hazards and privations. On the other hand, Alexander himself set sail by the sea-route with another

division of his army, and reached Persia. As the whole of the old Persian Empire had now formed a part of Alexander's greater demesne, he went to his capital, namely Babylon. But he did not return to the capital in that same triumphant spirit he had started on his Indian campaign two years ago, with a view to winning for himself the vauntful title of the Emperor of India. Not only did he not return like the Emperor of India, he did not even appear to be an emperor at all. He returned just like an ordinary commander of an army, despaired and worn out, after a long-drawn and hazardous campaign.

India was not Persia

73. The cause of this disappointment of Alexander was that the Greeks up to that time, knew only one empire worth the name—much more extensive than their own—that of Persia! When these Greeks marched upon that Persian emipre under their uncommonly brave and brilliant commander, Alexander, and when after only two or three campaigns the vast Persian empire fell before them like a paper palace, they were so much flushed with their victory, that they fondly considered their commander to be endowed with divine qualities, and as such unconquerable. Alexander himself could not escape the infection of pride. His ambition to win for himself the overlordship of the whole world soared to the sky. Bharat appeared to him just next to and as easy a prey as, Persia. So very vast a land and so very weak! So, he wanted to crown his Persian conquest with the glittering diadem of the Indian imperial authority. Greedily enough, he ran to have it with all haste.

74. But the experience he had was quite contrary to what he had expected. In India, he had to face the bitterest opposition at every step. Although he never lost a battle as such, his Greek army was completely exhausted and exasperated in the very process of winning them. These victories were far too costlier than the ones in Persia, and all their vauntful declarations of conquering India as easily as Persia proved to be empty words 'full of sound and fury signifying nothing'. And in the end, he had to return with the acquisition of only a small all of land along the Indus river.

75. Thus was Alexander disappointed and to a certain extent insulted. But that valiant emperor was not downcast. He was itching to return once again to India after stabilizing things in the newly conquered regions of India and annexing them permanently to his vast

empire like those of Syria, Persia, Babylon and others.

76. Alexander declared the annexation of the region from Hindukush and Gandhar to Taxila (Takshashila), half of the Panchanad up to the river Vyas, and that from the confluene of the Vitasta with the Indus to the sea. He appointed the Indian King Ambuj or Ambhi of Taxila his governor (satrap) of the Hindukush region, and King Porus as his governor of the Panchanad. To the third but narrow strip of land along the Indus were appointed his two trusted Greek generals, Philip and Nicanor, under whom he placed the mobile force of Greeks. He established in India some townships too, one of which was Alexandria in the direction of Taxila.

Alexander's Death

77. Before Alexander decided to stabilize things in the Indian territory he had recently captured, he learnt that the local democratic institutions refused to accept his overlordship. Even while Alexander was in Sind, he received intelligence of a revolt by the Indian subjects in Gandhar. He was about to send a fresh and large Greek army to Gandhar. But in quick succession followed another disturbing news of a fresh conspiracy being hatched in Punjab (Panchanad) to overthrow Alexander completely. But Alexander could at that time do nothing to thwart any such attempts at revolt. During his campaign against India not only his army but he himself was completely exhausted. To add to it, his addiction to drinking had grown beyond all limits of safety; he suddenly took ill and died in B.C. 323. That is to say, hardly within a-year-and-a-half of his return from India with all his army, the great Greek (Macedonian) Emperor breathed his last at Babylon.

Indian Politicians Conspire

78. As has already been told, as soon as Alexander began to retreat along the Indus, some of the Indian politicians began hatching out a secret plan against the Greeks in Punjab to win back their lost freedom. But it was not merely aimed at the recovery of the lost territory. It was essentially to overhaul and revolutionize the whole gamut of the political life of India and to bring about a sweeping change in the internal life of the country. Even if Alexander had not died so soon, the deep-laid Indian plot was destined to achieve this daring political revolution. This sudden death of Alexander, however, gave Indian political workers an

unexpected golden opportunity and they were quick enough to utilize it, for the overthrow of the Greek power.

Greek Governors Beheaded

79. Alexander had left behind Nicanor and Philip as the chief representatives of Greeks. When the news of Alexander's death reached India, the Indians in the republic of the Ashvinis suddenly fell upon the Greek Governor, Philip, and assassinated him along with his small Greek regiment. The second, Nicanor, was also similarly despatched, and all those monarchies and republics along the banks of the Indus, which had acquiesced in the Greek overlordship, shook it off at once and proclaimed their independence forthwith. Greek colonies, Greek ensigns and standards—whatever signified the Greek power—were completely destroyed on the spot. The whole of the tract along the banks of the Indus right from the Panchanad to Sindh, which Alexander had conquered and annexed for ever and anon to his empire, became independent within six months of Alexander's death.

80. Alexander had conquered states and countries and empires like Greece, Syria, Persia, Babylon, Egypt and the likes. There he founded Greek cities and Greek colonies, and even after the division of his vast empire, just after his death, his governors and military commanders and their descendants, ruled the respective regions like Babylon for centruries, together. Even now in some other countries cities exist with the name Alexandria, and Alexander's name is ever crowned with the honorifix 'The Great' throughout ancient histroy.

81. But what happened in Bharat? The small states and republics in the farthest corner of India, that Alexander had annexed to his empire under the impression that he had conquered them for ever and for ever, after fighting incessantly on various battlefields for two long years and shedding the blood of millions of Greek and Hindu soldiers—those very Indian states and republics and monarchies literally uprooted his power, his standard, the Greek colonies and every hateful sign of the Greek victory—and that too within six months or at the most a year!

82. At last, not to speak of the city of Alexandria, which he had established, his own name too is not to be traced anywhere in Indian history, as if there never was any invasion, any aggression on India's borderland of any Mlenchh (Yavan) emperor, named Alexander, who

dinned the ears of the people throughout Europe with his proud title, 'The Great'! Curiously enough, not even a stray reference has yet been discovered in Vedic or Jain or Buddhist ancient literature.

83. Writes Vincent Smith in his famous *Early History of India:* "All these proceedings prove conclusively that Alexander intended the permanent annexation of those (Indian) provinces to his empire.... But within three years of his departure from India (from 325 BC to 322 BC), his officers in India were ousted, his garrisons destroyed and all traces of his rule had disappeared. The colonies he founded in India, unlike those established elsewhere in Asiatic provinces, took no root. His campaign, though carefully designed to secure a permanent conquest, was in actual effect not more than a brilliantly successful raid on a gigantic scale, which left upon India no mark save the horrid scars of a bloody war. India remained unchanged. She continued her life of splendid isolation and soon forgot the passing of the Macedonian storm. No Indian author—Hindu, Buddhist or Jain—makes even the faintest allusion to Alexander or his deed." (p. 117)

84. Who were the most prominent leaders of this political conspiracy, which wiped out, within a period of six months or a year, the whole of the foreign political dominance caused by Alexander's aggression right from the Panchanad to Sindh? Histroy, as yet, is ignorant of their names! Still two of them, at least, have become immortal. They are the same two men whom I have mentioned while describing Alexander's advance up to Taxila. The first was a brilliant and smart youth, who had just completed his studies at the University of Taxila, Chandragupta. And the other was Acharya Chanakya, who had been a teacher at that University and who, later on, gave a practical lesson in political craft and political revolutions to the young Chandragupta! As they were to lead the whole of Bharat, hereafter, it is fit and proper that they should be introduced here.

The Story of Chandragupta's Birth

85. Like all other great men of the ancient world, Chandragupta and Chanakya have their life stories clouded with legends, anecdotes and imaginary accounts. Those who are interested in them for the sake of intellectual entertainment may profitably read Radhakumud Mukherjee's 'Chandragupta Maurya and His Times'. We shall give here only so much of their lives as appear to us to have historical sanction.

86. Some small bands of the Shakyas, amongst whom was born the

great Lord Gautam Buddha, had at one time to shift to far-off regions, because of some disastrous calamity that had befallen them. They called themselves Kshatriyas. However, in those adverse days, those displaced Shakyas began to follow other professions for their livelihood. There happened to be a plentiful breed of peacocks in the forest, where these tribes later on lived. To keep these peacocks and sell them became one of their professions. So they had 'Moriya' as their nickname, and the Moriya formed a class by themselves. One family of these Moriyas came back to settle in the vicinity of Pataliputra. One woman of that Moriya tribe named Mura (Mayura) somehow got access to the harem of the royal palace and soon became the concubine of the Emperor, Mahapadmanand or 'Dhananand', as he was generally called. Her son from this Nanda Emperor was the Emperor Chandragupta.

87. However, when Chandragupta became an emperor, the story of his birth might have appeared derogatory to his greatness and, therefore in some books of the time, the story was slightly altered to mean that Muradevi was the wedded queen of the Nanda emperor, not his concubine, which in consequence meant that Chandragupta was a legitimate royal prince and not an illegitimate one.

88. But a third anecdote seems to outdo both the above stories, saying that Mura and Emperor Nanda were in no way connected. Mura had a son from her husband of the same clan and that son was Chandragupta himself. Later on, with the help and guidance of Arya Chanakya and with his own valour, he raised his poor father and mother to eminence, and after wresting the imperial power from the Nandas, he founded the Maurya Dynasty.

89. It seems a common weakness among all human societies and communities, in a greater or lesser degree, to attempt to judge the greatness or meanness of an individual, not so much from his manifest virtues or vices as from the race, the community or the family he is born in. That is why, as the time passes, such inflated anecdotes about their family tradition are propagated and popularized through plays, poems and novels or through folk-lores. There are other anecdotes too besides the ones referred to above, which seek to ascribe greatness or meanness to Chandragupta. But for the reasons given above, they need not be mentioned here.

90. Was Chandragupta a concubine's son? Was he not a Kshatriya? What matters though! Chandragupta could have said with justifiable

pride, "More than any of you, nominal caste-born Kshatriyas, who bowed your heads to the Mlenchchas, the Greek emperor and his commanders, I, a 'peerless' Chandragupta, have a greater claim to being a Kshatriya in as much as with my sword, I have completely vanquished those very Mlenchchas in every battlefield." With the same haughty affront of Kama, he could have flung in the face of those railing enemies, the following words:

सूतो वा सूत पुत्रों वा यो वा को वा भवाम्यहम्
दैवायत्तं कुले जन्म मदायत्तं तु पौरुषम ॥

वेणोसंहार *of Bhatta Narayan, Act III, 37*

["Whether a charioteer or a charioteer's son, or whoever (else) I may be, (that is of no consequence!) Birth in a (noble) family depends on fate; but manliness depends on me!"]

91. The son of Mura is a Maurya! That is precisely why Chandragupta is called a Maurya. Proud of his maternal extraction, Chandragupta designated his royal family as Maurya and immortalized the name of his mother, Muradevi, in Indian history. The Maurya emperors accepted the same Moriya caste too (one traded in peacocks) that belonged to his mother. The guardian deity of the Maurya family is also a 'peacock'. This fact is corroborated by rock inscriptions. The Ashoka pillar found at Nandangad bears at the foot, a picture of a peacock. The stories from the life of Ashoka inscribed on the celebrated 'stupas' at Sanchi have similar figures of peacocks carved beside them.

The Emperor of Magadha

92. Mahapadmanand was the emperor ruling at that time over the vast Magadha empire. He was already very unpopular because of his many vices. His subjects were exasperated because of the heavy taxes, levied on them, in order to satisfy his lust for gold. People called him Dhananand instead of Mahapadmanand, in order to deride him for his excessive lust for money. He could come to the throne because he happened to be the brother of the earlier emperor, but he had not a single virtue, fit for an emperor. He would have proved his worth had he but taken up the challenge of Alexander and crushed him in the Panchanad, when the latter had marched on India, and when he had proudly declared his intention of conquering Magadha and becoming the emperor of India. He should have at least undertaken such a great expedition as to overthrow the Greeks, and free the Indian territory subujgated by them to deserve

the title of an emperor! But he did nothing of the kind, and meekly swallowed the insult hurled at him by Alexander! This cowardliness on his part made, on the one hand, every self-respecting and nationalist Indian despise him, while, on the other, made him crafty. He hated the selfless national politicians. In order to undermine their prestige, he insulted them publicly. A really capable person was invariably an object of his hatred and was subjected to malicious treatment.

93. From this Mahapadmanand, it is said his concubine, Mura, had the illustrious son, Chandragupta. Some anecdotes pertaining to Chandragupta's childhood are available, but they are far too few and merely hearsay stories. What appears to be certain is only this, that the cowardly but crafty Mahapadmanand began to fear the young Chandragupta, shining with his sharp wit, his daring and ambitious spirit, seeking to exercise his rights as the heir to the throne, bastard as he was. He feared that under the leadership of this unrestrained bastard son, his antagonists would not fail to dethrone him! Mahapadmanand very well knew how his very Nanda forerunners had vanquished the original Shishunag dynasty of Magadha and usurped the throne! Under some such apprehension, there appears to have occurred some clash that Mahapadmanand used as a pretext to banish Chandragupta out of the precincts of the Magadha empire. The intervening account is permanently lost to oblivion. Hereafter, Chandragupta makes his appearance in the University of Taxila (Takshashila) as a royal prince having his lessons in politics and the science and art of war. An anecdote that is current in that region viz. that he got access to this university mainly through the good offices of the renowned and learned Arya Chanakya may have some grain of truth in it. Chandragupta had already been studying in the manner described above at this university for about six or seven years when Alexander attacked India. There, for the first time, this illustrious disciple of Chanakya, this young Chandragupta, began to shine with his exceptional brilliance in the sacred national conspiracy, that was being hatched by the Indian patriots and politicians to avenge the insults heaped on the Indian nation by the Greeks and to liberate the territory lost to them.

A Marvellous half-hour in History

94. Young Chandragupta seems to have secretly wandered through the Greek camps in order to study the peculiar features of the Greek

armoury, the Greek military formations and war strategy. For, he was once caught by the Greek sentries on suspicion that he was reconnoitring in the emperor's camp. The report reached Alexander himself, and the Macedonian emperor summoned the disguised Indian youth to his presence. Some even think that the said youth went to see Alexander by previous appointment.

95. That valiant Macedonian supreme commander and emperor Alexander, in his thirties, and the future Indian captain-general and emperor Chandragupta just on the threshold of his twenties, but as yet merely a wandering nonentity, stood face-to-face, sizing up each other for a few moments! It appeared as if two lustrous suns, one fast approaching his zenith and the other, not as yet risen fully, out of the misty shroud of the early dawn, were staring at each other's eyes.

96. This strange interview is not likely to have lasted for more than half an hour. But it has truly proved to be a historical marvel of perennial interest!

97. Even while almost all the Greek writers allude to this strange interview, nobody can say for certain what exactly transpired between the two, or what words were exchanged between them. One or two of them write only this much that Chandragupta said distinctly that he was related to the royal family of Magadha, or something to that effect. This much is certain that to the question put by Alexander, Chandragupta answered boldly and resolutely! In that strange parley, something went wrong and Alexander ordered the youth to be taken out of the camp forthwith. Instantly, the fiery youth left the camp, but in the meanwhile, when Alexander changed his mind and called again for the youth in his presence, he was nowhere to be found again.

The Story of Chanakya's Family

98. Arya Chanakya was born in a Brahmin family and his name was Vishnugupta. His name Chanakya must have probably been derived from his native town of Chanak. But he is more particularly known by his name Chanakya, Koutilya is one more name by which he is equally well-known. His great and abiding work is known as *Koutiliya Arthashastra*. Koutilya must have been formed from his original family (गौत्र नाम) name Kutal. He was well-versed in almost all the sciences of the time and was renowned at the University of Taxila and also amongst the learned circles of India, as a great scholar. He

was ugly in apearance. Later on, when after the imperial revolution of Magadha, his name gained great fame not only all over India, but even in Greece and other foreign countries as the guide and preceptor of Chandragupta's early years, and later as the chief minister of the Indian empire, several hearsay stories sprang up as to his early age, as they did regarding Chandragupta and Alexander. Several references to them based on solid grounds or otherwise are to be found in many literary works, dramas, folklores written many centuries after the deaths of both Chandragupta and Chanakya. These references in Jain, Buddhist and Vedic literatures are not wholly reliable. Even in a Sanskrit drama, his character has been depicted in an unrealistic manner, for the sake of dramatic effect. As such, the ridiculous descriptions of his ugliness, or of his ungainly teeth, or the childish reports that he picked up from amongst the uneducated rustic children playing in the street one reckless Chandragupta, to be made the future emperor of India simply because he took a fancy for the child, or because his knowledge of palmistry guided his choice, cannot be taken as historical truths. However, more discerning research-workers should necessarily investigate if there is any basis for them.

The Perverted Report of Chanakya's vow

99. One such anecdote about Arya Chanakya should be discussed here as an illustration. For, it is being taught in the present-day schools in that very perverted form. The said anecdote purports to say that because he became famous as a great scholar in the University of Taxila (Takshashila) and the regions round about, Arya Chanakya was appointed the Chairman of the Grants Commission (दानाध्यक्ष) in the royal palace of Mahapadmanand at Pataliputra. While he was working in that high office, Emperor Mahapadmanand came there one day on his inspection rounds. But he laughed at his teethless ugly mouth and his unshapely body, at which Chanakya took a great affront. Therefore, Nanda pulled him down instantly and, as is written in some books, pulled his tuft of hair, till it was uprooted and finally ordered him to be driven out of the palace. The fiery Brahmin instantly retorted saying, "I shall drag you down from your throne and completely destroy the Nanda dynasty and then and then alone shall tie up my tuft of hair." With this grave vow, he marched straight out of the palace.

100. But let it be remembered that Emperor Nanda had come

there to inspect the work of the Charity Department, not to visit a beauty parlour! How is it plausible, then, that Mahapadmanand, who had himself appointed that learned scholar to the high office of the Chairman of the Charitable Grants Department, would now say that because of his ugly features Arya Chanakya was unfit for that post? The office of the Chairman of the said Grants Department required the expert knowledge of the religious sciences and judicial procedure, not physical beauty! But there is a more potent objection than this one to disprove this foolish anecdote. This anecdote implies that Chanakya revolted against Emperor Nanda, because of his personal insult alone, and that, had he not been thus insulted, he would have remained a loyal servant of Mahapadmanand, that the India-wide revolution that he successfully brought about, was not for the sake of freeing the Indian land from the foreign Mlenchcha domination, but only to avenge his personal insult! For this very reason, this anecdote is clearly perverted.

101. When as a strategy in politics, Shivaji went to Agra accepting the overlordship of Aurangzeb, the latter insulted him, and when there was a clash of words, Shivaji was put under arrest. But Shivaji slipped away most miraculously and skilfully, and declared war against Aurangzeb. If, after telling this story, any wiseacre were to conclude that it was because he was personally insulted, that Shivaji bore a grudge against Aurangzeb and established an independent kingdom for himself, that he had no higher motive of the emancipation of his religion and country, it would be the height of absurdity and foolishness. Equally absurd and foolish would it be to say that it was only to avenge his personal insult by Emperor Nanda, that Arya Chanakya brought about a political revolution by exterminating the Nanda dynasty.

That Anecdote should be Explained thus

102. It is not true to say that because of his personal insult, Shivaji revolted against Aurangzeb. On the contrary, Aurangzeb had taken a fright that it was to overthrow his alien religious domination, that Shivaji had taken arms, fired as he was with a glowing fervour for Hindutwa. That is why, he insulted Shivaji and relegated him to captivity! In a similar way, because Mahapadmanand had secret reports that, availing himself of the weakness of the reigning monarch, Arya Chanakya was busy conspiring against him so as to overthrow the Nanda empire, the Emperor Nanda insulted him in his royal palace,

and at that very moment, the illustrious Brahmin Arya Chanakya retorted boldly, "If I am a true Chanakya I shall see to it that your tyrannical rule is overthrown so that Bharat might prosper." This is how the anecdote should be explained.

103. A very solid proof for this is available to us in the very *Koutiliya Arthashastra* written by Chanakya himself. While introducing the writer, it is said (in the very book):

चाणक्य इति विख्यात: श्रोत्रीय: सर्वधर्मविद्

—मुद्राराक्षस उपोद्घात *Telang's edition p. 44*

येन शस्त्रं व शास्त्रं च नन्दराज गताच भू: ॥
अमर्षेणोरुधृतान्याशु तेन शास्त्रमिदं कृतम् ॥

—अर्थशास्त्र *p. 429*

"He who destroyed the Nanda and rejuvenated the national armed strength as also the national scientific advance which were decaying under the Nanda regime, and thus caused the uplift of his Bharatbhoomi, has written this treatise." He has not used even a single word in the introductory lines to say that he destroyed Nanda to avenge his personal insult. It is for the progress and prosperity of his own nation and motherland, that Nanda was destroyed! Chanakya's great work itself tells it clearly!

104. The anecdote that is told in a downright dramatic way perhaps means only this, that his original nationalistic animus towards Nanda was whetted more because of this personal insult.

Chanakya's Political Activities Preceded Alexander's onslaught

105. Chanakya had been living in the vicinity of Taxila for good many years before the aggression of Alexander. He had a first-hand knowledge of the political situation in the Bharatiya frontier territories right up to the Indus.

106. Just adjoining the borderland of India had stretched far and wide, the unitary and centrally well-organised nation, inimical to India. Chanakya was shrewd enough to understand that in the event of an aggression by such a well-organised and inimical country, the small native democracies and monarchies from the Panchanad to the Indus would utterly fail in the open battlefield, if they were to fight separately.

The Greek city-states too perished precisely for this reason

107. Just then a practical demonstration of the above-mentioned axiom took place in Greece. The moment the Persian Emperor invaded Greece, the small Greek city-states like their prototypes in India, were convulsed to their bones. In the end, it is only when Philip and Alexander conquered all of those separatist Greek city-states, forged them into a powerful empire, was it possible for them to vanquish the Persian empire. Chanakya was not slow to understand its significance.

108. He arrived at the firm conviction that *vis-a-vis* a powerful and extensive inimical empire as its neighbour, India had only one way to defend its independence and make its administrative machinery strong enough to withstand any foreign aggression and that was to boil down all the smaller monarchies and republics and to forge out of them, a centralized unitary and strong empire.

For the Entire Undivided India

108A. But there was not a single Indian monarchy or republic throughout the whole of the region right from Gandhar, Punjab to the Indus delta, which could execute this plan of Chanakya, who had already appraised their capability and inclination. Naturally, his next choice fell on the only mighty empire of North India, namely Magadha. His head full of plans for the future Indian revolution, Arya Chanakya came again to Magadha in order to study secretly the political situation, visiting every place right from a poor man's cottage to the royal palace. As such, he was trying to get access to the King's court on some pretext or the other. When the question of the appointment of Arya Chanakya as the Chairman of the 'Grants' Department' (दानाध्यक्ष) was mooted, Nanda did not object to it, because till then, he had known nothing else of Arya Chanakya, but of his scholarship. This appointment greatly helped Arya Chanakya perfect his secret revolutionary plans.

109. But before long, Emperor Nanda had reports that Arya Chanakya was not a scholar pure and simple, but an expert organiser of secret plots and was at that time busy plotting against him. Enraged at this, he publicly insulted Arya Chanakya as already told before, deprived him of his authority as the Chairman of the Grant's Department, and expelled him out of his imperial precincts. Being thus outlawed, Chanakya returned again to Taxila.

110. In the meanwhile, the young bastard son Chandragupta, being exiled, as has been already told, from the Magadhan court by Emperor Nanda, went to Taxila and joined Chanakya—an incident that proved most favourable to that patriot's ambitious plans of establishing an all-India empire.

Why did Chanakya back Chandragupta alone?

111. If he were to dethrone the weak and wicked Nanda, and crown in his place on the throne of the Magadha empire any outsider, the tradition-loving important persons from amongst the feudatories, the Indian princes and even the common people would probably have opposed vehemently, even though the chosen person had been endowed with the most excellent qualities, whereas Chandragupta, though not a lawful royal prince, had yet some native blood-relation to the throne as the bastard son of the Emperor of Magadha. He was, moreover, endowed with valour and other qualities of head and heart. As such, the arch-diplomat Chanakya shrewdly guessed that even these votaries of tradition were far less likely to oppose Chandragupta's election to the throne of Magadha. He, therefore, determined to champion the claim of Chandragupta to the emperorship of Magadha—why even to that of the whole of India.

112. While the grand plan of an India-wide empire of Chanakya-and-Chandragupta was thus being set afoot, the unfortunate event of a foreign invasion was reported towards Persia. Alexander had already destroyed the empire of Persia and had invaded India. Although as has been related in the foregoing pages, he was staunchly opposed by the Bharatiya valour and forced to retreat home, it was plain that Alexander's well organised imperial military might was not totally annulled.

113. Even out of this evil, some good did emerge. The republican subjects of the frontier regions, with their faith in democratic principles shaken rudely by the heavy knock of a foreign invasion and the bloody wars that followed, began to agree with Chanakya and other patriotic prophets that national independence was in peril, unless a countrywide Indian empire was established on the lines of the vast, highly centralized well-organized and unitary form of empire of the enemy.

114. The first happy sign of this revolutionary spirit was seen in the general uprising throughout the smaller states and republics,

conquered by Alexander and annexed to his empire and in the fact that hardly within six months or a year of Alexander's death, these Indian territories shook off the foreign rule and became independent. Justin, an ancient renowned writer, credits the leadership of Chandragupta with the authorship of this wonderful and noble collective uprising. "India after the death of Alexander had shaken, as it were, the yoke of servitude from its neck and put his governors to death. The author of this liberation was Sandrocottus." The 'Sandrocottus' of this quotation is Chandragupta. The Greeks pronounced the name of Chandragupta in this very way.

The only way to repel re-invasion?

115. Although the general rising in these frontier provinces was successful under the guidance of Chandragupta, Chanakya and others, the followers of Chanakya began to warn all princes and political leaders, that it had not as yet made Indian independence completely safe from the future Greek onslaught. They went on preaching everywhere that Alexander himself had vowed till the day of his death, that he would invade India once again and conquer it thoroughly, that the chief officers of his state and commanders were at war with one another for the division of the Greek empire, that the triumphant one among them who would ascend the throne at Babylon would not fail to attack India with an army more powerful than before, and that the first victims to that aggression would be these very people, if they remained disunited as separate Rajakas (monarchies) and Prajakas (republics). But if they availed themselves of this opportunity of the civil feuds of the Greeks, and they could merge the whole of India into a strong empire with an efficient administration at the centre, this new Indian empire, stronger than that of the Greeks, could very easily beat the Mlenchchas, were they to come once again aggressively. Hence, they said India should be built into one strong nation!

Invasion of Chandragupta and Chanakya on Magadha

116. Without wasting even a single moment of the golden opportunity of the Greek internecine wars, Chandragupta and other followers of Chanakya began openly to raise a powerful army to march first of all against Magadha, according to Chanakya's plan of the political revolution. A few but very telling references to this fact are to be found in

the critique named 'Mahavamsha'. From these and from other sources, it appears that this invading army of Chandragupta was mainly composed of the soldiers from Panchanad, the Pauravas and the republics that were inspired with the preaching of Chanakya for a unitary Indian empire. In order to enlist the sympathies of the Parvateshwara, i.e. King Paurav, who was a powerful king in those provinces, Chanakya is said to have met him secretly. As Alexander's sway had been completely thrown off from the Indian territories, King Paurav was no longer a subordinate satrap of the Greeks. From stray references in some books, it appears that not only King Paurav offered his support for Chanakya's cause, but some wealthy people too helped him actively. Chanakya offered the command of the whole army to Chandragupta. After establishing their hold on all possible regions of Panchanad, they marched speedily on Magadha. The Indian populace and the local powers disgusted with and enraged at the tyrannical and weak rule of Nanda, and inspired by Chanakya's ideal of a strong unitary empire of the whole of India, joined Chandragupta's army as it marched ahead fighting.

117. In this daring and stormy march of theirs, Chandragupta and Chanakya had many times to face very grave dangers to their lives. Once their whole army was routed by a violent knock of the opposing forces, and Chandragupta and Chanakya had to flee into the forest to save their lives. One night they had to sleep on the bare hard ground, but undeterred by any of these calamities, Chandragupta and Chanakya formed their armies again and again and kept on marching ahead, and in the end, entered the precincts of Pataliputra, the Magadhan capital itself.

118. The arch-diplomat, Chanakya had bribed the army and the people in the capital of Nanda. On the strength of this general sedition, the daring Chandragupta fell like an arrow-shot upon the city of Pataliputra.

Mahapadmanand Beheaded

119. When Chandragupta's army rushed into the capital, blocking it very rigidly from every side, there was a great havoc everywhere. Chandragupta himself entered the royal palace but Mahapadmanand had already left it in the general disorder that had ensued, and was trying to slip out of the capital secretly. He was, however, caught on the way and beheaded almost instantaneously.

Samrat Chandragupta ki Jaya!

120. Chandragupta was soon proclaimed Emperor of Magadha. He adopted Maurya as his family name after that of his mother, Mura. Hence, he and his royal dynasty came to be known for ever in history by that very name 'Maurya'. As soon as he publicly ascended the throne of Magadha, he appointed Chanakya the Chief Minister of the empire, approximately in B.C. 321.

121. Alexander died round about B.C. 323. It means, therefore, that within about two years, Samrat Chandragupta and Chanakya effected this gigantic revolution that established the independent and powerful Indian empire, dispelling all gloom of despondency and disintegration, while on the other side, the Greek feudal lords were quarrelling amongst themselves. In order to avail himself fully of this opportunity, Chanakya immediately busied himself with the establishment of internal peace and order.

The basic principle of Chanakya's Political theory—Military Might First

122. But the peace and order of even a unitary empire ultimately depends on its military strength alone, which forms the bedrock of the whole imperial structure. This was the basic principle of Chanakya's political theory. Warlike spirit and armed-strength, he said, were the very life-breath not only of the political but also of the civil life of a community. Let that warlike spirit mitigate itself a bit and all religions, all sciences, all arts why the whole life of a nation is doomed!

सर्वे धर्मा प्रक्षेययुर्विवृद्धा: । क्षात्रे त्यक्ते राजधर्मे पुराणे ॥

"In the event of the Kshatriyas forsaking their old kingly duty, all the religions are (bound) to perish." A huge building without a (proper) foundation, as also, an empire without an (adequate) military strength, are bound to topple down even with a stormy wave of wind. Arya Chanakya, who preached all this, first of all began to reorganize a huge powerful army, which was well-commanded and inspired with the ambition to win in order to defend the newly-born empire. This he did with such an amazing speed, that during three or four years, not only his subjects came to have faith in his great powers but also the enemies of India began to fear it.

123. What did this huge army of Chandragupta so well planned and so well organised, amount to?

124. Hardly four years earlier, when Chandragupta-Chanakya

vowed secretly to establish an independent Indian empire under a unitary command, their armed might was literally nil! That very Chandragupta who started with this 'nil', had now a well-equipped loyal army of 6,00,000 foot soldiers, 30,000 cavalry; 2,000 war-elephants and 4,000 chariots!

125. With this powerful army, Chanakya wiped out the chaos created by the separatist small states, republics and monarchies in north India, which wanted to lead an independent life of their own, and established peace and unitary organization. In the end, all the territory on this side of the Indus up to the Punjab, the Kingdom of the Pauravas and Sindh proper, were annexed to the Mauryan empire.

126. Had any political thinker and administrator or an Indian emperor felt proud to have established for the first time, such a unitary Bharatiya empire, it would have been but natural.

India's Frontier Hindukush not Indus

127. But Chandragupta and Chanakya were not satisfied with extending the boundaries of their empire up to the banks of the Indus only, they had vowed to establish the Bharatiya empire over the whole of India, and to annihilate the unruly Mlenchchas! At that time the (north-western) frontier of India did not rest with the eastern bank of the Indus. But it reached much farther beyond the Indus, so as to include among its fold the regions like the Gandhar and the rivers now lost to Afghanisthan, but once well-known to Vedic Aryans, like the Kubha (the Kabul of today), the Kramu (the Kurram of today), the Suwastu (the Swat of today), the Gomati (the Gumal of today) and others, right up to the peaks of the Hindukush mountains. To that far end, were spread our republics following the Vedic religion and born of a Bharatiya race! And over these regions had been ruling the traditional royal dynasties of India. As our people in that ice-cold regions were comparatively whiter, it was also called by some "White India". Naturally the national aspiration, as embodied in Chandragupta-Chanakya scheme of things, fortified its imperial boundaries not only up to the eastern bank of the Indus with a strong army, but it also busied itself with the planning and preparation and execution of the imperial boundaries right up to the natural geographic frontiers of India, the Hindukush mountain and yearned to hoist its flag on the top of that mountain!

"These also laboured in the cause espoused by the other sages."

Greek Feuds and the Division of the Empire

128. In the meanwhile, the Greek civil feuds had temporarily ceased by dividing Alexander's empire, ceding its vast portion from the Indian frontiers up to Babylon to Seleucos Nicator, one of the bravest and most experienced veteran of Alexander's military officers, who ruled it as an independent sovereign. He was supposed to inherit the claim to the region beyond the Hindukush, which was formely conquered by Alexander.

129. He, therefore, demanded the surrender of that region from Chandragupta, who had appropriated it to himself. Of course, Seleucos did not realize that now the Greeks had to face not an Ambhi of Taxila as before, nor any cowardly minister, but King Chandragupta and his minister, Chanakya! They not only scoffed at this frivolous demand of Seleucos, but demanded in return the surrender of the region from Gandhar to Hindukush beyond the river Indus.

Seleucos Attacks India with a Mighty Army

130. Enraged at this rebuff, Seleucos marched against India round about 315 B.C. with a Greek army, trained under Alexander. If we leave aside the little-known invasion of Gandhar by Alexander in B.C. 329, this was the second invasion of India by the Greeks after the famous one, already fully described, by Alexander in B.C. 326.

131. But this time, after he crossed the Indus, Seleucos was amazed to see that the region, instead of being divided into separate Indian republics as at the time of Alexander, had undergone a complete change, both political and military, because of the brave efforts of Chandragupta and Chanakya. He was confused. Right from the northern most part of Punjab on the bank of the Indus to the waters of the Western Sea (Sindhusagar), he saw erected, as it were, a steel wall of well-organized, centrally controlled fourfold Indian army to check his advance! And at the head of it was Chandragupta himself!

132. As soon as the two armies thirsting to fight met, a bitter war started. The Greeks did their utmost, but at last, the Indian forces on two or three battlefields somewhere on the banks of the Indus (the place or places are unknown yet), put them to such a pitiful rout that hardly four years earlier, when Chandragupta-Chanakya vowed secretly to establish an independent Indian empire under a unitary command, their armed might was literally nil! That very Chandragupta who started with

this 'nil', had now a well-equipped loyal army of 6,00,000 foot soldiers, 30,000 cavalry, 2,000 war-elephants and 4,000 chariots!

Seleucos could not help capitulating to the victorious Chandragupta.

Revenge of the Defeat of King Paurav

133. Thus was avenged by this decisive victory of Chandragupta over the vanquished Greeks, the old sore of the defeat of King Paurav and other atrocities and insults meted out to the Indians by Alexander! So...

The Vanquished Seleucos Meekly Accepted all the terms of the Victorious Chandragupta

134. According to these terms of the treaty, Seleucos relinquished his right to the Indian region this side of the Indus, which he had so far maintained. But when he was firmly told by Chief Minister Chanakya, that the war would not end unless the whole region from Gandhar to Hindukush, which was till then in the Greek hands, was yielded to the Indian Emperor, he submitted to it meekly and the thousands of Greek warriors, who proudly held their brave chests and their swords drawn up while crossing the Indus on their march against India, now returned crestfallen, with their heads and swords held down. They crossed not only the Indus backwards but retreated to the farthest end of the Hindukush mountain.

Love is Impossible Without fear

(भय बिन होय न प्रीत)

135. This singular victory of Chandragupta brought the Indian frontiers quite close to those of the Greek empire of Seleucos and the dividing line between the two empires was the range of the Hindukush mountain! The might of this Indian emperor and the personality of Chandragupta and Chanakya impressed the Greek Emperor, Seleucos, so much that he was fully convinced of the advisability of having friendly relations with such a mighty empire rather than to be on inimical terms with it! Secondly, Seleucos had enemies on the other frontiers, although they too were Greeks. Friendship with Chandragupta, therefore, was calculated to overawe them too! For these reasons, the Greek Emperor Seleucos wholeheartedly signed a treaty of permanent peace with Emperor Chandragupta.

136. Moreover, with a view to cementing this political and international friendship with a wedlock between the two royal families and personal affinities and ties, the Greek emperor celebrated the marriage of his daughter with Chandragupta.

137. This offer of the royal princess in marriage by Seleucos, erected a golden pinnacle bedecked with jewels over the magnificent temple of the success of Emperor Chandragupta!

The Glorious Treatise of Mahamatya Chanakya!

138. How very effectively and firmly with full regard to the propriety of the case and yet how very discreetly Chanakya managed the affairs of the state, can be clearly seen from his treatise on body politic named *Kautaleeya Arthashastra,* and from the far-reaching influence of the invincible Indian Empire, which kept on increasing for at least a hundred years afterwards. The account of Megasthenese, the Greek ambassador at the court of Chandragupta, also testifies to the part this treatise played in maintaining peace and order and affluence in the whole empire.

139. At times a single historical event happening overnight or within a single day, changes the whole current of history for over a thousand years to come. This decisive victory of Chandragupta over the Greeks had also had far-reaching effects. The English historian, Vincent Smith, has this remark to offer: "For almost a hundred years after the failure of Seleucos Nikator, no Greek sovereign presumed to attack India."

140. "...The first Indian emperor, more than two thousand years ago thus entered into possession of that 'Scientific frontier' sighed for in vain by his English successors and never held in its entirety even by the Moghul monarchs of the 16th and 17th centuries. "(*Early History of India, 4th ed. 1924* by V.A. Smith p.126).

Did Alexander Conquer India? No.

141. In the ancient period throughout the whole of Europe, the Greek civilization was the only one which was far ahead of others. Almost all the modern nations of Europe, therefore, rever it as their source. Naturally, the name of a valiant Greek emperor of that time like Alexander is, therefore, a source of living inspiration to them. The European histories, therefore, call him "Alexander the Great", and many anecdotes and legends in the mythical manner are colourfully taught

to the young pupils through their history textbooks. But the commonly educated European people—not of course the few learned historians—are blissfully ignorant of the then Indian antagonists of Alexander and his Greek empire, Chandragupta, and his minister, Chanakya! Such perversion of history can be overlooked so far as the Europeans are concerned. But after the establishment of the British rule over India in our schools and colleges too, the same disproportionate praises were sung of Alexander in the history textbooks and other types of literature. Because three or four generations of ours have been imparted the same English education, our educated classes are also impressed by the name Alexander the Great. But they too probably never knew who Chandragupta or Chanakya was. This perversion of history, and the misunderstanding it has created in the minds of our people, should no more be tolerated hereafter. We may not mind the other traditional anecdotes about Alexander, but those, at least that are connected with Indian history and that extol Alexander disproportionately to the derogation of the Indian people, must be deleted from our school textbooks and from our literature. Take for example, the one colourfully told in the school and college books of Europe and other types of literature, and which was widely published in our country also by the English.

142. The Greeks and other European people believed that Alexander was a world conqueror and he had conquered the whole of India. When that war-like Emperor returned home after his world conquest, he is said to have burst into tears at the sad thought that no more country remained for him to be conquered. This anecdote about Alexander is, proudly told not only in Europe but even in India! Now it can be very clearly seen how very absurd and ludicrous this belief is from the short account given earlier in these pages. To the great nation of those times, China, he never turned his face. But even if we leave this fact aside, we have already shown how he was baffled and made to retreat, when he came conquering to the Western frontiers of India with the ambitious design to conquer the Empire of Magadha and the rest of India, and how his aspirations were defeated. Alexander was brave; Alexander was a conqueror. But he was not a world-conqueror! Conqueror of India he never was!! If at all that valiant hero was really moved to tears, it was impossible that his tears should have been caused by the thought that there was no other country left for conquest. For, he himself knew that

it was false. His tears then must have been caused by the sad realization that he was not able to defeat India completely, which he longed so much to conquer. On the contrary, he must have been much disturbed by the thought that even the small corner of India he believed he was able to conquer, was also very likely to be wrenched from his hands by the rebellious Indians!

142A. As it is said in the poem "Gomantak":

अन्यकुणाचा असो शिकंदर, परन्तु भारत जेता ना॥
अंगण ही ना तये देखिले कला ही नाकुणाकुणा॥

[Of whomsoever else he might be the conqueror, Alexander was never the conqueror of India! He did not even see the courtyard (of the palatial edifice) of India, and to many others, he was never known (even by name)!]

Super Alexander!

143. Great men should ordinarily be never compared with one another. They are great in various ways, but if anybody tries to compare any such and extol the one to the derogation of the other, this hoax must be exposed and refuted completely. So long as Europe eulogizes Alexander alone as 'the Great' and tries to browbeat his antagonist, Emperor Chandragupta, by evading any reference to him, we Indians must need assert that if at all they are to be compared, Chandragupta was Super Alexander in comparison with Alexander! Alexander ascended the throne of a strong nation, already won by his father and commanded an army that was also formed by King Philip. On the strength of this ancestral inheritance, he bravely built up a strong Greek empire. But Chandragupta enjoyed no such heritage. He had not a single soldier under his command, besides he had been banished from his ancestral empire by his father! Only one man was at his side, it was Arya Chanakya!! Under these circumstances, he had to start anew. Yet he built up a mighty army, conquered the ancestral empire, and wiping out the Greek conquests under Alexander himself and under his general Seleucos Nicator, founded an Indian Empire mightier even than that of Alexander himself!

144. The epoch that starts with the conquest of the Yavanas by Emperor Chandragupta, the Super Shikandar is THE FIRST GLORIOUS EPOCH of Hindu victories over the aggressors.

□

2

Yavana—Destroyer, Pushy Amitra

145. Emperor Chandragupta expired in 298 B.C. He was succeeded by his son, Bindusar, who was also brave. He took for himself the epithet 'Amitraghat' (the annihilator of enemies). Even after the death of Chandragupta, the ministership rested with Chanakya at least for sometime. Naturally, Bindusar took upon himself the task of Chanakya and Chandragupta, which was left half accomplished at the latter's death (cf: paragraphs 108 to 127). According to the plan, the Yavanas were sorely beaten, the whole of India was once again free, and there was established, as far as north India was concerned, a centrally administered unitary form of strong empire. But there avowed objective was the consolidation of the whole of India under one supreme ruler, for the sake of which, it was his duty to assimilate South India into the Mauryan empire of the north!

146. Although the several states in South India at the time belonged to our own people, they were independent in their own ways and were absolutely free from any kind of foreign domination. It was, however, necessary that they should have merged their separate existence into the north Indian empire, if the whole of India was to be one indivisible nation with a central authority to guide its destiny. To do so was their national duty.

147. Once he started on his southern campaign, Emperor Bindusar made almost all of the southern states and principalities accept his sovereignty either by peace talks, by grants of money or by threats of violence or even by sowing seeds of sedition. It is recorded in history that he annexed seventeen capitals (with their states) between the eastern and western seas to the Maurya empire. It seems that he brought the whole of the northern, southern, eastern and western India under his sole command and accomplished the ideal of the India-wide unitary empire.

Besides this, the Maurya empire of Bindusar was unique inasmuch as, even according to the standards of history, India was the mightiest in its military sense, of all the nations of the then known world.

148. It was because of the invincible four-fold armed strength built up according to the precepts of Chanakya. that from Chandragupta's accasion to the throne of Magadha to the time when Ashoka courted Buddhism and even his death, i.e. for about a hundred years, no enemy from the outside world could give any kind of offence to this all India Maurya Empire, either by land or sea, or by crossing any frontier whatsoever!

Ashoka the Holy!

149. Samrat Bindusar died in 273 B.C. this son, Ashoka ascended the throne after him by putting aside his elder brother. Emperor Ashoka truly deserved to be included in the list of virtuous and holy kings not only of India but of the world. However, according to the criterion laid down in paragraphs 7 to 9 of this book, the Ashokan epoch does not fit in properly in the scope of the glorious epochs. Hence, we cannot do anything more than bypass him with only a slight reference.

150. But after his conversion to Buddhism, Ashoka carried out an excessive propaganda in favour of certain Buddhist principles like Ahimsa and the rest, which have caused so much harm to the Indian political outlook, her political independence, and her empire, that it has become absolutely necessary to discuss at some length here as well as in other chapters, not only the principles of Ashoka but also those of Buddhism and their practices.

Hail to Lord Buddha!

151. Before discussing here some of the anti-national Buddhist preachings and practices and their effects, I consider it my duty to state in the beginning—so that there may not be any misunderstanding or perversion of my views—that on the whole, I have a very high regard for Lord Buddha and his religion. In Indian history, there are several lofty Himalayan peaks of world famous personalities and the name of one of those sublime heights is Bhagwan Buddha! As regards this reverence for him, I, too, would gladly join his disciples in bowing down my head before his idol, saying. "Hail to thee, O Lord Buddha!" The

Hindu nation too, which gave birth to such a divine, considers him the ninth incarnation of Lord Vishnu.

Causes of Decline of Buddhism in India

152. The Buddhist cult for that matter was being preached in the vicinity of Magadha, at least three hundred years before Ashoka. It was mostly propagated, till then, by persuasion and conviction on matters of principles. Naturally, its progress was slow. It has already been pointed out in paragraph no. 16 that till the time of Alexander and Seleucos, Buddhist religion was hardly known in Punjab, Sindh, Gandhar and other provinces. The Greeks knew nothing of it. Good many historians are under the impression that because Buddhism did not regard the authority of the Vedas as the highest and because on the whole, it appeared atheistic, the followers of the Vedic religion at that time opposed it very vehemently and, as such, the Buddhist religion was exterminated from India. But this belief firmly established in the minds of the people throughout the ages till the very present day, is not wholly right; for, the belief that Lord Buddha founded any non-Vedic atheistic cult is in itself wrong. Round about the time Gautam Buddha was born, there were nearly fifty or sixty creeds in vogue, and this, the Buddhist books themselves admit as true. It was customary to hold intellectual debates of the Vedic and non-Vedic philosophies. Whoever was convinced by persuasion and discussion, adopted freely the religion he liked. Although it is true that Buddhism suffered a sort of defeat in this philosophical and intellectual warfare, that went on throughout the long period from the days of the Buddha to those of Shankaracharya, the disgust and hatred the Brahmins, the Kshatriyas and the other Hindu people felt for the Buddhist sect and the corrupt practices they followed, were mainly due not to the philosophical or intellectual, but to the national and political reasons. How all this happened will be explained, so far as the scope of this book will permit.

Ashoka Enforces Buddhism

153. After courting the Buddhist cult, Ashoka became such a great zealot of his new religion towards the end of his career, that he was not satisfied with persuasive type of religious conversion so far prevalent in society. He declared penal all those Vedic religious practices, which were taboo from the point of view of the Buddhists, but which were the very

foundation of Vedic religion. For want of space, we shall cite not more than two or three instances. He banned all those sacrifices throughout his empire, which admitted of violence. Sacrifice was the main stay of the Vedic religion, round which the Bharatiya civilization had flourished ever since the Vedic period. The discontent, therefore, that must have been caused amongst the eighty per cent of the population, which comprised Brahmins, Kshatriyas and other Vedic people, when those sacrifices were declared penal offences by the government, can best be imagined. Ashoka even banned hunting. The Vedic religion considered hunting one of the essential duties of a Kshatriya. Not only was it forbidden by Ashoka to kill fish and fowl for the food of millions of people, but simply for upholding the extremist principle of the Buddhistic 'total Ahimsa', it was also declared unlawful to hunt wild beasts like lions and tigers, which very often broke upon human habitations and caused great distress by carrying away men and animals. If practised sincerely and without making any exceptions, these principles prove utterly harmful to mankind. While he was, thus, tyrannically overriding the religious practices of the Brahmin-Kshatriya and Vedic people, Ashoka went on erecting great pillars and inscribed thereon his famous edicts, enjoining on his subjects to be tolerant to all religionists, to give respect to the Shramanas (ascetics) and Brahmins alike. It is really strange that an emperor, calm, cool, composed and considerate like Ashoka, should not be able to realize the inconsistency between his precept and practice.

154. Nearly fifty years before Ashoka, Chanakya had already visualized the inevitable, horriblle effect of some of the teachings of the Buddhist cult on the national strength and the foundation of the society as a whole. As such in his famous political treatise, "Arthashastra", on which was erected the whole edifice of the Maurya empire, he had laid down certain restrictions that were essential from the national point of view on those, who thought of leaving the wordly life and become 'bhikksu'. For instance, one of the Chanakyan rules forbade a minor girl to enter the Buddha 'Sangham' without the express permission of her parents and the government. Another of his rules prohibited every man from becoming a 'bhikksu', unless and until he had provided amply for the dependants, his wife and children.

But during the reign of Ashoka and later also, these restrictions disappeared, and every man or woman, young or old, became absolutely free to renounce the worldly ways to enter the Buddhistic Sanghas.

Thousands of these 'bhikksus' in the 'Sanghas' were allowed free food, clothing, beddings and abodes as charities, at the cost of the state. Ashoka spent crores of rupees from the imperial treasury on building gigantic viharas and on the maintenance of millions of such bhikksus living in them. The major part of the revenue collection of the imperial treasury was made from the estates of the Vedic Hindus, yet it was spent on the universal propaganda of the Buddhistic sect, which antagonised them. This squandering away of their wealth for the growth of their antagonists, naturally bred great discontent among the Vedic populace.

A blow to the Imperial Might!

155. This excessive propaganda for unrestricted 'ahimsa', which Ashoka carried on by the use of his political authority throughout his empire and the countries beyond it, cut at the very root of the Indian empire, and was even more harmful than any other acts of his for the national existence and national independence! Thousands of bhikksus, appointed and maintained by Ashoka, preached everywhere that armed strength of every sort was violent and sinful, and that all those who followed the life of a Kshatriya, were violent and so irreligious! Everyone who vowed to practise 'ahimsa', everyone who renounced the use of weapons and his family life and lived the life of a 'bhikksu' in the viharas according to the Buddhistic principles was greater, holier and so more praiseworthy than the brave Kshatriya soldier, who fought and bled and died in the defence of his nation. Naturally, the common people too came to think that any and every wandering parasite of a 'bhikksu' was more respectable and religious-minded, than the brave armed warrior.

156. Ashoka had precepts, commonly preached by other religions also, inscribed on his 'pillars': "Religious victory is more valuable than the one gained by means of arms." But was this religious victory possible in the earthly life? Was it practical? A draught of nectar is said to make a man immortal, maybe! But can anybody tell the whereabouts of the shop where that nectar is available?

156A. Whoever can satisfy his hunger by eating the rice and curry made of words?

बोलाचीच कढी बोलाचाचभात। जेवूनिया तृप्त कोण झाला॥

157. Was not the empire of Ashoka with the unlimited resources, power and wealth, with which he could carry out, throughout the whole of India and abroad, a vigorous propaganda 'that religious victory was

superior to victory on the battlefield', itself gained on the strength of the mighty and invincible four-fold army built up by Chandragupta and Chanakya? Had all that army forsworn arms and lived the idle parasitic life of the 'bhikksu' in the 'Viharas' embracing Buddhism, as soon as Ashoka ascended his ancestral throne, would it have been possible for him to sit there securely as an emperor even for a moment? Even at that time, the Greek states beyond the Indian border and farther off than these the more ferocious wild tribes of the Saka-Kushan-Hun type, who recognized 'violence' as the only mean of achieving their objectives were anxiously waiting for an opportunity to pounce, like a lion, on India, but they feared the four-fold invincible Indian army. Would they all not have taken this golden opportunity to throttle the 'bhikksu-ridden' India and Ashoka's religious triumph without the use of arms, and drawn its blood?

158. But it is hardly necessary to indulge in these 'ifs' and 'whens'. At that very time, India had unfortunately to suffer the grievous consequences of the preaching, not only of Ashoka but of the Buddha himself, as has been shown in my play, 'Sanyasta Khadga'. The miserable plight of the people and the successful resistance, which the Vedic Hindus offered, will be described hereafter.

159. While describing these sad consequences, I do not, at all, intend to analyse the comparative merits and demerits of all religious principles, practices or rituals of both the Vedic and the Buddhist religions like the sacrifices, penances, sanyas and the like, from the 'other worldly' point of view, nor do I wish to examine them thoroughly and comparatively from 'this worldly' outlook. To see how many of those principles are trustworthy today, or how many of those rituals are worth following at the present time, is also out of the scope of this book. So these points will not be raised. I, however, wish to discuss in this book, the nation-wide consequence of different religious principles and actions of their followers on political life of India of those days. For without any such historical analysis, the different currents and undercurrents of history of those times cannot be properly shown.

After the Death of Ashoka

160. This pious emperor, Ashoka, who till his end, laboured hard according to his own religious faith, for the ultimate good of mankind, died in 232 B.C.

161. His death proved to be the beginning of the end of that magnificent Maurya Empire!

162. During the last 25 years of his life, he had applied himself heart and soul to the propagation of the Buddhistic cult. His descendants, who succeeded him as emperors, were all honest Buddhists, and that is why, they turned out to be nominal rulers, weak in armed strength. Because of the criminal neglect of the imperial military might for these forty years or so by the 'extremists' among the followers of the Buddhist principle of 'non-violence' and their rulers, the whole military organization of the Maurya empire right up to the frontiers, and espeicially the north-western frontier, gradually went into complete disorder. This was allurement enough for the foreign foes, who had been so far kept off through the awe of the Maurya empire, to venture a fresh aggression on India hardly within thirty years or so of Ashoka's death.

The Aggression of Bactrian Greeks

163. Samrat Chandragupta had defeated Seleucos Nicator and driven away the Greeks far beyond the Hindukush mountains round about 315 B.C. (of. paragraphs 130 to 140). Seleucos had established his independent Greek kingdom in Bactria adjoining the western side of the Hindukush mountains, which was then the extreme frontier of India. As it was independent, it had lost every contact with the original distant European Greek state. If, at all, there existed any contact between the two, it was that of dire enmity. These Bactrian Greeks, therefore, were called Asian Greeks. Because of the break in the continuity during the intervening hundred years or so, these Bactrian Greeks had fallen off miserably in every respect from the high standards of the original Greeks of Alexander's time. They had now nothing of the spirit and vigour of their Alexandrian ancestors. Alexandrian ambition of conquering India, however, still goaded them on. As soon as they saw the degeneration of the military strength of the Maurya empire, these Bactrian Greeks were fired with the malicious ambition of Indian conquest, as has already been told above, and Demetreos, their king at that time, crossed the Hindukush and attacked India. As the Indian army offered no resistance worth the name, Demetreos reduced Kamboj, Gandhar and crossed the Indus, and conquering the whole of Panchnad, that Yavanadhip (the Greek King) proceeded with his army to conquer Magadha itself. The

whole of the Greek army was inspired with the warlike spirit and they began to declare that they were going to realize the dream of Indian conquest of Alexander.

Why this Sudden Degeneration of Indian Bravery?

164. How very strange it is that hardly before a hundred years or so, the provinces like Panchnad (Punjab) and others from the Hindukush to the Indus in which the brave Indian Kshatriyas, their republics, and soldiers and the common populace had all defeated and repulsed, with exceptional valour the aggressive Greeks under Alexander and Seleucos and drove them back, should now be overrun so very easily by the much too weaker and degenerated Bactrian Greeks! Owing to the constant dread of the brave fighting warriors of India, Alexander and Seleucos could not sleep soundly in their military camps, while fighting in these provinces. But these second-rate Bactrian Greek military leaders could sleep soundly in the royal palace of Ayodhya (Saketa) in the confident safety of their triumph.

165. This Greek invasion of Demetreos took place within thirty to forty years of Ashoka's adoption of Buddhism. How did the Indian resisting capacity and bravery in the valiant provinces of Gandhar, Panchnad and others deteriorate so suddenly during those intervening years? What particular event in those thirty to forty years necessitated this degeneracy in the high standard of Indian heroism?

166. Was the Bactrian Greek invading army, under the leadership of Demetreos, in any way superior to those of Alexander and Seleucos? Not at all. They themeselves admitted that their forefathers, under the leadership of Alexander and Seleucos were far superior to them, were endowed with almost divine powers. It clearly means that the reason, why these inferior and weaker Greeks should conquer the Indians so very easily, was not that the Greek prowess had increased since the time of Alexander, but that the Indian heroism and the Indian capacity to resist aggression must have deteriorated to a horrible extent.

167. Now, during the hundred-and-twenty-seven years or so that elapsed between the Alexandrian aggression in 327 B.C. and the one by Demetreos about 200 B.C., there occurred only one significant event, which was likely to bring about this grievous falling off in the high standard of Indian material prowess and their ability to repulse the enemy. It must have been the extremist propaganda of the non-

resistant, non-violent principles of Buddhism, which condemned the military might throughout these provinces. For, no other event of such magnitude took place at that time. We shall just consider here two points that throw some light on this issue.

Indian Mentality at the time of Alexander's invasion and that at the time of Demetreos!

168. At the time of Alexander, the Buddhist cult was never heard of in the provinces of Kamboj, Gandhar, Panchnad straight to Sind (cf. para: 16). The people there were hero worshippers of Vedic Hindus! States like the Youdheyas were proud of their war-like spirit and bore the attribute 'Nation-in-arms' (आयुधजीवी) with evident exultation! (cf: para 38). Not only the Kshatriyas there, but in some of the states, all the citizens, men and women, young or old, took the field to face the aggressive foreign enemy. Where, unfortunately, a certain republic got beaten, the brave Indian ladies there leapt into the fire with the dauntless children (cf: paras 40 to 55) at their breasts! One more thing can be adduced in support of the martial spirit of the Vedic Indians of the time of Chandragupta-Chanakya, who were ever prepared to protect the national boundaries.

169. It is interesting to note how martial prowess has been extolled in glowing terms in the famous treatise, 'Arthshastra' of Chanakya, which mainly guided the administration of the magnificent Indian empire of Chandragupta. According to Chanakya's treatise, all the varnas including the Brahmins, had free access to the military service.

अमर्याद प्रवृत्तेच शत्रुभिस्संगरे कृते।
सर्वेवर्णाश्च दृश्येयुः शस्त्रवन्तो युधिष्ठिर॥

(In the event of an extensive war with the enemy, O Yudhisthir, all the classes of people should be seen well-armed with weapons.)

This was the tradition of the Vedic Hindus! When such a large imperial army entered the battlefield in order to face the enemy, the emperor, dictates Chanakya, himself was to address the whole four-fold army in the following way:

''वेदेष्वप्यनुश्रूयते समाप्तदक्षिणाम यज्ञानामवभृतस्त्रानेषु या ता गतिः
शूराणामिति। क्षपेन तामाप्यतियान्ति शूराः प्रणान् युयुध्येषु परित्यजन्ति।
तुल्यभोगोस्मि भवद्भिः सहभेग्यमिंद राज्यम्। परान् हन्तव्यम्।''

(The brave warriors enjoy the same bliss as the one which is obtainable through the final ceremonial bath after the completion of sacrifices—it is vouchsafed by the Vedas! In the righteous war, the warriors sacrificing their lives go instantly to the same blissful state (in heaven). This kingdom is to be enjoyed by you as well as it is by me. Then, why wait. Fall upon the enemy, and annihilate them!)

171. Who can tell, even Chandragupta himself might have thus inspired his Indian fighting forces, when they marched upon Seleucos!

172. The war, which beats down unjustifiable aggression, protects the virtuous people and destroys the wicked ones, is never considered 'violent' by the Vedic religion. It is called a religious war (a righteous war!).

173. At the time of Alexander, the Vedic propagandists had been going round, kindling the fire of heroism and bravado in order to fight such a righteous war of liberation against the Yavan (Greek) enemy throughout that region, from Panchnad to Sindh. Many of such national propagandists, mostly Brahmins, were being caught and hanged by Alexander! (cf: paras 32 and 69 for Plutarch's citation).

174. After the valiant soldiers of Chandragupta, thus, routed the forces of the Yavan emperor, Seleucos, Chandragupta and Chanakya built a strong steel wall of the mightiest four-fold army in the world to protect the Indian empire right up to the Hindukush mountain. The dread of that armed might alone stopped the Bactrian Greeks beyond the Hindukush, from harbouring any thought of enmity towards India for about 125 years. So long as Samrat Ashoka called himself the follower of the Vedic religon, which means till about 252 B.C., the north-western frontier guards of the Mauryan empire remained well-equipped and invincible.

175. But as soon as Ashoka adopted Buddhism, this security of the empire fell to pieces! Had Ashoka abdicated from the imperial throne of Magadha, when he adopted Buddhism as Lord Gautam Buddha himself forsook the Sakya nation before him, and had he travelled around as a bhikksu propagating the faith, the Indian empire might have been spared a great calamity and Ashoka's loyalty to Buddhism, too, would have been truly tested. But till his death, Ashoka could not bring himself to abdicate this imperial throne. On the contrary, he turned his whole empire into a Buddhistic monastery to carry on the propaganda. Evidently enough in those frontier provinces, the dictums like 'Religious victory excels martial glory', 'Anger should be conquered by the negation of anger', "Non-violence is the supreme religious duty', 'Never kill any

animal' and such others, which had their roots in the Vedic religion, and which were beneficial to the society so long as they were practised with due regard to place, time and person, began to be preached in the Buddhist way, irrespective of any such consideration and in absolute terms without any reservations, bands of 'bhikksus' brought up and maintained by the imperial treasury of Ashoka began to preach in that region that armed might was a sin! Only the followers of Buddhism were appointed to high offices of Dharmamhamatra' (धर्म महामात्र), provincial officers, and the faithful government servants like the Rajjuks. All these were expected, according to the orders from Ashoka, to render every sort of help at government level to the precept and practice of the Buddhistic cult. Throughout the provinces like Gandhar and Panchnad, Buddhism was preached not only amongst civilians but also amongst the soldiers. Naturally, in those frontier provinces of India, the warlike spirit and armed strength began to decrease as speedily as the untrammelled propaganda about non-violence and other Buddhistic principles gained momentum everywhere with the avowed royal support. After carrying on such demilitarizing and anti-national propaganda for twenty years, Ashoka breathed his last. His successors, the Buddhist weaklings, surpassed Ashoka in the neglect of the invincible frontier guards, which had been so scrupulously and assiduously maintained in well-equipped military outposts since the time of Chandragupta. This was ignored to such an extent that the whole defence-line collapsed as would a whole turret, the base of which has sunk underground.

In Short

176. Because Ashoka and his descendants with their imperial support carried throughout their empire, the incessant propaganda of the one-sided extremist Buddhist principles, which derided martial prowess, and criminally neglected the intrepidity and valour which fought for national independence, and because they transformed the whole empire into a gigantic Buddhistic monastery, and converted the fighting warriors into saffron-clad Buddha bhikksu, the heroic spirit among the people of the frontier provinces and their staunch patriotism suffered a horrible debasement, and the military organization that had been the strongest in the world since the time of Chandragupta wore out completely because of this internal virus. And that is the reason why Demetreos' Greek forces, far inferior to those of Alexander and Seleucos, could so easily reduce the

whole region from the Hindukush to Panchnad and could march proudly towards Magadha.

177. With all the imperial authority and resources at the disposal of these Buddhists, none of the provincial governors, nor any administrator, nor even the Buddhist population, got excited and boldly came forward to fight in the battlefield these Yavan foes, who dared snatch away the independence of India and subjugate it. They were not enraged at this insult of India, nor were they ashamed of it. The very descendant of Ashoka in Magadha, who called himself emperor and was warming the imperial throne, the Buddhist King Brihadrath, never took a step to resist the advance of the Greek enemy!

178. Perhaps that Buddhist King was trying to win over the Greeks by his unrestrained observance of the Buddhistic principle of 'non-resistance' and the one that preached, "Anger should be conquered by the negation of anger" and was trying to succeed in the application of the Buddhistic doctrine by keeping indoors!

Wave of Nationwide rage among the vedic hindus: the Valiant Kharvela, the king of Kalinga, Marches on the Greeks

179. Although the Buddhists were neither enraged nor disturbed, nor for that matter, even ashamed of the fact that the Greek aggression was undermining the national honour of India or that it endangered the nation's liberty, the Vedic Hindus, at least, were highly enraged at this national insult and the imminent national calamity. Unfortunately, they had no political power left in the north of India, which could immediately resist this national calamity. But within a decade of Ashoka's death, the provinces of Kalinga and Andhra in south India had renounced the paramountcy of the Buddhist Mauryas, and established their independent kingdom. The kings of both these provinces were staunch followers of the Vedic religion and so equally staunch Indian patriots. Both of them had built up mighty armies, well-equipped with arms. The news that the Greeks had conquered northern India, and that the Magadha king, a weak Buddhist, could not at all resist it, caused a great furore amongst the Vedic population in South India. At last, the king of the independent state of Kalinga, the valiant Kharvela, decided to march himself at the head of an army against the Greek army of Demetreos.

The Yavanas Routed: their Hasty Retreat!

180. First of all, with a mighty army, he conquered Magadha and joined battle with the Greek forces somewhere near Ayodhya. The strong Indian army of Kalinga dealt such a crushing defeat upon the Greeks, that Demetreos immediately turned his face backwards, and marched off with all his army back to his home beyond Panchnad.

181. After driving the Greeks beyond the frontiers of India, Kharvela did not find much time either to pursue the fleeing enemy or to organize the administration of the whole of that region. Political emergency drove him back to Kalinga almost immediately. He did not dethrone the Maurya emperor of Magadha, King Brihadrath. As soon as he returned to Kalinga, Kharvela celebrated, according to the Vedic tradition, the horse ceremony to commemorate the brilliant victory he had gained against the Greeks in defence of the honour and liberty of India. This horse-sacrifice was particularly known to have a national and political significance. Besides owing to Ashoka's ban, the Vedic Hindus had not been able to perform any sacrifice whatsoever for the last forty or fifty years. But soon after the Vedic states were established in Kalinga and Andhra, this horse-sacrifice, the first of its kind, was celebrated in total defiance of all the injunctions of Ashoka on the Vedic religious practices, immortalising the crushing defeat inflicted on the Greeks, the national enemies of India.

Another Greek Invasion

182. Seeing that Kharvela had returned to the south, Menander, who had so far stabilized his position in Kamboj and Gandhar, and who was furious at the disaster met with by Demetreos on his march against Magadha, once again invaded India within a period of four years. As at the time of the invasion of Demetreos, so also at this time, the Greeks did not meet with any opposition worth the name in Panchnad, which was dominated by the Buddhists and, as such, had become pacifist, the weak descendant of Ashoka on the throne of Magadha, too, offered no effective resistance.

The Buddhists Sympathize with the Greeks

183. On the contrary, Menander could enlist the sympathy of many of the Buddhists in his campaign. For, he openly said that he approved of many of the Buddhist principles and that he was soon

going to become a convert to it. So, many Buddhist preachers began to publicise that the Greeks had come to fight with the Vedic Hindus alone, and that if they conquered India, there would be a Buddhist rule! The Buddhists were not much concerned with the alien nationality or the Greeks. Buddhism did not recognize the differences of caste, race or nationality! This was the anti-national and anti-Indian wicked way in which the Buddhist preachers began to delude the people of India! As their sympathetic assistance was so useful to Menander, he too began to circulate through his Greek agents, that this campaign of his was directed solely to nip in the bud the conspiracy of the Vedic Hindus to snatch away the imperial power from the hands of the weak Buddhist rulers of Magadha. Menander came once again, reducing Panchnad and other provinces right up to Ayodhya. In order to avoid the repetition of the sad plight of Demetreos, who had made undue haste at an inopportune time, Menander spent some time in Ayodhya, consolidating the newly won territories and replenishing his army before he launched an attack on Magadha and waited for the auspicious moment.

But there in Pataliputra...?

184. The Vedic community and their leaders in North India had already experienced a surge of heroic spirit because of the victory of the brave Kharvela of Kalinga. To add to it, the news arrived of Menander's menacing invasion! Besides, the Indian Buddhist populace showed clear signs of defection and betrayal of their co-nationalists to Menander. The nationalist Indian leaders, therefore, formed a revolutionary body with a view to dethroning the vacillating and weak Brihadrath Maurya from the royal seat of Magadha, and replace him with one of the Vedic sect, who was of proven mettle like Chandragupta Maurya. But everybody was confronted with the difficult question, as to who was there so bold and powerful, to take the lead in this national revolution and to destroy the Yavanas (the Greeks) completely.

Pushyamitra

185. Amongst the remnants of the Magadhan warriors in the army of the above-named Brihadrath Maurya was one, named Pushyamitra. He was a Brahimin by birth. He was, moreover, a staunch supporter of the Vedic religion and Indian nationality, and a devotee of Lord Shiv. His

family name was Shung. Even in the Magadhan army, he had attained so much importance because of his military exploits that Brihadrath Maurya himself had appointed him, not very willingly but only out of necessity, to the office of the Commander-in-Chief of the forces in the face of the deadly war with the invading Greeks. The moment he got the reins of the highest military authority, Pushyamitra began to enlarge and reorganize the army of Magadha, and equipped it with all the weapons. This focussed the attention of all the patriotic Vedic populace on Pushyamitra, the general of the army. Everybody anxiously hoped, if General Pushyamitra should lead the political coup...? Who else, they thought, was at that time fitter and abler than this valiant hero, to ascend the traditional imperial throne of the Indian empire?

186. From the historically established facts of this Magadhan political revolution, which are going to be related very shortly, it will be amply clear that General Pushyamitra must have accepted the leadership of the future conspiracy. It is very likely that he must have secured, in advance, at least tacit consent of his army and some of its leaders before he acted openly.

Assassination of Brihadrath Maurya

187. While all these preparations were going on, one day it was decided to hold a grand military review in the vast courtyard of the royal palace in the capital city of Pataliputra. Emperor Brihadrath Maurya was present there to witness the march-past and receive the salute of the army. But while as per Pushyamitra's orders, the ceremonial movements of the four-fold army and their different formations were going on with all pomp and show and noise and bustle, for some reason, not known to history, some trouble arose near the place where King Brihadrath was sitting. In the excitement of the moment, General Pushyamitra marched on Brihadrath Maurya, who had come to be merely the titular head of the empire, and beheaded him.

188. This chopping-off of the head of Brihadrath put a stop to the dynasty of the Mauryas! The Buddhistic Mauryan Empire met its doom that day.

189. This unexpected and horrible turn of events caused a great furore in the large crowd assembled there. But did any of the armed warriors or anyone from those of the royal household, who were sitting near King Brihadrath attack General Pushyamitra? No, not at all. On

the contrary, the whole army hailed him as their leader.

190. For, General Pushyamitra had done exactly what the soldiers themselves and many others wanted to do but could not, as nobody in the whole of India dared shoulder the responsibility for such an hazardous deed. Pushyamitra had simply done the unavoidable national duty of killing Ashoka's descendant, Brihadrath Maurya, who had proved himself thoroughly incompetent to defend the independence of the Indian empire.

Pushyamitra and Chandragupta

191. Chandragupta and Chanakya had to assassinate, as an unavoidable national duty, Samrat Mahapadmananda, who had proved himself thoroughly incapable of repulsing the Greeks for the protection of the Indian empire and its independence, at the time of the first Greek invasion of Alexander. Just for the same reason, Pushyamitra had to cut off the head of Brihadrath Maurya, the nominal Buddhist emperor, simply as a national duty.

Emperor Pushyamitra Shung

192. This momentous event took place round about 184 B.C., and with all the Vedic rituals, Pushyamitra was appointed Emperor of India on the throne of Ashoka in Pataliputra. It marked the end of the Maurya dynasty and the beginning of the reign of the Shungas.

Emperor Pushyamitra's Campaign Against the Greeks!

193. First of all, Pushyamitra stabilized the administrative set-up and consolidated his position in his capital and the regions around it, and after mobilizing a strong four-fold army, eager to fight, he fell upon Menander, who had so far dug in his feet safe in Ayodhya. Finding it extremely difficult to hold their ground before the mighty arms of the Indian army, the Greek general Menander began to retreat. Earlier, Demetreos had not been pursued, but this time, Pushyamitra was not going to be slack. He chased and hunted down the Greek army. Inflicting defeat after defeat on the Greek army and causing confusion in their ranks, Pushyamitra drove the dispirited and vanquished Menander far beyond the Indus. The Indian empire right up to the Indus was once again set free from the Greek political dominance.

The Greek sword was broken, the Greek shield shattered, the very root of their Political power dug up and Destroyed!

194. This was the last of the Greek aggressions on India. This terrible defeat inflicted on the Greeks by Pushyamitra consumed their strength so much, that they never had the heart to strike again at Bharat any time in future! Bharat, thus, annihilated this Greek enemy that had been a source of constant trouble since the time of Alexander.

195. Pushyamitra annexed all the territory liberated from the Greek hands to his own empire. He appointed at Ujjain his son, Agnimitra, as the viceroy of the region. General Agnimitra was a brave and able commander like his father. He forced the land up to Vidarbha in the South, to acknowledge his overlordship. But later Vidarbha refused to do so. Hence, Agnimitra attacked it. In the battle, Vidarbadhish (the lord of Vidarbha) was defeated. Amidst all this confusion, Princess Malavika, the daughter of the Vidarbharaj, was enamoured of the bravery and other virtues of Agnimitra, and was very eager to marry him. So with the consent of Pushyamitra, the King of Vidarbha celebrated her marriage with Agnimitra. This not only created the bonds of friendship but also the bonds of blood-relation between the two royal families. On this romantic theme itself, Kalidas composed his famous play *Malavikagnimitra*.

A Horse-Sacrifice in the very Pataliputra of Ashoka!

196. Pushyamitra, who had completely destroyed the Greeks, the age-old alien enemies of the nation, and rejuvenated the Indian empire, had acquired with his own splendid victories, the right to perform a horse-sacrifice according to the Vedic tradition. About this right of Samrat Pushyamitra, Vincent Smith writes in his *Early History of India* (1924), "The Yavanas and all other rivals having been disposed of in due course, Pushyamitra was justified in his claim to reign as the paramount power of north India, and straightaway proceeded to announce his success by a magnificent celebration of the Ashvamedha sacrifice at his capital (p. 212)."

197. This declaration of celebrating a horse-sacrifice by Samrat Pushyamitra thrilled the whole country, barring the minority community of the Buddhist with national pride and martial triumph. In the very capital of Ashoka, who had deprived the Vedic Hindus of their religious freedom by means of his supreme political authority, was

this Ashvamedha of Samrat Pushyamitra to be performed. This horse-sacrifice of Pushyamitra was, in fact, a public imperial proclamation of Samrat Pushyamitra, that all the restrictions imposed by Ashoka on the religious freedom of the Vedic Hindus were withdrawn.

198. Emperor Pushyamitra's grandson, Vasumitra, was also a spirited young prince, as his father, Pushyamitra's son, Agnimitra was a veteran army-leader and an efficient royal administrator. When Samrat Pushyamitra let his sacrificial horse loose on its triumphal march throughout the land, the task of protecting that horse with a strong army was entrusted to this brave young grandson, General Vasumitra. The horse was not obstructed in his free ramble right up to the banks of the Indus. But on the banks of the Indus, he was opposed by a certain Yavan King which, according to the conventions of the time, meant that the sovereignty of Pushyamitra was challenged. So the young General Vasumitra fought with the 'Yavan' enemy and after defeating him completely, got released the ceremonial horse. The boundless joy that was universally felt in the capital, when after a year the invincible and unconquered General Vasumitra tiumphantly marched into the city, can very well be seen in the formal invitation sent by Pushyamitra to his son, Agnimitra, which is still available to us in almost the very same words of the Emperor. Kalidas has practically reproduced it verbatim et literatim in his aforesaid play, *'Malavikagnimitra.'* That letter in the drama is so interesting, that everybody might read it with pleasure. It is a living document of the thoughts of Samrat Pushyamitra and the common feelings of the people of those triumphant days.

A National Festival

199. The festive occassion of the horse-ceremony was graced with the presence of the great sages and ascetics of India, Brahmins, well-versed in all the Vedic lore, the high-born Kshatriya kings and princes, the prominent officers and administrators of the empire, eminent citizens and leaders in towns. Patanjali, who was renowned as the greatest of the scholars, and who has now come to be listed with universal approval, among the world's greatest scholars—including the western ones—was also present on that glorious occasion. With the blessings and participation of such celebrities the festival of that horse-sacrifice naturally came to acquire the dignity and grandeur of the Indian national victory over the Mlenchchas.

Totally Annihilated Asian Greek Stock

200. After the Greeks were driven away beyond the Indus by Samrat Pushyamitra round about 190 to 180 B.C. and India was rid of all Greek dominance, the Greek race saw the beginning of their extinction. Beyond the Indus in Gandhar and Bactria (Balhik), they had some small states dragging on their uncertain existence. And about the beginning of the first century of the Christian era, when a great tide of the fierce war-like race of the Sakas from Central Asia dashed against Bactria, Persia and Gandhar, the Greeks knew not where to flee in order to escape the terrible impact of 'Sakas' sharp swords. They fled with wives and children, the old and the infant. At last, they crossed the Indus and entered India to save their lives. But now they came as displaced persons seeking shelter! What a tragic irony! This influx of theirs was a far cry from the triumphant entry of their forefathers under Alexander and Seleucos! The latter rushed in crying hoarse for war, while the present Greeks came in begging for shelter!!

201. But India gave them shelter very graciously in those most unfortunate days, forgetting all enmity. These runaway Greeks settled severally, wherever and whenever their separate batches could find any shelter. Some of them became converts to Buddhism while some courted Hinduism. But as Vedic Hindus alone had their states everywhere in India, these Greeks, whether they were Buddhists or Vedic Hindus, were not able to cause any sort of political trouble. They adopted the Indian languages, Indian customs and swiftly, they were merged completely in the Indian society. And because they had marital and other social relations with the Indians, within a century or two, they completely lost the sense of their separate existence as Greeks—the sense of their separate nationality! Just as a lump of salt dissolves swiftly into the torrential current of the Ganges, in the same way, their Greek extraction was totally merged into the tidal wave of Indian life.

The Mlenchchas Merged into our Civilization

202. Most of the western historians, and our own too, have completely missed one point in this connection, which, for that very reason, must be made explicit here. It is this, whether it was the Greeks or other foreign aggressors, whoever came flashing their swords, were ultimately conquered and engulfed, and completely submerged in our society, leaving not a trace of their separate existence behind. In every

case, it has been amply proved that it was only when the aggressor's insolent sword was beaten down—it was only when the aggressor was vanquished completely in the deadly armed conflict on the battlefield—that those foreigners became so very tame and pliable as to be easily overwhelmed and dissolved in our society. This was achieved not by peaceful persuasion, but by the stronger and deadlier weapons.

No Religious Persecution—
but the most Appropriate Punishment for Treason!

203. Some of the old Buddhist books, in the loquacious style of the Puranas, enlarge upon the cruel treatment meted out by Pushyamitra to Buddhist bhikksus, upon the outright massacre of some of them, and the destruction of some of the Buddhist monasteries. Even the European historians have set aside all these references as exaggerated ones! Still, some of them have stated, that there should be some grain of truth at the root of these exaggerated accounts that Pushyamitra might have been guilty of some slight persecution of the Buddhists by way of revenge. We also feel that Samrat Pushyamitra might have taken good many of the Buddhists to task, but not for any philosophical or theological difference of opinion.

204. The Buddhists were not persecuted as a class simply because they believed in nihilism or agnosticism, or because some of them were atheists while others were non-violent on principle and condemned the Vedas, or because their religious rituals were in many ways different from those of the Vedic Hindus. Lord Buddha himself experienced no obstacle in the propagation of his faith! Let that alone! The Buddhist faith had been more or less three hundred years old by the time of Chandragupta's succession to the throne! In his undivided all-India Hindu empire and also during the tenure of the ministerial office of the staunch Arya Chanakya, no Buddhist persecution of any sort was reported by the Greek ambassador, Megasthenes, who had stayed at the court of the first Maurya Emperor for years together. Megasthenes does not refer to Buddhism even by name, for they had not till then formed any anti-national and political alliances detrimental to the interests of the nation, either with Alexander or with Seleucos. It was not then possible for them! That is why, along with many other religionists, the Buddhists also could observe their own rituals according to their own beliefs and likings. Besides, they could openly preach by sweet persuasion and discussion.

205. Subsequent to the invasions of Alexander and Seleucos, when the Greeks came raiding for the second time under Demetreos and Menander, and when advancing as far as Ayodhya, they were about to dethrone the reigning king of Magadha and endanger the independence of the Indian empire, the Indian Buddhists played a brazen-faced treacherous role, as is seen from the fact that these Buddhists swore their loyalty to the Greek Emperor, Menander, whom they called Milind. When the latter adopted the Buddhist cult, they accepted him as the King of the region conquered by him. The Buddhist scholars and 'bhikksus' proudly struted in the Indian courts of those Greeks, as if they were moving in some national court. In order to put down as sternly as possible these highly objectionable treacherous acts of these Indian Buddhists, the plots hatched to undermine the national independence, and the open instigation to do anti-national acts, which went on incessantly through various Buddhist monasteries and viharas, Pushyamitra and his generals were forced, by the exigency of time when the war was actually going on, to hang Indian Buddhists, who were guilty of seditious acts and to pull down the monasteries, that had become the centres of sedition. It was a just punishment for high treason and for joining hands with the enemy, in order that Indian independence and empire might be protected. It was no religious persecution. As the supreme authority in the imperial administrative structure of India, it was Pushyamitra's duty—a religious and kindly duty, according national legal code—to chastise perfidy, whether it was on part of the Buddhists or on that of the Vedic Hindus!

Ashoka and Pushyamitra

206. In traditional historical writings, mainly based on Buddhist myths, Ashoka has been extolled as tolerant of different religious sects, while Pushyamitra wholly conniving at his efforts to establish religious freedom, is generally imputed with intolerence and persecution of the Budhists. This false notion has to be corrected. If any body is at all guilty of religious intolerance, it was Ashoka himself. For not only with verbal propaganda but with the abuse of his regal authority, he declared illegal all the fundamental religious rituals, such as sacrifice and hunting by the Vedic Hindus, who formed the majority of his subjects. But Pushyamitra did not issue any royal decree enforcing any performances of sacrifices in the Buddha Viharas or the worship of Vaishvadeva in every Buddh

household, even as a fitting retort to Ashoka's junctions. The Buddhists were as absolutely free as all other religious sects, to perform their religious rites and enjoy religious freedom, so long as they abstained from any anti-national foreign contact. It is likely that in the troubled times of national war, the chastisement of the disloyal Buddhists might have affected some of the innocent ones. But it was not a rule—but an inevitable exception!

207. What Pushyamitra really did was to reinstate the religious freedom, which was annulled by Ashoka. If anybody is to be called intolerant of religious difference, it should be Ashoka and not Pushyamitra.

208. In this context, the words of Vincent Smith, who shows no particular partiality for the Vedic Hindus, and yet writes judiciously, are worth remembering.

209. However, Vincent Smith, too, like other historians, has not realized that the main reason of the general animosity that the Vedic Hindus feel towards the Buddhists, and the persecutions that the latter suffered at their hands from time-to-time, culminating in the total annihilation of Buddhism in India, is that the Buddhists, often times betrayed the cause of Indian independence and Indian empire. In spite of the fact that Vincent Smith never realized this main reason of the downfall of Buddhism, he has held the Buddhists responsible for the religious persecution mentioned in various Buddhist writings. An extract from his *Early History of India* (1924) (P. 213-14) will bear out the above remarks:

209A. "The memorable horse-sacrifice of Pushyamitra marked the beginning of Brahmanical (Vedic?) reaction which was fully developed by centuries later in the time of Samudragupta and his successors... if credit may be given to semi-mythological stories of Buddhist writers, Pushyamitra was not content with the peaceful revival of Hindu rites, but indulged in a savage persecution of Buddhism.... it will be rash to reject this tale as wholly baseless, although it may be exaggerated.... That such outbursts after all should have occurred is not wonderful, *if you consider the extreme oppressiveness of the Jain and Buddhist prohibition, when ruthlessly enforced, as they certainly were by some Rajas and probably by Ashoka. The wonder rather is that the persecutions were so rare,* and that as a rule, the various sects managed to live together in harmony and in the enjoyment of fairly impartial official favour."

210. Pushyamitra who, with his armed might, completely exterminated the Greek intrusion, which from the time of Alexander had often caused great harm to India, and who, therefore, rightly deserves the title, 'Yavan-destroyer', protected ably for 36 years not only the independence of India, which he himself had won, but brought about the many sided development of his country, and then died peacefully in 149 B.C.

211. In the sense in which Chandragupta's rout of the Greek pockets of influence in India is said to be the first glorious epoch of Hindu victories over aggressors, this total extinction of the greeks in India at the hands of Yavan-destroyer PUSHYAMITRA becomes necessarily, THE SECOND GLORIOUS EPOCH of Indian History.

□

3

Vikramaditya, the Annihilator of Saka-Kushan Menace

212. After the total destruction of the Greeks, India saw another foreign aggression, which has to be reckoned with in the Indian history rather conspicuously, and which was in some respects more ominous and extensive than those of the armies of Alexander or other Greek generals. I mean the incursions of the Sakas and Kushans.

213. Although the Sakas and the Kushans in some respects differed very widely and although they fought each other very furiously, from the Indian point of view, they had such a striking similarity that they appeared almost identical. Hence their hordes, which dashed against India, like tidal waves, one after another, were generally called Sakas by the common Indian people. At some places in the Indian literature, they are referred to as 'Kushs'. For this very reason, in this book too, both of them are mentioned as Sakas.

214. The Sakas lived in Central Asia beyond Bactria (Balhik) in large wild gangs. The region beyond them was occupied by tribes, equally wild and ferocious. Even beyond this region right in China, there were still wilder, more ferocious, but braver nomadic tribes of the millions of Huns (Hsiung Nus), which were always at war with one another. These Sakas, Kushans and Huns entertained bitter enmity towards one another and were constantly at war.

215. About a hundred-and-fifty years before Christ, tribal feuds amongst these nomadic tribes flared up in such terrible manner as were never heard of before. One of these tribes, the Huns or Hsiung Nus of China, who were the most pertinacious desperados of all, fell with all their ferocity and might upon the neighbouring tribe of the Kushans, driving them off completely out of their homeland towards the west. So the Kushans in their turn, fell in repeated violent tidal waves upon their next

neighbours, the Sakas, who were then happily ensconced to the north of Bactria (Balhik), and after exterminating the latter from their abode, they founded there their own kingdom, instead. The Sakas faithfully forwarded that kick to the adjoining Bactrians, whom they attacked instantly. In Bactria (Balhik) were at this time, small Greek states, maintaining their precarious existence since the time of Alexander. But against the repeated attacks of these wild tribes in which the women too, on horseback, fought shoulder-to-shoulder with men, these Bactrian Greeks were absolutely unable to hold on any longer and were, therefore, completely destroyed, their land being overrun and occupied entirely by the Sakas. But even there and within a short span of a hundred years or so, came in hot pursuit their inveterate enemies, the Kushans, whose lives were spent, as those of the Sakas, more on campaigning on horses and in fully armed military camps, than in stabilized and prosperous cities. The Huns again attacked the Saka-Kushan and ousting them even from Bactria and other countries, established their own rule there. The exterminated Saka-Kushan, being blocked from behind and from the sides, had to descend into the region of Baluchistan, and along the route through the Bolan Pass they dashed avalanche-like on the Indian territories of Sindh, Kathiawad and Gujarat. They trampled under their horses' hoofs adjoining Indian territory, rushing violently, plundering and burning towns and cities, sparing neither women nor children. History, unfortunately, does not know for certain what Indian states existed there at that time, or whether or not, they could arrest this irrepressible aggression of these MIenchchas. However, it is not necessary to discuss the problem here as it does not fall within the scope of this book, which has been outlined in Paragraph 7. It is enough to state here that round about the beginning of the Christian era, these Sakas had occupied the Indian territory of Baluchistan, Sindh, Kathiawad, Gujarat and some parts of Aparantak (Konkan) to the south, right upto Ujjayini. And the whole of India was extremely uneasy at the gruesome prospect of the possible incursions of the Kushans and Huns, who were to follow the Sakas!

South India was absolutely free from the Mlenchcha Aggression

216. Foreign aggressions, at least in the ancient period of our history, being launched through the north-western frontiers, it was mostly our north Indian brethren, who had to bear the whole brunt, opposing them as best as they could and in the long arduous run, destroyed

them completely. That is why during this period, no foreign enemy could cross the Vindhyas and penetrate into the Southern half of India. Barring one solitary, transient and half-hearted Arab invasion. Southern India continued to enjoy unhampered complete liberty, sovereign imperial authority, and material prosperity; for almost since 500 B.C., no foreign aggressor had been able to cross the Vindhyas and stop into the South. Right from Kalinga to the Pandyas, the Cheras, the Cholas and other South Indian rulers of the time had always kept in readiness, strong naval forces, fleets and flotillas to protect the Western, Eastern and Southern seas against all foreign incursions. Naturally, the Indian seafronts remained absolutely inviolable throughout all this period. On the contrary, the strong South Indian naval powers had carried their invincible and conquering armadas to Burma, Siam and other countries right up to the Philippines and established their overseas political, cultural and commercial empire.

217. As the foreign aggressions through the north-west frontier were successfully opposed there and then, by our north-Indian heroes, those various enemies could not even reach the Narmada river. But the Sakas having entered India through the Bolan Pass in Baluchistan, the coastal provinces of Sindh, Kathiawad and Gujarat were comparatively exposed to their attacks. This foreign aggression on South India also proved abortive. Why?

The Awakening of the Andhras

218. Fortunately, at that very time, were rising to prominence the two States of Kalinga and Andhra, who were staunch followers of the Vedic religion and were nationalist in their outlook. Like all other nationalist Indians, the Andhras were beside themselves with mortification and indignation at the foreign Saka attack on the vast Indian region from Sindh to Ujjain, and at the sad and humiliating fact that there should be no Indian power to resist it. Moreover, since some of the Saka hordes had reached as far as Aparantak (Konkan) after having crossed the Narmada river, the safety of the Andhra kingdom itself was seriously endangered. For these various reasons, the rulers of Andhra marched with a mighty army against the Sakas with a view to annihilating them completely, and for the first time they challenged the Saka might, driving them back beyond the Narmada river. Simultaneously, with this impact of the Andhras, the Sakas, who had till then spread upto Ujjain in the north,

suffered another defeat at the hands of the Youdheyas and Malavas. It has already been described (in paragraphs 38 to 40 and 50 to 62) with what invincible valour, these two republics had offered sanguinary battles in the defence of Indian liberty, even at the time of Alexander's invasion. So, being attacked by the Andhras from the South and in the North by Youdheya-Malavas, the very sting of the aggressive fang of the Sakas was completely blunted and devenomed. Their progress stopped forever, they were never able to establish a unitary and powerful rule of all the Sakas anywhere in India, Whatever stray kingdoms they had founded so far in India were unable to face successfully the two-pronged drive of the Indian retaliation.

The Victorious Malavas

219. The above-mentioned Youdheyas and the Malavas attacked the Sakas, who had spread round about Ujjayini. An allusion has been found to have been made to the fact that the Malavas had invested the fort of 'Uttambhadra' round about the year 57 B.C. The then celebrated King of Sakas, named Nahapan, had forced the Malavas to lift the siege. But soon after, the Malava forces encircled Nahapan with his whole army from all quarters. Naturally, a decisive battle was joined, wherein the Malava republican army showed the limit of its valour, but not being content with the destruction of the Saka forces, which were considered to be second-rate, they killed in the war, their very King Nahapan.

Malava Samvat

220. Because of this crushing defeat at the hands of the Malavas, the Saka military might's morale was so much shaken that they seemed to have taken a fright of their lives to face pitched battles with the Indian armies. This battle is conspicuous in another respect too, inasmuch as the Malavas started a new era of their own in the year of this victory, to commemorate their signal success over the Sakas, which had resounded throughout the length and breadth of India. They named this era as 'Krut', but on the coins that they struck on this occasion, are inscribed in the Brahmi script, legends such as 'Malavajayah', 'Malavanam Jayah', 'Malava Ganasya' and so on.

This is the Same Vikram Samvat of ours

221. In our country, good many emperors started new eras in their

own names. It was a traditional ambition, and a kind of right of such victorious kings and emperors to style themselves as 'Shakakartas' (the starters of new eras). The latest instance that can be cited is that of Shri Shivaji Maharaj. He too commenced his own era, the 'Shiva-Saka'. Most of these various eras ended with the termination of these royal dynasties. However, of the two of three eras, which have attained a national character and which have been adopted by the Hindu world, although region-wise, and by which not only our mundane affairs but our religious rites also are dated for more or less two thousand years, the Malava Samvat should be remembered rather particularly, because this very Malava Samvat later on became our famous Vikram Samvat.

222. The celebrated historian, Dr. Jayaswal, in his 'Hindu Polity', has ably upheld the view that Malava Samvat is the same era as our Vikram Samvat. However, he maintains that Malava Samvat was also called Vikram Samvat (era celebrating a victory) from the very beginning. But from the historical incidents that we are going to cite here, it should be clear that another view of the matter is more acceptable. This second view claims that it was to celebrate the all-India character of the Gupta Emperor, Vikramaditya's victory over the Saka-Kushan, which wiped out their separate existence from the Indian soil, when the victorious king began to rule from Ujjayaini. That Vikram Samvat became, as years elapsed, more and more widely known throughout the nation and equally popular, so that throughout the whole of north India, millions of Hindus are even now observing it in their religious rites and ceremonies.

Origin of Vikram Samvat and Shalivahan Saka

223. It must be made clear here and now, that there is yet no agreement reached amongst the historians about the origin of this Vikram Samvat. There are very wide differences of opinion about the chronology of various important events in our ancient history. So are they on this point too! Even in respect of the birth of Gautam Buddha, the dates suggested by different historians vary at times by fifty or even a hundred years. The same can be said of Kanishka's times. Some maintain that he ascended the throne in 78 A.D., while others put up the date of his succession to the throne as 120 A.D. Even about this Vikram Samvat a third opinion is still sponsored by some historians that the Vikram Samvat, had nothing to do with the era started by the Malava

Republic; that it was the one started in 58 B.C. by Azes I, one of the Chief Kshatraps (Satrap) of the Sakas, who had by then entered India, and the one which later on people renamed as Vikram Samvat when the Gupta Emperor, Vikramaditya completely uprooted the power of the Saka-Kushan. There is also the fourth one that in 58 B.C., a certain valiant emperor, named Vikramaditya, who ruled there at the time, won a great victory over the Sakas and started this era in his own name to commemorate that victory of his. It had again nothing whatever to do with the Malava era or that started by Saka Satrap, Azes I. But as no rock inscription or any other evidence has been found that refers to Vikramaditya, who ruled at that time, or again as no coins of the Vikram Samvat have yet been found, this myth about the aforesaid era had not so far attained the veracity of a historical event.

224. If, however, any coins or rock inscriptions or other evidence were to come forth any time and if anybody were to propound a new theory about the origin of this Vikram Samvat, we shall be glad to accept it.

225. What is said about the Vikram Samvat can very well be said about the Shalivahan (Salivahan) Saka. The advocates of the first opinion about this era say that when the first King of the Kushans in India, Wima Kadphises [Wemo (Ooemo) in his Greek coin legends and Yenkao-ching of the Chinese historians—of Smith OHI p. 147], whom our people considered no other than a Saka, ascended the throne (of his father) in 78 A.D., it was he who started this 'Saka' era. But another class of historians hold that it was not Wima Kadphises, who ascended the throne in 78 A.D. but it was his successor Kanishka who did that, and that it was that Emperor Kanishka who started the Saka era in order to perpetuate the memory of his accession to the throne. Later on, when the Salihavan emperors of Paithan conquered the Sakas, they turned the Saka era into the Salivahan Saka to signalize their victory. Besides these two, there is a third opinion held by some historians that the Salivahan Saka is in no way connected with that of Kanishka or any other Kushan King. They maintain that about 78 A.D., King Hal, who wrote the Gatha Saptasati, himself won a glorious victory over a Saka Satrap in Gujarath or Sourashtra, and to perpetuate this monumental success over these Sakas, he started the Salivahan Saka.

226-229. Since there is no need to discuss this topic here at any great length, it will be quite enough to mention two or three important points from whatever little is written here about the Saka era. They are:

(a) Whatever opinion about the Saka and Vikram eras is accepted, it is agreed beyond doubt that both the eras signify the decisive victories the Indians won over the Saka-Kushan.

(b) *In our count of time, Samvat is a more acceptable term than Saka*—We have all along been using right from the Vedic times, Samvatsar and Samvat for the measurement of time. The word 'Saka' has not been generally used in that sense. It is quite clear, therefore, that the word must be a corruption of the name of foreign aggressors like the Sakas and the Kushans. 'Shalivahan (Salivahan) Saka' is not a pure name of Sanskrit extraction as Vikram Samvat is. So the name 'Saka' of our Mlenchcha enemies should be eliminated and only 'Salivahan Samvat' should be used at the time of the celebration of our religious rites and the words 'Shalivahan Saka' or merely 'Saka' as wrongly used in our religious ceremonies, should be banned.

(c) That both the national eras, namely the Vikram Samvat and the Salivahan Samvat, should be closely connected with the glorious memory of Indian victories over the Saka-Kushan is not merely a queer coincidence; it is of great significance. Many eras like those of the imperial Guptas and others, although greatly honoured during those particular periods, are lost in the abyss of time. Only these two, which recorded the Indian victories over the Saka-Kushan, have enjoyed immortality. This may give us a fair idea as to how our Indian Vedic people had to suffer grievously at the hands of the ungovernable hordes of the Saka-Kushan. For, otherwise, these Vikram and Salivahan Samvats, which were started to perpetuate the memory of the victories of the Salivahan and Gupta emperors over the diabolic atrocities of, and political subjection by, the Saka-Kushans, would never have attained so much importance *vis-a-vis* the extinction of many other victorious eras, and could never have been observed even after the lapse of two thousand years as the chief national eras of the Hindus.

Indian's Martial & Religious Victory over the Sakas

230. Just as the Malavas firmly checked the aggression of Sakas by killing their king, Nahapan (cf: Para 219), in a similar way and at the same time, did our Andhra warriors march from the south towards the north and destroy the Saka kingdoms in Gujarat, Sourashtra, and Sindh. Harassed by the repeated offensives opened against them by

the valiant Salivahan Kings like Vilinayankur, Gautamiputra Satkarni:, Vashishthputra Pulamayi and others, the Saka kings upto Ujjain ultimately reconciled themselves to the sovereignty of the Salivahan Emperors. There exists a rock inscription that tells us that a Saka Satrap 'Rudra' even gave his daughter in marriage to a Salivahan King as the Greek King Seleucos had years before given his daughter to Emperor Chandragupta!

231. It must also be borne in mind that because of incessant fighting with the Indians on various battlefields and the consequent destruction during this century or a half, of thousands of their original number of soldiers that came to India, the Saka power suffered great numerical losses.

232. As the Saka military might thus began to lose strength because of the Indian resistance, the highly developed Indian civilization began more and more effectively to impress itself on the foreign Sakas. As a natural result of the constant warfare with the Indians for over a hundred years, the Sakas seemed to have surrendered completely to the Indian civilization. From the common man to their royal families, the Sakas abandoned their own original Saka names and adopted purely Indian ones like Satyasingh, Rudrasen and others. It is strange to note that most of them embraced the Vedic religion. In fact, ever since the Sakas crossed the Hindukush and entered Baluchistan and Sindh and settled there permanently, they had come in constant contact with the Buddhist population and the Buddhist centres there, preaching and propagating the tenets of Lord Buddha from the time of Ashoka and Menander. Moreover, the Malava-Youdheya republics, which fought with them furiously at that time and defeated them, and also the valiant armies of the Satavahans were Vedic Hindus. The Buddhists had never resisted them with or without arms. Under these circumstances, it would have been but natural, had the Sakas hated the Vedic religion of their powerful enemies and accepted the Buddhist cult of those who ungrudgingly submitted to their political domination. But what happened was exactly the opposite of this natural expectation. The majority of the Sakas, right from the commoner to the royal prince, got themselves converted, most willingly to the Vedic religion. The raison d'etre perhaps was that the Sakas being originally of a warlike disposition, whose blood always rushed violently through their veins at the thought of a battle, looked with awe and respect at the valiant Vedic warriors, who fought and defeated them, enemies though they were,

and the Vedic religion, which inspired such fighting spirit amongst its votaries, that it must have exerted a great fascination for them.

233. The Sakas came to love the Sanskrit language too. The kings of two or three feudal Saka principalities that were left in their hands, patroinized Sanskrit studies. One of the Saka kings made Sanskrit the official language for all correspondence of his court and administrative department. Their correspondence with the other Indian states, big or small, was also carried on in Sanskrit. Their social customs and manners too, underwent rapid changes and they got themselves attuned to Indian Social life.

The Kushan Invasion

234. While the Indians were, thus, gaining victories over the Sakas in military, as well as cultural fields and were uprooting their aggression, the locust-like hordes of the Kushans dashed against the northern frontier of India towards the Hindukush. These Kushans were ousted from their homeland by the Huns along with their women and children. As such, fighting troops of millions of Kushan, men and women violently entered Southern Asia shedding blood, plundering and burning towns and cities and spreading destruction everywhere. Throughout the whole Asiatic region, right from the Chinese frontier beyond the Hindukush to that of Greece in the west, they literally played havoc. Some of their troops in hot pursuit of their old enemies, the Sakas, overran the Bactrian Kingdom, and, crossing the Hindukush, entered the Indian north-western provinces of Gandhar, and extirpating the smaller Saka principalities that still were there at the time, they pushed themselves ahead into Punjab. They founded there a kingdom of their own. The name of their first king in India was Wima Kadphises.

235. The might of the northern Youdheyas, Malavas and other republics and that of the Salivahanas in the South having been put to its last extremity of endurance in successfully resisting and ultimately putting down the Saka aggresion for more or less a hundred years, they could not immediately and successfully stem the overwhelming onslaught of the Kushans, who were crueller and more bloodthirsty than even the Sakas, till they came to occupy Punjab. However, even in those miserable days, the Indian resistance to Kushan aggression gradually became so hot and determined, that the Kushan hordes could not make any headway in the Indian territories this side of Punjab.

Emperor Kanishka

236. After the death of Wima Kadphises, Kanishka ascended the Kushan throne in 78 A.D. (in the opinion of some historians in 120 A.D.). His achievements were unrivalled; his ambition was boundless.

It is needless to give any detailed account in these pages. Some events, however, have to be recounted here so far as they fall within the scope of this book. Kanishka subdued all the nomadic, plundering and marauding bands of the Saka-Kushans on both sides of the Himalayas (Hindukush?), as also all the smaller or bigger centres of political power, and forged them all into an extensive empire. He proclaimed himself as the Emperor of the Kushans and founded his capital at Purushpur (Peshawar of today). Thereupon, he marched on the Sakas, who had established their power from Malava to Sindh and who, being defeated by the Andhras, had acknowledged their paramountcy. But the same Indian states that had been incessantly fighting the Sakas for over a century and had been by now thoroughly exhausted in their attempt to put down these aggressors, had to face this new calamity of the Kushan onslaughts and, as such, they found it extremely difficult to do so. Being defeated in one or two battles, the Satavahanas themselves had to withdraw their forces from the north of the Narmada river to the south, in order to build up a strong defence for their own territory against Kanishka's conquests. By that time, Kanishka had conquered all the Saka states of Malava, Gujarath, Sourashtra and Sindh. Naturally, the Sakas in those regions renounced their allegiance to the Andhras and paid the obeisance to their new lord, Emperor Kanishka. Over and above, Kanishka's army crossed the Narmada in order to march upon the Andhras themselves and subdued a corner of Aparantak (north Konkan). But mindful of the concentrated armed might of the Andhras, Kanishka dared not attack them. So, he withheld his southern conquests forthwith. Thereafter, he marched with a huge army to oppose the Chinese general who had invaded his north-Himalayan territories. After a series of battles, he vanquished even the Chinese general and annexed the Chinese provinces of Kashgar (Tashkand), Chaskand, and Khotan to his empire.

The test of a Nation's Prowess and its right to live

237. The propriety of recounting this whole incident here is to show

clearly that this sudden eruption of the Saka-Kushans throughout Asia did not convulse India alone; it discomfited even the then strongly-built and well-organised empire like China too for a time on the battlefield. But just as it is torn-foolery, born out of jealousy, to say that the Chinese nation had been weak throughout all these years and had never been better fitted for anything else than to be rotting in slavery simply because they suffered temporary defeats against the Saka-Kushans or at some such other times, it is equally foolish and jealously blind to say, as some of our enemies do, that the Indian national life was a series of defeats. It only shows that they cannot read history properly.

238. It is not the number of foreign aggressions over a nation that is the last criterion of deciding its vitality or virulity or the absence of both, but the query, whether that nation was destroyed as a result of those aggressions, or whether in the final phase of that national struggle, that nation was able to overcome those foreign aggressions, that determines a nation's prowess, its vitality and its right to live.

239. Let us see which of the three, the Sakas, the Kushans or the Indians, passed this test successfully, and who passed out of existence.

Kanishka Embraces Buddhism?

240. Although busy with his campaigns right upto China and the consequent wars, Kanishka's mind was always preoccupied with religious and cultural things. He, in the meanwhile, proclaimed his conversion to Buddhism. In consonance with this new creed of his, he built several stupas and vihars at various places in his empire. At that time also, as it was during the Ashokan regime, Buddhism was burdened with innumerable fads and fanciful therories. The different Buddhistic sects were at enmity with one another. So, in order to do away with all these differences and to bring about a general agreement, he, like Ashoka, convened a great council of all the Buddhist sects. But instead of a general agreement, there appeared a new sect called the Mahayan, which virtually changed the nature of the Buddhist cult. Since the all-embracing precepts and practices, which were agreeable to Kanishka, but which had no base in the original form of Buddhism, were incorporated in this new Mahayan sect, some others refrained from joining it and eventually founded a new sect, which came to be called Heenayan. Kanishka helped spread the Mahayan sect extensively in his trans-Himalayan demesne. This great council recognised Sanskrit as the

language of their religion. Hence, Buddhistic scriptures, which were formerly written in Pali and Prakrit only, were translated into Sanskrit. Many new books like the Buddha-charit and others on varied subjects were composed by learned scholars, who enjoyed the patronage of Kanishka. Naturally, not only in India but even amongst the Saka-Kushan population in the Asian empire of Kanishka, the old as well as the new Sanskrit literature and civilization began to spread briskly. Thus did this new Kushan world, which had come as a conqueror, willingly became subservient to this Indian civilization and culture, as did the Saka world before it, in respect of Indian religion, Indian language, Indian thought and Indian customs.

241. Since Buddhism itself was an Indian religion, India could boast of a religious victory when Emperor Kanishka embraced it. Although this was all well done, it must be borne in mind that Buddhism, which was embraced by Kanishka, was not the unadulterated original one of Lord Buddha nor that of Ashoka. It was the Kanishkan edition of Buddhism. For example, although the Emperor had surrendered his loyally to Buddhism, he still worshipped the Vedic deities like Rudra. Kanishka's Buddhistic faith had nothing to do whatever with the non-violence (अहिंसा) of Ashoka, which declared 'Abstain from violence to animals' or 'Not the victory of the battlefield, but the religious victory is the only true victory'. While, on the one hand, he was spreading the Mahayan sect, this avowed Buddhist was, on the other hand, attacking his enemies with huge armies. In order that he might be called the Emperor of China, he passed ten years of his life in bivouacs with armed soldiers all round him. In the end, tired of his lust for incessant warfare, his army revolted and killed him. Death alone could put a stop to his insatiate lust for war.

242. One more thing to be pondered over: How could Kanishka spread Buddhism in the Chinese territory beyond the Himalayas? It was possible because he had first conquered those provinces with his weapons of war. Spread of the Buddhistic cult there followed his martial glories on the battlefields! That is why it spread there so rapidly. He sent hundreds of missionaries there, built various vihars, fed and fostered thousands of Bhikksus! All this was possible for him, because he had under his command a very powerful empire i.e., he had a mighty armed strength. Wasn't it?

243. In fine, it will have to be said that the statements like, 'Armed

victory is superior to religious victory' or *vice versa* are untenable.

244. Without armed support, religious victory is tame and insipid, whereas martial glory without a strong religious footing becomes grossly diabolic! This alone is true.

Hereditary Disloyalty of the Buddhists

245. A Buddhist or a Vedic Hindu, Kanishka was after all a foreigner belonging to the Kushan aggressive tribe, and had founded an empire on the north-western frontier of India by force. His empire was, in fact, an aggression on India. His was, not at all an indigenous Indian empire. So the patriotic Vedic population of India fought furiously with Kanishka, as it did with the Sakas, in order to overthrow his empire and to liberate all those Indian provinces, which had the misfortune to grovel under his political domination. But what were the Indian Buddhists doing at that time? They tendered their submission to the Mlenchcha enemy, the Kushan emperor, as soon as they courted the Buddhistic cult and began to perpetrate acts of treachery against the Indian nation and the brave patriotic Vedic people, who were fighting for her liberty! As has already been described (in paragraphs 204 to 209), the Indian Buddhists had, formerly in the time of Emperor Pushyamitra, who fought for national liberty, sold their loyalty to the Greeks led by Menander and others, and committed treason against their native land. In the very same manner, they did not hesitate this time to act treacherously towards their motherland when the foreign Kushan aggression was at her throat.

246. Had the Indian Buddhists put down the Sakas and founded a kingdom of their own, the Buddhist King would certainly have had the rightful claim to the credit of liberating India like any other Vedic King, and like the Vedic King Salivahan or Emperor Pushyamitra, we would have gladly felicitated them. But how could the Buddhists ever show this staunch national spirit! Even when Vedic patriotic republics and states like the Youdheyas and Satavahanas were engaged in a life-and-death struggle with the Saka-Kushans for a hundred-and-twenty-five years or more, these Indian Buddhists did not trouble themselves in the least for the cause of national liberty. But as soon as the strongest of these national enemies, Kanishka, proclaimed his conversion, albeit half-heartedly, to Buddhism, the whole of the Buddhist population submitted their most affectionate loyalty at the feet of that national

foe. They extolled him like a God to the skies! They prayed fervently in their vihars for the everlasting existence of that Saka-Kushan MIenchcha State. What wonder, if the inevitable consequence followed! As a result of the extreme hatred, which the Vedic Hindus felt towards the Buddhists for their high treason, Buddhism continued to decline, as it had begun to do right from the time of Pushyamitra, in spite of the royal support of Emperor Kanishka.

Kanishka's Grandson Embraces Vedic Religion

247. Moreover, when Kanishka was killed, as has already been told, by his rebellious soldiers while he was fighting in China, the Indian Buddhists were in a miserable plight, as they found themselves utterly lost both ways. For, the successor of Kanishka, his son Emperor Havishka, remained comparatively cold in his sympathy towards the Buddhists. And after Kanishka, Kanishka's grandson, who became the ruler of the Saka-Kushans, actually abandoned Buddhism and embraced the Vedic cult with a public ceremony! He even changed his original name and took for himself the purely Sanskrit appellation, Samrat Vasudeo and struck coins with the images of Siva and Nandi imprinted on them!

After Kanishka's Death

248. As soon as Emperor Kanishka died, his Indian empire fell to pieces. His rule in India was not far extended even in north India. It was never very strong. It had covered only a small north-western strip of India, which comprised Punjab, Malava, Sourashtra and Gujrat and a small ribbon like piece of land from the north-Konkan, which had formerly been in the hands of the Sakas. Now after the death of Kanishka, the two or three Saka kingdoms that formed part of this Kushan empire threw away the Kushan sovereignty and once again became independent. During the century-old Saka-Kushan aggressive wars, the Satavahanas had maintained the independence of their entire Southern India unimpaired and now the north-Indian states also, who had so far accepted the nominal overlordship of Kanishka, renounced it and regained their independence. In this very confusion, the principality of Pataliputra in the eastern part of India also became independent.

Once Again rose the Sunken Sun of Pataliputra

249. Pataliputra has been called a small principality in the previous

lines. Our readers might feel that it is a slip of our pen. But it is not so. For during the deluge of the Saka-Kushan aggressions at the beginning of the Christian era, the throne of Pataliputra, which was adorned by the celebrated Emperors like Chandragupta, Ashoka, Pushyamitra and others, and from which were guided for centuries together the destinies of the all-India empire from the Himalayas to the southern seas, was lost all of a sudden, just as the setting sun vanishes while we are still looking on and know not when it has set. During the century-and-a-half of incessant Indian war with the Saka-Kushans that followed, the separate existence of Pataliputra or Magadha was never felt. Some non-entity of king from somewhere ruled and lived within the four walls of Pataliputra.

250. But about the year 300 A.D. was established on this very principality of Pataliputra, the rule of Lichchavi Republic, which was known in Magadha from the times of Lord Buddha.

251. The daughter of the chief of this Lichchavi Republic, Kumardevi, was wooed and married by a promising youth, son of a feudal chief named Chandragupta in 308 A.D., With the strong support of the same Lichchavi Republic, he established his sway over the surrounding territory and in 320 A.D. he founded an independent kingdom in Pataliputra. Let not this Chandragupta be confused with the famous Emperor Chandragupta Maurya, because of their similar names. Emperor Chandragputa belonged to the Maurya dynasty, while this promising Chandragupta was born in the Gupta family. His achievements, however, were as brilliant as would have befitted the glorious dynasty of Emperor Chandragupta Maurya. During his short reign of ten or eleven years, he extended his small kingdom of Pataliputra wide enough to include Magadha, Prayag and Ayodhya, so that the epithet of Maharaj should be applied to him deservedly. Entrusting his kingdom into the able hands of his son, Samudragupta, who was ambitious of uprooting the Mlenchcha power of the Saka-Kushans in the north-western part of India, and of establishing an extensive Indian empire, Chandragupta died in the year 330 A.D. This Gupta dynasty was a staunch adherent of the Vedic religion—Shree Vishnu being their chief God of Worship.

Emperor Samudragupta

252. As soon as he came to the throne, Samudragupta planned to conquer the several independent Indian states in the north as well as in

the south, and establish a strong Indian empire like the Mauryan Empire of Chandragupta and Chanakya, and then to sweep over the still lingering Mlenchcha power of the Saka-Kushans in the north-western part of India with all the might of his empire. Accordingly, he conquered Kamrup, Samatat, Nepal and all the region from north-eastern frontier provinces to the Vindhyas. Thereafter, crossing the Vindhyas, he entered South India with a powerful army. He conquered twelve prominent kingdoms in South India. Many of the defeated kings, after having been brought captives and after having accepted his overlordships, were granted their kingdoms and were allowed to go free. About these glorious campaigns of his in the north and south of India, many western historians have spoken with eloquent praise, giving him the best of their current phrases, 'The Indian Napoleon'. After such an extensive military expedition, Samudragupta returned to Pataliputra. Then in order to proclaim to the world his acquisition of this new Indian empire, according to the Vedic religious rites, he celebrated the horse sacrifice, on a grand scale and was rightfully appointed a Samrat (an emperor). Thereafter, he began his extensive preparations for his dash against the Saka-Kushans.

The Final Surrender by the Kushans

253. At the fearful reports of this impending attack of Emperor Samudragupta, whatever small kingdoms of the Kushans like Gandhar and others were, still leading a precarious existence in the north-western regions of India, voluntarily sued for peace and accepted the Gupta paramountcy. Our Indian ancestors at that time called these Kushans 'Kush' also. As a token of their surrender, those Kushans sent rich offerings along with their personal envoys to Samudragupta. Thus, after an incessant warfare for a century-and-a-half or two, the Indian sword ultimately cut asunder the very root of the Kushan power in India. The Kushan problem was finally disposed of, here and now!

254. But the Saka kings from Malava to Sindh who, as has been told in paragraphs 236 and 248, had thrown off the yoke of Andhra domination when the latter was engaged in a life and death struggle with Kanishka and later on, after the death of Kanishka, declared themselved free, did not on their own initiative talk of any submission.

Samrat Samudragupta's Death and After

255. While he was just preparing to march upon the Mlenchcha

power of these Sakas, this powerful Emperor Samudragupta breathed his last in 375 A.D. He had expressed his wish that after him, his younger but valiant and virile son, Chandragputa II, should be crowned emperor. But discarding this dying wish of his, the elder son, Ramgupta, ascended the throne on the strength of his seniority in age. But he was so weak that almost all efficient officials in his military and civil service and his ministers too began to hate him secretly. Just at this juncture, a strange thing happened, which galvanized the popular feeling against Ramgupta's feebleness. Although some historians consider this to be a hearsay anecdote, still ancient writers like Vishakhadatta and Banabhatta have credited it with truth, and a reference to it is to be found in the copperplate grant of King Amoghvarsha. Again as in the comparatively recent times, the Rajput warriors had faced a similar situation against Alla-ud-din in respect of Padmini, the opinion of some other historians that this anecdote about Ramgupta must be substantially true is more acceptable. The incident in question may be summarised in the following manner:

256. Emperor Samudragupta having died and a weakling Ramgupta having ascended the throne after him, the Saka kings became fearless and began to behave insolently with the Magadhan empire, which was at inimical terms with them. An impertinent and mean-minded Mlenchcha king of these Sakas commanded Ramgupta, in order to humiliate him, that he should send his young and beautiful wife, Grahdevi, to him or else be prepared for war. This insolent and wicked message convulsed the whole political atmosphere of the Magadhan empire with shame and indignation. But Emperor Ramgupta had become so utterly imbecile and shameless, as to start preparations to send his queen, Grahdevi, to that Saka Satrap with the sole intention of avoiding a conflict. This infuriated his younger brother, Chandragupta. Flouting Ramgupta's orders, he took Grahdevi under his protection. Then resorting to guile, Chandragupta sent word to the Saka king that, according to his commands, Queen Grahdevi was being sent to him, but that because of natural womanly bashfulness and modesty, she would like to go in a curtained palanquin. She was also to be accompanied by a retinue of her maids in similar litters. The Saka king was mad with joy to hear this message, and he replied that the queen might be sent that way. Chandragupta, however, himself donned the female attire and sat in the Queen's palanquin, while in the accompanying ones, too

sat the chosen warriors in feminine garb. As the train (procession) of those covered palanquins drew near the capital of that Saka King, the latter, beside himself with joy, came forward to the queen's palanquin to receive her in person; whereupon out came Chandragupta, in the guise of a woman, and pouncing on the unsuspecting Saka King, slew him instantly with his sword. From other litters too, issued forth the warriors with drawn swords, and before the shocking news of the slaughter of the Saka King could spread out, they vanished along with Chandragupta, quite out of the enemy's reach.

257. The whole capital and the nation itself was resounding with the praise for Chandragupta, when the glad news spread that Prince Chandragupta had returned to Pataliputra after accomplishing this unprecedented daring feat and punishing with his own hands the Saka King, who had insulted the nation, with instant death. There was a great agitation to dethrone the cowardly Ramgupta, who had ascended the throne of Magadha, setting aside the last wish of the deceased emperor, Samudragupta, and to crown Chandragupta in his place. In that commotion, Ramgupta was killed. Immediately Chandragupta was crowned emperor and he married the same Grahadevi, whom he had with his exceptional valour, saved from humiliation at the hands of the enemy. Later on, with a well-equipped huge army, Samrat Chandragupta marched upon the Saka satraps.

Saka Satrap Rudrasingh Killed: the last phase of the war with the Sakas

258. When the war came to closed grips on the Gujarat-Malava frontier of the Saka dominions, the Saka kings offered tough resistance at every place, and at every place, the Indian warriors crushed the enemy! In the last battle, the remaining Saka Satrap, Rudrasingh, the son of Satyasingh, himself was killed by Chandragupta.

Thus Ended the Saka Rule

259. Having thus vanquished the Sakas completely, Chandragupta liberated the provinces of Sindh, Kaccha, Sourashtra, Gujarat, Malava and others under their domination and incorporated them into his Indian empire. After such a total destruction of the Sakas, when Emperor Chandragupta entered the ancient and renowned city of Ujjayini, which till a little while ago was the capital of the Saka kingdom, the people there

celebrated his entry as a grand national festival. Samrat Chandragupta assumed the title of Vikramaditya. In order to immortalize his glorious and crushing victory over the Sakas, he renamed the so far universally current Malava Samvat itself as Vikram Samvat after his own name (cf: paragraph 222). He made Ujjayini the capital of the western part of his India-wide empire, and there he lived like a crowned King.

260. How far can one describe the satisfaction and pride that the people all over Bharat felt at this decisive victory won by Vikramaditya over the Mlenchchas? The whole of India became free from the foreign domination and became 'Ekrat', united under one King! How profound must have been the joy and pride of Vikramaditya himself when he saw that the strenuous efforts and successes and failures of a hundred-and-fifty years or so of the Youdheyas, Malavas Vilivayankur (Vilinayankur?), Satavahan and other great warriors for the destruction of the Saka power, and of the valorous achievements of his grandfather and the national aspirations of Vedic Hindus had, at last borne such glorious fruit!

261. Of this, the English historian, Vincent Smith says, though rather grudgingly, "We may feel assured that differences of race, creed and manner supplied the Gupta monarch with special reasons, for desiring to suppress the impure foreign (म्लेच्छ) rulers of Western India. Chandragupta Vikramaditya, although tolerant of Buddhism and Jainism was himself an orthdox Hindu, espeically devoted to the cult of Vishnu, and as such, could not but have experienced peculiar satisfaction in violently uprooting the foreign chieftains."

The Sakas too Vanished

262. In paragraph 230, it has already been described how the Sakas adopted the Vedic faith, Sanskrit language and Indian customs and manners. Now that Vikramaditya had utterly destroyed their political power with his 'mailed fist', they, hereafter, lost their separate existence as the Sakas as distinct from the Indians. Only within two or three generations, there was hardly any Saka to be seen in India, as it previously happened in the case of the Kushans.

263. In the historical past, there lived and ruled good many emperors in India, but there was hardly any as suprisingly popular as this Emperor Vikramaditya, who exterminated the Saka-Kushans so thoroughly, that not a trace of any of them is found today. Even a foreigner, the Chinese

traveller, Fa-hien (or Fa-hsien), who visited India in his reign, has paid a glowing tribute to the prosperity, happiness, wealth and contentment that had reached its height, throughout the whole of the Indian empire under the Guptas. Even today in the innumerable Indian villages, the name of King Vikramaditya, and his high sense of administration and justice is lovingly sung in folk-tales and ballad. After having defended the powerful unitary Indian empire and having developed it in every respect for more or less thirty-five years, Samrat Vikramaditya died in 414 A.D.

264. The epoch, which began with the royal seal of Samrat Vikramaditya, the proud Victor of Saka-Kushans, is THE THIRD GLORIOUS EPOCH of Indian History.

□

4

Yashodharma, the Conqueror of The Huns

The Hunnish Onslaught over the whole World

265. A reference has already been made earlier in this book to the Huns who routed all the Saka and Kushan tribes from their original homes and themselves occupied the vast tracts of lands. These very Huns, fiercer and far more cruel than their predecessors, now menaced not only the whole of Asia but also the whole of Europe. Every one of the then well-established, civilized, and strongly built nations and kingdoms of the world, right from China to Rome, was rocked to its bottom at the very thought of this impending doom. There was no limit to their number, nor were their raids limited to this region or that.

266. When their armies marched out, thousands of their men and women carried fire and sword to every city and every village they entered and to every human being, young or old, child or woman, whom they came across. Not only by day, but even at the very dead of night, did they carry on these nefarious activities, shouting wildly like beasts and engulfing the enemy lands like wildfire. At the end of every bloody battle, they celebrated their victory then and there, dancing wildly, and drinking strong liquors in cups made of the very skulls of the slaughtered enemy soldiers and their women or children.

267. Being very close to the original Hunnish territory, almost all the provinces of the vast Chinese empire were rendered desolate because of their terrible raids. The great China Wall of today is a glaring testimony to prove the incapacity of the Chinese Emperor to ward off these Hunnish locusts. The one great wonder of the world—this China Wall-is indeed the greatest monument to Hunnish Terror!

268. One of the leaders of these Huns, Attila, organized these

horsemen, who pillaged Central Asia and made straight for Europe. His various marauding armies dashed like an avalanche into European Russia through whichever inlet they could find and wrought havoc everywhere. Universities and art centres, houses and churches, the poor men's huts and rich palaces, towns and cities—whatever they could lay their hands on, these Huns went on reducing them to ashes. Whoever came in their way was ruthlessly cut to pieces. After trampling down Russia, they rushed into Poland, thence attacking the Goths in Germany and France. Army-after-army of the once invincible Roman Empire was put to rout. These Huns loved not victory so much as they did ruin and destruction for its own sake. Consequently, the whole of Europe was not only defeated in war but was virtually bathed in blood and laid utterly waste. For a harrowing description of this devastation of Europe at the hands of these barbaric Huns, one should read Gibbons, *'Decline and Fall of the Roman Empire'*. Even today, most of the European languages use 'Hun' as the foulest of abuses, indicating thereby, the horror they looked upon these devilish Huns with.

269. In the very same manner, did another avalanche of these Hunnish horses, which hovered for some time round about the Himalayas destroying whatever remained of the Saka-Kushan strongholds, dashed against regions like the Gandhar and others to the north-west of India. With the very same energy and devilish ambition with which they devastated the empires of China, Russia and Rome, did these Huns march impatiently to trample down India from end to end under their horses' hoofs, and began to force their way to the Indus.

But

270. But, fortunately, India was no longer being ruled by any coward like Dhananand, who brought disgrace to the land at the time of the Greek invasion of Punjab. It was now under the sovereignty of Kumargupta, the illustrious son of Emperor Vikramaditya, the avenger of the Saka-Kushan domination. India at that time enjoyed the century-old Golden Age of the Gupta era. The Mauryan Golden Age saw, towards its close, the Indian military strength disorganized and powerless, because of the foolhardy Ashokan policy of total non-violence (ahimsa). But the Vedic India of this time under the leadership of Kumargupta did not allow the imperial army to degenerate in the least. Being always aware of the avalanche-like Hunnish onslaught,

which was expected sooner or later, Emperor Kumargupta kept a very strong war-like and well-organized army, ever prepared to defend its frontiers.

The first Hunnish Onrush Paralysed

271. The moment he learnt of the Hunnish aggression on Gandhar, Kumargupta sent his valiant son, Skundgupta at the head of the four-fold (चतुरंग) army to uproot the Hunnish menace. With their special technique based on their unlimited number, which had so far been unmatched for its efficacy, these Hunnish invaders began to make short work of the Indian frontier guards. No sooner did the Indian soldiers destroy one Hunnish army at a place, than would they emerge up from all other quarters, like ants pouring forth from their anthills. Even if these were completely wiped out, there would appear a fresh one, creating confusion all over the land. The armies of Skundgupta fought battle-after-battle with the irresistible Huns, destroying them steadily but surely for years together. The result was that even the innumerable forces of these Huns gradually lost their strength and energy and dared cross the frontiers of the Gupta Empire no more. Why, they could not even defend the places they held so far against the aggressive and fierce impact of the Guptas. The remaining troops of the Huns, therefore, fled clean out of the Indian frontiers through the very passes they had come in. This crushing defeat kept the Huns away from India for the next forty years or so.

The Brave Skundgupta

272. After having fought continuously for years on end and having defeated the most powerful enemy, who had already brought to their knees the greatest empires of the world, Skundgupta proudly returned to his father at Pataliputra, where the victorious Prince was greeted with unprecedented enthusiasm, pomp and glory. Old Emperor Kumargupta's joy can easily be imagined. It knew no bounds. In order to celebrate this singular success, Kumargupta performed the horse sacrifice (अश्वमेध), according to the age-old Indian tradition.

Death of Kumargupta

273. Shortly after this, the old Emperor Kumargupta died, having satisfactorily fulfilled his life-mission. He was succeeded by his eminent

son, Skundgupta, many of whose memorable deeds showing his rare abilities cannot be recounted here for want of space and also because they do not directly bear upon the present theme.

274. While Skundgupta was thus ruling in India, another Hunnish adventurer, Khikhil by name, organized their scattered forces in Asia, as Attila before him had done in Europe, and founded another kingdom and styled himself a king. Towards the end of Emperor Skundgupta's career, this new Hunnish adventurer marched towards India at the head of a powerful army, with a view to avenging the ignoble defeat the Huns had earlier suffered here.

Second Hunnish Invasion of India

275. During the very first encounters, the Huns overthrew the imperial frontier guards and drove them back at one or two places. No sooner did he hear of this fresh Hunnish aggression than Skundgupta, in spite of his old age, left his capital and marched as far as the Panchnad (the modern Punjab). While he was thus preoccupied in his military camp, organising the overthrown imperial frontier forces for a counter-attack upon the enemy, he learnt that his step brother, Purgupta, was busy treacherously planning to usurp his throne. Nevertheless, the patriot Skundgupta, disregarding his personal interests, kept on fighting the alien invaders, instead of speedily returning to the capital to settle his domestic trouble, as some others in his place might have most probably done. Had he done so, and left the imperial army fighting without his guidance, the Indian soldiers would have, in all probability, lost courage and the invaders would have swept over the whole of Punjab and at least the half of north India. As he was convinced of this impending calamity, he rather preferred fighting against the barbaric Huns to returning home!

276. And even as he was fighting in the defence of his motherland, this aged warrior-king died about A.D. 471 in his military camp, like a true King that he was!

An Emperor must die Standing

277. An interesting anecdote is told about a well-known Roman Emperor who ruled in those 'palmy days of Rome,' that while he was lying on his deathbed in his royal palace, he once suddenly got up, sword in hand, and said to the frightened attendants, who suspected it to be a

delirious fit, that a king must not die in his bed. "A Roman Emperor", he said, "must die standing".

278. In the same manner did this great Indian Emperor, Skundgupta, die in a small military camp fighting relentlessly, in spite of his failing years, the very enemy on whom he had inflicted severe defeats in his earlier career. Renouncing all royal comforts and pleasures, he spent almost fifteen to twenty years of his life, suffering all the discomforts and hardship of a camp-life for the sole purpose of defending his empire and preserving the independence of his motherland. And when he did die, he did so fighting the arch-enemy of his nation, far away in a bivouac in the farthest province of Punjab—not in his royal palace in the capital! If ever there was an ideal emperor, it was he!

279. If the Huns were hemmed in one small corner of the Indus and if India was saved from all the indignities, massacres and wanton destruction at their hands to which Europe had been subjected almost contemporaneously, all the credit must go to the armed strength of Skundgupta. Although he died before the Huns were completely annihilated, his exemplary valour brought forth another generation of warriors, much stronger than before, to take the field against these once war-intoxicated but now enfeebled Huns.

280. Hence, we bow down to the memory of Emperor Skundgupta, with as much reverence and pride and a sense of national gratitude as we might do to any other conqueror like Vikramaditya.

After the Death of Skundgupta

281. Subsequent to the death of Skundgupta, the throne of Magadha was usurped by his rebel brother, Purgupta, whose lack of every sort of ability encouraged the Huns once again to push forward under their King, Khilkhil. In the reign of Torman, who succeeded Khikhil, Huns once again let loose the dogs of war and Kamboj, Gandhar, and Punjab suffered most from their horrible depredations and arson. The world-famous University of Taxila was razed to the ground. Thousands of its invaluable books only served to make bonfire for the Huns.

282. This is another instance that shows how even the national literature, civilization and culture are destroyed at the hands of foreign invaders, if they are not defended and supported by the nation's mailed fist.

283. In the meanwhile, those Hunnish hordes that had so far overrun

the kingdom of Persia, and in A.D. 484 put her King, Phiroz, to death, were now free to join the army of Torman in his work of reducing India to the same miserable state. With his army so suddenly augmented, Torman pushed ahead of Punjab into Malva and captured it round about 511A.D., along with its capital Ujjain. When tormans son, Mihirgula, who was braver and more atrocious than the father, succeeded to the Hunnish throne, strangely enough, he became a sincere devotee of the Vedic God, Rudra and held the cult of Buddha in the greatest spite.

Mihirgula, the Devotee of the Vedic God

284. Strange as it may seem, the Huns were speedily attracted to the worship of the Vedic God Rudra at least from the time they entered the north-western frontier province. Of these people, Vincent Smith says, "The savage invader who worshipped his patron deity Shiva, the God of Destruction, exhibited ferocious hostility against the peaceful Buddhistic cult and remorselessly overthrew the Stupas and Monasteries which he plundered of their treasures."

The Patriotic Vedic Hindus and Treacherous Buddhists

285. In this context, the readers are referred to paragraphs 182 to 209 and 245 to 246 of this book, wherein we have commented on the patriotic spirit of the Vedic Hindus and the treacherous attitude of the Buddhists. In order to vouchsafe this comment of ours, this incident of Mihirgula should be most significant.

286. Even when this Hunnish aggressor Mihirgula had accepted the Vedic cult of God Rudra and brutally oppresed the Buddhists, who had become inveterate enemies of the Vedic Hindus, the latter did not accept his political dominance, nor did they ever join him in his atrocities against their own rivals. In spite of his avowed acceptance of the Vedic cult, Mihirgula was looked upon as a foreign aggressor and as such, a national enemy by the Vedic Hindus. They avowed enmity towards him for the sake of making politically free those regions that had so far gone under his sway. It cannot be denied that even amongst the Vedic Hindus, kings like Kamoj and Jaichand did commit treason earlier or later, but on the whole, the Vedic community had all along been hating the non-Vedic people and had been giving terrible battles for protecting the independence and imperial power of their nation unimpaired. Even

the English historians like Smith could not help mentioning, maybe in malicious terms, *this strong national feeling of the Vedic people.* While stating in general terms that these Vedic Hindus were the born enemies of any foreign political power, trying to subdue the country, he says, "Those foreign tribes, Sakas, Pahlavas and Ionians (Yavanas), at the time, settled in Western India as the lords of a conquered population, were the objects of hostility of the Vedic King Vilivayankur II.... He recovered the losses his kingdom had suffered at the hands of the intruding foreigners and utterly destroyed the power of (the Saka King) Nahapan. The hostility of the Andhra (Vedic) monarch was stimulated by the disgust felt by all the Hindus, and especially by the followers of the Orthodox Brahmanical system of the outlandish foreign barbarians."

287. It should not surprise the reader if he finds in this observation of Smith, a faint echo of an Englishman's heartache at his painful experience of the British Imperial Colonies.

King Yashodharma

288. Under the undeserving and weak Purgupta, the suzerainty of Magadha began to be flouted and disregarded by almost every one. Most of the vassals of the Gupta Empire and even the provinces and principalities began to rule themselves independently. All these virtually subordinate but actually independent provinces and different feudal lords feared the political dominance of the Huns, which had by then spread as far as Malava. Everybody was seething with indignation at seeing a foreign tyrant like Mihirgula occupy the throne of the Great Vikramaditya at Ujjain, and every patriotic Vedic Indian was anxious to see the Huns overpowered and routed at the earliest oppurtunity. Yet, none of all these smaller states and provinces had the courage to take any aggressive move against these Huns. Nonody could broach the subject openly.

289. At such a critical time, an adventurous youth vowed to solve this knotty problem. He was not even a titular king or emperor. He was merely a small chieftain, Yashodharma by name, of a relatively small principality in the province of Malava. But his ambition, his sense of patriotism and his daring spirit were as lofty and powerful as to challenge the might of the mightiest and pompously styled 'King of Kings' of the Huns, Mihirgula, and dethrone him, and to destroy the Hanish influence root and branch.

A common front of the Vedic Kings

290. First of all, he organized almost all the neighbouring independent Indian states with a view to fighting out the Hunnish menace. Even Baladitya of Magadha supported this organized war effort, and under the leadership of King Yashodharma, all these kings marched against the Huns from all sides. This well-organized Indian Army could do what none else could think of doing single-handed, and the most powerful Hunnish army began to be slaughtered on the battlefields of India.

Defeat of the huns: capture of Mihirgula Himself

291. In the end, the Supreme Commander, Yashodharma marched at the head of a very powerful army on Mihirgula himself, and joining battle at Mandasore or Korur sometime about A.D. 528, overthrew the Hunnish dragon for ever. After a very savage man-slaughter, Mihirgula himself became a captive of King Yashodharma.

292. This singular success resounded thunderously throughout the length and breadth of India.

293. And in order to avenge the numerous atrocities that Huns in general and Mihirgula in particular, had so far perpetrated against the Indian population, King Yashodharma forthwith ordered the hanging of Mihirgula.

Baladitya's Anti-National Generosity

294. But as soon as Baladitya, the Emperor of Magadha, learnt of this death sentence passed on Mihirgula by king Yashodharma, he, as a member of the Combined Front, insisted that the Hun be spared and be handed over to him alive. Yashodharma did so only to avoid displeasing Baladitya. Whether according to a secret treaty with Mihirgula to serve some selfish end of his, or under some disastrous delusion of the so-called superhuman generosity consisting in the release of the deadliest enemy, who deserved nothing but hanging, a delusion that seems almost permeated through the very veins of the Indian people, Baladitya spared not only Mihirgula's life but even allowed him to go honourably to the remnant of the Hunnish territory to the north-west. A great many years after him, Prithviraj allowed another inveterate enemy, Mohammed Ghori, to go scot-free!

Milk offered to the Snakes Brings Venom only

(Payah-panam Bhujanganam Kevalam Vishwardhan)

295. Thanking his good stars, Mihirgula hurried straight to Kashmir, where he secretly organized the Huns and killed the king, annexed Gandhar, persecuted the people of the land, and especially liquidated the pockets of Buddhist influence after slaughtering wholesale thousands of Buddhist monks and nuns.

296. It is very difficult to say if fate had brought to life this Mihirgula, only to give a practical lesson to the Indian Buddhists who were intoxicated by the delirious idea, viz. 'Religious victory was greater than armed victory' and to show that without one's own armed support, even religion cannot survive the onslaughts of the barbarous enemy's fire and sword.

297. Nevertheless, these milkshops of the Buddhists who were sorely distressed at these persecutions, did not fail to use the only weapon they had to avenge themselves on Mihirgula. Only when Mihirgula died a perfectly natural death, these Buddhists recorded his death in their myths, sending him forthwith to hell. "When this demon of a Hun, Mihirgula, died", they wrote, "he went to eternal hell to atone for his hatred towards Lord Buddha and to suffer inhuman pangs, the Earth broke into two by the very shock. It rained as heavily as the Deluge of Manu, and the birds and beasts ran helter-skelter, crying horribly. Many other upheavals also took place."

297A. For these enfeebled Buddhists, was there any other way open for consolation than to imagine themselves, the unlimited tortures in the infernal fires of purgatory or the hell or the 'narak', as we Indians should like to style the place, for terrible enemy, whom they dared not think of harming in the least, while yet he lived in this world? But wasn't this consolation of these non-violent Buddhists violent? Is it kindness of extreme cruelty?

The Victorious entry of Yashodharma into Ujjain!

298. After vanquishing Mihirgula completely Yashodharma overthrew all Hunnish influence from the Panchnad and after having re-established Indian rule in this newly freed land, he returned to Malava with his victorious army. With great pomp and ceremony did this Yashodharma enter Ujjain, which had the reputation of being the

capital of India since the time of Vikramaditya, and which he had freed anew from the foreign yoke. Now he did not remain a simple king but had become the king of kings, Maharajadhiraj! He erected two pillars to commemorate the victory of the Indian patriots against the Huns. They even now testify to the gratification that the people of these times might have then felt.

What Happened to the Huns Next?

299. What else could have happened to them? They met with the same fate that their forerunners, the Ionians, the Sakas, the Parthians and the other aggressors did. Soon after Mihirgula died round about A.D. 540, the Hunnish states in the north-west region beyond the Indus valley dwindled into insignificance, within a generation or two, and perished completely. After wresting political power from the Huns, the Vedic Hindu kings once again began to rule right up to the Hindukush. The moment they lost political power, because of an armed might stronger than their own, the Huns became meek lambs. Dr. Jayaswal writes, "The Huns were fully crushed within a century by the successive (Hindu) dynasties." Because of the great losses in their ranks, suffered during a century of incessant warfare with the Hindus, Hunnish population diminished rapidly in numbers. Whosoever remained, took over willingly to Indian religions and languages and customs, and within a generation or two, merged so completely with the Hindus that they could never recollect their Hunnish extraction.

300. Vincent Smith has the following comments to offer on the far-reaching effects of this decisive Indian victory over the Huns: "After the defeat of Mihirgula and the extinction of the Hun Power on the Oxus, India enjoyed immunity from foreign attacks for nearly five centuries."

300A. It clearly means that after the defeat of Mihirgula at the hands of Yashodharma and after the end of the Hun empire beyond the Oxus, there had been no foreign aggression over India for nearly five centuries to come. Thus the whole of India, right from Pariyatra (Hindukush), Gandhar, Kashmir, Punjab and Sindh straight to Kanyakumari, enjoyed under the Hindu kings, prosperity and happiness for nearly five hundred years. The whole of Bharat was independent, powerful, wealthy and happy!

A Resume of the Ancient period in Indian History

301-307. If by the Ancient Period in Indian History, the one from B.C. 600 to A.D. 700—a period as large as 1300 years—and if the succeeding period is called the modern, it is in the fitness of things that here and now, should end that period so far as the subject-matter of this book is concerned. Some of the historical points pertaining to this ancient period—which should very carefully be impressed on the minds of our young men and women and the general reader, but which are generally lost sight of, are briefly dealt with here in this conclusion:

(1) *In this ancient period, no foreign aggressor could ever conquer the whole of India at any lime.* This fact generally escapes the notice of good many of the foreigners or our own men, while some deliberately neglect it or pervert it. On reading such titles of Chapters as 'Alexander's Invasion of India' "Sakas' Aggression of India", foreign as well as native readers are generally misled into a belief that the whole of India was overrun either by Alexander or by the Huns, and lost its independence. Under this delusion, many of the enemies of India and her so-called well-wishers have raised such objections and propounded such theory as to mean that the whole life of the Indian nation, i.e. the Hindu nation, has passed under foreign slavery. It is to bring to light and refute this foolish and wicked charge and to show that it is due to either unintentional ignorance or wilful malice, that such theories are ever propounded, that this book has been purposely written.

So from the foregoing narration, it should be clear that—(2) Right from Nepal to Eastern Sea (Bay of Bengal), the whole of northern and eastern India and southern India, that is to say, practically three fourths of this great continent of India, had remained completely independent of any foreign domination for these 1300 years. No aggressor by sea or land could ever reduce it completely to slavery.

(3) Of the remaining western and northern India, roughly about 1/4 of the continent was only once traversed by a foreigner. Sakas and Kushans held the north-western tract of land between Punjab and Gujarat for some time. The Huns could barely reach Ujjain. How miserably these national foes suffered at the hands of Indian nationals has been briefly decribed in the foregoing pages.

(4) Hardly any other contemporary nation of the world will be seen to have so successfully destroyed the foreign aggressors and maintained its national independence for such a length of time—not less than 1300 years.

(5) It is not only India that these Ionians, Sakas and Huns and other aggressors invaded. Some of them disrupted almost all the other nations of the then known world and brought in the so-called Dark Ages. They threw some of the other nations into complete oblivion--a fact that must always be kept in view, when comparing them with India in respect of these barbaric aggressions.

(6) These very barbaric aggressors, who came in such large numbers carrying powerful weapons, with the diabolic ambition of annihilating the whole of the Indian continent were themselves reduced by the Indian warriors to ashes in the conflagration of a general war, their beastly instincts being purified in the material fires and merged in the vast Indian multitude so completely, that even their name did not remain behind them!

308. Let us for a moment imagine that a certain Angel who had been oberving the affairs of this Earth at that time, has once again come down on the Himalayan peaks and is surveying the Indian scene. Not knowing what happened during the intervening years, he bagan to ask from the peak: "Well, are there still left over in this continent of India and of the Ionians (Greeks), who had once founded a kingdom in a small corner of this vast piece of land?" If any Angel does inquire this way, there is unfortunately no one left to tell him, ' *Well, l am he—their descendant*!" If again the Angel asks, "In one part of India, there were some kingdoms and communities of the Sakas and the Kushans. Is there anyone of them to be found here now?" To answer this question in the affirmative, there is unluckily none left. No one can be found today to say, "Yes, I am a Saka" or "I am a Kushan." Were he again to ask for the third time. "At least some of the gentlemen belonging to the Hun clan, who had once harassed the whole of the world and who had once advanced up to Ujjain must be found here! Are there any such?" Even to this question, no one can proudly say today: "Why not? Here I am their direct descendant."

309. But if the awe-stricken Angel asks again, "Well, tell me at least, if there is any yet left of those Hindus who fought bravely with all these foreign aggressors and ruled over India?" Then the answer, "Yes, I am that Hindu! I am he! would spring from more than three hundred million mouths in this country and prove, beyond a shadow of a doubt, the deep-rooted foundations and the *grand edifice of the Hindu nation and the Hindu State*!

310. So this can be fittingly called **The 4th Glorious Epoch** of Indian History, glittering in the lustrous martial achievements of the most daring and successful emperor, YASHODHARMA!

"The Mohamedan conquest of India is probably the bloodiest story in history. It is a discouraging tale, for its evident moral is that civilization is a precarious thing, whose delicate complex of order and liberty, culture and peace may at any time be overthrown by barbarians invading from without or multiplying within."

—*Will Durant: Story of Civilization.*

□

5

The Climax of Maharashtrian Valour! The Maratha Standard Flutters Proudly Over Attock

Nature of the Millennial Hindu-Muslim Struggle

311. The scope of this book, 'Six Glorious Epochs of Indian History', has already been explained in Chapter I (Paras: 4 to 8), from which it should be clear that a detailed account of the continuous, long-drawn fierce and gigantic Hindu-Muslim struggle is not intended here. What we intend to do here is to examine thoroughly and from the Hindu standpoint, this epic struggle and the period covered by it as searchingly, as faithfully and as fearlessly, as it ought to have been done—but unfortunately has not so far been done.

312. For even today, it is absolutely essential and beneficial to the interests of the Hindu Nation.

Two ages of our History: Ancient and Modern

313. We feel our History is naturally divided by the course of events into two great ages: the Ancient and the Modern; the first, ending with the seventh century, and the second, stretching from the beginnings of the eighth century to the present day. In the preceding four chapters, we have dealt with the vast ancient period of about a thousand years or so, while we intend to analyse, in the following nineteen chapters, the course of events in this modern age of Hindu History.

314. In doing so, detailed accounts of the many stray events supporting our main thesis will certainly be given, where necessary, and the chronological sequences will also be maintained. But the chronological details will not be allowed to crowd up the limited space

at our disposal, as they are easily available in various big or small volumes by many other writers. Hence, our whole attention will be focussed mainly on the bearing of different important points in the subject-matter in hand, rather than, though not without regard to, the chronological order.

The Epic Hindu-Muslim War

315. The struggle on the two fronts in all the bloody wars fought at every Muslim invasion, right from the beginning of this modern age was hitherto unknown and unheard of. For the Greek, the Saka, the Hun and other invaders, who came pouring in down the plains of Punjab, was political domination of this country as their sole objective. Barring this political aim, their raids had never been occasioned by any cultural or religious hatred. On the other hand, these new Islamic enemies, not only aspired to crush the Hindu political power, and establish in its place Muslim sovereignty over the whole of India, but they also had seen things' in their brains another fierce religious ambition, not heretofore dreamt of by any of the old enemies of India. Intoxicated by this religious ambition, which was many times more diabolic than their political one, these millions of Muslim invaders from all over Asia fell over India, century-after-century, with all the ferocity at their command, to destroy the Hindu religion which was the lifeblood of the nation.

The Outrageous Christian Incursion

316. To add to these catastrophic Muslim inroads over India, Christian nations like the Portuguese, the Dutch, the French, the British and others rushed upon our nation from the sea, round about the fifteenth century A.D.—even if we were to ignore the infiltration by the Syrian Christians in the Malabar during the 1st century A.D. This Christian offensive, like the Muslim one, was both political and religious and equally devilish. They also wrought havoc by converting millions of Hindus at the point of the bayonet—an account of which will be given at its proper place.

317. Although the two fronts of this Muslim aggression, viz., the religious and political, were only the two parts of the same epic Hindu-Muslim struggle, their original forms, their weapons of war and their ultimate end, were altogether different. Naturally, they have to be

discussed separately, as far as it is possible to do so.

318. Hence, we shall first examine the religious aspect of the Muslim-Christian aggression over our country in Chapters VI to XII, and then in Chapters 13 to 22 of this book, we shall discuss its political side.

□

6

Beginning of Muslim Incursion

319. We have already pointed out—and shall do so hereafter - how the histories written not only by foreign historians or those who are avowedly inimical to us, but even by our own people, ignore the glorious episodes of exceptional valour and monumental successes of the Hindus and in their stead, catalogue only the calamities that befell them and present them as the only true history of the Hindus, because they were never fearlessly written from the pure and simple Hindu standpoint. We have already referred to many such instances, in the first four chapters in support of our convention and will do even in the following pages. The period under consideration here is an instance in point.

320. Generally speaking in all histories, especially in the history textbooks used in schools, the writers invariably jump from an account of Hunnish onslaught to the first successful Muslim campaign on Sindh, without writing even a line or two about the intervening long period of these hundred years or so. Next follow in quick succession, the detailed narration of Muslim invasions one after another, so that a common reader, especially a pupil, catches an impression, which is very often carried even in his later life, that the history of the Hindus is nothing but a doleful tale of foreign subjugation and national defeats. Our enemies have publicized these false impressions as established facts all over the world for the last two or three centuries. For instance, a man like the late Dr. Ambedkar, burning with hatred against Hinduism, writes:

"...The Hindus' has been a life of a continuous defeat. It is a mode of survival of which every Hindu will feel ashamed."

321. In fact, historical evidence shows that after the total rout of the Huns, that is to say, since about A.D. 550, Hindu kings and emperors

successfully crossed the Indus at various places and reconquered not only what are now known as Sindh, Baluchistan, Afghanistan, Herat, Hindukush, Gilgit, Kashmir and many other regions from the Greeks, the Huns, the Sakas and other foreign people, but hoisted the victorious national flag of the Vedic Hindus far beyond the north-western boundaries of Chandragupta Maurya's empire upto Uttar Kurus! Why, even in Khotan in Central Asia beyond Kashmir, there ruled Hindu kings and in the opinion of many historians, even Ghazani was ruled by King Sheeladitya.

The Rejuvenescent Hindu Nation

322. Even the foreign historians like Vincent Smith are astounded at the enduring ability of the Hindu nation to rejuvenate itself after crushing defeats. For a detailed account of this period and Smith's glowing tribute to the successful struggle for independence of the Hindus, the curious readers are advised to refer to the concluding portion of Chapter IV of this book. Only one sentence will suffice here.

322A. "After the defeat of Mihirgula (by the Hindus) and the extinction of the Hun power, India enjoyed immunity from foreign attack for nearly five centuries."

323. Smith has thus completely refuted the extravagant and vulgar remark of Dr. Ambedkar on Hindu history.

The Beginning of the awful Muslim War with India

324. It is generally believed that Mohammad Bin Kasim was the first of the Arabian or Muslim invaders to march upon Sindh. But, in fact, it was at least fifty years before him, that other Arabian Muslims had started picking up quarrels with the Brahmin Kings of Sindh. They had even tried an armed aggression. Yet we do not intend to dilate upon the systematic and chronological account of these various skirmishes by armed bands or military detachments. It is enough for our purpose to bear in mind that all these attempts were foiled successfully by the Hindus. At length, Usman, the governor of the Grand Khalipha's distant province of Oman, openly attacked the Hindu state of Sindh. The then Brahmin King of Sindh, Chacha, vanquished not only these Arabs, but killed their very Commander-in-Chief, Abdul Aziz, in a battle. After these sporadic attempts till about A.D. 640, the Arabs did not undertake any important expedition with perhaps the only exception of the small distant province

of Makram, which they reduced to ashes° converting the Hindus there at the point of the sword to the Muslim faith. These Hindu Baluchistanian converts of those days became later on bigoted Muslims.

The first big Muslim Expedition against Sindh

325. Thereafter, it was in A.D. 711, that Mohammed-bin-Kasim launched the first large-scale offenive against Sindh with a huge army, fifty-thousand strong. The majority of the population of Sindh, then, was Vedic Hindus, with King Dahir at the head of the state, while, only a small minority was the follower of Lord Buddha. Formerly, when Sindh was under the Huns, their last King Mihirgula had persecuted the Buddhists very cruelly, because in spite of his Hunnish extraction, he had become a faithful follower of the Vedic religion and lulled Buddhism for its feebleness. (Chapter 4—Paragraphs 284 & 285). But after Mihirgula, when Sindh went under the sway of the Vedic Hindu kings, the Buddhists no longer suffered any such persecution. They were free to follow their own religion so far as it concerned only with their own selves.

The Buddhist Traitors

326. Nevertheless, these Indian Buddhists were elated to see the Muslim foreigners' march against the Hindu kingdom. These Buddhists, who bore malice towards the Hindu, perhaps thought that these new Muslim aggressors might embrace their Buddhist cult, as did their forerunners, the Greeks under Menander or the Kushans under Kanishka, and establish a Buddhist empire over India. So they went and greeted the Arabian-Muslim leader, when he captured Port Deval from the hand of King Dahir. They appealed to him in some such way saying following:

326A. "We have nothing to do with Dahir and his Vedic Hindu cult. Our religious faith differs very widely from theirs. Our Prophet, Lord Buddha, has taught us 'Ahimsa' (Total Abstinence From Violence). We never take arms and dabble with political affairs of the state. Whoever wins can be the ruler of the state, we obey him in all matters temporal. You are now the victor, so now you are our King! Never suspect for a moment, that we shall even enlist ourselves in Dahir's armed forces or help him in any way. So we pray that the Buddhist should not be subjected to any indignities or troubles at your hands."

326B. Complying with some such request of the Buddhists, which amounted to complete surrender, the arch diplomat Kasim gave them temporary assurance of safety.

327. On receiving the news of the fall of Port Deval, King Dahir, on the other hand, mobilized his army and took the field. Kasim too, on his part, went ahead subjugating some parts of Sindh. The Muslim writers or tarikhs (reports), who have recorded the details of this campaign, testify that the Buddhist in Sindh helped the Muslims in every possible way, while the latter marched onwards, by showing them difficult passes, providing them with foodstuff and fodder and supplying them secret military intelligence. Some few Vedic Hindus also were guilty of this treachery, but their attempts were individual and exceptional.

King Dahir dies Fighting on the Battle-Field

328. At last, the main forces of the Muslims and the Hindus joined battle at Brahmanabad. The Hindus fought fiercely. Although the Muslims then had no cannon, they had firearms of a new type the Hindus did not possess. Naturally, the latter began to find themselves weaker in strength. Moreover, the Arab platoons that were in the pay of Dahir rebelled, when the Hindu-Muslim armies came to close quarters; the Arabs informed him that they would not fight against Mohammed-bin-Kasim since the latter was a Muslim as they themselves were, and that it was a religious crusade against the Kafirs. What more, they even marched on their Hindu master himself. This artlessness of the Hindus in placing complete faith in the enemy met the same fate, whenever in future a Hindu King employed Muslim soldiers in his army. This very often caused the Hindu strategy to topple down and made their battle-arrays ineffective.

329. Nevertheless, without letting this betrayal of the Arab platoons cause any confusion in his ranks, King Dahir mounted his elephant and kept on fighting in the thick of the fray. But when he himself was killed in the battle, the Hindu army was routed, and the Muslims, in hot pursuit, entered the city.

330. However, the moment she received the horrible news of King Dahir's death on the battlefield, the Queen and hundreds of other brave Hindu women leapt into a great fire and burnt themselves to death. It was the limit of warlike spirit, the Kshatriya Dharma! The enemy's attempts to capture and molest the Queen and other women of high-rank were mostly foiled.

331. Even then, in the confusion that was wrought everywhere,

Dahir's two daughters named Suryadevi and Pramiladevi fell into the hands of the Muslims, who had dashed into the city, killing every captive soldier and every citizen. Mohammed Kasim took them and also hundreds of others away as courtesans. The looting and massacre of the Hindus and the large-scale arson in the city went on unhindered. But that was the fate of not only one city, but of every other city or town that the Muslims visited on their onward march through Sindh, which met with the same disaster.

But what were the Buddhists Doing in this National Catastrophe?

332. At the news of the fall of King Dahir and the victory of the Muslims, these Buddhists began to ring bells in their vihars to greet the Muslim conquerors, and prayed in congregations for the prosperity of the Muslim rulers!

333. But what they thus asked for as a boon proved to be an inexorable curse for them. After winning the final battle, when the Muslim rushed violently, like a stormy wind throughout Sindh, they went on beheading these Buddhists even more ruthlessly than they did the Vedic Hindus. For, the Vedic Hindus were fighting in groups or individually at every place and so they struck at least a little awe and terror in the minds of the Muslims. But as there was no armed opposition in Buddhist vihars and Buddhist localities, the Muslims cut them down as easily as they would cut vegetable. Only those of the Buddhists who took to the Muslim faith were spared, while all their vihars throughout Sindh and the innumerale shrines in them were knocked down, and hammered to pieces; for the Muslims hated these 'Buddhparastis'—these shrine-worshippers.

334. The very word, "Buddhaparasta", which found its way into the Islamic tongue, is itself a corrupt form of the original Sanskrit word of the Buddhists, "Buddhaparsata". The Muslims began to call the shrine-worshippers "Buddhaparashta" because on their way to India, they first found such numerous shrines nowhere but in the Buddhist vihars. To annihilate such shrine-worshippers was for the Muslims, a sort of religious commandment.

Buddhist Ahimsa and Muslim Himsa

335. This is now the place where the question that we have discussed at length in Chapter II (Paras 152 to 159) of this book, about

the downfall of Buddhism in India should be chronologically concluded. By the year A.D. 700, of which we are speaking in these pages, that is, before the Muslims could set foot in India towards Sindh, the Buddhists all over India were fast diminishing in numbers and dwindling into non-existence as is already shown in previous chapters. The successful theoretical refutation of the Buddhist philosophy and religious tenet by the stalwart Vedic theologians and 'pandits' is not the only cause of the total extinction of the Buddhists in India; many other social and political events also had a fair share in this momentous task. Of them only those, which have not received the proper attention from the historians so far, or which have not been given enough prominence they really deserve, will be conspicuously referred to at their proper places in these brief concluding remarks.

The first cause: the Buddhists' High Treason

336. We have already dwelt at length on this collective high treason of the Buddhists in India against their nation in Ch. II Paras 152 to 159; 182-209, and Ch. III Paras 242-246 of this book. Because of this treacherous mentality of the Buddhists, the whole of the patriotic and politically conscious Indian population was up in arms to destroy them root and branch. Being convinced beyond doubt by actual experience, that these Buddhist congregations (Buddhasangha) were inherently anti-national and unpatriotic, and treacherous institutions, the patriotic politicians and the kingly courts gave them hardly any support anywhere in India. Especially in the north about the year A.D. 700 as the new Rajput kingdoms, which were the staunch supporters of the Vedic religion, began to prosper, the Buddhist population and the Buddhist cult were rendered helpless, socially boycotted, weak and invalid everywhere in India.

The Second Reason: Fanatic Buddhist Ahimsa

337. Just as the patriotic and politically conscious population of India became impatient with the Buddhist cult, so was the general populace disgusted with the harassment of Buddhist ahimsa. At times—though few and far between—when the Buddhists gained the greatest political power over the major portion of India as in the times of Ashoka and Shree Harsha, they enforced the Buddhist tenets on the Vedic Hindus by misusing their political authority. The writings of the times are replete with copious references to, and illustrations of, the religious

persecution carried on by the Buddhists on those occassions. Yet, if passages are quoted from some Vedic books, some over-sensitive soul might doubt their veracity as they occur from an opponent's mouth. Hence, we are adducing a specimen, to show clearly how vehemently the foreign and non-Vedic historians have criticized it. Vincent Smith in his 'Early History of India' has this to say—

338. "It is recorded by contemporary testimony that in the seventh century, King Harsha, who obviously aimed at copying closely the institutions of Ashoka, did not shrink from inflicting capital punishment without hope of pardon on any person, who dared to infringe his commands by slaying any animal or using flesh as food, in any part of his dominion. Kumar Pal, a Jain King of Gujarat, imposed savage penalties upon violators of his (similar) rules. An unlucky merchant who had committed the atrocious crime of cracking a louse, was brought before a special court at Anilhawada and punished with the confiscation of his whole property. Another wretch, who had outraged the sanctity of the capital by bringing a dish of raw meat, was put to death. The special court constituted by Kumar Pal (for this purpose), had functions similar to those of Ashoka's censors. And the working of the latter institution sheds light on the unrecorded proceedings of the earlier ones."

The Martyr Louse!

339. Out of the proceeds obtained by selling the confiscated property of the offender, who committed the 'atrocious crime' of cracking the said louse, was built a big temple worth lacs of rupees and it was named 'Yukvihar'—the Temple of Louse!

340. Had this incident been decribed by any other writer, it would have been a parody of the Jain faith. But it is the Jain writers themselves, who cite it with evident pride. Hence, it has to be taken as true.

341. What a paradoxical practice! In order to save a louse in the hair of a man, to cut off the very head of that man! And this is called 'ahimsa'! As if to kill a man is no 'himsa'—violence! Man seems to have no life at all! It is because of this 'ahimsa', more ruthless and more violent than violence—'himsa'—itself, that millions of Indian hunters, fishermen, seamen, gamekeepers, foresters and others, who lived by hunting and fishing lost their professions.

342. When these millions of flesh-eaters jointly protested and demonstrated how they and their wives and children would starve to

death and how this would spell violence of an enormously grave nature, King Kumar Pal of Gujarat most graciously issued another order that these millions of people, who have been carrying on violent professions, ought to leave those professions themselves. However, as per their demand, the state was to subsidize them for three years.

343. But what after those three years! Starvation could not be completely ruled out in the case of these unfortunate millions. For, flesh and meat was their chief food, which could be had almost for nothing. But because this intolerant 'ahimsa' made flesh-eating punishable by death, this common mass of people was antagonized to the Buddhist faith. These millions of people shook off its tyrannical yoke, and sought refuge in the Vedic religion, which had now taken an all-embracing noble form, accepting a relatively considerate ahimsa, which allowed concessions for particular time and place and persons, concentrating mainly on human welfare!

Untouchability Aggravated by the Buddhist Religion

344. Even today, not only common people and good many propagandists, but even historians seem to be labouring under the delusion that the Buddhists did not recognize the principle of untouchability, and that no one was considered untouchable in the Buddhist regime. What is laid down in someone's religious texts is beside the point. What the actual practice was, is the most pertinent thing. One unavoidable result of the violent way in which the Buddhists tried to establish the principle of ahimsa, and of their declaring animal-hunting and flesh-eating punishable by death, of their over-enthusiastic and relentless efforts to search out such offender and give the harshest capital and other severe punishments, was that the practice of untouchability instead of being wiped out, became still more firmly rooted, widespread and most distressing. The limited space at our disposal prevents any further discussion of it in these pages, and, of course, it is needless! An unimpeachable proof can be found, not in the Vedic, nor in the Buddhist texts of the times, but in the account of the foreign, Chinese travellers who had espoused Buddhism and who had travelled all over India. They avow, "Whichever caste or community—as for example the 'Chandals'—did not give up the violent professions and did not observe ahimsa, according to the Buddha faith, were banished from the town as untouchables; they had to form colonies of their own

outside the towns and cities, like those of the lepers. If at all they had an occassion and were permitted to come to the town on some market-day, these untouchables had to carry in one hand a stick, to the end of which was tied a child's rattle or a small drum, which they had to beat while going along the road, so that the people in the streets might see them and avoid every possible contact with them."

345. Those, who ignorantly or maliciously blame the Peshwas for the evil treatment given to the untouchables when they entered the town, should also criticize, equally vehemently and for the same offence Ashoka, Shree Harsha and Buddhist kings, and all the Kshatriya kings right from Vikramaditya to the Rajput rulers, when they see this evidence. For this evil tradition of untouchability was not begun by the Peshwas, for the first time, but it had been prevalent even since the Vedic, the Buddhist and the Jain regimes, and in the Buddhist period, especially, instead of being weakened, it was most scrupulously and mercilessly observed. Even the untouchables themselves treated those below their own ranks as equally or even more untouchable. Those of the untouchables who are still under the delusion, that the Buddhists gave no quarter to untouchability and so extol that sect, should do well to remember that the Chandals, the Mahars and other untouchables were far more miserable under the violently non-violent Buddhists, than under the Vedic people, who accepted the principle of ahimsa with its limitations. The Buddhist, once again I would like to repeat, aggravated and not mitigated 'untouchability'. They should examine the validity of this statement in the light of the undisputed evidence cited here and then alone, should they choose whatever is beneficial to them.

346. They should remember that for the above reason, the untouchables like the Chandals and others preferred the Vedic regimes, a more congenial, to the unrelenting and uncompromising Buddhist ones, and those thouands of them who in the past had voluntarily (or helplessly and under pressure) embraced Buddhism, now renounced it and declared their allegiance to the Vedic religion. Thus, even before the Muslims set foot in Sindh, followers of the Buddha had begun to diminish in numbers by millions throughout all ranks of society, right from the highest to the lowest, and because of its inherent weakness, Buddhism had declined to such an extent that the Chinese Buddhist travellers, who had seen its sad plight with their own eyes, had been

moved to write that the holy and once prosperous places like Buddha Gaya, Mrigadava, Shravasti, Kushinagar, and the birthplace of Lord Buddha, Kapilvastu, which had been sanctified by the actual residence of the Lord and which had been the place of pilgrimage for the world-wide Buddhist followers, had been sadly rendered desolate and were overgrown with wild and thick forests.

347. Nevertheless, this moribund Buddhism was not altogether wiped out of India, before the advent of the Muslims. The Buddhists were more numerous in the north-western frontier states like Sindh and Kamboj, and even in Bengal in the east, than in the rest of India. It is said that the modern state of Bihar derives its name from the fact that there once existed far too many Buddhist viharas, stoopas and other 'Buddhaparasthas'. Since the Vedic states were prosperous everywhere, this Buddhist sect had no guts to carry on its traitorous activities or to enforce its religious rites and faith on non-Buddhists, whether it had their will to do so or not. And so long as they followed their religious faith harmlessly, they, their organisations, their institutions, and their viharas were never interfered with in any way by the Vedic kings. That they enjoyed complete religious freedom is admitted by the Chinese travellers open-heartedly.

348. What then made these millions of Buddhists, living in the various states of India before the Muslim onrush, dwindle into non-existence thereafter?

349. Some time ago, historians, and especially western historians, had a presumption that sometime in the past, or at frequent intervals, the Vedic rulers must have massacred these Buddhists and destroyed them root and branch, or reconverted them to Hinduism forcibly. In order to find some credence to this theory of theirs, they examined the historical records of the times most scrupulously. but even after taking into consideration a few trifling exceptions. they could find no proof to establish any deliberate, pre-planned, or systematic attempt on the part of the Vedic rulers to annihilate the Buddhists completely.

349A. At last, the more conscientious of these historians declared honestly, that this presumption of theirs was totally unfounded and the very idea of forcible extinction of the Buddhists at the hands of the Vedic people was basically wrong.

350. Who then was responsible for this total ousting of the Buddhist faith from India? The historians, foreign as well as native, do not seem

to have found an answer to this pressing question, or they have, at least, preferred to be silent on this point.

The third cause—Confrontation with Muslims

351 A. We have already briefly described in the foregoing pages how, in spite of their traitorous solicitations of the Muslims, these 'Buddhaprasthees'—the idol-worshipping Buddhists who preached extreme non-violence—were violently exterminated from Sindh by the Muslim aggressors under Kasim, owing to their innate hatred for that sect. For the same reason, and in the very same manner, the Muslims went on liquidating the Buddhist pockets of influence, as they advanced, conquering province-after-province in India. With a sword in one hand and the Koran in the other, every Muslim military chief broke down, demolished and razed to the ground the Buddhist 'stoopas', 'sangharams', 'viharas', the idols of Buddha, pillars, everything belonging to or relating to the Buddhists. As most of the Buddhists showed, through fear of death, willingness to embrace Islam, they were all converted. Not a single Buddhist remained alive in the northwestern provinces like Gandhar, Kamboj and others; everyone became a Muslim or was silenced by the victor's sword. On seeing Bakhtyar Khilji march on Bihar, several Buddhists took their religious books and fled to Tibet and China. The rest were polluted and taken over into the Muslim fold. Some might have preferred dying rather to being Muslims, but no one fought for life and religion. Nowhere, can one find evidence to say that some Indian Buddhist army or some Buddhist organization fought with the Muslim invaders any battle worth the name!

Majority of Muslims in East Bengal explained

352. The same is the case with East Bengal, where the majority of the population was Buddhist. With some honourable exceptions, the Buddhists there took to Islam en masse. In Delhi, where the Muslim sultans and emperors ruled for over five hundred years, the Vedic Hindus have all along been in a clear majority. The whole of Uttar Pradesh—the northern India—right upto West Bengal—whether under the Muslim administration or the British or the present one, the Vedic Hindus—has all along maintained its numerical superiority. For, even when the Muslims first came conquering, the Buddhists in these provinces were conspicuously few in number. It is only in East Bengal that the Hindus

fell into minority. How? Quite obviously! This province had numerically more Buddhists than the Hindus, and those numerous Buddhists became Muslims! It is natural, therefore, that this province alone should become, since then, a Muslim-majority province.

353. Thus, it is the social extinction of the Buddhists in India, which came to pass all of a sudden, which was the inevitable effect of the armed and ruthless might of the Muslim conquerors. The relentless and uncompromising Buddhist ahimsa was done to death by the equally relentless and bigoted Muslim violence!

354. But what happened to the Buddhist cult and Lord Buddha himself in India in the end? Just as a stream separated from the River Bhagirathi, should flow separately some miles away and once again should leap as a tributary into the same Bhagirathi, the Buddhist cult, born out of the Vedic Hinduism, merged in the end in the same Hindu religion; and Lord Buddha himself was established as the tenth of the Godly Avatars and was Hinduized.

The Neglected 300 years of Hindu Valour

355-356. In most of the 'Histories of India', by foreign as well as by our own writers, and especially in the textbooks of history for Indian schools, the Muslim invasions of India follow so thickly the one of Sindh in A.D. 711 by Mohammed Kasim, and the accounts of the subjugation of province-after-province of India are narrated so hastily, as in one breath, and the whole account is so cursorily given in a limited space of 20 or 25 pages, that a common reader or a small pupil is quite likely to think that the Hindus offered practically no resistance worth the name, that the Muslims were never halted in their advance. After the conquest of Sindh, the Muslim victor mounted, as it were, a magic horse and went on conquering the whole of India and never, till they reached Kanyakumari, did they alight from it. This is obviously childish!

The Intervening Period

357. To avoid this misconception and to nullify the injustice done to the Hindu nations, a true historian, whose avowed duty is to tell the truth, the whole truth and nothing but the truth, should effectively and proportionately, describe the intervals between any two Muslim invasions and the heroic resistance, successful or otherwise, offered by the Hindus. After the fall of Sindh in A.D. 711, Hindu kings most effectively

checked the Muslim advance outside Sindh for more or less 300 years. But this Hindu heroism quite easily escapes the notice of the common reader, because in almost all the textbooks of Indian History, it is not so impressively mentioned.

358. It is because we utter the words 'three hundred years' or three centuries within three seconds, that the enormous length of this intervening period quite escapes our notice, unless we are expressly told about it. We should, therefore, measure the period in question by generations of people. Five generations make up 300 years! The British rule over India, for instance, seems too lengthy to the present generation. But measured in centuries, it lasted only for one and a half. Compared with it, the Hindu valour in arresting the Muslim onslaught within the confines of Sindh for more or less 300 years, assumes a greater historical significance. The same holds good with regard to the other intervening periods.

359. One cannot say justifiably that the Muslim vigour or their ambition to conquer the world was on the wane. On the contrary, these both were at their full height during this period. During this very period of three hundred years, these very Arabs had overrun and vanquished nation-after-nation, right from Baghdad to the Mediterranean Sea and thence along the north African coast straight to Gilbralter, whence they subjugated Portugal and Spain and knocked at the gates of southern France. The name Gibralter itself testifies to the unrivalled Muslim conquest of the West Jebal-Tarik, which means the straits conquered by the Muslim Commander Tarik, which is the root of the modern corrupt form 'Gilbralter'.

359A. At last in A.D. 732, the valiant King of France, Charles Martel, gave a mortal blow to the Muslim aggression and repelled them for ever. It is this monumental triumph of Charles Martel, that saved the whole of Europe! In their triumphant march, the Muslims not only subdued the kingdoms in Western Asia and Northern Africa politically, but with the sharp edge of their sword, they also forced them all to embrace Islam. Even Portugal and Spain were forcibly converted to Islamic faith. Their womenfolk, too, were abducted and violently defiled. But both these nations freed themselves from the Muslim yoke some centuries afterwards. How they did so will be described a little later. Still the fact remains that the nations on the north coast of Africa are even today Muslims.

360. Well, it is not that during the years A.D. 700 to 1000 the Muslims did not try to march out of Sindh and attack the neighbouring Hindu States with the same devilish bigotry. They did try to force themselves on through Sourashtra and Gandhar many times. But every time, they were routed by the Hindus.

361. At that time from the eastern boundary of Sindh to the northern most boundary of north India, there was an unbroken chain of valiant Rajput Rajas which, like a mountain range, very difficult, though not quite impossible to cross, kept on resisting stoutly the Muslim onslaught. Consequently, in Sourashtra and in the north-west provinces, the attacking Muslim armies were put to rout again and again, by the staunch resistance of the Hindus. On the other hand, the mighty Bapa Raval of Chittod once attacked Sindh and after driving the Muslims clean out, annexed it to his own Kingdom. The Arabs did, no doubt, capture it once again, but ultimately, the Sumra Rajputs firmly established their rule over Sindh.

362. If the fanatic Arabs could trample under the horses' hoofs, the whole northern coast of Africa and two major nations of Europe, why could they not force their way out of Sindh? Thus, put in sharp contrast with contemporary history of the west, the heroism of the Hindus shines out all the more clearly and brightly.

363. Why couldn't another Chandragupta Maurya or a Vikramaditya channel out the whole of the Indian might, and drive the Arabian Muslims back right into the heart of Arabia, is a fact that disturbs us not a little.

□

7

The Peculiar Nature of the Muslim Atrocities [Sultans of Ghazni]

364. During the long period of nearly three hundred years, in which the Arab menace was being successfully hemmed in Sindh, and was finally overthrown by the Sumra Rajputs, different Muslim tribes were busy founding a strong Muslim power in Ghazni, further north of Gandhar. A Sultan of Ghazni, Sabakhtageen, was now preparing himself fully to attack his contemporary Brahmin king, Jaipal, whose forefathers had all along been ruling the whole of Punjab and Gandhar right up to the Hindukush, ever since the rout of the Huns.

365. Shrewdly anticipating the plan of Sabakhtageen to invade India, Jaipal himself attacked Ghazni, but unfortunately he was repelled, Encouraged by this success, Sabakhtageen boldly fell upon Jaipal, a few years afterwards, with a large army. In order to meet this fierce aggression more determinedly, King Jaipal formed a powerful alliance with the neighbouring Hindu princes, but he was again defeated and the whole region beyond the Indus river, including Gandhar, was lost to the Muslim invader. Soon afterwards, Sultan Sabakhtageen died and was succeeded by his son, Mohammed, a hundred times more fanatical and more crueller than his father, and an arch-enemy of the Hindus. This was the same Mahmud of Ghazni, who styled himself 'Butshikan', the Idol-breaker or 'Iconoclast'. At his accession to the throne of Ghazni, he had vowed in the presence of the highest religious and temporal Muslim authority, the Grand Khalipha, that he would wipe out the Kafir Hindus from India and in order to keep his word, he soon began a series of expeditions beyond the Indus.

366. It is from now onwards—i.e. about A.D. 1000—that the really great wars between the Hindus and the Muslims were to be fought for centuries together.

367. If the Muslim soldiers had gained great confidence, having twice defeated the Hindu forces under Jaipal, King Jaipal and his soldiers, without being disheartened and downcast even after suffering two defeats, speeded up their preparation for a still more determined stand against the Muslims. But fortune once again frowned upon the Hindu King. And when, notwithstanding all his valour and all his efforts to save his religion and his nation, he was again defeated in 1001 by Mahmud of Ghazni, Jaipal preferred entrusting the kingdom to his son, Anangpal, and burning himself to death in a great pyre, to a disgraceful life and a meek surrender to the enemy.

368. King Anangpal, too, carried on his father's arduous task of staunchly opposing the Muslim aggression. In A.D. 1006, Mahmud demanded passage through Anangpal's territory in order to invade Multan; but Anangpal refused to give any, whereupon the Muslim aggressor marched on Anangpal and defeated him. Anangpal had to retreat and when Mahmud went ahead to Multan, Anangpal again organized a united Hindu stand for protecting the Hindu religion. Once again, the Hindu-Muslim armies met in the vicinity of the Indus, in A.D. 1008, when the Hindus fought so furiously that in the afternoon, the Muslim formation was broken through and there was confusion in the Muslim ranks. Even Sultan Mahmud had prepared to leave the battlefield to make a retreat, when all of a sudden, Anangpal's elephant, scared by the shower of burning arrows, turned round and started running amuck. This was the most unfortunate thing, which had very often brought about the Hindu collapse, but no sufficient precaution was ever taken to prevent it. A great havoc was wrought by this retreating elephant among the Hindu ranks. Mahmud was quick enough to seize the opportunity of this decisive turn of the battle and reorganizing the choicest of his scattered soldiers, he once again fell upon the bewildered Hindu army and in a deadly struggle defeated it. But the Muslim army was no less worsted; so instead of pursuing Anangpal, Mahmud satisfied himself with the success he got and returned to Ghazni. But as it became quite clear to him that unless and until Anangpal was humbled completely, no Muslim power could be established in Punjab, he assailed the latter for the third time.

This time unfortunately, Anangpal had nobody to help him. Yet he went to war with the remnant of his loyal army and, as a brave King that he was, he died in the thick of the fray.

369. Thus, King Jaipal and his son Anangpal and thousands of their brave soldiers boldly faced, and fought against the early ferocious Muslim onslaughts in Punjab and laid down their lives for the protection of the Hindu state and the Hindu religion. They did their sacred duty of arresting the enemy thrust.

370. Soon after the death of Anangpal, Mahmud annexed Punjab to his kingdom of Ghazni, as he had formerly done with the north-west frontier province. Sultan Mahmud then marched on Thaneshwar and Mathura, the most renowned of the holy places of the Hindus; and after demolishing and burning as many of the Hindu temples, and killing as many of the Hindu male population as possible, and violating the chastity of hundreds of Hindu women and abducting them, Mahmud, like a ferocious wolf returned to his den, Ghazni. He also took with him immeasurable booty of gold and jewellery. In A.D. 1019, he pounced on the Pratihari capital of Kanouj and destroyed it in the same brutal fashion. The result was that the surrounding Hindu population took such a fearful fright for him, that when in A.D. 1023, he once again paid his sinister visit to Gwalior and Kalinjar, the princes there helplessly and meekly accepted his overlordship.

His Dash on Somnath

371. Next, when in A.D. 1026, Sultan Mahmud assailed the famous temple of Somnath in Sourashtra, he did it with such a huge army and with such terrible vows and declarations that Raja Bheem of Sourashtra and Gujarat fled away, leaving the kingdom exposed to every sort of humiliation and destruction at the hands of this appalling enemy, tainting his own name of Bheem with everlasting shame. Naturally, the Hindus had no army left, sufficiently well-equipped and well-organized to face this formidable Muslim assault. Nevertheless, even at this critical time, the priests of the Temple of Somnath offered to shoulder the responsibility of protecting the sacred temple as best as they could. They called upon the surrounding Hindu population to run to their aid in the sacred cause of defending the temple and their religion, and thousands of Hindus from far-off regions also, answered their call and ran to the rescue of the Temple of Somnath. The battle was to be fought not for any ruler or king; no Hindu soldier was to profit by it individually. It was a crusade, pure and simple. Moreover, these thousands of Hindu soldiers were not a trained and well-formed

army. It was a conglomeration of Hindu crusaders that was collected at the eleventh hour. Even then, they fought ferociously and desperately for the sacred cause without intermission or relaxation, by day and even by night, with the well-organized and stalwart Muslim soldiers! While the Muslim army climbed right upto the ramparts and barricades over the high walls of the temple, and even after it forced itself into the very temple, the toughest of Hindu resistance continued unmitigated. Muslim blood, too, was shed profusely. Not before did Sultan Mahmud completely put down all resistance, could he ever force his way right into the innermost chamber of the temple and break the idol of Somnath with his own hands. In order to celebrate this fanatical act, he took for himself the title, 'Butshikan'—Iconoclast!

Martyrdom of fifty thousand brave Hindu Soldiers

372. Even Muslim historians write that at least fifty thousand Hindus fell fighting in the defence of their temple. Had someone of these fifty thousand Hindus said, "I am willing to be a Muslim", he would have been spared by the Muslims, because it was one of their tactics in the religious war. But scorning such a base and defiled life, the Hindu volunteer force courted martyrdom; not one, not even a thousand, but fifty thousand of them sacrificed their precious lives on the altar of this holy battle!

373. While eulogizing an ancient Roman hero, Horatius, who fought with the enemy on a similar occasion, an English poet writes:

Thus outspake brave Horatius
the Captain of the gate,
"To every man upon this earth
death cometh soon or late,
And how can a man die better than
by facing fearful odds
For the ashes of his fathers and
the temple of his Gods?"

374. Which Hindu will be reluctant to shed his grateful tears for these fifty thousand martyrs, who died defending their religion and temples with the same fervour as is expressed in this verse?

375. But the most disgusting fact is that while narrating this invasion of Mahmud on Somnath, not only the foreign historians but many Hindu historians, ungrateful as they too are, have mocked at the

simple faith of the priesthood and other Hindu population of the place, and have not uttered a single word in praise of those Hindu warriors who made such a huge sacrifice, 'facing fearful odds, for the temple of their Gods'! If the wiseacres are not wise enough to appraise the jewels properly, can it be said that the fault lies with those jewels?

376. Even if it be neccesary to condemn the blind faith of those Hindus, yet those who do so, should also remember that, *albeit* blind, the Hindu belief in the mysterious divine power of their Gods was not a diabolic, fanatic, bloodthirsty religiosity like that of the Muslims, who attacked religious places of others with deadly weapons of war, slew the innocent men and women, young and old, forced them to embrace Islam at the point of the sword, and ran frantically, causing death and destruction everywhere. But such a statement born of boldness cannot be expected of these immature childish and cowardly writers! If the Muslim writers of 'Tarikhs' and the Mullah-Moulvis boast that the Hindu Gods were not the true Gods because they did not prevent the Muslim warlords from breaking idols and demolishing temples, and that theirs was the only true religion, they should be enlightened that the arch heretic Changizkhan and his deputies not only desecrated the very city of the Muslim-Khalipha, but ravaged it, killed the Khalipha, burned several masjids, turned others into stables for their horses, reduced the Bible to ashes and trampled the Koran under their horses' hoofs! The Muslim Allah could not stop the ravaging hands of Changizkhan! Hundreds of such instances can be cited. Are the Muslims ready to grant, on this account, the imbecility and falsehood of their Allah? Even when Shivaji slew the 'Butshikan'—idol-breaker—Afzalkhan, and offered his 'goat like head with thirty-two teeth', as a sacrificial offering to the Goddess Bhavani of Tulzapur, his hands were not staved off from doing so by the Muslim Allah!

377. After demolishing the temple of Somnath and loading the camels with the immense wealth, looted from it, when Mahmud set out for Ghazni, he learnt that instead of being cowed down into submission because of his wholesale destruction of the temple at Somnath, the Hindu population was even more enraged, and that the King of Malava with his large army was preparing to block his way back to Ghazni and had already entered the battlefield. As Mahmud was not prepared to risk this new battle, he took an unexpected and difficult route through the sandy deserts of Sindh, abandoning the usual way through Malava. While crossing the deserts of Sindh and Baluchistan, his army had to

face many dangers and unspeakable misery. Hardly within three or four years of reaching Ghazni, he died in A.D. 1030.

378. This fanatic but brave Sultan of Ghazni undertook at least fifteen major expeditions to India. Hindus too fought furiously on the battlefield every time. But no Hindu king could defeat him. But these invasions of Mahmud and his political conquests did not so much harm the Hindus, as did the forcible conversion of millions of Hindus in North-West Frontier Province and Punjab. That the Kingdoms, which were lost to the Muslims, were reconquered by the Hindus sooner or later, is plain history. But the Hindus could never bring back the millions of Hindus who were converted to Islam willy-nilly. We could free from the foreign yoke our geographical regions, but the enormous numerical loss of population could never be made up by the Hindu nation.

Change of Religion means Change of Nationality

379. We are now going to discuss at some length some of the religious concepts of the Hindus of those times; of the course of conduct and practices that were considered decent and in conformity with the religious laws of the Hindus of those times, and those that were declared to be against them; and particularly those that deeply concerned the large-scale forcible defilement and conversion of the Hindus that took place during the Hindu-Muslim war. It can be very briefly said here that if the millions of forcibly converted Hindus have remained Muslims even to this day, it is because of the perverse religious concepts of the Hindus of those times, which ultimately proved highly detrimental to the best interests of the Hindu community, viz.—caste-system, the fantastic ideas of pollution, the extravagant ideas of religious tolerance and many other silly notions. Why, these Hindu converts went on increasing enormously generation-after-generation and, as the later generations were born and brought up under the Muslim influence, they began to be more-and-more fanatical—so bitterly fanatical that they formed an appreciable part of the armies of the Iranian, Turkish, Mongol and other foreign Muslim invaders and, with equal hatred and bitterness, they attacked the Hindu Kafirs with a view to destroying them completely or force them to change their own religion and embrace Islam. One out of hundreds of such facts can be cited here to bear out the above remarks. A Hindu tribe, named Ghuri which lived, during the period

under discussion, beyond the Indus and which was forcibly made to change over to Islam under precisely the same perilous conditions, became later on, the bitterest enemy of the Hindus. The Hindu-hater, Sultan Mohammed Ghori, belonged to this very Ghuri tribe. In fact, the majority of the Muslim populations of Afghanisthan, Pathanisthan (Pakhtoonistan), Baluchistan were the converted descendants of the original Hindu natives of those places. But, later on, they did not even have the slightest idea that their ancestors were, once upon a time, Hindus. On the contrary, they were enraged at any mention of such descent of theirs and would say: "Bygones are bygones; today we are born Muslims and are Muslim nationals. We recognize no other relation with the Hindus than the one of utmost hatred and animosity." Such thoughts had turned their heads completely. Theirs was not merely a change of religion, but it was the inevitable change of nationality which necessarily forced itself upon the later generations of such converts. During the five or six centuries of the initial Muslim invasions of India, right up to Rameshwar to which we are referring here, the change of religion today generally proved to be the change of nationality for the future!

But what does Religion mean here?

380. But the terms 'religion' and 'religious conversion' in the above maxim, viz. the 'the change of the religion means the change of nationality', should first be defined clearly. They are not used here in the sense of comparative study of the various philosophical ideas and systems in different religions or the adoption of some of the agreeable ones in an individual capacity. The word 'religion' in the present context relates solely to the dogmatic and fanatical practices of those aggressive religious institutions, which insist that a particular book is apocalyptic, that whatever is told in its pages—and that alone and nothing else—is truly religious, that everything else is completely false and sinful. It then tries to enforce on people of other religions the strict observance, if not by advice and peaceful discourse and persuasion, even by skilful craftiness, cruelty and coercion, of not only the so-called philosophy in those religious books, but of the rules and regulations, of rites and rituals, of the language and social dealings prescribed by them. The religious conversion effected by such thoughtless and fanatical religious institutions is, in effect, the conversion of nationality.

Retaliatory Weapon of Ostracism

381. The Hindus could find no retaliatory weapon for this religious aggression of the Muslims. The weapon of ostracism, which they used for retaliation, turned on themselves like a boomerang.

382. In order that the reader should have a clear idea of this weapon of social ostracism, so far as it concerns the Hindu-Muslim war and how it affected, not favourably, but adversely the defence of the Hindu religion and Hindu community, it is essential to give first of all an account of the caste-system as briefly as it is possible to do so. Since such an account is absolutely esential for an analysis of the Muslim pollution of the Hindus.

The caste-system based on birth and Parentage and the National Penalty of Ostracism

383. Much earlier than the Muslim invasions of India, i.e. just after the Hindus conquered the Huns completely, hundreds of Hindu leaders tried on all sides all over India to restore political, religious and social stability in the society and the nation. The Hindu leadership of the time naturally devolved on them rising warrior class of the Rajput royalty, who were staunch devotees of the Vedic Hindu religion. In this very attempt at reconstruction, the vast Hindu community was being moulded with meticulous care into the framework of the parentage-dominated caste system. Slowly but surely, this caste system became an inherent and essential feature of Hinduism. Not only in the four former classes (वर्ण), but in more or less four thousand castes, born out of those four classes and many other accidental sources, sanctioned by the religious law, was the whole Hindu community everlastingly and almost unanimously divided internally. In a sense, the social transition of the Hindu nation was occosioned by the historical neccesity of the time.

384. The main principle underlying this caste-system was this: Only he who was born in a particular caste, could remain in it. To have food or to drink even water with or from one of another caste was considered liable for penalty. Is it any wonder then that the inter-caste marriages of boys and girls were strictly prohibited? To these very religious practices of the time, we have ascribed, in our various articles on the caste-system, the names 'Lotabandi (prohibition of drinking water), Rotibandi (prohibition of food), Betibandi (prevention of inter-caste marriages), Sparshbandi (untouchability) and the ones that we are going to discuss hereafter viz., Shuddhibandi (prevention of purification of religious

converts), Sindhubandi (ban on sea voyage) etc. These seven 'bandis'—or bans—which arrested not only the progress of the Hindus but also impaired their normal way of life were, in fact, seven fetters. These fetters were not forcibly fastened to the feet of the Hindu nation by any Muslim, Christian or other foreign power; they were so fastened by the Hindus themselves, in their extreme anxiety for the protection of their religion. That is why we have been calling them through spoken as well as written words not foreign shackles, but as 'seven native fetters'.

385. It is not necessary here in this book to discuss fully the caste-system of the Hindus, nor is this the place for it. Those desirous of getting themselves acquainted with our thoughts on this subject may profitably read the book, "Janmajat Jatyutchhedak Nibandha" (The Eradication of the Parentage-dominated Caste-system). Here, while describing the religious aggression of our foreign enemies, we shall discuss it only so far as it is absolutely necessary to do so.

386. First of all, it should not be forgotten that this caste-system must have facilitated the stupendous consolidation and remarkable stability of the Hindu Society under certain peculiar circumstances and in particular contexts. In evaluating it, it would be ungrateful only to point to the eventual harm that it has caused in its later stages.

387. It must also be admitted that the Hindus of those times created, or voluntarily allowed to be created, this caste-system with the sole object of protecting their racial seed and blood, preserving their caste-life and tradition, and keeping them absolutely pure from any contamination.

388. The structure of the caste-system was based on the principles of heredity, of the economy based on the division of labour, of social co-existence and of social ethics, so far as these principles were comprehended by the writers of different 'Smritis'. Thousands of years have rolled by, the Hindu nation has faced innumerable calamities and catastrophes, yet the hold of the caste-system and the influence that it has wielded upon billions and billions of Hindus throughout these tens of centuries, could never have been possible, if the roots of this birth-dominated caste-system had not gone deeper into the very foundation of this colossal edifice of the Hindu society. The Hindu faith—that the religious duties prescribed for the particular castes and sub-castes like Pariyas, Bhangis, Kolis, Bhils were the pious ways of attaining their earthly welfare, and heavenly bliss and Godly grace for them—would

never have otherwise remained so steadfast through all these perilous centuries, if the lifeblood, which ran through the veins of the Hindu Society, apparently most heterogenous and miserably disorganised, had not animated its diversified elements with some undying and unifying force with a certain consciouness of its true self.

388A. This powerful unifying national sentiment which so unmistakably held together these different and apparently autonomous elements of the Hindu society and fused them together was HINDUTWA! AND HINDU DHARMA.

389. What we should like to call today the seven native shackles, viz. Untouchability (स्पर्शबंदी) ban on dining together of the people belonging to different castes (रोटीबंदी), ban on inter-caste marriages (बेटीबंदी), and so on), did never appear to be shackles or fetters to the Hindus of those times, when the Muslims had begun invading India. To them, they were but the charmed amulets or protecting bands! Every caste, whether of the Brahmins or of the sweepers, was immensely proud of its separate entity.

390. These various castes and sub-castes of the Hindus punished even the slightest violation of the caste-laws with social ostracism—even if such a violation of caste-law was voluntary or involuntary, knowingly or unknowingly!

391. Today, we are apt to take this social ostracism quite lightly, but at the time of Muslim aggressions and thereafter, the very mention of such social ostracism would have unfailingly shocked to death every Hindu—whether he was a prince or a pauper—to be cut off from one's own caste, was to be cut off from the whole world and from life itself. So severe was this punishment of social boycott that the unfortunate person at once lost his parents and brothers, his kith and kin—the people of his own flesh and blood—and was thrown into abysmal gloom. It should be sufficient to say here briefly that this social ostracism was far more dreaded than any physical torture or a heavy fine involving any financial loss or even death. Consequently, the tendency to observe scrupulously, and in strict conformity with the prevalent social practices, the traditional caste-laws, sanctioned by the sacred religious books and the writers of the various Smritis, was ingrained into the very texture of the Hindu society for generations together.

392. Although we can gratefully cite many other things regarding the caste-system that brought about cohesiveness of the diversified Hindu

society and had lasting effects on it, it would be equally ungrateful on our part if we desist from criticising with sufficient severity, the unlimited harm done by this caste-system and the irrational and obstinate pride that the Hindus took in it, when the Muslims began to knock at their doors.

393. As a means of beating down the religious aggression of the Muslims, this counter-stroke of the Hindu caste system proved to be most ineffectual and useless like a blunted sword. On the contrary, these very caste-laws and the strict adherence to them brought about a series of disasters on the Hindu religion and the Hindu nation, making the conversion of the millions of Hindus far too easier for the Muslims than can be imagined, while it cannot be denied that they made the conversion of the Muslims to Hinduism, absolutely impossible.

394. Before they came to India, the Arabians and other Muslims forced the millions of Christian, Jewish and Persian populations of Iran, Turan, the kingdoms of the middle Asia and Africa, right from Egypt to Spain, to give up their own religious faiths and accept Islam at the point of the sword. But these various European and Afro-Asian people never for a moment thought themelves to be polluted, nor that their own original religion was lost to them, simply because they took food or drink with the Muslims. The Muslim rulers had to keep their swords constantly hanging over their heads to enforce their allegiance to Islam, and to ensure from them the strict observance of the Muslim religious rites and duties, for centuries together. If, by chance, the Muslim power at any place was uprooted and completely effaced, the forcibly converted Christians or Persians and others went over to their original religions en masse, throwing away to the winds the green Muslim shred of a flag and proudly fluttering their own in its stead. As such, it was very difficult for even the Muslim powers there to keep these unwilling converts tied to the Islamic faith, the Muslim armed soldiers had to keep a vigilant eye on these foreign converts and to see every time if their faith in Islam was shaken even a bit or whether they did not foment any agitation to go back to their own religion.

395-396. On the contrary, in Spain, Greece, Serbia and other countries, where the Muslims in their turn were forced to forsake Islam and court Christianity on pain of death, the Christian rulers there had to keep a similar strict watch on these Muslim converts. For the Muslims, too, never thought that they were anyway defiled because of any food they ate from the Christians or because they had marital or extramarital relations with them. These forcibly converted Muslims were on the alert, to see if the ruling power became weak at any place and immediately revolted, hoisting any green cloth that they could catch hold of as their flag and re-entered the Muslim fold. They would even compel, if possible, the Christians themselves to accept Islam, and thus avenge the wrong done to them. This experience elsewhere made the early Arabian and other Muslim invaders of India fear at least for a century or two, that they would be obliged to use military force alone to keep the newly converted Hindus tied down to the Islamic faith.

397-398. But when they invaded Sindh and forced conversion to the Islamic faith on the people there, these Muslim invaders came to realize soon enough that although the Hindus' pride for their religion and their loyalty to it was no less ardent than that of any other people, and that at times, it was far more fervent and irrepresible than that of all of them—why, for this very reason—it was very easy for the Muslims and others to enforce physical conversion on the Hindus, if, however, mental conversion was far too difficult.

399. This did not merely pertain to the time when the Muslims invaded India. Even before the rise of Islam, the Syrian Christians, who were very generously—in other words suicidally—given shelter by the Hindu kings in the Malabar, and who began to proselytize the Hindu community, also came to know very soon that it was quite possible to desecrate a whole village of caste Hindus by merely thrusting a morsel of grub into their mouths or by just throwing crumbs of half-eaten loaves of bread or biscuits or slices of beef or the meat of cows into wells and tanks, where people went to have drinking water; and that no one of them had any place in the Hindu community any longer.

400. Later on, when in the 15th and the 16th centuries, the European armies of the Portuguese and others rushed into India by the sea-routes, they, too, were pleased to find the above-mentioned superstitions of contamination and the absurd religiosity of the Hindus, and were fired with an evil ambition to proselytize the whole of India with no difficulty at all.

Fetters for the Miserable Hindu Proselytes

401-402. The Hindu armoury has all along been full of invincible weapons to beat back the political aggressions of the foreigners, and they had successfully crushed down such attempts on various occasions. But it had, at least in those times, no weapon to fight back this religious aggression. So the Indians had to rely on this sole weapon of social boycott, while facing this uprecedented Muslim religious aggression of polluting and converting the Hindus. They went on relentlessly with their policy of completely ostracizing every proselyte Hindu, according to the custom of those days. The then Hindu Society had kept no way open to purify a convert by some form of atonement for the sin of contamination and conversion. Although, by the time of the Muslim advance up to Punjab, the number of Hindu converts to Islam had already mounted to hundreds of thousands and although many of them earnestly wished to come back to Hinduism, this social ostracism of the converts was so very persistent with the ban on eating food from persons of another caste, the ban on inter-caste marital relations and the others, that it was at once accepted by the leaders of the Hindu Society without any thought about the consequences. Naturally, this ban on the repurification and adoption of the converts back to Hinduism, also automatically grew into a new fetter and instead of checking the foreign religious aggression, it hampered the progress of Hinduism itself.

Ban of Ostracism and self-seeking Converts

403. Well, it would have been quite proper and necessary to ostracize those opportunists among the Hindus, who had taken to Islam for their selfish ends, for power, or for avenging their private grudge against their own fellow men; for they had willingly severed all connections with the Hindu people, and no good could be served by readmitting these sinful people into the Hindu Society. But what, if they should later on, sincerely repent for this sinful act of theirs! This irrevocable ban did immeasurable wrong to those unfortunate tens and hundreds of thousands who, fearing social boycott, would never have dreamt of going over to Islam but who were absolutely unable and helpless to face the atrocities of the Muslim onslaught. For these miserable and forlorn thousands and for their offsprings, at least, there should have been some hope of redemption!

404. Again, the self-seeking opportunists, who willingly went over to Islam were much too limited in number. Precisely for this very reason, it seems extremely tragic that this punitive measure of ostracism fell like a bolt from the blue on the helpless victims of the avalanche-like Muslim

religious aggression, doing not the least harm to the real perpetrators of the crime. As it were, it was insult added to injury. They were already wriggling with excruciating agony at the loss of their religion and were even prepared to court death by way of atonement and yet, they were irretrievably condemned to permanent damnation, were never again to be received by their own parents, their husbands and sons and all their relatives, as their own. The very flesh of their flesh and the blood of their blood were now complete strangers to them, at least in this world!

A Strange Justice

405. While thus mercilessly penalising these innocent victims, the Hindus could not only do no harm to the malevolent and atrocious Muslim invaders with their counter-stroke of ostracism, but, on the contrary, helped them directly and enormously in their work of proselytization!

406-407. Unlike the armed vigilance that was necessary for hundreds of years to keep the converted Christians, Jews and other peoples of the west, tied down to the Muslim faith, the work of proselytization in India necessitated a day's labour for the Muslims. If once at the time of a battle, or an armed aggression on cities and villages, they took the trouble of defiling thousands of men and women either by food, drink or rape or mere association, the responsibility of keeping them in the Muslim fold for generations together was shouldered by the Hindus, as if it was a religious duty of their own! Thus worked the punitive measure of ostracism, serving the best interests of the enemy, whom it sought to counteract.

408. But the conversion of one Hindu to the Islamic faith meant the transformation of a man into a demon, the metamorphosis of a God into a Satan! This was the unpleasant reality of the cataclysmal Hindu-Muslim wars! How this demonization of the Hindus took place, is briefly shown in paragraphs 379 and 380.

409. Even then, the Hindu society turned a deaf ear and blind eye to this reality! To speak broadly, it can be safely said, that the Muslims had never to worry about the converts ever going back to their own religion, for they were convinced that the Hindus would never accept them!

410. The Hindus could never clearly distinguish the change of caste from the change of religion.

411. For instance, if a Vaishya had an illicit exchange of food or

matrimonial relations with one of a lower Hindu caste, say a Shimpi (a tailor), a Bhandari (a brewer), or someone else, he was excommunicated from his caste. Similarly, if a Hindu had perforce to take food, or drink water with a sinful (in their opinion) non-Hindu or if he or his wife was defiled or raped, and so had to live with the Muslims, he was banished not only by his own caste but even by the lowliest caste of the Hindus. It means the casting out of a Hindu from one caste, for having the so-called illicit relations with another, was considered on a par with the casting out of another from the whole of the Hindu society for similar reason! The fundamental national difference between the two, which in the long run was to affect, adversely and horribly, the numerical superiority of the Hindus, altogether escaped their notice.

412. An exile from any one caste of the Hindus never lost his Hindu society nor his Hindu religion; he could merge in any one of the many other Hindu castes or could form a new caste of similar outcastes. But this new caste of such outcastes formed an integral part of the Hindu society. There was a change of caste but never a change of religion—nor even a change of society. Why then speak of a change of nationality? The above-mentioned Vaishya, for instance, lost his Vaishya caste, but his being a Hindu remained unimpaired. Naturally, this sort of banishment from one caste to the other in the Hindu society, never caused any numerical loss to it.

414. Only one extract from the many 'Tavarikhs' (histories) written by various Muslim writers should serve as a sample to show how miserable the Hindu converts were!

415-417. Of the hundreds of Hindus taken as slaves and sent to Persia, Turan (Turkey) and Arabia, at the time of the invasions of Mahmud Ghazni, some could give the slip, individually or in groups, and would run away to Punjab, which because of the staunch Hindu resistance, remained the extreme limit of Muslim domination for over a century or so after Mahmud Ghazni. Thereafter, these runaway Hindu converts would escape even from Punjab and enter the neighbouring Hindu states of Rajputana for shelter, and were glad at heart that they were at last free from the Muslim clutches and that they would live happily in Hindu families, in their own temples and in their own society!

418. But when, according to the same custom, a Hindu, banished because of some sort of (so-called) illicit contact with any Muslim, would cease to be a Hindu altogether, and as thousands of such Hindu

men and women were, often enough being converted under coercion by the Muslim aggressors, and as they were all without any exception, thrown out of the Hindu society, it was the Hindu society that suffered huge numerical losses year after year!

419. But alas! they were grossly disappointed because of the ban on reconversion and rehabilitation of these caste-outs! These groups of runaway Hindu converts would come to these Hindu states only to find that not only their own, but no other Hindu state was prepared to accept them in their fold. If at all they wished to live in the Hindu states, these men and women of the runaway shelter-seeking groups had to live as Muslims alone! Later on, when after a century or so, the Muslim armies began to make successful expeditions upto Delhi and central India, they were very much surprised to see these people still living in these Hindu states as Muslims. If any such group or community of the Hindus were found to be existing in the Muslim states, it could never have been allowed to live as a Hindu community any longer! For, by force or by craft, it would have been converted to Islam. This was the experience of the Muslims! This was the Muslim religion!

419. Here, however, in Hindu states, the Hindus who were converted much against their will and who were willing to come back to the Hindu society, and to live as none else but the Muslims, because of the ban on their re-orientation! This was the Hindu Religion!

420. What wonder then, if in an unequal war, the Muslims defiled with craft or coercion, millions of Hindus, and thus inflicted immeasurable numerical loss to the Hindu nation.

The greatest wonder, however, is how this loss was limited to this much alone!

□

8
Perverted Conception of Virtues

421-422. Besides the silly superstitions of the Hindus about the caste-system, the various bans on exchange of food and drink, redemption of the outcastes and others, of which we have already written fully, and which had done tremendously more harm than the two-pronged religio-political Muslim offensive had done, another suicidal morbidity had completely possessed the Hindu mind for a long time. This morbidity paralysed their own offensive and counter-offensive might. Far greater than the Muslims could ever attempt, were the defeats inflicted on themselves by these morbidly virtuous Hindus! If a comparatively mild term is to be used for this infatuation—this mental imbalance of the Hindus, which caused disastrous losses for themselves—we have to call it a perverted sense of Hindu virtues.

423. In fact, virtues or vices are only relative terms. No virtue can be unqualified and absolute under every circumstance or at every place. Be it said briefly, that in practice or in ethical code, a virtue should be called a virtue only to the extent it is useful to the best interests of human society. And the moment it begins to cause harm to mankind, it should be considered a vice and as such discarded forthwith.

424. Some qualities at least are divided into three parts: Satwik (mild, gentle), Rajas (passionate) and Tamas (irascible, irritable); and even these should be viewed with reference to the peculiar conditon of time, place and person. The Hindu civilization had the noblest ambition of raising Man to the status of God and as such, it went in for an all-out attempt to inculcate and cultivate with assiduous care, these gentle qualities in him. But this worldly existence is not woven with one thread alone; its texture shows at least three different threads: the gentle, the passionate and the irritable. It is precisely for this reason that if a man, whosoever he may be, wishes to live in this world, wants to win or at

least does not intend to be vanquished by others, or does not want to see injustice triumph over him, he must have a three-edged weapon, which could successfully face these three-fold qualities. But at this time of the Hindu-Muslim war, the Hindu nation forgot even the Bhagwat Geeta, which preached the relative, and not absolute, values of these virtues. Why, they even twisted the message of the Bhagwad Geeta itself. The quintessence of the Bhagwat Geeta is the consideration of the fine distinction between man and man—of which the Hindus of those times seem to be divinely oblivious.

425. Of course, it must be remembered that all this argument applies generally and collectively to the Hindu polity made up of hundreds of millions of people, but it must also be remembered that there were to come to life, from time-to-time, thousands of exceptional groups of men and brave societies of dauntless people, who opposed this perversely virtuous Hindu society in order to bring about a social revolution. They will be referred to at their proper places.

426-427. To let go the vanquished and abjectly surrendering enemy, is said to be a virtue in some religious books; so enemies like the ungrateful Mohammed Ghori and the Rohila Najibkhan were set free. And what did they do in return for this noble act of the Hindus? The first brutally murdered his former benefactor, Prithviraj Chauhan, while the second conspired against the very Marathas, who let him go alive and brought about their unprecedented destruction at Panipat. Having only learnt by rote the maxim, to give food to the hungry and water to the thirsty is a virtue, the Hindus went on giving milk to the vile poisonous cobras and vipers! Even while the Muslim demons were demolishing Hindu temples and breaking to pieces their holiest of idols like Somnath, they never wrecked their vengeance upon those wicked Muslims, even when they had golden opportunities to do so, nor did they ever take out a single brick from the walls of masjids, because their religious teachers and priests preached the virtue of not inflicting pain on the offender:

'Never pay the tormentor in his own coin but bear the torments meekly and be patient that God will punish him.'

दिघलें दुःख पराने उसने फेडू नयेचि सोसावें।
शिक्षा देव तयाला करील म्हणुनि उगेच बैसावें॥

428. The vilest of vices recorded in the catalogues of the religious texts could never have been more detrimental to the welfare of mankind,

more harmful to the national interests and so, more detestable than such virtues as give rise to horrible atrocities and the greatest of sins. Naturally, whoever cultivates and lives upto such virtues thoughtlessly and foolishly and with slavish adherence to the religious texts, and also with fanatic obstinacy, is bound to perish individually and bring about disaster of the nation he lives. These qualities are not virtues; they are virtues distorted in the extreme. Whichever virtue is adopted thoughtlessly and without regard to the time, place and person is corrupted and rotten, and, like putrefied food, becomes poisonous.

429-430. Every Hindu seems to have been made to suck, along with his mother's milk, this nectar-like advice that religious tolerance is a virtue. But nobody never explains to him the essence of that precept. If that alien religion is also tolerant of our own religion, our tolerance towards it can be a virtue. But the Muslim and the Christian religions, which boldly proclaim it to be their religious duty to destroy most cruelly the Hindu religion and to eradicate from the face of this earth the kafirs and the heathens, can never be described as tolerant of other religions. In respect of these intolerant foreign religions, the very extremely enraged intolerance, which seeks to retaliate their atrocities with super-atrocious reprisals, itself becomes a virtue!

431. Even if we were to restrict our discussion to the period under discussion, it will be seen that every Muslim aggressor went on demolishing Hindu temples at Mathura and Kashi (Benaras). The most sacred idols in the various magnificent shrines from all over India right upto Rameshwaram were not only purposely taken to the Muslim capitals like Delhi and plastered into the portal steps of their royal palaces, but, for the sole purpose of hurting the feelings of the Hindus and insulting them, they were also used as the slabs and tiles for lavatories, water-closets, and urinals. To be tolerant towards those Muslims who called these and many other atrocities their religious duty, is the very negation of virtue, its sacrilegious perversion! Nay, for the Hindus to show such tolerance was the greatest sin to be punished in Hell! But the Hindus committed this very sin under the name of virtue! Even after overthrowing the various Muslim powers, i.e. even when the Hindus had acquired political ascendancy, they did not destroy the various masjids at Kashi (Benares), Mathura or Rameshwaram, nor did they use their ruins as tiles for the various building constructions along roads. At the most, the Hindus reconstructed and renovated their

old temples which were raised to the ground by the Muslims. They did nothing more! On the contrary, there are astonishing instances of grant of new lands for their maintenance and assurance of protection of the masjids, which had been built by the Muslim aggressors, by the Hindu powers. In this connection, one stray instance can be cited to show the confusion of the then Hindu thought. It affords a shameless exhibition of the perverted virtue of the Hindus, which makes any further discussion in this regard absolutely unnecessary!

432-433. After Mahmud of Ghazni demolished the temple of Somnath for the first time, it was rebuilt several times by the Hindus and destroyed by the Muslim conquerors as many times! Once, when a powerful Hindu king established his power in that region, he rebuilt it with all pomp and ceremony, and under his able guidance, the land also prospered. This Hindu ruler should have, in fact, debarred from entering into the Indian waters any Arab traders, who used the Indian ports in this region of Sindh as watering and fuelling stations on their way to the distant eastern and southern parts of India. For, the Hindus often had the bitter experience of the Arab armies and navies following these traders by sea. But in order to exhibit his religious tolerance and generosity, this Hindu ruler not only did not stop these Arabian traders from visiting the Indian coast, but treated them with such great deal of hospitality that they might feel quite at home there. Naturally, these Arabic traders, actuated whether by political trickery or by religious pride, thought of building by way of a challenge, as it were, a masjid just in front of the Somnath Temple, rebuilt by the Hindu kafirs. But under the circumstances, then prevalent there, they could not do so by force or bravado. Hence, with their usual craft, they applied in the most courteous and humble words to the King for permission to build the masjid. And O what wonder! That gullible Hindu King consented to it most willingly, and up rose the new masjid challenging the Somnath Temple. As a matter of fact, considering the highly miserable state to which the Temple of Somnath was reduced by Mahmud of Ghazni and others, that Hindu King should have wiped out of existence all the masjids, without exception, as soon as he conquered the land and then and then alone, could he have restored the Somnath Temple to its original glory. But instead of destroying the existing masjids he permitted a new one to be built up and bestowed an annuity on it for its maintenance. For this suicidal-religious tolerance (perversion of a virtue again!), he had very soon to pay dearly; because when after some time, the brutal forces of Alla-ud-Din and other Muslim aggressors attacked Gujrat and killed thousands of Hindu men and raped as many Hindu women, and pulled down hundreds of Hindu temples and marched straight towards Somnath, how did these Arabs and their descendants repay the religious tolerance of the Hindu King, who allowed the Arabian traders to build the said masjid? Did they allow the restored Somnath Temple to remain unmolested in return for the obligation of the Hindus—even if it were to tantalize the Hindu gullibility and simplicity? No! The Muslim armies battered the Temple to pieces once again, and outdid Mahumud of Ghazni in taking away the sacred idol and the slab inside this temple to Delhi and made them fit nicely into the pedestal for a masjid there.

434. Once again, when Hindu power was established in the region, Hindu temples rose up and once more, the Muslims like Sultan Ahmed Shah, ravaged the land with their usual religious ferocity and harassed the Hindus there with wholesale massacres, rapes, arson and other incendiary activities. Thousands of Hindus were taken prisoners and were sold as slaves in foreign countries. Somnath remained a heap of rubble, but the notorious masjid grew in importance. Besides the old masjids, which were preserved and raised to greater glory by the Hindu rulers, the Muslim rulers built taller and more spacious mosques.

435. It was this confused religious thought, the distorted sense of virtues and the blind religious tolerance, that culminated in the religious suicide of the Hindus. How many more incidents may one cite, which came off century-after-century at every place right from Kashimir to Rameshwaram, in the face of Muslim aggression? Still, one more instance may be narrated here to show the perversion of another virtue by the Hindus; generosity—misplaced genorosity!

435A. Siddharaj Jaysinh (1096-1143 A.D.) was a valiant king of Anhilwad in Gujarat. He had also a very keen sense of justice. But he was a Hindu king! He was deluded by the absolute values, without any regard to time, place or person of all the virtuous ideologies about justice and injustice, according to his own and the alien religion and especially generosity and large-heartedness! Once during his reign, there was some dispute between the Hindus and the Muslims near Cambay (Khambayat). Writes Muhammad Ufi—himself a Muslim writer—in his book *Jami'-ul-Hikayat.*

436. "In the reign of King Jai Singh, there was a mosque and a

minaret from which the summons to prayers was cried out. The fire-worshipers instigated an attack on the Musalmans, and the minaret was destroyed, the mosque burnt down and eighty Musalmans were killed..." A certain Muhammadan, a Khatib or a reader of the Khutba, by name Khatib 'Ali', escaped and fled to Nahrwala. None of the courtiers of the Rai paid any attention to him or rendered him any assistance. Having learnt that the Rai was going out to hunt, Khatib 'Ali' sat down behind a tree in the forest and awaited the Rai's arrival. When the Rai reached the spot, Khatib Ali stood up and implored the former to stop the elephant and listen to the latters's complaint. He then placed in his hand a "Kasida", which he had composed in Hindi verse stating the whole case. The Rai having heard this complaint, placed Khatib Ali under the charge of a servant, ordering him to take care of him... Later disguising himself in tradesman's dress, the Rai entered the city (of Khambayat) and stayed a short time in different places in the market-place, making enquiries as to the truth of Khatib Ali's complaint. He then learnt that the Musalmans were oppressed and were slain without any grounds The next day, he held a court. He said it was his duty to see that all his subjects were afforded such protection as would enable them to live in peace. He then gave orders that two leading men from each class of infidels—Brahmins, fire worshippers (sometimes applied to Buddhists) and others—should be punished. He gave one lac Balotras to enable the Musalmans to rebuild the mosque and the minarets. He also gave some clothes to Khatib." Muhammad 'Ufi: Jami'-ul-Hikayat, Elliot HIED Vol. II Pp. 162-163).

437. This Raja Jayasingh had gone on a foot pilgrimage to the rejuvenated temple of Somnath and was a devotee of Shiva and had implicit faith in the Hindu religion. Probably, because for this very reason, place of driving the inveterate and crafty Muslim enemies out of his own kingdom or instead of reconverting them to Hinduism, even if by means of force, he had the masjids—the masjids of those Muslims who had reduced to mere rubble, not only the temple of Somnath but hundreds of other temples in Gujarat and thousands in other parts of India—rebuilt at the cost of the Hindus, and offered them a special protection according to his Hindu creed of religious tolerance and generosity!

438. Was it ever possible for the Hindus under Mahmud of Ghazni or Muhammad Ghori or for those in the domain of the Sultan, who had gone on killing the Hindus and ravaging their lands—was it ever

possible for them to complain to any Muslim governor of the land against the destruction of their own temples? (Let alone the appeal for the restoration of such a demolished temple!) To complain in such a way would itself have amounted to a very grave offence of the kafirs, according to the Muslim religious code, and for this very offence, every one of the Hindu men and women would have been sold in Kabul or Kandhar as wretched slaves. But such treacherous and dangerous Muslims were allowed by the Hindu kings to live in large colonies, and were treated with special honour in order to bolster up their creed of religious tolerance. And in thousands of cases during the long period of Hindu-Muslim war, these very minority Muslims who had been living as refugees in the Hindu states, never failed to rebel or sabotage the Hindu war-efforts, as soon as there was any foreign Muslim invasion. Even while they were seeing all these treacherous activities of the Muslims, the Hindu kings went on practising and committing to their memory the precepts of religious tolerance and large-heartedness, in utter disregard of the proper place, time or person and, of course, they fell as miserable victims. This is verily the distortion of virtue itself!

The Grave Danger of the Muslim Abduction and Pollution of Millions of Hindu Women

439. One side-issue of the Muslim religious aggression, which caused a continuous drain on the numerical superiority of the Hindus, was the diabolic Muslim faith that it was a religious duty of every Muslim to kidnap and force their own religion into non-Muslim women. This incited their sensuality and lust for carnage and while it enormously increased their number, it affected the Hindu population in an inverse proprotion. To hesitate to acknowledge this hard fact under the guise of politeness, is simply a puerile self-deception. This abduction of thousands and millions of Hindu women by the Muslims is not such a trifling thing as to be dispensed with, by calling it religious fanaticism or simply by conniving at it. Even if it were a madness, there was a method in it! And the method in this Muslim madness was so horrible, that with the mistaken Hindu neglect of this so-called religious fanaticism, the Hindu nation came to have a perpetual bleeding sore. For, as a matter of fact, the religious fanaticism of the Muslims was not madness at all; it was an effective method of increasing the Muslim population with special regard to the unavoidable laws of nature.

440. The same law of nature is instinctively obeyed by the animal world. If in the cattle-herds, the number of oxen grows in excess of the cows, the herds do not grow numerically in a rapid manner. But, on the other hand, the number of animals in the herds, with the excess of cows over the oxen, grows in mathematical progression. The same is true of man, for at the core, man is essentially an animal. Even in the pre-historic times, the so-called wild tribes of the forest-dwellers knew this law quite well. The African wild tribes of today kill only the males from amongst their enemies, whenever there are tribal wars, but not the females who are eventually distributed by the victor tribes among themselves. To obtain from them future progeny to increase their numbers, is considered by these tribes to be their sacred duty! It is said of at least one of the Naga tribes that when they attack an enemy, they shoot simple unpoisoned arrows at the males, but if any women are seen fighting on the enemy side, highly envenomed arrows are used to kill them instantly. For they argue, to kill one woman who cannot be captured alive is as good as to kill five men.

441. This very natural law was adopted and obeyed openly by the aggressive but numerically poor African Muslim armies and their chiefs while attacking the major populations of North Africa. On conquering those kafirs, the ransom that was collected was calculated in terms of money and women in equal share, and these women, collected as ransom, were distributed by fives or tens amongst the most faithful followers of Islam. The future progeny of these conquered women was born Muslim and so amongst the Muslim environments became literally fanatical. The Muslim chiefs who thus multiplied their numbers rapidly were honoured as 'Ghazis' by the religious authorities. The law of the Muslim religious warfare granted the victorious Muslim army every right to own the kafir women as completely as their other movable or immovable property.

442-443. After Ravan abducted Seeta and Shree Ramchandra marched on him, some of his well-wishers advised the demon king, just before the war, that because of his unjust act, the demon kingdom was threatened with a terrible war and that he should send Seeta back to her husband, because it was highly irreligious to kidnap her. "What?" cried the wrathful Ravan. "To abduct and rape the women folk of the enemy, do you call it irreligious? Pooh; Pooh!"

—राक्षसानाम् परोधर्मः परदाराविघर्षणम्

(To carry away the women of others and to ravish them is itself the supreme religious duty of the Rakshasas.) 'Parodharmah', the greatest duty!

444. With this same shameless religious fanaticism, the aggressive Muslims of those times considered it their highly religious duty to carry away forcibly the women of the enemy side, as if they were commonplace property, to ravish them, to pollute them and to distribute them to all and sundry, from the Sultan to the common soldier and to absorb them completely in their fold. This was considered a noble act, which increased their number.

445. In every province where the Muslim rule established itself, the Sultan, the Nawabs and the Nizams—why even the meanest of Muslim officers in every town and village therein, levied on the Hindu population not only the Jazia tax for collecting wealth; but also the heinous tax of demanding openly the daughters and even married ladies from the Hindu royal families and others of high rank, and even carried them away forcibly and openly.

446. After Sindh, the Arabs did not attempt another invasion of India, yet the Arab bands did come here along with other Muslim armies, and like these Arabs, all those newly converted people like the Persians (Iranians), the Turanians, the Afghans, the Turks, the Moghuls and others fell on India with all the ferocity at their command. Obviously, they had not brought their millions of womenfolk along with them. But all those from the Sultans to the common soldiers, as a rule, began to settle down here with the kidnapped Hindu women, whom they either married or simply kept as their concubines. Let alone the vast numbers of Hindu women of high as well as low ranks, who led the most ignoble of lives in the harems of the Emperors, Sultans or Nawabs, but almost every Muslim kept at least three or four such forcibly pulluted women. Thus, women in this aggressive Muslim community came to be more numerous than men, and polygamy being an accepted practice sanctioned by their religion, these foreign Muslim communities began to grow rapidly year-after-year, from a few thousands to millions and more.

447. An interesting point to note is that Sultan Ghiyas-ud-din Tughlak, Sultan Shikandar, Sultan Phiroz-Shah Tughlak and many other devilish Hindu-haters were born of Hindu mothers!

Muslim Women too played their Devilish part in the Molestation and Harassment of the Hindu Women

448. Hindu women were considered kafirs and born slaves. So these Muslim women were taught to think it their duty to help in all possible ways, their molestation and forcible conversion to Islam. No Muslim woman, whether a begum or a beggar, ever protested against the atrocities committed by their male compatriots. On the contrary, they encouraged them to do so and honoured them for it. A Muslim woman did everything in her power to harass such captured or kidnapped Hindu women. Not only in the troubled times of war, but even in the intervening periods of peace and even when they themselves lived in the Hindu kingdoms, they enticed and carried away young Hindu girls, locked them up in their own houses or conveyed them to the Muslim centres in masjids and mosques. The Muslim women all over India considered it their holy duty to do so.

The Hindu Chivalry towards Enemy Women

449. The Muslim women never feared retribution or punishment at the hands of any Hindu for their heinous crime. They had a perverted idea of woman chivalry. If in a battle the Muslims won, they were rewarded for such crafty and deceitful conversions of Hindu women; lull even if the Hindus carried the field and a Hindu power was established in that particular place (and such incidents in those times were not very rare) the Muslim men alone, if at all, suffered the consequential indignities but the Muslim women—never! Only Muslim men, and not women, were taken prisoners. Muslim women were sure that even in the thick of battles, and in the confusion wrought just after then, neither the victor Hindu chiefs, nor any of their common soldiers, nor even any civilian would ever touch their hair. For, albeit enemies and atrocious, they were women! Hence, even when they were taken prisoner in battles, the Muslim women—royal ladies as also the commonest slaves—were invariably sent back safe and sound to their respective families! Such incidents were common enough in those times. And this act was glorified by the Hindus as their chivalry towards the enemy women and the generosity of their religion! For a sample, read the following incidents.

450. Even now we proudly refer to the noble acts of Chhatrapati Shivaji and Chimaji Appa, when they honourably sent back the daughter-in-law of the Muslim Governor of Kalyan and the wife of the Portuguese

governor of Bassein respectively. But is it not strange that, when they did so, neither Shivaji Maharaj nor Chimaji Appa should ever remember, the atrocities and the rapes and the molestation, perpetrated by Mahmud of Ghazni, Muhammad Ghori, Alla-ud-din Khilji and others, on thousands of Hindu ladies and girls like the princesses of Dahir, Kamaldevi, the wife of Karnaraj of Karanwati and her extremely beautiful daughter, Devaldevi. Did not the plaintive screams and pitiful lamentations of the millions of molested Hindu women, which reverberated throughout the length and breadth of the country, reach the ears of Shivaji Maharaj and Chimaji Appa?

451. The souls of those millions of aggrieved women might have perhaps said, "Do not forget, O, your Majesty, Chhatrapati Shivaji Maharaj, and O! Your Excellency, Chimaji Appa, the unutterable atrocities and oppression and outrage committed on us by the Sultans and Muslim noblemen and thousands of others, big and small. Let those Sultans and their peers take a fright that in the event of a Hindu victory, our molestation and detestable lot shall be avenged on the Muslim women. Once they are haunted with this dreadful apprehension, that the Muslim women, too, stand in the same predicament in case the Hindus win, the future, Muslim conquerors will never dare to think of such molestation of Hindu women."

451A. But because of the then prevalent perverted religious ideas about chivalry to women, which ultimately proved highly detrimental to the Hindu community, neither Shivaji Maharaj nor Chimaji Appa could do such wrong to the Muslim women.

452. It was the suicidal Hindu idea of chivalry to women, which saved the Muslim women (simply because they were women) from the heavy punishments of committing indescribable sins and crimes against the Hindu women. Their womanhood became their shield, quite sufficient to protect them.

453. Still worse was the ridiculous idea, which the Hindus of those times entertained, that it was a sin to convert a Muslim woman to Hinduism. They foolishly thought that to have any sort of relations with a Muslim woman meant their own conversion to Islam. Naturally, even in the midst of a Hindu community and the Hindu state, they were secure against any attempt by the Hindus at abducting them or their forcible conversion to Hinduism. Exceptions, however, were very rare.

454. Under these circumstances, the Muslim feminine class [fair

(?) sex] was left seraphically free from any chastisement or penalty for their share of the crimes perpetrated against the Hindu woman-world, and their work of enticing and ensnaring the Hindu women and forcing them to accept Islam, went on for hundreds of years, unhampered and unimpeded.

But if

455. Suppose, if from the earliest Muslim invasion of India, the Hindus also, whenever they were victors on the battlefields, had decided to pay the Muslim fair sex in the same coin or punished them in some other ways, i.e. by conversion even with force and then absorbed them in their fold, then? Then with this horrible apprehension at their heart, they would have desisted from their evil designs against any Hindu lady. If they had taken such a fright in the first two or three centuries, millions and millions of luckless Hindu ladies would have been saved all their indignities, loss of their own religion, rapes, ravages and other unimaginable persecutions. Our woman-world would not have suffered such a tremendous numerical loss, which means their future progeny would not have been lost permanently to Hinduism, and the Muslim population could not have thrived so audaciously. Without any increase in their womenfolk, the Muslim population would have dwindled into a negligible minority.

456. The sociological explanation for this contention has already been offered in paragraphs 439 to 446.

457. But haunted with the fantastic idea of chivalry to enemy-women and a blind eye to time, place or person, the Hindus of that period never tried to chastise the Muslim womenfolk for their wrongs to Hindu women, even when the former were many a time completely at their mercy.

Misplaced Chivalry to Enemy Womenfolk and the Consequent Miserable plight

458. Well, did this misplaced chivalrous idea of the Hindus have any salutary effect on their Muslim foes? Were the latter ever ashamed of their sin of molesting a Hindu woman in view of this Hindu religious generosity and high mindedness? Did the Muslims ever sincerely feel thankful to the Hindus for the safe return of thousands of Muslim women to their own kith and kin? Never! On the contrary, they again

and again reciprocated Hindu chivalrous behaviour with the same old treachery and atrocity, and thus held it to ridicule and scorn.

459. On the contrary, the Muslims were puffed up, perhaps with the thought, that if at all the Hindus were to show chivalry to anybody, it should have been to their own Hindu women! It was they who had the first right to such a chivalrous treatment! But if the Hindus could not rescue thousands of their own women who were being abducted, polluted and forced into Islamic religion in their very presence, through centuries, why should the Muslims not ridicule the Hindu chivalrous idea of civility to women, even enemy women? On the contrary, they perhaps thought that the Hindus dared not think of violating or even insulting the Muslim women for fear of horrible reprisals. Thus, they were more likely to misconstrue the Hindu idea of chivalry, than interpret it in the right sense as to have been born of cowardice than of strength and bravery.

The Hindus of the Pre-Islamic era never Interpreted Chivalry to Women in this Anti-National silly way

460. A serpent, whether male or female, if it comes to bite must be killed. The enemy women, who enforced conversion and heaped all sort of humiliation on our mothers and sisters, had by that very devilish act, lost their womanhood and their right to chivalrous treatment, and deserved nothing but only the most stringent punishment for their atrocious crimes. Hence, when Tratika, the she-demon marched on Ramchandra with other demons, he killed her immediately, without a moment's thought. When Shoorpanakha, another she-demon, rushed to eat away Seeta like cucumber, Laxman deprived her of nose and ears and sent her back—not honourably with generous gifts of ornaments, to show off his chivalay to women! When Narakasur carried away thousands of Aryan women to his Asur kingdom (Assyria of today), Shree Krishna marched upon the demon and killed him in the war. But he did not stop with military and political defeat he inflicted on Narakasur! He rescued all the thousands of imprisoned Aryan females, undergoing all sorts of humiliation there and brought them back to his own kingdom; and thus took a social revenge! Shree Krishna's army did not forsake their kinswomen, simply because they were forcibly polluted and violated—a dastardly thought that he never entertained for a minute. On the contrary, Shree Krishna as the Bhoopati—the Lord of the whole Earth—brought all those sixteen thousand or more women to his kingdom, rehabilitated them honourably and took upon

himself, the responsibility of feeding and protecting them. This very act of Krishna, as the Bhoopati has been fantastically construed by the writers of the Puranas as to describe him the husband of those thousands of women. He was later thought to have married all of them.

461. In the post-Puranik period, whenever our valiant and victorious princes vanquished the enemies like the Yavan, Shaka or Hun commandants, kings or emperors on the battlefield, they invariably married the enemy princesses. This seems to have been the tradition prevalent right from Chandragupta Maurya to the Gupta Emperors! Shalivahan kings too married Saka princesses. Not only our victorious kings but all Hindus, right from the Samants (feudatory princes) to common citizens, married unhesitatingly the Yavan, Saka or Hun women. The nation was valiant enough to absorb not only the progeny of those enemy-women, but the whole enemy communities in their own, and leave no trace of their origin behind.

Harmful effects of the ban on Purification and Rehabilitation

462. Under the illusion of preserving the purity of their own caste and religion, the Hindu Society of the Islamic era began to enforce as their religious duty, the bans on exchange of food, on inter-caste marriage and other bans, even when they were harmful to the society. In a similar way and for the same reason of protecting the purity of their caste and religion, the ban on re-purification of the converted Hindus and that on sea-faring, began to be enforced most scrupulously and rigidly as religious injunctions. Neither any single Hindu who was converted under coercion, nor even his progeny could ever come back to Hinduism: their sin (?) had no redemption, no salvation. For generations together, the Hindus believed this to be their inviolable religious injunction; with very rare exceptions, every Hindu, from sweeper to Brahmin, from Chhatrapati (the sovereign) to Patrapati (the holder of a parchment), from Shankaracharya (the Religious Head) to Shankhacharya (the prince of blockheads), whether learned or illiterate, held this opinion about the ban on repurification of the converts unanimously and unswervingly from Kashmir to Kanyakumari.

463. On account of these very bans, thousands of our Hindu ladies kindled the fires of johar, century-after-century, in order to avoid violation at the hands of the Muslims. To save themselves from this humiliation of violation by enemies, millions others leapt into rivers, lakes and wells,

all over the country and destroyed themselves along with their small children at their breasts. Most bravely, did many others die defiantly refusing to be converted to Islam, like Chahatrapati Samabhaji, Guru Teg Bahadur and many of our Sikh gurus like the martyr Bairagi Baba Banda, who kept on defying the Muslims till the last, even when his body was being cut off limb by limb. How can we ever forget this unprecedented martyrdom unless we are ungrateful to them? Few other communities in the history of the world could have sacrificed their lives on such a vast scale or with such severity as did the Hindus! This martyrdom of the Hindus was not altogether futile in respect of saving their religion from the Muslim onslaught. The heroic tales of their martyrdom have been inspiring generations of the nation to offer their life for protecting the religion, and this is not altogether insignificant.

464. Although highly detrimental to the interests of the nation as a whole, and as such deserving the severest of criticism, these various bans like those on exchange of food and sea-voyage and the custom of social ostracism, were all imposed by the Hindus of that period—let it not be forgotten—with the sole noble object of protecting the purity of their caste and creed. Millions of Hindus who, for generations, suffered unimaginable pangs did so with unswerving loyalty to their accepted creed. Were they ever happy to boycott an individual for having—although unwillingly and through force—taken water from a Muslim hand or for other such reasons? How can one describe the agonies and pangs of the parents and other relatives at the unavoidable separation of their sons and daughters, of husbands and wives, of brothers and sisters? How many of them might have courted death owing to this extreme grief when they closed their doors on them, simply because they were, although unwillingly and forcibly, converted to Islam? But they suffered all this with the grim determination, viz.,

त्यजेदेकम् कुलस्यार्थे। ग्रामस्यार्थे कुलत्यजेत्
ग्रामं जनपदस्यार्थे। धर्मार्थे पृथवीम् त्यजेत्॥

For the sake of the family, an individual is to be abandoned. For the sake of the village, a family has to be forsaken. For the sake of the state, a village has to be given up as lost, and, for the sake of religion, one should give up the whole world.

465. Should we not therefore be grateful to those Hindus for the unbearable pangs and unimaginable grief they suffered? They were misled into accepting those traditions of various bans as their religious

duties, but their loyalty to their religion was unmistaken, unshaken! What was considered to be an antidote turned out to be poison itself! But the object in administering it was to give an antidote, to save the life of the nation! How can we, then forbear writing a word or two of sincere gratitude for the harrowing mental and physical agonies they suffered, with the honest intention of saving their religion?

Anti-National illusory Platitudes!

466. An effective way of liquidating the Muslim religious authority could easily have been availed of by the Hindus of those times, if they had but done what the Muslims had been doing in their hundreds of offensives against Hindu states. The Muslims went on slaughtering wholesale the Hindu population. Similarly whenever the Hindus gained an upper hand, they could have retaliated by massacring Muslim population and making the region Muslim-less! Devoid of Muslims! Even their ban on re-purification (शुद्धि) would not have prevented them from doing this. For in doing this, there was no question involved of eating or drinking or of having any dealings with the Muslims. But –! But if not the ban on re-purification, the suicidal Hindu creed of religious tolerance was certainly a major obstacle! From the very ancient times, the Hindus had been boasting of their high ideals of religious tolerance, of the equal status they conceded to all the religions of the world, of preaching the sameness of Ram and Rahim, of allowing every one to follow his own faith! This they considered to be the height of their religion!

467. Instead of massacring en masse the hundreds of thousands of Muslims, who from time to time fell in their hands completely vanquished and utterly helpless, in order to avenge the untold wrongs and humiliation heaped by them on the Hindus, the Hindus, in their turn, refrained themselves from doing the Muslims even the slightest harm, because they were in minority and belonged to another religion. On the contrary, the Muslims were allowed to enhance the glory and scope of their own religion without the least possible hindrance. Not only like the Hindu citizens, but even more leniently and with more facilities were the Muslims allowed, by Hindu states of those days, to enjoy the legal rights—a fact that is borne out by pages after pages of Indian history.

468. Is it necessary to add that these 'cow-faced' followers of Hinduism, proud of their utmost tolerance of other religions, were not (in the least) likely to hit back the tiger-faced Muslims on religious grounds?

469. Religious tolerance! A virtue! Yes. It can be a virtue only where the other religion is tolerant of our own! But to tolerate the Muslim religion, the followers of which right from the Sultans like Mahmud of Ghazni and Ghori and others to the various Shahs and Badshahs, thought it their religious obligation to massacre the kafir Hindus to celebrate their accession to the throne, and had been carrying on horrible religious persecution of the Hindus for nearly a thousand years, was tantamount to cut the throat of one's own religion! It was not tolerance towards other religions, it was tolerance of irreligion! It was not even tolerance, it was impotence! But this truth never dawned upon the Hindu society of those days even after the horrible experience of a thousand years or so. They, on their own part, went on tolerating even such a hideous religion as the Islam and considered it a glorious virtue of their own—a special ornament in the crown of the Hindu community!

470. O thou Hindu society! Of all the sins and weaknesses, which have brought about thy fall, the greatest and most potent are thy virtues themselves.

471-472. Ahimsa (non-violence), kindness, chivalry even towards the enemy women, protection of an abjectly capitulating enemy, क्षमा वीरस्य भूशणम् (forgiveness, a glorious emblem for the brave!) and religious tolerance were all virtues no doubt—very noble virtues! But it is blind and slovenly—even impotent—adoption of all these very virtues, irrespective of any consideration given to the propriety of time, place or persons, that so horribly vanquished the Hindus in the milliennial Hindu-Muslim war on the religious front.

For

पात्रापात्रविवेकशून्य आचलि जरि सद्‌गुण॥
तों तोचि ठरे दुर्गुण, सद्धर्मघातक॥

[Every virtuous act done without the least regard to the propriety of the persons concerned—without the least thought, whether the other person deserves such noble treatment or not—becomes a glaring vice most harmful to the true religion.]

□

9

Super-Diabolic Counter-Offensive the Only Answer

473. It has already been shown in the earlier chapters how the Hindu Society was unable to recover its tremendous numerical losses suffered due to forcible mass conversions and tyrannical anti-Hindu laws of Muslim kings and sultans, because of its own silly, anti-national traditions of caste-differences, bans on reconversion of the helpless Hindu proselytes, and the like, and many other perverted concepts of virtue. Had it not been for some prophetic social and religious reformers, astute diplomats, gigantic thinkers and philosophers, and men of action among the Hindus of that time, who towered, though only from time to time, over the all-pervading gloom and guided their community, the Hindu society would never have escaped total extinction.

Maharshi Deval and Medhatithi

474. Two of these thinkers are Maharshi Deval and Medhatithi, the critic of Manusmriti, who unfailingly attract our attention because of their dazzling intellectual brilliance. Their extant writings show us, beyond any shadow of doubt, that even during those calamitous years, that intervened between the first Arab invasion of Sindh and the Muslim religio-political atrocities in the Punjab and its final occupation, they had pointed out to Hindus brave new ways, new religious thoughts, new weapons which were calculated to bring them success.

475-476. The Chapter on the pollution of religion in Deval Smriti, begins with the line

सिंधुतीरमुपासन्नम्! देवलं मुनिसत्तमम्!

It clearly shows that it was in Sindh first, that a section of Brahmins, Kshatriyas and others was organised. It determined to improve the code of social and religious behaviour of the Hindus as much, at least, as to recuperate the numerically stupendous losses suffered at the hands of the Muslims. For, they clearly saw that the laws of behaviour laid down in different smritis were in every way powerless to counteract the armed religio-political aggression of the enemy. The Hindu leaders, present in the hermitage of Deval on the bank of the Indus, once asked the sage, "Will it be possible to bring back to Hinduism, thousands of Hindu men and women, who have fallen victim to the religious persecution of the Muslims and have been forcibly converted to Islam, by some form of atonement and by repurification?" The verses in Deval Smriti clearly mention that such discussions were held at different times and the authoritative and final answers were given, and the rules of conduct propounded by Maharshi Deval favouring reconversion. These advocates and writers of this new Smriti and their followers declared as unlawful and irreligious in those adverse circumstances, the very religious act of banning reconversion as it was causing tremendous numerical losses to the Hindus.

Special Weapons for Special Occasions

477-478. In the armoury of our religious code of conduct, there always had been very special and progressive weapons for meeting very special and exceptional circumstances. All that was needed was a class of leaders to use them from time to time! If in the initial stages of adverse times of the Hindu-Muslim war, these special and exceptional weapons had only been unsheathed and sharpened, Hinduism itself might have completey routed Islam from the Indian soil, as it happened when the valiant (because they were attacking the enemy!) and victory-longing gods and the Aryans fought with the demons (dashyus). Even if the same religious resplendence was not uniformly shown by the Hindus, it was, in some measure, seen in the revolutionary religious reforms of Deval Maharshi of Sindh. Maharshi Deval is said to have lived sometime between A.D. 800 to A.D. 900.

479, Because of this religious resplendence alone, Deval Maharshi could kick away the traditional religious ban on redemption for the unwilling converts and propounded in his Smriti, an expedient of atonement for the sin of conversion. It has been laid down in the Deval Smriti, that if, within a certain period of his or her forcible conversion to Islam, a Hindu man or woman showed his or her desire to be reconverted to Hinduism with due atonement, he or she was to be administered simple and practical penance of fast or something else and absorbed once again in the Hindu society. The liberal attitude of this Smriti towards women, in the context of the times is specially laudable. It enjoined that the women forcibly converted to Islam, or those who served in the Muslim households as menial servants or slaves, be considered pure after their next menses and should be completely absorbed in the Hindu community. Even a pregnant Hindu woman, freed from the Muslim bondage, was to be considered as pure as a bar of gold after being heated in the goldsmith's chafing dish, once her foetus came out after delivery.

480. It is, however, really strange that even this Deval Smriti, which was so particular about the re-purification and reconversion of the fallen Hindu women, with a view to stopping the numerical losses of our community, should not have cared to do the same for their children born of the Muslim women. It is very difficult to explain why it should have failed to do so. We were reminded of this Deval Smriti when once we were told of a custom amongst the Bengali Hindus: if a child widow or an unmarried girl in a Hindu family gave birth to an illegitimate child, it was to be solicitously given over to the Muslims, who lived beyond the local river for being brought up as their own. This expedient was no doubt thought of by the Hindu priesthood with the best intention of saving the family from public humiliation and the society from every contagion of that sin. The Muslims too, thinking that these Hindu children increased their number, gladly accepted them. The simple god-fearing Hindus on the other hand, never for once understood that their own number decreased to that extent. It is quite evident that this Bengali custom must have been popularized by some Smriti like the Deval Smriti.

481. The basic cause of this cowardly arrangement made by even those reformers who condemned the caste division, ban on repurification of the 'fallen' and favoured reconversion, was the deep-rooted silly belief of the Hindus, that the purity of the caste was to be preserved at all costs and even at the risk of caste extinction. But the Hindu society of those days never understood that the very same purity of their caste was lost, when lakhs of their women fell into the hands of the Muslims, and that if those prohibitions on reconversion were to continue, the whole of the Hindu society would perish.

482. Another thing to be noted is that the portion, now extant,

of the Deval Smriti does not provide for the conversion of the original Muslims to Hinduism, as it did for the conversion of the unfortunate Hindu converts. The reason probably is only this, that the Hindus considered it a great sin to admit another community into their own fold. Even the religious laws gives up to the writer of the Bhagwat Geeta seemed to be extremely worried how to keep off the intermingling of the castes and subcastes within the Hindu Society itself.

483. In fine, we can say, the daring reformers at the Ashram of Maharshi Deval made at least some provision for admitting the forcibly converted Hindu men and women to the Hindu society. But it seems that the writers of Smritis and the warriors of the time dared not use at every stage, more violent means to beat down the monstrously violent Muslim aggression. Nevertheless, under the adverse circumstances, when the Muslim power had established itself firmly in the land, this religious revolt of the hundreds of Hindu leaders like Deval and others was not a small thing.

Check on Muslim Religious Aggression in Sindh

484. Strangely enough, the above-mentioned attempt of the Hindu leaders like Deval was supported by the Hindu society as a whole. The Hindu society, which was originally zealously fond of their caste-sysetem, reconverted thousands of convert men and women and absorbed them in their midst. Not only on the political (cf. para 357) front, but on the religious front, too, the Muslims were thus beaten completely in Sindh. This two-fold victory of the Hindus in Sindh—of reconquering Sindh within thirty years of Kasim's invasion and maintaining their grip on it for nearly two hundred years afterwards, and of the revolutionary redemption of the 'fallen', by Maharshi Deval and others—has to be stressed again and again, as it has not been adequately described not even mentioned at all, in Indian histories.

485. Although there is very slender evidence on our side to bear out this two-fold Hindu victory in Sindh, we can find a stronger proof in the writings of the enemy. The Muslim writers were vexed at their general rout in the reconquest of Sindh by the Hindus.

486. Al Biladuri (or Baladhuri) writes, "In the days of Tamim, the Musalmans retired from several parts of India and left their position... Hakim, son of Awanah al Kalbi, succeeded Tamim. The people of India had returned to idolatory, excepting those of Kassah and the Musalmans

had no place of security in which they could take refuge, so he built a town on the other side of the lake facing India and called it Al Mahfuza, 'the secure', and this he made a place of refuge and security for them and their chief town." (Elliot HIED, Vol. I., p. 126.)

487. History places Maharshi Deval somewhere between A.D. 800 and A.D. 900. Round about this period, i.e. about A.D. 850 to A.D. 950, was born fortunately for the Hindus, another upholder of this new surge of religious revival. He sought to overcome the disastrous Muslim religious aggression with still more disastrous counter-aggression. The weapon worship religious law given by Acharya Medhatithi, became the most effective guidance to the Hindus, like the *Arthashastra* of Arya Chanakya to the generation of the valiant Chandragupta Maurya. To the whole of Aryavarta, he wanted to teach once again the lesson of expansionism and victorious imperialism. Medhatithi, the new interpreter of Manusmriti, was the sole religious leader and perhaps the last of the writers of Smriti. He tried to erect before the perplexd Hindus of the 9th and 10th centuries, a huge lighthouse tower of the former Aryan imperialism and expansionism of Chanakya, and to regenerate into them, new courage to push ahead determinedly and strike hard at the aggressor. His intention was clearly to animate his society with the vibrant inspiration to repulse instantly the armed religious aggression of the Muslims of those times, in the same magnificent tradition of the Aryan empires of old and with their military strategy, in fighting down the aggressive rakshasas (enemies). He wanted the Hindus to establish not only the old empire of Aryavarta, but to conquer and annex the Muslim states even beyond the limits of Aryavarta and establish Hinduism there, if necessary, even with force. The Aryan slogan 'Krunvanto Vishvam Aryam' (We are going to make the whole world Aryan) of the Vedic times, resounds incessantly throughout his critique on Manusmriti.

488. There had been a great confusion wrought in the Hindu Society over a thousand years or so preceding Medhatithi's age by the anti-national and imbecile social traditions (which we have mentioned so far and will mention hereafter), about the differentiation of caste, religious tolerance and fear of pollution, which appeared as if laid down by the shritis (Vedas), and ruled as per the injunction of the Smritis. The critic Medhatithi was the only one, who on seeing the miserable plight of the Hindus determined to check their downward course and convulse the imbecile and intellectually stagnant Hindu society into its original Aryan

form. Naturally, he decided to criticise Manusmriti itself, which was considered to be the basic foundation of all other smritis. He ruthlessly tested the laws of political conduct propounded therein on the anvil of Chanakya's *Arthashastra.* In this way, with the original Manusmriti of the Aryans in one hand and the empire-worshipping conquest-loving Kautilya's *Arthashastra* in the other, Medhatithi declared irreligious all the codes of conduct, which had been rendered impotent because of the imbecile and intellectually sterile Hindu Ahimsa. With one stroke of remonstrance like the following:

489. या वेदब्राह्: यस्मृतमय: याश्च काश्च कुदृश्टय: ।
सर्वास्तान् विपरीतार्थान्, वेदविद् न समाचरेत् ॥

He rendered not only all the silly 'codes of conduct', but even the smritis that called them caste-laws absolutely defunct and valueless.

490. Most probably, Medhatithi might have seen and heard about all the religious persecution by the Muslims in Sindh and the Punjab and the failure of the Hindus, for various reasons already discussed, to avenge it or even to counteract it effectively. Naturally, in order to din once again into the ears of the then defeated, fallen and perplexed Aryan nation the echoes of the smritis of the old Aryavarta, which was on its way to glory and which, with the motto कृवन्तो विश्वम् आर्यम on its banner was conquering in all directions, Medhatithi picked up and extolled in his own critique as Manu's original commandments, only the warlike, arms-adoring and imperialistic religious rites and precepts. All others, he condemned as वेदब्राह्य: स्मृतय: (smritis against the Vedas)! His thundering sentences did not befit the then powerless Hindu kings, nor could those kings utter them with proper dignity and grandeur. Those precepts were really meant for an Emperor like Chandragupta or Emperor Pushyamitra!

491-492. Medhatithi clearly declares that to invade another kingdom—especially an enemy state—can never be an injustice in political science. It is, on the other hand, the duty of a king, he said, to pounce upon the non-Hindu enemy and crush him before he grows powerful enough to invade the former. In statesmanship, the protection of the Aryavarta is the supreme duty of a king. That is why he condemns as suicidal, dilatory and so adverse to the kingly duty, everything that the other imprudent foolhardy critics recommend as proper code of conduct: viz that while attacking a foreign kingdom and especially the Muslim kingdom, the Aryan kings should not strike till the other gives offence of some sort or the other. On the contrary, he says that the neighbouring king is an enemy is in itself his fault; at an opportune moment, he should be pounced upon and crushed. What more, if the neighbouring non-Aryan kingdom is seen to be getting stronger and mightier than our Aryan state, whether it is guilty of any tangible offence or not, we should ourselves form alliance with other friendly or unfriendly powers and go to war against this non-Aryan state, the moment we are assured of success.

493. Throughout the critical treatise of Medhatithi, one dominant aspiration makes itself felt on almost every page that the smaller states of Shreeman Bhojraj—the Rajput prince—and other Hindu kings should be united into a powerful kingdom and once again a mighty empire like the old—nay, an invincible and victorious Bharatiya Empire—should rise on the Indian soil. From this point of view, while writing about the other kingly duties, he has emphasized one, viz. that even before the Mlenchchas (non-Aryans) attack an Aryan state, the latter should march against the enemy kingdom. Once you are engaged in war with the enemy, you should throw kindness and generosity to the winds and crush the enemy outright. The crafty enemy should be struck down with super-cunning and skilful deception under any pretext whatsoever. In a war, the so-called virtues like honesty, simplicity, consistency in speech and action and politeness, gentility and generosity themselves prove fatal to the nation. Hence, a king should not fall a prey to them—should keep himself aloof from them.

494. Medhatithi has most powerfully expounded this sort of stern political theory (ethics). For, it was absolutely essential for saving the Hindus from complete annihilation at the hands of the Muslims, because of their simplicity. To teach them the arch-diplomacy of Arya Chanakya, was his sole aim. Medhatithi plainly says that the Aryadharma nowhere decrees that the Aryans should confine themselves to the boundaries of Aryavarta. On the contrary, the pith and marrow of the religious code of the Hindus, he says, is that if the mighty Aryan kings invade the non-Aryan kingdoms beyond the Aryavarta and conquer them, and immediately spread their Aryadharma there and finally establish their empire in those lands, then even those former non-Aryan lands should thereafter be considered Aryan lands and incorporated in Aryavarta!

495. At least some Hindu states of those times followed these precepts of Medhatithi and like Chanakya's ideal disciple, Chandragupta,

literally crossed the boundaries of Aryavarta and waged successful wars against the Muslim powers. Although to the north, the frontier Hindu states were forced not to cross but to defend their boundaries, yet till nearly one hundred and fifty years after the death of Mahmud of Ghazni, the Southern Hindu states remained independent and powerful. So the Indian Hindu States were able to carry out the victorious political experiments of the Mauryan era as per the injunctions of Medhatithi And that is why the Kalingas, the Pandyas, the Cheras, Cholas and other Hindu states sent powerful naval expeditions across the Western (often misnamed the Arabian Sea), the Southern and the Eastern Seas, carrying their victorious banner to the non-Aryan kingdoms, right up to the African coast on the one side and the Chinese on the other. The astonishing fact is that while in the north, Mahmud of Ghazni and Mohammed Ghori were ravaging and plundering capital-after-capital and temple-after-temple of the Hindus and trampling down their powerful kingdoms in the South, the colossal temples like the one at Bhuvaneshwar were being erected. Kings like Rajendra Chola marched with their mighty victorious naval forces, through Burma, Pegu, the Andamans and the Nicobars and other archipelagos in the Eastern Sea. They visited the Hindu confederate states in Java, Indo-China and Thailand, conquered the Lakshadiv and Maldiva island states in the Western Sea, and finally conquering Ceylon, hoisted their invincible flag on the Southern Ocean.

496. It is doubtless that on the strength of religious authority of Medhatithi, illumined by the glorious tradition of Chanakya, these victorious Hindu naval forces conquered kingdom-after-kingdom beyond the great seas and annexed them to the Aryan empire. This was accomplished not on the hobby horse to tight conventions and rigid injunctions which came into force a century or two before, but because of the enlightening and guiding commentaries of Medhatithi.

□

10

Intermittent Hindu Retaliation Against Muslim Religious Aggression

497. At the end of an earlier chapter, we had expressed our astonishment as to how the Hindu Society did not perish completely in spite of the various defects of class-differences, ban on reconversion misconceptions about virtues and the like, and how it escaped with the loss of only some millions of Hindus converted. For beyond the frontiers of India, wherever such Muslim religious aggression took place, the natives there were totally deprived of their religions. The northern coast of Africa up to Spain and the Asian lands up to the frontier India, were totally converted to Islam. But in India alone, then attempts were not completely successful. At the time of Muhammad Kasim's invasion of Sindh in the 8th century and then from the 11th century, i.e. for nearly a thousand years, from the marauding expedition of Mahmud of Ghazni and of Ghori to the complete overthrow of the Moghul empire by the Peshwas in the 18th century, the Muslim invaders violently converted lakhs of Hindus and tried to multiply their numbers. The circumstances in this land—most adverse for the Hindus—also favoured them. Why then did the Muslims fail to destroy the Hindu Society completely?

498. The first reason that can explain this strange occurrence is the political defeat, which the Hindus inflicted on these Muslims. In the initial stages, Bhim and Rana Pratap and other Rajput princes and next, the Hindu kings of Vijayanagar had rendered the Muslim power out of gear and crippled it. Lastly, the Marathas dealt it deadly blows and fluttered their victorious banner under the leadership of the Peshwa right up to Attock. This political defeat of the Muslims at the hands of the Hindus, which is well known to all, made it impossible for the Muslims to bring all the Hindus under their green flag.

499. But the other potent reason for this strange phenomenon is

that there arose from time to time, heroic men and women warriors, who staunchly opposed the armed religious aggression of the Muslims with counter aggression following the precepts of Maharshi Deval and Medhatithi. It is this counter-aggression on the religious front by the Hindus, that has really saved the Hindu society from total extinction. Some stray incidents are cited here to show how the Hindus did it.

500. (1) After the Muslims conquered Sindh, the celebrated Bappa Raval of Mevad attacked not only Sindh, but the Muslim strongholds beyond that land and annexed them to his territory. He even went further, as the Rasos (political biographies) of the Rajput princes tell us. He married a Muslim princess, who was captured at the final Muslim rout and kept her in his harem along with his other queens. His offsprings from this Muslim converted princess were respected in the society as born in the family of the Sun god. In respect of this progeny of the King of Mevad, the Hindus of that time did not always act with foolish religiosity of the Marathas, who refused to accept the son of the valiant Bajirao Peshwa from his Muslim wife, Mastani, and forced the child back into the Muslim society.

501. (2) Raval Chechak of Jaisalmir married the daughter of Sultan Haibatkhan named Somaldevi, and established her honourably in his Yadav race.

502. (3) When Kanwar Jagmal, the eldest son of Rao Mallinath Rathod of Marwad, heroically defeated the Muslim Sultan of Gujarat and annexed it to his own domain, he married publicly the daughter of the Sultan, called Gindoli, who was renowned for her exceptional beauty, and established his offsprings, born of her, amongst the high ranked Jagirdars of Marwad and assimilated them amongst the Rajputs completely.

503. (4) Besides all these, the Hindus here and there seem to have effected bold prudent counter-strokes to the terrible calamity of the mass conversions of Hindus by the Muslim aggressors, and foiled their attempts. For instance, Raimal, the King of Marwad captured 600 Muslim women, and after reconverting them to Hinduism, married them publicly to several noblemen of his court.

504. (5) Kumbharana of Mevad likewise defeated the Muslims, taking all the captured Muslim women to his Kingdom. He reconverted them and married them to his noblemen as per their wishes.

505. (6) The celebrated historian of Rajasthan, Major Tod, has

narrated many more instances of this type.

506. (7) The different political histories, called Rasos of the Rajput royal families, also mention many instances of this type of conversion and assimilation of Muslim women into the Hindu society.

507. (8) Raja Jayasthiti of Nepal also avenged Muslim religious aggression in like manner. He too followed Medhatithi's policy of rushing the wicked enemy. About A.D. 1360, Shamsuddin—the Nawab of Bengal—attacked Nepal and played havoc there, destroying many Hindu and Buddhist temples, converting violently hundreds of Hindu and Buddhist subjects. When this brave Hindu King came to the throne, he made Nepal a hotbed for the Muslims, drove them out completely and avenged the wrongs done to his subjects. Not only did he rebuild the ruined Hindu and Buddhist temples, but he even reconverted to Hinduism all the unfortunate Hindus and Buddhists, who had been the victims of the Muslim aggression.

508. (9) In the historical records of the times, like the Tarikhs, one curiously finds the Muslim writers themselves complaining that at the least opportunity, the Hindu kafirs converted even the Muslim women to Hinduism and married them in the Hindu community. Such events, of which no trace whatever, can be found in our Hindu historical books, are available only in the Muslim historical records.

509. (10) For instance, in Tarikh-i-Sorath, its Muslim writer says: "Even at the troubled times of Mahmud Ghazni's expeditions, the King of Anhilwad at the first opportunity, carried away several of the Turkish, Moghul and Afghan women who lingered behind and the Hindus married them unhesitatingly." He also puts it on record that whenever possible, the Hindus carried away Muslim women en masse and converted them to Hinduism! He has also given some interesting information on the purification and reconversion ceremony of Muslim women performed by the Hindus.

510. He says, "while converting the Muslim women as a class, the Hindu priests burned some barley over their heads. Then, they were given some water mixed with cowdung to drink. Then they were considered fit for all mutual dealings, and the Hindus married them as per their tastes and desires. At some places in the ceremonial mass conversion of Muslim women, these Hindus gave them purgatives and vomiting drugs, and thereafter, distributed them among the various Hindu castes and classes, according to their ranks. The fairest women

fell to the lot of high-ranking Hindus. Sardars and noblemen married those of decent birth and lineage, while the maids and slaves were wedded to the Hindus of their respective classes. The whole progeny of these women was completely merged into those respective classes of the Hindu society."

511. (11) When Arundevrai of Ajmer overcame the Muslims and ousted them from his land, he performed a great ceremony to purify the land which was rendered impure by the Muslim contact, and at that holy place, built a big temple and a lake named 'Anasagar'. All the men and women, who were converted at the time of the Muslim domination, were all reconverted to Hinduism by merely dipping into this Anasagar lake and moreover, it was given out as a religious precept, that whichever Muslim convert bathed in this lake, with due declaration of his intention and according to some procedure, was to be considered purified and could enter Hinduism.

512. (12) Amarsingh Maharaj of Jaisalmir also performed a similar ceremony and built a lake called Amarsagar. In this lake, sanctified by the great ceremony, thousands of Hindus in Sindh, who were formerly converted to Islam, dipped en masse, declaring their intention to enter into Hinduism, and chanted Mantras while they bathed, and the religious authorities recognised their purification and reconversion to Hinduism.

513. (13) A reference has to be made to Shree Vidyaranyaswami, who like Maharshi Deval and Medhatithi, tried to check the Muslim religious aggression by inspiring the Hindus to retaliate, by bringing forth revolutionary proof of religious authority and sometimes enunciating new religious laws for the purpose. Shree Vidyaranyaswami had accepted not only the supreme leadership (authority) of the religious institution of Shankaracharya at Shringeri, but also of the revolutionary institution designed to overthrow the Muslim power and to establish in its place, a Hindu empire in order to protect Hinduism. He produced not only religious authority for the reconversion of the unfortunate Hindus leading a miserable life under Islam, but he himself publicly reconverted the once forcibly converted Harihar and Bukka, and when these two great warriors defeated the Muslims on several occasions, and established in A.D. 1336, the Hindu State of Vijayanagar, he himself crowned the reconverted Harihar as the Hindu Emperor.

514. After the overthrow of the Muslim power in Gomantak, this very Vidyaranya Madhavacharya built at a holy place, a lake named Madhavteerth and effected mass reconversion of the Muslimized Hindus with ceremonial baths in it. He also provided a religious authority for the future reconversion and purification.

515. (14) Shree Ramanujacharya, his disciples Shree Ramanand and Shree Chaitanya Prabhu of Bengal, also purified hundreds of Muslimized Hindus with an administration of the vows of Vaishnavism.

516. (15) It is well known that the most daring and valiant Shree Shivachhatrapati, who avenged all the wrongs done to the Hindus by establishing a Hindu independent state, himself reconverted Bajaji, Nimbalkar and Netaji Palkar, who had been forced to court Islam.

A Counter-Aggression?

517. (16) Towards the end of his career, Aurangzeb opened, with his huge fourfold army, the most determined offensive against the Hindus. Before he fell upon the Marathas, he wanted to crush the Rajputs. But no sooner did he go away to the South, than the Rajputs retaliated with the same vehemence and vigour and made up for the humiliation and numerical losses of the Hindus. The glaring instance of Jodhpur may be cited here. Under the leadership of powerful Maharana Jaswantsingh and the brave Durgadas Rathod, not only the masjids, erected by Aurangzeb on the ruins of Hindu temples, but all other masjids also were razed to the ground and on their site, Hindu temples were built. The Jodhpurian Rajputs reconverted not only the Muslimized Hindus, but as many of the Muslims also as they could on an extensive scale. If the Muslim armies went on throwing beef into the Hindu temples and wells, the Rathod armies cast pork in masjid-after-masjid and paid them in the same coin. Hundreds of Muslim women were converted to Hinduism and married to the Rajputs or were simply kept as concubines, like the Hindu women by the Muslims before them. The whole of the Muslim society in Rajputana was horror-stricken to see this ferocious outburst of Hindu rage. Not merely for the sin of eating and drinking with the Muslims but for having cohabited with and married Muslim women, and even keeping them in their houses, Hindus were no longer socially ostracized. For, at least thirty to forty years, this Hindu retaliatory aggression on the Muslims had spread and glowed, and resounded through town-after-town and village-after-

village in the Hindu states in Rajasthan. It is, of course, needless to say that with the decline of the power of the brave Durgadas Rathod, this ferocious appearance of the Hindu society also vanished.

Reason?

518. The reason is only this, that the abiding state of the Hindu mind at that time, did not favour religious counter-aggression but social boycott.

The innate capacity of the Hindus for Rejuvenation

519. It is interesting to note how side by side with the repeated annihilating aggressions of Mahmud of Ghanzi and Ghori and other Muslims, and side-by-side, again with huge numerical losses suffered by the Hindus because of their morbid misconception of virtues and caste-differences, and the ban on repurification and reconversion, the age-old native missionary spirit and urge of the Hindu nation also burst into action elsewhere, acquiring not only political power but assimilating newer tribes of thousands of people. The story of the conversion of the Ahom tribe in Assam to Hinduism, can be cited here as a sample, noting at the same time, the spread of the Hindu empire in Indo-China and beyond, referred to already towards the end of the last chapter.

520. While hundreds of Hindu warships and merchant-marine were lording over the vast seas and oceans—the Gangasagar (The Bay of Bengal), the Sindhusagar (the Bay of Bombay) and the whole of the Indian Ocean—right from the Southern end of Africa to the very coast of China, it was impossible for any Hindu to have ever thought of the beggarly ban on sea-voyage! This conquest of the seas (by the Hindus), is also referred to earlier. The conversion of the Ahom tribe to Hinduism is described here as an illustration of how *vis-a-vis the* vast numerical losses suffered in the north because of the diabolic onslaughts of the Mahmud of Ghazni and Ghori, the Hindus went on winning religious victories and assimilating thousands of alien people into the Hindu religion.

521. Beyond Assam, many wild tribes had lived a nomadic life for generations together, subsisting on marauding and plunder. Ahom, a branch of one of these tribes, called Shan, began to press hard since the 8th century A.D. on the Hindu kings of Varman, Salstam and Pal dynasties adjoining Assam. In the end in A.D. 1228, King Sukapha

began to rule all these lands. He was the first king to call himself and his subjects Ahom—Ajod—i.e unrivalled! These new administrators of the land boldly and successfully faced even the Moghul might. Sukapha's kingdom was also called Ahom and modern Assam, in the opinion of some scholars, is the corrupt form of Ahom.

521A. The most astonishing fact is that among these various mountain tribes as among the Huns and the Sakas, the Hindu missions and missionaries then existing there, had planted the principles and rules of religious conduct as laid down by Hinduism, so deeply and firmly that as soon as he conquered Assam in A.D. 1554, another Ahom king along with many of his tribe accepted Hinduism. Gradually, that whole tribe of thousands of people merged itself into the Hindu society. That king changed his original name in the Shan dialect to Jaydhwaj Singh, a name among the Hindu Kshatriyas. All the later Ahom kings too took for themselves Hindu names alone.

Ban on crossing attock and sea voyage

522. While the brave tribes, like the above mentioned Ahom, were courting Hinduism even in its evil days, there was no likelihood of any ban on purification or any caste-differences, to stop them from doing so. For, these only made some new addition to the already existing numerous castes in the Hindu nation. Some of their customs and manners were limited to their particular castes, but all other rites and ceremonies were common to all, in strict conformity with the injunctions of the Hindu Smritis. The ban on purification and reconversion was being enforced more-and-more strictly only towards the north up to Punjab, solely because of the ruthless atrocities of the Muslims. The rest of the Indian continent was wholly free from the danger of Muslim domination. The Muslims had not yet made any further headway. Naturally, the ban on purification and reconversion had not so far presented itself to them in any urgency. It should be told here, that the ban on the crossing of the Attock, i.e. the injuction appearing in the later smritis, declaring it a sin to cross the Indus and to go over into the Muslim lands, must have been promulgated by our traditionalist priesthood, with the sole intention of saving Hinduism. For, it was impossible that crossing the Indus meant abandoning Hinduism (the Vedic cult) and being polluted, as it is now amply proved that even after the ravages of Mahmud of Ghazni, the whole of the region beyond the Indus even up to the Mount Pariyatra

(Hindukush mountains), was reconquered by the Hindus and the Hindu rule spread up to Khotan. Even up to that time, 'Krunvanto Vishwam Aryam' was the motto inscribed on our national flag. 'Traverse the whole world for spreading Aryadharma' was the supreme unqualified religious order of the day!

523-524. But it becomes clear from the historical facts mentioned above, that it is only when the Hindu states beyond the Indus were liquidated, thousands of Hindus began to be violently converted to Islam by the devilish Muslims, who subjected the followers of other religions to harrowing persecution. The ban on crossing the Attock must, therefore, have been enforced, owing to the helplessness caused by the lack of any armed support for the Hindus in those regions. Another proof of this is the provision in the (Smrityaite) smarta order (order-system-laid down by the smritis) for adding or deleting according to the times and circumstances, the religious duties beneficial or harmful to the nation. The verse:

"Different were the religious rites
and duties of the krit, Dwapar and
other epochs (ages) (But) owing to
the deterioration of the ages, the
duties of men have come to be different"

अन्ये कृंतयुगे धर्मा:
त्रेतायां द्वापरे परे ॥
अन्ये कलियुगे नृणाम
युग ह्रासानुरुपत: ॥

expresses the idea very succinctly.

525. Naturally, when the Hindu kingdoms beyond the Indus were lost and the Hindus and Persians and others were converted to Islam, under unbearable persecution by the Muslim powers established there, and, as such, when to go beyond the Indus became as horrible as to abandon one's own religion, it must have become absolutely necessary for the smritis to issue the new order of the darkest hour (adverse times), that it was sinful for any Hindu to cross the Indus, that the land beyond the Indus should be considered a Muslim land. From this time onwards, therefore, the ban on crossing Attock must have been strictly enforced.

526-528. The verse in Bhavishya Puran, which describes the new boundaries of India, and which I myself brought to light for the first time

"The Aryan nation is best called
Sindhusthan. The land beyond the
Indus is made the land of the
Muslims by that great soul".

सिंधु स्थानमिति प्राहु:
राष्ट्र भार्यस्य चोत्तमम्।
म्लेच्छ स्थानम् परं सिंधो:
कृतं तेन महात्मना॥

must have been appended to the smritis at this time, i.e. after Mohammed Ghori's invasion. This time is also mentioned in that verse itself. The then Hindu Maharaja—great King—who fixed this boundary, and who is referred to here by the phrase 'by that great soul', must probably be Maharaja Bhoj of Dhara (999 AD - 1054 AD), the greatest among the Hindu rulers of the time.

Smritis and the ban on sea voyages

529. Although the Muslim political conquests in the north brought upon the Hindu nation, this miserable calamity of narrowing the northern and north-western boundaries of India, yet it was limited to the north alone. The rest of India, on this side of Punjab, the whole of Sindhusthan was free to assimilate newer tribes beyond Assam, free to be the mistress of the eastern, western and southern seas and extend its rule right up to Indo-China and win new victories. Sinhaldweep (Ceylon) was also a Baby India—a satellite Indian state! For, the island of Ceylon had all along been ruled by royal dynasties of Indian extraction! The same is true of the Lakhadiv and Maldiv and other archipelagos in the vast ocean up to the African coast, which were under the authority of the Hindu kings. It is foolish to think of any order by the Smritis which claimed to follow the Vedic cult, banning sea voyage at that time. The greatest conquerors of all the quarters like the Emperor Rajendra Chola were strict followers of the Vedic cult, and took for themselves the title, 'Trisamudreshwar'—ruler of the three seas—as that of 'Samrat' in the north.

Sea Voyage and Fetters

530-533. The verse, 'अन्ये कृतयुगे धर्मा: त्रेतायाम् द्वापरे परे' ...cited above, indirectly points to the reason why helpless Hindu law-givers of latter days, labouring under political slavery, were obliged to clamp this ban on the voyage of the three seas in the South. The reason actuated in the north the prevention of crossing the Indus into the lands beyond, was no other than the religious persecution of the Hindus by alien religious fanatics. In order that the insertion into the old original smritis of new precepts and bans, calculated to meet the critical situations arising in future, might be possible, a new concept of the deterioration of the age and the chapter on rules of conduct prescrided in the कलिवर्ज्य प्रकरण was cleverly adopted. It is needless to say that this concept of the deterioration of the age and the theory of कलिवर्ज्य things, did actually affect adversely the immutability of the old smritis. But such an indirect change, in the best interests of the society, was unavoidable for the religious law-givers of the times, who sometimes modified or enlarged some old precepts, while they introduced some altogether new ones. The verse, अन्ये कृतयुगे etc., which occurs in most of the smritis mentioned above, bears out this remark very clearly. It is only in the smritis compiled or edited in this Smrityite fashion after the periods of Maharshi Deval and Acharya Medhatithi, that the unequivocal ban on sea voyage, denying every sort of redemption for one undertaking sea voyage, and making illegal the acceptance of such a person into his original religion or caste, seems to have been enforced strietly. That period synchronizes with the preponderance of Christians, more particularly the Portuguese, in our Western Sea, with the Portuguese persecution and proselytization of the thousands of Hindus in Gomantak (Goa), and with the Arab occupation of Java, Sumatra and Indo-China and the wholesale violent conversion of the Hindu-Buddhist population of those lands. This was the period when the sea-faring Hindu-Buddhist states of the greater Indian empire, staunchly supported by the gallant navies of the Cholas and the Pandyas, fell along with the whole of Southern India, devastated before the Muslim might. It was the same period when the Hindu ships stopped visiting those distant states and the Hindus lost all contact with them. It was the most miserable, the most wretched period in the religious and political life of the Hindu nation. Naturally, this must have been the period when the ban on sea-faring was strictly and universally clamped on the Hindus. And it is only in the latest smritis of this period, let it be remembered, that the verses about the ban on the crossing of Attock and that on sea-faring are to be found!

534. It is clear from the above-mentioned state of things that it

was only when every Hindu rover, crossing any of the three Indian seas, had to fall a prey to the rapacious Muslim or Christian crocodiles, with no Hindu power overlording the sea any longer, to protect him from that tragic fate, that their foremost leaders had to issue this ban—this order not to cross the seas on any occasion—with the noble intention of protecting the Hindu society.

535. A nation that obliged to suffer all sorts of humiliation heaped on her natives and the adherents of the native religion (one which is obliged to see helplessly foreign Muslim or Christian religions imposed on pain of death upon her people, and which sadly lacks the armed might to ward off this disastrous situation), has no other go than to forbid her people, of course, for self-preservation alone, from going to the enemy lands.

Self-imposition of the ban on crossing attock or the seas

536. The greatest mistake made was that when these various bans were interpolated in the older smritis, as the best means of serving the needs of the particular hour, the spurious verses dealing with these bans were also given the same sanctity, the same authenticity and the same inviolability by stamping them with the old authoritative seal of एष धर्मः सनातनः 'This is the old tradition', as was given to the genuinely old verses. That is why even after the particular adverse times, for which these bans on crossing Attock or the sea were originally designed, had passed off and more favourable times prevailed, inasmuch as when the Hindu military might under the Peshwas and Ranjit Singh was powerful enough not only to cross Afghanistan but even attack Persia, this anti-national blind faith in those bans, however, did not vanish. It was still boulking the credulous Hindu Society with the fear of committing a sin in crossing Attock. That means even when the once beneficial religious tradition had grown harmful to the nation, the Hindu Society was not prepared to give it up immediately for fear of the religious injunction. Even when to break that tradition would have definitely proved greatly advantageous to the nation and holy from the religious point of view, the blind faith in the old tradition that to break the old custom was to commit a sin was still maintained. It is, therefore, the sea, एष धर्मः सनातनः' that the modern writers of smritis affixed to these later interpolations, which acted as a bugbear, that played the greatest mischief.

537. Take for instance, the ban on seafaring! Had these writers of

smritis of later times specifically mentioned that in old 'Krit yug', our Arya nation was mighty enough to cross the (seven) seas and rule over other islands and archipelagos, that even up to the time of Rajendra Chola, we were the lords of the three seas (त्रिसमुद्राधीश) and that, as such, crossing the seas was essential for the spread of our religion and empire and was holy, but as the naval power and the lordship of the seas had now been unfortunately lost, crossing the seas and going into the enemy land in the helpless humble way, was highly injurious to our nation, and so sinful, and that it was, therefore, banned till we regained that lordship of the seas. Had they but said so in so many words! युग हासानुरूपत: should really be construed as शक्तिहासानुरूपत: 'because of the loss of might.' The bugbear of एषधर्म: सनातन: should be truly held up only to that extent. Had (once again we repeat) the writers of Smritis of that time announced this clearly, the tremendously harmful consequences of these bans on crossing Attock and the seas, which the nation had to suffer, could have been avoided to a large extent.

538. But because the new precepts about the various bans on crossing Attock and the seas and others, which were really introduced in the chapter on कलिवर्ज्य things by the new religious lawgivers of later days, were published under the name of the old writers of smritis, they were to remain in force till the end of the कलियुग (Kaliyug), i.e. permanently. Although, later on, breaking these bans itself would have proved advantageous to the Hindus, and although the Hindus had become strong enough to break them, it was impossible that the credulous Hindu Society would ever have been prepared to break them till the doomsday प्रलयकाल (the end of कलियुग), because of the specific Smriti order 'these five should be abandoned in Kaliyuga' (कलौपंच विवर्जयेत्). Again, when did the (कलियुग) Kaliyug begin? How long was it to last? And when was it to end? And after its end, when was the Age of Truth (सत्ययुग) to commence once again? The different opinions held on these points by many of our religious lawgivers made the confusion worse confounded.

The Christian Religious offensive against the Hindus!

539. In paragraph 399 of this book, is mentioned the antiquity of the first Hindu contacts with the Christians. According to the Christian mythology, when in the first century A.D. the Christian religion began to

be preached in Syria, the very Jews who had crucified Jesus of Nazareth began to persecute these handful of Christians. At that very time, some of the Christians, who knew the way to India, fled in groups to seek shelter with the Hindu King of Malabar Zamorin (the corrupt form of Samudriya). As a matter of fact, that Hindu King ought not to have unconditionally allowed these alien people to land on his sea-coast. But being afflicted by the disease of the morbidly erroneous conception of virtues, that Hindu king offered shelter to those Syrian Christians, and allocated a separate tract for their habitation. He even went to the length of offering a copper-plate (ताम्रपट) inscription recognizing their equality of right as a separate caste in the gram-panchayat (town-council). But, later on, when these Syrian-Christians came to know that even if the Hindus were forced merely to eat or drink with them, they would be polluted and could become Christians, these ancient Syrian Christians made an inauspicious start of the spread of Christianity in India, whereas during the first Christian century (1st Century A.D.), not a trace of Christianity could be found in England itself, in India, Hindus had already been begun to be forcibly baptized and made Christians! (It is worthwhile for every Hindu to read the history of the spread of Christianity in those days. Moreover, it seems that the customs and codes of conduct that were likely to facilitate the enemy in the work of proselytization, were firmly rooted in us as the basic religious conduct even as far back as the first century A.D. But we will leave this topic alone for want of space at our disposal, and because it has little bearing upon the subject in hand.

540. However, we should like to refer to one pregnant instance here. On seeing that a number of Hindu people in a town used to bathe in a holy lake, some of those Syrian-Christian missionaries thought that even here, they could try the device of polluting and Christianizing the Hindus, who considered themselves polluted by merely eating food or drinking water with the Christians. With this intention, these Syrian Christian missionaries stealthily went to big lakes where Hindu people used to go in large numbers for a bath and for carrying drinking water home. They bathed there along with all and drank its water. Then, after some days, these very missionaries themselves declared loudly in their congregations, "O you Hindus! We are Christians, the followers of Jesus! We are not Hindus! We have been bathing in your lakes along with you. After worshipping our Christian god, we drink the holy water of the

Christian religion and have been giving you the same water all these days and you drank it devoutly. As per your Hindu religion, whichever Hindu drinks the Christian water becomes a Christian for life. This is your religious injunction, so you all have become Christians. That your other brethren may not be deceived, we pious people are publishing this truth!' This news spread among the Christians and the Hindus of several villages in no time. There was a great havoc everywhere! All those Hindus became impure and so they began to be boycotted. In the usual way, all those villages and towns in course of time, were socially ostracized and became Christian villages and towns!

541. Now we shall cite just for fun—but fun that kills—another incident, showing how all the human races at that time were fanatics in the extreme.

541A. The early Syrian Christian migrants to India were also divided into different sects. They vied with one another as to which of them disseminated the Christian doctrine more truly in foreign countries. So the sects other than the one that had Christianized Hindu villages, protested against the latter and out of malice, informed the superior religious authorities in Europe that sect had converted the simple and foolish Hindu to Christianity by abominable lies and deception, and collected contributions, but had never preached any Christian doctrines, as such. Therefore, they pleaded, that the number of the converts should not be taken into account, and that they should be stopped from damaging the prestige of the Christian propagandists. Because of the incessant protests of these other Christian sects, those Hindu converts to Christianity had for a long time no legal status as Christians, although they thought themselves to be such, and their subscriptions to the church were not accepted, nor were they allowed entrance into the church. In the end, the knotty problem seemed to have been solved by way of sumptuous subscriptions. For, after some days, a directive was received from Europe that all the Hindu converts were now to be called Christians and subscriptions from all of them were necessarily to be collected. Later on, all the Christian missionaries, to whatever sect they belonged, declared it to be their religious duty to convert the Hindus not only by hook or by crook or by sly means, but even by force and armed force. Naturally, the elementary ways of conversion like making the Hindus eat or drink with the Christians, were beyond all range of dispute and doubt.

542. Thereafter, the Syrian and other Christians fell out in their own country, and there were fierce battles fought amongst the various Christian sects. Therefore, for two or three centuries, thereafter, the work of the Christian missionaries in India had practically stopped. But one thing must be remembered in this context, that because there was no attempt whatsoever on the part of the Hindus to reconvert the Christianized Hindus (Indian Christians), the latter kept on calling themselves Christians and ceased to have any relation whatsoever with the Hindus.

543. In this brief account, one great proselytizing movement in the fifteenth century deserves some slight reference. That is the rigorous proselytizing movement carried on by the Portuguese missionaries after the passing of Gomantak into the Portuguese hands, and the opening of the centres of Christian propaganda on the Malabar coast. Their first energetic and determined archbishop to convert the Hindus by means of any horrible atrocities was Saint Xavier, who came to the land of Gomantak by about A.D. 1540. After moving heaven and earth for the spread of Christianity (of course in his horrible way), he wrote several letters to the Emperor of Portugal about the obstacles in his way of proselytization.

544. In one of his letters to the Portuguese King, he complains that the Portuguese officers in India, in spite of the fact that they were Christians themselves, irreverently set at naught, his orders in respect of the propagation of their faith. They were entirely given to lustful pleasures and a life of luxury, and were always on the lookout for every means to grow rich. Money was their God. To the service of the true God, to which the missionaries like himself had dedicated their lives, those officers, never did lend any helping hand. "The Second necessity for the Christians", he wrote in his letter addressed from Amboina (Moluccas) to D. Joao III, King of Portugal on May 16, 1545, "is that your Majesty establish the Holy Inquisition, because there are many who live according to the Jewish law and according to the Mohamedan sect, without any fear of God or shame of the world. And since there are many, who are spread all over the fortress, there is the need of the Holy Inquisition and of many preachers." In one of his letters to the Society at Rome, he wrote, "If it were not for the opposition of the Brahmins, we should have them all embracing the religion of Jesus Christ." These Brahmins were alleged to hinder the progress of the Christian

proselytizing movement. While the Christian missionaries went on converting thousands of Hindus to Christianity, these 'wily' Brahmins were found to be secretly taking them all to the banks of the Mandvi river and bluffed them into bathing in the river; after reciting some verses, in order to wash off all sins of being converted to Christianity, they were declared to be original Hindus. Thus, with these and various other blatant lies, these Brahmins were alleged to be purifying a number of Hindu converts to Christianity. In spite of all attemps to intimidate and terrorise these Brahmins, they were said to be carrying on their activities nonchalantly. Xavier complains that the Portuguese officers in India did not inflict on these Brahmins such severe punishments, as he would have liked them to do.

545. Tired of these incessant complaints of the Christian missionaries like St. Xavier, the Portuguese Emperor issued stern orders to his Governors and other officers, that they should not neglect help in any way in the sacred (?) cause of the spread of Christianity, otherwise their whole properly would be confiscated. Even then not satisfied, St. Xavier went on complaining against the Brahmins. He, nevertheless, gloated at the tremendous success his proselytizing efforts had achieved. At the very sight of a Christian missionary, Hindu villages were taken alright and people there were said to be running away helfer skelter, for most severe were the measures taken against those of the Hindus, who did not court Christianity. Let alone the common Hindu villagers, even the high priests of big Hindu temples, the heads of Hindu monasteries and the rich in the cities, were all put into prisons and were subjected to so much physical torture, that the priestly class at many places is said to have made good their escape to places outside Goa, carrying their sacred idols with them. "Whenever I hear of any act of idolatrous worship", wrote St. Francis Xavier to the Society at Rome in 1543 A.D. "I go to the place with a large band of these children, who very soon load the devil with a greater amount of insult and abuse, than he has lately received of honour and worship from his parents, relations and acquaintances. The children run at the idols, upset them, dash them down, break them to pieces, spit on them, trample on them, kick them about and, in short, heap on them every possible outrage." He further wrote to the same society at Rome from Cochin on the 27th Jan, 1545, "When all are baptized, 1 order all the temples of their false gods to be destroyed and all the idols to be broken into pieces. "The cruelties',

writes a Goan Historian, J.C. Barreto Miranda, which in the name of religion of peace and love this tribunal (of Inquisition) practised in Europe, were carried to even greater excesses in India.... Every word of their's (of the Inquisitors) was a sentence of death, and at their slightest nod, was moved to terror the vast population spread over the Asiatic regions, whose lives fluctuated in their hands and who, on the most frivolous pretexts, could have been clapped for all time in the deepest dungeons or strangled or offered as food for the flames of the pyre." The harrowing atrocities of St. Xavier and his successors on the Hindus of his and later dates, cannot be described here for want of space.

546. In all the provinces in north India, the Hindus in general had to bear the brunt of the Muslim religious persecution only. But the Hindus to the South of Vindhyadri right up to Rameshwaram, had to suffer such horrible persecution not only from the five independent Muslim states, then ruling in the Deccan, but also from the even fiercer Portuguese, whose brutal treatment of the Hindus in order to force them to swear allegiance to the Christian faith, seems to have no parallel. Whoever wishes to understand the whole harrowing story should read [*'Os Hindus De Goa Republica Portuguesa',* by Dr. Antonio Norohna]. Although many great and small volumes of histories describe the horrible religious persecution of the Hindus by these Portuguese missionaries, before which the Muslim atrocities pale into insignificance, this book is particularly mentioned because *the writer Dr. Antonio Norohna happened to be a judge of the Portuguese High Court* in Goa. The Portuguese happily have the honest habit of preserving all the favourable and unfavourable documents regarding their history, right from the ancient to the modern times, and it is their ancient tradition to make all these available for study to any interested scholar. Naturally, he got every facility to read all those documents and books thoroughly, completely and publicly. That this Portuguese judge of the High Court should write this book after thoroughly studying all the documents, including the original letters of the then ruling Portuguese Emperor, the Portuguese Christian missionaries at that time in India, and the then Pope of Rome, deserves the special merit of this book!

547. Besides this book of Dr. Antonio Norohna, one is also recommended to read 'The History of Reconversion in Gomantak in Marathi'. It was written under the supervision of the late Shree Masurkar Maharaj, who reconverted more than ten thousand Hindus, formerly

made Christian under great coercion. The present book 'Six Glorious Epochs' is not really a history of India but a critical treatise, so the detailed account of this Portuguese religious persecution and forcible conversion of Hindus, cannot be given here at length. It is enough to say that the detailed discussion (which has here been recorded in the earlier chapters) of the thousand-year-old unprecedented and bitter Hindu-Muslim war since the invasion of Sindh by the Muslims, and the suicidal consequences of the various harmful and anti-national bans self-imposed by the Hindus on eating, drinking, touching, intermarrying and especially, that on re-purification and reconversion of the polluted Hindus, and many other foolish religious concepts of the Hindus of the time, is applicable, almost word-by-word to the various acrimonious battles of the Hindus with the Portuguese, after their arrival in India and the Christian missionaries in general, and the Christian nations also.

548. It must also be remembered here that at this very time, the Arab and the Christian nations established their rule over the South Sea (the Indian Ocean). They attacked our old Hindu-Buddhist states, that had spread far and wide up to Indo-China and deprived millions of Hindus of their religion, causing the Hindus, indirectly, to fetter themselves with the new shackles of the ban on sea voyage. This not only worsted the Hindu political and religious authority, but caused a great loss to them of their grand aspiration for the naval empire and foreign trade. They lost their whole navy and naval trade. Not only did the ship-building industry of the Hindus perish, but to maintain such seafaring naval force itself became sinful. Hindu religion and Hindu nation became literally narrow-minded because of its own blunders. Even if any daring Hindu tried to break this shell of narrow-mindedness on the Eastern, Western and Southern oceans, there was the prohibitive placard ''समुद्रयातु: स्वीकार – कलौ पंच विवर्जयेत्''—This was inviolable.

549. Heretofore, we have mentioned only some of the chosen events, violent or non-violent, regarding the Muslim-Christian two-fold political and religious armed aggression against the Hindus, and the way in which they faced it, and even of the revenge that the Hindus also took of those atrocities and humiliations during this violent thousand year-old Hindu-Muslim war. They can easily show according to the 'स्थाली पुलाक न्याय' (judging cooked rice by testing one cooked grain only), the enormity of the struggle.

550. Truly speaking, while religious leaders like Shankaracharya

Vidyaranyaswami, national heroes like Chhatrapati Shivaji, Durgadas Rathod° Maharaja Jaswant Singh of Jodhpur and saints and sages like Ramanand, Shree Chaitanya and others° gave the lead in carrying on counter-offensives on the religious front by individual or mass conversions, the Hindu society as a whole ought to have rocked the skies by effecting unceasing mass conversions of the Muslim men and women to Hinduism and reconversion of Hindu converts, who had fallen victim to the violence or guile of the enemy. They should have thrown to the winds, the old traditional views and customs. They ought to have made it the religion of the day!

550A. The Hindus were not averse to idolatory. Many of the Hindu seats and many of the Hindu religious tenets had been established by great personalities, and the Hindu society as a whole, had recognized them and adapted them to the framework of their religious code, at least so far as they concerned their followers. In their own individual capacity, the followers of those particular religious heroes, obeyed those particular codes of conduct. But the otherwise, highly idolatrous Hindu society did not follow these new idols—the new heroes—who effected individual and mass conversions and reconversions, carried on equally violent religio-political counter-offensives. They avenged the humiliation and persecution of the Hindu women on the Muslim women by similar treatment. The national heroes, who did all this, have all along been highly honoured and worshipped as idols among the Hindus, yet the way they showed as the most suitable for the age was not actively and enthusiastically followed, after they had passed away. As soon as those heroes died, their particular followers relegated to oblivion their practical lessons of violent or non-violent religious counter-aggression and their teaching in this respect. Why, while the particular sects of Chaitanya and others have been still alive so far as the other aspects of their teachings are concerned, and their eulogistic biographies like the भक्ति विजय have been written and read most devoutly, not the slightest mention of the armed revenge these very heroes took against the Muslims is to be found in them. Does it not sound very strange? Nor is any heroic ballad seen to have been composed on their counter-aggression or on their mass reconversions by any of the minstrels or bards or 'Charans' of those days! The Hindu society in general felt no urgency of handing down to the later generations, the anecdotes and legends of those heroic deeds.

551. FOR DEEP DOWN, THE MODERN HINDU MIND IS TOLERANT, WHICH IN THE VULGAR MEANS SHAMELESS OR CALLOUS!

THE MODERN-MOST EVENT OF THOSE TIMES, WHICH LENDS THE STRONGEST HISTORICAL PROOF AND SUPPPORT TO ALL THE STATEMENTS AND REMARKS THAT HAVE BEEN DISCUSSED SO FAR IN THE EARLIER CHAPTERS OF THIS BOOK.

552. Whatever instances we have quoted of the Hindu religious counter-aggressions so far in this chapter are, of course, only exceptions, considering the many centuries of the Hindu-Muslim epic war. They were inadequate attempts to patch up the shattered firmament. But it is because some Hindus performed brave deeds, befitting the valour of the Hindu nation, of retaliation to the Muslims on the religious front, that the Hindu side was not completely overthrown. The Muslim enemy always feared that even the Hindus also could avenge religious persecution on occasions. If without losing any time, the whole Hindu society had adopted the same military strategy on the religious front as these exceptions of Hindu heroes did in launching counter-offensive, not a single Muslim could have remained as a Muslim in this country—at least at that time. This, we have often shown in earlier chapters of this book.

553. But then why didn't all the other Hindus dare do so? Why were they afraid? Why did they feel it to be against their Hindu religion itself, to launch such armed counter-offensive against the Muslims? Why did they come to consider the various bans on repurification, sea voyage, eating and drinking and others, as the true religious codes of conduct for the Hindus? The answer to all these questions—the justification of their conduct—the Hindus of those times offererd, was that such an armed retaliation would not have been beneficial to the best interests of the Hindus, nor did it become the Hindu civility—Hindu culture! They meant to say that in those times of repeated terrific Muslim onslaughts if the Hindu kings and society had reconverted their unfortunate brethren, who were converted to Islam, or would have launched counter-attacks on the religious front and again, as we have suggested, converted the Muslim men and women to Hinduism, the Muslims would have been still more enraged and again-and-again in their fresh attacks, they would have wrecked far more appalling vengeance on the Hindus. It was this fear, they said, that prompted the Hindus to accept, as an exceptional code of conduct suitable for the adverse circumstances, those various bans

and the morbidly perverted concept of virtues, which amounted really to abject surrender.

553A. So, in order to refute these and other illogical arguments, and to support our arguments and opinions and the various references we have made in the foregoing discourse, we shall cite another event, which will go to prove conclusively our inference that the HINDUS HAD THE ABILITY AND STRENGTH TO LAUNCH ARMED COUNTER-OFFENSIVES EVEN ON THE RELIGIOUS FRONT BUT THEY HAD NOT THE WILL TO DO SO!

554. That event is the Maratha war with the Muslims in the South, that destroyed Tipu Sultan!

□

11

Tipu Sultan, The Savage

555. Towards the middle of the eighteenth century, the Maratha Empire had become so expansive and so powerful as to have brought about the *de facto* overthrow of the Moghul Empire at Delhi. The Hindu power had no Muslim rival state to oppose it effectively throughout the length and breadth of India, right from the Himalayas to Kanyakumari. But at this very time, Hyder Ali, an ordinary Muslim soldier, had been gradually rising to power in the army of the Hindu State of Mysore and had already become quite indispensable. Even after the sad experience of centuries together how the very Muslim servants, in whom the Hindu kings had placed complete confidence and whom they had brought to prosperity and power, had betrayed those very Hindu masters most treacherously ever since the times of Mahmud of Ghazni and Ghori, this Hindu King of Mysore committed the same blunder. Because of his usual artless, and almost unwise attitude of equality to all religions, which was imbibed assiduously amongst the Hindus in general, King Chikka Krishnaraj Vodyar or more particularly his Chief Minister, Nanjeraj, entrusted the supreme military command to this fanatical Muslim adventurer, Hyder Ali. The consequences were inevitable. Hyder Ali set aside Chikka Krishnaraj Vodyar, with a little pension and usurped the throne of Mysore. He once marched against the Marathas also but was so sorely beaten by them on the battlefield that he dared not give it a second trial again. He had also once attacked the English at Madras successfully. But as we are not concerned here with the other activities of his, it would be sufficient simply to add that after his death in 1782, he was succeeded to the throne of the Hindu State of Mysore by his equally unscrupulous adventurer of a son, Tipu Sultan-1.

556. As soon as he came to the throne, Tipu wiped out even the name of the original Hindu King and proclaimed himself the Sultan of

a Moslem state. Tipu was the last of the Muslim rulers to establish a new independent state, and style himself a Sultan during the millennial Hindu-Muslim war.

557. True to the usual Muslim tradition, Tipu performed his first duty as a Sultan of announcing publicly in the very first session of his court (Darbar), that he would see to it that all the kafirs were made Muslim willy-nilly. He commanded all the Hindus in his state to embrace Islam. He ordered his various officers of high and low ranks in every city, town and village to convert every Hindu to Islam. If the Hindus did not willingly take to Islam, they were to be forced to do so, or else the men were to be slaughtered and the women were to be distributed as slaves among the Muslims.

558-560. This campaign by Tipu of pollution and proselytization of the Hindus was so thorough and ruthless, and it was carried to such vast dimensions, that there was universal wailing and a sense of unimaginable horror throughout the Hindu community in the State. Not only the soldiers in his army but even the Mullah-Maulvis in the meanest of villages too, with the Muslim hooligans and ruffians to help them, began a systematic persecution of the Hindus! At a later date, Tipu invaded Malabar and at the first stroke, converted a hundred thousand Hindus in that one single coastal district. Then overtaking the Karnataka, he even marched on the Maratha territory. Millions of Hindus from Dharwar to Travancore were horror-stricken, and hundreds of men and women from all castes and sects of the Hindu society feeling thoroughly incapable of facing its armed attack of the Muslims, preferred death by drowning themselves in the Krishna and the Tungabhadra to all the indignities and atrocities of Muslim vandalism. Hundreds of others leapt into the fire but did not become Muslims!

Tipu's Arrogant Proclamation!

561. Puffed up by the speedy success of his atrocious aggressions upon the Hindus and diabolically elated at their miserable plight, Tipu once proudly declared in his court that his campaign of mass conversion of the Hindus was accomplished beyond all expectations. On one occasion, he said fifty thousand Hindus in his kingdom were converted hardly within twenty-four hours! No other Muslim Sultan before him, he proudly stated, could have achieved that stupendous success, but that by the grace of Allah, he had been able to perform that amazing

task of the spread of Islamic faith and the total annihilation of the kafirs!

562. In order to carry on this prodigious task, Tipu formed a special division of his army, which surpassed all other Muslim soldiers in enormity and vandalism. He manned it by the pick of the bitterest enemies of the Hindus and most lovingly called them his own sons. Whoever of those loving sons of his did some exceptionally brutal act of ravaging Hindu women, of forcibly converting Hindu families, of plunder and arson, or of wholesale massacre was rewarded with the youngest and most beautiful of the thousands of Hindu girls captured from different parts of the State.

563. The whole of the Muslim world was, no doubt, overcome with the highest gratitude to Tipu Sultan for his unprecedented success in the violent propagation of the Muslim faith. He was honoured as Gazi, the hero of the Islamic faith by his Muslim brethren all over. Naturally, the whole of the Muslim community was, thus, a party to this fanatical persecution of the Hindus by Tipu. Especially, the whole of the Muslim society from Karnataka to Travancore, which had collectively but actively participated in these artrocities, richly deserved punishment from the Hindu standpoint.

Now at Poona

564. Now on hearing the piteous cries and heart-breaking screams of the persecuted Hindus of Mysore, there arose a violent surge of fury at Poona, the capital of the Maratha Empire, which was duty-bound to defend Hinduism. The Maratha diplomats and warlords decided forthwith to invade Mysore in order to crush this new demon of a Sultan in South. The Chief Administrator of the Peshwas, Nana Phadnavis issued an instant order to all the available Maratha chieftains to march on Tipu from all sides with huge armies.

War with Tipu

565. Tipu was extremely annoyed to learn that the Maratha forces were proceeding against him. So, before the main Maratha battalions could arrive to their rescue, he maliciously attacked Nargund and Kittur in quick succession. These two very small Hindu states were very close to Mysore and far detached from the Maratha territory.

566. Tipu hated all the Hindus, yet more vehemently the Brahmins, who were foremost in trying to kindle in the Hindu Society, a burning

pride for their religion and self-respect. He had reached the limit of his brutality in persecuting the Brahmins more than any other caste of the Hindus. The great historian Sardesai writes: 'Brahmins were singled out for special indignities by Tipu.' The rulers of Nargund and Kittur were both Brahmins and both of them had spitefully declined his demand for immediate surrender. Furiously, therefore, did Tipu march first on Nargund and then on Kittur at the head of a very powerful army. The ruler of Nargund Bhave fought bravely to the bitterest end but for want of any timely assistance from Poona, his small army was easily vanquished. The moment the city of Nargund fell, Tipu, like a hungry wolf, rushed straight to the ruler's palace, his Muslim army burning and plundering the citizens and their houses. There he arrested the ruler Bhave himself and his valiant minister Pethe, and put heavy fetters on their hands and feet. They and their relatives, their families and friends were all subjected to unbearable torture. The brutal humiliation Tipu himself inflicted on the royal ladies in the palace and caused his followers to perpetrate elsewhere in the city, is beyond all description! The young and fair ones of the royal ladies were first put to inhuman torture and then brutally ravished. Tipu locked in his harem, the exceptionally beautiful young lady from the royal family and took her to his capital. The sight of the inhuman and disgraceful treatment meted out to her daughters and daughters-in-law, nieces and grand-daughters broke the heart of Pethe's grand old mother and she died instantaneously.

567. Tipu's army too spared no pains in torturing and violating the Hindu men and women in the city of Nargund and plundered to their fullest satisfaction, the palatial residences of the wealthy Lingayats as also every single house of the commonest of Hindu citizens. Finally, setting fire to their houses, Tipu carried away the select Hindu men and women as abject slaves.

568. Tipu next fell violently on the other Hindu state of Kittur and stamped it out of existence in the like manner. He himself repeated and made his army repeat to the letter all the infernal outrages, which were performed at Nargund, on the Kittur ruler, his family, all the men and women in his pay and all the people in the city.

569. By this time, the main body of the Maratha army was advancing rapidly, reconquering the regions and cities formerly subjugated by Tipu. Skipping over the other details of this campaign on Tipu, which are not quite pertinent to the topic in hand, we think it quite sufficient to say that

in the end, Sardar Patwardhan Phadke, Behare Holkar, Bhonsale and other Maratha Chiefiains routed the Muslim armies of Tipu on various battle, fields and after rescuing the whole of Karnatak, pressed him back up to Mysore and there, encircled him into a tight grip! Snatching this opporutunity of Tipu's distress, the English at Mudras too marched on him. As the strokes of the Maratha swords and the thrusts of their spears began to make bloody incisions on the back of Tipu's religious fanaticism, the devil in him began to relent and his haughtiness began to temper down. Tipu grew despondent.

And then Tipu fell at the feet of Hindu Gods

570. Whether to appease the Marathas or to win back the millions of Hindus groaning sorely under the yoke of his religious persecution, Tipu, all of a sudden, began to make munificent grants to Hindu temples. He even had new idols ceremoniously installed in the big temples, formerly smashed to pieces by his own Muslim hirelings. He requested the Hindu Brahmins lo pray to their gods in various Hindu temples that he might get success in this war with the Marathas. In order to please the very Brahmins he hated most bitterly and tortured mercilessly, he now paid them large sums of money. He had ceremonial prayers made. He himself paid great homage to Shree Shankaracharya (of Shringeri), to avert the imminent calamity and asked for his blessings, which the great man readily gave. Tipu not only attended the Chariot-festival of certain Hindu gods at Kanchi, but he himself walked in the festive procession. With his own hands, he ignited the fireworks to heighten the festive spirit of the occasion.

Demons Worship Gods

571. It is said that even devils start worshipping those gods, who have the weapons powerful enough to destroy the enemy.

But neither God nor Devil came to save the wicked Tipu from that calamity and at last, after two or three expeditions, the Marathas and the English forces subjugated the whole of his kingdom. Tipu himself was killed in 1799 and his dominions were divided. The small portion formerly belonging to the Hindu King of Travancore was returned to him, and the original royal family of the Vodyars was reinstalled at Mysore. Some of the remaining territory was taken over by the English, while the large tract from Karnataka to the Tungabhadra river was annexed by the

Marathas to their empire. All the Hindu states, which he had vowed to wipe out at the time of his accession to the throne, began once again to rule peacefully in their own places. If any one was totally ruined, it was Tipu himself with all his Muslim territory.

Hindus' Success

572. Thus, the violent religious aggression under Tipu's leadership, which the Muslims in South India had launched and perpetrated with a crescendo against the Hindus during the two decades or so immediately preceding the year A.D. 1790, was heroically and successfully put down by the Hindus politically, as well as, on the battlefield.

Muslims Gain

573. Maratha warriors, claiming to defend Hindu religion, smashed the Muslim military and political might, as has been already described. But they did not simultaneously deal any counter-blow to their religious front, in order to repulse and avenge their all-out attempt to disrupt Hinduism, their mass conversions of Hindus, their most heinous attacks upon the chastity of thousands of Hindu women. They did not severely penalize the perpetrators of these crimes. No, they did not do anything of the kind to attack the Muslim religion in return!

The Result

574-575. The inevitable consequence was that the two or three hundred thousand forcibly converted Hindu men and women and children remained groaning with agony in the clutches of the Muslim community in South India. Although Tipu's political power perished completely under the heavy counter-blows of the combined Maratha-English swords and spears, the religious domination he forced on the millions of Hindus grew ever stronger and stronger in the absence of any counter offensive. The future generations of these converted Hindus, in the absence of any immediate reconversion, went on adding rapidly to the numerical strength of the enemy of Hinduism, by at least one and a half times or twice as much. Being brought up from birth under the Islamic influence, this future progeny of the Hindu converts became the inveterate enemies of the Hindus, and instead of desiring to come back to Hinduism, they cherished like the wolf in the 'Aesop's fables,' the fiendish ambition of converting the rest of the Hindus to

Islam. They considered it their most sacred duty!

576. If the Marathas had so retaliated, all those two or three hundred thousand Hindu men and women recently converted during those four or five years of the war with Tipu, would have, in all probability, courted Hinduism most willingly because of the love they bore for their original families and relatives, and because of the pangs of separation they suffered. Their devotion to and fascination for their recently lost religion, their love and affection for their separated Hindu fathers and mothers, sons and daughters, relatives and friends, must have at that time been so acute and fresh as to cause them many a heartache, and to make them shed many an agonized tear at their slightest mention and recollection.

577. How very simple it would have been, at that time, to reconvert all those luckless two or three hundred thousand Hindu brethren and absorb them all in the Hindu society!

578. After Tipu's defeat, the victorious Maratha armies of Sardar Patwardhan, Holkar, Raste and other great chieftains were returning triumphantly to Maharashtra from their respective fronts and by different routes. Their multiple infantry, cavalry and artillery brigades were gaily fluttering their saffron-coloured banners and rending the skies with their war-cry 'Har Har Mahadev!' And in those very districts, towns and cities of Mysore, Karnataka and Maharashtra, through which these warriors paraded their victorious exultation, lay rotting and slaving in various Muslim houses, the thousands of abducted Hindu women, while men equally large in numbers, were leading a miserable life of shame and remorse for their forced conversion to Islam. The exultant war cries of 'Har Har Mahadev' of these Hindu warriors, following closely the glad news of victory and the downfall of the Muslim state of Mysore, must have informed them of the triumphal march of the Maratha conquering armies through their own towns, villages and cities. How eagerly these unfortunate Hindu converts—and especially the women—must have hastened to crowd the windows, doors, fissures and small openings of those Muslim prison-like houses and cottages, to have, at least, a fleeting glimpse of those martial processions! And how keenly must their sorely afflicted hearts have felt the happy yet acutely painful pangs of intense expectation of imminent deliverance from those satanic Muslim dungeons and confines! 'At last—at long last—they have come! 'They might have said to themselves, "Our/my Hindu brothers have come

trampling down the wicked hearts of the Muslim tyrants to deliver us from their abject servitude!' On occasions, some of them might have very probably seen their own fathers or brothers or husbands or relatives or at least some neighbours proudly strutting through the streets in their triumphal marches!

The lack of will

579. On such occasions, if only these proudly marching military detachments of Hindu warriors had simply willed it, they could have in no time set free those thousands of miserable Hindu men and women rotting in Muslim bondage. They could have simply gone on doing it just as they passed along the streets! So simple the whole thing really was. But...!

580. For, at that time, the Muslims, neither individually nor collectively, had any courage or strength left in them to oppose the triumphant Hindu army. At the approach of the Maratha soldiery, the Mullah-Maulvis and the rogues, knaves and brigands were at great pains to hide their faces into whichever nook or ditch they could find, in order to save their lives.

580A. If only one gay blast from the Maratha bugle had rung out and reverberated through every town and every village, assuring the people in some such manner! "Come, O you, Hindu mothers and sisters, come! You, who have been wickedly polluted and forced to do all sorts of menial and dirty wretched work in the Muslim household, come out, come under our protection! We, your foster-brothers, have come lo your doors in order to rescue you and take you to your respective families. Whichever Muslim comes to obstruct you, dies instantly. May that Muslim be then a man or a woman of high rank or low! Similarly, O you helplessly converted Hindu brethren come, join us when and where you can; join our conquering brigades! The moment you gather under this Saffron-coloured Hindu banner, you will have every sort of protection."

580B. If only such a reassuring blast was heard and echoed through towns and villages, thousands upon thousands of those ill-fated Hindu converts, men and women, mothers and sisters, would all have rushed most willingly, and of their own accord to join those Maratha warriors, and they all could have been most easily purified and reconverted to Hinduism, and the Muslim religious victory under Tipu's leadership would have been totally nullified.

But alas! Nobody ever thought of this!

581. Neither those Maratha warriors, nor their commanders, nor the Sardars and Chieftains nor the Shankaracharyas, nay not even the Peshwa at Poona, nor the Chhatrapatis of Satara and Kolhapur—alas! not a single Hindu soul ever dreamt of this simple way of reconversion of those ill-starred Hindus! Nobody of them ever felt ashmed of marching straight ahead, without casting so much as a sympathetic glance at the thousands of the brutally ravaged Hindu mothers and sisters! Their martial drums and pipes proclaimed to the world their military and political victory! The Maratha companies and battalions proudly paraded through the villages, towns and cities, supremely unconcerned about the two or three hundred thousand of their miserable Hindu brethren in Muslim bondage. No, no! not a single miserable soul was at that time reconverted to Hinduism!

582. The natural consequence of it all was that, those thousands of our brutally converted Hindu mothers and sisters anxiously waiting for the victorious Hindu armies to set them free from those hellish tortures and death-like humiliation in the Muslim prison-like homes, must have most probably turned away from the doors and windows in utter despair! To see none of the soldiers ever caring to recognize and pity them—let alone to rescue and reconvert them—must have rent their hearts in two! They must have resigned themselves helplessly to the Muslim bondage and rotted till death, bringing forth Muslim offsprings! What wonder if they might have borne the bitterest grudge against these unavailing Hindu brethren!

583. On the other hand, the Mullah-Maulvis and the Muslim hooligans and rogues, who had so far disappeared underground for fear of death, very soon came to know that neither those victorious armies, or their chiefs, nor even the rulers and administrators of Hindu states, were going to punish them individually or collectively for all the wrongs they had perpetrated against the Hindus. Being thus assured of safety, they came out boldly and began to move about freely and enjoy, as their legal right, the abducted Hindu women and the plundered Hindu property as their own. It also might have happened that many Hindus had the misfortune to witness meekly with their own eyes, their own daughters and nieces and daughters-in-law slaving as wives or maids in Muslim houses in their own villages and towns. But, strangely enough, neither the Hindu population there nor the Hindu administrators nor

again the officers at those places, ever thought of freeing any of those luckless ladies! Hardly any such instance is recorded in history. For, the Hindus had cultivated a shameless religious conceit for over centuries together, to suffer all the heart-rending humiliation without a prick of conscience. Nobody, as a rule, is ashamed of a thing that is not considered blameworthy by the society. Because of the one ban on reconversion, what was this shameless perversion of ideas and emotions to which the Hindu society had brought itself!

A heap of Contemporary Documentary Evidence

584. Abundant information in all details is now available about this war with Tipu. Histories written in English by Marshman and others, those in Marathi by Rao Bahadur Sardesai and the contemporary correspondence of the then English diplomats, administrators and political agents and ambassadors have been published. Research scholars such as Rajwade, Parasnis and Khare have brought to light heaps of letters by the Chiefs of the Maratha States, their subordinate officers and ambassadors and agents, of merchants and men of rank in the society, of various people in political, religious and social walks of life. A clear picture paints itself of the daily routine life of the Hindu Society of the time, its habits and customs, its codes of religious, political and social conduct, its ethics and philosophy, if one cares to read the dispatches of the great personalities of the times such as Haripant Phadke to Nana Phadnavis at Poona about his association with Lord Cornwallis at the battle of Shreerangpattam against Tipu, those about his high-level discourses on war-moves and treaties, down to the letters describing the raids of robbers and pilgrimages of devout pilgrims, letters of (Travels and those giving market rates, and also those of Shankaracharya complaining about the ransacking of his 'Ashram'!

585. But no evidence can be generally found in all this heap of documents to show if anyone was yearning to avenge the Muslim atrocities and their religious victory over the Hindus. No Hindu commander, nor a small troop of soldiers, nor even a group of men, is ever reported to have drawn swords to rescue the converted Hindu women and to cut down the Muslim miscreants. No one is reported to have felt any shame at the humiliation of these unfortunate women and at the Hindu failure to rescue them. These hundreds and hundreds of letters show a lamentable want of realization—not to speak of any anxiety about it on

the part of the Hindu society, that day by day, they were losing territory and power so far as their religion was concerned. Howsoever strange and sad it might appear, the fact cannot be gainsaid. Not a word seems to have been breathed or recorded about the retaliation of the Muslim atrocities—let alone its actual execution!

586. We may set aside the whole heap of contemporary documents, but we cannot help referring to one letter of Haripant Phadke in particular. The said letter was written to Nana Phadnavis, informing him of the two sons of Tipu, taken as hostages by the Marathas and the English, to ensure the prompt execution of the terms of the treaty, which was signed by Tipu after his defeat. Writes Haripant Phadke, perhaps casually, to show how they had brought Tipu to such a miserably low condition:

586A. "Lord Cornwallis sent the two sons of Tipu to me. When I saw them, they pleaded they were hungry. I sent them to a neighbouring tent and ordered that they should be well fed. Then after some time, they were returned to the English camp of Lord Cornwallis!"

586B. The incident referred to in this letter and the one we are shortly going to quote here, with reference to the Battle of Kharda hold as it were, to a searching analysis under the X-ray, the perverted sense of virtues, which had permeated, through centuries, to the marrow of the Hindu society, rendering it slovenly and inbecile, and insensible to all sorts of shameful humiliation.

587-588. Haripant Phadke's genial treatment of Tipu's two sons reminds us of another incident, which by contrast, will give us a practical illustration of our discussion of the perverted Hindu sense of virtues in paragraphs 405 to 471.

588A. In the first or the second decade of the seventeenth century, the tenth Guru of our Hindu-Sikhs, Dharmveer Shree Govind Singh found it impossible to continue the war with the Moghuls. He was at last besieged in the fort of Chamkaur along with his sons. Overcome with terror, some of his sworn disciples from the Sikh army conspired to desert their Guruji, renounce their Sikh religion and left the fort secretly. Two elder sons of the Guruji were killed before his eyes in the battle. At last, in the face of such grave danger, the Guruji advised all to leave battle and run for life, wherever they could. Finding a suitable opportunity, he made good his own escape. But in that confusion, two of his sons, of a tender age of 12 or below, missed the way and fell into the

Muslim hands. How did the Muslims treat them according to **THEIR OWN RELIGIOUS CODE?**

589. The Letter of Haripant Phadke referred to above shows how kindly and sympathetically, according to THEIR OWN RELIGIOUS CODE, the Marathas treated the two sons of Tipu, when they came into their hands.

590. On the contrary, as soon as the brave cubs of Guru Govind Singh fell into the Muslim hands, they were taken straight to their war council and asked: "Are you willing to be Muslims? If so, you will be given your life and everything you want. Otherwise nothing!" The children answered: "We won't be Muslims even if our life is not spared!" Immediately, the diabolic Muslim justice decreed that the two small children be forthwith built alive in a brickwall! While they were thus being built in, they were asked, as each brick was placed on the wall, "Do you become Muslims?" The two brave Hindu cubs would reply again and again: "No, we won't be Muslims!' The last brick was laid on the heads of both the young martyrs and they ceased to breathe! Then today, a true Hindu enters the vicinity of that scene of martyrdom, he will very likely hear the words reverberating the whole atmosphere there: "I won't become a Muslim: nay, not at all! I am a Hindu, I am a Sikh! I bravely court death!"

591. Supposing that by an adverse turn of events, two children of our Peshwas were to fall in the hands of Tipu or any Muslim ruler—what then? He would not have fed as the Hindu-hearted Haripant Phadke did, the two tender-aged children and returned them to the Peshwa! Such a behaviour would have been considered sacrilegious and cowardly, according to the Muslim religious belief; they would most probably have been built up alive in brick-walls or else would have been crushed under an elephant's foot. The Hindus, on the other hand, would not have avenged such brutality with any hyper-brutal retaliation, even if they had the strength and opportunity to do so. For, the virus the perverted sense of virtues had been flowing through their arteries and veins for centuries together.

592. It should be made clear at this very stage, that the ethics of war, which demanded that a charioteer must fight with another charioteer only, the sword should meet another sword alone, that the armed warrior ought not to fight with an unarmed one, till he has been armed equally, that a fallen senseless warrior was never to be attacked

till he had regained consciousness etc. etc., was perhaps quite suitable for the ancient times before Mahabharat. For both the contending parties obeyed the same set of rules: both worshipped the same ethics of war. The Pandawas themselves had violated, at the instance of Lord Krishna, many of these chivalrous rules of war! But the Hindus of these middle ages forgot the lesson taught by the Bhagwat Geeta, of giving due consideration to the time, place and person or persons concerned, while obeying these rules of war. They, on their own part kept on fighting the diabolic Muslim ways of war with the same old—originally sane and civilized, but now outmoded and so highly suicidal—tactics in war.

592A. Besides this incident of Tipu's two sons, we should like to cite another—equally shameful for the Marathas and the Hindus, inasmuch as it offers another illustration of the perverted sense of virtues of the Hindus of those times! It happened during the Battle of Kharda (1795 A.D.) against the Nizam, the last restlessly writhing remnant of the Muslim power at Delhi! The Nizam was at that time completely at the mercy of the Marathas; he would have been wiped out of existence and saved all further trouble, but for the shameless exhibition of this perverted sense of virtues, by the Marathas!

593. The Maratha forces with their excellent strategic moves had encircled the Nizam at such a desolate and dry place, that his vast army could get no food or water. The scarcity of drinking water was so acute that hundreds of Muslim soldiers drank stinking water from dirty pools, not fit even for animals. Nizam-Ali himself was almost in tears. And at this most critical moment, the big Maratha guns began to rend the skies with their thundering.

594. But at this most crucial moment, the Maratha war cabinet was seized with such a paroxysm of their age-old incurable disease of the perverted sense of virtues, viz. misplaced generosity to withhold the strokes and allow time to even the inveterate fainting enemy to regain consciousness, that had it lasted a little longer, the scales of war would have turned against the Hindus themselves and the Muslims would never have failed to annihilate them completely. At a time when the Nizam himself, the chief enemy of the Marathas, was dying of thirst and when the Marathas luckily had the best opportunity of capturing him alive and of destroying his whole army, the Peshwa, Sawai Madhavrao, was inspired with the grand idea that the true greatness of a warrior was to show mercy to the downcast enemy. He, therefore,

sent in consultation with his war-cabinet, a very valuable supply of water enough for the Nizam and his royal family from his own stock of drinking water, which was preserved with no less difficulty. And this was done in the thick of the fray—quite consistently with the maxim: क्षमा वीरस्य भूषणम् (Forgiveness is the virtue of the brave). [Remember for a contrast 'The Battle of Samugad or Shambhugad' (1658 A.D,) and the siege of Agra by Aurangzeb—Shahjahan was brought to his knees by cutting off the water supply to the fort of Agra.]

A fine illustration of self-contradiction!

595. A common belief seems to prevail that the Hindus strictly banned any reconversion of Muslimized Hindus or any conversion of born Muslims, because they dreaded fresh outrages from the Muslims in India and perhaps new horrible invasions of foreign Muslims, resulting in untold monstrocities and consequent horrible retribution.

596. It is purposely to show how erroneous, unrealistic and wholly improbable this belief is, that we have quoted the episode the Maratha war with Tipu, which provides ample historical evidence to support all the points we have made so far.

597. Setting aside that episode of the war with Tipu for a while, it is enough to pose a question: If at all the Hindus were so terribly and incessantly obsessed with the dread of Muslim retaliation, they would have offered no resistance, however slight it might have been! They would never have counter-attacked the Muslims on the political and military fronts and won at great odds. For, it is only in those Hindu states, which the Muslims conquered, that such religious persecution of the Hindus was, or would have been, possible for the Muslims. If at all the Hindus were to dread anything, they should have dreaded the Muslim armed political aggression first. But barring minor incidents and looking at this gigantic struggle in one broad sweep, the reader can clearly see that in order to protect their states and religion, the Hindus had fought grim and determined battles right from the times of Mahmud of Ghazni's and Ghori's demoniacal raids. They lost their states, they won their states! Defeat and victory, victory and defeat! The fortunes of the fields changed in quick succession! But for more than seven centuries, the Hindus kept on fighting the Muslims throughout the whole of India, fought every inch of it and finally brought the mighty Muslim enemy to his knees in abject surrender! To say that these Hindus

would have ever cared a two-pence for the fiercer rage of the Muslim revenge, is in itself, a fine illustration of self-contradiction!

598. Of course, the Muslims had never to worry in the least about the security of their religious domination in India! The Hindus were firm as regards one thing: never to convert any Muslim, not to counterattack the sphere of the Muslim religious influence; nor again to harm them in any way in matters religious; for, all these actions were completely contrary to the Hindu religious faith! The Muslims had only one anxiety as to how to spread the Islamic faith incessantly throughout the length and breadth of India, even if the Hindus had reconquered political power! We have already discussed at different places in this book, the tremendous loss to the Hindu nation this Muslim religious aggression had caused. Only two major points need a brief resume here.

Loss of thirty million Hindus

599. Even in those days, the Hindu society was quite aware of this numerical loss! But because of their morbid ban on reconversion, no effective remedy could be found against this drain of its lifeblood. Very like the invalid patient, meekly bearing the death-pangs of an incurable disease, the then Hindu world endured this blood-draining, deadly disease!

Loss of Territory!

600. But graver still than this loss of numerical strength, was another: the permanent loss of the vast territory snatched away by the Muslim religious incursions, slowly, bit by bit, but steadily, without the knowledge of the Hindus! THE MUSLIMS THUS SEIZED FAR MORE HINDU LAND THROUGHOUT INDIA BY CONVERSION THAN THEY DID BY CONQUESTS!

601. For, twenty to thirty million Hindu converts and millions of foreign Muslims that flocked to India to seek their fortune, settled permanently in India alone! The land—the cities and towns and particular parts of cities and towns and villages that were inhabited and were to be inhabited by these Muslims and their descendants to come in future—were permanently lost to the Hindus, never to be regained! On these tracts and patches of land fluttered nonchalantly, the green Muslim bands indicating the unimpeded sway of the Muslim religious faith all over! The Hindus, and more particularly the Marathas, wrested

away practically all the political power throughout the whole of India from the Muslims towards the end of this epic Hindu-Muslim war. Yet the Muslims retained their hold individually or collectively on the masses and on property too!

602. Again, as the Muslim population grew rapidly because of polygamy popular amongst them, and the spread of their religion by conversion, more and more land was to that extent being gradually but surely occupied by them and was passing for ever into the Muslim hands. In order to give some idea of the actual condition, it is enough to say that even after the establishment of the *de facto* sovereignty of the Marathas, every little town or village had a separate part known as Musalmanwada or Musalman mohalla! Why, even cities like Poona, Satara, Kolhapur, Nagpur in Maharashtra, Baroda, Devas, Dhar, Indore, Gwalior and Udaypur in Central India and Jodhpur, Jaipur, Amritsar, Lahore right up to Shreenagar in Kashmir in the north, each had a separate section exclusively colonized by thousands of Muslims and known as 'Muslim-pura' or 'Muslim-abadi'. The Muslims not only dominated these separate sections religiously, but practically became their owners!

603. And the fun of it was that this religious domination of the Muslims and their individual right to that land had been constitutionally and legally protected by the Hindu kings themselves, giving them equal civil status as subjects along with the Hindus! Especially, because of open and deep-rooted enmity between the Hindus and the Muslims in those days, and as change of religion was then tantamount to change of nationality, all the land that passed into the Muslim hands, this way or that, was in reality, permanently given over to the national enemy of the Hindus!

604. Thus, throughout the whole of India, in every village and town and city and province, big or small Muslim pockets (Muslimistans) were being created and fostered right from those days. That again means that from that time, India was being vivisected unwittingly between two parts: the Hindu India and the Muslim India!

605. **THESE BIG OR SMALL ISLAMISTANS WERE REALLY THE TIME BOMBS LAID BY THE CONVERT MUSLIM RELIGIOUS AUTHORITY IN THE FOUNDATION OF THE HINDU POLITICAL SUPERSTRUCTURE**!

606. Yet neither the Hindu rulers, nor the common people, nor even the historians of the time seem to have apprehended, acutely or even faintly, the instantaneous or the belated consequences of this tremendous loss of

numbers and territory. For, nobody else has so far tried, as we are doing here, any bold, lucid and comprehensive historical exposition of this loss of numbers and territory that the Hindu nation had to suffer because of the morbid Hindu religious concepts of various bans and their perverted sense of virtues! If at all there be any such attempt, it is bound to be an exception.

607-608. Moreover, had the Hindus at that time really understood the full significance of the above-mentioned evil consequences of the Muslim religion dominance, the Maratha government would have immediately and definitely launched a counter-religious aggression upon the Islamic faith in the south, the moment its leader, Tipu, was politically vanquished. For, the Hindus had never before had such a completely favourable opportunity as they had it then, to launch such a counter-offensive on the religious front. Throughout the whole of India, there was left no Muslim power at that time, which could even so much as think of opposing the Marathas, as we have already pointed it out, and as our contemporary bard sings in one of his heroic ballads with evident pride for Hinduism—

जलचर हैदर निजाम इंग्रज रणकरिता थकसे।
ज्यानि पुण्याकडे विलोकितें ते संपत्तिता मुकते॥

[The pirates (meaning the Portuguese), Hyder, the Nizam, the English all were exhausted fighting (with the Marathas). Whoever looked (with enmity) at Poona, lost their wealth!]

Devil can be Fought by arch-devil only

609. Suppose, as soon as this propitious time had come, the Maratha Chieftains such as Bhonsale, Holkar, Patwardhan, Raste and others, who had fought against Tipu, the Maratha administrators, the Peshwa and the Chhatrapati, had promulgated, in consultation with the prominent religious authorities, some such order (if not actually couched in the same words) as the following:

610. "Just as the valour of the Maratha warriors had trampled under their feet the Muslim rule of Tipu, in a similar way, in order to bring to the lowest dust the Muslim religious preponderance under the fiendish Tipu, which has so far inflicted every sort of brutality and humiliation on the Hindus and to chastise those guilty of these heinous crimes, our government had decided to attack in return the Muslims on the religious field.

611. "Faithfully following the interpretation of the religious

law and the religious code of conduct by Shree Shankaracharya Vidyaranyaswami, whose authority is considered next only to the Very First Shree Shankaracharya by the whole of the Hindu world, we hereby, for the first time, propose to break the psychological ban on reconversion, which has simply paralysed the Hindu society, so far as the retaliation of the tyrannical Muslim religion is concerned, and we hereby order every single official of whatever rank to make the necessary arrangements to enforce the strict observance of the following instructions.

612. "On learning about the forcible conversion of Hindu men and women in his particular jurisdiction, every village and city-officer shall gather together all such oppressed Hindus in some rescue camp under the government protection, and shall attend to all their needs.

613. "Every several Muslim man and woman in every town and village, in whose house or hut Hindu women, girls and children might be found slaving as oppressed converts, shall along with the whole family, be forthwith bettered and thrown into prison, and the miserable Hindu women and children after being immediately set free, shall be affectionately and courteously taken to the rescue camps.

614. "Similarly the warriors from Tipu's select company of the direst young Muslim scoundrels, whom he fondled as his 'sons', shall be fettered with very heavy shackles wherever they will be found in Maharashtra, Karnatak or elsewhere and locked in jails, and the fairest young and innocent Hindu women, who were given away as reward to those Muslim young rogues from this brigade for their brutal atrocities towards the Hindus, should all be rescued and sent with all civility to the said rescue camps.

615. "Finally, a national reconversion week will be announced by a superior officer, before which all the rescued Hindu converts from the rescue camps all over the particular region shall be conducted in large groups under military guard to the holy places adjoining their native places or to Dharwar or Badami or other places where the oppressive Muslim armies have been destroyed by the Marathas. At all these places, shall these oppressed Hindu converts be reconverted to Hinduism en masse. At all these places, sacrificial fires should be lit and offerings made for the repurification of all these millions of Hindu converts, and they should all be received in the Hindu Society ceremoniously with chorus-singing of praises for the Hindu religion. All those who are likely to be willingly, lovingly and honourably received by their original families,

should be escorted to their original homes and rehabilitated in those families. But the thousands of other repurified and reconverted Hindus, who may not find such a loving reception in their original sub-castes, should all be classed as a new warrior class in the structure of the Hindu society—अग्निकुल—a fire race according to the Rajput legend—and all the political and religious authorities in the land are hereby ordered to concede to them, all rights due to a Hindu as equitably and justly as the other caste Hindus enjoy.

616. "Then, in order, to reward the meritorious services of the choicest Maratha warriors in this Hindu-Muslim war, at least as many young and beautiful Muslim girls should be captured, converted to Hinduism and presented them, as were the Hindu girls distributed by Tipu amongst the daredevil warriors of his select brigade.

617. "Thereafter, the thousands of Muslim rascals and scoundrels, who have, in this Hindu-Muslim war, inflicted harrowing atrocities on the Hindus, raped Hindu women and girls, have broken holy images of Hindu gods and goddesses and have demolished their temples, and who will have been locked as per the above-mentioned order in various prisons, shall be conducted under strong military guard to the four or five chief cities that will be signified later on by the Superior Officers. They should, especially, be taken to Nargund and Kittur—the places where Tipu himself had inflicted inhuman atrocities on the Hindu men and women with the aid of his diabolic army, so that Tipu's devilish acts might be avenged with equal ferocity and with the harshest punishments meted out to the daredevil soldiers of his Islamic brigade in the very presence of the afflicted people there. On the appointed day, during the reconversion week, these hundreds of Muslim devils should be brought under strong armed guard of soldiers and cannons to the vast parade grounds and after the charge sheets against them, indicating their fiendish acts against the Hindus, have been read out to litem, they should be blown off from cannon-mouth before the joyful eyes of the thousands of Hindu spectators.

A National Homage to the Hindu Martyrs

618. "In the end, this reconversion week should be concluded with a national homage to the report of three volleys of guns from every fort and city of Maharashtra, in honour of the thousands of men and women, who courted martyrdom by leaping into the rivers like the Krishna or the

Tungabhadra or in some other ways, because they had no other effective means to save their religion and to escape the direct persecution at the hands of Tipu's soldiers, when thousands of them surrounded and blockaded whole towns, carrying on wholesale conversions with fire and sword."

The Echoes of Religious Retaliation

619. If at all, the Marathas had dealt such a crushing counter-blow on the Muslim religious front, the echoes and re-echoes of the guns, thundering from every fort in Maharashtra, would not have been heard in the valleys of the Krishna and the Tungabhadra alone; they would also have reverberated throughout the Gangetic, the Indus, nay, far beyond it, the Vakshu (Oxus) river-valleys and the whole of the Muslim world. The barest news, that the Hindus too, had been reconverting the millions of converted Hindus, breaking away the fetters of the ban on reconversion, would have shocked the Muslim world far more fiercely than the report of thousands of guns fired simultaneously, and their very existence would have begun to dwindle. This is not mere historical guesswork but a guarantee of historical probability.

620. But this historical probability remained only a probability! The Hindus never broke the ban on reconversion, nor did they allow it to be broken. Naturally, the Islamic religious dominance in India could not be overthrown.

621. The virus of the caste-differences caused by birth had already permeated the whole blood-system of the Hindu society long before any Muslim aggressor could come to India. Perpetual Muslim atrocities aggravated its effects all the more, and the Hindu Society lost its original susceptibility to change, its expansionism, its ability to absorb newer elements and its strong inclination to retaliation even in the religious field. How could the Hindu leaders, then, hit back the Muslim foreigners or absorb them in their Hindu Society?

622. 'How could a man', they thought who was a born Muslim, ever become a true Hindu by merely dipping into the Gangetic waters?' 'For', they argued, 'the caste is decided by birth'.

623. रासभ धुतला महातीर्थामार्जी।
नब्हे जैसी तेजी शामकर्ण॥

'Even as a donkey washed in the holiest of water can never become a spirited horse...'

How can we then admit these born non-Hindus to our original

castes, merely because a certain scented pigment betokening Hinduism is applied to their foreheads? Are we to dine with them? And if that person be a woman, are we to marry her simply because an auspicious kumkum tilak from a Hindu box is applied to her forehead? And that too openly? Impossible! Impossible! Irreligious! Irreligious!

623A. Such were the religious ideas of not only the Brahmins and the Kshatriyas but the Mangs, the Dhors, the Bhils and other so-called 'low castes' and wild tribes too! They considered this to be the only true Hindu religion. The main principle underlying these ideas of caste-differences was that whichever Hindu went over to the Muslim fold, willy-nilly—whether by persuasion or by coercion—was polluted and damned—irrevocably damned for life—nay, for all his generations to come!

623B. What wonder then, if hundreds of millions of Hindus who, cherishing such absurd ideas about religious behaviour had stoutly opposed any reconversion of the oppressed Hindus or of the born Muslims!

The only Fortunate thing was...

624. The only fortunate thing was that at the beginning of the Muslim onslaughts on India, no couplet in Anusthup metre was interpolated in some smriti by some Brihaspati (wiseacre) or another banning territorial conquests as others were, in respect of bans on food-exchange, inter-caste marriages, reconversion, sea-faring and many other things! If the forcibly converted Hindu could not be reconverted to Hinduism, if a man dealing with a Muslim himself became a Muslim, how could a land or territory once conquered by the Muslims be again a Hindu land? Whoever tried to win back that lost kingdom would himself become a Muslim! The land, however, would never become a Hindu land again! If some learned Hindu fool had argued this way, and promulgated such a ban on reconquering the lost territory, the Hindus would have been rendered as absolutely powerless to overthrow the Muslim political dominance, as they were to overthrow the Muslim religious ascendancy, because it would have become equally irreligious, and so impossible, owing to such a ban. And like Afghanistan, Iran, Babylonia, ancient Egypt, Turkey and Morocco in the far west, India in the east would also have been completely Muslimized! It would have become both politically and religiously an Islamistan! That would have been the last line written about the Hindu History. But India was at least

saved that horrible fate then, and once again was written a new chapter of the rejuvenation of Hinduism, illuminated by dazzling valour of the Hindu warriors.

625. The history of India as also of all the parts of the rest of the world, wherever the Muslims had established religio-political ascendancy, amply proves that not only those several nations that were incapable of overthrowing the Muslim religio-political dominance became completely Muslimized, but even those other non-Muslim nations which smashed the Muslim political might but left their religious hold untouched, could not escape the constant horrible pestilence of the Muslim onslaughts. Only five or six or at the most, ten nations that precipitated the Muslim religious downfall soon after their political and military defeat and rid themselves of every single Muslim, could—these and these alone could—free themselves completely from the Muslim pestilence! For want of space, only one instance of Spain should suffice to illustrate this point.

Emancipation of Spain from Muslims

626. Simultaneously with their raids on India, the Arabs under the Omayyads had overrun Spain and had established a powerful Muslim state there. Naturally, as elsewhere, the Muslims began the religious persecution and conversion of the Spanish Christians. Countless Christian men and women were violently and mercilessly converted to Islam at the point of the sword or killed outright. Later on, after some centuries, when there were internecine wars amongst the Muslims themselves, the much too oppressed Christians of Spain rose in revolt against the tyrannical Muslim Government under one of their own old royal dynasties, and with the help of a growing Christian nation in France and with encouragement from the Papal seat of Rome. After many years of bitter warfare during the 11th and 13th centuries, the Spanish Christians delivered most of their country from the Muslim rule and finally with the conquest of Granada in A.D. 1492, they wiped out the Muslim power altogether. But as in India so in Spain too, even after the loss of political power, the Muslims had their firm religious hold unimpaired on the converted Spanish Christians and the land they had actually inhabited. Nay, this Muslim religious hold was getting more and more explosive and terrible, so as to cut asunder the whole of the Spanish nation at some future date. Those of the Spanish

Christians, who could clearly foresee this impending danger and who had always awaited an opportunity to wreak their revenge, decided to root out the Muslim religious influence from Spain, as they did with their political overlordship.

Christians were never fettered as Hindus were by any Religious bans on food Exchange, Reconversion and so on

627. The task of reconverting the countless Muslimized Christians was, therefore, so easy as to be readily accomplished, the moment these Spaniards simply willed it.

The only difficulty was that of the Muslim political and military might. No sooner was the Muslim army destroyed than the Spanish Christians started the complete rout of the Islamic faith in one holocaust throughout Spain. Thousands of Muslimized Christians began to be rebaptized incessantly and speedily. The sporadic Muslim resistance infuriated the Spanish nation all the more. The Spanish Government, the Spanish Christian Church and the Spaniards at large vowed openly that in their country no person calling himself or herself a Muslim, nor any structure known as a mosque be allowed to remain unimpaired any longer

628. The newly independent Spanish Government gave an ultimatum that before an appointed date, every sundry Muslim—man or woman had either to court Christianity willingly or to leave the country forthwith, with family and friends, bag and baggage. Whoever failed to do either, after that date was to be beheaded mercilessly and unhesitatingly.

629. What? A Christian Government order! How atrocious! But it must be remembered that when the Muslims conquered Spain, they had imposed their faith far more brutally on the Christian populace there and flooded the street with Christian blood. Now the Christians were to rewash the streets with Muslim blood. As soon as the stipulated time elapsed, the Spanish Christians rose violently against the remaining Muslims at various places and put everyone of them—man or woman, young or old—to the sword! The Christian Church of Spain became pure with a Muslim bloodbath. Spain was rid of the Muslims entirely. And so Spain remained Christian! It was not turned into another Morocco!!

630. The same fate awaited the Muslims in Poland, Serbia, Bulgaria, Greece and other Christian nations. They all rid their once Muslim-dominated countries of every single Muslim!

□

12
A Resume

631. The various points that have been discussed at length in the foregoing chapters, viz. Ch. V to XI of this book, can now be briefly summarized here into a consistent whole.

632. In the historic past, India, too, like all other great nations, had been invaded by the Ionians, Sakas and Huns and other non-Hindu wild people. But after centuries of violent struggle with them, all the Hindu nations stamped out their political dominance by smashing their armed might on the various battlefields and became independent again and again. Moreover, it converted the millions of the Ionian, Saka and Hun foreigners who settled down here in various provinces during the years of those hard struggles, and taught them the Vedic cult, the worship of the Vedic gods and goddesses, and the Sanskrit civilization and culture, so as to merge them so completely amongst its own people as to leave not a single trace of their original non-Hindu races and names behind.

633. When the unprecedented calamity of the Muslim aggression fell on India, the Hindus kept on stubbornly fighting the aggressors for over a thousand years or so, and ultimately shattered the Muslim power as completely as they did the non-Hindu Saka-Hun empires; and once again, they established their political independence! Yet, they could not recover their tremendous loss of numerical strength, which was brought about by the forcible conversions nor could they regain the Indian areas actually occupied by the Muslim settlers here, nor even could they Hinduise the Muslims as completely as they did the Ionian, the Saka, the Hun and other non-Hindus! Why?

634. The answer to this main vexing question is chiefly and thoroughly discussed with adequate historical proofs in chapters V to XI of this book. The conclusion that one arrives at after evaluating the contemporary events and circumstances is that as soon as the Muslim rule was overthrown,

or was in the process of being overthrown, neither the Hindus at large, nor the Hindu rulers ousted the Muslim religious dominance even when proper opportunities presented themselves, and although they were far more strongly armed than their Muslim opponents. They did not convert even a single Muslim to Hinduism by persuasion—let alone by force!

635. Had the victorious Hindu nation instantly broken off all bans on food-exchange, inter-marriages, (re)conversion, seafaring and other refractory social and religious traditions and reconverted all the Muslims—whether converted or original—and absorbed them in the then prevailing caste structure of the Hindu society, of course with due regard for the status and qualifications of the persons concerned (as they had already done with the Saka, Hun and other subjugated foreigners, in the by-gone days), like Spain, India would immediately have been rendered Muslimless! Hindusthan would have been at that very time, the place of the Hindus in the truest sense of the term.

636-637. This treatise deals with the Muslim invasions of India during the period covering over a thousand years from A.D. 700 to A.D. 1800 and the chain of consequent Hindu-Muslim wars. Naturally, the points raised in this discussion apply only to the conditions prevailing during that period. Therefore, while reading such historical dissertations and treatises, the reader must always bear in mind one important fact that the actions and the codes of conduct, which are, or seem to be most proper, beneficial and necessary in the context of the particular conditions obtainable during that period and in respect of persons and places concerned, may not necessarily be proper, beneficial under different conditions or during another period. They might even be highly objectionable, detrimental and so unnecessary at times under different conditions or with different persons. May those actions then refer to religion or politics or other walks of life! Samartha Ramdas Swami, well-versed in religious and political sciences, has succinctly made the same point in the following words:

समया सारखा समयो ये ना।
नेम एकची चालेना
नेम धरिता राजकारणा
व्यत्ययो पडे।   श्री दासबोध दशक 18-6-6

"Conditions are not exactly similar, nor can one rule prevail (for ever)! If one rule is followed (every time) in politics, difficulties arise.

[Ramdas—Shree Dasbodh - 18.6.6]

□

13

Hindu War Policy on The Religious and Political Front

638-639. It is made amply clear in chapters V to XII of this book that in their religio-political war with the Muslims, which the Hindus fought most tenaciously for centuries together, the Hindu war-policy had not been sufficiently strong to defeat the Muslim on the religious front. Why, it proved to be definitely weak and suicidal in comparison with the diabolically ferocious war-strategy of the Muslims on that front. For, the Hindu nation had completely forgotten, at least in respect of the religious side of it, that a nation has, as a rule, to adopt a war-strategy far stricter, crueller and more unrelenting than that of the unscrupulous enemy it wants to conquer.

640. During the Vedic and the Puranic (mythological) period, the ancestors of the Hindu Nation had to fight the Daityas, the Danavs and the Rakshasas, the cruellest, most atrocious and cunning cannibals of the time. It is because (as the Vedic and Puranik stories show) those of our ancestors, our gods, our emperors, the Vedic Rishis who chanted war canticles, the epic poets of the Puranans and all those who actively participated in the war could become more atrocious, more deceptive and cunning, and far crueller than those enemies like the Rakshasas and others. It is because they could formulate an adequate war policy to meet the ever-changing guiles of the enemy and practise it effectively so that they could always succeed in those various wars, and our nation too became stronger and more expansive than before.

641. It was not on the political front alone, but on the religious front too, that the enemy had to be faced in those times! When Vishwamitra took Shreeram to the forest to protect the Rishis, the latter was told at great length how those Rakshasas destroyed the religious rites of the time, viz. the sacrifices, and how the daughters of the Rishis were kidnapped.

Later on in, Dandakaranya, Shreeram came to know what great havoc had the Rakshasa army of Ravan wrought upon the hermitages of the Rishis, who were in a minority there, with their sacrificial rites, with their colonies and even with their lives. Ram was also shown at various places the heaps of bones of those Rishis, whose blood those cannibals had drunk and whose flesh they had eaten. This will clearly show that this long-drawn mythological war of our ancestors with the Rakshasas was fought not only on the political but also on the religious front. And at that time, those gods and god-like emperors, too, considered it the holiest religious duty to show super-savage cruelty to beat down the cruelty of the Rakshasas, to be arch-devils against the devils! (For a fuller discussion of the point, please refer to paragraphs 460 to 461 of this book). It is enough to mention here that the incarnation of Nursinh, who appeared in the most terrifying form in order to protect the great devotee Prahlad and who tore to pieces his religious enemy, the wicked Hiranya Kashipu with his leonine talons was—

A God-Head of our Nation

was our leader! The story of Kacha also shows that in the war, our gods followed the policy—

642. व्रजन्ति ते मूढधियः पराभवम्। भवन्ति मायाविषु ये न मायिनः॥

To fight the crafty enemy with super-craft, to destroy barbarism with hyper-barbarity, as the only effective means of annihilating the foe, was the praiseworthy principle of religious warfare of our ancestors till, at least, the close of the Puranic era.

643. However, when gods fought against other gods, or when there were internecine wars like that of the Kouravas and the Pandavas, the war strategy differed completely. No single charioteer was to be attacked by many charioteers; the submissive or surrendering warrior was to be given his life. Such considerations for justice and injustice were to be actually shown on the battlefield. This ethics of war was preached because it was honoured by both the contending parties.

644. But, as we have already pointed out in paragraph 315, the invasions of varying magnitudes of the Persians, the Ionians, the Greeks, the Sakas and the Kushanas and the Huns, which began at the close of the Puranic period and continued during the early part of our historic past, were all made mainly for political ascendancy and not for any religious enmity. Their own religions were more or less like the offshoots

of Hinduism itself. Later on, after their defeat by our Hindu ancestors, the millions of these foreign invaders, who chose to settle here, merged into the Hindu society completely. So during this early historical period, in the absence of any religious aggression by these foreigners on our religion, our ancestors fought pure and simple political wars with them with effective strategical counter-moves and vanquished them completely. As these wars were purely political in nature, the question of religiosity or irreligiosity, of extreme kindness, truth, violence or non-violence or other fine distinctions of principles never arose! Naturally, the tendency to retaliate in the same fashion even on the religious front—to face religious aggression with counter religious offensives—to meet cruelty with supra-cruel blows, craft with super-craft, violence with extreme violence and to consider this war policy to be a highly religious duty of a brave warrior—lay dormant in our national mind, because there was no occasion for them to use such war tactics on the religious front long after the religious wars with the Rakshasas.

645. Moreover, during this intervening period, the different religious sects that were really the offshoots of the Vedic religion, and had a strong propensity to Sanyas (renunciation or asceticism) and extreme non-violence like the Ajivakas, the Jains, the Buddhists and others, preached to the society that true religion meant extreme non-vidence, kindness, love and truth and nothing else. Among the rest of the Vedic population, class distinctions and their development into caste differences and the religious traditions about food-exchange, touchables and untouchables, which cut to pieces the composite life of the society, were growing stronger and these very, really anti-social traditions came to be considered as true religion. Later on, flesh-eating was prohibited even in the sacrificial rites. The fact that the extreme forms and manifestations of truth most often prove to be the harmful vices was lost sight of by the religious ideology of the time, while the excessive inopportune and suicidal use of virtues, which ruined the nation, was itself considered the highest form of religious conduct. Generally speaking, truthful conduct is a virtue. To satisfy a promised gift or word is also a virtue! But when in the heat of extolling virtues to the skies, the Puranas (mythological stories) told the story of Harishchandra, who made good his promise given to Vishwamitra in his dream by presenting him with his kingdom and such other childish stories, they definitely changed the national war-policy into an imbecile, weak and suicidal

one. No words can adequately condemn this influence of the Puranas. More respectable than this truthful conduct was considered the practice of non-violence as the highest form of virtue, not only by the Jains and the Buddhists but in some of the Vaishnav texts also, which later on hastened our terrible downfall as determinedly and as enormously as even our enemies, the Muslims, could not perhaps accomplish. Manliness and valour came to be condemned as the vilest of vices. The unmanly, the imbecile, the valour-lacking coward, not only lacking the ability but even the desire to avenge the national insult and injustice, came to be highly respected in religious circles as the greatest and most magnanimous saint, ripe for an honourable place in heaven.

646. This point has already been adequately discussed with sufficient proofs and illustration in chapter VIII under the caption 'Perverted Sense of Virtues' and in other chapters also; and it will be touched again, while we shall be narrating the events on the political front. Here, it has to be remembered that as all the invasions on India after the Puranic times had been political and not religious (at least not of such huge dimensions as those of the Rakshasas so as to shake the very foundation of our religion), we had completely forgotten the old war-strategy to meet such terrible religious aggression. Our very definitions of virtues and religion and their practice had undergone a complete change. The war-strategy of Nursinh of the ancient times, which sought a tooth for a tooth and an eye for an eye had now become vegetarian, submissive, tolerant and shameless!

647. Naturally, when Islam invaded Hinduism with far more ferocity and bitterness and with more dangerous weapons than the Rakshasas of the Puranic age, our Hindu ancestors of the seventh century had no other war-strategy to face it with than the imbecile, impotent and suicidal—one which offered milk to a venomous serpent. To encounter the wolf, the sheep had preferred its own neck! All this, as also our consequent enormous losses on the religious front, has been clearly shown in the earlier chapters. Hence, we shall now begin a critical study of the political side of this Hindu-Muslim epic struggle.

□

14

The Age-Long Relation of the Arabs with India

648. When I first read the word मुसल (Musal) in my student days in 'Mousal Parva' in one of the secondary Puranas like the Hariwansh, and wondered how the huge rushes uprooted by the Yadavas from the seashores became big pounding pestles, which crushed their bones as some lethal weapons would, I at once hit upon one probable explanation that perhaps the word, 'Mousal', might be an attempt at pun on the word Musal (मुसल) by the Puranic punsters, and that it might have been suggested by the word Musalman given to the Arab traders of the past after their conversion to Islam. But this fanciful explanation could not then be supported by the time-sense and other coordinating historical events.

649. Much later in the Andamans, when I began reading a lot of Bengali literature, 1 remember to have then perused an essay about the passing away of Lord Krishna either by Shree Madhusudan Datta, the famous Bengali poet, of the narative 'Meghanad' and the promoter of the 'Amitrakshar' metre, or by Bankimchandra, the poet who sang the national song, Vande Mataram! The said essay tries to offer a plausible explanation of the final exit of Balaram, after the death of Lord Krishna, along with his followers into the sea in his original form of Shesh (शेष), a snake. It meant to say that Balaram entered the Western sea at Dwarka in his ships and went away to some foreign island in a serpentine fashion. I then remembered to have read a parallel instance mentioned by an Arya Samaji traveller in the account of his travels. About fifty years ago, this Arya Samaji traveller had visited Arabia to see the actual condition of the Hindu residents of the place. After enquiry, he found there is a small section of people who grew tufts of

hair on the top of their heads (as the Brahmins and other Hindus here did till very recently). They told him that, according to a very sacred legend handed down to them by their forefathers, they were supposed to have gone there from India at some very ancient time. It is believed that at the time of a great war in India, they had left for Arabia and established a colony there, but never got themselves mixed up with the factions of the natives there, nor with their feuds and wars. That was why they could be seen in their much the same original state. The inference that the said traveller has drawn from this, is that these strange people must have been the same Hindus who had left India at the close of the epic struggle of the Kouravas and the Pandavas in Mahabharat.

650. If we then assume from the foregoing statements that Yadavas led by Balaram had gone to Arabia and formed a big colony there, two more things seem to support such an assumption. The first is that Tamil was originally called अरवी (Aravi). The aborigines of Arabia were mostly Shaivites, worshipping the (Shiv) ling (as most of historians agree) and their priests were called Druids (Dravid द्रविड़) in English, the same class that seems to have existed in Britain and Ireland as per the old legends told by the historians.

651. This is not the place to relate all these and other legends bearing on this topic, but it can be fairly assumed that Arabia and India had very close ties and trade relations from very ancient times, and there must have been Indian colonies established in that peninsula, and we can infer that like those in Java, Sumatra and other lands in the Eastern Ocean, in this land in the Western Ocean too, now known as Arabia and others, there must have once thrived Indian (especially South Indian) colonies, kingdoms and civilization. But we cannot offer it here, as yet, as any proven fact or theory. Only the various details leading to this conclusion have simply been summarized here briefly, so that they might be of some use to some future student of history, who might be attracted to it.

652. It is only pertinent here to write about the relation of India and Arabia during the seventh century when the Arabs had already courted Islam. Islam was born after the birth of Muhammad in A.D. 570, and it took at least forty to fifty years for the Arabs to join it. They had civil wars on the question of adopting this new faith. Yet the Muslim history is believed to start from their Hizri era in A.D. 622 and

we might as well accept that belief for the present discussion.

653. Even before these new Arabic Muslim aggressors crossed their borders and fell on their neighbouring Persian empire, the Hindu states had practically spread once again to the very distant borders of Chandragupta Maurya's empire beyond the Indus. The Chinese traveller, Huen-tsang entered India from the north-east about A.D. 629 and has left an eyewitness account of whatever he saw here. According to him, the Hindu borders had stretched far beyond the Indus to include what are now called Kabul, Ghazni and Gandhar. Almost all the Chinese, who came to India during those years, had to cross these Hindu states and the Indus, before they stepped into India.

The Chinese of that era called the Hindus 'Shintsu'

654. That is why, they in China are referred to India by its most ancient name of Sindhu, and the Hindu people as 'Shintsu'. It is quite plain that this 'Shintsu' was a Chinese corruption of Sindhu. This is yet another proof on the Chinese side that the word Hindu is derived originally from the word Sindhu.

The first Arab invasion of Sindh and their defeat

655. Most of the modern histories refer to the Arab invasion on King Dahir as the first invasion, wherein the Hindu King was completely defeated. But this is a blatant falsehood. The first Arab invasion of Sindh took place in A.D. 640, in which the invaders were completely vanquished and their commander-in-chief was killed by the Hindus (cf: paragraph 324).

The second major invasion of Dindh by the Arabs

656. But in A.D. 711, however, Mohammed Kasim marched on Sindh at the head of a fifty-thousand-strong army and while facing it bravely, Maharaj Dahir of Sindh was destroyed (cf. paragraphs 327 to 331).

657. But immediately within fifty years of this fall of King Dahir, the Rajputs and specially their leader, Bappa Raval of Chitod, wrested it away from the Arabs and he and other Hindu kings pushed their boundaries right from the Pariyatra Mountain, i.e. Hindukush mountains, Kashmir, Gandhar (which is now called Afghanistan) straight up to Sindhusagar (which we now shamelessly call Arabian

sea). This Hindu sovereignty over the vast region lasted for three hundred years.

Three hundred years amount to about seven Generations

658. Even when the Hindus held their sway over such a vast region for more than three hundred years and even when Sindh had been reconquered by the Rajputs within twenty-five years of its loss to Kasim. most of the English, as also the Hindu historians, never so much as mention it. On the contrary, great historians, litterateurs, well-known professors, all the world over as also the school-going children, have all along been repeating blindly that right from the time Kasim conquered Sindh, the Muslims began their onward march right up to Rameshwaram and for all these twelve hundred years or so from A.D. 711, to the time the British left India in 1947, the Hindus had been rotting in slavery. This assumption is as false as it is insulting to the Hindus. This is an unbearable perversion of facts.

659. Hereafter, at least a truth-loving writer of history should scrupulously avoid this falsehood, this perversion of facts from school or college textbooks as also from those of a greater worth and importance.

These three hundred years

660. For during these three hundred years i.e., up to A.D. 1000 or so in the whole of India, right from Hindukush to Ceylon and to Burma in the east, the Hindu Sovereign states ruled proudly. At such an early date as that, the Hindu kings in the south such as the Cher, Chowl, Pandya, Rashtrakut and others, sometimes the one, at others the next, ruled the vast southern seas so powerfully as to call themselves Trisamudreshwar. To say that the whole of India sweated in slavery under the Muslims or some other rulers, ignoring its prosperous and independent sovereign status, is to belie history.

From A.D. 1000 To A.D. 1030

661. All of a sudden, like a comet, rose Mahmud of Ghazni at this time. At his accession to the throne, he vowed to Muslimize the whole of India and as has been already described in paragraphs 365 to 375, carried on a series of depredations and arson, religious persecution and rapes, and pollution and conversion, throughout the vast tract

from Multan in Punjab to Someshwar in Sourashtra.

662. But it is because, at such cataclysmal times, the Hindus showed exemplary valour and perserevence and forbearance in facing all these calamities, never losing self-respect or courage, that Hindu states could again raise their banners overthrowing the Muslim ascendancy hardly within twenty-five to thirty years of Mahmud Ghazni's death in A.D. 1030, with the sole exception perhaps of the northern part of Punjab beyond the Indus. This can surely be cited as the astonishing illustration of the tenacity of any nation for that matter.

663. Secondly, it must be remembered that during the thirty or forty years of the political havoc wrought by Mahmud of Ghazni in the north, the whole of South India had been displaying daring and adventure while enjoying independence, prosperity and the mastery of the three seas as nonchalantly as before.

664. This is why even during those thirty or forty years of Ghazni's raids, India as a whole can never be said to be slaving under the foreign heels. Of course, we do not deny that a small part of the north-western Punjab was annexed by Ghazni, establishing political as well as religious ascendancy firmly over there. However, it must also be borne in mind that even at that time, Kashmir was a Hindu state.

Hundred-and-Fifty years after the death of Mahmud of Ghazni in A.D. 1030

665. A hundred-and-fifty years, i.e. about five generations after A.D. 1030, the whole of India, right from Kashmir to Assam and Burma in the north and Rameshwaram in the South, was politically independent, powerful and prosperous as before. Great preachers, saints and mahants and priests following the path of Shree Shankaracharya were, along with Smritikars Deval and Medhatithi, leading the cultural life of the whole of India and its overseas colonies. Sanskrit was the Indian priestly language throughout. Kashi was the cultural centre of the whole Hindu nation. The great wounds suffered by our Hindu nation on the political front during the raids of Mahmud of Ghazni were healed up by rulers dining these years. If the temple of Somnath was rebuilt on this side, new sky-high temples like that of Bhuvaneshwar and religious centres in Orissa and Assam rose to their full glory. The Hindu mastery of the Eastern, Western and the Southern seas, their trade and commerce, to-and-fro movement of thousands

of their troops, their royal visits and return visits up to Maxico in the far east and to Africa in the west, continued unhampered and, therefore, the Indians overseas could keep constant contact with their motherland, and thereby prospered materially as well as culturally.

666. Can any Hindu-hater dare say, therefore, of this period at least, that the whole of India was rotting in abject slavery?

□

15

From the 12th Century A.D. to the end of the 13th Century A.D.

667. After the death of Mahmud of Ghazni, the Muslim power there grew far too weak because, in the first place, the population there consisted mainly of the aboriginal tribe converted quite recently by craft or coercion to Islam and secondly, because the Arabian Muslim States were being destroyed completely by the Mongols and the Turks, the two great Asian tribes that had not yet sworn allegiance to Islam, during their sweeping raids through the vast tract of Central Asia right up to Europe.

668. As has already been pointed out, many big and small Hindu communities and royal families ruled this region for a long time. Ghuri was one of these Hindu communities round about Ghazni, which was wholly converted to Islam during the Muslim religio-political aggressions. Being forced to follow the Muslim socio-religious practices for generations, this originally Hindu community of the Ghuries became too staunch and bigoted in their faith, that they ardently desired to rule the other Muslims in Ghazni. From the same Muslim (yet originally Hindu), Ghuri community rose to power one Mohammad Ghori, who, subjugating all the warring tribes during the internecine battles that broke out after the death of Mahmud of Ghazni, finally proclaimed himself, the Sultan of the State. In order to enlist the loyal support of all the Muslims, he made everywhere the stock-in-trade proclamation, which reverberated throughout that region and the northwest region of Hindusthan, that he would force all the kafirs (meaning Hindus) in India to accept Islam and would found an empire there.

669. However, in spite of his ambition, he could not do anything of the kind Mahmud of Ghazni had done before him in his seventeen horrible predatory raids because of the adverse circumstances. In A.D.

1176, Mohammed Ghori first captured the strong fort of Ooch near the confluence of the Panchnad with the Indus. Enraged at the weakness of her husband, the queen in the fort killed him and married her daughter to the victorious Mohammed surrendering the overlordship of the region at the same time.

670. Then in order to size up the Hindu kingdoms, Mohammed Ghori marched on the weakest one of Gujarat by proceeding stealthily along the borders of Rajasthan. For, the King of Gujarat having died, the Queen and her military chief enthroned a minor. This led Mohammed Ghori to think that it was weak enough to be attacked. But he was misled by appearances. For, in learning of Ghori's ensuing invasion, the Hindu army of Gujarat, augmented by those of other sympathising Hindu Kings, marched forward to the mountain-ranges of Abu. The Queen herself fought in the battle most valiantly, urging all the soldiers to defend the infant king whom, she said, she had delivered to their care. Inflamed by her words, the whole Hindu army fought so furiously that the Muslims were routed completely in all directions. Mohammed Ghori himself escaped narrowly and fled straight to his domain beyond the borders.

Second major defeat of Mohammed Ghori by the Hindus

671. Mohammed Ghori, however, was not to be daunted by adversities. So, without being discouraged by his recent defeat at Abu, he once again marched on India in A.D. 1191, invading this time the territory of Prithviraj Chouhan, whereupon that gallant monarch of Delhi along with as many Hindu rulers as he could then gather, advanced against Ghori and joining battle at Tarayan to the north of Karnool near Panipat, dealt a crushing defeat on the invader after a bloody day. Mohammed Ghori himself was captured alive by Prithviraj. This battle is known as the Battle of Talavadi.

672. Emperor (Samrat) Prithviraj and his feudatory princes were after all Hindus by birth and belonged to the topmost Rajput ranks. Hence, they sincerely believed that to let go the captive national enemy alive, however treacherous he might be, to give back his kingdom with all pomp and show, was the highest form of religious conduct, conducive to heavenly bliss as regards a true warrior was concerned.

673. सांप बिखारी देशभूमिचा ये घेउं चावा।
अवचित गांठुनि ठकवुनि भुलवूनि कसाहि ठेचावा॥

Were a serpent (an inveterate national enemy) to come with a view to biting the motherland, he should be smashed to pieces with a surprise attack, deceit or cunning or in any other way possible. Although this war-strategy of Shree Krishna and Chanakya was taught to the Hindus long ago, at that time, it appeared to them like one of the five deadliest sins. For, as we have already shown in paragraphs 397 to 454, the whole of the Hindu nation was at that time utterly infatuated with the perverted sense of virtues. But the Muslims, however, followed this very war-strategy most scrupulously.

674. See how: Had Prithviraj Chouhan, instead of Mohammed Ghori, invaded Ghazni and had the Muslims defeated the Rajputs (as the Rajputs had actually done with Mohammed Ghori), they would have not only killed Prithviraj but would also have converted, by using force and cunning, all the captive Rajputs to Islam, would have made them their wives and children slaves for the whole of their lives in their houses, and the beautiful among the Hindu captive women Ghori himself might have taken into his harem and ravaged. To such a damned, demoniacal enemy of our religion like Mohammed Ghori, was mercy shown by Prithviraj and the other confederated Rajput rulers, following sheepishly the textual maxim क्षमा वीरस्य भूषणम् (a maxim to be used only in the case of some noble and magnanimous enemy!) without the slightest consideration being given to the propriety of time, place and the circumstances and persons involved! Nay, they showed mercy not only to Mohammed Ghori but even to the whole Muslim army, only to respect the noble Rajput tradition of assuring full protection from fear to those who surrendered meekly. Only an oral promise was obtained from Mohammed Ghori that he would not again invade India and he was allowed to go alive. His domain of Ghazni, too, was returned to him and proud, more of their suicidal and credulous generosity than of their having defeated the Muslim army of Mohammed Ghori, those Rajput warriors marched triumphantly to Delhi and celebrated their victory!

But what did Mohammed Ghori do on Reaching Ghazni?

675. Did Mohammed Ghori forget his enmity to the Hindus because of this generosity of Prithviraj Chouhan? No! On the contrary like a snake, provoked by a slight injury, Mohammed Ghori and all the

Muslims in his kingdom, without any sense of gratitude for the Hindu imbecile generosity were all the more embittered, and resolved to crush the Hindus altogether. And with a huge army, Mohammed Ghori once again attacked Prithviraj in A.D. 1193.

The Rajput 'rasos' and the best among them the 'Prithviraj Raso' of Chand Bhat

676. In fact, it is impossible and improper to write any trustworthy history of the Rajputs without closely studying the contemporary historical accounts written by the Rajput Bhats, Charans in their heroic and, to some exent, poetic style and known in that region as 'Rasos'. But it is doubtful whether amongst our historians, there be five or at the most ten such as have read them with any scientific curiosity! That is why none of the histories written of the Rajputs of the times or, for that matter of the whole Hindu society of that age, with the solitary exception of that of Col. Tod, really deserves to be truly called histories. They are mere translations or transliterations of stray incoherent remarks and disconnected and perverted accounts of the Muslim or the English writers. Independent 'Rasos' seem to have been composed on valiant Rajput Ranas, proud of their religion (Hamir Raso, Chhatrasal Raso, etc.). The 'Rasos' are not pure, unadulterated histories! But the forceful and vivid descriptions of the various events, their high fervour and the fact of their authors' participation to a lesser or greater degree, in those particular historical events, make those grand incidents live, as it were, before the imagination of the reader, as the above-mentioned sketchy outlines of chronological accounts can never do. 'Prithviraj Raso' by the famous Chand Bhat, who was in the pay of Prithviraj, bears out the above remark by its epic serenity, calm dignity and moving pathos in the descriptions of the Hindus of the time and of its account of the first Muslim raids from the north-west.

677. The Story of the fire race (अग्नि-कुल)

678. The Nagari Pracharini Sabha had undertaken to republish this 'Prithviraj Raso' in 1922-23, when 1 was in prison at Ratnagiri, where some parts of it were sent to me on request by my brother for my essay on Hindutwa. I do not know, however, whether this whole book was ever published.

These non-Hindus are Shameless, we Hindus, fight shy!

निर्लज्ज म्लेच्छ लजै नहीं, हम हिन्दू लजवान्

679. The 'Prithviraj Raso' describes the Hindu-Muslim skirmishes and frays in the epic style of Mahabharat, and the poet has praised the Hindus highly for vanquishing Mohammed Ghori again and again and then setting him free to go alive, because this noble act of the Hindus, he thought, added to their glory! But when Mohammed Ghori again attacked Prithviraj in A.D. 1193, violating his promise that he would never again invade India, Chand Bhat wrote wrathfully, "We Hindus are scrupulous about religious and irreligious conduct, about truth and falsehood, we fight shy of sinful acts, but these non-Hindus (meaning Muslims) are utterly shameless!"

680. But the breach of promise, which could Muslimize the whole of the kafir state, was a highly religious duty for the Muslims, and because Mohammed Ghori broke his promises again and again, he became a Gazi among the Muslims! This fact also must be engraved on the hearts of the Hindus that (the Muslims who acted irreligiously according to Chand Bhat were blessed with success by God, whereas the Hindus who never broke any promise but showed the quixotic greatness of setting the enemy free alive, were crushed outright owing to their steadfast adherene to their so-called religious conduct!

681. There was another reason why Mohammed Ghori thought it to be the best opportunity to march against Prithviraj, Jaychand the King of Kanouj, had secretly given a solemn promise to help him against Prithviraj, his direst enemy, a promise that later proved fatal to himself. In A.D. 1193, the Hindu-Muslim armies met at 'Sthaneshwar, where in the thick of the fray fell in the hands of the Muslims dead or alive the Rajput princes, Chamundrai, Hamir, Hada and good many other warriors! Muslim losses in lives were also terrible. All this detailed account should really be read, if possible, from the 'Prithviraj Raso' itself, because in the historical accounts by the Muslim writers, nothing but censure and condemnation of the kafirs can only be met with, and with the exception of these poetical Rasos, histories written by Hindu writers, do not simply exist. The Muslim writers vouch that Prithviraj was, at length, killed in the battle and the Muslims were victorious. Soon after this victory, Mohammed Ghori marched straight to Delhi, because he had to perform his diabolically pious deed of demolishing the Hindu temples, of slaughtering the masses of Hindus,

of arson and especially of ravaging the young wife of Prithviraj, the daughter of Jaychand, Sanyogita, who was well-known at that time for her exceptional beauty. Fast as Mohammed Ghori made for Delhi, faster still went the tragic news of the defeat of Prithviraj and of his death or probable capture by the Muslims, to the royal palace of Delhi, whereupon, according to the pre-arranged plan, perhaps the empress Sanyogita lost not a minute to face the danger boldly in the traditional Rajput way. At once, leaving aside all consideration for wealth, parental love, fraternal affection, the attachment to her earthly existence and breaking all ties of love and duty, she jumped from the top-most floor of the palace and killed herself with the word Jayhar (जयहर) --glory to God Shiv! on her lips, she performed Jayhar—Johar! What of the empress, Sanyogita, hundreds of other Hindu women leapt one after another into the Yamuna (Jamuna) and drowned themselves before the Muslims could even touch or pollute them!

682. On reaching Delhi, Mohammed Ghori immediately set to plunder and destroy the royal palaces and the citizens with fire and sword to his heart's content. Proclaiming next the establishment of the Muslim power there, he appointed a trusted slave of his, one Kutubuddin, as his chief administrator and went straight off to Ghazni. Later on, within two years in A.D. 1195, Mohammed Ghori attacked Jaychand. With his administrator Kutubuddin to assist him, he marched on Kanouj, where in a furious scuffle, Jaychand was utterly vanquished and killed. In a sense, the Indian King received a fitting reward for his high treason against the Hindu nation!

683. Nearly a hundred years or more had elapsed since the dreadful raids of Mahmud of Ghazni and as such their recollection was growing fainter like an evil hallucination or dream in the Hindu mind. So, with these two invasions of Mohammed Ghori, every Hindu King, Emperor, Saint, dignitary of every sort, down to the hut-dweller was shocked to the marrow of his bones at this miserable plight of Hindu courage and strength. Mohammed Ghori, too, was elated at this unexpected victory, and hearing of Kashi (Benares) as the holiest of Hindu places of worship, he headed straight for it in order to destroy Hindu religion.

684. The people at Kashi were taken unaware by this fanatical and bloodthirsty raid and, as such, had no arrangement to face it. Naturally, Mohammed Ghori captured Kashi in no time, started forthwith to slaughter Hindu men and women, to plunder the Hindu houses, to ravish

Hindu women and specially to force countless Hindu men and women to accept Islam and slavery. Above all, he raised to big heaps of rubble and brick every Hindu temple and broke the idols within it to bits.

685. But he immediately heard the news that in the Hindu states beyond and especially in Rajasthan, plans were being chalked out of encircling him; and having the bitter experience of the united Hindu swordsmen twice before, he satisfied himself with whatever he could achieve during one sweep from Kanouj to Kashi (Benaras) and went back to Ghazni. As before, he appointed his versatile, brave and trusted slave Kutubuddin himself as the Governor of the recently won territory up to Kanouj.

686. And alas! At this very evil, unpropitious moment, our age-old Capital of the Hindu empire since the days of Yudhishthir, this our Indraprastha, Hastinapur or modern Delhi was lost to the non-Hindus and there was laid the foundation stone of the Muslim empire for centuries to come! Delhi became the centre of servitude and remained so, rotting under the foreign rule for the next five or six hundred years (with very short breaks in between), till at last, the Marathas triumphantly hoisted their saffron-coloured flag at Attock, and overthrowing the Muslim imperial power beyond, made it the handmaid of the Hindu imperial authority.

687. Soon after he reached Ghazni, Mohammed Ghori was killed (in the opinion of some Muslim historians) by a small band of soldiers in his army, but Chand Bhat gives a colourful and detailed description in his Raso of how Prithviraj seized the one unique opportunity to kill him and avenged his defeat. Although no other support for this folklore can be found, as yet, it is not unworthy of a mention here. The essence of this superbly described folklore in the poetical 'Prithviraj Raso' is that Prithviraj was captured alive by Ghori and was not killed in the battle. Mohammed Ghori took him to Ghazni as a captive and struck out his eyes, making him blind. At this shocking news, Chand Bhat went on his own to Ghori's court at Ghazni in order to do his traditional duty as a Bhat of laying down his life for his emperor. Charans and Bhats were supposed to bear a charmed life—they were not to be killed—and the Muslim rulers also could not generally break this convention! Sultan Mohammed Ghori too asked Chand Bhat to have his say. Chand Bhat was a well-known and ready-witted, facile poet, who sang out at the top of his sonorous voice a heroic ballad

to mean, "My master is your captive and you are sure to end his life as best you please. But my sole request is that I should also be killed with him in the same or any other manner. Secondly, I submit that the Sultan should himself witness a demonstration of the exceptional skill of my master in the wonderful art of hitting the sound (शब्दबेध) in archery. "This request made the Sultan curious about this wonderful art. Even then, with every precaution, the necesary arrangments for the demonstration were made. Twenty-one pans were hung in a row. Sultan Mohammed sat eagerly with his select retinue and his noblemen at a high place in the court to witness the feat. Chand Bhat and Prithviraj, the last Hindu Emperor of Delhi, were made to sit before the pans in the wake of a strong military guard. Then, as each pan was struck, the stroke rang clear and loud. As soon as the sound rang out, the blinded Emperor Prithviraj took an unmistakable aim at the pan concerned and hit the mark. As this feat was repeated with exceptional accuracy of aim for twenty-one times, the whole court was thrilled with wonder and admiration and the clapping of hands went on unceasingly and finally the Sultan himself shouted aloud 'shabas' shabas'—bravo, bravo!! At that very moment, the captive Chand Bhat sitting near Prithviraj composed a couplet (दोहा) on the spur of the moment, telling Prithviraj to shoot, without wasting a moment, the Sultan sitting at a particular distance, shouting 'shabas, shabas—Bravo, bravo'. At this, the blinded Emperor Prithviraj took an aim in the direction of the Sultan shouting 'Shabas, Shabas' and killed him with a sharp arrow. At once, there was an uproar and confusion everywhere, but before the guards of the Sultan could fall upon them with their weapons, Prithviraj and Chand Bhat drew out their own swords and cut off their own heads!

The Slave Dynasty

688. Soon after the death of Mohammed Ghori, his slave (governor) administrator in India, Kutubuddin, himself became the Sultan and established his independent kingdom at Delhi. Kutubuddin was a Turk by birth, but as he was a slave of Mohammed Ghori, his dynasty is called the Slave Dynasty.

The fictitious story of Kutubminar

689. The legend that he built the famous Kutubminar as a memorial

to his victory is altogether false. This pillar of victory was built as Vishnu stambh—the pillar of Vishnu—by a certain Hindu emperor, most probably by Samudra Gupta and was dedicated to Lord Vishnu. Recent excavations have discovered an ancient idol of Shree Vishnu near the pillar, which supports the above assertion. Thereafter, Prithviraj Chouhan improved it to a great extent, so in the Rajput period it was sometimes called Prithvistambh. The Muslims had grown very much fond of obliterating the names and all other traces of the old monuments and stamping them with their own seals wherever they went on with their expeditions. Hence in India, too, they changed the old original names of the capitals they conquered, the holy places of pilgrimage, the important sites, works of art and gave them all their Muslim names. According to this mischievous habit, Kutubuddin named this very monument of Vishnustambh, Kutubminar. At many places on that pillar, he got the hymns and aphorisms from the Koran engraved in Arabic, and added some new features to the pillar here and there. But the blocks of stones that were required for this purpose were intentionally procured from the demolished Hindu temples and the idols therein.

Raids on Chitod and Hindu Victories

690. While Kutubuddin was conquering the Punjab, Delhi, Kanouj and other Hindu states, he was uneasy about the Rajput states. Soon he learnt of the death of Rana Samarsingh of Chitod and of the succession of his minor son, Karna, to the throne. He was not a fool to let go this fine opportunity to subdue it. But the mother of the minor king of Chitod, Karundevi, was very brave and of great ablilities. That young mother-queen took the leadership of the army and inspiring the other neighbouring Hindu states to fight on her side, dealt a memorable defeat on the Muslim army in a battle near Ambar (Amber or Amer). In order to avoid complete destruction, Kutubuddin retreated to Delhi. Later on, when Rahup succeeded Karna to the throne of Chitod, Kutubuddin's army once again marched on Chitod. But once again, the Rajputs put the Muslim army to rout. Rana Rahup proved to be a very able ruler. The Muslims, therefore, never thought of invading Chitod till his death.

691. But it must be remembered here that even while the Muslims launched repeated attacks on the Hindu states, the Hindus as a rule, never invaded them nor ever pursued the fleeing Muslim army, nor

again besieged the Muslim localities left behind and destroyed them or their masjids. It is because the Hindus never thus retaliated the Muslim aggression owing to their perverse sense of virtues, the latter again and again perpetrated these crimes against the former.

692. After Kutubuddin's death in A.D. 1210, one or two incapable Sultans came to the throne of Delhi, but as they were soon deposed, Sultana Razia began to rule. She was well trained in the affairs of the State by Kutubuddin himself. She attended the court or her army in the guise of a man. Later on, she fell in love with a trusty slave of hers, named Jalaluddin, who chiefly manoeuvred things in the court and began to live openly with her. This was, however, most detestable to the Turkish noblemen of her court, because Jalaluddin was a Negro. The Turks thought themselves to be of high rank and despised the Negroes as lowbred.

693. This will make another point clear to the reader that although the Turks, the Mongols, the Arabs, the Pathans, the Negroes (Abyssinians) and others called themselves Muslims, and proudly proclaimed the absence of caste differences and exhibited in place and out of place, the equality of status for all in order to belittle the Hindus on that account, they were not altogether free from those caste differences. These distinctions were on the contrary, far too pronounced amongst them and caused a good deal of trouble.

694. Shortness of space compels us to refer the reader to a chapter in our book, 'Essay on Abolition of Castes' (जात्युच्छेदक निबंध) named 'Sects and Factions Amongst the Muslims'.

695. In the end, the Turkish noblemen rose in rebellion against the Negro J alaluddin and Sultana Razia under the leadership of Altunia, the governor of Sarhind, and defeated Razia in a battle, whereupon, Razia cast her spell upon the victor Altunia and married him. The newly-wedded couple marched on Delhi once again, but were defeated and killed by the noblemen and the army there. After considerable court intrigues and plots, and counter-plots a nobleman named 'Bulban', usurped the throne and became the Sultan of Delhi.

Mongol Raids—Chengeezkhan

696. During the reign of this very slave dynasty, Mongol raids on India's farthest borders through Central Asia were causing constant trouble. Like whirlwinds, great armies from Mongolia who had not so far sworn their allegiance to Islam, went on trampling over, and crushing,

all the nations and countries from the Pacific to the Black Sea. Their leader, in those days, was the world-famous Chengeezkhan, who till the last moment of his life, heaped all possible ignominies and insults on the Muslim and Arab States and the Muslim religion. He deposed and killed the Khaliph of Baghdad, whom the Muslims highly respected as the political and religious representative of God, and razed to the ground the city of Baghdad. Yet the Allah could do absolutely nothing against him. With his ploughshare of destruction, he furrowed the vast territory right up to Russia without the least obstruction; he overthrew the kingdom of Kiev in Russia, ravaged the whole tract straight up to the Black Sea with massacre, plunder, arson and annexed it to his trans-continental empire. But no power on this vast earth dared restrain this destructive hand of Chengeezkhan! On their way back from Russia, these Mongol armies were obviously to dash violently against India. But quite mysteriously, he went straight off to Mongolia, after first subduing the Muslim kingdom of Ghazni and quite suddenly died there in A.D. 1227. Later on, this extensive empire passed into the hands of one of this Mongol race—Kublai Khan. These Mongols had already reduced the whole of China and Korea. Kublai Khan made the age-long Chinese capital of Peking his own.

697. One after-effect of this Mongol-Turkish struggle was that they had a mixed progeny, which was called Moghal or Mughal. These Moghals frequently tried to rush into India and finally reached Delhi. Some of them took to Islam, but the old Muslims did not treat them equally; they considered them to be low-born. These Moghals founded in Delhi, a separate colony of theirs, named 'Moghalpura'. Some others of them went to the Rajputs for shelter because the old Muslims scoffed at them. Especially, some two thousand of them sought employment in the army of the valiant Hindu king of Ratanbhor.

698. Sultan Bulban of the Slave Dynasty was, in a sense, the most powerful and able; he called himself the true representative of Allah. But as regards his hatred towards the Hindus, he surpassed everybody from the emperor to the meanest of servants. He imposed various heavy taxes on the Hindus, forbade their pilgrimages to the holy places while their forcible conversions and massacres went on unceasingly from village to village.

699. Bulban died in old age in A.D. 1286. There being no able person from the Slave Dynasty to succeed him, within four years, a nobleman from the Khilji family, Jalaluddin, slew the sons and grandsons of Bulban

and proclaimed himself the Sultan of Delhi, putting a stop to the Slave Dynasty for ever, and starting his own.

Khilji Dynasty

700. This Khilji dynasty of Jalalluddin called itself Pathans (Afghans), if at all it was of Turkish extraction. Jalalluddin himself was, as the other Sultans and Muslims were, fired with the devilish ambition to destory the Hindu political, as well as religious power, root and branch. He was just, as regards other departments of administration, but was partial to the Muslims. Seeing the tremendous loss of Muslim lives in the siege of Ratanbhor, he raised the siege and decamped saying, "I value a single hair of a Muslim more than a hundred such forts." But this wisdom of his was so belated, that the cause for this action of his has to be sought in the unbeaten valour of the Rajputs. After this failure, he never again troubled the Rajputs.

701. The old Jalalluddin really wanted to enthrone his one ambitious, brave and staunch Muslim nephew, Allauddin after his own death. So he had sent him with a large army to face the Rajputs. But not content with this assignment, which seemed too meagre for his daring Hindu-hatred, he marched straight off without the Sultan's permission to conquer the southern Hindu states and rob them of their reported fabulous wealth, of which he had lately grown covetous beyond every limit. The first Hindu state to fall a victim to this unexpected attack of Allauddin was that of the Yadava of Devgiri.

702. There is one special point to be noted as regards this southern conquest of Allauddin. The Hindu society of the south had, for more or less two thousand years, from the early beginnings of the modern history, i.e. from 500 or 600 B.C. to the 13th century A.D., been enjoying complete political, religious and social independence and had been economically highly prosperous. It had never been successfully invaded throughout these two thousand years. Whoever of the foreign invaders dared to do so, was ruthlessly crushed on the borders themselves. So, this invasion of Allauddin was the first of its kind and was bound to be successful with far-reaching harmful effects. Because of this special revolutionary and harmful character of this invasion of Allauddin, it has to be dealt with in a fresh chapter.

□

16

Muslim Invasions on South India upto the Beginnings of the 14th Century

703. Right from the beginnings of known history, i.e. from about 500 to 600 B.C. to the beginning of the 14th century, South India never knew any great foreign invasion either by land or sea. The Hindu states there enjoyed their political liberty and power almost unhampered and unimpeded. On the contrary, millions of Hindu people and armies of the Kalings, Pandyas, Chers, Chols, Andhras, Rashtrakuts, Chalukyas, Yadavas and others up to Dwarka had victoriously spread their political and commercial supremacy, their theological and scientific knowledge, their art and sculpture up to Mexico on the one side and to central Africa on the other.

704-705. But this glorious achievement of the Hindu states of the South of maintaining their independence for over two thousand years has never been so specifically and forcibly stated anywhere in history! We, however, challenge if any country or state of such magnitude as that of the continent like South Indian peninsula can be found on the face of this earth, which has valiantly maintained its independence, power and empire and kept foreign invaders either by land or sea, off its territories for such a long period!

706. And such a country like India, more than half of whose territory enjoyed such a glorious past, is derided by some half-crazy jealous historians, foreign as well as Indian, or by some Hindu-haters like Dr. Ambedkar or by some quite ignorant writers, so as to say, "Indian history from the beginning is a history of a slavish people sunk deep into foreign bondage and constantly trampled under foreign heels. "The word 'slavery' sums up the whole history of the Hindus who have been

dragging on the poor existence for tens and scores of centuries!"

707. At least, from now onwards, every Indian or non-Indian historian must, for the love of truth, mention specifically this glorious peculiarity of South India! Then alone, their writings would deservedly be called history!!

The Credit due to the Hindus of the North

708. Of course, while speaking of this glorious achievement of the South of India—of maintaining its independence and vast empire over such a long period—due credit must be given to the Hindu warriors, who tenaciously fought for more than six or seven hundred years the bloody and disastrous wars with the Arabs, the Pathans, the Turks, the Moghals, millions of pillaging aggressors of numerous nations and communities of almost the whole of Asia and halted their all-sweeping advance there in the North for such a long period; and to those millions of Hindu martyrs who gave away their lives for defending their religion by leaping into the hungry flames, into the bounding waves of the Hooded rivers or in the wholesale man-slaughter carried on by the enemy, but never forsook their religion as per their various beliefs! The Hindus, history can never forget—must never forget—these immeasurable obligations of those generations of Hindus of the North over the whole of the Hindu nation-obligations which can have no requital whatsoever!

709. However, world history itself tells us that even the greatest of nations, too, fall victims some time or the other, even if after a very long lapse of time, to some foreign domination. Similarly, towards the very end of the 13th century (in A.D. 1294), this sub-continent of South India was overcome with this calamity of the foreign Muslim aggression.

710. But it must be remembered here that the only nation in the then known world, which could be fairly compared with India as regards its extent and greatness—the Chinese nation—was overrun from end-to-end, and subjugated by Chengeezkhan nearly a hundred years prior to the 14th century; and simultaneouly with the first invasion of South India by Allauddin—of which we are going to write very shortly—it had already become the footstool of the foreign throne of the Mongol Emperor, Kublai Khan! But can any profane, abusive writer make bold to say that the Chinese nation has all along been rotting in foreign bondage?

Modern History of South India

711. The relevant and sufficient portion of the ancient history of South India has already been referred to in an early part of this book. We can safely assume that with the downfall of the Shalivahan dynasty in A.D. 236 or thereabout, began the modern history of South India. Thereafter, the gallant Chalukya Emperor, Pulakeshi shone like a light-house tower, counting the passage of time, in the history of the South. He too has been mentioned in the earlier chapters. To his court had come the famous Chinese traveller, Huen-tsang (or Yuan Chwan), who has first used the word Maharashtra to describe Pulakeshi's kingdom. That is the first important recorded use of the word in history. Emperor Pulakeshi fell fighting with the Pullav King, Nursinh Varma, of the South in A.D. 642 and his kingdom was conquered by the Pallavas. But very shortly afterwards, it was reconquered by his son, Vikramaditya I, after defeating the Pallavas in a furious battle.

712. To this very Chalukya dynasty, belonged Vikramaditya II, who later on in the 8th century A.D., sent a huge army to Navasari and defeated the Arab invaders there!

713. Various such Hindu conquests over the Muslims are not even mentioned in modern histories. History, of late, has become too partial and vulgar. The various such incidents of Hindu supremacy and superior craft, that have been mentioned heretofore, can very rarely be found in the contemporary histories written by Muslim writers. Hereafter, at least Hindu writers should describe such glorious acts of valour of the Hindu kings and warriors after careful research.

714. The above-mentioned royal dynasty of the Pallavas was one of the valorous and prosperous ones of the South. They had their capital at Kanchi (Kanjivaram) for some time. At the end of the ninth century A.D., a Chol king of South India itself, named Aditya, overpowered Aparajit Pallav and subdued his kingdom for ever.

The Rashtrakuts

715. After the Chalukyas, the Rashtrakuts had established a prominent and very powerful kingdom, bringing practically the whole of the South and even the southern part of Gujarat under their sway. For some time, they had their capital at Malkhed. By far, the most important achievement of theirs is getting the famous Kailas cave carved at Verul (Ellora).

716. After the 10th century A.D., there were only two prominent kingdoms in the South: those of the Cholas of Tanjawar (Tanjore) and the Pandyas of Madura. Fortunately, we have the eyewitness account of the political independence of the South, their prosperous state, and their gallantry, by a third party, namely Marco Polo, the celebrated, discerning, learned European (Italian) traveller and writer, who had spent many years of his life in the court of Kublai Khan in China and who on his way back, had at this very time, stayed for some days at Madura, the Pandya capital. His testimony as to the Hindu mastery of the three seas and their overseas empires, which we can find in his book of travels, is the most important. For when he came from China to India, he came via Indo-China and visited the Hindu states in Sumatra and other islands. At the time of his sojourn in Sumatra, the island was ruled by one Hindu King, Shree Vijay, who gave equal protection to the Buddhists also. Marco Polo, thereafter, went back to Venice, his place of birth, about the year A.D. 1295. Two or three other foreign travellers had come and stayed in India at that time, and have left behind them some account of their travels, which, along with that of Marco Polo, bear important and independent witness to the fact of the complete political freedom of the Southern Hindu states, of their political, commercial and religious supremacy over many other nations around them, of their overlordership of the Eastern, Western and Southern Seas, of their powerful navies and merchant marine, which traversed the tides of the three seas unopposed, and of the unrivalled title of 'Trisamudreshwar', which these Southern Hindu kings proudly took lor themselves.

717. 'Trisamudreshwar' emperor Rajendra Chola died in A.D. 1042 and after one or two powerful kings after him, the Chowl dynasty and the Chowl empire perished at the end of the 13th century.

Religious Preachers like Shankaracharya and others

718. During these years, South India saw not only the rise of royal heroes like Rajendra Chowl, but also the glorious heights reached by religious heroes, the foremost among them being Shreemat Shankaracharya, defeating the various so-called heretical views that were being advocated throughout India against the Vedic religion. At Kalindi in Karal, was born this great personality of Shankaracharya in a Nambudri Brahmin family. Being well-versed in the Vedic lore and having taken the vow of Sannyas (having renounced the worldly life)

even before the tender age of sixteen, he began to preach and conquer the heretics in all quarters. Kumarilbhatta, the well-known exponent of the Karma theory, who successfully refuted the Buddhist religious opinions, was also preaching throughout the four corners of India round about this time. Another preacher Diggaja (दिग्गज)—(the elephant defending the directions)—Mandanmishra, was also the contemporary of this young Shankaracharya. In order to establish his theory of अद्वैत (the non-existence of duality between—the unison [unity] of—Jeevatma and Paramatma) and to hoist the victorious banner of Vedic religion throughout the whole of India, Shankaracharya went on searching out and completely defeating in religious debate not only the followers of the absolute theory of karma, but also the other non-Vedic beliefs and even the renowned leaders of the Buddhist religion. Finally he paraded the victorious Vedic banner througout India and established authoritative religious institutions of his order at four places in the four directions of India: at Shringeri in the south, at Dwarka to the west, Jagannathpuri in the eastern quarter and at Kashmir to the farthest north. These religious seats (institutions) received full Government support so long as Hindu states existed in those various places. Having accomplished this wonderful work of religious propaganda and having written the (unparalleled) unrivalled book, 'Shankarbhashya', he entered the cave-took a living samadhi—(ended his life by restraining his breath).

The Political Activities of the Shaivite sects like the Pashupatas

719. Even before this period was resuscitated, the Shaivite Sect of the Pashupatas, which being militant like the Shaktas, extremely hated the meek अहिंसा—'non-violence'—and renunciation of the worldly life of the Buddhists and Jains. It fomented and fanned to red heat', at least indirectly, among the Hindus, the tendency to oppose the non-Hindu religious aggressors and a love for war. Shree Lakulesh was their apostle, who was born in Gujarat and whose great work and Influence made the Hindus take him for the very incarnation of Lord Har (Shiv), and whom even Shankaracharya mentions proudly.

Bengal during these years

720. Till 700 to 800 A.D., Bengal was ruled by the Pal kings, the first of whom was king Gopal. He was a Buddhist. He had from his queen Deddadevi, a son, named Dharampal, who ruled from 800 to

825 A.D. He too was a Buddhist and had been married to Ranadevi, the daughter of the Rashtrakut king Govind, who was most famous in the South. By about A.D. 1095, the Sen dynasty destroyed the Pal kings and founded their own kingdom. These Sen kings were the Kshatriyas from karnatak in the South, who had their silent access to the royal circle perhaps through the retinue of the above-mentioned Rashtrakut princess, Ranadevi. Whatever that is, as these Sen kings were the staunch followers of the Vedic religion, they suppressed Buddhism in Bengal and vigorously revived the caste-system, rendered chaotic by intermingling of different castes during the Buddhist period as also the Vedic lore and other Vedic religious institutions. The book on Sanskrit grammar, Mugdhabodh, written by Bopdev was very popular in Bengal at this time.

The contemporary history of Gujarat

721. The famous King Karnaraj, who built the extensive lake of Krishnasagar, ruled Gujrath from A.D. 1063 to 1093. The original capital of his royal family was at Pattan, which he shifted later on to a new place and named it Karnavati, and it remained the capital of Gujarat even afterwards.

722. But later on, when Gujarat was overcome by the Muslims, Sultan Ahmedshah, who persecuted the Hindus most cruelly, changed the historical Hindu name of Karnavati to Ahmedabad in A.D.1412, befitting the traditional Muslim malignity towards the Hindus, and added to it, a newly built suburb. And the meek and submissive attitude of the Hindus of those times has been fondling that name ever since as their own.

The first Invasion of the South by the Foreigners and Non-Hindus

723. Sultan Jalalluddin's nephew, Allauddin crossed the Vindhyas with a huge army without any permission from his uncle and attacked the south of India, to loot the fabulous wealth, of which he had so long been receiving tempting reports. This invasion was so unexpected and the negligence, conceit and narrow-mindedness of the South Indian Hindu Kings of that time were so profound and criminal, that perhaps it is after his kingdom was actually attacked that the king of Devgiri, Maharaja Ramdevrao Yadav, came to know of it, and being thoroughly

unprepared to face it, was utterly confused.

723A. Is it not really strange that even while the Muslim states were being founded everywhere in the north of India, while they had been so very cruelly ravaging the Hindu religion and Hindu states for two or three centuries, while thousands of Hindu temples were being continuously and insultingly demolished, while Kashi was almost turned into Mecca, while Dnyandev, Namdev and other saints and their followers and millions of travelling Hindu pilgrims were going right up to the Punjab to visit the holy places and were returning aggrieved at the sad plight of Hindu religion there, while the Muslims were openly swearing and voicing their ambition to invade the South and convert it to Islam, the Hindu kings of the South should be so very careless and negligent, that instead of collecting their armies and sending them to the north to help the Rajputs face the Muslim aggression, Ramdevrao's forces under some of his chieftains, should have gone far to the South, and Ramdevrao himself should have been wandering most frivolously with his small army, hunting wild animals away from his capital? But...

724. Let alone Ramdevrao's state of Devgiri, but didn't even a single spy from the secret intelligence service of the four or five prominent Hindu states in the south go to the north and observe and inform his king or kings anything even while the north-Indian Hindus were so pitifully groaning and rending the skies with their miserable cries? But! ....But!!

725. Under these circumstances, it is no wonder if Ramdevrao was utterly vanquished. Allauddin extorted from Ramdevrao a huge ransom, made him a mandatory prince and went off hurriedly to Delhi because of some political urgency. It was really fortunate that, according to the Muslim custom, the whole state of Ramdevrao was not immediately turned Muslim.

726. For, Allauddin was busy with his plans to dispatch his uncle. Jalalluddin as soon as he reached Delhi and to usurp the throne. Accordingly, he hatched up a big conspiracy and had Jalalluddin killed and himself became the Sultan in A.D. 1296.

727. Immediately after he became the Sultan, he invaded Gujrath in A.D. 1298 and overcoming the Hindu king there, conquered the capital of Anhilwad. In the confusion of the battle, the beautiful Hindu queen, Kamaldevi was captured while she was trying to escape, but

the defeated Hindu king could slip away with his daughter, Devaldevi. Allauddin thence marched straight into Sourashtra, again demolished the newly built magnificent temple of Sorti Somnath and took away the idol therein to Delhi and used it as a stepping stone for his throne, only to add insult to the Hindus' injury!

728. On reaching Delhi, he married Rani Kamaldevi perhaps with her own consent. That harlot of a woman was not satisfied with mere cohabitation with Allauddin, but requested the Muslim chieftains marching on the south to search out and capture her young, pretty daughter, Princess Devaldevi, and bring her to Delhi into Muslim captivity.

729. At this time of Allauddin's invasion of Gujarat, there was a most handsome, smart, and young lad working as a slave with a wealthy banker. Him Allauddin asked for as lustfully as if he would be a girl in marriage. But as the banker refused to part with the young slave, the Sultan angrily seized the lad and carried him away forcibly. In those days, the Muslims had inherited the vice of sodomy—an unnatural form of sexual intercourse with fair-looking boys instead of with girls—from the Arabs, which became an accepted custom in the Muslim community as a whole, being never considered to be irreligious! According to this general practice, Allauddin too had such unnatural sexual relations with this young handsome slave. But that smart slave turned out such an expert swordsman and politician, that he actually began to lead the armies on the battlefields himself with as much ability and skill, as Allauddin himself. The ageing Allauddin began to call the slave Maliq-Kafur. Later still, he began to run the whole administration of the empire with the latter's advice.

The second Muslim campaign on Ratanbhor

730. It has already been told that Jalalludin was defeated by the Hindus of Ratanbhor. In order to avenge that defeat, Allauddin marched again for the second time on the fort of Ratanbhor in A.D. 1301. Even the then Rana Hameer of Ratanbhor fought to the last, and laid down his life along with thousands of his soldiers in that furious battle, and on seeing the fall of the Rajput warriors, hundreds of Rajput ladies including Hameer's queen standing on the ramparts of the fort, leapt into the blazing fire according to a pre-settled plan and burned themselves to death. How often have the Hindu warriors and their brave wives done

such magnificent deeds of valour and sacrificed their lives! That is the only reason why the Hindu nation could still remain alive!

Invasions of Chitod Subsequent to the fall of Ratanbhor

731. The most beautiful daughter of the Rajput king of Ceylon, named Padmini, was married to Rana Bheemsingh of Chitod. According to the shameless but proud vaunt of the Muslims in general that to kidnap the non-Muslim beautiful women openly was a Muslim's religious duty, Allauddin openly demanded from Rana Bheemsingh his charming queen, and as the Rajputs spurned it, Allauddin marched on Chitod round about A.D. 1302. While describing the battles at that time, the Rajput history tells a story how in order to deceive Allauddin, the Rajputs promised to send Padmini to him but actually sent armed gallant fighters disguised as women in several palanquins and successfully executed a daring plan of rescuing the captured Bheemsingh, but the paucity of space prevents us from narrating it in any detail. Finding it impossible to crush the mighty Rajput valour even in that furious battle, Allauddin had to return to Delhi. This incident clearly shows that Rajputs, too, could resort to cunning.

732. In order to avenge the defeat inflicted by the Rajputs in this battle and for the sake of Padmini, Allauddin once again invaded Chitod in A.D. 1303, when once again the brave Rajputs donned the ' Kesaria' (saffron garments) and fought till the end, slaying hundreds of Muslims, and died to a man. Seeing the victory smile upon the Muslims and fortune darken upon the Rajputs, about ten thousand Rajput women, including Rani Padmini, leapt into the blazing fire with their children at their breasts. Allauddin conquered Chitod, only to collect the ashes of Padmini! When the Hindu warriors and Hindu women fought, they fought thus!

733. It must be told here that before the old Allauddin breathed his last, this defeat of the Hindus was avenged under the very nose of Allauddin in A.D. 1313 by the famous Rajput, Hameer, who conquered Chitod, after inflicting a crushing defeat upon the Muslims. He even captured a son of Allauddin alive—but he was not converted to Hinduism. He should have been, at least, to pay the enemy in its own coin! This is the very same suicidal generosity of the Hindus.

734. In A.D. 1307, this Maliq Kafur, Allauddin's famed general, was sent by the Sultan to invade the South. Ramdevrao was once again defeated, but he made peace by paying off the accumulated ransom. But during this turmoil, the runaway Princess Devaldevi of Gujarat, who was

married to Ramdevrao's son Shankardev, was captured and sent to Delhi by Maliq Kafur. Soon after in A.D. 1308, he invaded the Deccan for the third time and defeated in a bloody action Raja Pratapdev of Varangal, the heroic king who had once vanquished the Muslims. Raja Pratapdev had to swear allegiance to the Sultanate at Delhi.

735. Flushed at this success, Maliq Kafur marched on the third Hindu State in the Deccan and defeated the Hoysal king there likewise. Kafur's victorious sword then subdued the remaining Hindu kingdom of Madura.

736. Thus, for the first time, during the past two thousand years, practically the whole of the Deccan passed into foreign and non-Hindu enemy hands! The independence and prosperity of the Deccan came to an end in this year! At the Southern-most end of the Deccan, Maliq Kafur built a fine Masjid as if to commemorate this Muslim conquest of South India. But the Hindu reaction to it was to precipitate the successful Hindu conspiracies against Muslim bondage.

737. Ramdevrao's son, Shankardev, succeeded him to the throne of Devgiri, and soon repudiated the oath of allegiance to Sultan Allauddin, whereupon Maliq Kafur swooped down on the Deccan once again. Shankardev did not surrender till the last and fought furiously till he was killed.

738. As Allauddin and Maliq Kafur stamped out the Hindu political power from the Deccan during their frequent invasions, they likewise crumbled to dust the huge and magnificent Hindu temples of the South, cut up their golden pinnacles and in majority of the cases, built palatial masjids on their sites, forced thousands of Hindus to be converted. These innumerable converted Hindus made big farming and feudal estates in this Deccan itself. But Hindus, however, did not massacre these Muslims nor did they destroy them outright as and when they subdued the Muslim power later on. This is what we call the perversion of the concept of virtues!

Most often the Hindus used the same War strategy of the Muslims, according to the Military Science of the time

739. On the religious front, the Hindus were, thus, being vanquished mostly because of their own foolish religious concepts and traditions, but on the political front, they were fighting with the Muslims as they ought to have done! Even after being completely overcome, they rose again and again and defeated the Muslims! Craftiness and cunning were

generally matched with the same strategic moves by the Hindus!

740. Allauddin surpassed every other Sultan before him in cruelty in the persecution of the Hindus. He would have reached greater heights in cruelty in respect of his treatment of the Hindus, had he not been forced to fight on the other front with the Mongols, who unceasingly hurled their armed might against the western borders of India and caused a great turmoil throughout Mongolia and Cenral Asia. A few of them took to Islam and formed a new Muslim colony in Delhi itself. At last, the enraged Allauddin cut off the whole of this new Muslim colony to a man!

Death of Allauddin

741. Allauddin was the first and the last Muslim Sultan to rule over practically the whole of India with the exception of some Hindu states like those of Chitod and others. Neither Akbar nor even Aurangzeb can take that place, as their territories never equalled those of Allauddin.

742. But in his old age, Allauddin was surely afflicted by his bodily diseases, which were the outcome of his physical vices. Naturally, he became a tool in the hands of Maliq Kafur, and in that miserable state, this valorous but Hindu-hater Sultan died of dropsy in A.D. 1316 or as it is said, Maliq Kafur killed him or had him killed. His 'Allah' could not bless him with a happy death because of his virtue of Hindu-hatred! In a few days Maliq Kafur, a one-time slave of Allauddin, usurped the whole power of Allauddin, but in the political chaos that ensued after Allauddin, he was soon killed. In the turbulent days that followed, a certain Khushrukhan of exceptional abilities, who had been shining in the diplomatic circles at Delhi, rose to the highest seat of power. From the point of view of the Hindu nation, his story deserves a separate chapter in the history of India.

□

17

Khushrukhan and Devaldevi

743. If the millions of students who are learning history in all the states in the Indian Union today are asked what they know of Khushrukhan, a unique unforgettable character, who was acclaimed as the Sultan of Sultans in the Muslim Sultanate at Delhi, and who was worthy of high praise from the point of view of the Hindus, it is more likely than not, that at least 93 per cent of these millions of students will reply with evident surprise, "Khushrukhan? No, we haven't come across any major reference to such a man as you describe!" Let alone the students, but even if you were to ask the same question to the teachers in general, to the whole editorial staff of the newspapers in India or even to any educated man or woman, at least 75 per cent of them will very probably reply in the same manner; 'who is this Khushrukhan? We have never heard even of his name!'

744. It is for this very reason that we are attempting to give a brief sketch of his life and work, as far as we can do so with the available evidence. For, although he is a unique character in the modern Indian history, his name has been obliterated, as it were, by the Muslim historians and their blind foreign and Indian, Hindu followers, from the textbooks of history used in schools, for his sole offence of putting the Muslim Sultanate to shame in order to avenge the wrongs and insults hurled by them at the Hindu nation. Wherever he has been mentioned, he has been given the most insulting and abusive attributes like, 'low-bred', 'depraved', 'a knave', 'a hell-hound' by the Muslim writers.

The early history of Khushrukhan

745. When in the reign of Allauddin, Gujarat had to face the first onslaught of the Muslims in A.D. 1298 and the governing authority of the Hindus was much shaken down, in the chaotic conditions then

prevailing, a very tender, attractive but very brilliant Hindu youth had been captured and made a slave by the Muslim noblemen and was offered into the service of Allauddin, much the same way and for the same reason as Maliq Kafur was made a slave. This youth was originally a Hindu, belonging to the untouchable caste of Paria of Parwar (sweepers) in Gujarat. One or two Muslim writers deny that he was a Paria (sweeper), but emphatically assert that he was a Rajput. Alter having been captured and converted to Islam, he was first called 'Hasan'. When he was taken in the service of Allauddin at Delhi, in keeping with the social vice of the Muslims (viz., sodomy; paragraph 729), the greatest noblemen and generals of the court had unnatural sexual relations with him, and so they were extremely solicitous about serving his whims! When after Allauddin's death in A.D. 1316, Maliq Kafur became the chief administrator, he also came to have great regard for his abilities. Very soon, Hasan was given the title of Khushrukhan. For, even in the days of Allauddin, he was being sent independently on some small military expeditions in charge of small troops. That Hasan should become Khushrukhan and then a general in the army so rapidly, bespeaks of his exceptional qualities. But more than these qualities of his limitless love that Mubarik, the son of Allauddin, bore towards this charming young man, was responsible for such a spectacular rise. So after both Allauddin and Maliq Kafur died or were dispatched as the case may be, Mubarik got the Sultanate of Delhi mainly with Khushrukhan's assistance and quite naturally, all the reins of the government passed easily into the hands of Khushrukhan, the dearest, ablest and the most trustworthy young nobleman of Mubarik's court, and young Khushrukhan, too, proved wholly efficient in the discharge of his responsible job. Mubarik was vicious and pleasure-seeking by nature. Therefore, he considered it a godsend gift to have such an efficient assistant in the person of Khushrukhan to run the whole administration, and especially, a loyal executive to manage his private affairs in the harem.

Devaldevi

746. When in the court of Delhi, the attractive Maliq Kafur, who was born a Hindu but converted by Allauddin to Islam, became later on the commander-in-chief and an astute politician, practically at the same time, rose in status another young, handsome, Hindu convert, Khushrukhan, who after the death of Maliq Kafur, wielded all authority

at the court of Delhi. In a similar way and simultaneously enough, rose a third figure in the political circles at Delhi, who was equally important, able, and who managed the affairs of the state only with the twitch of her eyebrows, and her sidelong glances—I mean the former Hindu princess of Gujarat and the sometime wife of Shankardev Yadav of Devgiri, namely Devaldevi.

747. Of these three Hindu converts, Maliq Kafur seems later on to have wholly turned a Muslim even mentally, completely forgetting his Hindu origin, the Hindu blood running through his veins, his Hindu parentage, let alone his love for all these! But Khushrukhan and this royal princess of Gujarat, Devaldevi, seem to have borne in their mind not only the memory, but a love, a fascination for their Hindu origin, their Hindu blood, and their essential Hindu make-up—there seems to be rankling in their hearts, intermittently or continuously, the atrocities inflicted on them by the Muslims. It seemed to burst out through their actions. At last, it is because of their irrespressible yearning to avenge the wrongs done to their 'Hindutwa' that in Delhi itself, broke out that great conflagration which like the wild fire of Khandav forest of Mahabharat, reduced to ashes the Muslim Sultanate which had under its sway practically the whole of India, if only for a short while!

748. In the very first expedition of Allauddin against Gujarat, after the Gujarat ruler's defeat, his crowned queen Kamaldevi fell into the hands of Allauddin while she was fleeing for safety. But the ruler, however, could effect his escape along with his princely daughter, Devaldevi, a mere child then. Used to all sorts of royal comforts and pleasures till the very previous day as she was, how hard and unbearable might this tender and beautiful royal princess have found it to undergo all the calamities and privations and exertions of wandering for days together through forest-after-forest, and trying to evade the ever present possibility of capture by the pursuing Muslims, might easily be imagined. In that tender age, hatred for the Muslims must have been engraved deeply on her bosom, because of other people's and her own actual experience. Her very mother, Rani Kamaldevi, had become the beloved queen of Sultan Allauddin at Delhi, and that very mother of hers was now out to seize her and make her a Muslim! How painful must this news have been to her tender heart! In order to evade this terrible fate, she was married, even a little against her father's wishes, to Ramdevrao's son, Shankardev, the staunch follower of Hinduism. But her evil star did not

leave her alone there. In one of the invasions of Maliq Kafur against the Hindus, she was caught and carried away to Delhi as a captive. She must have been smarting with pain and humiliation a hundred thousand times in that moment of despair! At last, on reaching Delhi, she was forced to marry Khijrakhan, the eldest son of Allauddin. Some writers vouch that Devaldevi and Khijrakhan greatly loved each other. But this seems to be the flattering way of the courtly writers. Her subsequent course of action makes it abundantly clear! But that shrewd Hindu princess seems to have affected her love for Islam and for her husband till she got the desired opportunity.

749. It becomes crystal clear from the latter part of her life that after all the atrocities and persecutions, she was constantly worshipping the Hindu god.

750. Even after being forced to marry Allauddin's eldest son, the mental agonies of Devaldevi did not cease. For, immediately after Allauddin's death, there was a revolution, in which Allauddin's second son, Mubarik, attacked and blinded his brother along with his followers and then put them to death. Installing himself as the Sultan, he seized his brother's wife, Devaldevi, and forced her to marry him.

751. This alone seems to be the civilized and polite tradition of the Muslim Sultans and Emperors to marry again the fairest of queens and wives of the late Sultans or Emperors, dead or put to death!

752. This way did the former Hindu princess, Devaldevi rise to the highest status of a Sultana! However, she abhorred Mubarik most bitterly, yet she had, per force, to keep marital relations with him. Although her precious body was thus continually defiled, she had the most favourite opportunity of her life owing to this marriage of hers with Mubarik.

753. In gaining the Sultanate of Delhi, Mubarik had mainly to depend on the former Hindu slave, who later on was forced to become a Muslim, and who now had become the commander-in-chief of the whole Sultanate of Delhi—namely Khushrukhan! Mubarik himself had willingly entrusted the whole administration to Khushrukhan, for he had no time to mind other things except every sort of depravity and vice. For instance, he was extremely fond of dressing like a woman, going to the greatest noblemen of the court with the whole band of dancing girls, and there dancing himself, or having dancing and musical concerts there. So, while this licentious Mubarik was fully engrossed with his various

vices, his chief minister of state, Khushrukhan, who had the burning memory of his former Hindu wife, and his present wife but the former Hindu princess, Devaldevi, who had similar thoughts and tendencies and similar mishaps in life as the former—both being Gujarati Hindus originally—had the greatest opportunity of coming into closest contact, of developing the strongest love-ties and the greatest confidence in each other. They could carry on the day-to-day political intrigues and plans authoritatively and with impunity, even to the solitude of the innermost secret chambers of the Sultan's private palace.

754. It has to be taken for granted from the latter course of events, that it is there, that they must have hatched some important conspiracy for the benefit of Hinduism.

755. The first proof that contributes to this assertion is that Khushrukhan appointed his former Hindu Paria or Parwar brother to the governorship of Gujarat, his native province.

756. The second very important pointer: Khushrukhan appointed openly in Delhi itself, for his own protection, thousands of his former Hindu warrior compatriots—at least twenty to thirty thousand strong—in the Muslim army.

757. The Third Pointer: These manoeuvres of his were highly resented to by many of the Muslim grandees. But the innormost intention behind them all was kept so very secret that, it is doubtful, whether, it had by that time, become so crystal clear to Devaldevi or even to Khushrukhan himself, let alone the others! Faintly and slowly, yet surely enough, was that intention taking shape in their minds.

758. The Fourth Pointer: Khushrukhan incited the most incapable Sultan like Mubarik to lead an expedition to the South to put down in good time, the rebellions of the conquered Hindus in the Deccan, and he himself accompanied him second-in-command. The Hindus were worsted a lot. Their immeasurable wealth, taken as spoils of war, filled the Sultan's treasury. Most probably, it was during this expedition, that after the death of Shankardev of Devgiri, his relative, King Harpaldev, rebelled and founded the kingdom of Devgiri once again, for which he was defeated and ordered by the Sultan to be skinned alive and then put to death! And for the defence of his religion, the royal Hindu warrior bore it bravely.

759. Thereafter, Mubarik returned with his army to Delhi. Because of these deeds of valour of his for the sake of a Muslim Sultan and

the Muslim state, and because of his devastation of the Hindus, his rival Muslim grandees, too, could not breathe a single word against his unshakable faith in the Islamic religion. They could at the most, only whisper that there was danger of his overthrowing Sultan Mubarik and become the Sultan himself in his stead. But that, he would be a Muslim Sultan and none else, there was not the least doubt.

760. But if at this very time that future conspiracy of a Hinduistic revolution, which was very strange and unheard of before, had germinated in the minds of Khushrukhan and Devaldevi, it must have been kept highly secret with utmost caution.

761. Very soon, Mubarik sent Khushrukhan to the Deccan for an extensive conquest but he himself did not go with him. So complete was his faith in Khushrukhan! In this expedition, Khushrukhan subdued the King of Malabar too, and exacted therefrom immeasurable plunder in the name of Sultan Mubarik!

But

762. But in this very campaign of South India, various open or secret Hindu conspiracies against the Muslim empire began to brew up from various quarters of the South Indian peninsula. The royal Hindu families of Varangal and Gujrath, the valiant Rana Hameer, the redeemer of Chitod, and other Hindu Chiefs, the religious leaders and propagandists in the various religious institutions and monasteries like those of the Shankaracharya and even the common people were becoming restless and agitated with a common antagonism to the Muslim domination. And anonymous complaints by Khushrukhan's enemies had reached the ears of the Sultan of Delhi to the effect that Khushrukhan was in some mysterious way and most secretly connected with this universal discontent!

763. So, scanty and self-contradictory bits of information are available in the writings of the contemporary Muslim writers about this Khushrukhan, the conqueror of Malabar, and the whole of the Muslim empire, that we have to correlate them into some sort of consistent account, only as far as it is possible from the later happenings! Once in the open court of the Sultan at Delhi there was a rumour, which apprehended that instead of coming back to Delhi amongst the ring of his adversaries, Khushrukhan was about to escape to some neighbouring foreign island by sea with the immense wealth he had amassed in

the South. One Muslim writer has gone to the length of saying that Khushrukhan was brought back to Delhi in fetters!

764. With an exceptional daring and ability to cut off the strings of the net of inimical conspiracies with one stroke, Khushrukhan at once declared his intention to go back to Delhi in the grand manner of the conqueror of the South with all his army. For, his secret accomplice, the former Hindu princess but now the Muslim empress, Devaldevi, must have been keeping him posted with every detail of the daily happenings at Delhi!

765. From the few English translations of the Muslim books of the time that are now available, even those who do not know either Persian or Arabic can have some information. Most of the Muslim writers mention Khushrukhan with utmost scorn and finish him within four or five lines only. The reason is plain enough. The Muslim historians can never bear with equanimity Khushrukhan's taking the conceit out of the Muslim rule at Delhi. Even these Muslim historians have found it at places improper to distort and garble up the truth about Khushrukhan or to suppress it altogether. Their manuscripts, especially the recently published ones, prove very useful in this respect. Even the account by the recent Hindu historians, who based their conclusions on the above mentioned old Muslim books, is to that extent useless. The Hindu writers have done nothing more than merely repeating the obloquies like 'mean-minded', 'shameless', 'dastardly', hurled at him by the Muslim writers. But there are two honourable exceptions to this general tendency: one is that of the veteran historian Riasatkar Sardesai and the other of Shree Munshi. These two historians, however, have given a comparative account of Khushrukhan and Devaldevi, too, and have attempted to appraise, though very faintly and cursorily, the great revolution they had finally effected to etablish a Hindu empire. But theirs is a half-hearted attempt, which fears its own conclusions, and which could never fully grasp nor could explain the real implications and nature of that unprecedented revolution. A contemporary Hindu writer, who could elucidate the Hindu side of this great event is, obviously enough, not to be found! For, no Hindu of the time could have been dared to express his own independent opinions or judgement.

766. Under these circumstances, it is only possible to give in the form of a connected narrative, the obvious conclusion that can be drawn from what little consistency can be found in the disconnected reports in the

above-mentioned original Muslim writings, and the actual undisputed acts of the leading personalities like Khushrukhan, Devaldevi and others.

767. As already told above, Khushrukhan went to Delhi with his victorious army and the immense spoils he had gathered in the Deccan, But why did he go there? Not only in Delhi but even in the Deccan a political rumour was secretly disseminated amongst the Hindu political circles that the Hindu leaders, who were organizing Hindu revolts in the south against the Muslims, were in collusion with Khushrukhan about some deep-laid conspiracy to disrupt the Muslim empire. In Gujarat, Khushrukhan's brother himself was the *de facto* ruler, while all the Rajputs were inspired by Rana Hameer to overthrow the India-wide unitary Muslim empire, the first of its kind, at least till that day. And most wonderful of all, was the fact that Sultan Mubarik's supreme commander and chief administrator, Khushrukhan himself, working as he was directly under Sultana Devaldevi's confidential orders, was taken in confidence by the Rajput leaders in respect of this daring plot to establish a Hindu empire! Such a rare concurrence of opposing forces is bound to astound history itself! Stand to reason, it never can, till at least something miraculous happens.

768. But something of the kind did begin to shape itself at the time. In the fiery brains of Sultana Devaldevi and Khushrukhan, there really was seething some such extraordinarily magnificent and by its very nature almost an incredible idea or plan, which seemed possible only to some mysterious intrigue and daring of a Nurshinh!

769. But neither their enemies nor their friends could breathe it openly! For with what magic wand was this supreme commander of Mubarik–the commander, who had brought all the Hindu states in the Deccan to meek submission before the Muslim Sultan-who had very recently devastated the wealthy Hindu kingdom of Malabar and hoisted there the green Muslim flag of the Delhi Sultanate—and who, above all, had come to Delhi to lay down all that success, all that glory, as an humble homage at the feet of the Muslim emperor—how was he, the sole supporter of the India-wide foreign and non-Hindu empire—he, who, born though he was as a Hindu, had become converted to Islam—how was a man of such a status likely to transform so suddenly the whole Muslim empire into a Hindu one? No staunch Muslim could even dare express it openly. Khushrukhan and Devaldevi had been keeping up till the last, the pretence of their being diehard Muslims and of their

greatest loyalty to the Muslim Sultan and his empire so scrupulously and thoroughly, that even their direst enemies who had dark suspicions of their having underground connections with the Hindu rulers, feared that were they personally to charge Khushrukhan before the Sultan in Delhi or in the open court, the Sultan would point out proofs to the contrary and outwit them forthwith. Even the top-level Muslim officials feared this eventuality. Whatever complaints had reached the general populace of Delhi of the ears of the Sultan himself were so baseless and completely anonymous, that nobody credited them with any more veracity or seriousness than they would do hearsay report or false accusations by some mischief-mongers!

770. As soon as he came to Dehli, Sultan Mubrarik did not put him under heavy fetters and custody, as his Muslim enemies had expected, but being extremely pleased with the immense treasure Khushrukhan had laid at his feet and the unlimited power he had gained for the Delhi Sultanate, Mubarik, on the contrary, conferred upon Khushrukhan the administrative, military, civic and all other residual authority. And if he had put anybody under arrest, it was the great Muslim noblemen and Khankhanas of the court, who were dismissed for charging Khushrukhan unreservedly.

770A. On the other hand, in the regime of Khushrukhan as the chief administrator, the strictest bans against the Hindu introduced by Allauddin in former days were now being gradually relaxed; the exploitation of the Hindu-Muslim farmers, and the people in general, also was stopped; the Hindus, too, got much relief in matters religious; the common discontent amongst the subjects against the tyrannical rule of the emperors was on the wane. And the whole credit of this comparatively happy state of things began to go very naturally to Khushrukhan, who was the chief of the imperial administration at that time. Gradually, by Sultan, the common people came to understand, not the vicious and good-for-nothing Mubarik, but his all-in-all, valiant and popular administrator, Khushrukhan, and behind him loomed the Sultana, Devaldevi, with whose internal and open support he could wield this authority.

771. The Hindu began to look upon Khushrukhan as their saviour; even though he was still a Muslim, because he had set them free to a great extent from the vexatious taxes and restrictions imposed on them by Allauddin and the untold humiliation they had to undergo.

Khushrukhan began to be popular amongst the Muslim farmers and other citizens, because of the relief they got from heavy taxes. And, above everything else, because of his military exploits, which had resounded throughout the whole of India and his superb adroitness in statecraft, many of the high-ranking Muslim noblemen had enlisted themselves on his side.

772. Seeing such a favourable opportunity, Khushrukhan and Devaldevi thought the right moment had come for them to proclaim boldly their grand scheme of a political revolution—for one who hesitates to undertake this hazard under favourable circumstances must be a coward, who would accomplish no daring feat! It was not merely a coup d'etat in a small state; it was an imperial revolution, which sought to subvert the India-wide unitary and danger-free Muslim empire of the late Allauddin and of the present Mubarik, and to establish in its place overnight, most unexpectedly, a Hindu empire all over India. It was a religious revolution inasmuch as it sought to pull down the enthroned Muslim religion and to supplant it by the Hindu Vedic religion.

773. That such a perfect revolution was most difficult—almost impossible—to be accomplished, even if Hindu-Muslim wars were to be fought continuously for five hundred years, was quite plain from the Arab invasions of Sindh in the seventh century and the later history of Muslim invasions, till the time of Allauddin. But such a complete revolution was in fact brought about by the exceptional genius of Khushrukhan and Devaldevi, even if it was only for a short while!

774. Had not the Muslim Sultanate conquered the Hindus completely by hard fighting for centuries together and turned their country wholly Muslim? Then if Khushrukhan were able to wrench the imperial authority from the single Sultan and if he were to ascend the throne of the Delhi Sultanate in the name of Hinduism, then the whole of the empire would necessarily be a 'Hindu' one, with one stroke! Then the Muslim Sultan would necessarily become a Hindu emperor. This feat was as daring in planning as it was easy in execution under those circumstances! It was quite possible too. It is this magic wand that Devaldevi, originally a Hindu princess, and Khushrukhan, the original Hindu Paria youth wielded, which worked as an unparalleled miracle not only in Indian but in the whole human history!

775. Having arranged every minute detail of the future revolution

most secretly, Khushrukhan humbly requested Sultan Mubarik, who had willingly allowed himself to be governed completely by the former: "The thousands of Hindus of my caste whom I have stationed in Delhi want to be converted to Islam with proper religious ceremony; but they are fighting shy of doing so openly in the city. Some of them are really afraid to do so. Hence, I wish to bring the choicest amongst them into the palace today and convert them in due course." Under this pretext, Khushrukhan brought the hundreds of his bravest Hindu warriors in Delhi into the palace and housed them in the barracks for the imperial guards. One day in A.D. 1319, at the dead of night, suddenly there was a great turmoil in the palace in the midst of which Sultan Mubarik was killed.

776. But many had been the tumults and turmoils, causing change of rulers before this. Sultan Allauddin himself, was similarly dispatched. Sultan Mubarik had dealt with Maliq Kafur in this very way. The city of Delhi, which was quite used to such turmoils, began to whisper the next morning: "What terrible things happened in the palace last night?"

777. Within a very short time, only a single proclamation of a political nature gave a violent shock, as that of an earthquake, to the whole capital and brought to it the rude realization that the previous night Khushrukhan's people had effected at one and the same time, an imperial and religious revolution by putting Sultan Mubarik to death, and it was immediately followed by another that Khushrukhan had installed himself as a Sultan!

778. However, there was nowhere to be seen any immediate, open and organized opposition amongst the people to this unprecedented revolution. The fact that the new Sultan Khushrukhan married Sultana Devaldevi, the queen of Mubarik, as soon as the latter was killed, stirred the revolutionary curiosity of the people but did not overawe them!

For, that was the age-old tradition of the earlier Sultans! Kutubuddin's widows were married to the latter Sultans who succeeded him, while Allauddin's and his son's, Khijrakhan's widow, this very Devaldevi, was espoused by Mubarik himself. Quite consistent with this time-honoured tradition was this act of Khushrukhan of marrying Devaldevi, the widow of the late Sultan Mubarik, with whom he had established very close contacts much earlier and who was really his partner and perhaps a source of inspiration! Why should it not then seem quite natural to everybody in the state?

But...!

779. But more startling than this was another proclamation made authoritatively and with every political formality by Khushrukhan and Devaldevi, which suddenly turned this political revolution in the royal palace into a religious one of a unique nature. Everybody in India right from the Kings and Nawabs to the Parias and Parwars, Mahars and Mangs was thrilled with a strange sensation at this unique proclamation! The Hindus were thrilled with unlimited joy while the Muslims were filled with the darkest apprehensions. The said proclamation made by Sultan Khushrukhan himself from his throne on the 15th April, 1320 meant to say:

780. "Although till today I was forced to lead the most detestable life of a convert to Islam, I am originally a son of a Hindu. The mainspring of my life is Hinduism and the blood that throbs into my veins and arteries is that of a Hindu. Now that I have won independent and powerful status of a Sultan for myself, I am hereby breaking off the shackles of conversion to a foreign religion, and I do hereby declare that I am a Hindu! I have now ascended publicly the throne of the vast and entire, undivided India as a Hindu Emperor! Similarly, Sultana Devaldevi till very recently was originaly a Hindu daughter. Her husband, the Raja of Devgiri, Shankardev Yadav, was most brutally murdered and she was treacherously captured from her father sneaking miserably through dense forest to avoid seizure by the enemy. She was brought to Delhi and put to shame and ignominous disgrace by being forced to marry Khijrakhan, in the first place, and secondly after his brutal murder, Sultan Mubarik, who was killed in the coup d'etat last night. That Devaldevi is my queen, the empress of Hindusthan of today! Being originally Hindu in flesh and blood and a Hindu royal princess, she also hereafter re..ounces disdainfully her shameful conversion to Islam and henceforth will lead her life strictly according to Hindu religion! May this solemn vow of ours absolve us both of our former sin of forceful conversion!"

781. To refute or to challenge a proclamation of this nature came forth no stronger Hindu, nor even a single Muslim!

782. Hence, hereafter, we are going to address Sultan Khushrukhan as a Hindu Emperor and Devaldevi as a Hindu Empress!

783. This Hindu Emperor did not, however, disclose his original Hindu name of his young years! Most probably, he had no recollection of

it whatsoever; today it is eternally lost. The imperial title that he adopted for himself was also a Muslim one, viz., Nasir-ud-din! The reason for this, perhaps, was that the whole of the Muslim world and even the millions of Hindus who were used to Muslim titles for generations together, might not be scandalized in respect of these minor details also. Nasir-ud-din, roughly speaking, means a sort of a defender of faith or religion! Hence, this Hindu Emperor made it clear in the said proclamation that 'Din' or religion that he was going to defend was not Islam! Naturally, it must be the Hindu religion! It is, therefore, proper that his name Nasir-ud-din should be translated as the Defender of Hindu Religion—Hindu dharmarakshak!

The Unprecedented Revolution!

784. As soon as this unheard of revolution, transforming the India-wide Muslim Empire into the Hindu one, suddenly within a day, was accomplished, this Hindu Emperor disbursed amongst the thousands of soldiers of his caste, the immense wealth, which he had pillaged in his conquest of Malabar by vanquishing the Hindu states and which had filled the coffers of the late Sultan Mubarik, along with the unlimited wealth accumulated during the regimes of the former Sultans. Similarly, he increased the pay-scale of both the Hindu and Muslim soldiers. Having won over his soldiery in this way, he introduced new reforms, gave to the farmers and common Hindu-Muslim citizens facilities, and allowed them concessions they were never allowed to enjoy by any of the former Sultans! Likewise, he set free thousands of Hindu prisoners who were interned as a diversion in religious persecution and the hundreds of Muslims, who were imprisoned simply because they were repugnant to the former Sultans for one reason or another. No wonder if this Hindu Emperor, Dharmarakshak, immediately became popular amongst the Hindus as well as the Muslims throughout his empire!

785. It is needless to say that he also absolved all the Hindus of all the humiliating bans on their pilgrimages and holy baths. The Jizia tax was repealed and other degrading conditions that had been enforced upon them by Sultan after Sultan were ameliorated forthwith. What wonder then if the whole Hindu world felt a thrill of joy and freedom that at long last, they had a saviour!

786. Even when this Hindu Samrat was fighting in the guise of a converted Muslim, victoriously in the South and reducing Malabar, he

had been formulating the scheme of the future revolution. So, all the big Hindu-Muslim officers and generals in the fighting forces, who depended on his patronage and who had risen mainly because of his support, of course, remained loyal to him for safeguarding their own selfish interests and also for protecting themselves from the malice and enmity of the old Muslim Khans, Nizams, and other co-religionists of theirs. For, as a natural consequence of intermingling of the two religious communities, Muslims serving in the armies of many Hindu States had come to form a habit of rendering loyal service to their Hindu masters! The political service of a Hindu King was taboo formerly when the Muslims first came to India, but by this time, the taboo had lost its intensity and in its stead such a loyal service rendered to a Hindu master came to be considered quite in conformity with the Muslim religious code! Many incidents illustrating this point have already occurred so far, and will occur in the following pages too. Although acceptance of any high office under a Hindu ruler was no more considered contrary to the Muslim religious law, the staunch moulanas and moulavis, however, looked upon such acts as necessary exceptions and bore a secret grudge in their hearts that they were time bombs laid under the Muslim political power! Never from the very beginning, did the Hindus consider it contrary to their religious code to fight in the Muslim army on the side of the Muslims! It was only the exchange of food and women in marriage with the Muslims which endangered the sanctity of their religion! How foolish and suicidal to think so!

786A. This Hindu Emperor did not rest with the mere declaration of his adherence to Hinduism, but he fearlessly began to bring it into action in the presence of the Muslims. Idols of Hindu gods and goddesses were immediately installed in the holiest of places of Muslim civilization, the Diwan-i-Aam and Diwan-i-Khas in the royal palaces of Delhi. All the worships and all the religious rites in royal palaces began to be performed according to the Hindu ritual. Loud chanting of Hindu mantras and singing of Hindu devotional songs took the place of the 'Ayats' in the Koran! This Hindu Emperor himself and the hundreds amongst his old Hindu battalions, who had remained Hindus from the beginning and who were guarding the royal palace, paid scrupulous attention to the protection and proper worship of these new idols of Hindu gods and goddesses. The enthusiasm and vigour of the Hindu citizens and especially of the Hindu soldiers in the capital knew no bounds! Just as formerly the aggressive Muslims completely demolished the godly idols in the Hindu temples and turned them into Muslim masjids immediately after they conquered any Hindu capital, so did these counter-revolutionary Hindus install new images of their gods in every masjid as a retaliatory measure, and most ceremoniously converted the masjids into Hindu temples and filled them with loud chanting of mantras. It is only by this counter-attack of the Hindu Parias that the fanatic Muslims could ever have had any idea of the pangs of humiliation and grief that might have rankled in the hearts of the Hindu community, which had grown feeble because of their malady of religious tolerance, when the Muslims polluted the Hindu temples by cow-slaughter and turned them into masjids.

787. It might be true that in the heat and excitement of this unheard of and unprecedented religious revolution, the Muslim scriptures, some Muslim writers charge, might have been exposed to ridicule or shame. But at least the Muslims, who considered to be Gazis, those scoundrels, who destroyed the whole university of Nalanda in flames and sat warming themselves at that bonfire and laughed scornfully and shamelessly as the valuable religious books of the Hindus were being reduced to ashes, had no moral right whatsoever to blame this incendiarism against the Muslim religion!

787A. This Hindu Samrat converted with their willing consent the young wives, daughters and nieces of the earlier Sultans and other Muslim women to Hinduism and married them to his Hindu Paria followers.

788-789. But more than this, this Hindu Dharmarakshak did not do!

Even the Muslim historians do not mention any atrocities or religious persecution or plunder as having been committed by this Hindu Emperor as the Muslim aggressors were wont to do after overpowering any Hindu State. As against the wholesale forcible conversion of the Hindus, the brutal ravaging of Hindu women, the reckless destruction of Hindu property and temples, the Muslim historians have no grievous crime to attribute (impute) to this Hindu Emperor! Even if he had committed the very same atrocities on the Muslim community as a revenge against the Muslim diabolism towards the hapless Hindus, it would have been not a bit derogatory, but all the more glorious for this revolutionary Hindu Emperor! The non-Hindu aggressors would have taken the fright of their lives as never before, and it would have proved a deterrent to their perfidious activities! We have already made it amply clear that it is only the fierce retaliation that destroys atrocity, root and branch!

790. But the main reason why this Defender of Faith (Dharamarakshak Nasir-ud-din) did not commit any such revengeful atrocities on the Muslims must probably be his keen sense of the strength and weakness of his side. Were the whole of the Hindu community in the Indian sub-continent and the ruling Hindu kings of the time to lend him their immediate and active support—had his example in Delhi of reconverting to Hinduism the converted Muslims at their own free will, of turning masjids into Hindu temples and of other revolutionary activities of his, been copied in various towns and cities of India from Rajputana to Southern capitals—and had the Hindus risen openly against the Muslims and if the proclamation of the success of Hinduism were published openly, this Hindu Emperor would have persecuted the Muslims as were the Hindus actually before them and would have also launched a special military offensive against the Muslims and would have made it impossible for them to live as Muslims!

791. But the Hindu kings and Hindu people in general did not openly support this Hindu political revolution. They were, however, inwardly proud of it and overjoyed at it. They did appreciate this utter humiliation and ruination of the Muslim Sultanate at the hands of this Hindu Dharmarakshak 'Nasir-ud-din'. The Hindu kings and the Hindu society at large nevertheless refrained from attempting any open revolt. The one reason why the Hindu Society failed to attempt the establishment of a Hindu Empire at this most opportune moment, was that the Hindus harboured serious doubts whether this undreamt of revolution would succeed. If that revolution were to fail, they feared, the followers would never escape complete annihilation. So, the Hindu community only waited. Secondly, the entire Hindu society never approved of the mass conversion of Muslims to Hinduism that was effected in and around Delhi as a sound religious practice! The Hindu Dharma of the day meant ban on reconversion, not reconversion! Religious tolerance had been their religion because of their perverted sense of values; their religion never brooked either the demolishing of masjids or converting the Muslims to Hinduism. This sort of reactionary measure was considered by the Hindus to be the greatest sin! So, who could have predicted that the Hindu society itself would not oppose

tooth and nail this religious revolution? That possibility could not be ruled out altogether! Muslim opposition to this revolutionary change, however, in the imperial government and religion was quite natural.

792. Under these circumstances, Dharmarakshak (Nasir-ud-din) refrained from any further atrocities or revenge upon the Muslims in Delhi or elsewhere in the empire, considering that his religious and political revolution in Delhi was in itself so daring as to put the Muslim power to shame, and so he was satisfied that the Hindu society had now become strong enough to relish and digest such a revolution! And this was not a small achievement! The next step could be deferred to a later date! The next favourable opportunity would most certainly be availed of. He did not, therefore, think it wise to stretch things too far so as to cause a complete break.

793. On the other hand, as had already been told (in Paragraph 784), he allowed the Muslim soldiers and peasants and civilians equal rights to the new facilities and exemption from taxes, which he did in the case of Hindus. Moreover, he kept on sending extremely valuable presents to those Muslim officers and Mullah-Maulvis, whom he suspected to be secretly despising this religious revolution of the Hindus and the Hindu Empire, as often as he sent them to those Muslim officers, who were loyal to him and with a extremely polite treatment, kept them under his obligation.

794. It is because of this exceptional skill of his at diplomacy that even after the successful realization of this religio-political revolution of the Hindus, immediately or for months together thereafter, there was not a single Muslim revolt—no riots nor brawls—throughout the length and breadth of his vast empire. His whole administration was working as smoothly as it did in the days of the old Muslim Sultans. Revenues, taxes or ransoms were collected from all provinces and remitted to the imperial treasury at Delhi without any default. In Delhi itself, the greatest of Muslim knights and feudatory princes, generals and sardars and other courtiers and officers attended the imperial court on the orders of this Hindu Dharmarakshak and took their appointed seats. Of the great Muslim noblemen reported by the historians of the time to be attending the court of this Hindu emperor, Nasir-ud-din, some may be mentioned here: they were Ain-ul-Mulk Multani, Yusuf Safi, Hatim Khan, Kamaluddin Sufi, Faruk-did an-Tughlak, Mulgati, Mohammed Shah, Baharam Anayya, Yuklakhi, Hoshang, Kaphur Saheb. Because

of the presence of these big shots in the Hindu court of Nasir-ud-din and because of written letters promising allegiance to the emperor from governors, and administrators and Muslim officers in the army, peace throughout the whole of India was never broken for months together.

795. On the other hand, the Hindu kings from Rajputana to Madurai did not protest, perhaps according to some previous secret pact, against the revolution effected by this Hindu emperor. Why, availing themselves fully of this military coup in Delhi, they began to rule the Hindu States independently as before. Their chief fault was that at this greatest and rarest of opportunities, they did not make a well-organized effort to proclaim the independence of the Hindus and establish a united strong central imperial power at Delhi.

796. Under the circumstances, the shrewd 'Dharmarakshak' (Nasir-ud-din) well knew that although at first his Hindu administration was running smoothly, his revolutionary Hindu empire depended on no other thing than his armed might. He, therefore, kept the thousands of his choicest of Hindu soldiers stationed in the capital in all readiness! At every vital centre of defence in his empire, he drafted his most faithful Hindu battalions and also the Muslim troops, which had sworn loyalty towards him. For, he knew perfectly well that although the Muslims everywhere in his empire obeyed him implicitly and swore alligance to him, sooner or later some rebellious faction amongst them was bound to organize itself and stage a counter-revolution against his pro-Hindu authority!

797. Want of space obliges us to skip over many intervening events. Suffice it to say that the imperial administration, which nobody could have expected to work smoothly even for a day, ran most efficiently, not for a day, nor a month, but for nearly a year, overthrowing the Muslim domination and turning the very same Muslim 'Takhta' (throne) which means a 'Sinhasan' of a Hindu emperor, and replacing the green Muslim Chand, which had been flaunting almost over the whole of India by the victorious Hindu flag. Millions of Muslims, rich or poor, liege or serf, throughout the whole of India, accepted without a murmur the overlordship (sovereignty) of the Hindu empire. For, at least a year, the great Muslim governors and officers obeyed implicitly the orders of this Hindu emperor and made the common Muslim community do likewise. This itself was a great wonder that glorifies the Hindu history of the times.

798. And another equally great wonder, which condemns the Hindus of the time and those of later times also, is that in the histories written of the Hindu people and by the Hindu people no major reference, let alone grateful reference is made either to this Hindu imperial and religious revolution and to its architect and engineer Dharmarakshak, (Nasir-ud-din)! Whatever few words are written about him are full of censure and ridicule for him and for his acts, in strict pursuance of the Muslim historical writings!

Ghyasuddin Tughlak

799. But before this year of amazement elapsed, one or two top-ranking Muslims ventured to hatch a conspiracy to overthrow the yoke of this Hindu Emperor. Secret provocative pamphlets were being circulated and bigoted moulavis were already instigating sedition secretly in their masjids, that it was a grave insult to the whole Muslim world that the Muslim imperial throne should be turned into a Hindu one, and that the Muslims should be forced to bow down meekly before a 'kafir', and finally, that it was highly essential for the Muslims to go on a crusade against the Hindu sovereignty in order to end the utter degradation of Islam. But no Muslim 'amir', nor military chief, nor any superior officer offered to lead the insurrection. Ultimately, the administrator and governor of Punjab under the Sultan of Delhi, by name Ghyasuddin, aspired to shoulder that responsibility. He began sending secret emissaries and epistles to that effect to various higher Muslim authorities under Sultan Nasir-ud-din. Ghyasuddin himself had sworn allegiance to the Sultan and was appointed military Governor of Punjab, while one of his sons was an officer at Delhi itself under the direct control of this 'Hinduised Sultan'. Ghyasuddin called this son of his for a private visit under some pretext, and gathered every sort of minute detail about the situation in Delhi in his private interview with that son. Whereupon he came to know for certain that after the murder of Allauddin, his sons and relatives were either killed or deprived of their eyesight and thus rendered useless. When he was thus satisfied that there was no proper heir of Allauddin's for the Sultanate at Delhi, he was all the more elated to declare boldly, that as there was no proper heir left from the house of Allauddin's, it was only some powerful Muslim who could lay claim to the throne at Delhi. That kafir Hindu Paria was not to be suffered to touch it even. That kafir had married all the widows of all the earlier sultans and the

young Muslim girls and maidens from the royal palace to the Parias (sweepers), whom he had formerly raised to eminence, and converted all those ladies of the Muslim royal families to Hinduism. As no Muslim dared to dethrone such a sinful Hindu kafir, he himself was going to shoulder the responsibility.

800. For the first time, these secret letters of his were turned down with spite by the top Muslim officers, while some others placed them into the hands of Dharmarakshak Nasir-ud-din himself, who having already apprehended such an eventuality and undaunted by it, calmly prepared himself to crush this rising of Ghyasuddin immediately. Good many Muslim generals, who had acknowledged him as a Sultan, enlisted their forces in his service while the Hindu section of that imperial army was always ready to fight at the cost of their lives under his standard.

801. At last, depending chiefly on the Muslim battalions, which were employed under his command for the protection of Punjab and the frontiers, Ghyasuddin decided to march upon Delhi. Some Hindu soldiers, too, were amongst those advancing Muslim forces. No sooner did he hear that Ghyasuddin was marching towards Delhi than the Hindu Emperor—Dharmarakshak Nasir-ud-din himself—attacked him with his whole imperial army. Along with this Hindu Emperor, marched the great Muslim generals, too, with their battalions to fight under his command. When the two armies met on the first day, the imperial army of Sultan Nasir-ud-din won the field, and Ghyasuddin had to retreat. But the latter did not lose heart. Knowing that depression of heart at this time meant utter ruin, and that success depended briefly on enterprise and intrepidity, Ghyasuddin rearranged his ranks and made ready for another battle. Fortunately for Ghyasuddin, on that very day, one or two Muslim chieftains in the Sultan's armies conspired to betray the Hindu Emperor Nasir-ud-din and let the former know of their decision most secretly. Encouraged by this, Ghyasuddin himself fell upon the forces of Sultan Nasir-ud-din (Hindu Samrat, Shree Dharmarakshak). In the melee that ensued, the betrayal by the Muslim forces brought about the utter defeat of Sultan Nasir-ud-din. So the Sultan—Shree Dharmarakshak—left the field and started for Delhi. But mad with victory, Ghyasuddin marched straight towards Delhi, and in that hot pursuit, Shree Dharmarakhak—Sultan Nasir-ud-din—fell helpless in the hands of the enemy.

802. When the victor, Ghyasuddin, ordered the captive Sultan, Nasir-

ud-din, to be brought before him and charging him with the murder of Mubarik and decided to sentence him to death, he asked the captive the last question: "Setting aside the question of political expediency or the bid for the throne of the Sultan and considering only the personal aspect of this act of yours, what personal wrong did Mubarik do to you, that you might seek to avenge it by his death? To this, the captive Nasir-ud-din (Khushrukhan) replied to this effect: "Of course! He was guilty of a such personal wrong to me! For the most heinous crime of inflicting homosexual and other unbearable atrocities that this mean and vicious Mubarik had perpetrated on my body ever since my tender age and for the humiliation that he had heaped upon my life. I had long vowed most solemnly that at the earliest opportunity, I would avenge all those personal wrongs upon that villain with murder!"

803. Thereupon, Ghyasuddin dispatched him instantaneously.

804. That was the tragic end of Shree Dharmarakshak (Nasir-ud-din). But the last of the accredited Hindu Emperor of Delhi, the valiant Prithviraj Chouhan, was also equally tragically murdered by the Muslims after his utter rout in the last battle!

805. And the dountless Shree Guru Banda of Punjab! After inflicting several crushing defeats upon the Muslims, when at last he fell into the hands of the Muslim monarch, was he not locked up in a cage like a wild beast? Didn't red-hot iron pikes and pincers pierce his body and pull out large pieces of his flesh and was he not after so much torture, put to cruel death by the Muslims?

806. But is any thoroughbread Hindu likely to forget the gratitude that we all owe to those various Hindu gallant warriors for their glorious martyrdom in the cause of Hinduism, simply because they were defeated in the end? It is this grateful memory of such martyrs that becomes the perennial source of inspiration for the nation for ages after ages!

807. O You! Hindu Samrat 'Shree Dharmarakshak! This martyrdom of yours, too, has become a freshwater spring of inspiration for the Hindu nation! It is to atone for the sin of failing to utter a single grateful word for you, to preserve some souvenir, some memento of yours, that the Hindus of your own times or those of the later generations have committed, and it is again in expiation of the sin of our Hindu ingratitude towards you, that we have most reverently offered you this separate chapter in this book.

808. Had you but chosen to remain a Muslim Sultan, you could

easily have perpetuated the Sultanate of the whole of India down to your descendants, generations after generations, as it happened in the case of the Khiljee or Slave dynasties after Allauddin or Ghyasuddin. But with glowing respect and pride for the Hindu religion and the Hindu nation, you purified the very Muslim Title of Sultan, turned the Muslim, 'Takhta' into a Hindu 'Sinhasan', and slighting the Muslim Sultanate, proclaimed yourself Hindu Samrat (Emperor)!

809. After Emperor Prithviraj Chauhan, it was you alone who made a gallant bid to occupy the imperial throne of Delhi as a Hindu Emperor! In spite of your birth in an humble and miserable Hindu family; in spite of your being defiled and converted to Islam and made an abject slave by your Muslim enemies at your tender age, you became the Sultan of Sultans by the dint of your valour, your versatility, your military exploits, your arch-diplomacy and your adroitness in engineering deep-laid plots, and made the whole of India resound with the glory of Hinduism! We have done our duty to relate with proofs, your (in a way) peculiar life to the Hindu Nation and the world at large, so far as it is possible for us to do so.

The Peculiar Character of this Hindu Revolution!

810. Although in this millenial Hindu-Muslim war, the Hindu Nation had been fighting on the political and military fronts more or less on equal grounds, using effective counter-offensive and tactics and ultimately overpowering the Muslim sovereignty, it was incessantly overwhelmed on the religious front, because of their own hateful bans on re-conversion and the like—fetters, which prevented the Hindus from opening any counter-offensive on the Muslim religion as such! But, this Hindu Emperor, Shree Dharmarakshak (Nasir-ud-din), successfully launched a counter-attack upon the Muslims, both on political and military as well as on the religious fronts, using the same means and weapons. To counter-balance the forceful conversion of the Hindus by the Muslims, Shree Dharmarakshak (Nasir-ud-din) brought about hundreds of Muslim reconversions to Hinduism and their republication ceremonies under the protection of his armed might.

Just as the Muslim used to rush headlong to ravage and convert the Hindu women to Islam, in the same way, the Hindus broke into the harems of the Muslim Sultan and converted the willing Mohamedan women to Hinduism and married them to their Hindu followers. If the Muslims demolished the Hindu temples, Shree Dharmarakshak, in the excitement of this victory, turned the very Muslim Masjids into Hindu temples. It was this Dharmarakshak (Nasir-ud-din) who, for the first time in Hindu history, showed so very successfully and on such a large scale, how the Muslim armed aggression upon Hinduism and the religious persecution that they perpetrated before and after, could be retaliated and how the Muslims could be routed completely on the religious front too. If from the beginning, the Muslims had to face such bold opposition and been forced to suffer such powerful counterstrokes on the religious front, they would never have dared to strike, in spite of all their military might at Hinduism. This first blow, which the Hindus delivered to Islam in Delhi, shook the Muslims so very severely! And this is the peculiar character of this Hinduistic revolution brought about by Shree Dharmarakshak (Khushrukhan Nasir-ud-din).

811. We have intentionally called this account of Khushrukhan's life and achievements as based on proofs! Although, as we have pointed out in Paragraph 744, nobody barring some honourable exception, has written any good word about you, O Khushrukhan, the very inconsistent and confused and oblique reference to you, tell a story which is all the more glorious for you! As such, although your life and career as painted by us too has so far not any 'written' or 'oral' 'basis' or any strong proofs, even then there is another equally strong and unimpeachable legal evidence, which, at times, sets aside even written or oral ones, in such historical and judicial matters of daily occurrence. That evidence is called circumstantial evidence!

The Authority of Circumstantial Evidence

812. In the science of logic the authority of circumstantial evidence is considered, at least in certain cases, to be the better mode of reasoning than inference, the word of the elders, or illustration. Especially, when the intentions and feelings or emotions of the engineers of deep-laid political conspiracies and plots are to be ascertained, circumstantial evidence is considered to be the only strong basis for it and it should be thought so, and rightly too! The written confession of the accused under their own signature can be refuted by the circumstantial evidence of bodily persecution and torture; so does written evidence!

813. Your life, O Dharmarakshak, therefore, has been based more on the strictly logical circumstantial evidence than on your own words

or the writings of your contemporary and later day historians, hence it is based on solid proof. Even if your words are not available, your very act and deeds are in themselves far more telling.

814. The brother of this Shree Dharmarakshak (Nasir-ud-din) was himself a very great warrior and an able administrator. The original Hindu name of this brother of Shree Dharmarakshak is also not known as yet, for in his very early childhood, he too was converted and made a slave. When this Hindu Emperor appointed him the Governor of Gujarat, he openly accepted Hinduism and canvassed for it. In order to overthrow the Muslim government in Gujarat, he raised a Hindu revolt and sent twenty to twentyfive thousand brave warriors of his parwar (community) to help his brother at Delhi. What ultimately became of them all is not known to history. He too deserves place of honour in Hindu history.

815. And on the same basis of this circumstantial evidence, does that former Hindu royal princess and the Yadav Queen, Devaldevi, who was equally responsible for bringing about the unprecedented Hindu revolution of Shree Dharmarakshak (Nasir-ud-din) and who was his important accomplice in the secret plot, and who became, after the successful accomplishment of the said revolution, the Hindu Empress of Shree Dharmarakshak, deserves even a greater place of honour, like that of Devi Padmini of Chitod, for the unimaginable mental agonies that she had to suffer in the most adverse circumstances! She deserves the honour of a brave warrior Rajput Princess, burning herself on the pyre or in Johar!

816. Her end, too, is clouded in mystery! One of the writers of the time has said that she was provided for Ghyasuddin after he became the Sultan of Delhi.

Not a Fruitless Martyrdom!

817. Thus were the two valiant associates of the Hindu Emperor, Dharmarakshak (Nasir-ud-din) forced to court martyrdom! But their martyrdom lent a wonderful strength to the morale of the Hindu Nation. For, the fact that in Delhi itself, was established a Hindu Empire, which could powerfully and effectively govern the Muslim States, Nawabs, and Muslim populace throughout India for nearly a year, helped the Hindu kings and the Hindu people to shake off the dominant influence of the Muslim political superiority, which had for centuries overawed the Hindu

mind. The myth of this Muslim political superiority as at once exploded and a rare confidence was inspired amongst the Hindus that, were they but to run a little risk, they would also be able to crush the Muslim political hold on them. Shree Dharmarakshak courted martyrdom in 1321; it was soon followed by the risings in Hindu States in the north and south of India. The Muslim provinces round about Delhi, too, began fighting with the Muslim imperial power at Delhi in order to establish their own dynasties in their own provinces. In the end, hardly within fifteen to sixteen years of the martyrdom of Shree Dharmarakshak, the Muslim imperial authority at Delhi became extremely weak, and a powerful Hindu revolt culminated in the establishment of a completely independent Hindu Kingdom of Vijayanagar, the detailed account of which must necessarily be deferred to next chapter.

□

18
The Beginning of the Final Overthrow of the Muslim Empire

818. Soon after slaying Shree Dharmarakshak (Nasir-ud-din), Ghyasuddin Tughlak ascended the throne of the Delhi Sultanate in A.D. 1321 and issued a proclamation to that effect. This was the end of the Khilji dynasty and the beginning of the Tughlak rule.

819. Ghyasuddin too was old. Naturally, he treated the Muslims leniently. But although born of a Hindu jat mother, he strangely enough did not fall short of any type of religious persecution of the Hindus perpetrated by any or all of the former Muslim Sultans!

820. Ghyasuddin died in A.D. 1326 and was succeeded by his son Mohammed Tughlak, who has gone down in history as 'crazy'. He once had a strange whim of shifting his capital from Delhi to Devgiri in the south. Immediately, he changed the name of Devgiri, according to the Muslim tradition, into Doulatabad, just as Warangal had been changed earlier by the Muslim into Sultanpur. But this change of capital from Delhi to Devgiri caused him and his subjects so much trouble, disrupted his already confusion-fraught revenue system so completely, and so many insurrections and political risings were brewing in the royal families and the people at large in the Deccan (as already pointed out in the previous chapter) that this 'crazy' Mohammed was ultimately forced to have another whim of shifting the capital once again back to Delhi. But this short interlude cost millions (crores) of rupees and thousands of lives.

820A. With a view to getting out of this financial trouble, he introduced the copper coins, which drained his treasury completely; but he blamed the farmers and the other gentry for it, saying that they did not pay the taxes. He, therefore, issued orders to his fighting forces to collect the revenue under compulsion, but while the Muslims were shown all leniency in the collection of taxes, the Hindus were most cruelly forced to pay them. Just as the beasts are surrounded on all sides in a hunting expedition and are held at bay and then massacred, similarly a number of Hindu towns and villages were besieged and the Hindu population therein was mercilessly put to the sword. (This sort of persecution devastated numerous Hindu towns and villages, while whole province like Kanouj were rendered desolate!)

821. Nevertheless, there darted from the bow of the Hindu nation a Ram-ban [an arrow of Ram—an (unerring) unmistakable shot!], which put a stop, even if temporarily, to the Ravan-like atrocities by the Muslims perpetrated under every Sultan over the Hindus for centuries together!

822. The diabolic Muslim ambition to spread the unitary Muslim empire to the ends of Hindusthan (Paragraphs 636-737) received a death blow in the very hour of its fruition. For (as it is shown in the previous chapter) with the first vigorous blow struck by the Hindu Emperor, Shree Dharmarakshak, the extensive Muslim Empire had already begun to dwindle, while the Hindu discontent, especially in the Deccan, culminated into a powerful insurrection, which shattered the already dwindling Muslim empire into small fragments.

New Hindu State

823. For, in A.D. 1336, was established the new, independent, and powerful Hindu State of Vijaynagar, defying the Muslim might in the very lifetime of this 'crazy' Mohammad Tughlak, a detailed account of which will be given in the next chapter.

824. Immediately after this momentous event, the Deccanese Muslims under Hasan Bahamani rose in rebellion against the Delhi Sultanate following the age-old separatist tendency of the Muslims, which had been exhibited in their fratricidal wars ever since the times of Mohammad Paigambar. Hasan Bahamani was crowned with success in this attempt, and so he founded the Bahamani kingdom in A.D. 1347 and proclaimed himself to be an independent Sultan.

825. This act of Hasan Bahamani will explode the popular misconception of the millions of credulous gulls amongst the Hindus, that the Muslims always showed a united front in their political as well as religious wars, that they never fought amongst themselves and that they had no separatist tendencies—a baseless misconception, which is

not only foolish in the extreme but which falsely extols the foreigners and undeservedly runs down our own Hindu community. A number of such instances have already been cited in this volume and many more will occur in the pages that follow. The history of the Muslim community all over world is replete with such instances.

A Grievous fall and Breaking of the Dream of an Unbroken Muslim Empire

826. Just as perhaps some adventurous mountaineer should, in the excitement of his almost impracticable ambition to scale the highest peak of the Himalayas and to hoist his national flag there before anybody else does it, climb on and on, and after reaching some altogether different peak should victoriously cry out, 'This is the very same highest peak!' when all at once, the seemingly highest peak should give way under the heavy load of his ambition, being made as it really is, not of any solid rock, but of a frozen heap of snowflakes, and the ambitious climber should topple down and fall headlong from crag to crag into the deep ravine of destruction along with the bits and fragments of his signal victory—in the very same way, the Muslim ambition to establish the centralized paramount Muslim power over the whole of India was beguiled for a while, and ultimately came to naught. All the Asian Muslim States right from the Arabs to the Mongols invaded India one after another and carried on for seven or eight centuries continuously the bitterest, bloodiest and cruellest wars and at last, when in the regime of Allauddin, practically the whole of India passed under the Muslim sway round about the year A.D. 1310, the Muslim ambition seemed to be almost fulfilled! But, as it is already told, with a hard knock from the resurgent Hindu valour, the Muslim rule collapsed from the highest peak of success attained by Sultan Allauddin and was shattered to pieces within only seven or eight years, never to rise to that giddy height again! The Hindu might went on increasing like the crescent moon!

Death of 'Crazy' Mohammad and after

827. This 'crazy' Sultan Mohammad died in A.D. 1351 and his tottering crown with the disintegrating Sultanate of Delhi passed on to his cousin 'Pherozshah Tughlak'. This Pherozshah's mother was the daughter of the Rajput King Malbhatti of Deepalpur. When Pherozshah's

father demanded her (that Rajput Princess) in marriage, King Malbhatti flatly refused to give her up, whereupon Pherozshah's father marched on Malbhatti and began to persecute the Hindus most cruelly. The princess could not bear the inhuman sufferings of her father and her Hindu brethren in the kingdom. So, she volunteered to marry Pherozshah's father. However praiseworthy the tenderness of her heart might be, it has permanently stained her father's family. Had she swallowed fire like some Padmini of Chitod and followed the path of martyrdom for the sake of religion, her life and her family tradition would both have been for ever glorified!

The Superstitious Muslims!

828. An anecdote of this time of the Tughlaks, which is recorded in history, may be related here so that the reader might have some idea of the extent the superstitious nature of the Muslims could go to, and of the influence the religious credulity and fanaticism of the Arabs invariably had over the Muslims of later days, ever since the inception of Muslim religion.

828A. In order to atone for the crazy religious acts and the harassment of the subjects by the 'mad' Mohammad (setting aside the religious persecution of Hindus, which was deemed harmonious with the tenets of the Muslim religion), Sultan Pherozshah interned with the bones of the late 'mad' Mohammad, the original papers regarding the reimbursement of the unjust land revenue collected by him, refund of fines and compensation for the other unjust acts of his, or their governmental acknowledgments along with other original papers signed by Mohammed himself. This action of Pherozshah was perhaps prompted by his credulous belief, that on the strength of this written record of the compensation for all his crimes, the great Allah would forgive Mohammad on the last day of the judgment! And, be it remembered that Pherozshah was well-educated, according to the standards of the time! What to say, then, of the common people!

829. Although in the beginning, Pherozshah proclaimed himself as the Sultan of Hindusthan, everywhere in India, with the only exception of Delhi and a small region around it, the Hindus and the Muslims began one after another to repudiate his imperial authority. In the South, the celebrated kingdom of Vijaynagar had openly asserted its freedom. Under these circumstances, Pherozshah Tughlakh decided finally to

acknowledge the independence of the recalcitrant people under him in order to assuage their political bitterness, and to consolidate whatever little he could retain rather than lose all. He, therefore, gave an official recognition to the independence of the Bahamani Kingdom in the south and to that of the valiant Hindu Kingdom of Vijaynagar, which was founded by the great Hindu leaders, who were fired with the bitterest hatred for the Muslim domination and were bent on driving it away right out of India.

830. Thus was the Muslim imperial power, which had reached its zenith round about the years A.D. 1310-12 in Allauddin's times as a result of the incessant Hindu-Muslim wars for about six or seven centuries, and which had spread over almost the whole of India, dissolved by the very descendant of the same illustrious Sultan, for he could not help yielding to the powerful Hindu resistance. The Muslim empire over the whole of India was completely shattered in the hour of its fruition, never to be rebuilt on such a vast scale. Now the Hindu resurgent independent power had begun its inroads on the Muslim might, which were never to cease again!

831. In fact, the moment Pherozshah Tughlak recognized the political independence of the South, the Muslim imperial power came to an end! He, as it were, rang the death knell of the Muslim ambition of an imperial power!

The Direct Evidence

832. This explicit recognition of the political independence of the Deccan, including that of the newly established Hindu state of Vijaynagar by the Sultan of Delhi, Pherozshah Tughlak himself, conclusively proves the statement that we have made in paragraphs 807 to 817 and that has so far escaped the notice of the writers of Hindu history. It is the two-fold politico-religious aggression of the Hindu Emperor, Shree Dharmarakshak, (Nasir-ud-din) in Delhi itself on the Muslim power, and especially his frightful revenge of the religious persecution of the Hindus over the Muslims in much the same horrid way, and the terror it struck in the minds of the Muslims, which inspired this political rising of Vijaynagar, which in its turn dashed to pieces the Muslim ambition of an all-India empire!

833. Although Sultan Pherozshah helplessly surrendered his overlordship over the Deccan, he still mercilessly continued to persecute

the Hindus in the big cities like Delhi under his direct control. The Hindus, too, persisted in their staunch resistance in the defence of their religion, even at the risk of martyrdom. Numerous instances of the varied kinds of this Hindu reaction to the Muslim atrocities are recorded, one of which might be given here on the authority of the Muslim writers themselves.

833A. Sultan Pherozshah hated the Brahmins far more bitterly than the other Hindus. He said, "Brahmins are the veritable keys to the strong fortress of the Hindu religion." It is the Brahmins who organised a resistance movement against the Jizia tax, freshly imposed on the Hindus by Sultan Pherozshah. They organized collective hunger strike before the royal palace and announced their determination to swallow fire and court martyrdom. But the Sultan heeded it not. So, many Brahmins, no longer able to bear the humiliation, died in that horrible manner. In the end, the Hindus of other castes paid up the tax for such staunch defenders of their religion that still survived and saved their lives!

834. But the account of one of those Brahmins is the most remarkable for his martyrdom. In the city of Delhi itself, this old Brahmin openly worshipped an idol. Now the diabolic religion of Sultan Pherozshah Tughlak had absolutely banned any such idol-worship throughout his kingdom. But in order to protest against this ban, that Brahmin collected all the Hindus in the courtyard of his house and worshipped the idol with such great pomp that many Muslim men, women and children, too, became the devotees of that idol. The rumour quickly spread far and wide that this Brahmin's God always came to the rescue of his devotee. The news that this Brahmin openly worshipped idols painted on a wooden plank reached the ears of the Sultan, who immediately had him brought as a captive, along with his idol, before him. Thereupon, he called all the ulemas (the Muslim religious priests) and asked them: "What punishment should be inflicted on this Brahmin?" They replied: "This Brahmin should either be a Muslim or be burnt alive to death." The Brahmin, thereupon, chose to die that horrible death by burning. In Delhi, just before the king's court, a big pile of wood was made and the Brahmin was placed on it, bound hand and foot, with the idol painted on the wooden plank. The Muslim demons set fire to that pile of wood from all sides. Still, the Brahmin would not consent to be converted to Islam. In a few cruel moments, the fire blazed very hot on all sides. But without even a faint sigh of pain or grief, the Brahmin remained bowing

down to the idol. Within a moment, the hungry flames swallowed up the devoted Brahmin!

835. This arch-enemy of the Hindus, Sultan Pherozshah Tughlak, died in A.D. 1388, followed by an utter chaos in the meagre remains of his kingdom, whereas on one occasion, two of his grandsons fell out and at the two ends of the city of Delhi, there ruled two Sultans at one and the same time, Mohammadshah and Nasratshah, the two grandsons of Pheroz. Half the city of Delhi became the capital of the one, while the other half, that of the other!!

Invasion by Taimurlang

836. Under these chaotic conditions, Delhi fell a prey to the inhuman ravages of the notorious Taimurlang, the Sultan of the far off Samarkand.

837. Taimur was a Turk, and not originally a Muslim. After conquering the city of Baghdad, he burned to ashes the whole library of literature and at many places, he even burned Masjids! In A.D. 1369, he became the King of Samarkand. Following the lead of Chengeezkhan before him, he had conquered not less than twenty-seven crowns from Russia in the West to Afghanistan in the South-East! Because he had lost a leg in one of the battles, he received the nickname 'lang' (lame). Thereafter, he happened to cast his eyes on India, not simply because of any allurement of political power or the lust for victory, but because he had formed a bitter hatred towards India. For, he had in the meantime become a Muslim. His original destructive tendencies now received this new ghastly impetus! Says he in his autobiography: "My intention in marching upon India is to massacre the Kafir Hindus there, destroy the idols of their Gods, convert them all to Islam and thus win the title of a 'Gazi' in the court of the Allah."

838. So, immediately in A.D. 1397, he invaded India. He had under him a gigantic force of ninety thousand strong. He marched straight up to Punjab. Still nobody came forward to oppose him. He, therefore, swooped down straight on Delhi, where a small force came to oppose him in the name of the Sultan of Delhi, but it was soon put to rout. An interesting point to note is that this veteran army of Taimurlang, which had trampled over half the world, was scared to death for a time by the mere sight of elephants in this ludicrous army of the Sultan of Delhi, for they had seen such huge beasts for the first time in their lives.

Yet it got over the fear very soon and as soon as the Sultan's forces were completely routed, it dashed violently into the city of Delhi, letting loose the orgy of wholesale massacre, plunder and arson. Millions of lives were lost this day. After having thus quenched his thirst for Hindu blood to some extent, Taimur turned further to Meerut and Haridwar, smashing to pieces Hindu idols at many places on his way. At Haridwar, he reached the pinnacle of his cruelty in the Hindu bloodbath. How many instances is one to quote of the harrowing atrocities which the Hindu community had to suffer simply because of their dire determination and holy resolve not to forsake their religion! From Haridwar, this fiendlike Taimur went further to the north, raining Hindu blood on the Shivalik hills, Nagarcote, Jammu and demolishing Hindu temples on the way. On his way, he got the news of his native capital of Samarkand being threatened by the rebels. So, mad with fury and mental anguish, he hurried straight off to Samarkand with the whole of his army.

839. In this Taimurlangian deluge was washed off the little that was left of the Tughlak Sultanate. In the chaotic conditions that then prevailed in north India, the Sayyads usurped the nominal Sultanate of the Tughlaks.

840. Availing themselves of this miserable condition of the Muslim power at Delhi, the veteran defenders of the Hindu religion, the independent Rajput kings, went on setting free the territories formerly conquered by the Muslims.

For that matter, the holy places of the Hindus like Kashi, Prayag and others hand, even before this time, been reconquered from the Muslims. But!—Although the political power there was defeated and uprooted, their colonies and their religious centres like their Masjids and mosques were not destroyed—as did the Muslims, whenever they conquered the Hindu territories, slaughtering the Hindus irrespective of their age or sex and pulling down the Hindu holy places of worship, so as to make mere existence impossible for them. But because the Hindus did not emulate the Muslims in this respect, these local Muslims, who were left alive and unmolested, turned traitors, like serpents fed and fostered as pets, and invited again and again the Muslim aggressors for help and made life miserable for the Hindus in those holy places and cities. But the Rajput malady of the suicidal generosity even now persisted without any moderation. (The reader is referred to the detailed discussion in this regard in Paragraphs 421 to 426).

Rana Kumbha

841. Most notable among the Rajput heroes of the time was Rana Kumbha, who excelled not only the great leaders of Chitod but even those of Hindusthan in respect of valour and success. He went to war with a powerful neigbhouring Muslim Sultan, Mohammad Khilji of Malwa, who had become independent by renouncing the overlordship (paramountcy) of the Sultan of Delhi, and in a battle near Sultanpur, vanquished the latter completely. Sultan Mohammad Khilji of Malwa was at last caught alive by Rana Kumbha. But grossly affected as he was by the age-old malady of the perverted sense of virtues, as the other Hindu heroes before him were, he allowed the Sultan to go free, considering it a noble act on his own part. Had but Rana Kumbha been taken captive by the Muslim Sultan, Mohammad Khilji, he would very likely have been deprived of his eyesight, as Prithviraj was, and brutally murdered according to the diabolic war-ethics of the Muslims. In fact, this diabolic war-ethics is the only one that is beneficial to a nation in such fiendish wars and hence is highly pious and thoroughly sound!

842. This battle was considered so unique and unparalleled in the Hindu history of those days that in order to celebrate it, Rana Kumbha erected a colossal and artistic pillar of victory at Chitod, which still stands to the admiration of all visitors! In a like manner, did Rana Kumbha beat down Sultan Kutbuddin of Gujarat when the latter attacked Kumbhalgad, and Kutbuddin had ultimately to sue for peace and save his life.

843. Even after Rana Kumbha, Rajputana claims so many brave and capable leaders of men that whole volumes ought really to be devoted to the generations that produced each of them. But, our recent histories are so much haunted by those of the Muslim and European nations, that they fight shy of recording the glorious acts of the Hindus—it is, in fact, a clear proof of the absence of any independent research made by them and of their glaring ignorance! Fortunately, the contemporary Rasos, written honestly and with a rare literary flavour, and inspired by the exceptional valour of the Hindus of the times, are available here and there. Prithviraj Raso, Hameer Raso, Chhatrasal Raso and many others—beautiful heroic ballads and narrative poems of varied lengths—are to be had even today. But God knows if these historians know them even by name! Again, modern historical research has discovered many rock inscriptions not only in Rajputana, but in the caves at various other places. They also are likely to help a lot in re-writing the history of these

Hindu heroes. But the present doesn't seem to be the proper time to undertake that work on a major institutional basis! Till such a propitious time comes, smaller institutions or individual scholars can start, if not the actual research work, at least, the work of collection of this vast deal of source material. Such a fond hope can safely be entertained, if we remember the celebrated name of Rajwade alone!

Lodi Dynasty

844. After the end of the Sayyad Dynasty in A.D. 1450, some Lodis of Afghan extraction ruled as Sultans at Delhi for some time. Of them all Shikandar Lodi tried to consolidate his power during A.D. 1485 to 1517. This Shikandar Lodi again was born of a Hindu mother, but like every other Muslim ruler, he always had a stern eye upon the Hindus. He again enforced the ban on the Hindu pilgrimages, which the Hindus had begun to make in the meanwhile. He even forbade collective baths in holy rivers on Parvani days. Nevertheless, as elsewhere, the Hindus resisted stubbornly even at the cost of their lives. The following account of a great martyr should suffice to illustrate the foregoing remarks.

845. At a certain town near Lakhnau (Lucknow) lived a Brahmin, named Buddha, who preached that whatever just and virtuous religious code one followed, so long as one followed it sincerely, was equally acceptable to God. In spite of all the harassment caused to him by the Muslims on this account, he propagated his views so very vigorously that even the Kazi of Lakhnau had to give way. In the end, the authorities committed this complaint to the Sultan, Shikandarkhan, thereupon, had a full-dress debate between this Brahmin and nine other learned moulavis. But the Brahmin, loyal as he was to his own religion and to truth, would not give in. So the Sultan himself threatened him: "Be a Muslim or you will be put to instant death." And as the said Brahmin spurned his threat, he was killed forthwith.

Rana Sang

846. After the death of Shikandar Lodi in A.D. 1517 his son Ibrahim Lodi ascended the tottering throne of the Sultan of Delhi. For the disintegrating Muslim power at Delhi experienced excruciating death pangs at the hands of the Rajputs of the time, who had in Rana Sang a very great, valiant leader. Even the smaller Muslim rulers took great offence at the brave deeds of Rana Sang. The ruler of Idar expressed

his malice against Rana Sang by naming a dog at his door Sangrana. In order to chastise this monkeying of the Muslims, Rana Sang marched with a large army against Idar, and vanquishing them completely at every place, he avenged in full the wrongs done to the Hindus. This battle caused no harm to the Hindus round about. On the contrary, they looked upon him with evident pride and pleasure as their Godsend saviour and protector. Registering his conquests over the Muslim foes at every place with triumphal marches amidst popular applause, the loud beats of his war-drums and the gay fluttering of his victorious flag, he returned to Chitod in A.D. 1519. He had, by this time, liberated Ratanbhor, Gagrone, Walpi (Kalpi?), Bhilsa and Chanderi from the Muslim domination and annexed them to his own kingdom.

Defeat of Sultan Ibrahim lodi by Rana Sang in the battle of Khanoli

846A. In order to improve the decaying condition of the Muslim power, constantly harmed by the Rajputs, Sultan Ibrahim Lodi gathered all his strength and invaded Rana Sang. The two parties joined battle at Khanoli, where in a bloody action, Rana Sang put to rout the Sultan's army and sent him back to Delhi downcast and crestfallen.

Babar's Invasion

847. Beset with such calamities, Subedar Daulatkhan Lodi of Lahore became, along with other Muslim chieftains, quite pessimistic about their own safe existence. As a last resort, they invited Babar, the then powerful ruler of Afghanistan, to help them put down Rana Sang. Babar, too had been waiting for such an opportunity, for as a descendant of Taimurlang, he claimed a direct right to the sovereignty of India. So Babar hastened to help Daulatkhan Lodi in A.D. 1526.

848. Seeing this allied Muslim army come menacingly, the scared Sultan Ibrahim Lodi sought the help of the valiant Hindu King of Chitod, Rana Sang, in spite of the fact that the latter had very recently inflicted a crushing defeat on him. But the Muslims were never ashamed of eating the humble pie before the Hindus on such occasions. Again, it has been already shown and will, hereafter, be shown, how foolish and baseless are our popular notions that the Muslims never fought amongst themselves, or that they never sought help from the Hindus to fight with their fellow Muslims, should such an eventuality arise! Sultan Ibrahim's is a glaring instance in point. With the help of Rana Sang, Sultan Ibrahim fought

with the invading Babar at Panipat in A.D. 1526. But as Ibrahim himself was killed on the battlefield and his army took to flight, Rana Sang too had to retreat. While wandering through forest-after-forest, organising a strong army to meet Babar again on the battlefield, this high-minded Maharana Sang succumbed to incurable diseases in A.D. 1530, and the Hindus lost a precious diadem.

Moghul Dynasty founded at Delhi

849. After this signal victory, Babar grasped the Sultanate of Delhi for himself in A.D. 1526, setting aside the original aspirant to that place, Subedar Daulatkhan Lodi of Punjab. This was the beginning of the Moghul Empire of Delhi.

Notable Events in the Remaining Provinces of North India at the Time

850. SINDH: The reconquest of Sindh from the Arab hands by the Hindus has already been noted (cf. Paragraphs 655 to 656). Those Sumer Rajputs retained Sindh in their hands till A.D. 1336. In A.D. 1336, a Rajput King named Jam Afra, was ruling there as an independent potentate. There were constant wars between this Hindu monarchy and the Sultans of Delhi. From A.D. 1367 to 1380, a Hindu monarch was succeeded to the throne by another Rajput Prince, who, however, because of many maladies, lost his balance of mind and voluntarily became a Muslim.

851. BENGAL: When ultimately in A.D. 1192, Mohammad Ghori subjugated the Sultanate of Delhi for ever, he sent many valorous chieftains under him to subdue the Hindu states round about. One of them, Bakhtyar Khilji, overcame the Hindu rule in Bihar and Bengal in A.D. 1195 and founded the Muslim rule there for the first time. Of his persecution of the Hindus and especially of the Buddhists and their wholesale conversion to Islam, we have already said enough in Paragraph Nos. 342 to 356. On this very occasion, this wild fiendish commander of the Muslim forces razed to the ground the world famous University of Nalanda, which had a glorious tradition of over five centuries to its credit. The Muslims set fire to the vast and invaluable collection of innumerable books, which had kept burning, it is said, for six months. But the Muslims never allowed anybody to put the fire down before it quenched of itself, and every written record was reduced to ashes!

Want of armed might renders the power of Science as also the power of Religion Miserably Helpless—one more illustration!

852. In that vast burning library, there were innumerable valuable books of the Vedic, Buddha, Jain and other religions. But to protect them from fire came neither the Vedic Gods, nor Lord Buddha, no, not even Lord Jain! The actual armed might of the devotees is the only armed strength the Gods seem to have!

853. In the end, Bakhtyar Khilji conquered the last of the Sen Kings and after annexing Bengal, started his campaign of the wholesale conversion of the Hindus to Islam.

854. The Muslim Subedars themselves rebelled from time-to-time against the paramount power of Delhi and calling themselves the Sultans of Bengal, ruled the province independently. Fakruddin was the first of them to announce his independent sway over Bengal in A.D. 1347. Since then, these Afghan Sultans had ruled the province till A.D. 1576. Once in the meantime in A.D. 1386, a Hindu Jamindar named Kans overthrew this Afghan rule and established Hindu power in Bengal. When this King Kans died in A.D. 1392, his son Jitmalla came to the throne of Bengal. But to the greater discredit of the Hindus there, this Hindu King Jitmalla once had the wanton caprice to court Islam, and he changed his name to Jalaluddin! And to the greater shame of the Hindus, be it said that not a single Hindu throughout the whole of Bengal came forward to chastise Jalaluddin for this national crime. They acquiesced in the Muslim domination without a murmur!

855. One more capable Hindu Jamindar, who was a proud adherent of Hinduism, had nearly managed to do as much. But his efforts too ended in disaster. Of the few brave Hindu warriors who rose in rebellion against the Muslims and fought tooth and nail, the only one who can be ranked along with Rana Pratap and Baba Banda was Maharaja Pratapaditya of Jashodhar. Although his sphere of activity was not very large and although for want of active and potent support from the Hindu community, he was in the end defeated, his name will ever be remembered in the history of Hindu independence movement!

856. KASHMIR: For want of space, it is enough to say here that while the Muslims were wantonly subjugating Gujarat, Malwa and other provinces of north India, Kashmir was completely immune from the Muslim influence till the fourteenth century of the Christian era, being governed by the Hindu Kings, sometimes vigorously and potently

enough, at others mildly but always independently! The last of its Hindu Kings was Sendev. The history of Kashmir is written by Pandit Kalhan under the name 'Rajtarangini'. This Sendev had appointed one Muslim, named Shahmir or Mirza, to be some official of the state and later on raised him from post-to-post, until he was made the Chief Minister of the State. What happened elsewhere in the history of many Hindu States also happened here, and after the death of Sendev, this very Muslim Minister treacherously destroyed this Hindu State on the strength of a very cleverly preconceived plan, and usurped the throne of Kashmir under the title 'Shamsuddin'.

857. Of course, just as the Hindus ultimately liberated the whole of India from the Muslim hands, similarly our Hindu Sikhs and Dogras not only freed Kashmir from the Muslim bondage, but they also marched victoriously to Laddakh, on one side, and to Gilgit, on the other, and proudly planted the Hindu standard there—but after fighting many grim battles and in course of time—some centuries afterwards!

□

19

The Establishment of the Glorious new Hindu Empire of Vijaynagar

858. For the better convenience of the reader, it is advisable to recall at the very outset, the chronology of certain events. The first foreign—especially non-Hindu—large-scale aggression on the Deccan was the one by Allauddin on Devgiri in A.D. 1294. It was followed with precipitate haste by three or four such tremendous military expeditions up to A.D. 1318 under the intrepid yet cruel Muslim commanders like Maliq Kafur and Khushrukhan, who ruthlessly forced conversion upon thousands of Hindus. During these twenty-five years or so, the Muslims overran practically the whole of the Deccan and wiped out of existence, five or six ancient, famous and strong Hindu Kingdoms from Devgiri to Malabar.

858A. Howsoever shameful and stigmatic this historical fact might be to the prestige and self-respect of the Hindu Nation, the Deccanese Hindu heroes, too, swallowed up, as it were, in one draught, as their ancient ancestor, Agasti Rishi, did of yore, the doomsday flood of the Muslim warriors and hardly within a decade or so, shattered the Sultanate of Delhi to pieces! They raised in its place, at least in the Deccan, a grand victorious Hindu Empire of Vijaynagar. The lightning-like speed, with which they achieved all this, is also so creditable to the Hindu Nation, that we should for ever, be proud of them and grateful to them.

859. For, even before the whole of the Deccan was subjugated in A.D. 1318, some of the indefatigable Hindu leaders, highly ambitious of re-establishing Hindu sway over the Deccan without delay, had already begun establishing secret contacts with Khushrukhan himself. The Khan cherished in his mind daring plans of dispatching Sultan Mubarik after reaching Delhi and crowning himself as Sultan in his

stead. But he knew full well that in this courageous bid for power, even the bitterest of the Muslim enemies of the ruling Sultan would not have helped him in the least. But he could expect passive, even active, support from the Hindu chiefs or sirdars. For, Khushrukhan himself had become most impatient to tear off his tawdry guise of Mohammadanism, which was forced upon him, very much against his will, and to appear in his original Hindu form. Naturally, secret reports and slanderous complaints constantly reached the court of Sultan Mubarik at Delhi, that Khushrukhan was in collusion with the recently overpowered Hindu chiefs and leaders of Hindu Society, and that some deep-laid mysterious plan was afoot. The reader should refer to a connected and plausible account of this whole affair, so far as it can he deduced from these various scattered bits of information, that are so far available to us (Paragraphs 754 to 782).

860. The founders of the Empire of Vijaynagar, Harihar and Bukka, were the two sons of Sangam of the ancient Yadav family. They were employed at the court of Anagondi. During the turbulent times following the Muslim conquests of Devgiri and Warangal in the reign of Allauddin, the Kingdom of Anagondi, too, was overpowered by the Muslims. Anagondi itself or some place nearby was the former city of Kishkindha of Wali, as the folklore goes. After the downfall of Anagondi, Harihar and Bukka were taken as captives to Delhi in A.D. 1327 and were converted there to Islam. Later on, being pleased with their behaviour and exceptional ability, the Sultan sent them both with a new expedition to fight with the Hindus in A.D. 1331, with higher authority and responsible posts. But as soon as they came to the Deccan—

Most probably as per a pre-conceived plan

861. They paid a visit to the then chief preceptor of Sankeshwar Math, Shree Shankaracharya Vidyaranyaswami, who was a skilled politician too. Immediately, the Shankaracharya himself re-converted these two converted Hindus who promptly raised a Hindu army and defeated the Muslim host, which they themselves had led a short time ago. Soon in consultation with Shankaracharya, Vidyaranyaswami and many other brave Hindu leaders, it was decided to found an independent sovereign state on the banks of the river Tungbhadra. The Capital was established at the newly-founded city of Vijyanagar, which bespoke of Hindu victory. The reins of this kingdom were placed in the hands of

Shree Harihar in A.D. 1336, while Shri Vidyaranya himself became his chief minister.

862. At this very stage, it is advisable to explain one enigmatic episode, which is not yet so explained by historians. The event in question is the transfer of the capital from Delhi to Devgiri by Mohammad Tughlak, who is considered 'crazy', but who was, in fact, a learned fool, without any practical sense. His decision to shift the Capital of his Empire from Delhi to Devgiri is considered to be his wayward caprice. But it was not a pure whim of his. It was to consolidate his victories in the Deccan that were gained by his generals and to rule that region effectively, that he thought of having his capital in its very midst. Again, his precipitate decision to shift his Capital back to Delhi, which resulted in untold sufferings for the people was also not his pure caprice. In fact, it was for the last ten years or so that the Muslim rule seemed to have stabilized itself in the Deccan, but it was most humiliating and so most hateful and unbearable to the Hindus. So, all the Hindu kings, all the Hindu religious preachers and lawgivers and Hindu people at large, were preparing feverishly though secretly to overthrow that alien rule, and the Muslim army had also grown panicky about such an armed rising. The Sultan realized the grave danger of his being involved in the meshes of this Hindu revolt and the possibility of his being destroyed completely. That is why he hurriedly shifted his Capital back to Delhi, far to the north—not simply because his caprice dictated it! As a matter of fact, it was the panic about this growing armed strength of the Hindus that caused all these crazy and contradictory moves of his!

863. One more important event of this time has equally baffled the historians, but it is far too strange to be set aside. It is this Sangam, whose young sons, Harihar and Bukka, were taken captives by the Muslims, was in fact, closely related to the Kings of Anagondi and Warangal. Naturally, these two sons were also fairly well connected with these royal families. It was for this particular reason that Mohammad Tughlak took them to Delhi and converted them to Islam. On many Hindu kings and princes had fallen this calamity of being forcibly converted to Islam, but even if they escaped afterwards from such a calamity, they had, unfortunately, no hope of being absorbed in the Hindu Society. The stumbling block was that of the ban on reconversion to Hinduism (Paras 379 to 403). How then and from what source, did this inspiration arise, which actuated the two young warriors, Harihar

and Bukka, to seek reconversion to Hinduism, which again emboldened Shankaracharya Vidyaranyaswami to preside over and effect this reconversion, totally disregarding the staunch public opposition and all the rules and regulations laid down in the interpolated chapter on Kalivarjya Prakarna, and which finally made many other Hindu men of action to follow up this new movement?

864. The answer to this riddling question is to be found in the unprecedented politico-religious revolution brought about some ten or twelve years ago by the Hindu Samrat Dharmarakshak (Nasir-ud-din) at Delhi. For, Sultan Nasir-ud-din himself was originally a Hindu, who was forcibly converted to Islam. But because of the fondness and infatuation of Alauddin and his son, he was given the title of Khushrukhan and was gradually raised to be the commander of a huge Muslim army to invade the South. Till the moment he became sufficiently powerful, Khushrukhan outwardly maintained his Muslim garb; but as soon as he returned from his southern campaign, he cut off the Muslim Sultan, Mubarik, and crowned himself as Hindu Emperor, proudly proclaiming that he was originally a Hindu and that he was re-embracing that religion once again. Not content with this, he reconverted hundreds of such unhappy converts to Hinduism, and changed the Muslim masjids into Hindu temples! The exciting news of this unheard of but successful attack of Hindutwa (हिंदुत्व) upon the Muslim empire and Muslim religion had already reached the farthest corners of India. Naturally, when Harihar and Bukka were stationed at Delhi as captive Muslim converts at the orders of the Muslim Sultan, they must have heard the excited discussions about this very recent happening, which must have egged them on to attempt some such seemingly impossible feat of escaping to the Deccan with a large army. So, they must have simulated to Mohammed Tughlak that they were staunch Muslims and as such deserved his fullest confidence, and that is why Mohammed Tughlak appointed Harihar and Bukka at the head of Muslim army in that region. When Mohammed Tughlak shifted his capital from Devgiri to Delhi, he could not keep sufficient army in the South to protect the imperial territory in the Deccan. So, when the news of the probable rising of the Hindus came to his ears, he decided to send these two warriors to strengthen the imperial position in the south, because in the first place, they were closely connected with the royal Hindu families of the Deccan and secondly, because they were now trustworthy Muslims. Harihar and

Bukka, too, got the wishes for opportunity and showed all the eagerness to execute the tasks set to them. It was an established practice of the Sultans of Delhi to send the converted Hindus to extend the imperial boundaries and such attempts bore rich fruit, as can be seen in the case of Maliq Kafur and others. With the apparent determination to destroy the Hindu revolts in the Deccan, Harihar and Bukka took leave of the Sultan and with the Muslim army, went straight to their own States of Anagondi and Warangal.

865. In all probability, they must have passed on to Shree Swami Vidyaranya and the rest of the Hindu kings in unmistakable terms, the information as to their secret plans and their real intention, long before they reached the Deccan. They had given Sultan Mohammed Tughlak the slip and were now to embrace Hinduism openly. Hindu Samrat Nasir-ud-din's successful military coup in Delhi had already given the impetus to the Deccanese Princes and the priests like Shankaracharya. Naturally, with the approval of Harihar and Bukka, Vidyaranyaswami and other Hindu leaders decided to reconvert them to Hinduism with the ceremonial rites.

866. Our observation at the end of the Seventeenth Chapter that the political revolution, which Shree Dharmarakshak (Nasir-ud-din) effected at Delhi, had far-reaching consequences can also be proved by the influence that great event exerted on the establishment of the Empire of Vijaynagar. Even then, that great event has been so far referred to with contempt and in insulting terms! It only shows that modern historical textbooks lack the Hindu point of view, and hence they are merely blind to some such events!

867. The proud achievement of the Hindu generation which established the new Hindu Empire of Vijaynagar has not been sufficiently glorified in Hindu histories. The case of Madhavacharya, the Shankaracharya of Sankeshwar, Vidyaranyaswami is the one in point. It has already been pointed out how great a political revolutionary this exceptional personality was! But the fact that he was an equally great revolutionary in matters of religion, can be proved by his repudiation of the old traditions by re-converting the two princes, Harihar and Bukka. In a similar way, he was the synacure of the then learned-world. He wrote several treatises on several subjects, of which 'Sarwadarshan Sangrah' and 'Panchadashi' are the most renowned. No other abler Shankaracharya seems to have ascended the seat of Shringeri or any

other monastery after the First Shankaracharya! Especially, his arch diplomacy and political wisdom seen in the rapid growth of the Hindu Empire of Vijaynagar in the teeth of Muslim opposition, bears no comparison!

867A. Indeed, the names of Vidyaranyaswami, of the warrior kings, Harihar and Bukka, Harihar the second, who took the proud title of Maharajadhiraj, and his Chief Minister Sayanacharya—the brother of Vidayaranyaswami, whose critique of the Vedas is still accepted as an authority, Maharajadhiraj Krishnadevray and the last but not the least, Maharajadhiraja Ramrai also, who had inflicted crushing defeats in rapid succession on all the five Muslim States in Maharashtra viz., Adilshahi, Nizamshahi and others, but who was in the end, killed in the forefront of the bloody battle against the combined Muslim forces, should really be honoured in every home and be remembered by everybody as are those of Rana Pratap, Raja Chhatrasal, Govind Singh, Chaitanya, Banda Bairagi and other great men of those times. But today, North-Indian Hindus seem to have never heard of them, while in the South, hardly one in a thousand seems to know them but faintly. This is most shameful for the Hindus and this state of things must be changed forthwith.

The establishment of the Bahamani Kingdom

868. Seeing the disintegration of the sovereign power of the Sultan of Delhi, set afoot by the Hindu State of Vijaynagar in the South, Hassan Gangu, the Muslim Governor of the Southern Muslim possessions, revolted against the Delhi Sultanate and proclaimed himself Sultan of the so-called Bahamani Kingdom in A.D. 1346. His domain spread from the Narmada in the north to the Krishna in the south. The rulers of Delhi completely lost their hold on the south, which was now to be ruled by two prominent powers. The Bahamani Kings and the Hindu Princes of Vijaynagar. The name Bahamani, which Hassan Gangu adopted for his kingdom, is explained away by the historians in two different ways. It seems that this Hassan Gangu was a domestic servant with a Hindu Brahmin, named Gangu, when the former was but a slave. Pleased with his loyal service, the Brahmin looked into his horoscope and prophesied that the slave Hassan would, sometime in the future, become a king. Mad with joy to hear this prophesy, Hassan began to style himself as Hassan Gangu and when he actually got the sovereign power over the Deccanese sector of the Muslim empire, he designated it as the Bahamani

kingdom, thinking it to be the fruit of the blessings of his former Brahmin master. Some other historians suggest another derivation for the name Bahamani Kingdom. They say that perhaps Hassan Gangu might have felt that he belonged to the Bahamani stock, a princely lineage from Persia. If it be so, why did Hassan continue till the end to call himself Hassan Gangu which clearly referred to his Brahmin master? Moreover, what proofs are there to show his descent from the Persian Bahamani royal family? There is none forthcoming so far!

869. This Bahamani Kingdom and the Vijaynagar Empire had a common boundary, the Tungabhadra river. Naturally, intermittent warfare between these two rival states was the result. Those who want to read a more detailed account of the Vijaynagar Empire and its wars with the Bahamani Kingdom should read with profit two books viz.: (i) 'The Forgotten Empire' by Robert Swell and (ii) 'The Never To Be Forgotten Empire' by Dr. S. Krishnaswami Aiyangar. The second book, so to say is an answer, at least to a certain extent, to the first one by an English scholar.

870. As this one, far from being a book of history, is in fact an interpretation of history (as we have been saying from the beginning), we shall restrict ourselves to those events only, which are relevant to our purpose. For, there is no room here for any detailed historical account.

Foundation—the building of the City of Vijaynagar

871. The site selected on the banks of the Tungabhadra for the capital city of Vijaynagar by the great Hindu leaders of the day, such as Vidyaranyaswami and others, was from the architectural and military points of views so beautiful and well fortified, surrounded as it was by hills on the three sides and a deep river on the fourth, that the architectural and military acumen in the selection of this site has been highly praised by several foreign travellers, well-versed in these two sciences. There were as it were a natural fortification for this vast city, seven strong enclosures, one within the other, round this city of Vijaynagar. In every one of these enclosures, there were majestic buildings, beautifully carved temples, and rich palaces and pleasant lakes. On all these buildings, temples and royal palaces, flew the saffron-coloured flag masked with a golden cup. For the authorized standard of Vijaynagar was the same traditional flag of the Hindu Nation, the saffron-coloured banner!

872. Of all these temples, the grandest, most magnificent and

spacious was that of Shree Nursingh, for he was the presiding deity of the royal family of Vijaynagar. Inasmuch as very few temples are found to be dedicated to this God. Nursingh, throughout the length and breadth of India, represents the genius and practical sense of those kings of Vijaynagar who chose for their daily worship, this incarnation of Nursingh from amongst many others of the Hindu pantheon, which is undoubtedly praiseworthy.

873. For, in those days of bitter warfare between the most cruel and diabolic Muslim invaders on the one hand, and on the other, the tolerant Hindu Society emasculated to suffer persecution and indignities to the last limits of endurance from the days of Gautam Buddha himself, it was this incarnation of Nursingh that could inspire in the spineless Hindus of the day, instinctive and effective reaction to retaliate every wrong done to them and also violent valour, which could strike terror in the hearts of the enemy.

874. ब्रजन्ति ते मूढधियः पराभवन। भवन्ति मायाविषु वे न मायिना ॥:।
साध्वाचारः साधुना प्रत्युपेय। मायाचारो मायया बाधितव्यः ॥

(Those dull-witted, who do not behave knavishly with base and crafty rogues invariably court failure! A polite person should be treated politely while a crafty scoundrel should be destroyed by super-craft.)

[THE SELF-SAME STORY OF NURSINGH ITSELF TELLS] that not with the perverted virtues of Prahlad but with the cruel, crafty measures alone could that demon, Hiranayakashipu, be killed.

875. Shree Shankar had blessed Hiranyakashipu with a boon that he would not be killed by any man or beast, with any weapon or missile, ordinary or charmed with magic power, on the earth or in the skies, neither by day nor by night, neither in nor out! But mysteriously enough, an effective expedient was found for every one of these thoughtless terms of the equally thoughtless boon and the enemy of the Gods, the invincible demon, Hiranyakashipu, was killed by an incarnation, which was neither purely human nor purely beastly, but a mixture of both, at twilight, on the threshold, taking him on the lap and by cutting open his stomach with his sharp talons!

875A. It is this frightful incarnation of God, whose whole body has been besmeared with the spouts of blood emanating from the dying body of the wicked demon, rending the whole universe with his horrible war-cries, and at whose furious visage, made ten-times more terrible by his beard standing erect, even the Gods themselves were alarmed and began to request him to calm down, that a Nation wishing to keep itself alive in this diabolic warring world, should worship as the emblem of the high peak of national valour!

876. This story also implies another noble principle that although the outward appearance of this violent incarnation of Nursingh was fierce and repellant, its heart was that of a human being made of the 'milk of human kindness'. Its merciless valour also is most essential, even unavoidable, to the development of 'human kindness'! For this violent act of tearing open the entrails of Hiranayakashipu, a reckless tyrant, a terror to Gods and demons alike, was performed solely to protect a devotee of the Gods, Prahlad, and that too as the last remedy! It is for the sake of free development of human virtues that the principle of अहिंसा (non-violence), which emasculates human beings with the curse of weakness, should at times be killed by cruel violence! It itself becomes a truly righteous, a truly religious act, leading to the development of human culture! At a particular stage of development of the human society throughout the world, and in the tumultuous times when it was surrounded by different warring nations, fired with the inordinate selfish ambition and diabolic violence, the Hindu nation, too, ought to have chosen Nursingh as its God of worship, if it wanted to preserve its free existence or even its invincibility!

877. The magnificent temple of this Nursingh, whom the kings of Vijaynagar had offered their devout hearts, does not stand there today in its original form. When the Muslim invaders attacked and devastated Vijaynagar in A.D. 1565, they also demolished and razed to rubble this royal temple of Nursingh. However, whatever ruins are left over of that old idol of Nursingh in that temple, are even now sufficiently clear to signify the originally huge, magnificent, furious figure of that Godhead, and we can easily imagine how very majestic and awe-inspiring the temple in its original form and glory might have been, distinguishing itself from the other huge, magnificent temples all over India by its inimitableness.

Bahamani Sultan defeated by the King of Vijaynagar

878. After the death of the valiant Harihar, the brave Bukkarai ascended the throne of Vijaynagar. This Bukkarai too was of a daring and aggressive nature. He not only saved his own kingdom but also waged counter-offensives on the Muslims round about the year A.D. 1374 and defeated Majahid Shah, the great Sultan of the Bahamani

kingdom. There is proof to show that this King Bukka had sent a friendly mission to the King of China.

879. In A.D. 1379, this brave monarch of Vijaynagar, Bukkarai, died and was succeeded to this ancestral throne by his son Harihar II, born posthumously to his queen Gowri. During his reign, the Hindus inflicted frequent and crushing defeats on the Muslims and extended the boundaries of Vijaynagar empire, whereupon Harihar took for himself the title of Maharajadhiraj with a grand ceremony to grace the occasion with the brother of Madhavacharya (Vidyaranyaswami) Shree Sayanacharya himself as the Chief Minister of his and Sudha, Isag and Gund, the well-known commanders in his army. Maharajadhiraj Harihar ruled prosperously and extended the boundaries of his Empire to include Goa, as is borne out by a copper plate inscription dated A.D. 1391.

[गोवाभिदां (भिदानाम्) कोकण राजधानीम्]

880-881. It is impossible and unnecessary to give the lineages of the Vijaynagar or any other royal families in this volume. It is enough to say that the kings who succeeded Harihar II also added to the glory of Vijaynagar. There was only one unhappy exception of a weak and imbecile king named Devrai, who came to the throne in A.D. 1406. He did hate the Muslims, but he found a strange expedient for destroying the Muslim powers, that of employing Muslim warriors in his army, as the Muslim rulers employed the Hindus! But seeing his weak and vacillating nature, those Muslim warriors in his employ became so very conceited, that they refused to bow down to him in his very courtly assembly, as they never bowed their heads before any mortal! So, for their satisfaction, Devrai had the Book of the Koran placed on a high pedestal beside him, so that when they bowed, the Muslims were satisfied that they did so to the Koran and not to the King, whereas the King was satisfied that the decorum of the assembly was not violated! He even went to the length of building a masjid in Vijaynagar in order to please those Muslims. It is needless to say that these pampered Muslim soldiers did not fail to betray Devrai in the very thick of the battle, and Devrai was defeated at last by the Bahamani Sultan, Phiroz Khan, who faithful to the demonic Muslim tradition, asked for the daughter of Devrai at the signing of the treaty and the latter had to concede the demand most shamefully and helplessly! Fortunately, during those two or three hundred years of Muslim ascendancy, hardly five or six kings followed this tradition of abject surrender of the Rajputs. Of course, it must be remembered that no Hindu conqueror even laid down this condition for the vanquished Muslims in the great victories that the Hindus gained in those days over the Muslims! The reason is plain enough! For, whoever thought of marrying Muslim girl, would himself have been converted to Islam! The evil effects of this perverted virtue of the Hindus have been dealt with in the chapters on the ban on reconversion (Paragraphs: 413 to 473).

Retaliation by the Hindus

882. However, after the death of Devrai, the kings of Vijaynagar began to avenge this ignoble defeat on various battlefields and once again, the Muslim powers were overawed. Especially in A.D. 1417, when Phiroz Khan invaded Telengan, the Hindus routed the Muslim forces killing their very Vazir.

882A. Round about A.D. 1460, there was a bitter struggle for power in the royal family of Vijaynagar in the reign of Virupaksha. Availing himself of this opportunity, a mighty Vijaynagar Chieftain, Shalva Narsingh by name, dethroned Virupaksha and thus ended the original Sangam dynasty by assuming sovereignty and establishing order throughout the kingdom.

Advent of Western Nations in India

883. During this very period, the European, Portuguese discovered a sea route to India and entered the Indian political arena. Their first entry was not effected in Vijaynagar; it was the coastal Prince Samudrin (Zamorin), to the southern corner of India who was their first host. This seemingly insignificant event is recorded here merely for keeping up the time-sequence. The new locust-like aggression of the western powers that followed it, will have to be reviewed in a separate chapter.

Maharaja Naresh

884. Following the thread of the history of Vijaynagar, it must be said that during one or two generations, this second royal dynasty of Shalva Narsingh was in its turn overthrown when another military commander, Naresh by name, assassinated the then ruling monarch, and established the third ruling dynasty of Vijaynagar in A.D. 1507. In all these three political revolutions, one remarkable thing is noticeable that even when the Muslim States were waiting most anxiously to destroy

this Hindu Empire, and even when these Hindu-Muslim states were constantly at war, these political revolutions took place amongst the Hindus themselves. The surrounding Muslim states got no opportunity to lend a helping hand to one contending Hindu side against the other and thus force their grip on it, nor had they the courage to do it.

The Break-up of the Bahamani Kingdom

885. Before the third political revolution in Vijaynagar was effected, the Bahamani Kingdom of the Muslim was broken up into five. The Bahamani Sultans first of all extended their boundaries from the Narmada to the Tungabhadra, but as its boundaries reached those of Vijaynagar, there was constant warfare between the Hindu-Muslim States. The many victories that the Vijaynagar kings won over the Muslims effected the annexation of Gomantak to the Hindu Kingdom and the extension of its boundaries right up to Orissa. As a natural consequence of these Hindu victories, the Bahamani power weakened considerably. Moreover, the last of its monarchs were absolutely worthless. Mohammed Gawan, the last Bahamani Vazir, however, was able and warlike in spirit. Because of his honest and diligent service, his valour and prudence, that Muslim state managed to exist somehow between A.D. 1484 and 1526. But some Muslim noblemen, who were Mohammed Gawan's enemies at the court, contrived to have him killed by royal order. It must be remembered that, however great Mohammed Gawan might be, like practically every other Muslim ruler, he never left anything undone to persecute the Hindus in the Bahamani Kingdom. Yet he met his doom, not at the hands of the Hindus, but at those of his own Muslim colleagues.

886. Even before the death of Mohammed Gawan, the Sultan's capital had been shifted to Bidar, and after his death, that feeble Muslim power was broken up into the following five parts:

1. Adilshahi of Vijapur.
2. Imadshahi of Berar (Varhad or Vidarbha (1484-1503).
3. Kut-b-Shahi of Gowalkonda.
4. Nizamshahi of Ahmednagar (1489 to 1637).
5. Baridshahi of Bidar.

887. Two remarkable things about this break-up of the Bahamani Kingdom should well be remembered, especially by the Hindus. The first is that the founder of Imadshahi of Berar (second in the above list) was originally a Telangi Brahmin. His father lived in Vijaynagar. In

one of the battles with Vijaynagar, this son of a Telangi Brahmin was captured by the Bahamani Muslims, who, true to their wicked custom, converted him to Islam. He was, thereafter, raised to a higher status by the kindness of Gawan. At last in A.D. 1484, he divorced himself from the Bahamani Kingdom and as a Muslim, took for himself the proud title of Imadshah and proclaimed himself an independent ruler of the Province of Berar, relegated to his charge.

888. The second remarkable fact is that of the foundation of the Nizamshahi of Ahmednagar, the fourth fragment of the Bahamani Kingdom. At Vijaynagar, there was a Brahmin named Timmappa Bahiru (Bhairao?), whose son was taken captive and converted to Islam, when Ahmedshah was at war with Viaynagar. He was renamed Ahmed. When this convert Ahmed was posted at the command of a big Muslim army, he utilized his authority to break loose from the Bahamani domination and established his own Sultanate in A.D. 1489. Because of his title of the Nizam, his Sultanate came to be known as Nizamshahi. In his domain was situated the famous fort of Shivneri. Somewhere between Daulatabad and Junner, there was a small village called 'Binkar'. Finding it suitable for his capital, he named it as Ahmednagar after his own name Ahmed in A.D. 1494.

889. This break-up of the Bahamani Kingdom was mainly due to the internal dissensions of the Muslims. The original Bahamani Kingdom had vowed to destroy Vijaynagar. But the latter survived to see the break-up of the Bahamani Kingdom into five fragments and continued to fight adamantly with all those five Muslim states, and proved to be more than a match to all of them for at least seventy-five years to come!

890. The claim that the Muslims never fought amongst themselves is once again belied by this five-fold fragmentation of the Bahamani kingdom, which was caused by their internal rivalries. That the Muslim Sultans looked for help at the mighty Hindu empire of Vijaynagar in order to put down their Muslim rivals, gives the lie to their second boast that they never sought help from the Hindus!

Maharajadhiraj Krishnadevrai

891. To the above-mentioned Tuluv dynasty of Naresh of Vijaynagar, belonged the mighty emperor Krishnadevrai, who ruled from A.D. 1509 to 1530. He was well-educated and his address was clever and pleasing. He impressed even the greatest of scholars of the time. The

learned scholars of Sanskrit, Telugu, Tamil and Kannad literatures were generously patronized by his court. In his court were eight great poets, whom he called 'अष्टदिग्गज' ('Elephants of the Eight Directions'). He himself was a great writer. His Telugu book named 'अमुक्ता माल्यदा' is very well-known. Maharaja Krishnadevrai was equally fond of architecture and sculpture. It was he who got the famous Ram Mandir of Vijaynagar built, besides the many forts, ramparts, temples, courtyards, monasteries and caravan sarais throughout his empire. He made munificent grants to the Brahmins and temples. His career shines with his various virtues such as courteous behaviour, dexterity in discourse, prudence in politics, his long-range view in chalking out plans and formulating policies, and last but not least, his sternness and valour in respect of the enemies. Western and other foreign historians have unanimously praised him as an unrivalled great ruler!

892. If Maharajadhiraj was most civil with the gentle folks, he was unrelenting and merciless when he fought bravely with the enemies of his religion or those of his nation! Victory graced him in his bitter war with Adilshah, whereupon, the treaty he effected with the Adilshahi Sultan, laid down such acid terms as completely crushed down the Muslim swaggering claims of invincibility, established the superiority of the Hindus, and were accepted by the abject Muslim rulers with great reluctance.

893. His army was vast and powerful. It comprised seven hundred thousand foot, twenty-two thousand cavalry and five hundred and fifty-one elephants, ever prepared for war.

894. The glory of Vijaynagar reached its zenith in the times of Maharaja Krishnadevrai, which can be proved beyond doubt by the various detailed accounts written by many foreign travellers, who visited his court. Many of them have even described his appearance. He was very handsome to look at, a man of action and a very powerful personality to impress at first sight any visitor.

895. He was a Vaishnav himself, yet he gave the same sympathetic and tolerant treatment to the Vedic Hindus, who were in a majority, and to the other minorities like the Jains, Lingayats, Mahanubhavas and other Hindu, sects, avoiding every sort of clash of dissentient opinions and thus tried to cultivate amongst the Hindus the feeling of oneness by means of his compromising attitude. From the inception of the Empire of Vijaynagar, the great Hindu leaders like the Shankaracharya

Vidyaranyaswami and Sayanacharya and others had adopted a wise policy of assimilation, equality and tolerance that precluded every sort of clash between any two religious sects, while their religious preaching fostered high respect for their Hindu religion and their Hindu national sentiment. Foreign travellers refer most admiringly to this religious tolerance and the sense of equality that the Vijaynagar kings always showed.

Prosperity and Glory of Hindu Empire of Vijaynagar

896. Foreign travellers have very highly praised not only the civic and religious liberties that the people of Vijaynagar enjoyed, but also its overall prosperity and glory and the powerful influence that it wielded far and wide. For instance, when the Portuguese traveller, Duarte Barbose, visited Vijaynagar and stayed there for a while, he was very much astonished to see its exceptional wealth and glory.

897. The ambassador from the Shah of Persia has clearly said, "The like of this city is nowhere to be found on the face of this earth." Adjoining the royal palace, there were four-fold extensive market places for jewellery and pearls. Foreign travellers have written that thousands of citizens were to be seen adorned with ornaments of gold, jewels and pearls, Portuguese traveller Paes asserts that the area of Vijaynagar was as extensive as that of Rome.

898. Even before the reign of Maharajadhiraj Krishnadevrai, the Hindu Empire of Vijaynagar had been renowned as the most powerful in the whole of Deccan. The five fragments of the former Bahamani Kingdom were beset with internal dissensions and fratricidal wars, to the immense advantage of Vijaynagar Empire, and the then Hindu political leaders did have the sense to utilize this opportunity for the extension of its boundaries and for teaching a lesson to the Muslims. The Muslim Sultans could do nothing independently without the help or consent of the 'Rais' of Vijaynagar! Every one of the Muslim cliques laboured hard to secure the support of the Hindu rulers of Vijaynagar. As has already been said above, the absurd patronization by the Hindus and their indulgence of the Muslim soldiers, as in the times of the weak and imbecile King Devrai, had been abandoned. Those of the Hindu Kings, who built masjids for the Muslims in their own capital, did so in order to win them over and to parade their religious tolerance. But now that 'cowardly' religious tolerance had given place to valiant

aggression on the Muslim States and the retaliatory demolition of the Muslim mosques and masjids. Forbearance, due to the perverted sense of virtues, began to give the palm of honour of the real virtue of retaliation!

899. Maharaja Krishnadevrai died in A.D. 1530; just four years before it, Babar had captured Delhi. Rana Sang was his contemporary. He was succeeded by his brother, Achyutdev with Salur Timma as his Chief Minister, who for all practical purposes ran the administration. Achyutdev died in A.D. 1542 and then after an insignificant King Sadashivrai, the nephew of Achyutdev, ascended the throne. But Ramrai, the son of the Chief Minister, Timma had done so much in helping Sadashivrai become the king that within a very short time, all the real power passed into his hands. This Ramrai himself is called Ramrajah.

Ramrai, the valiant defender of Religion!

900. All the five Muslim States in Maharashtra tried to obtain help from the powerful army of Ramrai to fight their fratricidal wars. Although these five Muslim rulers knew well enough that Shree Ramrai was a strict adherent of Hinduism and hated all Muslims alike as equally treacherous enemies of the Hindus and looked down upon them with scorn, they had fully realized that without the powerful support of this valiant Hindu hero, they could hold no ground before their adversaries.

901. In A.D. 1543, the Nizamshah of Ahmednagar and Kut-b-Shah of Gowalkonda jointly thought of teaching a lesson to Adilshah, the Sultan of Vijapur. They implored Ramraja himself to take the lead. Accordingly, the three together marched on Vijapur and went on slaughtering the Vijapur forces. The most noteworthy was the fact that even the Muslims came to know that the Hindus had been cured of the one hateful vice of the 'perverted virtues', which we have so far condemned in this volume (Paragraphs 401 to 473). For, on the religious front, too, the Hindus overcame the Muslims and in order to avenge the demolition and molestation of the Hindu temples, they razed numerous masjids at various places to the ground. The houses of Muslims, the localities and townships, where the Hindus were persecuted and Hindu women were treated most insultingly as slaves, were burnt and destroyed completely. This religious retaliation by the Hindus struck new terror in the hearts of the Muslims, and quite contrary to their age-old practice, the Muslim

community no more dared to tread upon the Hindu populations, as they would have upon ants. It dreaded the resurgent Hindu society as it would have dreaded a poisonous snake. Naturally, the Adilshah of Vijapur had to sue for peace and to please every one of the three.

902. This temporary compromise did not end the Muslim feuds for ever. The Adilshah of Vijapur felt sore about the two forts of Kalyani and Solapur appropriated by the Nizamshah of Ahmadnagar. As such, he decided to invade the Nizamshah in 1557 and entreated Ramrai to help him. So now along with the Vijapur army, the Hindu forces of Vijaynagar, which had gone out to help the Nizamshah, marched on the Nizamshahi lands. Needless to say, that the very idea that all the five Muslim states should seek help from the Hindu State of Vijaynagar thrilled the hearts of the brave, while the common people came to lose their former fear-complex about the Muslim might. In this war with the Nizamshah too, the Hindu forces punished the Muslims in the Nizamshahi lands and avenged the atrocities on the Hindus in earlier times on a larger scale and even more sternly and mercilessly than before. Not only on the battlefield, but even during their marches, the heretofore arrogant attitude of the Muslims to the Hindus was also punished by way of reprisals in the form of plundering of their houses and property. The Muslim masjids were destroyed in the very same way as the Hindu temples had been demolished. On the battlefields, the Hindus simply routed the Muslim forces.

903. This fierce retaliation by the Hindus to the Muslim fanaticism and devilish treatment of the non-Muslims, which had gathered momentum during the last forty years or so, struck terror in the hearts of the Muslims, and they, in their turn, formed a new fear-complex about the Hindus. They began to complain most piteously that the Hindus perpetrated insults and atrocities on them and even exposed their religion to ridicule and shame.

The Destruction of Vijaynagar

904. All the five Muslim States in the Deccan and the Muslim society in general took a great fright at the defeat of Nizamshahi at the hands of Ramrai, and especially, the fierce reprisals that the Hindus had newly begun, and were excited with extreme fear and anger. They came to realize that if they wanted their kingdoms to last and if at all they wished to live as Muslims, it was absolutely necessary for them to

forget their mutual grievances, and launch a united and determined attack against the proud kings of Vijaynagar. For, they knew that none of them by itself was a match for the Vijaynagar Empire. So, Adilshah of Vijapur and his Vazir Kishwarkhan decided to take the lead in this daring project. Kishwarkhan personally went and interviewed the Nizamshah and Kut-b-Shah at their respective capitals, while all prominent Muslim Sardars and Manasabdars, and army chiefs and Mullah-maulvis preached jihad (crusade) everywhere. In order to cement their mutual trust and newly-formed friendship, these Muslim Sultans intermarried their daughters and formed family-ties, and, thus, after a thorough preparation the joint forces of all Muslim States marched on Vijaynagar.

905. Ramrai himself was not quite idle. Every now and then, he got details about this secret plot of the Muslim States. He was, in fact, an old man of seventy at that time, but his passion to fight with the Muslims had not grown a bit less in intensity than what it was in his youth. Undaunted, he, too, equipped his army in every respect and made ready to meet the Muslim attack. He posted two big divisions of his forces under the command of his two brothers—Tirumalrai and Vyankatadri—on two sides of the city, and he himself took the centre.

906. The Hindu-Muslim armies met for a savage struggle at Rakshasbhuvan (Rakkasgi-Tangadgi) near Talikot on Friday, the 2nd of January, 1565. Both the sides had many good cannons and they were arranged before the armies, tied fast with strong chains. The fact that for some time after the first shots were fired, there was fierce fighting and that the Muslims had a very hard knock, which caused confusion amongst their ranks, is admitted even by the Muslim historians. Enraged at this unpleasant turn of event, and thinking that the slightest slackness might bring upon them all total ruin, Sultan Husen Nizamshah dashed right on the centre and forcing a breach amongst the Hindu ranks, he made straight for Raja Ramrai. The historians have no consensus of opinion about what exactly happened at the moment. Some say that a Muslim soldier in the pay of Ramrai himself treacherously killed him. Others declare that Raja Ramrai got down from his palanquin, sat on a jewelled throne in the centre of his army rewarding the feats of valour of his soldiers with gold and jewels, and encouraged them incessantly. Some others avow that when the battle reached its high pitch of ferocity, the Muslims, drove an intoxicated elephant against the royal palanquin and slew him. Whatever that is, one thing is accepted on all hands that

as soon as Raja Ramrai was encircled by the Muslims, they slew him and on the orders of Nizamshah, his bloody head was exhibited on the sharp end of a long spear through the entire army. The sight of that gory head unnerved the Hindus and the Muslims closed in upon them with triumphant war-cries.

907. In spite of all this confusion wrought amongst the Hindu ranks, Tirumalrai, the brother and Commander of Raja Ramrai, made haste to reach the capital city of Vijaynagar with many of the royal family, and before the Muslim forces arrived there, he left for the south with whatever royal treasure he could load upon five hundred and fifty elephants, and the remnant of his army, foot and horse. Mad with triumph, the Muslim armies soon came in hot pursuit of the defeated Hindu ones and not only did they capture the city but destroyed it completely with their traditional cruelty and animosity. They razed to the ground grand palaces, temples, town-halls, beautifully laid-out gardens, market places and colossal statues. Libraries of books were burnt to ashes; crores of rupees worth of treasures were pillaged. The Muslim writers themselves state with evident pride that the infernal fires started in Vijaynagar by the Muslims kept burning for five or six months together. Thus perished the grand city of Vijaynagar at the hands of the Muslim demons in human form.

908-909. It is frivolous to say that the Muslims ravaged Vijaynagar only to avenge—only as a reaction to—the religious atrocities committed by the Hindus in return for the similar atrocities of Muslims. It is not tenable against the mass of evidence now available.

910. But these writers, both the foreign and Muslim ones—and also the Hindus with a perverted sense of virtues—do not see—do not remember—when they say so, what cause had the Hindus given to Mahmud of Ghazni, Mohammed Ghori, Taimurlang, Babar and others to invade them. They had never harmed any of them in any way. How many masjids in Ghazni had the Hindus burnt? How many of the Muslim subjects in the lands of Ghor of Ghazni had been oppressed and how many of their womenfolk had been raped by the Hindus? How many millions of the Muslim women had been kept by the Hindus as concubines or maids? What atrocities did the Hindus commit first on the Muslims for avenging which, the above-mentioned Muslim leaders marched towards India? Did they not, each one of them, declare openly in their courts that it was sotely for the sake of completely destroying

the Hindus, for wiping out their race from the face of the earth and for converting them forcibly to Islam, that they attacked the Indian continent?

911. While reviewing this destruction of Vijaynagar, it is enough to see if even the Muslim writers have the face to say that before the mighty armies of Allauddin and Maliq Kafur marched against the Deccan, the South Indian Hindus had perpetrated any atrocities on non-Hindus in the north. If they cannot do so, they should explain why did the Muslim armies attack the Hindus in the South and brought wholesale destruction on state-after-state from Devgiri, Warangal to Madurai, much in the same horrible form as was meted out to Vijaynagar? Why did they hurl insults and indignities at the Hindu religion and why did those Muslim demons persecute the innumerable Hindu men and women? Nobody can say by any stretch of imagination, that it was to avenge the religious atrocities of the Hindus over the Muslims of the North. It was due to the fact that extirpating the Hindus was itself considered to be their religious duty—a holy faith as it was!

912. The unhesitating, shameless and open stand of the Muslim writers of the times, and of those before and after, is: "We believe that it is our chief religious duty to annihilate the non-Muslims. To conquer the kafir Hindu states, to rape the royal Hindu ladies, to enslave millions of other kafir women and men, and to massacre others, to burn, devastate and demolish the Hindu capital cities, their temples, the idols of their Gods, to reduce to ashes their libraries of religious books and do all sorts of wrongs to them were all the 'holy acts' of the Muslim Gazis—the defenders of the Muslim faith! All these 'holy' acts were done to chastise the kafirs strictly according to the Muslim religious and ethical code, for their inexcusable (unpardonable) sin of being kafirs! When the kafirs call these holy acts atrocities, they must be plainly told that they were not atrocities at all! They were all righteous and virtuous acts! It is the bounden duty of every faithful follower of Islam, that he must thus chastise the kafirs whenever, and to whatever extent, he might be able to do so.

913. "But for the Hindus to call our religious chastisement atrocities and to retaliate against our holy religion as a reaction against our so-called cruelties, to burn our pure masjids because we have burned their temples—it is simply diabolic!—atrocious in the extreme!"

914. It is because the Muslims had this perverted conception of

their religious duty that they marched upon Vijaynagar primarily as it was a Hindu State, and as the Hindus stubbornly refused to become Muslims. Even if the Vijaynagar armies had not invaded the Bahamani Muslim States, as they often did, and even if they had not retaliated with equal vehemence against the usual Muslim atrocities by burning their masjids and houses and plundering their property, all the Muslim Sultans would have attacked Vijaynagar Hindus simply for their fault of being Hindus. They would have committed the same inhuman atrocities, even if the Hindus of Vijaynagar had not done them any harm, had they but got an opportunity to do so!

Why did the Muslim Armies go back after the Pillage of Vijaynagar?

915. The underlying reason why the Muslim armies drew back after pillaging Vijaynagar and did not pursue *the fleeing* Hindus is that they dared not do so; for the state of Vijaynagar had broken away from the old Hindu tradition of meek submission and tight-lipped endurance and had begun to reciprocate atrocities with counter-atrocities and reprisals with super-reprisals!

916. As has already been told above, Ramrai's brother, Commander Tirumalrai, had already left Vijaynagar with his army into the South and was re-forming his forces for another knock. Had the Muslims advanced further they were bound to meet with strong opposition from Tirumal's army. Partly owing to this fear, the Muslims retreated from Vijaynagar, content with whatever they could sack there.

917. Another reason that was responsible for this speedy retreat was the opening of the 'old sores' among the Muslim Sultans! Their belonging to different sects, like the Shias and Sunnis, had always created bickerings amonst them. Naturally, as soon as the hostilities with the Hindu state of Vijaynagar ended, their temporary alliance went to pieces and fresh warfare ensued. A little later, when their arch-enemies, the Muslims in the North, the Moghal Emperors, Shahjahan and Aurangzeb, invaded them with their invincible armies, they could not help looking for support from the then growing Maratha chieftains and their sturdy followers in Maharashtra. Being most mercilessly hammered from the North by the powerful Moghal armies and being internally eaten away by the very Maratha Sirdars who were called for help, these Muslim powers in the South perished one after another!

Shahaji, the Valiant!

918. The most prominent of all these Maratha Sirdars, and the one in whom always blazed the secret ambition to establish a Hindu power was Shahaji, the valiant of the Bhosale family.

919. It has been already stated that after the collapse of Vijaynagar, Tirumalrai and other Hindu princes fled to the South and established another independent Hindu principality at Penukonda in A.D. 1567. Shreerang, Tirumalrai's son, removed his capital to Chandragiri after his father's death. Other princes, too, founded their small States, but they were in fact, the fragments of the old Vijaynagar empire, now set adrift after the deluge of the different 'Nayaks' (Subhedars) of the Vijaynagar empire; a few now consolidated their power and ruled independently. Some called themselves 'Palegars' and founded the states of Jingi, Tanjawar and other 'small Hindu states. So, even after the collapse of Vijaynagar, the whole region south of the capital right up to Rameshwaram was under the Hindu sway. Later still, with the nominal suzerainty of the Sultan of Vijapur, Shahaji, as a Vijapuri Sirdar, established his *"de facto'* overlordship in the south and brought them all under his unifying control. Shahaji exerted a great influence as an able political and military leader, because of his victories, right from Ahmednagar to Rameshwaram under every Muslim power, from the Moghals of Delhi to the moribund Sultanate of Vijapur. He was equally known everywhere as the staunch supporter of the Hindus! His was the deciding vote in respect of the political manoeuvres in the south. A line from a contemporary poet, which became a common saying in those days, stated that the earth was ruled by the two guardians of directions'; उत शाहजहां इत शाहजी है। (Shahajahan in the North and Shahaji in the South)

920. For Shahaji, thus to conquer the remnants of the Vijaynagar Empire in the name of a Muslim, would at the first sight, seem highly preposterous and would even smell of high treason against the Hindu nation. But it should, at the same time, be remembered that it is because he brought all these scattered and vanquished Hindu states under his unified control, that he could overawe his very Sultan and rule the South like an independent Hindu King at Mysore.

That he did this in order to root out all the Muslim Sultans from the Deccan and to found an all-embracing powerful Hindu Kingdom can amply be proved by the act that very soon, one of his sons could set up an independent, powerful and conquering Hindu Empire and that he could help him secretly in that great cause. That this 'insignificant rebellious' son of his could not have grown into a successful empire-builder without, not only the benevolent connivance of Shahaji, but also his active but secret assistance and guidance, requires no further elucidation. Although for reasons of chronological sequence, we may not name this illustrious son of Shahaji just yet, it must already have flashed like a lightning in the hearts of the readers! There can be no doubt about it!

921. In similar circumstances during the years A.D. 1316-1322, Khushrukhan commanded the Sultan's whole army at Delhi as a Muslim, because the Hindu military help was readily available, and conquered and consolidated forcibly the Southern Hindu States, which never united of their own accord, as parts of the vast empire of a Muslim Sultan (Ch XVII). And, only after he succeeded in perfecting the plans for his coup d'etat, did he kill the Sultan of Delhi overnight, ascending the throne himself as a Hindu monarch. He merely brushed aside, as it were, the label 'Muslim' from the imperial throne and wrote in bold letters 'Hindu' over it. Within a day, the all-India Khilji empire became a Hindu empire! Again, a little later, when Harihar and Bukka were captured and made Muslims and were rotting in captvity at Delhi, they first employed the same Koutileeya code of ethics to win the confidence of the Sultan of Delhi under their Muslim garb. They invaded the rebellious Hindus of the South as Muslim commanders at the head of a Muslim army and aided by Muslim wealth; but at the earliest opportunity, they joined the rebellious Hindus themselves, and being reconverted to Hinduism, founded a strong independent Hindu empire at Vijaynagar. The same Koutileeya strategy was used by Shahaji in conquering the Hindu States right up to Jingi and Tanjawar with the Vijapur army and at the Vijapuri expenditure, and bringing them under the nominal sovereignty of the Sultan of Vijapur. Immediately after the fall of the Vijaynagar empire, Shahaji was consolidating the Hindu might to overthrow the Muslim domination and to establish a sovereign Hindu government, which was going to be far mightier than any gone before it, and which was destined to bring the final victory for the Hindus. This was the momentous job of laying the foundation of the

future Hindu victory that Shahaji was engaged in those perilous times!

922. Because of these heartening events, the indomitable Hindu national aspiration could easily survive the grievous fall of Vijaynagar, whereas the Muslims could not avail of it in the least, so as to shape the future in their favour!

□

20

The end of the Sixteenth Century and After

923. After having so far reviewed Indian History from the standpoint of the Hindu nation, we shall now take up some connected events of the sixteenth century and thereafter.

Swarm of European Pirates Invade India

924. The first of the European nations to invade India was Portugal. It was Vasco De Gama, the Portuguese navigator, who first rounded the Cape of Good Hope and discovered a straight sea-route to India. He was, however, guided by one of the captains of the Indian mercantile morine. who plied to and fro between the Indian and the African coasts. In A.D. 1498, he first landed in the port of Calikat on the Western coast of India, professing purely commercial interests, which subsequently served to be a very fine pretext for the other Portuguese and European nationals, who followed suit, to camouflage their secret territorial ambitions in India. Accordingly, immediately after two years in A.D. 1500, came Padro Alvaira's Cabral, another Portuguese admiral with thirteen warships fitted with guns and weapons under his command. Seeing that the Muslim traders had already established themselves well in Cochin, he went there first to undermine their preponderance in inter-continental trade. Since the beginning, the Portuguese had cherished inveterate enmity towards the Muslims as a result of the horrible religio-political aggression of the latter on Spain and Portugal as has already been referred to in Paras 539 to 546. Later in A.D. 1509, Albuquerque was made the Governor of the Portuguese possessions in India. It was he who conquered Goa and the surrounding territory from the Muslim Sultans of Vijapur in A.D. 1510. It was he again who encouraged his Portuguese compatriots to marry, even with force and deceit, if necessary,

Hindu girls in order to ensure the permanent Portuguese settlements in India. About this time, the Portuguese priesthood claimed that it was their supreme religious duty to proselytize the Hindus even with force and made their king issue a royal order to that effect. It is under this royal sanction that the Portuguese in Goa perpetrated the indescribable atrocities, rapes and various other outrages on the Hindus—men and women—there as are mentioned in Paras 539 to 546 of this book.

925. The patron-saint directing these blood-curdling Portuguese religious formalities was the Jesuit missionary, Saint Francis Xavier, whom the persecuted Hindus called Satan incarnate! He came to India in 1540.

925.A. This so-called 'Saint' Xavier himself proudly states in one of his letters his triumphant success in the devilish persecution of the Hindus (see Paragraphs 539 to 546). He himself and hundreds of other missionaries, who came after him, converted innumerable Hindus to Christianity with all sorts of brutalities and vandalism. Countless Hindu men and women committed suicide to escape this violent persecution. The Portuguese gradually conquered Div, Daman, Sashti, Vasai (Bassein), Choul, Mumbai (Bombay) on the Western coast of India and Saint Tome near Madras, and Hugh in Bengal, of which Mumbai (Bombay) was presented to the English King as a dowry in 1668 (1661-2?) by the Portuguese King Charles II. It was subsequently made over the King Charles II of England to East India Company for a nominal rent of 4-10 a year. The rest of the region round about Bombay in the Portuguese possession was released by the Marathas. Goa was the only major possession left in the Portuguese hands.

926. The Dutch: Quick on the heels of the Portuguerse, the Dutch of Holland entered India. The Dutch East india Company was formed in A.D. 1602 for the purpose, but they could not find a firm footing in India. Jawa and Sumatra, however, proved congenial to them. Hence, they directed all their attention to that region and made it their stronghold. When the English began to dabble there, the Dutch cut them all but one at Amboina, and ruled practically the whole of the Indonesian archipelago unhampered.

927. The English: Although the English East India Company was formed in A.D. 1600, it could not open its first factory in India till A.D. 1608. Jahangir gave them permission to open one at Surat in A.D. 1613. After a while in 1689, the monopoly of the British East India

Company was cancelled because of many malpractices and rivalries in the Company's servants and another company was formulated to carry on Indian Trade. But when it was seen that such competition was detrimental to the interests of the British Nation as a whole, the two companies were amalgamated.

928. As the British East India Company was later on to enlarge the scope of her activities to such an enormous extent as to encompass a foreign stupendous Indian empire, it is out of place and even impossible to discuss its extensive history in these introductory remarks. Moreover, as the English were to meet the Marathas on the battlefields amidst the clash of arms, the boom of cannons and the swaggering wagers with empires as the tempting stakes, we would rather discuss it a little later so far as it will be possible to do so.

929. The French: Of the European nations that followed suit after the Portuguese and tried their hand at the eastern trade and the overseas empires, the French, were the last to appear on the scene. For the French East India Company was floated as late as A.D. 1664. But they prospered quickly in their commercial activities. Why, if credit is to be given to any European, who thought for the first time of acquiring not only small scattered footholds but large empires in India and who tried to realize these ambitious schemes of his by large-scale military intervention in Indian politics, it was French Governor Dupleix. The next claimant to that honour is that vagabond and tempestuous English youth, Robert Clive, who entered India as a common soldier, but who soon came to command large armies and to lay the foundations of the vast British Empire in India. The basic idea underlying the schemes of these two far-sighted young men was that with proper training, great drilled and well-disciplined armies could be formed here in India out of the very Indian soldiers within a very short time, and that, with competent, efficient and uncorruptible European military officers and commanders at the head of this very Indian army, they could easily build up their strong Empires in India. It will be discussed in its proper place, how great was the harvest that these daring schemes reaped in the years to come.

930. It is, however, proper to discuss the French affairs in India to a certain extent. For, although for a time, the French and the English fought amongst themselves on the Indian soil and although they took opposite sides in the internecine civil wars of the Indian Kings and Princes, in the end the French were on losing grounds. Again their defeat at the hands

of the English in the European theatres of war rendered the French authorities in India thoroughly incapable of defending their positions against the ever increasing severity of the English attacks. The leaders like Dupleix, Busie, Suffren and others, who worked hard and spent the best of their energies for the expansion of the French empire in India, were very shabbily treated at home by the French people and the French Govenment. Nobody appreciated their best efforts at the proper times nor gave them any support. Again, this Indian army of the French fought against the Marathas, on a few occasions, only to receive stunning blows and as such when it was clear that the chances of the French empire in India were almost nil, they began to help the Indian princes and especially the Marathas, particularly in respect of the training of the army and the use of the new guns. The English were very reluctant to help any native ruler create a disciplined army or to sell them newer weapons like the guns and cannons. But the French were only too willing to do that in exchange for large sums of money or substantial grants of land, and especially so, if that purchasing authority was engaged in a struggle with the English. The Marathas, in particular, realized the inevitable greatness of the European type of training of troops and the production of the efficient new weapons of war like the various types of small and big firearms. Hence, they employed veteran French military officers and their satellites in their armies. Ibrahim Khan Gardi, the famous artillery commander in the Maratha army at the battles of Udgeer and Panipat, had received his training in that field in the French artillery divisions. Later on, Mahadaji Shinde (Scindia) employed French officers like De Boyne and M.Perron as the chief commanders of their artillery and other divisions and formed a well-equipped, well-trained, mechanized army of his own. With this well-trained strong army, Mahadaji could overawe the whole of the antagonistic north and vanquish the enemies in various military engagements. But after a while, the European nations working in India had come to a certain unwritten understanding, at least as regards India, that in the event of any Indian ruler fighting against any of the European nationals, no European army leader should take sides with the Indian and help him with his army. As such, later on when Shinde (Scindia) was engaged in a deadly struggle with the English, De Boyne, who had been receiving thousands of rupees by way of salary, and the army trained by him flatly refused to fight. The Marathas, too, were conscious of such a treacherous behaviour on the part of these salaried foreigners some time or the other. Hence, the Marathas, on their part, had begun to open factories to manufacture similar guns and to prepare Indian officers to train and drill the army on European lines. But in those stormy days of incessant warfare, it would have been unwise to depend solely on nothing but such trained army divisions. Even second rate states like the Jats and the Sikhs maintained such battalions. On the whole, the existence of the French military might in India, helped here and there check the onward march of the British imperialistic power, and the Marathas, Tipu, the Sikhs and other Indian rulers did not fail to utilize it to that extent.

The Simultaneous Attack of all the non-Hindu Nations of the World on the Deccan (South India)

931. When the European powers, mentioned above, invaded India, they all did so by the sea. Naturally, their first tremendous onslaughts had to be borne and resisted by the Deccan and especially by the Marathas. Earlier, North India had to bear for six or seven centuries, the whole brunt of the fierce and marauding attacks of the fanatical Muslims like the Moghals, the Turks, the Afghans, the Arabs and others, and had to offer them the sternest possible resistance. Eventually, all these Asiatic Muslim nationals and the barbaric tribes fell violently upon the South with a view to conquering it for ever. Even while all these enemies were repeatedly invading from the North and the Deccan was engaged with them in bloody and deadly wars, in which thousands of Hindus were offering their precious lives for the sake of defending their religion, as they did in the North, the South Indian people were invaded, by the sea, by the new European Christian nationals, as numerous as the locusts themselves. The enemies crowded in upon the Deccan not only from the north-west or the north-east but also from the west. Not only by land but by sea also, did all the combative, marauding, aggressive and fanatic Muslims and Christian nations had simultaneously attacked the Deccan at the time, to overrun the Hindu states there and to eradicate Hindu religion from the land.

932. North India had to face only the Muslim nations, which itself was not an easy job. The deadly war that the Hindus had been fighting with the Muslims for centuries was as fierce and beset with all sorts of dangers as to exhaust even the Gods who had fought against the demons! But the Deccan had the misfortune of facing not only all those

Muslims but also the European Christian nations like the Portuguese and others, who were even greater enemies of Hinduism than the Muslims, and who tried every form of cruelty to proselytize the Hindus. And the South Indian Hindus—and especially the Marathas, who had assumed their leadership in this war—showed the rarest tenacity and irresistible daring to repel single-handed, these waves of aggression rising all round them. While thousands of Hindus had been sacrificing their lives along with those of their wives and children on the religious front against the Muslims and the Portuguese Christians, as many others were fighting battles after battles and wars after wars on the political and military fronts. This exceptional struggle of the Hindus against foreign aggressors is worth a glorious mention in the history of the world.

Hindu Vikramaditya, Hemoo

933. The many Rajput and Muslim states, which had collected together under the leadership of Rana Sang, and who had aspired to re-establish the Hindu empire had joined battle with Babar at Kanvah. But after fierce fighting, Rana Sang was finally defeated and Babar laid the foundation of the Moghal empire at Delhi. Soon in 1530, Babar died and was succeeded by his son, Humayun, who in his turn was overcome by Sher Shah, the founder of the Sur dynasty. As Sher Shah Sur captured Delhi, Humayun had to wander in exile through various countries such as Kabul, Kandahar, Persia and others, of which we need not give any detailed account. It is enough to say that even in the royal dynasty of Sultan Sher Shah, the upheavals, usual and inevitable in every Muslim regime, took place and after violent rebellions and bloodshed, Mohammed Adilshah was at last installed as the Emperor.

934. This Mohammed Adilshah had enturested his administration to an able Hindu Vazir named Hemoo. Hemoo, too, without ever endangering his Hindu religion in the least, appropriated the *de facto* power of the Sultan to himself and ruled his dominions efficiently.

935. But this roused the jealousy and anger of other Muslim sirdars. In the meanwhile in 1542, while he was yet in exile, Humayun had a son, named Akbar, who was later on destined to be a great emperor. With the help of the Shah of Iran (Persia), Humayun invaded India and burning the eyes of his faithless brother, and inflicting exemplary punishments on other enemies, he reconquered Delhi. But soon after

his regaining the throne of Delhi, he slipped over the marble staircase of his palace and died in 1556, giving rise to anarchy everywhere. The last emperor of the Sur dynasty, Mohammed Shah Adil, who was defeated by Humayun, had fled to the north-west frontier. But his able minister, Hemoo, however, lingered on in Delhi itself, trying to avail himself of that opportunity.

936. A very scanty reference has been made in the Muslim historical writings about the past or future life of Hemoo, the valiant Hindu leader. A Hindu historian was an impossibility at that time and whoever tried his hand later on at writing history has not said anything independently about Hemoo. But we have already shown in Chapter Seventeen about Hindu Emperor Dharmarakshak (Nasir-ud-din), that his actual heroic deed is far more important and reliable a proof than any written record. Similarly, we shall try to give here the account of the Hindu Hero, Hemoo, as far as we can do so with the same unassailable logic.

937. It is to be noted that even while he aspired to form a Hindu Empire, he received help from many Afghan sirdars, who had fallen foul of the Moghal Muslims and especially of the Babar faction.

938. It is obvious that the life and career of the earlier Hindu Emperor, Shree Dharmarakshak (Nasir-ud-din), must have served as an ideal to be followed before Hemoo as regards the original inspiration to found a Hindu empire and the formation of a detailed scheme of his war of independence was concerned. An undying fire of freedom which sought to overthrow the Muslim rule and found a Hindu Empire in its stead had once inspired Shree Dharmarakshak (Nasir-ud-din) to bring about a glorious yet unsuccessful military coup, spurred Rana Sang and other Rajput warriors to cross swords, although not successfully, with Babar at Kanvah and at hundreds of places earlier and later, had stimulated millions of Hindu men and women to undergo all extremities of fortunes, to fight horrible battles or to immolate their lives to save their religion. The same blazing fire of freedom glowed clear and bright in the Hindu heart of Hemoo, the ambitious Hindu leader.

938A. As has been said above, he secretly prepared for a decisive battle, organized the Muslim dissentients against the Moghals and the Hindu army marched against Delhi. All the Hindu-Muslim officers at Delhi had served under him when he was the Chief Minister (Vazir). There, other politicians and the Hindus in general, offered him no opposition worth the name, surrendering to his once dreaded influence as a Vazir.

His conquest of Delhi, the chief capital of Moghal empire, caused a great commotion everywhere.

939. Hemoo was born a staunch Hindu. During the Sultan's regime, he rose to political eminence by sheer dint of his merit without the slightest slur on his Hindu individuality. In the end, assuming responsibility as the weak Sultan's Vazir, he began to control the whole imperial administration and consolidate power into his own hands. And now he had openly hoisted the standard of Hinduism, boosted up a Hindu imperial power trampling down the whole of the Muslim Sultanate! Quite naturally, the whole of the Muslim world was rocked to the bottom with the cry that Islam was doomed and that kafirs flourished!

940. Immediately after capturing Delhi, he publicly ascended the imperial throne as a Hindu emperor with all the adequate pomp and glory and assumed the title of Vikramaditya for himself. Then after stabilizing and introducing efficient management of the affairs of his state, he started new conquests. Formerly as the Sultan's Vazir, he had won fifteen to sixteen battles, crushing down the revolts of the Muslim and other chieftains. As such, he had a great self-confidence in his abilities, as regards the efficient conduct of war was concerned. At the first stroke, he stormed and seized the second great Moghal fort of Agra, which was considered to be impregnable and the city around it.

941. At this time, the future emperor Akbar was a mere lad of thirteen or fourteen years. His Vazir, Bahiramkhan, was his guardian and the *de facto* head of his administration. On hearing the news of Hemoo, he at once resolved to crush down this bold rising of the Hindus. But right from Rajputana to the Deccan, numerous Hindu-Muslim states, both big and small, had risen in revolt against this newly-formed Moghal empire. Hence, the other Muslim sirdars advised Bahiramkhan to put these down first and to keep young Akbar at Kabul in safety. But the discreet Bahiramkhan firmly asserted that Hemoo's rising in the name of a Hindu empire had to be put down firmly. Accordingly, Bahiramkhan marched on Hemoo at the head of a powerful army, and instead of sending young Akbar to Kabul, he took him along to the battlefield. The armies of Bahiramkhan and Hemoo met near Panipat. Vikramaditya Hemoo's warriors fought with exceptional bravery and skill. It seemed for a time that Hemoo had won the battle, but as ill-luck would have it, in the very hour of glory, Vikramaditya Hemoo was struck in the eye by a

stray arrow from the army of Bahiramkhan and he fell from his elephant unconscious! This created a havoc in the Hindu ranks of Hemoo, while the Muslim soldiers in Bahiramkhan's army, being quite mercenary were in a way let loose. With a determined attack, Bahiramkhan made this confusion worse confounded and vanquishing the leaderless Hindu army, captured Hemoo alive. Taking him to young emperor Akbar, Bahiramhan requested the latter to behead Hemoo with his own royal hands. But young Akbar could not bring himself up to do such a cruel deed. So the enraged Bahiramkhan himself unsheathed his sword and cut off Hemoo's head.

942. This martyrdom that Vikramaditya Hemoo courted was as obviously (manifestly) done in the cause of Hindu religion, and the greater glory of the Hindu nation and Hindu welfare as any other. The Hindu nation must always bow down its head in all reverence to this hero, who unfortunately is not so remembered amongst the very few so-called martyrs and warriors in the Hindu world. Well be it so! But even if the millions of these self-deceived and ungrateful Hindus have forgotten him, the Hindu nation as a whole must always remember that the undying Hindu aspiration to free itself, which was kept continually ablaze through a succession of generations and over centuries together and which ultimately rent to pieces the Muslim imperial power, planting on its dead remains the glorious banner of an India-wide Hindu empire, was fed on the now forgotten martyrdom, and the sacrificial offerings of their lives on the altar of war, of the numerous brave heroes like Hemoo, who were दिल्लींद्र पदलिप्सव (ambitious of being the lords of Delhi).

943. Here itself, may we offer our reverential tributes to the glorious memory of Vikramaditya Hemoo, the great, and proceed futher!

The Valiant Queen Durgawati

944. Bahiramkhan, thereafter, took Akbar straight to Delhi, later they two together reduced all the rebels up to Gwalior (Gwalher). But they soon fell out and Akbar assumed supreme authority, whereupon Bahiramkhan rebelled, but was defeated. Even then, Akbar did not kill him outright, but sent him away to Makka. Bahiramkhan, however, fell a prey to a revengeful enemy of his of the earlier days.

945. In A.D. 1564, the independent Rajput King in Gondwana, named Veer Narayan, was attacked by Akbar. King Veer Narayan was a minor. Yet his mother, the dowager Qeeen Durgawati, decided not to surrender

but to fight the well-equipped imperial army of Akbar, and offered such a tough resistance that for a while, the invaders were astounded. She bravely defended the cause of Hinduism till she was overwhelmed by the vastly superior numbers of the Muslim emperor. But did she sue for peace and lay down arms? Did she ask for the imperial clemency as for a powerless woman? Or, did she send a 'Rakhi' to Akbar and abjectly request him to treat her as a sister and show mercy to her as did some other Rajput ladies, off and on? No, not at all! Knowing full well from hundreds of such cases how these Muslim wolves ill-treated and molested the royal Hindu ladies, who fell captives in their hands, Rani Durgawati staunchly refused to do anything of the kind. She, on the contrary, offered her body, along with many other ladies of the court, to the 'sacred' fire of the battle. She left strict orders to her attendant to burn her dead body and not to let the Muslim infidels touch it. Even after her death, Raja Veer Narayan continued to fight with the Muslims, but his resistance was put down by the vastly superior Muslim forces and in A.D. 1562, his small state of Gondwana was annexed to the Moghal empire.

946. Akbar then began to entice the softer ones of the Rajput rulers, who had been disgusted with incessant warfare with the Muslims over generations, together with very alluring promises of honourable and friendly treatment to the Hindus. But on seeing that, even when these docile Rajput rulers were prone to accept Akbar's terms, they often hesitated and fought shy of doing so in the face of the high sense of honour and pride in their religious and racial purity, which made the belligerent Rana of Chitod staunchly turn down all overtures of peace from the Moghal Emperor. Akbar decided to subdue the fort of Chitod first and accordingly, laid siege to it in A.D. 1567. The Rana of Chitod at that time was Uday Singh, who had not even a small percentage of the dauntless valour of his celebrated father, Rana Sang, who had earlier fought with Babar. But the one courtesan who was at that time wielding real power in Chitod inspired the Rajputs to extraordinary valour. Even when Uday Singh fled away to the forest, the great feudatory lords of Chitod like Jaymalla, Patta and others continued to fight with the Moghals. Later, when Jaymalla and Patta were killed on the battlefield and defeat was absolutely certain, the Rajput Hindus of Chitod, instead of becoming dispirited and disheartened, were touched to the quick and infuriated to the extreme. All the soldiers desperately entered the battlefield and with the war-cry 'Har, Har Mahadev' heaped

up mounds of the massacred Muslim warriors. But ultimately, when the Rajputs themselves were almost killed in the battle, all the Rajput ladies of Chitod set ablaze the big fire, which was kept ready for the purpose and leapt therein from the ramparts of the fort, according to their age-long glorious tradition, with small children at their breasts and the acclamations in praise of their religion on their lips. These brave ladies reduced themselves to ashes but did not allow the hateful Muslim-touch to defile their pure bodies! This was the third great self-immolation by the ladies of Chitod.

947. It was the same heartless Akbar who caused such a great havoc amongst the Hindus, but whom the spineless Hindu historians of today call the most liberal of monarchs; the one, they say, who yearned to bring about amity between, and unity of, the Hindus and the Muslims; the one, in their opinion, who treated the Hindus far more honourably than any Muslim ruler, before or after him; who was according to them a veritable Raja Ramchandra amongst the Muslims!

948. But let it also be remembered that, as if not content with this blood-curdling sacrifice of men, women and children of Chitod, Akbar entered the blood-stained city of Chitod, put to sword every one of the bewailing Hindu citizens that remained there—and mark well—he made no exception for the Hindu women. Thirty thousand Hindus lost their lives in this one battle of Chitod. Eventually, it seems the stones and other inanimate objects of Chitod appeared to him as deadly enemies of the Muslims as the Hindus there, and hence this devilish destroyer Akbar went on pulling down the Hindu temples, prayer halls, palaces, houses—everything that came his way, and reduced them all to heaps of rubble and ashes. The temple of the presiding Goddess of Chitod, likewise, was razed to the ground, the idol of the Goddess and all the courtyard being completely destroyed. The beating drums, the fifes, the lamps, jewellery and ornaments, door frames and every sort of valuable or grand articles of Hindu interest were sent away to Agra. Only after quenching his fiendish fanaticism a little with such an inhuman destruction of the Hindu capital of Chitod, did this Muslim Emperor Akbar return to Delhi, calling himself 'Gazi' for this virtuous and pious act of his.

949. On the other hand, Uday Singh, who had been wandering in the forest for four years, unable to avenge the brutal destruction of his kingdom and the capital city of Chitod, died of grief in A.D. 1572.

Rana Pratap Singh, the jewel among the Hindus

950. Uday Singh's son, Rana Pratap Singh, immediately ascended the non-existent, imaginary throne of Chitod! But, as he was offered the truly great throne in the hearts of all the staunch Rajputs and as he was considered the very emblem of their invincible courage and valour, this Rana Pratap Singh shone with more dazzling glory than many enthroned kings. He turned out to be the one such Rajput Rana, who would never, under any odds—even at the peril of his life—leave the traditional high sense of honour of the Rajputs. Instead of seeking the humiliating friendship with Akbar and the moments of peace and ease that it would have offered, he preferred to be the direst enemy of the most powerful of Muslim Emperors, regardless of untold miseries and calamities that such an enmity devolved on him. He considered it to be the hallmark of true Hinduism and true Hindu kingship to do so?

951. As Chitod was in the hands of the Muslims, he kept his capital moving with him through villages and towns, in those perilous times, and gradually rescued a large portion of his lost kingdom. He also formed a staunch army of desperate but devoted followers, who held their lives at naught. It is a pity that we cannot describe his thrilling exploits and pitched battles here, for want of space.

952. In the end, his influence grew so powerful and so widespread, that Akbar himself had to send his imperial army to subdue him. Shameful as it is, Raja Mansingh of Jaipur, who had surrendered himself to Akbar and the Rajput convert Mahabat Khan, committed an unpatriotic act of joining Prince Salim's army, marching against Rana Pratap at the Emperor's orders. And at this time, it was that the celebrated battle of Haldighat was fought. In the heat of fighting, Rana Pratap rode his horse straight at the elephant of Prince Salim and that unrivalled horse, Chetak, without the slightest hesitation, made straight at the trunk of the Prince's elephant and planted his front feet on it. With lightning speed, Rana Pratap's spear whizzed past Prince Salim's throat so dreadfully as to stun the latter for a moment. But seeing that his dart missed the mark, Rana Pratap retreated with equal speed and got mixed up with the army the very next moment, and was not to be singled out.

953. Soon he retreated from this undecided battle with thousands of daredevils for his faithful followers, who were sworn to his cause and captivated by his valour and carried the swift guerrilla warfare throughout Mewad, destroying the Muslims and freeing the whole of Mewad except

for the capital city of Chitod. In the end, Rana Pratap stabilized his moving capital at Udepur, which never till the end, fell to Akbar. The latter dropped peace-feelers, but Rana Pratap never paid any heed to them. His regime is so replete with chivalrous and romantic adventures, deeds of exceptional valour done by common folks, as those by the great warriors and the Rana himself, that our young generation should delve deep into them and learn them by rote as reverentially as they would, the stories from the Ramayan and the Mahabharat. Fortunately, the romantic Rasos of Rajput Bhats up to the date of the great poet Bhooshan, are still available, which should really be appointed in the secondary schools as compulsory textbooks. But alas! in this critical historical survey of ours, there is no place for citing any passages from them.

954-955. Nor now in the fading light of my last days, is any time left for them!

This Rana Pratap Singh, a great ornament to the Hindu society, died in A.D. 1581.

The rise of the Sikhs in Punjab—
a new awakening of the Hindu might

956. A saintly person, by name Guru Nanak, started a new religious sect in Punjab by the end of the fifteenth century, the followers of which soon organized themselves into a homogeneous group calling themselves Shikh [Sikh—शिष्य—The disciples of Guru Nanak] Shree Guru Nanak was not a sanyasi—a recluse—but a man with a family to bring up. He preached that the worship of God and the service of humanity was possible through devotion. "Every man can follow this path of devotion!", he asserted.

956A. At that time not only in Punjab but throughout the whole of India, the Muslims had waged a total war against Hinduism and resounded the whole country with the clash of swords, the twang of arrows and the beat of drums. But throughout the whole of India, Hindu rulers and the Hindu populace had been bravely resisting the Muslim aggression on every battlefield. Allauddin's almost completed India-wide conquest and the consequent Muslim empire, was precipitately broken into numerous fragments and free and strong Hindu States like the Vijaynagar empire had already been established. In Rajputana and Gondwana, too, the Hindu Kings with their daring armies had frequently worsted the Muslim forces!

957. But in Punjab alone, there was left no Hindu strong enough

to challenge the Muslim government. At such a dark hour SHREE GURU NANAK began to preach in the Punjab that from the point of view of God, both the Hindus and the Muslims were the same. Both the communities could attain bliss through his path of devotion. Both the communities were one common fraternity. In his sect, he said, he did not recognize any distinction between the two. Yet with all his preaching of this common accord, very few Muslims could be found amongst his disciples. All the others were Hindus. Shree Guru Nanak himself was a Khatri. He died in A.D. 1538. Although he had sons of his own, they did not follow his tenets. So, he installed his disciple Angad as the chief priest after himself. This sect of Shree Guru Nanak, however, was at least up to his death, nothing more than a mere devotional group, a singing choir of devotional songs and mattered very little politically. Still, his grief at the miserable plight of the Hindus, found echoes in some of his writings. For example:

958. क्षत्रियां ही धरम छोडियां, मलेच्छ भाषा गही।
सृष्टि सब इकबरन हुई, धरम की गति रही॥
नील बरन के कपड़े पहने, तुरक पठानी अमल भया॥

The Kshatriyas have left their religious duties (of protecting the land), as the Muslims have flourished. The whole universe has taken on itself one colour, and religion is in danger; people have begun to wear blue garments and so the Turks and Pathans have become rulers.

959. Many other similar lines ascribed to him have been very popular. Like all other Hindu saints, he also has condemned many blind superstitions and foolish customs.

960. After Guru Angad, the third was Guru Amardas (A.D. 1574) and the fourth Guru was Ramdas. It is said he had an interview with Akbar, and the emperor is said to have bequeathed a large tract of land to him. On the same land, Guru Ramdas dug out a beautiful lake and built a temple on its bank, which is now known as 'Amritsar'. Guru Ramdas died in A.D. 1581. The fifth Guru was Arjundev, in whose times Sikhism grew rapidly, for they now had a central rendezvous at Amritsar. Moreover, the growing need of a religious text for this growing sect was satisfied by him by collecting whatever sayings of Guru Nanak he could get hold of along with those of other contemporary saints, and thereby creating an authorized religious book for the Sikhs! This very authorized religious textbook was called by him 'Gurugranth' or 'Adigranth'. In it are to be found the sayings of Kabir as also those of the

Maharashtrian saint, Namdev. While the Maharashtrian saint, Namdev, was on a pilgrimage of Punjab, his teaching of the path of devotion (भक्ति मार्ग) and his 'Abhangs' (hymns) had a widespread influence there. The striking similarity between his teachings and those of Guru Nanak prompted the inclusion of some of Sant Namdev's Marathi poems in this 'Gurugranth'. This 'Gurugranth' is in Prakrut, which is now called in Punjab as Punjabi. It was not written in the Devnagri script, which was then called 'Shastri Lipi', as it was mostly employed by the learned 'Pandits' for writing about scientific topics. Just as for ordinary day-to-day affairs, 'Modi' script was employed in Maharashtra till very recently, similarly in Punjab at that time in general correspondence of the common people, a Prakrut script was employed and it served for this 'Adigranth'. The script was commonly called 'Lundimundi'. But after the 'Gurugranth' had been written in it, the Sikhs began to call it Gurumukhi, as it was adopted by their Gurus!

961. When Jahangir became the emperor, his eldest son, Khushru, rebelled against him, and fled to Punjab. As the Sikh Guru Arjundev gave him shelter, the enraged Jahangir captured the Sikh Guru and slew him. In the Sikh history, Guru Arjun was the first heroic martyr who laid down his life while fighting with the Muslims in the cause of his religion. In the days of this very Arjundev, a separate organization was set afoot and a tradition of compulsory religious tax to be paid to the Guru by every Sikh was established, and in order that Sikh sect might grow powerful, a military front was also initiated.

962. The violent death of Guru Arjun secretly rankled in the hearts of the Sikhs, giving rise to inveterate hatred for the Muslims. Most of the Sikh followers in those times, as also later on, were Hindu Jats by caste. As these Hindu Jats were the main support of the Sikh sect and that too, quite strong, the Punjabi Hindus in general had affection for, and a feeling of oneness with them. The militant tendencies and the military organizations began to grow amongst the Sikhs and as a sect of the Hindus, they happened to be staunch defenders of Hinduism against the increasing ferocity of the Muslim religious persecution. So, the Moghal government began to look upon that sect as a troublesome centre of Hindu resistance.

963. Soon the son of Guru Arjun, Guru Hargovind refused to pay taxes to the emperor. He was, therefore, captured and interned in prison for twelve years. Later on, when he was released from captivity, he

rebelled against the then Moghal emperor, Shahjahan, who dispatched a small detachment to crush this apparently meagre opposition. But at Sangram, the Sikhs fought with such fierceness that the Muslim detachment was completely vanquished. Although this astounded and pleased the Hindus in Punjab, the Emperor did not mind it. Guru Hargovind died in A.D. 1645 and was succeeded by Harrai, Harkrishan and Teg Bahadur as the high priests of the Sikhs. But it is the exceptional and glorious sacrifice of Teg Bahadur in the cause of religion, that has given dignity and splendour to the seat of the high priest of the Sikhs.

963A. Guru Teg Bahadur lived at Anandpur. Whenever the atrocious conversions of the Hindus to Islam took place in Punjab, Guru Teg Bahadur, with his Sikh warriors, had often fought and opposed them fiercely. And then Aurangzeb, the veritable demon in human form, vowed to root out the whole Hindu world. Naturally, throughout the whole of India, the Hindus too, opposed him violently. Aurangzeb, particularly, aimed at the top-ranking Brahmins of Kashmir, and enforced on them the Jizia tax, if they did not opt for conversion. This caused a great commotion everywhere. At this time, Guru Teg Bahadur told the Hindus boldly not to pay any such taxes and preached that they should sacrifice their lives rather than forsake their religion. When the Hindus began to give such bold replies, Aurangzeb was aflame with rage. He captured Guru Teg Bahadur and commanded him to court Islam on pain of death. Guru Teg Bahadur thereupon staunchly refused to be a Muslim and defied Aurangzeb, who immediately had him beheaded. This horrible tragedy took place in A.D. 1675. Along with Guru Teg Bahadur, several of his Hindu disciples also were caught and they all suffered horrible deaths after all sorts of atrocities and torments, but they defied the tyrannical Muslim emperor by boldly refusing to be Muslims. The heads of some of the prominent Hindus were actually cut asunder with a big saw. Among these martyrs was Bhai Matidas, whose family was lovingly given the title 'Bhai' by the Sikh Gurus and in this very family was born the latter day Hindu patriot, Bhai Parmanand. The son of this very brave Guru was the holiest of the holies, the Hindu national hero, Shree Guru Govind Singh!

The Hindu National Hero—Shree Guru Govind Singh

964. To Shree Guru Govind Singh goes all the credit of militarizing Sikhism and to create out of that sect, a militant and invincible organization, which gave a strong impetus to the establishment of a

strong and independent Hindu government in Punjab at the time of Maharaja Ranjit Singh. He was called Tenth Emperor—दशम बादशाह—because he was the Tenth Guru from Shree Guru Nanak, not only by the Sikhs but even by all the Punjabi Hindus. From innumerable daring and thrilling events in his life, which well illustrate the above remark, only one might suffice here for want of space for others!

965. As inevitably happens in the case of every big religious organisation, Guru Nanak's disciples also came to be divided into many sections and sub-sections, but they were all living a Hindu way of life. In respect of marriages and other religious rites and social customs, they were not in any way separated from the Hindu society. In the 'Gurugranth' itself, the sayings of Hindu saints like Sant Namdev and Kabir were incorporated along with those of Guru Nanak himself. And from the beginning till this day, that 'Adigranth' has always been read with equal reverence for all these sayings. But a son of Guru Nanak himself had started a separate branch of Sikhism.

965A. In course of time, when the Hindus and Sikhs began to be atrociously persecuted by the Muslims, it was felt that an armed force of the Sikhs for self-protection was absolutely necessary, and Guru Govind Singh began to dream of establishing an independent kingdom of the Sikhs. To that end, he wanted a band of daredevils of inviolable loyalty to their Guru.

966. Guru Govind Singh, therefore, called a big assembly of all the Sikhs. Such incidents in his life have been described a little later in poetical compositions, much on the same lines as the colourful descriptions of the Hindu Puranas. But we shall give here only the historically relevant part of it.

967. In that big assembly, Guru Govind Singh invited volunteers, who were prepared even to lay down their lives in the defence of their religion and willing to spend their whole lives in the army, take it up as their profession, for, he said, he had to build a standing army of the Sikhs. It was a very austere vow. Of the many, who thus volunteered, the Guru himself chose for the first time only the best five who were expected to be as sharp and as unbending as steel. To imbibe this principle on their minds, the first religious rite that was performed was the sprinkling on their heads of the holy water that was churned by a sharp steel sword as the mantras were chanted. Then it was enjoined upon them that they were always to have a sword fastened to their waist; they were never to

cut the hair on any part of their body. They were asked ever to gird up their loin, to wear kaccha or langot—a loin-cloth, and to wear steel rings round their wrists as a mark of their stern military vow. A comb was also considered to be a must for every Sikh. Thus hair (केश Kesh), a comb (कंग-कंगवा—Kangha), a loin-cloth (कच्छ-लंगोट—Kaccha), a steel ring (कड़ा—Kara) and a sword (कृपाण—Kripan) became the five inseparable marks of every true Sikh, and were called 'five kakkas'. The military wing of the Sikhs, specially chosen by the Guru has since then been called the 'Khalsa', which has become an honourable appellation throughout the whole of India. Khalsa is originally an Urdu word meaning 'chosen'!

968. As soon as this Khalsa army reached a desired magnitude, Guru Govind Singh began to conquer smaller Hindu-Muslim States or to sack them. Quite naturally, the Moghal Emperor, Aurangzeb, who had most brutally murdered his father, Teg Bahadur, for not renouncing his religion, sent a detachment of his army to capture Guru Govind Singh. Because of the actions that were fought with the Moghal army, the Guru enclosed himself in the fort of Anandpur, which was immediately invested by the Moghals. Amongst the soldiers fighting with Guru Govind Singh from the fort, were two of his sons below the age of eighteen. In order to boost up the courage of the army, the Guru sent his two sons with other soldiers out of the fort to fight with the Moghals. While these two sons were being done to death in this unequal battle, this strange father was crying words of approbation 'Wah-wa! Wah-wa!' At nightfall, the fighting stopped as a matter of course and the remnant of the Khalsa battalion entered the fort very stealthily. But of that Khalsa (chosen) soldiers, many had lost hope. So, the Guru plainly told them all, that those who wanted to save their lives should leave the Khalsa army and forsake him immediately. He, however, was determined to fight on from inside or, if neccessary, out of the fort. Thereupon, from the best chosen (the Khalsa), many Sikh warriors resigned their membership and deserted Guru Govind Singh. Soon on that dark and dismal night, Guru Govind Singh bade adieu to those who remained of his Khalsa army and escaped through the Moghal siege, along with his wife and two sons, who were under twelve.

969. While after leaving the fort, Guru Govind Singh was thus wandering through the forest on that fateful night, he lost track of his two tender children, who unfortunately fell in the enemy hands. Those wicked monsters gave the young kiddies an ultimatum 'Forsake

Hinduism and become Muslims, or else we will kill you with all sorts of tortures!' Prompt came the reply from the young mouths, thundering dauntlessly—lion's cubs as they were—'We are prepared to die for our religion!' They had refused to forsake their Hindu religion. Highly enraged at this defiant reply, the Muslim authorities pronouned their direst sentence. Building a wall round them to suffocate the two children to death was the horrible punishment given. Straight stood the two tender children and brick-upon-brick rose to their very neck, when they were again asked, 'You kafirs, don't you forsake your Hindu religion even now?' 'No, no never!' came the smothered voice! And even as the two kids were shouting slogans in praise of Hinduism as loudly as they could in that horrible position, the last bricks were laid, to bury them for ever.

970. This is truly a glorious incident of martyrdom for the sake of Hinduism that has to be honourably listed amongst others in the annals of Hindu nation. It is a true historical fact but is to be found only described in the poetical form.

971. **Kumar Haqiqatrai**—At this very time, a Hindu lad, by name Kumar Haqiqatrai, happened to draw a picture of the Hindu Goddess of Learning, Saraswati, on his slate for worshipping it. But for this very atrocious deed! the Muslim officers there sentenced him to be converted to Islam. On his refusal to do so, he was threatened with a horrible death. When he defied that threat too, he was killed forthwith. The Hindus of the Punjab even today celebrate his memory every year as a religious and austicious occasion.

972. **The End of Guru Govind Singh**—After the horrible death of his two sons, Guru Govind Singh sent from his exile a conciliatory letter to Aurangzeb as a strategic move in politics. The Emperor, too, sent a reply and after a certain mutual agreement, Guru Govind Singh was allowed to leave the Punjab. Guru Govind Singh thereafter came wandering to Maharashtra and settled at Nanded. Here it was that two Pathan disciples of his conspired and attacked him while he was soundly sleeping. The wounds that he received in that struggle proved fatal and soon he died.

973. Guru Govind Singh had passed his boyhood days, not in Punjab but in Patna in Bihar, for reasons of safety. As such, he grew fond of the Bihari Hindi language, in which, later on, he became well-versed. His autobiography, 'Vichitra Natak', is written in the Bihari Hindi, not in the

'Gurumukhi' Punjabi. He also composed a heroic poem on the Goddess, 'Chandika'. He symbolised the sword as Goddess 'Chandika' herself and has writen a hymnal song on it. We have already cited some of its warlike passages in our other books under the caption 'Jay Tegam' (Jay Khadgam). As the writings of this tenth Sikh Guru, Guru Govind Singh, are in Hindi, and the duties he had enjoined on the Khalsa sect were not so very palatable to the traditional devotees of Guru Nanak, they did not find a place in the 'Adigranth', whereas the sayings of all the former nine Gurus were included in it. So the writings of Guru Govind Singh were collected in the so-called 'Dasham Granth' (दशम ग्रंथ), the tenth book.

974. Another fact that is important from the point of view of the Hindus must be mentioned here. Because of the creation of the Khalsa sect, there have been two divisions amongst the Sikhs: Sahajdhari and Keshdhari. The Sahajdharis follow the path of Guru Nanak. They don't allow the hair to grow uncut, nor are they particular about following the other 'kakkas'. Thousands of such Hindu Sikhs fall under this Sahajdhari sect. But it must be remembered that it was Shree Govind Singh who, by giving them a martial garb, built the Sikhs into a virile sub-Hindu nation, which could ultimtely oust the Muslim rule from the Punjab at the point of the sword.

975. **Shree Veer Banda Bairagi—**The name, which can never be omitted from the list of the brave martyrs of Hindu history, is that of Veer Banda Bairagi, who for the first time avenged the wrongs done by the Muslims on the Hindus and even boldly attacked them. He was originally a Vaishnav saint known round about Nanded, where he happened to meet Guru Govind Singh, from whom he gradually learnt of the miserable plight of the Hindus in Punjab, of the harrowing calamities that befell Guru Govind Singh's own family and of the relentless war he himself had carried out in spite of all odds. He was particularly much moved to hear the despairing complaint of the Guru that there was nobody left in Punjab to avenge the tragic deaths of his four sons. His blood began to boil and he once again took the bow and arrows of his former vocation in life. Guru Govind Singh wrote a note to all his former disciples to render Veer Banda every possible help. Taking that note and vowing terrible revenge upon the Muslims for the inhuman atrocities committed by them on the Hindus, this brave Hindu soul made his way to the Punjab.

976. But alas! want of space and my own old age makes it imperative

that whatever is written so far should be somehow rounded up. Else I would certainly have described, if not in full, at least briefly the havoc Veer Baba Banda wrought amongst the Muslims of Punjab, their grand slaughter, the most appropriate retaliation of the molestation of the Hindu women, the capture of the same Sirhind, where Guru Govind Singh's two sons were buried alive behind the brick-walls, and the eventual burning of the Muslim locality there, not to speak of the abject parade of Muslim men, women and children, barefooted. In the hot sun, the same atrocious tortures of the Muslims as were visited upon the Hindus for not renouncing Hinduism and finally the proclamation of a Hindu State in the whole of Punjab. We have already shown in the sixth chapter of this book, how the Muslim community was panic-stricken whenever the Hindus opened up religious aggression on the Muslims. Baba Banda also struck terror in the hearts of the Punjabi Muslims by his retaliatory aggression. At last, the Emperor of Delhi sent a big army to Punjab. Resorting to the guerrilla warfare, Baba Banda defeated it at various places. But as ill-luck would have it, the Khalsa Sikhs began to be jealous of the epithet 'Hindu commander', which Baba Banda Bairagi had chosen for himself. Ultimately, that jealousy grew to such an extent that the united Hindu army of Veer Banda broke into two factions, and the one consisting of the Khalsa Sikhs deserted him. The Khalsa Sikh faction was by itself not able to conquer the Muslims. Naturally, the Moghal army grew stronger and in a desperate action, valiant Banda Bairagi fell into the Muslim hands with his only son and close followers. The Muslims were haunted by a false fear that Veer Banda possessed some magic power, and the higher Muslim officials, too, feared that even when he was bound hand and foot with strong iron fetters, Veer Banda Baba would transform himself into a cat and would escape through the ranks of a powerful army. So, he was sent to Delhi, locked in a strong cage, like a wild beast, along with many other captive Hindu warriors. What a horrible scene it was when he was, brought in the presence of the Emperor! How hellishly inhuman the torture of Veer Banda, his only son and his hundred or so Hindu followers, and the streams of blood that flowed! Veer Banda was not beheaded or killed straightway. He was pierced scores of times with red-hot iron bars and lumps of his flesh were cut out every time with a view to making him suffer extreme torture before he died—but there is no scope to describe this harrowing scene here. But every true and grateful Hindu should rather read it from the books written by the Sikhs and Muslim writers themselves.

977. **The History of the Sikhs Written by me—**I am very sad that I cannot refer the reader to the History of the Sikhs I had written years ago. It is necessary that the reason be explained here. Round about the year 1909, in the thick of the revolutionay activities, when I happened to go from England to France, I stayed for a month or so with Madame Cama. During that short period, I wrote out in Marathi the thrilling history of the Sikhs, running to about two hundred pages or so, based on the proven material It had at my disposal at the time. I had studied almost all the Sikh literature right from the first book of Sikh literature, named 'Bhai Balaki Janamsakhi'—the lifestory of Guru Nanak written by his disciple 'Bhai Bala'—to the tenth book—Dasham-granth of the tenth Guru Govind Singh in the original, not to speak of the Histories of the Sikhs by Cunningham and other English writers. I had brought the account of the Sikhs up to the establishment of a new Hindu Kingdom by Maharaja Ranjit Singh right from the river Shatadru (Sutlej) to the Sindhu (Indus) and much above towards Jammu and Kashmir by uprooting the Muslim power from Punjab and avenging the defeats of Jaypal and Anangpal. But even today, it pains me to say that the manuscript of that book must have very likely fallen into the English hands who destoryed it. Else, the person with whom I had entrusted it to be taken to India for being printed and published, must have drowned it into the sea for fear of the search by the English police somewhere on his way to India. Doubtless it is, that Marathi book of mine has been lost before it could be published—has been destroyed!

978. Even then whoever has a mind should read my poem composed in the Andamans on this tragic, yet imperishable and resplendent martyrdom of Shree Veer Banda, which is available even now.

979. According to the belief prevalent among his disciples, Veer Banda's body was thrown away into the debris on the outskirts of the city under the impression that he was dead. But with his magic power and some miraculous herb that his disciples made him eat, Veer Banda Baba came to his senses and he was secretly and immediately taken to Punjab. Further on, an institution grew up in his name and hundreds of his Sikh followers have kept it running to this day under the name 'Bandai'. Like the Kuka followers of Guru Ram Singh of a later date, these 'Bandais' call themselves Hindus.

980. After the tragic death of Veer Banda, there was no armed force left either of the Khalsas, Bandais, Sahajdharis or any other Sikh or Hindu sect. Every one of them was disorganized and disgruntled. But on the contrary, the Muslim political power had begun to crumble down by the time it was fighting with Veer Banda. Throughout the whole of India, a new resurgent Hindu power—the Maratha military and political aspiration—was dealing knock-down blows to the Moghal imperial power and the latter existed only nominally from Delhi to Punjab, Multan, Kashmir and Kandahar. Only the local ruffians terrorized the general populace with their bands of scoundrels!

981. How the Sikh power grew thereafter and how, at last in the times of Maharaja Ranjit Singh, it spread throughout the whole of Punjab and Kashmir, obliterating every vestige of the Muslim rule and how the Hindu independent empire came into existence—we can only just hint at here! For all these events fall out of the period under discussion here.

982. However, two or three statements about this period of Punjabi History can be made here briefly and it is necessary to do so.

983. The first successful attempt to overthrow the Muslim rule in Punjab was made by the Marathas. The belief prevalent in the histories of the Sikhs and in the other loosely written history books of India that the Sikhs ousted the Muslim rule from Punjab for the first time is erroneous. Even when the Sikhs were at the height of their glory, they could not conquer the neighbouring Muslim capital, Delhi. In bringing this to light, we do not in the least mean to disparage the Sikhs, but we do certainly want to stop every attempt at belittling the national glory of the Marathas, by pointing out false things. No doubt, the credit of overthrowing the Muslim rule, at least in the precincts of Punjab and establishing there an independent Hindu State, like that of Maharaja Ranjit Singh, goes primarily to our Sikh organisation. But it is equally true, beyond any vestige of doubt, that the Maratha valour which, lunging, as it did, from Poona, fluttered the victorious and resplendent flag of the Hindu nation to the South right up to Tanjawar (Tanjore) and to the north to the very banks of the Sindhu (Indus) and beyond, fighting battles after battles and reducing the Muslim Emperor of Delhi to a nominal existence—a thing of shreds and patches—can have no parallel at least in the Hindu history of that long period of seven centuries.

984. **The Independent Hindu State of Nepal:** In our history books and the school textbooks of Indian history, almost every Indian

region is mentioned. But strangely enough, the state of Nepal and the valiant Hindu Kingdom there is never mentioned—or if at all, only in passing over the campaigns of Ochterloney—as if Nepal is in no way connected with Hindu India. But, in fact, Nepal is as much an indivisible part of India as are Maharashtra, Punjab or Madras. These regions might have been governed by different rulers at different times, but the term Hindu Nation is equally applicable to all of them. The rest of the Indian continent was subjected to aggressions by Asian Muslims and European Christians during the last nine or ten centuries and there were constant wars. But fortunately, Nepal was singularly immune to all the political and religious aggressions. On the whole, in Nepal alone, could Hindu religion and Hindu culture maintain its independence unimpaired against the incursions of the foreigners. As such, Nepal must really be considered to be the best part of Hindu India, and should be given the palm of honour in the history of our Hindu Nation! But because of our thoughtlessness, the result is just the reverse. Only because Nepal did not get lost in the mire of foreign domination and slavery and because it kept itself aloof from the political upheavals in India, our frivolous history books mention that nation only in passing or never at all!

985. In order to rectify this spineless (dishonourable) perversion, we started a movement in India as soon as we were released from the Andamans in 1924 in respect of Nepal, as people well know. At that very time, we wrote a book on the History of Nepalese Movement! (नेपाली आंदोलनाचा इतिहास) and in it we gave an account of the brave history of Nepal and its role in the protection and maintenance of the independence of Hindu religion and culture. But now in this discourse on Hindu history, paucity of space prevents any such detailed account--and there is no need for it. In the early part of the tenth century and onwards, Nepal was governed by Newari Hindus. Thereafter, it was captured by some of the Rajputs who left Rajputana because of the Muslim aggression to seek fortune elsewhere. Gradually, these Rajputs spread up to Kathmandu, which they made their capital. The strong Hindu government which these Rajputs established there is the modern Nepal. This much reference is enough here to attract the attention of the Indian Hindus to its importance and to the homogeneity of race of Nepal with ours.

986. These Rajputs being strong worshippers and protectors of the cow (गोरक्षक), eventually came to be called Gorkha by caste.

986A. Although it refers to the more recent times, we should like to make a special mention of the fact that while the whole of India was being governed by the English, thousands of Gorkhas (Gurkhas) had joined the English army and in both the great world wars, they showed so much prowess and bravery and exceptional skill in fighting, that even the best soldiers in England, America and Germany, too, were astounded. Hence, today a Gurkha soldier has proverbially come to mean an excellent warrior!

The latter half of Akbar's life

987. It has already been shown, in Paragraphs 946 to 954 of this book, what cruelty and atrocity Akbar resorted to in order to crush Hinduism and the Hindu rulers. Even those passing references alone are quite sufficient to prove that he was as fanatical and as fiercely inimical to Hinduism and the Hindu nation, as was either Allauddin or Aurangzeb.

988. European writers on Indian history slowly hint and our Hindu writers slavishly and thoughtlessly imitate them. When they say that Akbar was not like other Moghal or Muslim fellows, meaning thereby that he did not hate Hinduism and the Hindu nation, that he was just, and never differentiated between the Hindus and the Muslims, that he ruled equitably and, as such, the Hindus must be highly grateful to him. This eulogy of Akbar is utterly false. We, Hindus, can either show respect, gratitude and affection for Rana Pratap or for his dire enemy, Akbar. How can we show equal affection and respect for both of them? How can we worship God and the devil at the same time? How even can we compare the fanatical Akbar who deprived the independence of the Hindu kings like Rana Pratap and thrust the yoke of slavery on their necks, who demanded the Hindu royal princesses as queens and concubines in order to add insult to their injury and attacked with his vast armies those, who declined to do so, and crushed them completely—how can we compare him with those thousands of martyrs and valiant Hindu leaders like Rana Pratap and Rani Durgawati, who laid down their lives on the battlefields in defence of Hindu Nation, Hindu states and Hindu religion?

989. Another important point that has so far escaped the notice of many of our gullible and slavish Hindu writers, is that to say that Akbar treated all his subjects equally and sponsored equality of status for the

whole humanity—as is being taught in schools—is absolutely erroneous and is the result of bad habit of extolling the Muslims unproportionately. For, being a Moghal Emperor, he never hesitated to crush down ruthlessly anyone who refused to bear the yoke of his sovereignty—might he then be a Muslim or a Hindu! Now all the Muslims were not Moghals. As a matter of fact, many of them hated the Moghals bitterly, because he had extended his empire by destroying the old Afghan and Turkish Sultanates. It means that like any other ambitious adventurer, Akbar fought for the sake of his own Moghal glory not only against the Hindus alone but against others also. Obviously enough, he did not treat even the Muslims equally. He liquidated and annexed many Muslim kingdoms. Only with a view to safeguarding the interests of his empire, did Akbar in his later life repeal the revolting religious taxes like the Jizia and refrained from opening campaigns of mass conversion of Hindus. There was no such intention of behaving equitably, the Hindus and the Muslims behind this policy, as is generally supposed. On the contrary, he knew quite well that whenever such atrocities were committed on the Hindus, in the name of religion, by the former Sultans, they were followed with disastrous revolts. Sometimes, even the whole Sultanates were consumed in the conflagration of the Hindu wrath. In order to avoid this disastrous end for his empire, and to establish a tranquil administration of his own, did he treat all his subjects, whether they were Hindus or Muslims, justly so far as their individual life was concerned and much more leniently and harmlessly than other emperor like Allauddin or Aurangzeb. But once again, let it be remembered that it was not because he believed in the equality of men or the equality of the Hindus and the Muslims irrespective of their religion, certainly not because he did not consider the Hindus to be kafirs!

990. Once he became the all-powerful and absolute monarch in temporal affairs of his empire, his ambition goaded him on to found a new religion to be another Paigambar and lord of the spiritual life of the people! To that end, he thought of starting an absolutely new religion quite different from either Hinduism or Islam. But here, also, it must be remembered that as he knew it would be disastrous to force it cruelly on the people, as had other Muslim Sultans done earlier or as Aurangzeb did it later, Akbar very slyly tried to undermine Hinduism through his Din-e-elahi; for the Chief Paigambarship of this religion was to be ceded inevitably to Akbar himself. No Hindu could greet

others with a 'Namaskar', he had per force to say 'Allah-o-Akbar!' The accredited language, too, of this new religion 'Din-e-elahi' was Arabic! It may, however, be noted in passing, that this quixotic ambition (idea) of Akbar of becoming the spiritual lord of the human race came to nought. For, beside the flattering sycophants in his court, none of the Hindus or the Muslims accepted it as their creed; the sycophants themselves had nothing to do with it the moment Akbar died.

990A. However, of the many great emperors that lived at the time in Europe or Africa or Asia, Akbar was the greatest in respect of his strategy, his wielding of the widest power, bravery, founding of a vast empire, his patronage of learning and arts and crafts. Although, according to some writers, he was illiterate, he patronized great authors and encouraged the writing of famous books! This comparative greatness history can concede to him, and we do not hesitate to call him great as he really was. But with all that greatness, he was, from our Hindu point of view, foreign, belonging to another religion and mean-minded and, as such, he should be decried by us, Hindus!

□

21
Come the Avengers of the Atrocious Muslims' Rule: The Marathas!

991. It is a common belief that the writing of history must be a prosaic account of bare facts describing them as they have actually happened, and it is mostly right. There ought to be a marked difference between the descriptions of something that is purely imaginary and poetic and of something that has actually happened. The one can best be well expressed in a faithful and matter-of-fact way.

991.A. Yet merely to list out the correct dates and years of historical events, to note the deaths and births of certain individuals, and to keep a record of battles fought or the occurrence of famines and floods cannot be called history, although such a bare record of these various events is the basis of history. It may, at best, be called a chronological account. But there is a borderland between pure history and pure unalloyed poetry, which can adequately and effectively be expressed by a fine blending of history and poetry. Without such a blending of history and poetry, descriptions of such events can never be living. While describing such events, history itself becomes poetry. Such occasions and events can never be effectively described without resorting to mythological and romantic metaphors and grand poetic style. Simple events can be described as truthfully as they happen in prose, but human nature demands that everything that is unique, everything that is stupendous and splendid and exciting, must be expressed in a highly emotional and ornate style, be it an event of a very recent occurrence. Simple dry prose will never be able to sustain it. It is these exciting events that make a man roar with laughter, groan with sorrow, dance with joy or get wild with rage—in short, exciting events make him speak the language of poetry! It may be prose, but poetic prose, often bedecked with dazzling ornaments of simile, metaphor and other figures of speech, as is the prince of princes adorned with the real ones!

992. निषादविद्धाण्डज दर्शनोत्थः
श्लोकत्वमापद्यत यस्य शोकः

"His grief at the destruction of the bird by the hunter took the form of a four-lined verse—a श्लोक"

993. Is it not testimony enough that the very first quatrain by the very first poet should be born of a highly exciting sentiment, which could never be conveyed in simple words?

994. Precaution, however, must be taken that the poetic description of such exceptional yet exciting events should not pervert the original facts. A well-authenticated history should express itself through all this emotional display.

995. The period of Indian history, which we are now going to discuss in this book is from the point of view of the Hindu Nation so glorious, so thrilling, and so full of daring events that the poetic style of writing alone can describe it adequately and in a living manner.

996. In the twentieth chapter of this book, the Hindu-Muslim war, which had been going on for six centuries, had entered the seventh. But even when such a long time of bitter warfare had elapsed and even when the Hindu Nation had been sorely plagued and profusely bled by the ferocious religio-political aggressions of all the Asian Muslims—the Arabs, the Afghans, the Pathans, the Turks, the Moghals—yet even by the beginning of the seventeenth century, the Hindu Nation had, neither in the north nor in the south, been completely vanquished! Nay, it was still fighting on bravely on the battlefield itself, although sorely smarting under the countless wounds it had so far received. On the contrary, the aggressive might of all the Asian Muslims had been steadily but surely getting weaker and weaker after their incessant warfare with the Hindus right from the beginning of the eighth century to the death of Akbar. We have already shown, in Paragraphs 818 to 857 of this book in the chapter named 'The Beginning of the Fall of the Muslim Power', how that 'beginning' was made from the 14th century and how the ground was being prepared for the establishment of the victorious Hindu Kingdoms, like that of Vijaynagar.

997. The same resurgent spirit of the Hindus grew steadily every day and ultimately by the time which the course of our story has now reached, the presiding deity of the Hindu Nation seems to have felt the dire necessity to use the histro-mythological phraseology, of bringing

forth an extraordinarily, illustrious Hindu family which could ultimately lead the ever-growing Hindu might throughout the whole of India. In the old times when that deity felt a similar need of extirpating the Saka-Hun and other Mlenchhas, she performed, according to Chand Bhat in his epic 'The Story of Agnikula', a great sacrifice on Mount Abu and brought forth four Indian Hindu heroes. But unfortunately, it was not sufficient to bring forth four such valiant heroes to meet the exigency of the times of which we are telling here, to extirpate the Muslim political power throughout India. A whole generation of such divinely blessed heroes was needed for such a stupendous task! As such, to use again the metaphorical style of Chand Bhat, the presiding deity of the Hindu nation glanced all over India. That enraged deity sprinkled her holy water on the heights of Sahyadri thinking, perhaps, that region alone was the fittest one for the final overthrow of the Muslim power after a millennial war with it. How could a small sacrificial pit at Abu be equal to that stupendous task! And all of a sudden, the whole of the Sahyadri mountain was aglow with the fire of war and resonant with the beat of the drum. And there arose a whole class, a whole generation of brave warriors. Each one lighted his individual torch on the general conflagration and traversed the whole of India with the war cry, 'Har, Har Mahadev' on his lips to wipe out the Muslim political menace. The name of this national race? It is—

'MAHARASHTRA BORN OF THE TIMES OF SHIVAJI'

Hindu Maharashtra alone fought with the whole Muslim World

998. At this time in the millennial Hindu-Muslim epic war, such a great catastrophe befell the whole of India—and especially Maharashtra—as had menaced perhaps a very few nations of the world. To add to the Muslim maelstorm, from the north European nations like the Portuguese, the Dutch, the French and the English dashed on India—and especially the Deccan, with an avalanchine force, and it was practically the lot of the Maharashtra, born out of the times of Shivaji, to face all alone all these terrific aggressions. Stranger than this is the fact that this Maharashtra, born as it was from the sacrificial fire of dire calamities, faced them all successfully and was a match for all the enemies! The Muslim imperial throne of Delhi was hacked to pieces by the Marathas and the Muslim power was finally rooted out throughout the whole of India.

999. The legend of this exceptional glory and valour of Maharashtra has now been generally known in its true perspective and form, to the common people in Maharashtra at least. The credit of making it widely known in its grand and spectacular aspect, in its all-India context, must necessarily go to the great research-scholars and writers of history like Rajwade, Ranade, Khare, Itihasacharya Sardesai and others. But with the exception of Ranade, others have written their books in Marathi. Histories of the Marathas written in languages other than Marathi have been mostly written by our age-old enemies like the Muslims, the Portuguese, the English and others with horrid perversion of facts, and unfortunately, our Hindu writers from the other Indian States have echoed them mostly through ignorance.

1000. Hence I, at least, felt, right from my student days, that this post-Shivaji history of Maharashtra should be written in English, based on the research-work done in this field till today; so that non-Maharashtrians and other foreigners might know! But, as I had selected warfare with the then enemy of our nation rather than that of the past, as the field of my action, I was more and more involved in the revolutionary activities against the British. Hence, till the time I was released from the Andamans, I had no time to write about the past history of Maharashtra. Again I thought people like Sardesai who had devoted themselves to the writing of history should better undertake that job and it was, I thought, proper from the point of view of division of labour. So off and on, I tried in that direction.

Sardesai Himself sees me

1001. By the way, it would, I think, be proper to relate just here a small incident that bears on this topic. I had an earnest desire to see the late Shree Sardesai from my very young days. For, his books on Indian history, we had been reading constantly. But we were all revolutionaries, while he was a high placed servant of a king—although that king happened to be the ruler of a feudatory state like Baroda—subordinate to the British government! Again, he was older; I was younger! Later on, I was transported to the Andamans and was eventually released from there in 1924. I learn from other people that Sardesai praised my revolutionary activities as brave deeds. So up to the time I was at Ratnagiri, I sincerely felt that Sardesai should write a History of the Marathas in English. As such, I sent oral messages to him to that effect, because every letter of mine was a burning spark of fire, which was most likely to reduce to ashes the whole house of a government officer like him. Such things often happened in our revolutionary life. So I kept quiet. And one fine morning, an old gentleman appeared at my doorstep, my rented tenement in the house of Shree Nana Patwardhan at Ratnagiri. I got up in deference to his grey hair and asked, 'Whom have I the pleasure to receive?' 'I am Sardesai from Baroda', came the answer, 'whom you know as the writer of Indian history'. I was surprised. 'What? Riyasat-Kar Sardesai?' When he nodded his head in assent, I told him how I had cherished high respect for him ever since I had read his big volumes on Muslim Riyasat. I told him that I had read all of his books. But having had a chance of mixing with non-Marathi scholars, I could authoritatively say that they had no knowledge of the greatness of nor even a nodding acquaintance with, the essence of Maratha history: that many of them bore a sort of grudge towards the Marathas. So I requested him to undertake the writing of an authentic, handy history based on solid facts so that non-Marathi world might know it in its true form and perspective; upon which he said that some one else should do it now. So I said, 'No, at least today, you are the only authoritative writer who can possibly do it. Although your old age may present difficulties, you should undertake it as the crowning glory of your life work. Possibly it will be completed! You seem to have been blessed with a long life. At least, you should begin at once to write such a history in English.' Then after some casual talk while seeing him off, I expressed my gratitude at the visit of such a great historian at my residence. Before even my sentence was completed he said 'No, No, the real pleasure is mine! We are all the writers of history; but you are the makers of history! When you make history, we note it down and I came here with a sincere desire to see you as the maker of history! And then we took leave of each other with thankful hearts.

1002. And I think it would be proper to set down just here that some fifteen years or so after this visit of ours, he wrote as the ripe fruit of his life, a detailed history of the Marathas in English in three volumes.

1003. As soon as I came to Ratnagiri, after being released from the Andamans, I was forbidden to take any active part in politics and because of the ban on the change of district, I was forced to set limits to my movements. So in this restricted life of mine at Ratnagiri, I decided that I myself should write a discursive book although without any help from reference books that would interpret and explain the unrivalled valour of the post-Shivaji Maharashtra and the freedom of the Hindu nation that it effected by destroying the Muslim domination. Why, before the end of February 1925, I completed the writing of that book.

Hindu Padpadshahi

1004. The very name of that book I chose as 'Hindu Padpadshahi' rather than merely the history of the Marathas. For, in my opinion, the Marathas in general did not fight only for Maharashtra, nor for their household land or their fields. Their sole objective was to liberate Hindu religion and Hindu Nation—of which Maharashtra was known to them to be only a part—from the yoke of Muslim domination and to establish all over India, a sovereign Hindu power. The inner urge of the new resurgent Maharashtra was to dethrone the Muslim imperial power at Delhi, and to hoist in its place the Hindu imperial standard. The anguish that rankled in the hearts of the Hindus and that found expression in Shree Ramdas's famous couplet—

1005-6. या सकल भूमंडला ठायी।
हिन्दू ऐसा उरला नाही।

('Nowhere on the face of this whole earth is there left any Hindu')

was mainly responsible for all the future glory of the Marathas! The heartache of the Hindus as expressed by Shree Ramdas.

1007-8. प्रस्तुत यवनां चे बंड। हिन्दू उरला नाहीं चंड।
बहुत दिसां चे मुंड। शास्ता न मिले तयासि।

(At present, the revolt of the Muslims has come to stay, and no daring Hindu has been left; no one is able to curb and subdue this long standing evil)

set aglow the whole of Maharashtra. The Maharashtrian movements in that century spread far and wide throughout India, the invasions and campaigns, the battles and pursuits and retreats, consistent or inconsistent historical events, which so far baffled the greatest of historians, can well be explained by the magic words 'Hindu Nation' and 'Hindu Imperial Power'. Hence, it is, that I named that book as, 'Hindu Padpadshahi', the name which stamped its own seal on the history of the millennial Hindu-Muslim war, by gaining ultimate victory over it.

1009. Even in this book of mine, the history of the Marathas has not been given in all its details, because historians have already done that work most painstakingly and on a larger scale. Jadunath Sarkar, who wrote in English, and Riyasatkar Sardesai, who wrote in Marathi, had already written books collocating all the available research-work most laboriously done by several research scholars and assimilating and interpreting it in the best way they could. It is, therefore, to avoid needless repetition that I did not attempt to write a detailed history of the Marathas. Moreover, sitting as I was in the small room, made available to me for my residence in a small village of Shirgaon near Ratnagiri, by my friend Shree Vishnupant Damale, even in those days of local detention imposed on me by the British Government, I could not think of writing such a big volume without the aid of reference books!

The Hindu Nation

1010. Just as a man lost in a dense forest on a dark night can see everything in its true perspective, in its form and colour, as soon as he throws around him a flashlight from the electric torch in his travelling kit, and in that enlightened state of his mind can very easily find his way out, similarly very early in my college days, when I threw the electric searchlight of the Hindu national point of view on the then extensive but chaotic mass of details about the history of the Marathas, my mind, too, became suddenly enlightened. Viewed in that brilliant light of the national Hindu outlook, that whole incoherent, loose and chaotic mass of historical details regarding the Marathas' enterprise appeared to me absolutely consistent and well-defined. Then alone was it that its essential greatness and unique character became apparent to me. The import and essence of Maratha history is most certainly not as it appeared to most of the historians, including Jadunath Sarkar, who read it simply as the history of the Marathas and found it self-centred, self-seeking, marauding, bellicose and mediocre. On the contrary, I could well see in it the grand manifestations of a Maharashtra (a great nation), which had singly accepted with a grave determination, the onerous responsibility of meeting and beating down the challenge for the supremacy over our country, thrown by all the foreign powers in the three continents of Asia, Europe and Africa—i.e. the whole of the then known world—by the non-Hindu aggressors who had attacked our great Hindu Nation. Especially, when even after continuously fighting, although not unitedly, severally, yet grimly enough, with these aggressors, for over ten centuries, no other Hindu state nor any other

Hindu community seemed to win that epic war, annihilating the enemy completely, it is significant that Maharashtra should do it.

The Hindu War of Independence

1011. It is, therefore, as a sacred national duty, that I earnestly request every loyal Hindu, setting aside all false humility to read the above-mentioned book of mine, viz. 'Hindu Padpadshahi', which surveys the Hindu War of Independence, carried on by the Marathas from the seventeenth century, from the Hindu national standpoint. For looking at it, as impersonally as it is possible to do so, this one of all the extant books on the history of this period, appears even to me as the most stimulating, most searching and teeming with the national spirit imbued with Hindutwa. *Ranade* forever closed the mouths of the foreign as well as our own historians, which derided the Maratha history of the times of Chhatrapati Rajaram as the anarchy of the rabble, and called it the Maratha War of Independence.

1012. But the all-India war, which the Maratha fought for nearly a century subsequent to the times of Rajaram, was not merely a Maratha War of Independence, it was an all-India war of Hindu Independence. My book 'Hindu Padpadshahi', is really the golden temple of the survey and appraisal of that great war—an enthralling piece of sculpture in colour and solidity, of the Goddess of that great war, like any in the Caves of Ajantha.

1013. And still every paragraph in that book is based on solid evidence not because extracts from the writings of other renowned historians of acknowledged authority have been freely used therein, but because the very sentences uttered by the heroes who actually fought on the various battlefields and by those who actually played the political and diplomatic game are cited. Extracts from the letters fresh from their hands, written just after the events have been profusely used. As such, the book is as authoritative, as it is interesting to read. The genius of the historians, Rajwade, does not seem to have altogether missed this all-India character of this Maratha history. But in his writings, it did not receive the all-round treatment it deserved. Perhaps his writing itself was so extensive and varied as to preclude even the vast intellectual capacities of the man from grasping its full significance and import. His incidental and desultory discourses on the subject appear, by the very nature of their topics, incomplete and inconsistent. About the English, the Muslim and other historians, we had better not say anything. Under such circumstances, therefore, my book Hindu Padpadshahi estimating this great Hindu-Muslim War through the Hindu national angle of vision is the only one of its kind. That is why I recommend it whole-heartedly to every Hindu nationalist.

1014. That is why, again and because of my failing health, I do not propose to go in for that review of the war in these pages. The curious readers might advisedly read it from those pages. It is only necessary here in these pages of the 'Six Glorious Epochs of Hindu Victories over the Aggressors' to display the golden chain of events that led ultimately to the pinnacle of glory that the Hindus obtained by finally subduing the Muslim power at the close of this millennial Hindu-Muslim war of epic dimensions.

A Chain of rare and remarkable events

1015. The first of such rare and remarkable events, which at the outset appears trivial but, viewed now from the telescope of historical studies, assumes exceptional importance and which follows immediately after the account of this Hindu-Muslim war given in this book up to Ch. 20 is The Birth of Shivaji either in 1627 or 1630 A.D.

1016. Shivaji's father, Shahaji, was reckoned among the petty Maratha chieftains and noblemen, who took active part in the political movements of the time. But all of them had to owe allegiance to some one of the five Muslim Sultans that they might enjoy their own knighthood or 'Jagirdari'. Not a single Hindu independent State—not even the smallest that can be thought of—had remained throughout the whole of Maharashtra. But the son born to the above-mentioned Shahaji Raje, was, however, destined by Providence to lead the Hindu War of Liberation and to be honoured with the auspicious red mark, applied to his head, of the gushing blood of the mortally wounded Muslim power, heralding the advent of Hindu independence!

A wonderful coincidence

1017. Whether because of good fortune or because it was the will of God, whether again owing to mere accidental coincidence or as the extraordinary harvest reaped from the well-coordinated sowing of the seeds of gigantic efforts—call it what you will—but ever since the birth of Shivaji from the womb of his mother Jijabai, there was a strange turn given to the technique of the national front in this Hindu-Muslim War.

1018. Generally speaking, right from the beginning of the eighth century to that of the seventeenth, wherever the mighty armies of the Muslims and the Hindus fought, wherever the Hindus and the Muslims were engaged in decisive battles affecting the destinies of the states and the Hindu Nation as a whole, it was the Hindu who usually, barring honourable exceptions, suffered crushing defeats with heavy losses in men and material, sometimes because some leader sat in 'Hawda' on the elephant, while at others one sat in palanquin—sometimes because there was treachery in the Hindu ranks, at others again when victory was almost in Hindu hands—mere chance coincidence deflected it towards the Muslims. This cruel verdict of the Goddess of War was, as it were, predetermined. The resistance offered by the brave Daheer, the one offered by the valiant Jayapal or his son Anangpal or the last battle given by Veer Prithviraj or again the one fought by Maharana Sanga, in every decisive action fought throughout, through all these centuries up to that fought in 1565 A.D. at Talikot by the dauntless Ramraja of Vijaynagar the scales of war turned always against the Hindus—the Hindus alone were unmistakably defeated!

But since the beginning of the 17th Century

1019. That means from the birth of Shivaji, so to say, the same cruel Goddess of War began to show a highly astonishing difference in her verdict regarding the same Hindu-Muslim struggle. And it was this! Just as formerly, it seemed almost predetermined that the Hindus were bound to be defeated in every Hindu-Muslim struggle, similarly now onwards, wherever the Hindu-Muslim armies met, the Hindu victory was almost assured and the Muslim defeat a foregone conclusion! From this seventeenth century onwards, wherever they met the Muslims in a state of war, the Hindus invariably vanquished them! Whether they were the decisive battles shaking the very foundations of states or nations or whether they were only fleeting skirmishes, the victory for the Hindus and the rout of the Muslims was the result! Every Hindu young man should necessarily read the long list of Hindu victories from the same book of mine viz: Hindu Padpadshahi, the victories which swell our hearts with pride, the victories again that were won not only on land from Punjab to Kanyakumari in the south seas but in hundreds of naval engagements from the Western (the so-called Arabian sea!) to the Eastern (the Bay of Bengal) seas!

The guiding principle of the new Maratha strategy—Aggression—not merely defence

1020. The most important reason why since the time the Marathas assumed the military leadership of the Hindu nation, the Hindus alone went on winning victories, as has been already shown above, all over the vast subcontinent of India whenever they joined battle with the Muslims, was that these Marathas with their daring valour, had at once purged the Hindu mind of that pernicious epidemic of the perverted sense of virtues, which had afflicted and paralysed most of the Hindu society all over India and which had given birth to the false notion of chivalry, deeming it highly despicable from the ethical point of view, a veritable sin, as it were to lead a military attack—even against the direst enemy.

1021. In fact, the creed of every national army is to march upon the enemy even before the latter attacks—to lead a blatant aggression, not merely to stage defensive formations! The first successful attempt to inspire this aggressive mentality amongst the Hindus was made at the time of the establishment of the Vijaynagar empire against the Muslims, even before the Marathas took the lead. But it was restricted to the south alone and the terrible defeat at Talikota deterred the Hindu mind from invading the Muslims. It was then that the Marathas inspired the Hindus with a new war-like spirit by successful inroads upon the Muslims.

1022. To invade the enemy territory is the chief aim or the chief duty of a national military strength. The nation that maintains armed forces just strong enough for the purposes of defence—and does not build it up so as to be capable to undertake an invasion and considers it improper to do so—is either basically coward at heart or is labouring under a delusion. Perhaps it is to camouflage that inward cowardice that such high sounding declarations are made. A nation, whose armed might is evidently built up on the basis of its aggressive capacity, is certainly capable of self-defence.

1023. Again, the Hindu aggression against the violent and unjust political domination of the Muslim rulers was basically not an aggression at all. The really unjust aggression was that of the Muslims who had invaded the territories of the Hindus. The aggressive risings of the Hindus against the outrageous Muslim rule can never be called revolts or rebellions. For, the aggression of the Muslim rulers against the independent and rightfully established Hindu states was itself mutinous and revolting. The rising of a robber against the rightful owner can be called mutinous, not the taking up of arms by the rightful owner to chastise the rebellious freebooters! It is, therefore, to inspire with indomitable courage the majority of the Hindu society all over India, which had taken fright of these Muslim freebooters that Shree Ramadas raised his war-cry from every peak of the Sahyadri.

'प्रस्तुत यवनांचे बंड'

"It is the Muslim-insurrection!"

"The insurgents are the Muslims and not the Hindus! In order to punish them severely invade them from all sides all at once!"

1024. 'धर्मासाठी मरावें। मरोनि अवध्यांसि मारावें।
मारितां मारितां ध्यावें। राज्य आपुले।'

(One should court death for the sake of religion (But) while dying, one should kill (the enemies) and by thus killing them, one should win back one's kingdom.)

1025. The most important weapon of this aggressive war policy of the Marathas was at least, till that time a new one to the Hindus. It was not used so far by any before them. That weapon is

Guerrilla Warfare

1026. This type of war is called in Sanskrit' Vrikayuddha' (वृकयुद्ध).

This Vrikayuddha (वृकयुद्ध) of the Marathas humbled the vast armies of the Muslims. According to the peculiar mode of this guerrilla warfare, the Marathas never faced the highly well-equipped fourfold armies of the enemy. Whenever the Maratha force were small in number, they attacked the enemy from the right or the left flanks or from behind.

1027. Yet, it should be borne in mind that while thus harassing and cutting off the huge armies of the Moghals with their meagre numbers and inadequate arms, they never hesitated to offer pitched battles standing face-to-face at the most unexpected moments, if they found that their own military strength had grown sufficiently strong to do this. As even when the Maratha forces went on increasing in number and quality, and their responsibility about the various states, smaller or greater in size, about the forts and territories that fell in their hands, began to assume enormous dimensions, they did not lie idly in their different capitals, guarding their own positions. Everyone of them had always a keen eye on the neighbouring or the distant Moghal territories and pushed on into those territories as soon as the monsoons were over, even before the enemy had time to come aggressively against the smaller Maratha feudal lords and Jagirdars or their forts. The Maratha forces attacked even the Muslim Nawabs and Nizams, who never gave them offence under some pretext or another. Moreover, they were hardly to be found in their usually known capitals, great or small, or in their forts or caves known to be their usual resorts. On the contrary, they seemed to carry their so-called capitals on horse-back while they started on their campaigns against the Muslims. The *de facto* address of the various Maratha warlords and their brave followers was not their homes or fortresses; it was invariably their ever shifting camps or bivouacs in the Moghal territories.

1028. Even a solitary instance in the times of Rajaram, regarding Aurangzeb, may be suffcient to show clearly what great havoc was caused amongst the vast and unwieldy Muslim armies, harassed, hacked and hewed by these Maratha guerrillas! The huge armies of Aurangzeb pursued the Maratha force right up to Jinji (or Zinji) in the South, reducing their territories as they went. But? - the moment they turned their back, they saw that smaller bands of the Maratha irregulars had already crossed the Narmada and after having entered Gujarath, they had frightened the Subhedar of that province out of his wits. Farther off, the Marathas were often reported to have attacked the central provinces to the utter dismay of the already confused Moghal Emperor. In the end, giving up Maharashtra as precipitately as they would have dropped a glowing cinder from their hands, those huge Moghal hosts hacked, harassed and harried by the indomitable Maratha warriors retreate, crestfallen, back to Delhi.

1029. It is not correct to assume that the Marathas had resorted to this aggressive war policy only so long as their martial power and their administrative machinery had not had a sound footing or had not grown sufficiently strong. On the other hand, they renewed their aggressive incursions into the remaining Muslim territories under the command of the invincible veteran war leaders, like Bajirao I, with greater rigour and zest, when every one of the several Sardars and Chieftains had tens and scores and thousands of soldiers under them, fighting, conquering and establishing Maratha rule right from Jinji to Gujarat and even Malwa and Central India! If at all, they were to establish Hindu-Padpadshahi throughout the whole of India, the defensive war policy of preserving whatever they had, would have been of little use. They had necessarily to adopt the bolder policy of making new acquisitions. That way, those brave and indefatigable Maratha warriors had an insatiable desire to assail their religious enemies whenever and wherever they could!

The aggressive war policy of the Marathas stopped the inroads of the Foreign Enemies beyond the Himalayas

1030. The reports that the bold thrusts of Bajirao I right up to the gates of Delhi, had convulsed the Moghal imperial power to its very foundations and rendered it disjointed, and that the mighty Maratha armies were about to invade the territories even beyond Delhi up to Punjab, did not fail to give a rude shock to the Muslim powers of Kabul, Ghazni, Iran, Turan, Balkh, Bokhara, Arabia and other countries beyond the Himalayas!

1031. It has already been shown in this book how, before the rise of the Marathas, these very Arab, Iranian, Durani, Turk, Moghal and other Muslim tribes had often swooped down the Himalayas into the Indian plains with all the ferocity and barbarity at their command; how some of these Muslim aggressors overran the Hindu states, dashed towards the south, worsting the Hindu religion, heaping up inhuman religious persecutions and untold devilish atrocities on its adherents; and again, how some other of them established their own independent stable Sultanates at Delhi and like Alauddin, made straight for the southernmost end of India.

1032. The then Hindu Kings themselves could not invade Iran, Turan or Arabia beyond the Himalayas even before those diabolic Muslim aggressors could trespass the Indian territory. They could annihilate those Muslim invaders in their very homes!

Nadirshah and Abdali

1033. But as soon as the Marathas assumed the Hindu leadership all over India in this millennial Hindu-Muslim epic war, and so soon again as the ramparts of Delhi began to crumble with the forcible thrusts of the Maratha arms, this age-old notorious habit of the Muslim aggressive tribes and states in Asia of attacking every now and then, like Mahmud of Ghazni, with vociferous vows of complete destruction of the Hindu and their religion was for ever broken! Since the time the Maratha arms brought Delhi under their control, and the imperial administration at Delhi began to obey the dictates of the valiant Peshwa, like Bajirao I, only two—Nadirshah of Iran and Ahmedshah Abdali of Ghazni—dared cross the Indian borders from beyond the Himalayas, putting on the pompous airs of the former Muslim invaders swearing terrible wrongs unto the people herein and longing in vain to become the Emperors of India. But really speaking, none of them had come upon India, like the former invaders, on their own initiative and with an irresistible itch. The full knowledge that the Marathas had succeeded in establishing the Hindu rule all over India up to Delhi or that they could do so, had overawed both Nadirshah and Abdali, too! It was only at the supplications of the Muslim Sardars of Delhi and Punjab and at times, the secret invitation of the Emperor himself, that Nadirshah and Ahmedshah made bold to cross the Hindukush and march upon India. The Rohillas, the Pathans and the Moghals secretly pleaded that the Marathas had practically usurped the whole power, that the Kafirs were gradually becoming dominant throughout the whole of India and that they were approaching those foreigners as the defenders of the Muslim faith in order that they might invade India to save the Muslim imperial power at Delhi. They even offered to make those foreign Muslim leaders, the Emperors of Delhi. It was on the invitations of these Indian Muslims and depending on their strength and assistance, that the above-mentioned violent aggressors could think of attacking India.

The Invasion of Nadirshah

1034. Of the Muslim Sardars, Emirs and Khans who secretly invited Nadirshah to invade India in order to crush the Marathas, Nizam-ul-Mulk was the most prominent. As Bajirao I had vanquished him completely, he fondly hoped that the Marathas would be squarely punished and destroyed by Nadirshah. He did not care what would happen subsequently. Nadirshah crossed Attock and reached Lahore in 1732. The Emperor of Delhi made a grand show of opposing him with his army. But in the very first battle, he was routed entirely. Nadirshah called him and put him in his prison. Nizam too was similarly reprimanded for suffering the Marathas to be so very powerful as to engulf the imperial power of Dehli, and because he did not pay the several crores of rupees that he had promised, Nizam, too was put behind the bars. Then, Nadirshah marched straight to Delhi. On the 10th March, 1739, Nadirshah liquidated the Moghal imperial power and proclaimed himself the Emperor of India. With precipitate haste, he not only followed the age-old Muslim imperial tradition but far outdistanced it with all sorts of monstrocities and orgies of blood and fire. Plunder, arson and man-slaughter ran riot in the streets of Delhi. The Muslims, however, hoped that Nadirshah would at least annihilate the Marathas. But deliberately or knavishly, Nadirshah did not offend the Marathas. Why, in his rage of Delhi, he never spared the Muslims. Nadirshah himself seated the Nizam on the back of a donkey and forced him to undergo the humiliation of a parade throughout this city.

1035. Soon the news came headlong that the Marathas had inflicted a great defeat upon the Portuguese and the well known sea-port of Bassein (Vasai) had been conquered from the latter and that the Portuguese Governor of the place and his army had laid down their arms and sued for peace with the Marathas, and that feeling himself free, therefore, to do as he liked, Bajirao I had started with huge preparations and was heading towards Delhi.

1036-37. अरे बघतां काय: चला जोरानें चाल करून !
हिंदु पदपादशाहीस आतां उशीर काय !

"Why do you look so amazed? March on to Delhi (My Boys!) What can now delay the establishment of Hindu Padpadshahi?"

—*Bajirao Peshva I.*

The Maratha Sardars in the North and the various diplomats and political workers that Bajirao I had stationed everywhere also felt keenly that Nadirshah had to be taught a lesson. From various different places, they informed Bajirao about the movements of Nadirshah and the state of affairs in the north. Of those reporters one writes:

तहमास्प कुलीखान (नादीरशाह) कांहीं देव नाहीं जे पृथ्वी कापून काढील। जबरदस्तार्शी सुलुख करिल। म्हपून मातबर फौजे निशी यावे। आधी जबरदस्ती नि मग सुलुख। आता (सारे) राजपूत नि स्वामी बाजीराव एक झालिया निकाल पडेल। समस्तास बुदेले वगैरे एक जागा करून मोठा भाव दाखविला पाहिजे। नादीरशाह तसा माघारा जात नाहीं, हिंदु राज्यावरी निघेल। रायाचे सवाई जयसिंग मनी राणाजी उदेपूर चा महाराणा दिल्लिचे बादशाही तख्तापर बसवावे आसे आहे हिंदुराजे सवाई आदि करून स्वामीचे स्वारीची मार्ग प्रतीक्षा करतात। स्वामींचे पुष्टिबल होताच जाट बगैरे फौज दिल्ली कडे पाठवून सवाईजी आपण दिल्लीस जाणार॥

Tahmaspa Kulikhan (Nadirshah) is not after all a god who will devastate the whole world! He will surely come to terms with a mightier adversary, hence come with a mighty force. Pressure (should be applied) first and peace treaty afterwards! Now it is only the combined might of all the Rajput kings and princes and your Excellency (Bajirao I) that will settle the matter for ever. Boundella Princes and all others should be brought together and the invincible power (of the Hindus) should be manifested on a grand scale. Nadirshah is not likely to go back unless he is forced to do so. He will (most surely) assail the Hindu States, Rai (Sawai Jaysingh) is of the opinion that Ranaji (Maharaja of Udaipur) should be installed upon the imperial throne of Delhi. Sawai (Jaysingh) and other Hindu kings are eagerly waiting for a mighty campaign under your Excellency's leadership. With the strong backing of your Excellency's forces, Sawai (Jaysingh Ji) decides to send the Jat Battalions to Delhi first and then to follow them himself thither!'

1038. Other Maratha leaders from North India also sent similar spirited letters full of confidence and urging bold action! On the basis of those letters, Bajirao addressed in these stirring words those dignitaries at Chhatrapati Shahu's court, who had always tried to disparage every one of his heroic and aggressive moves and bring all sorts of impediments in his progressive measures, O! You brave warriors, why all these doubts and apprehensions? March on united and the glorious dawn of the founding of Hindu-Patpadashahi is a certainty beyond all measure. I, for my part, am determined to cross the Narmada (river) and deploy my troops everywhere right up to the Chambal (river). I shall see then how Nadirshah dares descend southwards!'

1039. As soon as he received the news that the Marathas were already on an aggressive march to the north against him, Nadirshah lost all his enthusiasm to push forward with his conquests to south India as did the former Irani, Turani, Turkish and other Muslim aggressors before him; and with a view to pack off before the Marathas reached Delhi, he voluntarily relinquished the imperial authority, reinstalled the former Emperor of Delhi on his throne and admonished all the courtiers and feudatory princes and vassals to obey the Moghal emperor. Thereafter, Nadirshah hurriedly went back to Persia with the enormous plunder of about five to six hundred million rupees worth of treasure and the peacock-throne and other pieces of art. And that, too, he did because of the fearful apprehensions of a counter-attack by the Marathas!

1040. Along with the letter that he sent to other princes and Kings and vassals of India. Nadirshah sent one to Bajirao Peshwa, commanding him peremptorily to be always faithful to the Moghal Emperor and with a stern warning of the consequent punishment, in case he failed to do so. Foolishly enough did Nadirshah write this letter, but wisely he retreated! It goes without saying that this preposterous letter of Nadirshah, was shown its way to the waste paper basket, and in A.D. 1739, Chhatrapati Shahu unequivocally declared in his court that Nadirshah took a fright of the Maratha retaliation and fled away out of India.

Ahmadshah Abdali becomes the Emperor of Kabul

1041. In Nadirshah's army and under his command had been rising on the strength of his own merit, a certain Afghan Sardar (Emir) called Abdali, who ultimately became the former's right hand man. Abdali had accompanied Nadirshah in his above-mentioned raid against India. After his return to Persia, Nadirshah was soon killed in 1747. In the confusion that was caused subsequent to Nadirshah's death, Ahmadshah Abdali usurped all power and since he was an Afghan, Ahmadshah proclaimed himself an Afghan Emperor making Kabul his capital (1747 A.D.).

The Rohillas and the Pathans

1042. Now, there had been an incessant internal rivalry about the acquisition of the imperial throne of Delhi and consequent mutual hatred between the Moghals and the Afghans (Pathans), who chiefly led the Muslim administration throughout the large tracts of India from Punjab, Delhi, Farukhabad to Rohilkhand—sometimes quite openly, at other times covertly! The former Sultanates of Delhi were Afghans. It was after extirpating the last of the Afghan dynasties, that the victorious Moghal conqueror, Babar, had attained the imperal power over Dehli (as has already been shown in this book earlier). Nevertheless, several Afghan Sardars dominated even this Moghal administration. Amongst these Afghans, the Rohillas and the Pathans had their own states of varying sizes. Later on, when the conquering Maratha armies soon began to establish, one after another, Hindu state all over the Northern half of India and reached Delhi and when in the political affairs of Delhi, practically not a blade of grass could move without the Maratha support, all those Muslim factions became absolutely one at least in the early years of the Maratha preponderance in order to subvert it. Yet later, still the dissentient and scheming amongst these Muslim leaders, secretly sought for the Maratha help for the destruction of their co-religionist opponents.

The first invasion of India by Abdali

1043. Abdali was closely watching these developments in Delhi. He knew full well that the Pathans over there were highly perturbed lest the hated Marathas might leave a vestige of their own existence, unless in the meanwhile, the Pathans overthrew the Moghal imperial authority over Delhi, and on its ashes raised their own. They could find only one way out of this predicament: to invite the new Afghan emperor, Ahmadshah Abdali who had all along supported their political moves. So, the Pathan-Rohilla leaders sent letters to Abdali, importuning his armed help, if at all Islam in India was to be saved. Abdali, too, had cherished the ambition to strangle the moribund Moghal imperial authority in Delhi and to revive in its place the Pathani rule, as of yore. But earlier, he had visited India along with the warriors of Nadirshah's invasion and was fully conscious of the growing Maratha influence in the imperial administration at Delhi. So, he was far too cautious in making his moves. After having secretly supplied all sorts of armed help to the Pathans and the Rohillas in the Doab, Abdali himself came aggressively in the month of January 1748 up to Lahore and captured it. This was the first of his invasions of India.

1044. But the Moghal imperial army defeated Abdali's advance guards just near Lahore and blocked his way to Delhi. Just at this time, he got reports that his enemy, the Emperor of Persia, was preparing to invade Kabul and that at the invitation of the Moghal Emperor to help arrest his onward march, the Marathas had set out with a large army towards Delhi. So considering it to be inopportune to press onwards to Delhi, that shrewd general Abdali retreated immediately to Kabul. But before his departure, he had it proclaimed throughout India that the whole of Punjab was subject to the sovereign Afghan rule under him.

The first treaty of surrender by the Moribund Moghal Empire with the Marathas

1045-46. In the meanwhile, the Moghal Emperor at Delhi had delegated most solicitously all administrative authority over the whole of India right from Bengal, Bihar, Orissa to Sindh (including the Subba of Multan), the whole of Punjab, Rohilkhand, Doab and all the South Indian divisions of the Moghal empire to the Marathas by a special treaty.

1047. By this treaty, at least by this written consent of the Moghal emperor, the Marathas had become since that date the *de facto* sovereigns of the whole of India, and the Moghal Emperor himself had been reduced to a non-entity.

1048. The tremendous reponsibility that devolved upon the Marathas because of this change in the imperial administrative authority was, of course, the onerous one of defending the Moghal empire against all internal as well as external dangers—against internal rebellions and revolts as well as against foreign invasions. Gigantic as this responsibility was, it was only the Maratha sinews that could bear it efficiently—the sinews that had almost realised the dream of the foundation of Hindu—Padpadshahi! That is why they accepted that condition of the treaty quite readily as if it was a boon.

Abdali's second invasion of India

1049. Abdali had been secretly given reports of this forthcoming imperial treaty with the Marathas six months or more before the actual event. That is why in 1749, he invaded India for the second time simply to oppose the Marathas. So the imperial governor of Punjab, Mir Mannu, himself ceded helplesssly Thattha, Sindh (Multan), Punjab and other adjoining territories to Abdali and accepted the overlordship of the latter over that region. Satisfied with the thought that the Maratha authority over that region, relegated to them by the imperial treaty, was wiped out by the abject surrender of Mir Mannu, the imperial officer-in-charge of that part, and that the time for further advance was not yet, Abdali once again went back to Kabul.

1050. But the Marathas were highly infuriated at this duplicity of the imperial officers and the reported mute consent of the Emperor himself to the treacherous act. The Marathas vowed to avenge Abdali's usurpation of the regions between Sindh, Thattha and Punjab, in defiance of the Moghal-Maratha treaty just as furiously as would a cobra, whose tail has been trodden down wilfully. But they were at this time preoccupied with the South-Indian Muslims, the westerners like the Portuguese and also with the domestic political troubles at Satara. As such, Nanasahib Peshwa ordered Malharrao Holkar and Jayajirao Shinde, and the two Maratha leaders crossed the Jamuna and fell upon the fifty-to sixty-thousand-strong army of the Rohillas encamped at Kadargunj on the 20th March, 1751. The Pathans fought tenaciously, but in the end, the Marathas completely routed and destroyed the joint army of the 'original and legitimate' Pathans and

Rohillas. Quickly following this signal success, the Marathas fought the Pathan, Ahmadkhan Bangash, who had come on a hot scent to Farukhabad with his army. Ahmadkhan took shelter in Farukhabad and was timely joined by the second mighty army of the Rohillas. But again, the Marathas besieged the conjoint army of these 'true born' Rohilla-Pathans in the month of April, 1751, and fetching them in open field, inflicted a crushing defeat on that huge army on the 28th of April, 1751. About twenty to twenty-five thousand Pathans and Rohillas were cut off in the battle. Everything belonging to them including their camp was plundered. Thousands of horses, elephants, camels and the battery of guns were all captured. Jayappa Shinde writes in his letter, "The devotees of Hari appropriated that booty to themselves."

1051. When the Peshwa received the news of these battles, Shreemant Nanasahib himself felt elated at the exceptional valour of the Marathas. In his congratulatory reply to the Sardars and soldiers, he himself wrote:

1052. शाबास तुमच्या हिमतीची नि दिलेरी रूस्तुमीची
दक्षिणच्या फौजानीं गंगा यमुना पार होऊना पठाणांशीं
युद्ध करून फते पावावें ठे कर्म लहान सहान नन्हे
तुन्ही एकनिष्ट कृत कर्मे दौलतीचे स्तंभ आहात
इराण तुराण पावे तो लौकिक झाला वझीर पव्ठाला असता
फिरोन फतेच्या मसनदीवर बसविला

(Bravo, well done! All praise to your intrepidity and valour! That the Southern armies should cross the Ganges and Jamuna and win a glorious victory over the Pathans in the open battlefield, is neither a small nor a commonplace thing! You are single- minded loyal men of action, the pillars of the (Maratha) Empire! Your fame has spread far beyond Iran and Turan. While the Queen (on the chessboard) had run astray, (you) have installed her at the vantage position once again!

The Marathas humbled time and again the Hauteur and pride of the true-born and the greatest Muslims too!

1053. A common misleading statement is very often to be seen in the histories written not only by the Muslim, the English, the Portuguese and such other writers who are naturally inimical (hostile) towards the Marathas, and have always tried to disparage them and to detract from their glorious deeds, but also by some of the Hindu writers who evince a slavish mentality and only 'look' and 'write' (without using any independent judgment of their own)—a statement that purports to say:

'One important cause why later on the Muslims were often defeated in India and why the Maratha could set in the process of disintegration of the Muslim empire under their crushing blows, was that the Muslims of the latter days had lost much of the 'original' and 'real' blood and spirit of the early Arab, Mongol, Turkish, Irani, Durani, Afghan, Moghal invaders. Because of the racy climate beyond the Himalayas, big, rushing rivers, hilly and snowy territory and their hardy and robust constitution, which was the result of their spending whole lives in constant warfare, and such other reasons, the comparatively more civilized and 'hence' milder and 'feebler' Hindus could not withstand their earlier invasions. But as those wild and valorous Muslims from beyond the Himalayas began to settle down here for centuries together, generation-after-generation, and as many of their dynasties ruled here, they, too, were victims of laziness, mildness, and proclivity towards luxurious living. They could not retain their former sturdiness, endurance and savage strength, which could stand them in good stead on the battlefield. The 'unhealthy' climate of India did not fail to tell upon their originally strong wild bodies! On the whole, the descendants of those very Muslims came to be weaker and 'not true to their mettle'. That is why the Hindu, especially the Marathas could vanquish only those Muslims!

1054. How very imperfect and unrealistic is this statement! Only one instance of the Maratha offensive against the Rohillas and the Pathans in the Doab and the fact that the Marathas killed as many as twenty thousand of the enemy in the action is quite sufficient to prove the falsity and platitude of the above estimate of the Muslim failure! The Pathan-Rohillas ruling from the Doab to Rohilkhand at that time considered themselves to be 'high-born' Afghans of the finest mettle. Even the Moghal imperial power and the Turkish Nawabs and chieftains dreaded them most. These Afghans had even at that time close and uninterrupted blood relation and family ties with the 'original' stalk of the Afghans beyond the Himalayas. Every year, hundreds of those 'true-bred' and 'real' Afghans came to reside in this Pathanistan in the Doab, while the Afghans here went over to their original homes. It clearly means, therefore, that the thousands of the Pathan-Rohillas in the long tract between the Doab and the Rohilkhand were till that time, at least, 'real' and 'original', 'true-born' and 'thorough-bred' Pathans and Afghans! And the Marathas?

They belonged, after all originally and traditionally, to that country—India—which her enemies called sterile-born and brought up there for generations together!

Even then, did they not often prove these so-called 'true-born' and 'thorough-bred' Pathans and Afghans to be of baser mettle in the final test on the field of battle? Even when Nadirshah fell upon Delhi with an army of the thousands of his 'true-born' and 'thorough-bred' Pathans, crowned himself 'Emperor of Delhi' and threatend to march to the South like Mahmud of Ghazni, is it not because he realized in his heart of hearts that the times had then changed—that it was not the India of Ghazni's times—that now it was the Marathas, whom he had to face, that he retreated so hastily and went clean out of India! Simply because of the dread of the Marathas? In his wake, followed Abdali invading India thrice or four times, every time with an army of not less than fifty thousand strong, made up of the pick of Turkish, Iranian, Durani, Pathan soldiery. But how every time he had to go back crestfallen, because of the armed counter-offensive of the Marathas, how even in the turning of the scale of fortune and even after the terrible losses for the Marathas at Panipat, he had to sign a treaty that the direction of the Moghal imperial affairs at Delhi be left into the hands of the Marathas, how he agreed not to interfere with it, in the least, and how, relinquishing his high ambition to be the absolute and unlimited Emperor of Delhi, he had to submit to the Marathas and go back, never to return, can best be read by every Hindu from our book, Hindu Padpadshahi. It is going to be referred to again in the following pages.

1055. Physical build, height and breadth and weight do count as important and decisive factors in matters of personal combats. Even then, it cannot be made a rule without exception! The grave of the monstrous Afzalkhan at the foot of Pratapgad is evidence enough! But in the struggles of nations, the chances of success or failure can never be assesed on the strength of physical build, enduring capacity and the stubborness of constitution. Didn't the dwarfish Japanese lay the gigantic Russians low on the battlefield in the first Russo-Japanese war—the towering and sturdy Russians in comparison with whom the 'true-born' and 'thorough-bred' Pathans seem absolute midgets? Our Hindu Gorkhas are veritable Marathas in respect of stature. But haven't these very Gorkhas vanquished the Italian, the Austrian and the colossal Hitlerian German armies on various occasions and on various battlefields in the last World War? The whole world still resounds with the fame of the Gorkhas—'A Hindu Gorkha means a gallant fighter' is a common place adage nowadays who once ruled as the invincible Emperor of all the European nations like Germany, Russia and others, renowned for their tall and sturdy soldiers, if not the 'short' Napoleon and his small French army?

Abdali's third invasion of India

1056. The Moghal Emperor had made Gazi-ud-din his chief minister (Vizier), who went all the way along to Sarhind in Punjab in February, 1756, to appoint Adina Beg as the chief imperial officer there. Gazi-ud-din acted in this case depending solely on the Maratha support, and this act of his clearly meant that the whole of the province of Punjab, which was reduced by Abdali, was once agian seized by the Moghal Emperor. Even in Delhi, the Afghan influence was ineffectual and Gazi-ud-din, strongly supported by the Marathas, spoke for the Moghal Emperor. Under these circumstances, Malika Zamani, the old and crafty chief stewardess in the Moghal imperial household, who was frightened out of her wits (at this all-enveloping Maratha hold on the Moghal Empire) and Nizibkhan Rohilla, who was then a prominent leader of all the Rohillas and Pathans in India and who was the bitterest enemy of the Marathas, secretly wrote letters to Ahmadshah Abdali to the effect that if at all Muslim power in India was to be saved, it was Abdali alone who could save it, and that, as such he should forthwith march on India with a well-equipped army. They had also mentioned the fact that the Maratha armies were occupied in the south and that Delhi was practically defenceless. But the Moghal Emperor, they wrote, had already sent word to the Marathas to come to Delhi in all haste. So, if Abdali was late, they argued, the Marathas were very likely to establish their authority right up to Punjab, Thattha and Multan (Sindh) as per their treaty with the Moghal Emperor and that they were to march with mighty armies on Delhi and Punjab.

1057. At this news, Abdali was enraged beyond measure. It was to nullify the imperial charter (Sanad) which entrusted the government of Punjab and the neighbouring region to the Marathas, that he had recently invaded India and annexed that region to his kingdom. He, therefore, took it highly amiss that Gazi-ud-din should reincorporate that part into the Moghal empire, without any sort of appeal or reference made to him. Naturally, once again, he came to Peshawar in November, 1756, with a view to invading India sending his son, Taimurshah and his General Jahankhan to take Lahore. The Moghal general Adinabeg fought with Taimurshah, but was defeated, and there was nobody to beat down the orgy of sword and fire which the Afghan force indulged in, while they rushed headlong from Lahore to Sutlej. Emboldened by this Moghal infirmity, Shah Abdali advanced straight to Delhi without stopping anywhere for rest, with an army of eighty thousand strong in January 1757 A.D. Delhi fell into his hands practically without any resistance. Immediately, he took over the imperial authority and began to run the government in his own name.

1058. And he precipitately performed what the Pathans and the Muslims of the time thought to be their first and foremost duty, according to the religious code of every Muslim Emperor. In order to make it suit his dignity, he even fumed and fretted at the slightest pretext and ordered a horrible general massacre of the citizens of Delhi, so that they might submit meekly to his rule over Delhi. Within a few hours, 'true and high-born' and 'thorough-bred' Afghans beyond the Himalayas slaughtered more than eighteen thousand people, and according to the second universally acknowledged notion of the time, regarding the regal function in accordance with the Muslim religious code, he proclaimed forthwith that as an humble and royal adherent of Islam, he would completely destroy all the Kafirs and their temples and all religious institutions throughout India!

1059. Without any loss of time, he brought his horrible announcement into action. Under his orders, the Hindu temples, shrines, idols and their houses began to be pulled down and set ablaze. Emperor Abdali was particularly infuriated against the several Hindu holy places like Mathura and Prayag, which the Marathas had rescued from the Muslim hands. So he began to defile them all, one after another. On such occasions, Mathura, which is very close to Delhi, was the first to fall a prey after Delhi, to all sorts of vandalism of the monstrous aggressors and stoically enough, did that holy city offer itself, time and again, as sacrificial oblation, as any brave lady in the famous immolation (Johar) of Chitod or the very city of Chitod itself. But this time, it did not merely submit itself to the Muslim religious persecution, without fighting, as it had been doing till this time. Although detailed description is not possible here for want of space, it must be told here that nearly five thousand Hindu Jat citizens fought to the last drop of blood left in them that innumerable and well-organized Muslim army. Every brave Hindu, who died, did so only after killing as many of his Muslim foes as was possible for him to kill. After bathing Mathura in blood and burying it under heaps of the rubble of its demolished temples and shrines and idols, Abdali attacked another neighbouring holy place of the Hindus, Gokul Vrindavan. This also had been the object of Abdali's fury for the simple reason that the Marathas had recently snatched it away from the Muslims. In order to halt this monstrous attack, more than two thousand valiant 'Gosavees' (Monks), from the famous gymnasium of 'Nanga Gosavee', suddenly fell upon the Muslim army with a grim determination to fight unto death. This assault of the Gosavees was so sudden, so well organized and so ferocious that Abdali's forces reeled back all of a sudden at the first knock. Thousands of Muslim soliders were killed outright, and the brave gosavees, too! After the fierce fighting that continued throughout the day, the Muslims left the town and retreated while the wounded and bleeding city resounded joyously and thankfully with praises for those Nanga Bairagees (naked ascetics), who had defended its Gokulnath. If at all, one wishes to be a naked ascetic (Nanga Bairagee), he should be one such!

1060. Abdali then marched against Agra and invested that strong fort. In this very fort was fighting the direst enemy of the Pathan party in imperial court, and one who sincerely tried to save the Moghal imperial power, namely Gazi-ud-din, and he was every moment expecting reinforcement from his protectors, the Marathas!

1061. But what were the Hindu kings and princes of Jaipur, Jodhpur and Udaypur and other neighbouring states, the sardars and noblemen of courts and the million of their warriors and subjects doing at this critical time for the Hindu religion? While Abdali was indulging in reckless and ruthless bloodshed of thousands of Hindu warriors, who sacrificed their lives in the defence of their religion, and while all the Hindu places of pilgrimage were being turned red with the blood of these innumerable Hindu martyrs, it was the common people in north India, and not their rulers, who anxiously waited every moment for the arrival of the Marathas and the relief at their hands from all these atrocities! But the rest of Hindu kings and princes and landlords (jagirdars), who had in their pay large fighting forces, wasted their time cherishing malice towards the Marathas. All the Rajput princes were secretly longing for the destruction of the Marathas at Abdalis's hands. Many of the Hindu rulers there—significant as well as insignificant—had been carrying on secret negotiations with Abdali's. But what, if Abdali had wiped out the Maratha influence from Sindh-Multan to the end of Rohilkhand and Nepal in the north, according to the wishes of the Hindu and Muslim rulers in the north! The appalling answer to this question doesn't seem to have disturbed them a bit. Except for the Marathas, who else were there of these Hindu princes and kings, who could have proved to be the destroyer and conqueror of the Muslim domination? None at all! What, then, could these incompetent Hindu Rajputs and others have gained, if the Marathas had been destroyed by Abdali and the latter had once more established Muslim imperial power throughout the North of India? All that would have happened was perhaps that, a new wave of bloodshed of millions of Hindus and atrocities at the orders of another imperial power of a new Allauddin or a new Aurangzeb would have swept the Hindu world.

1062. But perhaps it was because of the earnest desire and heartfelt longing of the above-mentioned millions of the Hindu commonality, who themselves being disorganized, were utterly powerless to do anything in the matter, except secretly wishing for the speedy arrival of the Marathas, who, in their opinion, were the only ones to smash the Muslim power completely or perhaps because of the original sustaining power of the Hindu nation in general, that nothing of the kind happened.

1063. For, on receiving letters from the Maratha Sardars and Gazi-ud-din and others, Peshwa Nanasahib immediately sent Malharrao Holkar under the chief command of Raghunathrau Dada, with a large army. Urgent letters were also sent to the Maratha Sardars such as Govindpant Bundeley, Barve and others, who were already in the North to render every sort of assistance to Raghunathrao. Before Raghunathrao left Indore and marched ahead, news arrived that hearing the reports of the Maratha advance, Abdali had left Mathura, Vrindaban and other Hindu places of worship and pilgrimage, and gone to Delhi and thence to Kabul, taking away all the booty he had acquired. But he had vested, before his departure to Kabul, the supreme command of that region in the hands of his son, Taimurshah, stationing ten thousand soldiers under him at Sirhind and installing his officers at various important places in Punjab.

1064. While on this side, the Maratha forces under different military leaders in the North, which had gathered together under the one command of Raghunathrao, began to punish severely all those who had begun anti-Maratha activities, relying on Abdali for support. Sakharam Bhagwant, Gangadhar Yeshwant and other Maratha Sardars entered the Doab and once again beat down the Pathan-Rohilla malfactors, released and brought into their fold Vazir Gazi-ud-din, who had been made a captive by the Abdali party. Vithal Shivadev himself marched on Delhi, and after about a fortnight's fierce fighting, entered the city triumphantly, crushing down the Abdali faction completely. The greatest of the triumphs was that the direst enemy of the Maratha and Abdali's right-hand man, Najibkhan Rohilla, was caught alive. Eventually, Abdali's settlement of the region under his suzerainty was toppled down completely. The Pathan army of ten thousand strong, which Abdali had stationed at Sirhind under the command of Abdul Samad in order to maintain his hold on the region, itself lost courage. Consequently, when the Marathas themselves advanced menacingly towards Sirhind, there was a great commotion caused in the Muslim ranks even before a regular battle was joined, and they were completely routed in the initial skirmishes and their commander was caught alive. This news made Taimurshah, the son of Abdali and his governor of Punjab, and his commander-in-chief, Jahankhan, leave off their original plan of defending Lahore and in the face of this forceful and precipitate Maratha counter-offensive, both of them struck an honourable retreat to Kabul along with all their army, hardly daring to face the Marathas on the battlefield. Abdali had strictly urged upon them that they were under no circumstances to let the vast treasures of millions (crores) of rupees, which was still in their possession, to fall in the enemy hands. As such, they tried utmost to carry it safely, retreating in as orderly a manner as was possible. But the Marathas not only pursued them even beyond Lahore but they played such a havoc in the Muslim ranks that Traimurshab crossed Attock and fled to his own province, leaving behind at various places all his elephants, horses, camels, and all the treasure in cash and jewellery, gold and silver. He had nothing to carry home of the vast plunder from India, except his own life! Whatever else belonged to him, was either sacked or destroyed by the Marathas. Whatever little of his Afghan army escaped only with their lives to Kabul like their governor, were the only ones that remained alive! All of the veteran Pathan army of fifteen to twenty thousand strong, which was kept behind in Delhi and Punjab by Abdali to annihilate the Hindus and the Hindu religion throughout India, was attacked group by group and massacred by the Marathas in the battles and skirmishes fought with them.

1065. Thus, by inflicting crushing and humiliating defeats on Emperor Ahmadshah Abdali and by reconquering from the Afghan empire the whole vast region from Sindh to Multan and Multan to Sirhind, the Marathas once again gained the *de facto* control over the governance and administration of this extensive province which they had earlier gained by a paper treaty with the Moghal emperor! But the then Moghal emperor and his Vazir, Gazi-ud-din, themselves knew very well that in their own interest, too, it was essential that the Marathas should do this. Hence, the Emperor himself gave order that Raghunathrao's formal triumphant entry into Lahore for the settlement of the affairs there, was to be celebrated publicly with all pomp and festivities. All the Hindu chieftains of Kashmir, Dogra nobles, Missals of the Sikhs and the so-called Muslim Empire, Umraos, 'Nizams and Nawabs', who had been so far engaged in riotous actions and ravaging the country to their own sweet will, were so much overawed and struck dumb by this extraordinary heroism of the Marathas in recapturing the whole of Punjab and the adjoining territories, that they began to join the Maratha General Raghunathrao as subordinate allies. The Sikhs had been recently gaining control over things in Punjab and they were infuriated by Abdali's wanton act of demolishing their at Amritsar and filling up their holy lake round it with filth, mud, stones and bricks during his retreat to Kabul for fear of the Marathas. They had, therefore, become inveterate enemies of Abdali, and mighty leader of one of their powerful 'Missals', namely Alasingh Jat (whom the Maratha correspondence of the times referes to as 'Ala Jat') had joined the Marathas openly in the battle of Sirhind. Hence, as almost all these leaders and parties who had been then active in the political movements in Punjab were favourable to such a grand ovation to be given to Raghunathrao, it was agreed on all hands that the imperial ceremony felicitating the triumphal entry into Lahore of Raghunathrao at the head of his army should be celebrated after the Maratha general's successful campaign towards Sindh.

The Triumphant March of Raghunathrao Peshwa in Punjab

1066. Taimurshah, who fled beyond the frontier, tried to carry with him the immense treasure the Muslims had plundered in India, and it was to seize that treasure that Raghunathrao entered Punjab in hot pursuit of the Pathan army, which ran helter-skelter. Conquering more than half of Punjab of Abdali, Raghunathrao drove them off to the frontier. Leaving the rest of the work of regaining the frontier to the other Maratha companies and brigades, he returned to Lahore, the Capital of Punjab, in order to consolidate the Maratha gains and settle the affairs there and lay a firm foundation of the Maratha power in the newly accquired territory. On the 11th of April, 1758, he made his triumphant entry into Lahore with all the regalia and his victorious army.

1067. A magnificent ovation was given to him in order to glorify this victorious entry of his, attended with feasting and dancing. Raghunathrao sojourned in no less a place than the imperial palace itself. The other prominent Maratha warlords had also put up in big palaces in Lahore or the camps in the vicinity of the city. Everywhere, hundreds of well-adorned elephants, horses, camels and fatted bulls paraded through the streets. Various big Hindu-Muslim from different places, Emirs, Umraos, the so-called Nawabs, Nizams, Raos, Kings and courtiers presented themselves in the magnificent Darbar in the afternoon. Everyone of them, the political as well as the civil administrators, nay, even the imperial army in Punjab, vowed allegiance to the Peshwa at Poona and Raghunathrao was honoured as the representative of that Peshwa. Every one of them tendered his homage in the form of rich gifts to Raghunathrao. At night, the whole city was gloriously illumined. Dazzling fireworks were displayed everywhere. Even the neighbouring cities round about Lahore celebrated that feast of light and fireworks display.

1068. What was the setting or the location of this triumphant assembly—this feast of light? It was no other than the recreation grounds of the greatest of the Moghal Emperors, like Akbar, Jahangir, Shahjahan and others—the extensive courtyard of the most famous Shalimar gardens of Lahore!! The Marathas had thus reduced the Muslim imperial power to serfdom!

1069. At the news of this glorious Maratha victory, there was literally a shower on Raghunathrao of the congratulatory letters written not only by the numerous Kings and courtiers, Sardars of various ranks and the learned Shastri-pandits, who were openly or secretly endeavouring beyond all measure in the cause of Hindu-Padpadshahi throughout the length and breadth of India, but by the self-less ascetics, also. As has been said in Paragraph 991, the various writers of these multifarious congratulatory letters were so much overcome by a sense of pride and jubilation over this unconceivable Maratha victory, that they could not convey their feeling in simple prose. These could only be conveyed through some mythological imagery, a sample of which can be had in this one sent to Raghunathrao on the 5th of May, 1758, by a Maratha General in Delhi, Antaji Mankeshwar, who was in the habit of writing nothing but simple political reports and yet who was one of the higher officers in the Maratha army.

1070. "Received your Excellency's favour (of 13th April). How can I express adequately the excessive joy I felt at the news in your Excellency's letter about the victory at Lahore, the destruction of the enemy and the acquistion of the terrirories there? (Your Excellency's) fame has spread far and wide in Hindusthan (North India). The high-born Emirs and Umraos and Governors, all are overawed! It is your Excellency alone who avenged the wrong of the whole of Hindusthan (North India)! As such, your Excellency's success vies with the mountains! Your Excellency is (destined to be) successful. How can this poor servant of your Excellency have the ability to dilate upon this topic? The Vazir was extremely pleased to hear these tidings (and said) "His Excellency is truly an incarnation of God. How can a human being praise Him sufficienty'? Your humble servant (i.e. I) has no other safe shelter anywhere except at your feet. If your Honour is likely to encamp at Lahore, I will come there with the Emperor and his Vazir. The Vazir and all others, great and small, fear that in case your Excellency were not to encamp, the Pathans are likely to return to Lahore in the rainy season. I have just set down here what the people say. Your Honour's is the right to decide upon the course of action to be followed. May your Excellency be kind enough to let this humble servant know whether the proposal of bringing the Vazir and the Emperor there is fair or otherwise, and your Excellency's orders in this respect are awaited. Vithal Shivdev would escort them there if Your Honour so pleases. Krishnarao (Kale), too, might come, and put before Your Honour everything."—5.5.1758.

The report on the conquest of Punjab sent by Raghunathrao Peshwa Himself

1071. Now letters-after-letters followed in quick succession from Shreemant Nanasahib at Poona asking Raghunathrao to return along with his army to the South before the monsoons set in. But as Punjab had been very recently conquered, it was absolutely essential that proper system had to be urgently laid down for the governance and administration of the vast territory. As such, it was desirable that Raghunathrao should entrench himself there with all his army for another four months. All the ablest Maratha leaders and army commanders thought and urged that Raghunathrao had better not to go to the Daccan along with Malharrao Holkar. But Raghunathrao Dada and Malharrao Holkar, too, were in their heart of hearts inclined to go to the South. Now that Nanasahib had 'called' him back, Raghunathrao himself sent an authentic report, penned by himself, to Shreemant Nanasahib about the unprecedented success in Punjab, and began his return march towards Poona. Many other Maratha Sardars, including the one of the status of Malharrao Holkar, returned to the Deccan along with Raghunathrao. Of course, in order to maintain the Maratha rule unhampered in Punjab the requisite Maratha forces were stationed at different places by Raghunathrao under some Sardars.

1072. Although it was quite possible to describe the valour of the Marathas in this campaign in Punjab in the grand style of an epic or heroic poetry, Raghunathrao, however, it is especially to be noted, put the whole thing in the report he sent of this campaign to Poona in the most direct matter-of-fact way, befitting his solider's profession, without any long-winded digressions or self-adulation or exaggeration of any sort. Hence, we should like to cite his very words.

1073. Writes Raghunathrao in his despatch of the 4th May, 1758, to the Peshwa: "As regards the bandobasta of (resettling the affairs or re-establishing firm control over) the provinces, the Lahore, Multan, Kashmir and rest of the territory this side of Attock, I should like to say that a part of the work is done and rest of it I shall do very shortly. After hotly pursuing Sultan Taimur and Jahankhan, we have routed and plundered all their army. Fighting some skirmishes here and there and being beaten, they have fled to Peshawar beyond Attock. Abdali marched against Iran but the Persian emperor despoiled his whole army. Abdali then came (back) to Kandahar, followed by the Irani army in hot pursuit. Jabardestakhan and Mur-r-rubkhan, the Sardars and Landlords of this province, who had tendered their loyalties to Abdali because of the latter's threatening might (or tyrannical treatment), have also now changed their side and are promising to serve faithfully and to chastise Abdali. Abdali himself has lost courage. In short, it does not seem that he can muster strong from that front. He has been, already, chastised by the Shah of Iran on the other side. It would be proper if you send reinforcements and establish His Majesty's control beyond Attock. His nephew and heir to the throne, who had approached Your Excellency and whom Your Excellency had sent to us, will be given some territory this side of Attock to establish himself and then will be appointed to the Subha of Kabul, Peshawar beyond Attock. The chief of Abdali's forces, Abdul Samadkhan, who was in Sirhind, is captive of our state. I shall send him and some Moghal and Irani forces from this province. They will manage the affairs there. By virtue of Your Excellency's greatness and piety, they will bring pressure on Abdali and punishing him severely, they will establish our control beyond Attock. Renake Anaji and Rayaji Sakhadev have been posted in Lahore. Gopal Ganesh (Barve) also is quite at home in this region. He too will stay. The Emperor of Iran had sent the letters to me and to Malharrao (Holkar) calling us precipitately to Kandahar to destroy him (Abdali) and to fix up the frontier at Attock. But we, at least on our part should like to send Abdul Rahimankhan of Kabul, whom your Excellency had sent to us, and we shall help him with some armed forces and other sinews of war. The provinces of Kabul and Kandahar, beyond Attock, have been a part of Hindusthan from (the times of) Akbar to (that of) Alamgir; why should we then give these away? For the present, we shall establish Irani control over the region and send a pleasant reply. Ambassadors from all the neighbouring powers like Jammu and Kashmir have come. We shall settle about the territory this side of Attock; further beyond, it is not yet possible (to do anything of the kind). Efforts (in that direction) will be made. For the present, I shall do whatever is most urgent. Whoever stronger person will lead the next expedition will effect a permanent settlement. The province has a revenue collection of about two to four crore (twenty to forty million of rupees). But the landlords and Jamindars are very powerful. We collect only a nominal revenue. It is difficult to realise even two hundred thousand rupees from a province with a yield of at least two and a half million. For the present, we are staging a comeback under Your Excellency's orders. As such, we do whatever is possible; we do not stretch matters too far. For the time being, the governance of the territory has been entrusted to Adina Beg alone. To him we have given Lahore and Multan on lease. This year, the whole (of the revenue collection) will be consumed by the occupation army (garrison army); even fitting out such an occupation army will be difficult; things would be favourable after two or three years. With compliments to Your Excellency!!"

1074. THE ONLY DISGRACEFUL PART OF IT IS THAT WHILE RETURNING TO THE DECCAN, THE MARATHAS DID NOT TAKE REVENGE ON THE MUSLIMS FOR THEIR RELIGIOUS PERSECUTION!

1074A. In Chapter 8, on the 'Perverted Conception of Virtues', of the book, it has already been shown in greater detail how the Hindu society (of the time) was haunted by a false and perverted sense of virtues and as such how the Hindus did not even slightly avenge the unbearable and unlimited persecution and the diabolic atrocities perperated by the Muslims on the Hindu religion. Unlike Spain, Portugal, Bulgaria, Greece and other (European) nations which saved Christianity from extinction (from their lands) by ridding completely their homeland of Muslims, the Hindus did not extirpate the Muslims from India. They refrained from inflicting similar, not to speak of greater atrocities even on the enemy, like Muslims who considered religious persecution and diabolic and heinous atrocities themsleves to be their religious duties! Every drop of blood in the Hindu veins and arteries was surcharged, as it were, with the false and suicidal and perverted conception of religious tolerance towards the aliens. The notion that whatever the nature of atrocities of the aliens on our religion, we should not, even for resisting them, retaliate against these very aggressive alien religionists, was the essence of their religious tolerance. And it was considered by the Hindu to be their religion! It is because of this suicidal notion of religious tolerance that Hindus, even when they had gained unparalleled victories over the Muslims on the battlefields and in the political arena, did not oppose them in the least on the religious front. Naturally, on this religious front, the Muslims in India were not extirpated, nor were they subdued. Root them out completely the Hindus never did, as they had done with the Greeks, the Sakas, the Huns and other ancient aggressors.

1074B. I should be failing in my duty if I were to proceed without referring to one more illustration of this incurable disease of the Hindu mind—of this perverted sense of virtues—which has proved highly injurious to the Hindu valour and Hindu political victory had reached its zenith in Punjab.

1075. Just at the time when Raghunathrao had started from Poona with his army and reached Indore round about 14th February, 1757, the malevolent Adbali had heaped untold humiliation and outrage on the Hindu religion and Hindu women. He had sent some of the cruellest of the commanders to Mathura, Vrindavan, Kurukshetra and other Hindu holy places, in order to avenge their rescue by the Marathas from the Emperor's clutches. Abdali had given these Muslim commanders strict order that—

1076. It was their religious duty as true Muslims that they should devastate every one of the so-called Hindu holy places like Mathura and massacre as many Hindus there, as was possible and to heap up the chopped-off heads together. Whoever from amongst them would chop off the heads of the Hindus as those of Kafirs, were to be rewarded by Abdali at the rate Rs. 5 per such Hindu head.

1077. How mercilessly those savage Muslims wolves, instigated by Abdali's order, attacked Mathura and other holy places of Hindus has been described in Paragraphs 1059 and 1060. Accordingly, the Muslims fell upon the Hindu religious centres at Mathura and slaughtered the innocent Hindus there. Gigantic Hindu temples were toppled down one after another. Streams of blood of the Hindu men and women, children and old people, began to flow through every house and every street. Not a single young Hindu woman escaped kidnapping. Not a single cow was spared her life. The innocent blood of the cows, too, flowed like water. Those Muslim demons were neither satisfied with nor tired of this brutality. On the country, in order to adorn these devilish acts of theirs with their diabolic artistic sense, they travestied the ceremony of the Hindu Rangpanchami, which happened to be at that time. And how? Big cauldrons and vessels full of Hindu blood newly shed, were kept at different places at short intervals, and the Muslim solidiers with large syringes in hand went on drenching the Hindus in every street and every home in their own blood. The same was the miserable fate of the next town of Gokul, Vrindavan. But the moment he got the news that Rughunathrao had left Indore and proceeded with a large army to destroy him, that self-styled Shahenshah, Abdali, hurried for life to Delhi with all his army and thence to Lahore and onwards straight to Kabul!

1078. Although the very same Maratha force that had beaten back Abdali's army straight beyond the (North West) frontier (of India) were now returning to the Deccan after glorious victories in Punjab and were visiting the same holy places of Mathura [wrongly spelt Mattra, CHI (1939) and by other writers] Gokul, Vrindavan, and while they were performing their religious rites and having ceremonial baths in the holy rivers, while again they were listening to the harrowing accounts of the Muslim atrocities on the Hindus and their religion, perpetrated only a year ago, while still the Hindu blood spilled profusely by the Muslims on the well-built banks (घाट ghats) of the Jamuna at Mathura had not yet completely dried away, while again the ditches filled with the beef of cows (slain by the Muslims) had been putrefying along the streets, the heads of this Mathura army were not excited with anger at these Muslim brutalities! Nobody of them was beside himself with shame and indignation! None of them was infuriated and none of them vowed revenge of this religious persecution! The victorious general of the Hindus, the brave Raghunathrao, did not issue any order to his army to the effect that they should retaliate with the same atrocities on the Muslims as were indulged in by the latter, that the Muslims as a whole were to be slaughtered, that just like (the ruined) heaps of the Hindu temples, the Muslim masjids should be pulled down without any exception, that the Muslim women should be put to the same indescribable humiliation and shame as the Hindu women folk were done by the Muslims, that it was their duty to take such a revenge for the wrongs done to Hindu religion and Hindu society! Abdali had but done it!!

1079. We have explained the inestimable wrong done to the Hindu society by this suicidal disease of the perverted conception of virtues so fully in Chapter 8 of this book, that it is needless to repeat it here again. We hereby urge upon every reader to read the above-mentioned Chapter 8 over and again and very carefully.

1080. The most fortunate thing for the Hindus was only this, that the catastrophe, which threatened to extinguish very flame of life of the whole Hindu nation, as a consequence of the silly Hindu religious notions (as the ones described above), was averted by their retaliatory deed of valour and more especially by those of the Marathas on the political and military fronts. Although the Marathas are guilty of not taking revenge of the Muslim vandalism on Mathura-Vrindavan, while on their triumphal march from Punjab, the glorious victory that they won on the Muslims in Punjab in this continuous millennial Hindu-Muslim war and the terrible blow that they gave to the Muslim imperial power, establishing the independence of the Hindu nation and their own political hegemony in the north incapacitated the Muslims from completely destroying the Hindus in India, just as they had completely annihilated the other ancient nations in Asia. Babylon became Baghdad, but Mathura could not be transformed into another Mecca! Fighting incessantly and indefatigably for ten long centuries, Mathura still exists as a holy Hindu place. The traces of Muslim domination have been wiped out! From the millions of Hindu throats, the triumphant chants of the divine valour of Shree Krishna still resound the Ghats of Jamuna and the temples unmitigated!

□

22

Not Only Attock—Even Beyond It!

1081. सरदार पदरचे कसे कुणि सिंह जसे कुणि शार्दुल गेंडे।
अरे ज्यानी अटकेंत पाव घटकेंत रोविले झेंडे॥

—प्रभाकर

(Of what caliber were the Sardars under (him)? Some were veritable lions, others were tigers, whereas some others were rhinoceroses indeed! Why, within a quarter of a 'Ghataka' (a period of 24 minutes), they planted their flags in Attock!'

1082. As has been told in the previous Chapter, while Raghunathrao was returning to the Deccan after his unprecedented triumph in Punjab, along with his numerous Sardars and warriors, the tidings of his victory had already been reaching Maharashtra from time to time. One day, all the Maratha forces gathered together at Indore, the next day they were collecting the Chauth and Sardeshmukhi taxes from all over Rajputana; later on, they were reported to be rushing into the Antarvedi, punishing the Rohillas and Pathans for joining hands with Abdali; then conquering Delhi and performing the obsequies, as it were of the vaunted imperial authority of Abdali and releasing the Moghal Emperor from his captivity and esablishing him on the throne of Delhi as the puppet in Maratha hands; then again immediately invading Punjab, routing Abdali's Afghan army of ten thousand strong, which was kept there for the protection of Punjab at Sirhind. Then Abdali's son Taimurshah and his general Jahankhan were reported to have fled from the Marathas without giving any battle, and fled straight to Kabul leaving Lahore to the tender care of the Marathas, and the armies of Raghunathrao were said to be mopping up Punjab clean of the Afghan domination and driving the enemy far beyond Attock. Then came the news of the triumphant entry of Raghunathrao into Lahore! With such heartening news and reports pouring in daily of the Maratha victories and the worsting of the enemies at their hands, the mighty heart of Maharashtra was filled with justifiable pride. Raghunathrao had already earned for himself a name fit to be ranked with the greatest in the world in his single victorious campaign right from Poona straight to the Indus! The whole of Maharashtra began to call him, willingly or unwillingly, but lovingly enough Ragho-Bharari, in order to express its wonder and pride about this unhampered and undeterred spring of his, about this eagle-flight of his, towards the Himalayas! This informal title of the victorious general, Raghunathrao, had become immortal!

Soon arrived the news of the Crowning Glory of the Marathas

1083. Raghunathrao, the commander-in-chief of the Maratha force, had posted some of the Maratha Sardars to punish severely all the Muslim Emirs, Umraos, gangsters and marauders, fakirs and parasites of every sort, who were creating anarchical conditions in Punjab and especially towards the Indus Valley, plundering the peaceful populace there, and establish the Maratha hold in that territory firmly and to collect the revenue and the 'chauth' and 'Sardeshmukhi' taxes from the territory. Of those Sardars, Tukoji Holkar, Sabaji Shinde, Gopalrao Barve with their soliders attacked the fort of Attock, which was the pride of the Indus valley, and snatched it away from the Muslim hands in the month of July, 1758. The Muslim green flag was uprooted and in its place was hoisted in the tumultuous war cries of 'Har Har Mahadev!' of the Marathas, the saffron coloured 'Jaripatka' of Hindus—on the fort of Attock. The Marathas and so the Hindu-horses once again drank the holy water of the Indus!

1084. On that glorious day, at last, was the ban (Atak—अटक) of a thousand years enforced by the religious law of the Hindus themselves, broken by the Hindu arms! Why, the Maratha warriors pursued the Muslims even beyond Attock upto Kandahar!

1085. It is already explained in Paragraphs 522 to 535 how this town was named 'Attock' and why.

1086. When the news arrived in Maharashtra of the conquest of Attock and of the hoisting by the Marathas of the Hindu Jaripatka on that fort, the universal joy felt there knew no bounds. The Marathas had taken revenge of the wrong done to the Hindus over a thousand years by routing and driving the Muslims right up to Kabul and Kandahar and wrenching the *de facto* sovereignty of the whole of India from the Muslim hands.

And this itself is the fifth Glorious Epoch of Hindu Victories over the Aggressors

1087. The page in the history of the Hindu Nation, which records this unique event of the conquest of Attock and the final victory of the Hindu in the epic millennial Hindu-Muslim war and the establishment of the *de facto* sovereignty of the Hindus over the so-called Muslim empire, is really the Golden Page in Hindu history and that day is truly the Red Letter Day in the life of Hindu nation!

However

1088. Just as a man on his deathbed, too, breathes a little longer and sometimes even makes a violent effort to rise in epileptic fits, but dies at last; or just as the whole body of the enormously long snake, twenty feet or more in length, gigantic in thickness vying with the broad trunks of the Vat (Indian fig- Ficus Indica) tree, moving dangerously at large in the forests, does not lie lifeless all at once in a moment, even if its head has been smashed completely, but keeps on moving convulsively and even at times seeks to leap ahead, yet ultimately, the dying body does die at last, similarly, in spite of the fact that the Marathas had smashed the head of the Muslim imperial power and left it gasping for its breath on the battlefields of the Indus valley, the moribund Muslim power did continue to make feverish efforts to rise again here and there for sometime more; that dying body did in fact take a long leap like that of the Panipat, but ultimately, it could not avert its fast approaching death.

1089. And in the end, throughout the whole of India began to flutter the flag of independent Hindu power! Not alone from the Indus but right from the bank of the Kabul river, spread throughout the whole of Punjab, up to the frontiers of Jammu and Kashmir, was established the Hindu-Sikh empire of Maharaja Ranjit Singh! Further on, from Delhi right up to Rameshwaram in the rest of India, was established the paramountcy of the Marathas, and to the north was the independent Hindu State of Nepal!! Thus, everywhere in India began to rule once again the Hindu political power: the Muslim power could not recover its fall!

1090. That is why it must be said that on the day on which the Marathas uprooted and flung away the green flag of the Muslim political dominance from the fort of Attock and hoisted in its place their own triumphant saffron coloured Jaripatka, the Hindus gave a really mortal blow to the Muslim power in India and caused its subsequent death!

1091. Even a historian like Sardesai, who was wont to make understatements, wrote: 'All Maharashtra felt electrified with the proud performance of Raghunathrao and his bands having reached the extreme frontier of India and bathed their horses in the Indus.' (New History of Maharashtra: Vol. II, page 401)

1092. As soon as the reports of the final victories of the Hindus over the Muslims in this millennial Hindu-Muslim war reached Maharashtra, the Charans, the Bhats, the Gondhalees, who were the chief exponents of the poignant national feelings of the people at large, began to surcharge the atmosphere of every village in Maharashtra with triumphant joy, by means of their heroic poems and ballads, imbued with the most warlike 'spirit'. There was not to be found any self-respecting Maratha who was not enthralled and inspired to hear these deeds of his own army. Since it is only in the imaginative vein, that a true picture of the romantic mood of the Maharashtra of that day can be drawn. I have tried to express it in my poem 'Gomantak' through the mouth of Maharashtrabhat, a typical representative of the Bhats, Charans and Gondhalees! A few couplets from the same poem are translated into English from the original in Marathi and cited here for the perusal of the reader.

1093. **A Panegyric**

By Maharashtrabhat

Here, O Hindus, hear you all
Comes the news of our victory in War,
Wrongs of a thousand years aveng'd
Down is the victor vanquish'd again'
Celebrate the day with feastings and dancing
Yours is the right by martyrdom seal'd
But mind, th'task is not yet done!
Only the ramparts so far're won;
The rock's to be clim'd, the fort's to be storm'd
The wish'd for summit is safely to be made!
Dawn'd today is the moment auspicious
For Hindu-padshahi happy and glorious!

Still the solemnities aren't over
Impending dangers overhead hover.
Like Starters of Eras have we won this glory
Like Starters of Eras must we hold it grimly
Once again o'th banks of the Indus
Proudly carrying the crest of gold
Stands the horse of a Hindu warrior
To quench his thirst of a thousand years!
Come with the seas, ye, Gangamaiyya,
Waters pure of Caveri come;
Sindhu, Shatadru, Triveni, Jamuna
Goda, Krishna're welcome here!
Holy places'nd pilgrim-resorts
Spread o'ver India, come, you, all.
Haridwar, Kailas, Kashi'nd Puri
Dwarka'nd Mathura come in a hurry!
Hear, O, hear the tidings clear
Victory on th'field is pure, O, dear,
Wreck'd we our vengeance on the foe
Delay'd though 'twas for a thousand years,
And Look! The vaunting victor lies, how low!'
God has indulged Hindu warriors
With their cherished dream of life.
Proudly flutters on Attock today
Again the Hindu Jaripatka.

(Translated from the couplets numbered 1, 112, 116, 117, 118, 127, 128, 129, 130, 131 from the original poem)

□

23

The Sixth Glorious Epoch of Hindu Victories over the Aggressors

India freed from the British Domination

1094. This Chapter on the Sixth Glorious Epoch of Hindu Victories Over Aggressors is the last one.

1094A. The scope of this book has been defined in Paragraph 7 of the first chapter of this book. That delimitation itself suggests that in this chapter on the Sixth Glorious Epoch of Hindu victories, it is not at all necessary to give a detailed account of how, while the British had firmly established their mighty empire on the whole of India, the Hindu nation could make itself independent and how it has taken a place of pride as an indigenous and sovereign republic amongst the nations of the world. The only object of this chapter is just to examine and assess only salient points in this exciting war of liberation of the Hindu nation from the British, which have been purposely overlooked by almost all the foreign as well as the independent historians, notwithstanding the fact that they are highly important from the point of view of Hindutwa.

1095. But that too, I have done for the most part in my other books, as far as it was necessary to do so:

1096. (1) It is already mentioned at the end of the last chapter that the Hindus had completely uprooted the foreign Muslim empire from India and Hindu States had once again, been established everywhere and the Muslims did not, in fact, wield any imperial authority over the land of Hindusthan. But while the Hindu nation was thus inextricably involved in a gigantic millennial war to root out the Muslim imperial power from India and while all its energies and time were utilized in that direction, European nations like the Portuguese, the French, the Dutch and especially, the English had already commenced their efforts at establishing their rule over India secretly or even openly. The Marathas, who had assumed the leadership of the Hindu nation at that time, had simultaneously to face all these European nations, just when they were carrying on a life and death struggle with the Muslims! Although they had been mostly successful in the end in arresting the progress of the Protuguese, the French, the Dutch, the English, however, shrewdly availabled themselves of the opportunity, they got, when the Marathas were engaged in the struggle with the Muslim powers, and gradually but firmly established their foothold in Bengal trampling under their feet the weaker Muslim Nawabs over there. Thereafter, they pushed on their aggressive moves and established, though not *dejure*, yet, *de facto* sovereignty over the territory right up to Delhi. Naturally they soon came to grips with the Marathas, who had to lead the Hindu nation at that time. In my book, Hindu Padpadshahi (originally written in English and now translated in Marathi) I have sufficiently discussed, from the standpoint of the Hindu nation, how and to what extent the Marathas worsted the English during the First and the Second Anglo-Maratha Wars. The curious readers should do well to read it.

1097. That discussion will make the following two broad points absolutely clear. The first is that from the time the English stepped on the Indian soil, the Muslims never fought with them for national political independence. With the short exception of those with the Mysore State of Haidar and Tipu, all the wars, that the English fought for the sovereignty over India had to be necessarily fought with the Hindus alone. This clearly shows that the Hindus had practically destroyed the political power of the Muslims and had snatched the imperial authority. Another equally important point to be remembered is that the English, too, had maintained the nominal dignity of the puppet Moghal Emperor for fifty years after they had established their *de facto* sovereign power over India in the very same manner as the Marathas had, as a political expedient of the time, kept on recognizing the same 'king of shreds and patches' as the 'Emperor of India'.

1098. It again exposes the snobbery and ignorance of the Anglicized people who ridicule the Marathas for this 'political expedient' of theirs, of a nominal recognition of the Moghal Emperor. For the English, too, found the same political expedient useful to them. These Anglicized people, however, do not criticize the English for this same 'weakness' of theirs!

The Anglo-Sikh Wars

1099. No sooner did the English destroy the sovereign Maratha power over India in A.D. 1818 and no sooner did they force the rest of the Maratha states to accept their overlordship than they had to cross swords with another newborn Hindu power. That Hindu power was the great kingdom of Maharaja Ranjit Singh, which rose to prominence after 1818. It was after the death of Maharaja Ranjit Singh, that the English took the field against the combined Hindu might of the Sikhs, the Jats and the Dogras spread far and wide from the river Kabul to the river Shatadru (Sutlej) and to the north up to Kashmir and Ladakh. In the end, the English were successful and the English sovereignty was established from Punjab to Kashmir round about A.D. 1850.

My book on the History of Sikhs—the one that was Destroyed

1100. As I have surveyed the period of Indian History covered by the Maratha Empire, in my English book Hindu Padpadshahi, smilarly I had written a discourse on the period following the Maratha epoch in that book of mine, the History of the Sikhs, written in Marathi. But while I was in the thick of revolutionary political activities against the English in Paris, round about 1909-10, the manuscript of my book, 'The History of the Sikhs' fell into the hands of Government of India's Secret Intelligence Department and was destroyed before publication. However, in my books "Prushthabhumi" and this one "Six Glorious Epochs of Hindu Victories Over Aggressors", I have discussed from the Hindu standpoint all the important events in the Sikh history up to 1850—the time when the mighty kingdom of the Sikhs was virtually destroyed! The curious reader should read it.

The Anglo-Nepalese War

1101. The third great power, with which the English had to fight for the sovereignty of India, was the then mighty Hindu state of Nepal. Although the English ultimately won that war, their success was not so great as to destroy that Nepalese Hindu State completely. Barring the English paramountcy as regards the external affairs, their internal independence was unimpaired. Again, this existence of the Nepalese Hindu State was essential for the continuance of the English sovereignty over India for a long time afterwards. For, Nepal was a fertile field, which ceaselessly provided staunch and brave Hindu Gurkha soldiers for the English army. This Hindu Gurkha army proved itself quite capable of, not only in India, but also in Europe, successfully facing the even numbered white army of either European countries. Moreover, in the face of a plausible aggression from the mighty Empire of Russia, which was not only capable but anxious to invade the northern frontiers of the British Indian Empire, the English wished that the warlike state of Nepal should serve as a buffer state in order that such a Russian aggression might not come too unexpectedly.

1102. Only after defeating the Hindu power of the Marathas, the Sikhs and the Nepalese, could the English claim complete sovereignty over India.

1103. The scrambling little East India Company of overseas traders in England, which was established round about the rise of Shivaji Maharaj and which had begun its activities with two meagre factories at its disposal, went on enlarging the sphere of activities and thus acquired the sovereignty of the whole of India about 1850! Originally started by about a dozen Englishmen of pluck, the obscure trading company thus became, within a short period of two centuries or so, the mistress of a mighty empire! During the same period rose and fell many royal dynasties vying with one another for the sovereignty of India. Many sundry states were founded soon and found themselves engaged in internecine warfare and destroyed. But, ultimately, it was this East India Company that struggled and fought on and ultimately supplanted all those rival powers to become the sole mistress of India. How very insignificant a commercial body was this East India Company on the day on which it was started by a handful of shareholders! But all its yearly reports of its assets and liabilities, of its income and its expenditure, right from its first year of inception to the year of its dissolution, carrying forward its previous year's balance and new sources of income and new items of expenditure every year, till after a hundred and fifty or two hundred years it came to include towards its credit side the very empire of India, had all been very scrupulously and systematically preserved in its secretariat in London. And when in 1858, it was dissolved and the British Government itself took over the Empire of India in the name of Queen Victoria, it was most systematically and legally wound up like any commercial or professional concern paying every shareholder his dues as per its last balance-sheet of that year and after paying off all other liabilities!

1104. This continuous process of British administration, this neatness and precision in its work, its capacity to organize and govern, to run a vast and complicated administration, shine all the more gloriously when contrasted with the confused way of doing things, prevalent in our country at that time, our lack of order, political instability and our complete disregard for well organized work! Although it is unjustifiable to show the similarity and difference between the British nation and our own, as they at the time were, by such a solitary and comparatively insignificant instance as this, it may still serve as a pointer—and a very effective pointer at that—to show how the once petty East India Company could become in the end, the Honourable Company Sarkar Bahadur, which ran the imperial administration of India.

1105. Although the total defeat of our Hindu nation at the hands of the British had always been rankling in our hearts like a deep-rooted and envenomed arrow, we had never repudiated it or glossed over it, not even detracted from the victory of the British people over us by scolding and railing at them under false pretexts. For, we had the courage and ability, which had never died away to avenge that defeat of our Hindu nation. On the contrary, we sincerely believed that in this bitter war between the Hindu and the British nations, it was on the whole natural that the British, who were at that time superior to us in the art of war and strength, should succeed over us. We knew that the success or defeat on the battlefields never obeyed the dictates of the code of justice or injustice.

1106. For this reason, as soon as the British imperial power was established in India, the innermost heroic spirit in the country took up the gauntlet to vanquish the British nation on the battlefield itself, by resorting to some Nrusinhian act of aggressive heroism.

1107. After the British snatched away the imperial authority from its hands, the defeated Hindu nation lay for some time dazed and pale-faced. Even the volcano lies dead and cold for sometime after every eruption. But unless that particular eruption is its last, the terribly explosive substances in its womb smouldering inwardly become unbearably hot. Similarly, the Hindu Nation was merely defeated by the British—it was not yet dead. As such, in its mighty heart, there soon began to seethe and smoulder the explosive elements of many valiant souls, in order to go full tilt once again against the victorious English!

(OUTBURST)

The first Great Indian Bombardment Sgainst the British Regime

1108. Hardly a dacade elapsed after the British had conquered the last Hindu State of Ranjit Singh in Punjab, when there was great outburst of Hindu-Muslim joint effort to uproot the British imperial power from India. And there flared up the first conflagration of the War of Independence against the British in 1857!

1109. The one remarkable aspect of this revolutionary war was that the Hindus and the Muslims had organized themselves into a joint national front and waged a nationwide war against the British, forgetting their age-long enmity of centuries together!

1110. But I have already written some time in 1908-1909, a detailed history of this revolutionary war in my book of about five hundred pages named, "Indian War of Independence of 1857". In it, I have reviewed that war from the standpoint of the Hindu nation. As such, it is not necessary to repeat the same here again.

1111. During those two or three years of this war of Independence, the English suffered such heavy losses that the English casualties far outnumbered those suffered by them in all wars with the Marathas, the Sikhs and the Nepalese taken together, for the sovereignty of India. The brave revolutionists killed so many British warriors and white men! Let alone the petty English captains, lieutenants, collectors, magistrates and such like second-grade officers, but such eminent personalities like General White, General Neill, Sir Henry Lawrence, General Outram, Commander-in- Chief Anson and others too had to pay the penalty with their lives. The revolutionaries dispatched most of them on the battlefield! The English too killed nearly a hundred thousand fighters from amongst the revolutionaries, as per the statement of Nanasahib Peshwa, the leader of that revolution!

1112. At the end of this revolutionary war, the British terminated "The Honourable East India Company", which was to the revolutionaries a virtual British Government, and which they hated for the same reason. The British thought that the abolition of The East India Company and its rule would pacify the Indian revolutionaries inasmuch as their wishes had been honoured in this respect! So the British Government proclaimed it with all the fanfare and grandiose display that the administration of India had been taken over from the East India Company and that the latter had been dissolved and further, that the British Queen, Victoria, would, thereafter, take for herself the title, The Empress of India, assuming full sovereign power over the country. Thus, the clash of arms on the battlefield, by the Indian revolutionists for about three years had put an end to the hated 'East India Company'.

1113. Over and above this, the British issued throughout India a proclamation in the name of the new Empress of India, Victoria, the Queen of England, in which, for the sake of the revolutionists and with a view to pacifying them a bit, it was said that after the issue of that proclamation, whoever of the 'mutineers' would stop fighting openly or covertly and return to their homes never to harass the English people and would begin living a peaceful life, would be shown, without exception, royal clemency, irrespective of anything they might have done in respect of the 'mutiny'.

1114. After the British had, thus, surrendered, though not explicitly yet doubtless implicitly, to the revolutionists in repsect of the above-mentioned two points, there was included in the said proclamation of the new Empress of India, a further important promise that neither the British Government, nor any local white-skinned officer, nor even any British missionary would be suffered to interfere with the religion of their 'natives', that the Empress of India wished to treat all her subjects, the Hindus, the Muslims, the Christians and others, impartially and that she, as the Empress of India, would protect every religion from the tryrannical persecution at the hands of every other religion. This express promise was included in this famous proclamation in order to eradicate one of the most potent causes of the outbreak of the War of Independence, namely, the Indian apprehension that the company's government was out to destroy the native religions and to convert all the Indians to Christianity with the use of force. And this was, too, a tacit submission of the British to the revolutionists!

1115. Yet another important submission was implicitly made to the revolutionists in this proclamation. It was the discontinuation of the obnoxious practice of denying the Indian rulers the right of adoption and liquidating and annexing their territories to the British possessions in India. For, it was expressly promised in the said proclamation that the traditional right of Indian rulers to adopt heirs to their estates would be honoured. Their adopted heirs were promised the same political and administrative rights as they enjoyed under the old tradition.

1115A. Thus, the British had tried by means of this Queen's

proclamation to remove almost all the causes, which in their opinion, had led to the horrible revolt of the Indian revolutionists. Nevertheless, the most important promise—of course, in the British opinion—and the one that they thought would give complete satisfaction to the Indian people—was that—

1116. All the Indian subjects of Queen Victoria would be treated as respectfully as the British—and that they would be selected for appointment to all the official posts in the British empire, irrespective of caste, creed or religon!!

1116A. BUT THIS PROCLAMATION HAD NO EFFECT WHATSOEVER UPON THE REVOLUTIONISTS!

1117. Why, a parallel proclamation was issued by the revolutionists as a pungent and trenchant rejoinder to the Queen's proclamation! How appropritate and poignant it was, has already been clearly shown in my book, 'The Indian War of Independence of 1857'. The very basic statement made in it was that the revolutionary war that had been fought so far was not fought because they wanted the rule of the British East India Company over India to be replaced by that of the imperial authority of the British Queen. They did not want any foreign power—and certainly not that of the British—to dominate over India! They wanted a completely indpendent self-rule! That is why, they said, they were fighting on the battlefields. Although the Queen's proclamation was exhibited on every wall throughout India, thousands of revolutionists, including General Tatya Tope, Shreemant Nanasahib, Balasahib, 'Jalka Rambhau', Amar Singh, Ferozshah and other eminent leaders of the revolution kept on fighting for months together! Only after the heroic fall of almost all of them in the all-consuming flames of the revolution, fighting and fighting till the very last, could that sacrificial pit smoulder low and cool down subsequently!

However!

1118. However, the last two or three promises given in the Queen's proclamation did not fail to have the desired effect on the new generation of Indian people, which was later on educated in the English schools and colleges that were shortly opened thereafter and on that of the thousands of Indian officers and servants, which thrived on the Government salaries. Especially in Calcutta, Bombay, Madras and other cities, where the illusory British reforms had already spread their cobwebs much earlier than 1857, the then Indian leaders were so much elated by the promise in the Queen's proclamation that the British Empress would allow her British as well as Indian subjects to enjoy all civic rights equally and without any invidious distinction, that they declared openly in the public meetings held to celebrate the total extinction of the 'mutiny', that now on, the British empire belonged as much to the British as to the Indian people! This proclamation of the Queen was just another peaceful device that the British had found out, as they had used the other one of 'violent repression' simply to put down the Indian revolutionaries. They had not the least intention to follow in future the political or administrative policy outlined in it. This, I have amply proved by quoting the words of the British statesmen themselves in my books written on later history. But the credulous and converted minds of the above mentioned class of Indian people who were educated in 'English Schools' and who were earnestly busy serving their British masters, could never grasp this secret and crooked ruse of British diplomacy. On the contrary, being deluded by the preposterous proclamation of the Queen, who mad with victory, had the audacity to ascend to the imperial throne of India, these simple gulls of Indian leaders hastened to glorify that 'proclamation' as the Indian Magna Carta in press and public meetings. How absurd and foolish it is to compare that original "Magna Carta" in English history, with which the English people, after fighting successfully with their King, had forced him to concede to them their fundamental civic rights, with this deceitful and profane 'proclamation of the Queen', which tightened the shackles of slavery on the Indian hands and feet even more forcibly than before, only gilding them outwardly so as to pass them on as ornaments.

1119. But in my Background to my 'Autobiography' I have already dealt, at greater length, and from the point of view of the Indian people, with the period of Indian history, after the temporary pacification of the War of Liberation of 1857 was achieved and the foundation of the British administration in India was firmly secured. Hence, it need not be repeated here!

The Peculiar Character of the period the Political Movements of the Loyalists

1120. The peculiarity of the period following the pacification of the national rising of 1857—i.e., roughly speaking from 1860 to 1900—is that, it is dominated by a nationwide movement under the leadership of those who believed that India would once again see national prosperity and development only by remaining in the British empire and she must achieve it that way alone! Hence, this period can be generally called an age of the loyalist politicians. However, even in this age of avowed loyal politicians, the age-old tradition of heroism, which vehemently advocated armed revolt to free the motherland from British domination, was not altogether extinct! It did flare up secretly or even openly, in some daring risings! Even those momentary explosions of that traditional heroism did not fail to convulse the British administration in India and to excite and inspire the Indian people at least for the time being. Only two illustrations of these armed revolts would suffice. The Hindu rising under the leadership of Ramsingh Kuka in Punjab during 1870-74 A.D. against the British and the Muslims for politicial independence and for defending our religion, is the chief of them. And the second, far more extensive and even more effective than the first, was the one in Maharashtra under the leadership of Vasudev Balwant Phadke. It was a violent armed revolt against the British for the complete independence of India! These incidents, too, are reviewed in detail in the Background to my 'Autobiography'.

1121. Thereafter, dawned the age of Lokmanya Tilak, which was synchronized by the lethal attacks of Chaphekar brothers on the English officers and the feverish activity of secret revolutionary societies for liberty.

The Political Movements in India after 1900

1122. At the end of 1900 or thereabouts, terminated the era of loyalist political movement and began the one of Lokmanya Tilak which might fittingly be called—though not revolutionary—conducive to revolution. To this very period were inextricably tied up in my very childhood, from the time of the martyrs, Chaphekars' sally at the British, my heartstrings and later on my whole life was dedicated to that revolutionary activity. As such my life-history itself became an expensive chapter in the war of liberation against the English. Naturally, whatever might be said about these nation-wide political activities during this period, from the point of view of Hindutwa, has already appeared in the written part of my 'Autobiography' or will perhaps in the one, which might be written hereafter. As such, even when I was in my teens to come in closer contacts with almost all the elder reputed leaders of India in respect of this independence movement.

1123. When I had been to England in my very young days, I had come in contact with the eldest of the Indian politicians of the time and the earliest founder of the loyalist political front, namely Dadabhai Nawroji, in his eighties. Why, there my revolutionary party had to cross swords with his British-loyalist party in our tug-of-war for the leadership of Indian political movement in England. Next to him, I had developed in England itself closer relations with the respected staunch Bengali freedom fighters from amongst those belonging to the generation following that of Dadabhai Nawroji, like the late Shree Surendranath Bannerjee, Romeshchandra Datta and others. With most of the younger leaders of the same period belonging to the staunch nationalist party fighting vehemently against the loyalist front, I had developed personal friendship and ideological kinship. With the active political workers from Pandit Shyamji Krishan Verma, Lala Lajpat Rai, Bipinchandra Pal, Right Honourable Gokhale and such other all-India figures to hundreds of the leaders belonging to different provinces, I had either developed friendly ties or had to fight political battles on many occasions. Lokmanya Tilak, Shivrampant Paranjpe, Shreemant Dadarao Khaparde, Dr. Moonje and the other Maharashtrian leaders of that line were individually so closely acquainted with me that some of them and the staunch nationalist leaders from other provinces, too, bestowed parental affection on me. For example, while Bipin Chandra Pal was in England, I was staying with him for sometime in company with his son, Niranjan Pal. Bipin Babu himself had more than once cooked fish and flesh in the Bengali style and had served them to me with great importunity and had added to his moral credit the meritorious act of polluting a strictly vegetarian Maharashtrian Brahmin like myself. With the future exponent of the 'non-violent truth-assertion' (Satyagrah), 'non-coperation movement' who later on came to be widely known as Mahatmaji—I happened to be closely acquainted in a fiendly way when he had come to England, where he was then known simply as Barrister Gandhi and thereafter throughout our lives, we came together and many times in conflict—in the political arena in India. And my relations with armed revolutionary party in India are too well- known to be recounted here! The All-India leadership of the post-Chaphekar revolutionary activities had by chance devolved on me at least in the beginning—first in Maharashtra and thereafter in England. Need it be told, that I had developed very close acquaintance with thousands of brave martyrs and gallant fighters of that party? Shyamji Krishan Verma, Madame Cama, Barrister Rana and many other elder and eminent personalities were among those who were converted to our revolutionary views through my propaganda and guidance. Thus, I had very close contacts and personal friendship with various great personalities from all over India. To the thousands of members of my revolutionary secret society, the Abhinav Bharat Samastha, right from its original nucleus at Nasik and Bhagur to its innumerable branches in many foreign countries, I had myself administered the oath of all allegiance in person. The martyr Madanlal Dhingra, Lala Hardayal, Bhai Parmanandji, Chattopadhyaya, Senapati Bapat, the great historian, Dr. Jayaswal, Tirumalacharya, "Rishi" Aiyar—how many names can one recount? Thereafter, when I was sent to the Andamans on transportation for life, I had the company of Pulin Bihari Das, the Chief of the Anushilan Samiti, Barindra Ghosh of Yugantar Samiti, Upendranath Bannerjee, Ashutosh Lahiri, Hemchandra Das and other Bengali revolutionary conspirators, as fellow-convicts. Nearly a hundred or more Sikh and non-Sikh revolutionaries of the Gadar Party and other societies, who were originally sentenced to death but whose sentence was later on commuted to deportation, also came along with us, to the Andamans to serve their terms and stayed there with us suffering unbearable innumerable hardships and torture for years together for the sacred cause of the liberation of our motherland. Subsequent to my release from the Andamans, I again came into very intimate contact with the millions of the avowed believers in Hindutwa in the great organizational movement for the solidarity of the Hindus as a staunch opposition to the fanatic Muslim activities, which was a natural concomitant to the armed revolutionary work against the British. For want of space, it is impossible even to mention their names! But a special request has to be made just here, lest the omission of their names might be misunderstood to be due to their work being less important in comparison to that of the others whose names are herein mentioned.

1124. Ever since the sixteenth year of my life—the time when I began to take part in politics—I have been personally and closely connected—at times as a vehement adversary—with all the above-mentioned four phases of Indian political life—the Loyalists, the non-violent but vehemently nationalistic, the revolutionist and finally the

Hinduistic—subsequent to the defeat in the war of Indepenedence of 1857. As such, the compilation and interpretation from the Hindu standpoint of the history of the period has been fully done in my writings and speeches made on every occasion during these fifty or sixty years. Now I don't think it necessary for me to add even a single word to the published work of mine running to about seven to eight thousand printed pages in the form of books or otherwise, leaving aside hundreds of my speeches, interviews, articles and the written work that is now lost beyond recovery and now at this age—the eightieth year of my life—when I am confined to bed, I have not the physical strength left in me to go on repeating it once again!

Conclusion

1125. During this ceaseless and relentless war with the British, which India had carried on so consistently and so resolutely with violent and non-violent means for more than a hundred years, from its first volcanic eruption in 1857 to the year 1946, when the Second World War had come to an end—in order that it might free itself from the tyrannical bonds of British slavery, our Hindu nation ultimately got the golden opportunity of achieving the greatest success as the war-drums began to thunder and rend the European skies!!

1126. If we have received any real and effective help from any nation, it was from Hitler, the dictator of Germany and General Tojo, the militant leader of the Japanese! It is these countries, Germany and Japan, which gave substantial help in up-to-date arms and ammunition for the army, navy and air force to the revolutionary party from the very beginning, that is from the violent agitation in Europe by the Abhinava Bharat Samstha to the declaration of war against the British by Netaji Subhash Chandra Bose in the Second World War. That is why an army of hardly forty to fifty thousand strong, could rise in revolt against the British near Malaya and Singapore and could march against India under Netaji Subhashbabu to free it with the war-cry 'Chalo Delhi'. At the same time, the British came to know that in India too, the Indian army, navy and air force under the British had hatched out a conspiracy to go in for a revolutionary war of independence. Of the Indian citizens, millions were just waiting to raise a standard of revolt against the British. Some had gone underground and begun subversive activities, while others openly raided the British armouries in surprise attack and sacked them thoroughly; others still, started prototype governments and rooted out the British control over those particular regions. Thus harassed on all sides and paralysed by incessant fighting in the two world wars in Europe, the crippled and mutilated British power lost its hold on India. The English people had lost the vigour and strength needed to hold the empire in ice! At last, in 1947, the British Viceroy began talks with the Indian leaders saying that they would recognize Indian independence and leave it and go back.

1127. Of course, the British naturally recognized those political parties alone as the leaders of India that were originally labouring under misconceptions and delusion as regards their political theories, were generally chicken-hearted and pro-British on the whole, frightened of the Muslims and still very eager to have anyhow, by fair means or foul, whatever little political power they could grab, and with them alone, they carried out all their talks on the transfer of power! These parties, too, no doubt, were patriotic in their actions; they, too, had laboured for the cause of freedom constitutionally and non-violently.

1128. But the British had laid down one crafty and far more dangerous condition. The British statesmen insisted that India be vivisected into two because they wanted to reward those Muslims who had consistently and treacherously helped the British throughout the Indian War of Liberation ever since 1857, and who demanded a unified state of the Muslim-majority provinces cut out from the rest of India, as a price for that help. The British statesmen conceded to this anti-Hindu, highly perfidious and anti-national demand of the Muslims with a still deeper and more sinister motive of creating an everlasting enemy for the Hindu nation.

1129. This insistence of the British was basically the Muslim demand for a separate sovereign state over the Muslim-majority provinces, which had been supported quite vehemently by all the Muslims in India. But all the Hindus in India, strongely enough, did not oppose this Muslim demand for a Pakistan so vehemently! With only one exception, all the political parties in India were for granting the Muslims Pakistan, and ending the strife forever. It meant that the whole of Punjab and Bengal should be ceded to Pakistan. Over and above this, the Muslims demanded a corridor to connect their two Muslim states of Punjab and Bengal, a strip of land right from the Punjab to Bengal through the heart of North India!!

1130. The only party which staunchly and consistently opposed these Muslim demands throughout India was avowedly a pro-Hindu party! Under the leadership of the Hindu Mahasabha, these Hindus started an all-India agitation against the vivisection of India, and protested against it as bitterly as possible. The anti-Hindu elements, the Muslims, the British Government, all persecuted them, tortured them, locked them up in prisons, shed the Hindu blood at various places, to crush this great agitational movement of the Hindus. But throughout the whole of India, these avowed pro-Hindu (Hindutwa-nishtas) faced boldly all the atrocities of the enemies, even when they were in a minority. They even did not refrain from avenging the spilling of Hindu blood by shedding the enemy blood and by beheading those who proved treacherous to the Hindu cause!

1131. Fortunately, this retaliation by the loyal Hindus, done at the risk of their lives, did not prove quite futile. For, although the British Government decided much against our wishes to partition India, they had to concede to the least of our demands that instead of giving over the whole of Punjab and Bengal to the Muslims, as per their demand only, the Muslim-majority part of those provinces should be included in Pakistan while the rest of Punjab and Bengal with Hindu majority should be joined to India as Eastern Punjab and West Bengal. The demand of the loyal Hindus (Hindutwa-nishtas) 'Let us vivisect their proposed Pakistan before they vivisect our Hindusthan', thus proved successful. And as for the more dangerous Muslim demand for a corridor—a passage through north India to join Punjab and Bengal—not a word was ever spoken nor considered during these talks of the transfer of power mainly because of the bitterest opposition of these 'loyal' Hindus!

1132. And when during the election for the central and provincial legislatures of India, the majority of the Indian voters elected those very candidates and parties who gave their consent to create Pakistan, they proved themselves to be the greatest sinners, responsible for the horrible national crime of eternally harming the undivided India!

1133. Again the 'loyal Hindu' knew in their heart of hearts that this creation of Pakistan was the necessary consequence of the great sins of cherishing perverted conception of virtues, of banning reconversion of the polluted Hindus and many other such religious and social vices imbibed in us from our old ancestors. These very anti-Hindu and anti-national practices of the Hindu had already created big and small "Pakistans" in every city and every village. It was inevitable that we had to suffer the horrible consequences of these, our social sins and crimes. A detailed discussion on this point is available in the foregoing pages (of Chapter 8, Paras 421 to 472.)

1134. While all these momentous movements were going on in India, the British Cabinet itself, after taking into account the general trend, tabled a bill in the British Parliament, named "Independence of India Act," which was unanimously passed. Accordingly on the 15th of August, 1947, the British Governor-General in Delhi declared, at last, with the consent of the elected representatives of India, that the British nation was on that day liberating India from their imperial domination and making it politically free, that of the Muslim majority districts of West Punjab and East Bengal separate independent Muslim State, called Pakistan, would be created. While the rest of India would be founded as an independent Indian State!

1135. Thus was India liberated from the domination of the British Empire and this great Indian republic was established! The practical politicians amongst the 'loyal Hindus' satisfied themselves, whatever was obtained was not meagre! Though not the whole of Bharat, at least three-fourths of it was liberated in an undivided state! Quite a great boon indeed! After about a thousand years, a great new age of national importance has dawned in the history of the Hindus. As such, the real strategy for the Hindus from the point of view of their own benefit and the greater glory of Hindutwa is first to make the newly won Bharat wholly their own. The fragments that were left in the foreign hands could be attended to later on!

1136. Immediately, the British Union Jack which had been fluttering proudly over the Red Fort in Delhi—over the heart of India as it were—for the last hundred or a hundred and fifty years with overbearing imperial haughtiness, was pulled down and in its place was hoisted amidst tumultuous applause and the deafening cries of "Hail, Indian Independence, all Hail to thee!" the tri-coloured flag of the independent, sovereign Government of India, with the Sudarshan wheel imprinted on it!

1137. From the Western Seas came the British imperial power marching on us with the supercilious vanity that with the sword alone, they would conquer empires and with the sword alone, would they run them, and straightway it climbed the Indian imperial throne of Delhi.

But, at last, from the very same throne of Delhi was it dragged down, its vaunting sword being cut to pieces! To the shores of the very same Western Seas, it was driven back and was ultimately submerged into the very same Western Seas! The last defeated British soldier, we saw with our own eyes going back to the same Western Seas with his head long down and back towards us.

1138. Thus of all the foreign aggressions over India that took place during the last two thousand years, the greatest and mightiest one—the sixth in order—that of the British was in the end, utterly defeated by India and its political domination crushed to pieces!

This victory over the English which deserves the Commemoration by a Horse-Sacrifice is *The Sixth of the Glorious Hindu Victories* over foreign aggressors!

□

Oh Martyrs

The Battle of Freedom once begun
and Handed down from sire to son
Though often lost is ever won!!

Today is the tenth of May! It was on this day that in the ever memorable year of 1857, the first campaign of the War of Independence was opened by you, Oh Martyrs, on the battlefield of India. The Motherland, awakened to the sense of her degrading slavery, unsheathed her sword, burst forth from the shackles and struck the first blow for her liberty and for her honour. It was on this day that the war-cry 'Maro Feringhi Ko' was raised by the throats of thousands. It was on this day that the sepoys of Meerut, having risen in a terrible uprising, marched down to Delhi, saw the waters of the Jumna, glittering in the sunshine, caught one of those historical moments which closed past epoch to introduce a new one, and 'had found, in a moment, a leader, a flag and a cause, and converted the mutiny into a national and a religious war.

All honour be to you, oh Martyrs. For it was for the preservation of the honour of the race that you performed the fiery ordeal of a revolution when the religions of the land were threatened with a forcible and sinister conversion, when the, hypocritc threw off his friendly garb and stood up into the naked heinousness of a perfidious foe breaking treaties, smashing crowns, forging chains and mocking all the while our merciful mother for the very honesty with which she believed the pretensions of the white liar, then you, oh Martyrs of 1857, awoke the mother, inspired the mother, and for the honour of the mother, rushed to the battlefield terrible and tremendous with the war-cry 'Maro Feringhi Ko' on your lips, and with the sacred mantra of God and Hindusthan on your banner! Well did you do in, rising. For otherwise, although your blood might have been spared, yet the stigma of servility would have been the deeper, one more link would have been added to the cursed chain of demoralising patience, and the world would have again contemptuously pointed to our nation saying, 'She deserves slavery, she is happy in slavery.' For even in 1857, she did not raise even a finger to protect her interest and her honour!'

This day, therefore, we dedicate, oh Martyrs, to your inspiring memory! It was on this day that you raised a new flag to be upheld, you uttered a mission to be fulfilled, you saw a vision to be realized, you proclaimed a nation to be born!

We take up your cry, we revere your flag, we are determined to continue that fiery mission of 'away with the foreigner', which you uttered, amidst the prophetic thunderings of the Revolutionary war. Revolutionary, yes, it was a Revolutionary war. For, the War of 1857 shall not cease till the revolution arrives, striking slavery into dust, elevating liberty to the throne. Whenever a people arises for its freedom, whenever that seed of liberty gets germinated in the blood of its fathers, whenever that seed of liberty gets germinated in the blood of its Martyrs, and whenever there remains at least one true son to avenge that blood of his fathers, there never can be an end to such a war as this. No, a revolutionary war knowns no truce, save liberty or death. We, inspired by your memory, determine to continue the struggle you began in 1857, we refuse to acknowledge the armistice as a truce; we look upon the battles you fought as the battles of the first campaign—the defeat of which cannot be the defeat of the War. What? Shall the world say that India has accepted the defeat as the final one? That the blood of 1857 was shed in vain? That the sons of India betray their fathers' vows? No, by Hindusthan, no! The historical continuity of the Indian nation is not cut off. The war began on the 10th of May, 1857, is not over on the 10th of May, 1958, nor shall it ever cease till a 10th of May to come sees the destiny accomplished, sees the beautiful India crowned, either with the lustre of victory or with the halo of martyrdom.

But, O glorious Martyrs, in this pious struggle of your sons, help. O help us by your inspiring presence! Torn in innumerable petty selves, we cannot realise the grand unity of the Mother. Whisper, then, unto us by what magic you caught the secret of Union. How the Feringhi rule was shattered to pieces and the Swadeshi thrones were set up by the common consent of Hindus and Mahomedans. How in the higher love of the mother, united the difference of castes and creeds, how the venerated and venerable Bahadur Shah prohibited the killing of cows throughout India, how Shreemant Nanasahib after the first salute of the thundering cannon to the emperor of Delhi, reserved for himself the second one! How you staggered the whole world, by uniting under the banner of mother and forced your enemies to say 'Among the many lessons the Indian Mutiny conveys to the historian and administrator, none is of greater importance than the warning that it is possible to have a revolution in which Brahmins and Shudras, Mahomedans and Hindus were united against us and that it is not safe to suppose that the peace and stability of our dominion in any great measure depends on the continent being inhabited by different races with different religious systems, for they mutually understand each other and respect and take part in each other's modes and ways and doings. The mutiny reminds us that our dominions rest on a thin crust ever likely to be rent by titanic fires of social changes and revolutions. Whisper unto us the nobility of such an alliance of religion and patriotism, the true religion whichever is on the side of patriotism, the true patriotism which secures the freedom of religion.

And give us the marvellous energy, daring and secrecy with which you organised the mighty volcano; show us the volcanic magma that underlie the green thin crust on which the foe is to be kept lulled into a false security; tell us how the chapati, that fiery Cross of India flew from village-to-village and from valley-to-valley, setting the whole intellect of the nation on fire by the very vagueness of its message and then let us hear the roaring thunder with which the volcano at last burst forth with an all shattering force, rushing, smashing, burning and consuming into one continuous fiery flow of red-hot lava-flood! Within a month, regiment-after-regiment, prince-after-prince, city-after-city, sepoys, police, zemindars, Pundits, Moulvis, the multiple-headed Revolution sounded its tocsin and temples and mosques resounded with the cry 'Maro Feringhi Ko'! Away with the foreigners! Meerut rose, Delhi rose, rose Benares, Agra, Patna, Lucknow, Allahabad, Jadagalpoor, Jhansi, Banda, Indore—from Peshwar to Calcutta and from the Narmada to the Himalayas, the volcano burst forth into a sudden, simultaneous, and all consuming conflagration!!

And then, oh Martyrs, tell us the little as well as the great defects that you found out in our people in that great experiment of yours. But above all, point out that most ruinous, nay, the only material drawback in the body of the nation, which rendered all your efforts futile—the mean selfish blindness which refuses to see its way to join the nation's cause. Say that the only cause of the defeat of Hindusthan was Hindusthan herself, that shaking away the slumber of centuries, the mother rose to hit the foe, but while her right hand was striking the Feringhi dead, her left hand struck, alas, not the enemy, but her own forehead! So she staggered and fell back into the inevitable swoon of 50 years.

Fifty years are past, but, oh restless spirits of 1857, we promise you with our hearts' blood that your Diamond Jubilee shall not pass without seeing your wishes fulfilled!! We have heard your voice and we gather courage from it. With limited means you sustained a war, not against tyranny alone, but against tyranny and treachery together. The Duab and Ayodhya making a united stand, waged a war, not only against the whole of the British power but against the rest of India too; and yet you fought for three years and yet you had well-nigh snatched away the crown of Hindusthan and smashed the hollow existence of the alien rule. What an encouragement this! What the Duab and Ayodhya could do in a month, the simultaneous, sudden and determined rising of the whole of Hindusthan can do in a day. This hope illumines our hearts and assures us of success. And so we allow that your Diamond Jubilee year 1917 shall not pass without seeing the resurging India making a triumphant entry into the world.

For, the bones of Bahadur Shah are crying vengeance from their grave! For, the blood of dauntless Laxmi is boiling with indignation! For, the shahid Peer Ali of Patna, when he was going to the gallows for having refused to divulge the secrets of the conspiracy whispered defiance to the Feringhi said in prophetic words: 'You may hang me today, you may hang such as me everyday, but thousands will still rise in my place—your object will never be gained.'

Indians, these words must be fulfilled! Your blood, oh Martyrs, shall be avenged.

VANDE MATARAM

□

Letters From Andamans

D/15-12-12

Dearest brother

Thus it is *after 18 months I have a chance to touch pen and ink again.* At this rate one can quickly unlearn the art of writing altogether! You must have been very anxious about this delay but as you had received a letter from our dearest Baba in July, I thought it would be more assuring to you to hear from us a few months later than at about the same time. How glad I was to learn that you have joined the medical course and are doing well. How do you like that course? To me it is a noble course. I should like you to take not only Medicine but the Science of Physiology itself as your special province. Please do follow it up not only as a profession but as a pursuit. It opens out inexhaustible field for charity and benevolence. It is respected all over the world, in the Hotenttots as well as in the Aryans. The study of body—a temple wherein the soul lives—is next to the study of the soul itself.

Your choice of books last year was simply capital. Moropant, Bharat, Vivekanand—all standard books. Out of the books asked for by me only ज्ञेयमीमांसा and अज्ञेयमीमांसा did not come why? I have sent a list for this year, but *do not spend* more than 10 rupees on my books. If the list comes to more than that please go on omitting from the bottom. You need not buy all books new. You can send some second hand ones if you like.

And how do you like Bengal? By this time after the Puja holidays you are back to Calcutta and must have grown quite into a Bengali Babu—is not it? Forgotten Marathi language? Please take care you do not lose something else. For, I am afraid I might hear at any time that some one in those clever Bengalis has stolen your heart away! Though I for one should like so much to have found a dear little Bengali sister-in-law. I am as strongly in favour of these inter-provincial marriages among the Hindus as I am deadly opposed to the practice of marrying the European girls *at this stage* of our national life.

And now my dear Bal, something about me here. My health is all right. Ever since I came to this jail, I never had a serious illness and have managed to keep my weight just what it was when I came here. I am both physically and mentally doing well—believe me, dearest, in some respects so well that I had hardly ever done so before; for life in a jail, for good, for evil, is a unique chance. Man can never go out of it exactly as he came in. He goes out far better or far worse. Either more Angelic or more Fiendish. Fortunately, for me, my mind has so quickly adapted itself to the changes in circumstances. It seems so strange that a nature so restless and active, roaming over continents, should so quickly feel quite at home in a cell hardly a dozen feet in length. And yet one of the kindest gifts of the Providence to Humanity is this plasticity, this adaptability of human mind to the ever changing environments of life.

When early in the morning and late in the evening, I try a bit of Pranayam and then pass insensibly into a sweet sound-sleep. Oh how calm and quiet is that rest; so calm that when I get up in the morning, it is long before I can realize again that I am in a prison cell lying on a wooden plank. All the common aims and allurements of mankind having receded far, the conscience is perfectly pleased with itself with the conviction of having served under *His* banner and served to some purpose. A calm, a sweet equanimity is left with my soul and it lulls my mind in an intense peace. *There are exceptions* but this is the general rule. In fact, if I be suddenly dropped in the midst of Bombay or London I think I will have to shout with the hermit in 'शाकुन्तल:—'जनाकीर्णं मन्ये हुतवहपरीतं गृहमिव ॥'

And even if hearing the market gossip, your mind sometimes sighs: 'Oh still his life would have been more useful and dazzling outside', even then remember that those who work outside, work much; but those who work in the prison, work more; and after all, my dearest Bal, don't you think that suffering is in itself work intense because it is subtle!

I get up in the morning when the bell goes on at 5 A.M. At

its sound, I feel as if I have entered a higher college for a higher study. Then we are doing our work of rigour till 10 A.M. while my hands and feet are automatically doing the given task, my spirit avoiding all detection is out for a morning trip, and across seas and oceans, over hills and dales, it roams sipping only pleasant things, and things noble, like a bee amongst the flowers. Then I compose some new lines. Then we dine at 12 noon, work again. From 4 P.M. comes rest; reading & c. This is the usual round of life here.

In your answer, please inform me how our dear Motherland is getting on? Is the Congress united? Does it pass the resolution for the release of the political prisoners from year to year as it did at Allahabad in 1910? Any remarkable Swadeshi enterprise like the iron works of Tata or Steam Navigation Company or new mills? How is the *Republic of China?* Does it not sound like *Utopia realized?* A Romance of History! Don't suppose that China's work is a day's. No! from 1850, they have been strenuously at it, though the world knows not where the Sun is making its way—till it is risen: and Persia, Portugal and Egypt? And are the Indians in south Africa successful in getting their demands? Please do mention if any important law has been passed by the new Councils, e. g. the Education Bill of the Hon. Mr. Gokhale. When the great Tilak is due to be released?

Did you show my letter to my beloved Yamuna? Please translate all to her. It is only a few years more not more than 5—when a better day will dawn. So my beloved wife, hold on as nobly as you have done. My most respectful pranams to my dearest Vahini—she who had been and is still through her blessings—a mother, a sister and a friend at the same time. I cannot name, for obvious reasons, others with whose memory my heart is now overwhelmingly full. Tell them all that I remember each and all of them. How can I forget them? No, a man in a prison cannot forget. The mind, shut up from the new impressions can only feed on the old ones, and so in a prison, so far from forgetting old acquaintances, one vividly remembers and begins to love even those who were before forgotton. My sweet friends, in a prison one weeps and weeps and vainly waits for some one to come to wipe the tears—to speak a word of affection and love. Oh in a prison how can I forget? To all those please give my affection and love who you know were my sweet friends and comrades and dearer than life to me, and to those who even when some were not ashamed to disown the ties of blood, *are still* standing by *you* and remember me, *my deepest obligations* are due. They know that a letter from a jail must be more or less stereotyped, and hence no names. Please give my ashirwadas to dear Mai, my only sister and Vasant, my only hope. Also remember me to dear Mami and little Champi.

with all love

I remain, your own brother

TATYA

□

Cellular Jail
15-2-1914
Port Blair

My beloved Bal,

And now come along. A year has rolled by and the happy day has come back again! Only those who had been in a jail can fully appreciate what a soul-entrancing blessing it is to hear from home, to write to home!! Sweet-sweet something like the sweetness of conversation in the moonlight, by the sea-beach, with one whom one loves and adores! But wait, the bell is gone and I must go to take my food—it is 10 A. M. ...yes, now I have come back again, after having taken my food in the general file of the denizens of the jail. Yes I said it was sweet; in fact the day of a letter to home is to me always the real पाडवा, my new year's day; I count my year from that day; for I get a stock of energy and enthusiasm from the communion with my chosen few, which enables me to breathe and live and laugh a year further on. I was sorry not to write earlier and to compel you to undergo the troubles of sending a telegram. The authorities had kindly informed me of it. But you see, brother, though a year was past and I was entitled to send a letter, yet the antediluvian spirit of our postal system here does not carry a letter to Calcutta from this place unless some five or six weeks after it is written, so I am told. That is why a letter cannot be sent unless some fourteen months go by. But then any letter that you send reaches here almost as soon as in this twentieth century it ought to. From your letter, I am so glad to learn that you are in sound health and passed the examination with credit. Examination or no examination, you must not neglect your health. No. I long to see you robust, bubbling with health and freshness and vigour. The dawn of youth, that is just breaking upon you, is the very fountain of life and energy. So do not waste it by overwork of any one member in excess of the rest. But grow in harmony, brain and body. You are a Doctor yourself and it is a bit of presumption on a layman's part to insist on good health. But then youth is blind and forgets to lay by, a fund of energy and life, while the vital forces are still welling up from within, and the organism is growing so that when the winter age comes, they may have abundant fund of vitality to draw on. Otherwise, if your eyesight is weakened, if you look like the willow of a man—I will shout out: 'Physician, heal thyself! (Don't laugh in the sleeves—for I am not a physician and so I can afford to have a bad eyesight! For, all lawyers have it—at least ought to have!) And how proud am I to know that some of my pet lambs have come out first class B.A. and M.A. That is noble! But then nobler when the field of duty that faces them now, is also well fought and well won, and they are hailed therein too, as deserving of its gold medals, for before the gold medals of that great corporation of man, the gold medals of these so-called 'universities' are as of tinsel! I should be so glad to hear from them personally—for some of them are never absent from my memory even down to this day. About those who inform you voluntarily to do so, write to me by naming and particularizing.

The books that you sent are simply capital. The महात्मा परिचय—what a fine translation.—and the introduction of two lines how modest and appropriate—'फोडिलें भांडार धन्याचा हा माल। मी तव हमाल भार वाही'!!! I liked it awefully. And the 'जाईचा मंडप!' No sooner did I go through a dozen of pages, then each time, each word began to pulsate harmoniously with my heart, and I knew who could have written it! The language is worthy of the sentiments, the sentiments so poetic and sublime, worthy of the theme, and the theme worthy of both. I wish that such popular series as the भारत गौरव माला realize their responsibility of guiding and not only tickling the popular fancy and so publish every now and then political history, science and economy, e.g. Mill's Representative Government etc. About the books on Vedant philosophy, well, I fear it is not opportune that such men should be busy with such things. The Americans need Vedanta philosophy, and so does England; for they have developed their life to that fulness, richness and manliness—to Kshatriyahood and so stand on the threshold of that Brahminhood, wherein alone the capacity to read and realize such philosophy can coexist. But India has not. We are at present all शूद्र and cannot claim access to the Veda and Vedanta.

That is the underlying idea why शूद्र were not allowed to read Vedas, not certainly not, for cruelty, nor for narrow or vested interest—

otherwise "पुराण would not have been written by the very Brahmins expounding the same philosophy more lucidly. We, as a nation, are unfit for these sublime thoughts, for it is well known that Bajirao II was a great Vedantist and that is why, perhaps, he could not see the difference between a kingdom and a pension. Let us study history, political science, science, economy, live worthily in this world, fulfil the "गृहस्थाश्रम—the house-holders's duties—and then the वानप्रस्थाश्रम and its philosophic dawn might come. And whatever these works are meant to do, they might be left to be written by widows, old men and pensioners out of offices. *They* should live in the past old works and old puzzles of God and soul and man. The young, the youth—why not live in the future? Talk of Vedanta—Benares has not produced a single martyr and they cannot give up a farthing for their fatherland!!!

And now, something about myself here. Well, during the last year, I had no illness, whatever. My health is excellent and my weight, as yet, unreduced and that is a feat, is it not? In this tiny cellular sanitarium, I get up early, take regular amount of food regularly, and go to bed early—in fact *have to do* all these things and so early to bed and early to rise is making me healthy—(though not)—'wealthy and wise'! In fact you, Oh! would-be-Doctor Saheb! could not have devised a better time table for your patients. And, good as is the health of my body, the health of my mind is better still. Any work hard or mean, I ply myself to humming every now and then, 'स्वे स्वे कर्मण्यभिरत: स्त्रंसिद्धिं लभते नर' : or 'यत: प्रवृत्तिभूतानां येन सर्वमिदं ततम्। स्वकर्मणा तमभ्यचर्य सिद्धि विंदन्ति मानवा' or 'सर्वारंभा हि दोषेण धूमेनाग्रिरिवावृता:!! And every evening—for nowadays I am in a cell, a bit of the sky is visible from—I watch the glorious sunset and the pomp of light and shade and loose myself in the rose and the lilly, and the lilac of the west; thinking now this and now that; from the poets 'एकतस्तटतमालमालिनीम्। पश्य धातुरसनिम्रगामिच' or 'तेन मानिनि ममात्र गौरवम् to the profoundest fancies of idealist philosophers, that all that seems is but subjective affection and there is nothing objective to correspond to it—at least we do not know of it. And my mind is perfectly happy—happy even as it was in his company there—with her company there!! And if at times, the mind like a child gets silly and simply will weep—then the Grand Reason steps in and smiles 'well sweet heart, what ails thee? What un-known you suffer? How silly! Did you want to ride on the crest of ambition, drive in the chariot of self-glorification yourself? If you did, well, then you deserved to be baffled and defeated in such a selfish and demoralising ambition! But God and I know you did not covet any reward personally—no, neither fame nor name nor land nor lucre, nay, not even happiness. The only thing you wanted was to be privileged to *suffer most*! At least, that is what you used to say in my presence—to sacrifice most, for others, for humanity. Then lo! where is the disappointment? you have done 'यज्ञम् सर्वस्वदक्षिणम्' are suffering without end, without limitation of time! Not a minute, not an action of yours that is not dedicated to the purification of the race through suffering. Then rejoice! What *could you* have done better than this? And the mind plumes its feathers again, and soars, and rises and sings once more! But if ever the mind still goes on still puffing up its little ego, then the Grandam takes it out and showing the world says: 'There are the Himalayas! There was a time that they were not there and a time there will come when they shall not be there!!! And this moon and this solar system and the Sidereal!! It is too much then for that little mind; it forgets itself, is absorbed in the Universe—ashamed of its self-importance and self-care!!!'

So my beloved Bal, both of us here are in perfect health of body and mind. Do not care at all about us. The only thing that we feel still individually attaches us to this world is thy health and safety. So if you guarantee these two—of course, try your best and then we do not care for the result—we shall be happiest. As yet jail has left no mark, no shadow on us for anything, worse—and all this health is *in spite* of circumstances and not in virtue of them. You have written about the petition you sent to the authorities here enquiring about the time of visit. Well, in fact, I ought to have been, according to the practice here, released from this Cellular Jail and allowed to live on the island. My 'behaviour' is admittedly good. But then neither of us is released. I am trying to request the Government to reconsider this and you, too, whenever you know anything be writing to the authorities here. Very soon our dearest Baba will have done his 5 years and you can then claim a visit. But our release and permission to bring our relations here to live with us, the authorities here can do very little, though they can do every thing in the case of other convicts. Nor are they very much to be blamed, for orders we suppose come directly from the Indian Government. So, you better send a petition to the Indian Government whenever you fail to know anything directly from the authorities here. But even as it is, do not worry yourself about any arrangements concerning us. The Government will do in all likelihood all that justice demands themselves. And we shall be reminding them every now and then. What else have we to do? You only care for your health and safety. I am glad you remember what I told you in the High Court.

Assure our beloved Yamuna that these four years will not pass without ushering the dawn of a happier day. So let that noble heart and that heart—our dearest Vahini hold on! Hold on even as they have been doing up to this time!! Let them read all मराठी literature and not only the old mythological works but new and current and living streams of life's expression in the West and the East. It was a sad pride that I felt when I heard the noble death of our noble comrade and brother Sakharam.[1] You know it was in the High School days that we first saw each other! He lived bravely—died bravely. What more can one wish for oneself! His wife—dear Janki Vahini—well I have not seen her and yet have seen her through your pen-pictures. All that I feel for her is that she is *not* poor, *not* ill-starred—but called upon to play the holiest part in life even because it is the lanliest! Remember me to her. And how is tiny Vasant? Will the great little man write me a word? He is now some 7 years old, is he not? And his mother? Oh! I saw her for the last time in the Dongri jail A sister is one of the richest gifts that a man can have!! Give my love to her and a sweet kiss to that great little gentleman—my Vasant! Also remember me to all our relations—one and all—and above all to her who though not a relation and even *because* she is not a relation, whom I used to call jokingly the mother of the party and whom now in all seriousness and gratefulness, 1 call my own mother, and who is standing by you and remembers me—give her my most grateful regards and loving remembrances—names not to utter which seems a sacrilege and yet which cannot be uttered, *for their own sake,* from a prison wherein not only legs but tongues too are fettered! Well you know them all. I told you who were nearest to

1 Sakharam Gorhe—he was one of those accused persons in the Nasik revolutionary conspiracy trial who stated in the High Court to have been subjected to police tortures and morpolurs starvatonary to wring out confessions from them so as to implicate other persons as well. The High Court held that the story was an exaggeration and partly a fabrication! History in the long end may record who was right and spoke the truth. All that can be said now is that Sakharam did not implicate anyone else, was sentenced to 5 years' imprisonment and died while in a jail, a martyr's death.

my heart as my most intimate friends—to all of them give my love, my fresher love! If some of them voluntarily ask you to be particularized in letters to me from you, I will then umburden my heart and name them. The books that are to be sent to me, I write down here. The time is up and so my sweetest Bal, I am, with most reluctant steps receding and tearing myself away from you.

Your own brother

TATYA

□

Celluar Jail
9-3-1915
Port Blair

Best beloved Bal,

And once again, my pen after a Ripvanwincle's sleep is wakened and hastens to acknowledge the receipt of your letter received some 7-8 months ago. To have a letter from you is like to see you: for partly owing to the cinematographic flashes with which your letter abounds and partly owing to the wonderful faculty, with which the solitude of a prison, endows the power of hearing in man-faculty, which enables one to visualize the thing heard, as in the case of those born blind. Whenever I hear from you, I succeed in almost seeing you and all those dear faces and dear scenes that constitute our happy little home on the banks of the musical Godavari. Our dearest brother Baba and myself are happy in seeing you doing well and as long as you take care of your health and try your best to lead a life, at once noble and happy and healthy, you need not be anxious about our health, mental and physical. The books that you sent last year were 16 and this year's 13 (4 English 2 Oct. 2 Nov. The rest Sanskrit and Vernacular. Please do write whether this is correct. Next time you send a parcel, please do send a list with it in your own handwriting, so that we may be able to check the postal delivery. 1 was glad to read समाज-रहस्य (why you sent two copies of it?). It is a very good novel. One thing more—among the social institutions—the greatest curse of India is the system of castes. The mighty current of Hindu life is being threatened to perish in bogs and sands. It is no good saying: 'We will reduce it to four caste-system first. That would not and should not be. It must be swept away, root and branch.' The best means to that effect is a crusade against it, in all forms of literature, especially drama and novel. Every true patriot should cease to have double dealing and speak out his mind clearly and *act* up to it. The only care to be taken being not to pay so much attention and not to create so much fuss in this side-issue and our internal relation as to forget and hamper and thwart the issue—our relation with the world—but for the right adjustment of which, no internal questions can be satisfactorily solved, or solved to any substantial purpose. So, I shall like to have a number of goodly written novels like the समाज-रहस्य, which would attack this effete and unjust social curse. It had done much good in the past, but it is dead now. So let us bury it, with tears if you like. I am glad to hear that the Government is going to allow you to see me this year. Please do thank the authorities for it. But I am firmly of opinion that dear Vahini should not be put to troubles of the voyage this year. You should come alone and when you see all the facilities or otherwise here and know the best way to bring her, then the next time you come to see me, you may bring her, and dear Mai too. I feel it a duty to forego the inestimable pleasure of seeing those dearest ones this year for the sake of their convenience. So, please come alone this year.

It sent a thrill of delight in my heart to hear that the Indian troops were allowed to go to Europe, in their thousands to fight against the best military power in the world and that they had acquainted themselves with such splendour and were covered with military glory. Thank God! Manliness, after all, is not dead yet in the land! And what a funny thing! We have been trying our best to encourage foreign travel and used to congratulate ourselves if a dozen could be sent a year! And now Providence has done what we could not—thousands of Hindus, orthodox like the Gurkhas and Rajputs and reformed like the Shikhs have crossed the sea and under the Government patronage! Now let our Pandits sit hatching over the eggs of शास्त्रार्थ to see if foreign travel is permissible to the Hindus or not. Permissible or not, the Hindus *have* crossed the sea, and in crossing it, they have crossed an epoch! What the crusades have done for Europe by bringing it in contact with the superior civilization of Asia, this conflict with the Europeans of our Hindu troops across the seas will do for India—for Asia.

As for the petition, that is made for the release of Political prisoners in the Punjab we can hardly thank them sufficiently for this, their charitable deed. You may be knowing by this time that some of us have already volunteered, to go to the front of the War and I am glad to inform you that Government have made a special note of it, though no answer could come as yet.

By the by, please do write of the rumour that some M.P. had asked a question in the Parliament about me, or some of us before the war broke out, be true and if so the particulars of it. Did you get the poems on Guru and Ravi?

It pained me very much to hear, that Hon. Gokhale was dead. He was, after all, a great patriot. True, at times, especially in panics, he used to say and do things, which he himself must have been ashamed of a few months after, to own. But then, his life was dedicated to the service of Motherland and there was very little personal and selfish about him. All along his life, he served Her and for the good of Her, as he saw it. How anxious I was to see him, before death parted us; and to compare notes as he had said to me in London, when we saw each other for the last time. We could not agree on certain points and he said 'well Mr. Savarkar, come! We will see each other after some six years and then would compare notes'! Maharashtra must send some one—worthier than he—to his place in Councils. If every Indian could do at least as much as he did!

Next time you send books, please send the novels जन्मभूमि and गौतम, which brother is very eager to read. I was very much afraid that owing to the invasion of France, you would be unable to hear from Madame Cama-who had been ever since my coming here a second mother to you and who had so nobly and so faithfully stood by us in the darkest hour of our life. But I was very glad to be assured that she, even in the midst of this world-hubbub, remembered you and had regularly been sending letters to you. At the touch of one such faithful, noble, unshaken loving hand, one's heart recovers its belief in Humanity—belief rudely shaken by the disappearance of the closest and by the treachery of the truest and by the indifference of the dearest. It is a pity I can not write to the dear lady and tell her how I esteem her noble life and her solicitude for the needy and the distressed and love and long to see her once more: but as it is, please give to her all my esteem and respects, before you give them to any of our relatives: for what wonder they do something for us? Wonder is how she does and does so much.

While I am reading the books you sent, I see that in the Telagu provinces, the new life that is struggling to find expression all over India, has been sweeping over our bretheren there. The Andhra-Sabha आंध्रसभा is a great and grand movement but the question of getting that province separated from the Tamil one is not ennobling. But what pained me most and what was but a natural corollary from the desire of petty provincialisms was that the national shouts were आंध्र माता की जय! In this little thing and straw, we see the direction of an ominus wind to come. This is one of the unhealthy reactions of the grand Swadeshi movement and must be corrected before it is too late. The Swadeshi connected in Bengal with the little partition question brought in this reaction. Every province wants to be separated, and shouts and invokes long life to itself! But how can the province live unless the Nation lives? They all—Maharashtra, Bengal, Madras—are great and will live long but through Her-India! So let us not say आंध्र माताकी but भारतमाता की जय of whom आंध्र is only a limb, and let us sing not 'वंग आभार' but 'हिंद आभार'! All provinces and petty languages, instead of asking to be separated, should try to get amalgamated and remove the barriers that yet remain and destroy the confusion of tongues and not to hug to it. Smaller nationalities! Is not Belgium a sufficeint warning? The greatest good that the British Government has done without meaning it, is to, melt and mould the disintegrating factions of our Motherland and hammer us into one people. Now instead of trying to remove whatever stands in the way of its consummation, we are, on the one hand, hugging to the fetters that were the necessary price of this boon and trying to turn the very boon into a curse, on the other.

Now I think I had written all that I felt and wanted to ask about your letter and the books you sent. Next time you please send me the books the list of which I subjoin. Instead of sending a parcel, you may bring them with you if you come before September 1st. If not, send a parcel. Please do answer this letter as soon as you have carried the necessary communication with our friends. I am extremely glad that you could see the gentleman, you refered to in your letter. I knew you would like each other very soon, for birds of the same feathers gather together. Please give my affection and best remembrances to him. I remember him every now and then. How is our dear Professor getting on? My heart gladdens at the thought that by this time, one more bird must have come back to that dear little nest after sustaining a night through dreary deserts of burning sands, where no drop cools the thirsty heart and no dew vivifies the parched flower of hope. In his release and the release of so many of them, I feel as if my own partial release had come. If poor dear Sakharam too would have been there today! Though foolish and almost dishonourable to feel he should have been living, who has done better to die in such a cause—still the heart feels.

As far as we are concerned, I again assure you not to be anxious about us at all. All the term-prisoners of our case had been sent back to India, and we lifers (life-transportees) only remain. As long as the war is going on, I, on principle, have made up my mind not to ask for anything so as to embarrass the authorities here; and at present both of us are keeping good health and Captain—now Major Murray is superintending the jail affairs. As long as he is here, you may rest assured that nothing that evinces a personal rancour will be done or said; no underhand pinpricks, beyond what the regulations require. Every letter and every book you send will be duly delivered. As far as our daily life is concerned, well, it is going on in the same even way as it did last year. In a prison what happens on the first day happens always-if nothing *worse* happens. In fact, it seems to be the essence of prison discipline to avoid all novelty, all change. Like specimen and curios in a museum—here we are each exactly in the same place and same position, bottled and labelled with the same numbers with more or less dust about us; and the guide book that I wrote to you in my last year's letter may serve the purpose of description as long as 1 am here. We get up early—work hard, eat punctually—at the same time, at the same place and the same amount and kind of food prepared with same match-less prison-skill and medical care. I read much in the time that can be spared from work and sometimes in the evening attack many flowers-now remembered only in names-and flower-like themes with blank verse and then sleep. Here one thing must be said. Although it is true that prisoners are not free to do or say what they will, yet to the credit of the jail authorties, it must be admitted that everyone is absolutely free to dream what he likes. And I assure you I take the fullest advantage of this concession. Almost every night, I tell you, I break jail and out by dale and down and by tower and town, go on romping till I find some one of you—some one who somewhere had been held close to my bosom! Every night I do it but my beneficient jailors take no notice of it. You have only to wake in the jail, that is all they say.

I hope just at the end of the war, you send a public petition for the release of us. The thing is this. Not only in India but even in any free and self-governing country, the Government *cannot* release political prisoners unless the Government are backed up and supported by the wish of the people to that effect. An exercise of the right of amnesty cannot be made by the king or the president unless the people are willing to have the prisoners back. If Indians are willing and petitions to that effect go at the end of the war, we may be released and if Indians are not willing to have us back, neither the Government can release us nor it is worthwhile to have that release. Port Blair is willing to have me, and I am here. I have no wish to thrust myself on any people unwilling to have me back. At any rate you may ask for our being sent out of this jail just as all other prisoners—even those who had been sentenced here additionally—are allowed to go and settle on the island and bring their family here. In short, all the concessions that the prisoners get under the regulations here in force. In this, we ask nothing special and this by repeated petitions from you and us both, we in all probability will succeed in getting.

Last year in the letter of our dearest Vahini, she had not written how the little Dhondi was? Is She married? Please give my best love to our beloved Yamuna—how is her health? Does she read? In what class or college is my dear Balvantrao? And the other children? Give my best love and respects to my dearest elder sister-in-law—whose life is a record of self-sacrifice and noble enduring and calm and silent suffering for no fault of her and for the good of others, and also to my younger Vahini whose kind remembrances of me I got last year through our Mai's letter. I remember them and all other beloved friends every day. At every corner that my mind takes in its aimless rambles, their dear image is sure to be met and then my mind is sure to stop and build a new temple of a sweet and a sad tear and hold them there a while and worship them, who made my life as it is and pray they do not forget me. Whoever allowed, maybe for a minute—the right of *loving and being loved* by me—I worship them all in the same temple and on the same pantheon my *petts* and *boomfriends,* my *comrades* and *chums!!*

Well my dearest brother, I am glad your study of medicine is promising to be fruitful. Do not *injure health* for the sake of study. Let me know your weight. Now my dearest Bal with all my love and with my choicest आशीर्वाद to you and our dear little Vasant and our sister Mai, will you allow me to tear myself from your sweet mental communion.

Your own brother
TATYA,

□
+

Cellular Jail
6-7-1916
Port Blair

My beloved Bal and sweet Shanta,

Please accept my and my brother's heartiest congratulations upon your entering the second stage of life—the life of wedded love. Nobly hast thou, dear Bal! fulfilled the first stage of your life—the stage of self-culture and self-sacrifice. Thou possessest the golden keys to the treasured wealth of knowledge, both ancient and modern, in the acquaintance with Sanskrit and English languages. The final examination that you have passed in Medicine is bound to stand you in good stead, in any part of the world and in spite of any laws passed by a narrow misguided legislature; while your pen has already made its influence felt in Maharastra in both the fields of prose and poetry. On the other hand, the responsibilities and duties of that stage could not have been better discharged and fulfilled. When the storm began to gather over our Mother, it found you unmoved and firm at your post—it burst and left you undaunted and true, and among the many faithless yet faithful! The enthusiasm, to awaken which amongst their youth, Europe has been holding before their eyes the glories of iron crosses and Victoria crosses and unrolling rolls of honour—that enthusiasm and faith had been displayed by you, who discarded even the reward of public acclamation; nobly therefore hast thou completed the first stage of your life and now enter ye-, dear Bal and beloved Shanta!—on the happiest and most exalted stage of life, the life of wedded love. May thy path, dear Bal, be strewn with roses and may thy youth, dear Shanta, blossom forth in Amaranthuses and gold! Domestic happiness—the only bliss of paradise that has survived its fall' may bless your nuptial shed! 'मधुनक्तमुतोषसि मधुमत् पाथिवं रज: (The dawn, the evening sweet and grateful be the Earth)!!

You perhaps remember that in one of my letters, I had just dropped a suggestion to the effect that it would not have surprised me if some one amongst the clever Bengalis had stolen your heart! After all, the expected had very nearly happened. For though I long to see the day, when inter-provincial marriages amongst the Hindus would throw down the artificial and harmful barriers of castes and creeds and the Great River of Life—our Hindu life would, having freed itself of all bogs and sands, flow in an ever fresh and mighty current-uninterrupted and interruptible—still the first and foremost thing to be effected in that direction is to restore to love her sole privilege and right of presiding over the wedding rights. Indeed, we can no longer be blind to the fact that we care more for the good breeding of cattle and fowls than for the Eugenics of man. Centuries of child marriages and marriages by proxies! Centuries of love banished from its legitimate sphere of influence to attract and develop elements that tend to the betterment of body and mind and soul; and the inevitable result is a race puny, debilitated, all vigour and manhood sapped out of it. Thousand things have wrought this and the marriage customs that prevail in us are one of the few important factors contributing to it. Authorities should come in to sanctify but not to silence love altogether. And glad was I, therefore, that the age, the education, the part that mutual attraction and esteem played in welding your hearts together and above all, the sanction of all those who feel drawn towards us should have enabled you to have realized that in which I thought our family should not lag behind. Or in short, when dear Bhau has sanctified it with his blessings, it goes without saying that it must have been just after my heart.

And now Doctor Saheb, where are you going to settle? Only yesterday, I was told to write this second letter as the first had been lost in the post office by accident. Although it must have cost you a lot of anxiety, to me it enabled to know your present address. From that, I see you are in Bombay, at present. Would you settle in that unhealthy and cramped in city! Would not the rising free Baroda suit better where the enlightened prince Sayaji rules? But all that as you choose and not I—for you are on the spot and *know* how to judge best. One thing only I would insist upon and that is you must not in any case risk your health and freedom personal freedom. This is—depend upon me—perfectly not only permissible but positively commendable in *your* case and the case of those who stand as you do. In other cases, too much attention to personal considerations is undoubtedly demoralizing; but you cannot pay too much attention to it. Be anywhere in the world—in the forests of Africa—in the republics of America—the medical knowledge that you possess is sure to serve a passport and a safeguard to you. For, indeed, wherever death is, doctors also can be -(Ugh! Seen very angry? Of course, 1 mention this with all due respect to the Majesty of Medicines—in fact in order to exalt it.) Therefore, do nothing that would do injury to your health and also, nay more so, health of Shanta. She should, of course, be encouraged to read more and to write even if she chooses; but the first and foremost consideration of a young lady should be her health. It is a trust she holds for others, a debt she owes to generations not yet born. Every atom of health that a young lady dissipates is so much that is taken away from the strength of souls that are yet to rise. She is a golden link that joins the yesterday to tomorrow; a promise that holds in it the possibilities of her race. Therefore, the first care of a wife should be her health that would harmonise the beauties of her body and mind and soul. So neither study nor pleasure should entice her away so as to tax her energy too much, but both should be indulged in only so far as to render that health perfect and that beauty transparently pure.

Now something about me; and yet I wonder what that something is! For there am I, as you left me after you finished the last letter you got from me. Change is a word that is not found in prisoner's dictionary—especially in its Port Blair edition. The great war that you say has shaken your hemisphere has left totally untouched me and my Port Blair. This, our little kingdom here, is about the only state that can with a justifiable touch of egoism claim in its yearly speech from the Throne of having maintained its interests intact in this world-earthquake. Our imports and exports are unchanged. We keep our lights all night up. While our international communications are as peaceful as they had been ever since this little kingdom rose out of its Oceanic Night! Mr. Asquith has every reason to be jealous of us. Our citizens have not been forced to subsist only on a reduced scale of meal and potatoes as the Germans are said to die for the simple reason that we never ate any! Whatever we eat, we grow—grass and such other edibles, while these solid and aspiring walls of my jail have reduced the very walls of China to a mere heap of debris. Those walls could, and that too not very effectively, stop the outsiders from rushing in but these walls while doing that can also effectively prevent anyone inside from going out. No! On pain of death, no! Thus we, like a little world organized to serve as a prototype and a foretaste of the hope of the Humanitarians, when the war shall have been banished from the realms of man, live—I beg your pardon—exist—as peacefully and quietly as to put to shame the very realm of death.

As to the interview, I think it is best to wait till this war be over. For, to a certain extent, we can understand the hesitation of the Government in granting it now. And even after the war, the letters that you may write to them for the interview should be only on the ground that every other prisoner is allowed a visit, so should I after five years and not on the ground of any anxiety of our hearts to meet. For, in that case, even if they do not grant it, we shall at least have the manly satisfaction of not having displayed the most sacred and the most human of all wounds—the wounds of separation—to an alien and unsympathetic eye. Again, whatever you wish to write in amelioration here should be written directly to Delhi. For almost nothing lies in the hands of the authorities here as far as change, especially for the better, is concerned in my case and whatever they can do, they are doing and I would request them to do if possible, when it be left undone. I know that some of you, though sure and certain that I shall not break down under this imprisonment, are still grieved to think that I should have been suffering all this and should have been forced to desist from *all work,* social or political or even literary. But brother just think—is suffering no work? Who worked more for Christianity—they who suffered in silence and unknown or they who worked? Surely both; but I suspect that those who work for a good cause outside, work much—but they who suffer for it in prisons and fields work more. *At bottom,* work, if true, is suffering and suffering, if true, is work. Suffering is the motor, the power that moves, and goads and propels a people. Unless the best amongst them suffer, the rest cannot work. Both are grand, both are indispensable, and if both be indispensable, then what grief if we be chosen and ordered to guard this post rather than that? I bless myself that—*this* fell to my lot! Do not grieve, brother, that I sit in darkness and simply waiting, while everyone else is lighting his or her lamp to shed light on the path of man.

Do you not remember that 'Her State', is queenly thousands at her bidding post—they also serve who only stand and wait!

And how much more then do they who not only wait but suffer and yet *stand!!* The worker is great for he puts stone upon stone and chisels and moulds; but then the *cement* of the Church?—is the sufferer! The martyr that bleeds!!

And indeed, Bal! You can hardly believe how happy I feel from moment to moment—strange breezes of bliss pass and repass, kissing all the inevitable physical worry and weakness into ever fresh and ever blossoming joy of the soul at rest. I feel just as I used to feel in the college days after some final examination had been satisfactorily gone through and went to stay home quietly but confident by expecting the welcome news of passing. This Great Trial, This Test, to achieve the deliverance of the Mother!—and so satisfactorily gone through as far as I was concerned! and now I have come Home here and am confidently expecting the Great News that must come! Oh! how I sleep soundly—how sweet the thing; for I worked so strenuously in the day and while I was required at Her headquarters that as soon as this night came, sleep fell as gently on my eyelids as dew. There are moments when ugly dreams trouble desire to shine and see light—but at the first touch of analysis, the self stands revealed and the dreams melt away, are swept away—and calm once more sets in. Oh, when some times after such a sleep, I wake in my cell and hear the waves idly breaking on the beach just outside my little, high-placed and barred window, I remember the lines of Kalidas प्रासादवातायनदृश्यवीचिः। प्रबोधयत्यर्णव एवं सुप्तम्! and fancying myself like that king, I laugh and play and joke—all with myself! Such thoughts are suggested by that consciousness of a rest, that is at the same time the intensity of work—and they in their turn guiling away the mind from the too real hideousness of a prison, strengthen that consciousness of that rest. And thus, it is a fact that *on the whole,* I am and so is our brother happy, satisfied and willing to live as long as that must be in the atmosphere of frowns and frettings and harshness, of constant clash and constant discipline, every step in which reminds you that you belong to a race of slaves.

The account of your marriage ceremony was very graphically written. As to the writer—he is indeed a very gifted man but with him, self-diffidence is a great drawback. I think he should first try to write small popular stories and short novels and get them *published* in some of the magazines, for that would give him confidence in himself. Take, for example, the question of caste system. Let him by suggestive stories paint the harm it is *now* doing, *how* it is retarding us from the great goal, to which all mankind is moving. Then let him write bigger works and so on. To him and to the Sahodar Yamaraj and to all of them, give my most affectionate remembrances—my companions of childhood and chums of the college days and comrades in the field, all they whomever I called mine and to whom I pledged my word, I remember them all with fresh affection and esteem. I was glad to know the whereabouts of my dear Rishi! Is he still in the 'Service'; holds the same office? And my new friend! I remember him so much; for he had been so considerate and kind under—even under *these* circumstances, even when he himself had been undergoing the same trial! And then he is so intelligent and active. I have missed the name of our Professor in the account of your marriage ceremony? All my best wishes for him, and my dear and very esteemed Madame Cama! She must have suffered a lot of worry owing to the war! Give her my best and freshest love and tell her that those whom I saw in Paris while I was with her then, are ever foremost in my memory—especially the Sannyasin! The photos that you sent have been a constant source of happiness to us. My dear Yesu, Vahini looks so calm and ever bearing and ever true 'like a Devata,' as one of the officers had said to me when she came to see me in the Bombay jail! My deepest love to her and my Tai and my Shanta. I am proud of them all! Next time do not forget to forward the translation of my beloved Yamuna's letter—Noble girl! poor girl! a thousand pities! and yet a thousand glories for her silent and yet intense fixity of purpose. Do not press her to come to Bombay if her parents object. Their judgment and love must be respected. How are all her brothers? My most humble प्रणाम to my mother and aunt मावशी.

With all love

I am yours—TATYA

□

Cellular Jail
5-8-1917
Port Blair

My beloved Bal,

I was extremely glad to get your answer to my last letter, which I sent to you in July 1916. How grateful we felt to hear in your latest that you with all our friends are getting on well, and are healthy and happy. Thus, it has pleased Providence to spare for you another year of bliss and especially of that tender and pure bliss, which is only to be found in the bosom of a devoted and dear family life. You see, my Bal, the times and the climes, in which the lot of our generation has fallen, make it so imperative for all noble and honest hearts to choose the path that leads through sorrows and sighs and separations which is the path of duty, that the heart so hardened and accustomed to the hard and merciless blows of fate comes to look upon disasters and disappointments as the very order of nature at any rate of our part in the nature's scheme, and when a delighting event takes place, its attention is more fixed on how temporary such a good luck must be than how good that luck is. To me, a joy is ever a solution of tears. Well, any how the days are changed and with changing fortune, friends too are returning. When I left you in the dock in Bombay High Court, and had a last look of you not being allowed even to shake hands, waved my hat and parted, my child, at that time the sting of the whole scene was in the thought that we—Dear Baba and I—could not do anything for you, our nearest and dearest charge. So young, so humble and having already suffered more than a man in his whole life does, you, my brother, were cast adrift, befriended by none, hated by many, suspected by a powerful Empire! The family hearth seemed extinguished for ever, the family gods broken to pieces. And although even all that could not deter us from the right nor make me ally myself with the wrong, yet it was with a bleeding heart that I wrote 'जो वंशबाग उध्वस्त झाला। संततपुष्प तोचि एक' (the garden that has shed all its flowers for the garland of the Gods, is in blossom for ever.) Even the evergreens of hope stood withered and blasted. Only dear

Vasanta, that was the bud, a melancholy memory of the past. But now a few kindly touches of the spring have revived the sap and the creepers are putting forth new buds. We had dear Vasant, and we have our Ranjan and God willing, we may be blessed with one more messenger of new life. The lamp of love is burning cheerfully under thy roof, and its warm and kind reflections have lightened the utter darkness of my cell here. And the new name of little Ranjan brings do mind the all suffering, the all loving, mother, his grandmother, my dear Mavashi. What a joy it must have been to her! Please to give my love to that dear little child, whom perhaps I may never see! And tell me whether it understands it or not! And why did you not write to me about Shanta herself? You left it to Vahini to do it for you. It is typically Indian but in your next, you must write to me directly about your child and everything else. It is this extreme modesty that makes the generality of Indian babes grow rather in the shade than in the full light of their parents' eyes. No, No! you must look upon it as a special and a sacred charge. It was a pity that our dear Vahini should have been suffering from plague. I thought that this dire epidemic had at last, by this time, left our shores but it seems that it rages there still. Please be very careful of it. Is it a little less rigorous than it used to be? Has not medical science as yet been able to find some reliable cure for it? You should better leave Bombay as soon as it appears there. Nothing can be too costly to avoid its dire claws, if indeed we cannot blunt them.

The last parcel that I got was in January 1916 and our dear Baba in March 1916, so neither of us has received any parcel for the last eighteen months or so when we ought to have received two. Now this was the reason what made us very anxious about your safety and I had to ask the permisison of the Superintendent, who so kindly gave it, to wire to you. But I think we should take as much care as it is possible to avoid any such necessity. The best way would be that letters and parcels should be posted by you in fixed months, if not dates, ...

This much, so far as we are considered. But then there is the other party in the game-the post or the Government, and we cannot help suiting things to their pleasure. In your last letter, you have written of a parcel lost in the post and last year, my letter also was lost. Now what is the meaning of this? Thousands of parcels and letters come all right to this place; only our letters and parcels should be so mysteriously spirited away! Is it the post? If so, please do leave no stone unturned till they give some definite explanation for the loss of this parcel. You must have registered it; then it would be clear whether and through whose indulgence or malice, my letters and parcels are tampered with. This much for the post office. But if not the post—It is the Government! Well; if so, then, mum!!! Mum is the word!! As I have learnt to do without so many things which make life worth having, so also I shall and can learn to do without a yearly parcel too! But one should have thought that when a dozen censors have followed a book from the printer's office to the clearance house and when powerful microscopes have searched the very anatomy of the pages, the books, at least, those that are found unobjectionable, should have been returned to their owner!

The Nasik conference was really a success. The resolution about the release of the political prisoners has delighted even us, the forlorn and forgotten, and our deep gratitude to those who dare to remember us still. One wonders why the Congress should fight shy of any such thing even after its union. Perhaps the leaders of that body are too much weighed down by the sense of self-importance. Perhaps they think themselves too immaculate—far more responsible a band of statesmen and patriots than General Botha whose Government has released *the leaders, the rank and file of the Boer rebellion or Redmond, whose nationalists have never ceased to try for the release of the Irish prisoners* till they succeeded in having it. Nor can it be said that 'that was a general participation in a rebellion', as Mr. Bonarlaw has attempted to state; for firstly in the Indian political prisoners also, the overwhelming majority are convicts of general participation and secondly, the suffragists though admittedly and case for case had been convicted of 'individual' charges, were released by Mr. Asquith long ago. But leave the Congress alone! At any rate as soon as the war ends please do see if a public Petition for our release could be sent. *Such petitions and resolutions do not in themselves bring such a release, but they at any rate make it more acceptable* if it ever comes. For, I for one would indeed *feel it a shame* to go back to a people which dares not, or for all I know wills not to remember those who *loved and love and will never cease to love the land of their birth and rightly or wrongly but fell fighting for Her!* See, see if the petition could be sent. That would be far more significant than any resolutions or meetings.

While together for a minute or so, I said one day to our dear Baba, that there is said to be a पितृऋण Pitrarina and देवऋण Devarina and ऋषिऋण Rishirina & C. So, also there is Putrarina पुत्रऋण (debt due to a son). After the receipt of your letter, I felt myself fully acquitted of it! For, after all, you are now fully educated and fully fledged. Now come what may, at least two years of joy have been bestowed on you by the kind Providence and through you on us. *No day can shine forever.* The life on this earth is like a *three petalled flower;* one is coloured with pleasure, the second with the colour of pain, the third mixed or colourless. Now the petal of pleasure and then that of pain gets wormed and thus this vain round of recurrence goes on. Take any letter or any life or even History itself, it is more or less a book of mere statistics of so many births and so many deaths, so many weddings and so many mournings, so much colour and so much shade. So, while there is a brief respite, a passing ray of joy, a single touch of the spring, let us not forget the hardship of the winter or foolishly depend upon and get addiction to these wines of spring, while they are dancing in the cup. No, No, our, ...of those who are born in India in this age ...our constant companion is winter and not spring! Let us not forget that our life is a vast Sahara, unbearable and still to be borne, sandy, burning. And while we are keeping to the path of duty that passes through this parched desert, if the grace of God places in our path such an 'oasis' as this, with which we have been recently blent, then let us not forget that it is an accident, an art of grace; and without haste and rest, must continue our way on this holy pilgrimage of life. Let us pray in all humility as the old saints prayed: 'Give unto us what thou wilt and when thou wilt and how much thou wilt! And also *take away* from us what thou wilt and how much thou wilt.' After all, the fine ideal for a young man is not to acquire but to sacrifice, not to rear but *'the garden that sheds all its flowers for the garland of the Gods and* **thus** *is in blossom for ever.'*

How is my dear Mai getting on? What a silly idea that I could forget my only sister! I may as well get angry and cease to speak with myself. While the day lasts, try to save something and invest in some safe form in the name of dear Shanta or dear Ranjan for we can never tell when winter may come again!! Nothing could match the ideal constancy of affection of our dear MadameCama. Even the war has not made her forget you! Thus, it is that many a time the blood is *not* thicker than choice and there are affections, which noble hearts alone can know, of which neither the lack of blood nor of interest can cool and which growing up in an ideal land flourish and are nursed on forces so subtle that the every day and matter of fact world fails to see or comprehend.

How are also my beloved Mai (Yamuna) and Vahinis, getting on? My love to them all. How is dear Balu? When I saw him in the Bombay jail he seemed so upright and so loving a boy! Now he must be quite a respectable gentleman? And so also Anna. I expected him to be a clever and able youth and shall be very glad to know how far my guess has been correct. I wish I could know everything about all my brothers, including dear Dattu and Nana and what they do. But it is not and cannot be owing to my forgetting them as my dear Yamuna seems to think, but for other reasons, which she can well understand by her past experiences that refrained me from mentioning in my previous letters. If there be any man or any famity next to dear Baba, to whom I owe that is best in me, and owing to whose noble patronage and winning solicitude I had unusual chances and facilities of assimilating the noblest things of this world and even of doing something for our common Motherland, then that man and that family is theirs: (Chiploonkers). But the sense of having been the cause of so much worry and loss and pain to them with whom the dearest ties of blood and love and mutual respect have bound me, has already been so keen a source of sadness and mental unhappiness to me that I do not dare to add an inch more to it all. And so have denied myself the gratification of expressing my thankfulness or love. Otherwise, who cannot be proud of those fine youths such as my own brothers-in-law are—at any rate promised to be? And of him who brought me up as dearly as them? and of that saintly dutiful mother!! The same thing is true of all my friends! I remember them all! But for their own sake and *not for my own sake,* dare not acknowledge them all. I could not understand who the pleader was, who came to you as my contemporary but if really so, please do thank him on my behalf for remembering me still. By the by, be very careful of men who may come to you as acquainted with me or even claiming to have seen me here or having had talk with me here. You are too experienced to be cautioned but nevertheless, I assure you, I send no word or message through anyone to you. Hear all but believe none, except what stands to your reason without my recommendation and on its own merit. Now the time is over and I must finish. I am all right, the details you asked would be sent in dear Baba's letters. Love to all from both of us. *Do not worry for our health.* As far as possible, take care of your own health. If in spite of all human efforts, the worst comes to the worst, well then we are quite ready to face it all! Do not worry.

Yours affectionately

TATYA.

□

4-8-1918
Port Blair

My dear brother,

I was very glad to read your letter. This year owing to the regularity with which your parcels and letters had been despatched, we could get them all at the expected time and were, thus, able to get rid of a lot of anxiety and trouble and petitioning. The answer to my letter, then the parcel to brother and then his letter—all these enabled us to get your news almost every three months. Please do follow up this plan as regularly as possible. The news that the Maharashtra provincial conference had passed a strong resolution and that with greater unanimity in favour of the release of *all* political prisoners was very welcome! In fact, the Bombay provincial conference has been doing its duty with greater vigour, consistency and persistence than any other P.C. in India. Last year, so far as I could know, the provincial conference of U.P. and especially the Andhra Conference had also passed resolutions in favour of this release. The resolution of the Andhra Conference was very definitely and comprehensively worded and showed that the heart of the Andhras beat in thorough and honest sympathy with those who, with the means *they* thought best to effect the Great Deliverance had, maybe rightly, maybe wrongly but in utter sincerity and indisputable selflessness, offered themselves to pine away in prisons. You write that many of the papers write constantly for the release and magazines too press on do the point that the release of all political prisoners is one of the conditions, under which the removal of Indian discontent is possible. If all this be true, then I really fail to understand why the Congress, so far as I know, should still be fighting shy, should still be trembling to utter a syllable that might smell of sympathy, nay even of ordinary humanity for the political prisoners, of the people in whose name it poses to speak! Last year, they passed a resolution for the release of the interned, forgetting totally and very conveniently that the sufferings which brought tears to the eyes of the patriots sitting comfortably in the well-aired and well-decorated pandal had been indefinitly multiplied and incessantly faced by other men—not one not two, but thousands of other men whose services or sacrifices cannot, at least, be less than our interned brothers and who, because their misery cannot automatically end with the war as in the case of the interned and therefore demand a greater and more persistent agitation on the part of those who are pasing as responsible leaders of the people! 'Responsible' that is the thing! They talk of the 'interned' only, because they know that it is *safer* to do so and they dare not talk *of the* rest because they might be losing their responsible positions in the eyes of their boss! Otherwise, when the different provincial conferences have so clearly and so often made it obvious that the majority of the provinces heartily wish to effect the release of the political prisoners, one fails to understand why the Congres should fail to do so. The business of the Congress is not to voice the sentiments of the few that dominate its proceedings but of the many, who give it its weight and support and in whose name ought to derive its right to be a 'Congress' at all. When so many provinical conferences have passed this resolution and so often, when the leading papers and magazines have incessantly pressed this point, when many of the leaders of the Congress itself, when it was their turn to be rotting behind the prison walls had expected and had thought they had a right to expect the sympathetic mention of them by the people for whom they fought, above all or rather least of all when the very Austrian people, not to mention the Irish, the Boers &c. had been bold and honest and grateful enough to agitate for the release of all their political prisoners and succeeded in getting it done, when all these things are known and admitted, then I think that the Congress could be and should be immediately forced to pass as bold and as comprehensive a resolution as that of the Andhra or Maharashtra Conferences this year. If some old hags tremble, let them absent themselves from the sittings that adopt this resolution. Why should you all share in this guilty silence because a handful of 'Responsible' are shaky about it?

Secondly, one or two precautions should be taken in case of any such resolution or movements, if to be effective. Many papers write about 'political prisoners' but the language is so conveniently dubious that the Government and even the people are quite likely to fail to understand what is meant by that omnibus term, 'political prisoners.' Some times it means interned, at others the detenue, then deported or the state prisoners, but hardly it ever means those also who are convicted for offences of political nature. I pointed out to you last year that Mr. Bonarlaw himself made a distinction in Irish cases that the rebels were not guilty of 'individual acts'! Now that gentleman knew well that suffragists were all 'convicted' for 'individual acts' including arson! Yet they were released as soon as the war broke out by the very Government Mr. Bonarlaw works in. Then I don't see why the word 'convicted' should be a bogey to the Indian 'Responsibles' and the 'individual acts' a screen to hide the Government anomalies in the hands of Mr. Bonarlaw. Botha is a prime minister and Redmond the constituted Leader of a Parliamentary Party and yet they released their own opponents and actual rebels, against their Governments. But the Congressmen think *they* are 'responsible men'! The pariah that stands begging at the city gate is more responsible citizen and belongs to a higher caste than the Sheriff and the Chairman of the city itself! So, in the future resolultion and articles, this point should be clearly and definitely pressed that *'political prisoners means all those undergoing imprisonment whether convicted or not, whether for individual acts or acts in general'* (I indeed fail to understand it altogether!!!)—*for actions which proceeded from purely and admittedly political motives.'* The term political can be distinguished from private only by the criterion of the motive of the act and not by the act itself. No act is or can be by itself political. For, even a rebellion if that proceeds entirely for my own bread and butter is not political and ought not to create any sympathy in others, unless indeed my cause was only a case in hand and was fought out for establishing a general privilege or in vindicating of a general right. The thugs fought battles and were not political in the sense of sacrificing for the general good. But even the arson cases or flogging the prime ministers by a suffragist in England had been recognised by the British Government itself as political because the *motive* was neither personal aggrandisement nor revenge but the advancement of some social good. The means may be wrong, even criminal or not, the motive counts so far as the moral value, and here national aspect of the act is concerned. I write this with special stress for the reason that in case of an amnesty being granted—which I expect not—this point will be a stumbling block in our path, for the Government might adopt some anomalous distinction and interprete the term in any sense convenient to them but not just in itself. Try your best to make this clear to all you can approach and let our journalists and leaders keep this constantly before them.

(a) Please do write to me in your letter whenever any of the provincial conferences have passed any resolution to this effect, whether last year's Congress had deliberated on it in the subjects committee; how many papers write wholeheartedly about it, and if something could be done in this year's Congress. When you write about it only mention those cases in which the general amnesty is asked and not only that of a few interned etc.

(b) Then again what had come of the movement of sending a general and mob petition—of which you did not speak in your last. That idea should not be dropped at all. I believe you have only postponed it in order to put it foreward more effectively at the end of the war. If it is so, all right. In the meanwhile, I saw in one of the letters here that a petition for the release of P.P.s had been forwarded to Montague, while he was in India. How far is this correct? (c) The campaign of the meetings of which, once you spoke, should be kept in view and not only once but almost every year, it should be carried on. (d) The Congress, the P. conferences, the petitioning of the individual members, families, special series of meetings arranged for this purpose, the constant attention of the press, questions in the Viceregal and Provincial Councils and in the Parliament: all this and each of this must be *systematically* and *persistently* carried year in and year out till, the amnesty question becomes a necessity of the politics there. In each of your letter, please give me a summary of what could be done in each of these directions, and forget not to make clear the meaning of the 'political prisoners' whenever resolutions and articles talk about it to the people and the Government as well.

Throughout the discussion, I must frankly admit, I have aimed not so much at the result of the agitation as to the moral effect of it. I know and have clearly written to the Government in one of my petitions last year that the question of a general amnesty of the political prisoners is closely and inevitably bound up with the question of the establishment of a progressive and *really* constitutional Government in India. So, the chances of such an amnesty being actually granted are not and cannot be immediately and primarily expected. But though, thus, we should fully realize the impossibility of any actual results being attained, yet we should not lose sight of the moral ones, which would reward our efforts immediately by an elevation of the national tone and character and which, by reminding the nation of the sufferings of their martyrs and soldiers and victims that fought for the success of the common cause, and more enthuse the people to see the fight continued and fought out to its ultimate victory. Gratefully remembering the soldiers, who fell, is the most effective way of recruiting more soldiers to continue the fight.

In the petition, to which I referred to above, I had put before Mr. Montague and the Viceroy, a frank statement of the case of such an amnesty as this. The main points being that while they were considering the question of the reforms in India, they should not fail to recognise that if they aimed at the establishment of any responsible Government in India, they should thereby render it utterly futile to continue to lock us in jail. For, if a real responsible Government be given and still the amnesty not granted, then the latter fact would act as a millstone round the neck of such a system as that. For, our presence behind the stone walls and cells cannot fail to keep the memory of the old suspicion and embitterment between the people and the Government living and would take away much from whatever claims and confessions the Government might make, as to change of angles & efforts for co-operation and mutual trust. For, even if Home Rule be granted to the people unaccompanied by a general amnesty of the P. Ps, how is it likely to touch the real roots of discontent in the land? How can there be peace and contentment and trust in a land where a brother is torn away from a brother, where thousands upon thousands are rotting in cage cells and stand exiled and in jails, and where every other family has a brother or a son, or a father, or a friend, or a lover snatched away from its bosom and kept pining away his life in the parched and thirsty Saharas of Separation!! While on the other hand, it would be as futile; *I stated this for the sake of entire honesty and truth, though it was against my personal interest*—to release the political prisoners unaccompanied with a sincere and substantial effort to a responsible Government in India. For, it would be intolerable for us to live in a land where all paths to progress are barred by a 'trespassers would be prosecuted' or to move there without treading on suspicious paths, where every step forward is an affront to the Sultans ahead and every step backward an affront to one's self-respect and conscience, which is no less Sultanic in its exaction. Therefore, Home Rule and Amnesty go hand-in-hand and in order that the one may be effective, it should and must be accompanied by the latter. I also stated in it that my motive and aim in sending the petition being the Grant of a General Amnesty,

I should be the last to be dissatisfied if that could be done by omitting my own name, if that alone be a thorn in the way of its fulfilment. If such view be ever taken by the Government and I see that the recently published Draft of Mr. Montague's Scheme has in a striking paragraph expressed the hope almost in it—a way of answer to a corresponding question—that the revolutionists would now find something to be constitutionally done to the realizing of their hopes and aspirations and would change their minds and return to useful paths of activity; and a really Responsible Government meaning thereby *at least a substantial majority* in the Viceregal Council—without of course the fetish of a Council of State kept presiding over it and mixing a curse with every blessing the first may confer on the land—if I say a substantial majority of the elected be granted in the Viceregal Council, and such a grant be accompanied with a graceful and general amnesty of the P.P.s, including the Exiles in other lands such as America and Europe—then I for one and many whom I know, would *consciously* accept such a constitution as that and would, if thought fit by our people and given a chance to do so by the Government, work under it and try to fulfil the Mission of our life through the council chambers, which have up to this time been bearing nothing but ill will towards us and have spared nothing to embitter our hearts against them and their policy. Where is the man who would run the ordeals of fire or would tread the paths of furies with bleeding feet-for sheer amusement! That is rare, and rarer it is to find true patriot and humanitarian, who would indulge in reckless and bloody and necessarily outrageous revolutions—if but and even when a safer, nobler, more certainly moral because entirely effective and employing least resistance, if but such a path, the path of constitutional progress be open and accessible to him? It is a to talk of constitutional agitation where there is no constitution at all; but it is worse than a mockery—a crime to talk of revolutions as if it was a work of Rose-water even when there is as elastic and progressive a constitution as say there is in England or in America.

This word for word, I wrote in October last to the Government and the recent changes give me a hope that if properly and organisedly pressed, the bill when it comes before the Parliament would grant us acceptable scheme. And I would like to bring this to the notice of the Viceroy once more and ask whether the Indian Government have come to any definite decision as to my petition.[2] I received an answer on 1-2-18 from the Viceregal Government that the 'petition for the Amnesty of political prisoners' is being considered by the Government. After that I have reason to think that the Government mentioned to submit the question of such a release immediately after the war. Please do enquire directly yourselves, as it takes a lot of cajoling—the Red Tape System for me—to enquire often.

You asked in your last letter about the advantages we reap in being promoted to the second class; Well, going out of the jail? No! Being allowed to keep writing material? No! Being allowed to live with or even to speak with my brother? No! Being exempted from the compulsory and hard labour? No! Being promoted to be a warder or cease to be locked up in the cell? No! Better and hospitable treatment? No! More letters? No! Any visits from home?—others get it after five years and I am in the 8th—No! Then if you still ask what advantages in being promoted to 2nd class—well the great one-that of being promoted to the second class!! Do you understand, Doctor?

So far as to the advantages in the jail: but all this was bearable to me when my health was comparatively sound. But this year, I must tell you that great and counting disadvantage has been added to my lot, for my health is utterly broken. You know I could not have used such language but I feel it my bounden duty to do so. Confident am I that a student of Geeta and my own brother would not be shaken under any calamities that the blind dame may bring to us in her usual rounds and would stand squarely firm facing all winds as they last. Brother! each year, one day which was joy unalloyed—that was the day of writing the letter Home. This year even that is a partial joy, for though I am writing to you to the immense delight of memory—all the pleasant scenes and dear faces and grateful remembrances being made alive—yet am feeling the strain of penning even such a letter as this! The

---

2 This petition expressing the political views of the revolutionaries in general and Mr. V. D. Sawarkar in particular was written to the Government chiefly with the intention of pressing no sooner than the passage of the Reforms through the Parliament. For, Mr. Savarkar had several reasons to believe that the Government was then anxious to know what effect the bill would have on the revolutionist attitude. He was several times approached by the authorities there and invited to express his views. He was convinced that the Reforms were chiefly addressed to the revolutionists.

flesh complains and I could not go on without a rest! Last year March, I weighed 119—this year, I weigh 98! They take the weight with which we come here as the normal one; that is a wrong test for we come here after rotting for years in the jails and custodies there. But even when I came here, I was 111 lbs. Chronic dysentery due to disregard of the medical treatment in the beginning has reduced me to a skeleton. Eight years I bore the burden well. Innumerable and unknown hardships taxed my mettal and an atmosphere of frowns and threats and sighs of demoralising and disheartening stench tried to stifle the noble breath of Life—but God gave me strength to stand and stand firm, and face it all for these eight years or so. But now I feel the flesh has received wounds that are hard to heal and is day by day pining away. Recently, the Medical Superintendent has been paying a little special attention to my weakness and though I am still on 'duty', i.e. work and not in the hospital, yet I get hospital diet that is better cooked, and eat only rice and am allowed milk and bread at present. It is better a bit and hope it may improve. But what is likely is that this constant debility may end in some fatal malady or that inevitable friend so well known in jails, specially in Andamans—the Pthysis. Only one thing and one thing alone could assure me of my recovering and that is a change—not in the sense of jail technicalities where a change means always for the worse—but a change for the better to a *better climate* in some Indian jail. The monotony is getting appalling! And yet be not over-anxious, trying it is but it cannot be decisive. For jails as such have great sustaining power. They corrode but they do not kill. They petrify but they preserve. And cases are not wanting of prisoners living with slender chances of life for 80 years and more. So however weak the body be, still there is no fear, at any rate unless some further complications arise of any fatal event.

And all this again so far as the flesh is concerned. For although one cannot afford to be flamboyantly defying fire while one is bound to a pile of leaping flames—yet I may mention that the spirit is still willing and able to dominate the quivering flesh, willing to suffer even further and even all not only ungrudgingly, but even unflinchingly. Brother's health is relatively better, though, the headache has reduced him to 106 lbs.

Please do give my reverence and love to my dear Madame Cama. Hope she takes care of her health. How aweful for her to pass her days in exile when one should have thought of passing them attuned to the music of sweet smiling children? Then what of Mai? Our sister! Never mind whatever troubles she has to face—let her remember first that her brothers are facing greater troubles for Duty and secondly, come what may, her Vasant is with her and the sight of his face should make her forget and forgive all the miseries of her life. Nevertheless, the love of a brother goes out to her and his sympathy and hope that may be a little cheering news for her. My love to my dear Yamunabai, and my dear sisters-in-law. Glad to hear Shanta improves. And about the friend—the Dear and kind hearted Doctor, whom you mentioned in your letter, please ask him to forgive me. If ever I see him, he could know how I prize him and friend-few indeed—but so constant as he—sorry, I could do nothing for him or for my brothers-in-law Balu, Anna, and others or for my chosen chums of College days or for my dear and faithful comrades—except to—send forth my hearty grateful memory of them all. How is my little Ranjan? Does he know me? I hear that plague is likely to break out once more. So, be watchful and take care of your health which is life to us!!

Yours affectionately
TATYA

□

Cellular Jail
21-9-1919
Port Blair

My dear brother,

I expected to hear from you as soon as you reached Bombay and so I waited longer than usual. But as I have not heard from you uptil now I have decided not to wait further in writing to you. Ever since my last letter to you, my health has been just as it was when you saw me. After your going back, for a week or so, it continued to be well and then again, either a malarious fever or an attack of dysentry upsets it and takes a toll of lb. or so, causing my weight to fall yet more and again it continues well for a week or a fortnight further. Thus, have I been going on and on and consequently my weight, which last year, when I wrote to you, was on the average at 99 lbs., has for the last couple of months been at *96 lbs. and 95 lbs.* In fact, my health would have been worse but for the little better food and little better cell that have been allowed to me though too late, and although my weight is rapidly going down yet, on the whole, my appetite is improved and my stomach causes less complaints owing to the hospital diet that I have been getting for the last 10 months or so. Moreover, in consideration of my weakness and chronic malarious inroads, I have been treated as a hospital patient and have been exempted from rigorous work. So far as this jail life is concerned, I gladly state that the Superintendent has been trying to put things as straight as he can after I wrote to you about the rapid breaking down of my health. But it is, therefore, all the more necessary and is all the more forcibly demonstrated how necessary it is to remove me from this unhealthy and malarious climate, where in spite of much attention of the jail superintendent, my health and my weight are ever on the decline, and not a fortnight passes without a fever or some attack of stomach complaints. I can assure you that the climate of this place is acknowledged as a very unhealthy one and the life in a cellular jail in such a climate as doubly dangerous to the health of even a strongly built man used to hard labour throughout his life by the medical authorities themselves.

I do not know whether you in India know anything about the order that was read out here on the day of the peace celebration in England, concerning the Amnesty of prisoners. On that day or owing to the remission granted on that day—some convicts have up to this time been released from this convict colony. But so far as the political prisoners are concerned, nothing beyond the vaguest promises was done, not a single day's remission has been as yet positively granted to any of them barring a couple of Bengali P.P.s. An order was read out in the name of the Secretary of State and the Government that so far as the political prisoners were concerned, the Government was considering the question of granting some remission to them. The above consideration being guided by the opinion of the respective provincial Governments in the first instance and secondly, by the local recommendations of the jail authorities based on the jail conduct of the prisoners. Moreover, the *personal opinions* of the individual prisoner would be carefully weighed before any decision is arrived at! Now this language may mean much or what is more likely may mean nothing. No time is mentioned as to when the decision would be arrived at. And, when, in addition to that, one remembers that four years ago, the Indian Government had been pleased to assure me that they were even then having the question of Amnesty 'under consideration', one hardly can help suspecting that this reiteration of the same words may be asking for another four years hence. Again the clause referring to the personal opinions is very likely to be the curse of almost anyone who falls under the head of P.P.s., for if personal opinions means the opinions of the individual about the political situation in India—then, of course, that is quite sensible and natural—but how the Government is going to know about them? If by the statements of the individual concerned then, there could be no objection to that at all. But if—as is more likely to happen by hearsay or secret reports, then it would be better if the Government and the public would be frankly telling that they do neither wish nor want to consider this question at all. For being forced to live amongst such a distinguished company such as thieves, robbers and habitual convicts and in such a company alone—what chance is there that these would be reporting only truth about our opinions on politics, when these neither understand a bit of what opinions on politics mean, nor are ever wanting in the gift of instinctively hating anyone who is spotted out to them by the authorities as one whose opinions they are required to report. No sooner does an officer ask these 'gentlemen' in the jail to know and inform about A or B, than do these people come to the conclusion that a report against that individual would be more likely to increase their importance in the eyes of the authorities. And even the highest officers in an institution like jail cannot but depend on the reports of these men, who have themselves been convicts and criminals and raised to higher posts in the jail through sheer double dealing and in general, this is the case. So, I think unless the public makes all these matters clear to the Indian Government *in time* and even now, even with the best of intentions on the part of the Secretary of State, little or nothing will come out of the promise that the Government has made.

Do you know anything about this promise? Is it made public? If so, are the provincial Governments already approached and have they submitted their opinion? Has anyone attempted to get the time fixed or at any rate approximately but definitely indicated by the Government? I again submit that unless the public makes it quite clear and that not spasmodically but systematically that there is an unanimous, hearty and determined desire in the hearts of our countrymen to effect an Amnesty of the political prisoners before this opportunity of the peace celebration passes by, the Indian Government can neither be in a mood and even if in a mood, yet not *in a position* to do much in this direction. The promise, vague as it is, is made to feel the public pulse, and if the people do not *before hand* express their will and sympathy with this projected Amnesty, I for one could not find much cause to blame the Government for not having granted it.

If the charge of 109, 302 is true against me, it is truer against all. And, if for that, I am not going to be released as a political prisoner, then there is no political prisoner in India at all! I simply indicate the line of argument knowing pretty well that you would fill it in much better way than I can do it here. Secondly 'jail conduct.' Well for the last five years, there had been no occasion of being cased even once. I am sure, the authorities here, would not have anything particular against me, on that score, to say.

Thirdly, so far as my *personal opinions* are concerned, well I had been definitely and clearly stating them to all concerned—the Government itself not excepted. *So early as 1915 and again in 1918,*

I had sent, and sent voluntarily a clear statement of my thoughts knowing full well that misunderstood, they were quite likely to deprive me of any chance of release. The statement sent to the Government is exactly like what I wrote to you in my letter last year and which had already been before the public eye. So, neither the public nor the Government can be in any way unacquainted with my opinions. I believe that as soon as the reforms are effected, and if they be soon effected and at least the Viceregal Councils are made to represent the voice of the people, then there would be no hesitation on my part—infinitestibly humble though it be—to make the beginning of such a constitutional development a success, to stand by Law and Order, which is the very foundation and basis of Society in general and Hindu polity in particular. Do not the Scots or ever the Majorities of the Boers choose to maintain a partnership in the Empire when that Empire opens better facilities for their respective developments than otherwise? India too and for the matter of that, any other people ought to and naturally will join in forming a Commonwealth and an Empire. Why should they be against it? When such a common life promises to be more fruitful than divided petty and lonely individuality? As man is Social animal, so is also a state. And Empires had been and would be as natural a development of the inherent tendencies of the social nature of man as nations and families had been.

Well my dear Bal, I have been getting fever for the last two days, as I have caught a cold and so find it necessary to leave much that I meant to write to you. Please *take care of your health,* and do not worry on our account or any other account. Take things easy. Please not to forget what I told you about our family affairs when you met me, try to save a little and spend less. Dear Yamuna promised me to send a very very big parcel of almonds and candy and sweets and what not at an early date. But being very very big, it is quite natural that it is taking months to pack it up. It was indeed a pleasure to see her and know how she is as courageous and as sweet as ever. But poor Vahini! Half the joy of any release fades into apthy at the thought of my going back to a home, where she is not likely to come to welcome me! My earliest friend, my sister, my mother and my comrade—in one, all at once, she really died as dies a suttee! Did she not immolate her silent soul and even at the altar of our Motherland? Ah! as truly as martyr dies for his Land or Religion, do these Indian girls of today die panting, withering, watching for the return of their lovers who are not destined to meet them, suffering in silence, serving though unknown, paying though unacknowledged—do these Hindu girls pine away and die for their Motherland, for their religion. Woman in general is sweet beyond measure! But a Hindu girl—good, good good. She inflames not but soothes, remembers though forgotten each and an ever newly-published edition of the Immortal Story of Sita! Dear Baba asks me to tell you to console Mathutai especially on his behalf; he feels more for her than our dear Vahini herself. Nothing pleased me so much as to find you quite healthy and bubbling over with life when I saw you here. Always try to be as healthy and more. I am totally unable both owing to the intensity of my feeling and the circumstances, under which I have to pen this letter to express faithfully my and our thanks and sense of gratefulness to all those, who, through a personal or public concern had felt such deep sympathy for me and for us and tried to bring some relief or other to us. To tell you the truth, I honestly believe that this consciousness alone had been the only medicine that has enabled me to pull on without being worse and in fact made me live throughout this year in spite of dysentery, malaria and jail—this consciousness that there are so many men in my Bharatvarsha who are ready to share my sadness and lighten my burden—friends that enquire and papers that wrote—those who are moved through personal friendship or acquaintance and much more than that those who felt out of a genuine and simple humanity. How is my dear Shanta? Don't you trouble her much for any reading or writing. But do trouble as much as you can my friend Yamuna on that score—she has promised me to act as a typewriter and a clerk—of course, without any pay and out of sheer patriotic fevour! When, and if, I ever come back and my love to dear Babu, Anna and all my brothers-in-law.

Yours affectionately
TATYA
□

Cellular Jail
6-7-1920
Port Blair

My Dearest Bal,

Your letter to dear Baba, dated 2-6-20, reached us and made us glad by removing the sense of anxiety caused by your constant postponing your coming over here. My health is just as it was when you left me. It is not worse either. But after your going, the health of our brother has been going from bad to worse. It is his turn now. The complaint is the same. Digestion troubles and consequent liver disorder. His weight is 106 Ibs. Because I write this much, do not imagine that our health must be worse still. Not so. I write exactly as it stands. If something worse happens, I shall inform you of it.

After all, the general amnesty has come! Hundreds are being released. Thanks chiefly to the great exertions of the Bombay National Union and of our leaders and of our patriotic country-men, who organised, supported and signed the mass petition for the release of Indian political prisoners. That huge petition signed by no less than 75,000 people at such a short notice as that must have certainly put an immense though unacknowledged pressure on the Government. At any rate, it elevated the moral status of the PoPs and, therefore, of the cause for which they fought and fell. Now, indeed, our release if at all it comes is worth having, as the people have expressed their desire to have us back. We cannot sufficiently thank our countrymen for sympathy and solicitude for us all. They had really shown greater regard for us than we honestly believe to have deserved. Nor have their efforts been entirely fruitless. For, although we two have been declared to fall outside the scope of the Amnesty and are still rotting in the cells, yet the sight of hundreds of our political comrades and co-sufferers' release makes us feel relieved and repaid for all the agitation that we have been carrying on for the last eight years or so, through strikes, letters, petitions, the press and the platfrom, here and elsewhere.

On 2-4-20, I put in a fresh petition to the Government of India on the subject of Royal clemency recently granted. Therein, after thanking the Government for the release of hundreds of political prisoners and for thus partially granting my petition of 1918, I have pleaded for the further extention of the Royal clemency to those who are yet in jail as well as *to the political exiles abroad.* I had once more defined my personal position as regards the political situation in India, especially with reference to those questions, which from time-to-time are still being discussed and debated upon in the official circles and have been personally pressed before me by some of them only very recently.

We believe in an universal state embracing all mankind and wherein all men and women would be citizens working for and enjoying equally the fruits of this earth and this sun, this land and this light, which constitute the real Motherland and the Fatherland of man. All other divisions and distinctions are artificial, though indispensable. Believing thus that the ideal of all political science and art is or ought to be Human state in which all nations merge their political selves for their own fulfilment even as the cells in an organism, organisms in families and tribes, and tribes in nation-states have done; and believing, therefore, that humanity is higher patriotism and, therefore, any Empire or Commonwealth that succeeds in welding numbers of conflicting races and nations in one harmonious, if not homogenious whole, in such wory as to render each of them better fitted to realize, enrich and enjoy life in all its noble aspects is a distinct step to the realization of that ideal I can conscientiously co-operate with any attempt to found a *commonwealth*, which would be neither British nor Indian but which may, till a better name be devised, be styled as an Aryan Commonwealth. With this end in view, I ever worked in the past. With this end in view, I am willing to work now. And therefore, I rejoiced to hear that the Government has changed its angle of vision and meant to make it possible for India to advance constitutionally on the path to freedom and strength and fulness of life. I am sure that many a revolutionist would, like me, cry halt under such circumstances and try to meet England under an honourable truce, even in a halfway house as the reformed Council Halls promised to be, and work there, before a further march on to progress be sounded.

For, it was this very principle that humanity was a higher patriotism that made us so restless when we saw that a part or it should aggrandise and swell like a virulent cancer in such wise as to threaten the life of the human whole; and forced us for the want of any other effective remedy, to take to the surgeon's knife and feel that severity for the moment would certainly be mercy in the long run. But even while combating force with force, we heartily abhorred and do yet abhor all violence. *For violence is force aggressively used—force that is life killing.* I never cherished, not even in my dreams, any aggressive ambition for personal or national aggrandisement, and so far was I from being a party to violence, that actually kept opposing it tooth and nail whenever I saw it used by powerful combinations against their weaker but righteous rivals. I heartily abhorred violence resorted to in days gone by—by ambitious men and nations not only outside India but even in India herself. I felt as rebellious against the caste systems and the untouchability inside India as her being dominated by foreigners from outside.

Thus, we were revolutionists under necessity and not by choice. We felt that the best interests of India as well as of England demanded that her ideals be progressively and peacefully realized by mutual help and co-operation. And if that be possible even now, I shall take the first opportunity to resort to peaceful means and rush in the first constitutional breach effected by revolution or otherwise, however narrow it be, and try to widen it so as to enable the forces of evolution to flow in an uninterrupted procession.

If the reforms wholeheartedly effected and worked out by the Government would serve the purpose of such a constitutional breach as that then revolution ceases and evolution becomes a watchword and a rallying cry of us all. And I, as one humble soldier in Her rank, would honestly try my best to make the reform successful, that is, work them out so as to render them a stepping stone to the realization of the great mission of our generation of making India free and great and glorious, leading or marching hand-in-hand with others to the appointed destiny of man.

Such were my views when I was working in the revolutionary camp. And such are my views after 12 long years of being pent up within the four walls of a solitary cell. True it is that we found it impossible to bear love and loyalty to laws that were dictated by the sword, and constitutions that serve as masks to conceal the hideousness of tyranny, yet it is equally true that we honestly felt and still feel ourselves in duty bound to stand by the side of Law—that is the expression of the righteous resolve of a free people and Constitution that holds together, harmonizes and fuses the efforts of free men and women towards the good of man and the glory of God.

As to the question so often put to me and others by officers no less exalted than the members of the Indian Cabinet: 'What if you had rebelled against the ancient kings of India? They used to trample rebels under the feet of Elephants.' I answer that not only in India but even in England and all other parts of the world, such would have at times been the fate of rebels. But then why did the British people fill the whole world with a howl that the Germans had ill-treated their captives and did not allow them fresh bread and butter? What if the Germans had reminded them—Fresh bread and butter! There was a time when captives were flayed alive and offered as victims to Moloch and Thor and such other Gods of war!' The thing is this that this advanced stage in civilization attained by man is the resultant of the efforts of all men and therefore their common inheritance and benefits all. *Speaking relatively* to Barbarian times, it is true that I had a fair trial and a just sentence and the Government is at liberty to derive whatever satisfaction they can from the compliment that they give a fairer trial and a juster sentence to their captives than the cannibals used to do. But it should not be forgotten that if in olden days, the rulers flayed their rebels alive then the rebels too when they got the upper hand flayed alive the rulers as well. And if the British people treated me or other rebels more justly, i.e. less barbarously then they may rest assured that they too would be as leniently treated by the Indian rebels if ever the tables are turned?

Please do not hope much from this petition so far as our release is concerned. We never pitched our hopes too high and if not released, we shall not be very much disappointed. We are quite prepared to face it either way. You have tried your best and it is mainly due to your unceasing efforts that the release of P.P.s became such a burning question as that and though not we two, yet hundreds of others have won back their liberty.

Hoping to find you in good health and with best and loving regards to all our friends and relations.

I remain dear brother
Yours affectionately
TATYA

□

Miscellaneous Statements and Writings

The Nepal Movement (1925 A.D.)

Our doubts are traitors.
And make us lose the good we oft might win.
By fearing to attempt.

—*Shakespeare*

It is very gratifying to note that the Nepal movement has recorded a satisfactory progress during the last year. A couple of years ago, Hindusthan as a whole and even the leaders of Hindu thought in general, were totally unconscious of the far-reaching influence, which the movement is likely to exercise, if well and ably handled, on the future of the Sanghatan movement. The Hindu press was too busy in writing columns after columns about the duty of Hindus owed to the Khalifa in Turkey or the famine-stricken poor folk in Constantinople. The Hindu public was too much moved at the news that certain mosques in Syria had fallen in a dilapidated condition and was busy gathering funds with M. Shaukat Ali to rebuild it and the Hindu leaders led by the ablest of them, Mahatma Gandhi, who always knows how to lead and who never knows where to lead, were straining every fibre of their pinny hands to prop up the Khalifa on the throne of Turkey, whom his own people wanted to get rid of and were too much occupied in their efforts to save Mesopotamia and Arabia and Egypt and Syria and, in fact, all the great world but Hindusthan—to care how Nepal, that only independent Hindu Kingdom fared.

When the independence of Afghanistan was formally recognised by the British nation, there passed a wave of enthusiasm over the Hindu press and the Hindu platform and thousands of Hindus took part in the anniversary celebrations in memory of that event. But for months, the formal recognition by the British nation of the independence of the Hindu Kingdom of Nepal remained entirely unnoticed by the Hindu press. Even the news did not appear in the majority of the Hindu papers. The Anglo-Indian papers knew what the recognition meant and noticed it with few suggestive remarks. A khadi shop opened somewhere in the village in Assam, used to receive more prominence in the great Hindu dailies and weeklies in Bombay, Madras, Calcutta and Lahore than the terms of this important treaty, that was signed between Britain and Nepal, did. We are not exaggerating; matters stood exactly like that. Nay, even today, a section of the Hindu press is groping as hopelessly in this suicidal blindness to our own interests and what is worse, is sticking it up as a feather into his cap. The Mohamedan will swagger to know about his Amir and Sultan but ask a Hindu if he had ever heard of an independent Hindu Kingdom that still flies its flag, unsullied and unbeaten, he will give you a blank look. Even when you mention Nepal, he will at the most, shrink his shoulders and crowl out: 'Oh! the Gurkhas! what traitors they are!'

Against this criminal apathy that Hindus exhibited towards Nepal and as a reaction Nepal had been guilty of exhibiting towards the Hindus outside Nepal, it was the Maratha press that was first to raise a powerful and vigorous protest. It opened the eyes of the Hindu public to the far-reaching consequences that the general awakening amongst the Hindus of Nepal and outside was likely to have, if the forces of Hindudom as a whole were made to work towards a wide, definite and well-outlined common goal. Sindh and the Hindu press in Calcutta followed. The Arya Samaj papers soon caught the flame. The Hindu Mahasabha nearly offered its presidentship to the Maharajadhiraj of Nepal and although His majesty could not accept it for weighty reasons, and although the question was dropped before it was pressed to the last stage, the special session of the Mahasabha unanimously passed a resolution at Belgaum congratulating His Majesty on the recognition of the independence of the Hindu Kingdom by England and France as well and expressed in significant words the hopes and aspirations which the strength and the greatness of Nepal aroused in the hearts of Hindu patriots all over India.

This general awakening of Hindu mind naturally called forth opposition. Attempts to misguide and divide by raising false issues in the name of solemn history and disinterested sophistry, which wanted to assure us that Nepal was not, had never been a part of India nor the people there had anything common with the Hindus outside Nepal, were not wanting. But such disingenuous attempts to alienate the Gurkhas away from their brother—Hindus in India—only intensified the interest of the general public on the question and the Nepal movement began to loom even larger and larger on the horizon of Hindu hope.

Just then, the anniversaries of birth of the Majesty, the King of Nepal and Excellency, the Prime Minister of that kingdom furnished an occasion that proved the movement had entered on the third stage of its existence. For the interest that the Hindus had begun to take in the affairs of Nepal, has at last roused the Gurkhas to the sense of their own importance and strength and let us hope of their duty too, which as the foremost section of the Hindu people, they owe to Hindudom as a whole. This year the citizens of Nepal, Gurkhas and Newaries observed in Calcutta the birthdays of their King and Minister as national festivals and several distinguished Hindus took prominent part in the proceedings. The National banner of Nepal was raised and all Hindus worshipped the colours of the only independent Kingdom with a fitting devotion and ceremony. National songs were sung by the Gurkhas, which exhorted them to organise and serve their Motherland and strive as champions of the Hindu Dharma and the Hindu race. These are the first signs of the awakening of a great people. That even the little interest and love that the Hindu outside Nepal manifested and extended towards our countrymen and the brethren in Nepal, should have within a year's course, roused the Gurkhas and made them respond so deeply, it all augurs well for the Sanghatan.

The Hindu Sabha of Ratnagiri and Nasik and Bombay and Sindh and Poona and Calcutta set the example, which was quickly followed by other Sabhas at Delhi and several other places by organising public meetings and conveying public congratulations to His Majesty and His Excellency on their respective birthdays and assure them of the deep love, regard and pride that the Hindus feel and cherish as regards the Hindu Kingdom and the confident hope that it will, God willing, serve as the main mast of the movement of Hindu Sanghatan.

Thus, the work of a year is not disappointing, it is even gratifying, for not only the Hindus have grown conscious of Nepal but what is far more important, Nepal, too, has grown conscious of herself. Let us not forget that what is done is as nothing in respect of what is yet to be accomplished. For all movements that are at present agitating the heart of Hindudom, none is so pregnant with results, great and glorious, as is the movement that aims at bringing the Hindus of Nepal in line with their co-religionists and countrymen outside Nepal and enthusing them with one hope and inspiring them with a great ideal, wield all Hindudom into an organic and mighty whole. This is what Hindu Sanghatan aims at.

□

Awaken Nepal (1926 A.D.)

या भूमंडळाचे ठायीं। हिंदु ऐसा उरला नाहीं।
हिंदु राष्ट्र राहिलें काहीं॥ तुम्हा कारणें॥

The 19th of July was the twenty-first birth anniversary of His Majesty the King of Nepal, Rana Tribhuwan Veer Vikramdeo.

Hindudom heartily sends forth, to thee, oh Ranaji! its loyal greetings in loving homage on this auspicious occasion.

Some three hundred years ago, a hermit saint of Maharashtra went round on pilgrimage to all the four Mahadwars of Bharat Varsha from Attock to Kanyakumari, Dwarka and Jagannath. Having thus surveyed the whole Hindusthan, he came back to Maharashtra with a bleeding heart and bewailed that throughout the world, there was not a place where the Hindu banner could raise its head anew, no Hindu could champion the cause of his fallen race! While his heart was bleeding thus with unutterable grief and anxiety, his eyes caught the sight of a rising youth and his heroic band. Patriotic joy swelled in his hermit bosom and the prophet pointing out that heroic Hindu youth, with his brave band of followers, exclaimed. But there! Even though no Hindu is left throughout the world who could lead his race to greatness and glory, there in thee, oh Maharashtra, I discern some signs of hope in that heroic youth and his brave band! Our nation and our faith may yet live through them.

या भूमंडळाचे ठायीं। हिंदु ऐसा उरला नाहीं।
महाराष्ट्र धर्म राहिलें कांहीं॥ तुम्हा कारणें॥

Saying so, he handed over a gerua (भगवा) kerchief to them as a token of his divine blessings.

The hermit saint was Ramdas, the rising youth was Shivaji and the brave band of his followers were they, who and whose descendants raised the kerchief as their banner and carried it to Attak till it came to represent the strength and glory and the mission of a mighty Hindu Empire.

This was three hundred years ago.

But if the spirit of that patriotic saint troubled at the news of this second calamity that has befallen his Hindu race, comes down to visit our Earth today, then standing once more on the debris of crowns and coronets of Hindu kings and kingdoms and reviewing with a bleeding heart, the whole situation with a view to discerning if possible a point, which may yet serve as a position of vantage to start anew the movement, with means ever changing to suit changed circumstances but with the ideal full in view, Ramdas is sure to lay his unerring finger on thee, oh Nepal, as he did on Maharashtra then, and exclaim in prophetic accents anew.

या भूमंडळाचे ठायीं। हिंदु ऐसा उरला नाहीं।
हिंदु राष्ट्र उरहें काहीं॥ तुम्हा कारणें॥

Amidst this general wreck of Hindu crowns and coronets of Hindu aspirations and ambitions, I still discern enthroned and living in thee, oh, Nepal, the seed of Hindu hope! God has not spared thee in vain. Through thee, the Hindu race and the Hindu Nation may yet scale the Himalayan heights of its ancient glory.

Destiny at times loves to conceal mighty meanings in ciphers that seem but trifling. Can it be then that, if what tradition tells be true and that gerua kerchief handed over by Ramdas to Shivaji has through strange vicissitudes receded to the strongholds of Nepal and is being preserved and worshipped along with the gadi of Peshwas in a temple at Khatmandu. Can it be that emblem and insignia that once authorised the Marathas to lead the cause of the Hindu race and religion have now been handed over to thee, Oh Nepal, to invest thee with the same rights and responsibilities to champion the cause of Hindudom under changed circumstances with means necessarily changed? If the tradition is true, the Marathas are glad to find that these relics of their past should have been spared the humiliation of being exposed to the impudent and vulgar foreign gaze in one of the museums in the capital of their conquerors and should have found a safe and honourable asylum in Nepal where the standard of Hindu independence is still holding its own.

Our drooping hands hand over to thee, Oh Nepal, the standard of Hindu cause. Hold it aloft! Awake to thy new and mighty responsibilities! Lead the Sanghatan! We will follow thee! May the guardian Deities of our Hindu race inspire thee with mighty aspirations and high designs, add ever increasing strength to thy arms and may glory follow thee till Hindudom is restored to its rightful place in the commonwealth of man and shines once more, even as it did in the days of Shri Ram or Ashok the Priya Darshin.

***

Nepal in the Bombay Session of the Hindu Conference (1926)

Another, yet more significant feature of the conference that deserves to be specially emphasised was the presence and the thrilling speech of Shriyut Agamgiri, a Nepali leader, who came all the way from Calcutta to Bombay with a set purpose of representing the feelings of our Nepali Hindu brethren towards the Sanghatan movement.

The Sanghatan movement cannot be said to be the spokesman and cannot claim to represent the Hindus as a whole as long as it fails to enlist not only the sympathy but the actual and active participation of the most powerful and prominent and the only organised section of the Hindus—the Hindus of Nepal. The moment Nepal steps in and assumes the lead of the Sanghatan, it will be a power that could no longer be safely despised or neglected by any one in the world. Nepal as the only organised Hindu power owes it as much to herself as to us all. Whatever affects us Hindus as Hindus, must affect our brothers and co-religionists in Nepal too. This pan-Hindu consciousness must be instilled down into the heart of the humblest of the humble of the Nepali Hindu. With this end in view, for the last two years or so, constant attempts have been made through the press and platform to rouse amongst the people a sense of the importance of this Nepali question. Last year, a proposal to offer presidential chair of the Mahasabha at Calcutta to His Majesty the King of Nepal or to His Excellency the Prime Minister was deliberately put forward from the chair and was unanimously adopted at the special session of the Mahasabha at Belgaum, congratulating the King on his progressive policy and assuring him of the feelings of deepest love and loyal pride that all Hindus cherish towards our brethren in Nepal. This interest that the Hindus on our side began to evince in Nepal naturally disturbed some people whose energy is ever employed in one single mission—to keep the Hindus divided in castes and creeds and provinces and sects and sections. Queer and mischievous theories were cooked up insinuating that Nepal was no more a part of India than Tibet was. Nor was she racially, communally or any way organically connected with us, the Hindu outside Nepal. The mischief was transparent and yet unfortunately some Nepali Hindus too did fall a victim to its spacious reasoning and said, 'We are not Indians; we are Nepali. The Sanghatan has nothing to do with us.'

To defeat this ignoble attempt to alienate Nepali Hindus from Sanghatan and open the eyes of those simple-minded Nepali Hindus who fell a victim to it, required that some prominent Nepali Hindus should come forward, publicly participate in the session of the Hindu Sabhas and respond to the cause of Hindu Sanghatan in no uncertain terms. With this end in view, the leaders of the Bombay Hindu Conference acting on a request submitting to them through a resolution passed by the Ratnagiri Hindu Sabha, sent a special invitation to our Nepali brothers in Calcutta, requesting them to send some prominent gentleman who could grace the assembly by his presence and acquaint us with feelings of our Nepali brothers to some extent or the other as regards the Sanghatan movement. They were fortunate in securing a man of Mr. Agamgiri's standing, who had been one of the moving spirits in organising the Gůrkha Sanghatan Society in Calcutta, and who wrote in the Krishna-Sandesh, a leading weekly in Calcutta, every now and then exhorting our Nepal friends to participate in the pan-Hindu movement. His speech in the conference was the most effective rejoinder that could be given to those who hoped to alienate Nepal from the Sanghatan Movement. In the very opening sentence, the Nepali gentleman emphatically declared that the Gurkhas and the Nepalis look upon Bharatwarsh as their fatherland and their Holy land. Nepal is and will ever continue to be an inalienable part of Bharatwarsh, of Hindusthan. Whatever, he said, affected the fortunes of Hindus outside Nepal must affect her too. Socially, culturally, religiously, communally in all aspects of life and in all questions that relate to Hindudom and Hindu Society as a whole, it was impossible to think of Nepal apart from Bharatwarsh. As a Nepali, he movingly assured the assembly that the deepest sympathy was being felt with the Hindu sufferers who had been subjected to wanton attacks and humiliation and declared that Nepal would not only remain unaffected but would stand shoulder-to-shoulder with her Hindu brothers all over India in defence of Hindu culture, Hindu religion, the Hindu temple and the honour of Hindu race, whenever and by whomsoever they be attacked. The reception that was accorded to him when he rose and the way his speech was received by the assembly must have proved to all, who have sense to understand

and honesty to acknowledge, that Nepal is sure to fall in rank before long and boldly respond the cause of Hindu Sanghatan. On points of civil, communal, cultural, religious and racial interests, we Hindus all, whether Punjabis or Pahadis, Marathas or Madrasis, Nayars or Nepalis are one, feel as one and mean to make a common stand, long before they will come to realise this all.

Godsend Books and How should man read them?

One day, while I sat in the night reading History and comparative sociology, I could not help being overwhelmed by the thought that of all superstitions, which outliving their utility, continued to block human progress, the superstition that attributed Divine origin to a set of books and consequently held every word in them as infallible, as God's truth, was most responsible for perpetuating senseless animosities and ignorance, which hampered rational advance of mankind not only in science and social solidarity but even in religion itself and ranged man against man and creed against creed with deathless enmity and schism. Verily there have been in human history, more men victimised to death and disaster in the name of God and the Gospels than in the name of the Devil and the Dollar.

Nevertheless, it cannot be gainsaid that the greatest boon that mankind could have ever received at the hands of its creator would be a book emanating directly from him setting forth in unmistakable accents His will and command, which he meant us to follow, either for man's good or God's glory or for both. In that case, instead of groping from error to error in the dim and fickle light of our unaided human reason, we could have treaded on this fair earth under the Divine Guidance with surest steps and in full confidence that it led us to bliss here and hereafter. We know for certain that this generous hope had actually prompted many a prophet in his search after truth and anxiety to receive a revelation directly from the supreme source of wisdom. Had all the prophets succeeded in receiving their commands from the Creator of man in words and substance uniform, unequivocal and uncircumscribed by time and place or if so mentioning clearly the limitations that defined and determined them, our difficulties and controversies with regard to the authenticity of the revelation would have been very much simplified, if not altogether eliminated. But as it is, revelation differs from revelation in the God-sent books as much as in any man-written books and it is due to the explosion of these mines of discrepancies and contradictions which the God-sent books carry within themselves, that the citadel of orthodoxy is often shattered and the forces of doubt and disbelief rush through the breach to complete its ruin.

While I was thus overwhelmed by forces of scepticism and sat sorely afflicted in heart, I felt a strange lassitude creeping over me and sealing my eyes with sleep. But the train of thought that occupied my mind nevertheless continued in subconscious or superconscious state and I fancied as if a Pandit stepped forth and accosted me thus: 'Listen', said he, 'you wished you had a revelation to enable you to know the right path and to dispense with the erring and confused guidance of human reason. Well, there is such God-sent book as that—the most ancient and the most infallible, emanating as it did from the all-wise and Almighty God Brahma Himself. The only reason that makes you doubt the authenticity of a God-sent book seems to be that it contradicts and even controverts other books that also severely claim to be God-inspired; but it only proves that all of them cannot be really so. It does not rule out the possibility of one of them being a really God-inspired Gospel. Well, that real Gospel, that only true revelation, is this 'Veda.' If other Gospels contradicted it, it only proves that they are not really reliable. Their refutation of this Veda, the first and foremost word of God, only refutes themselves.' While our friend, the Pandit had not even finished this exhortation rushed in the High Priest of the Golden Temple at Jerusalem and with a solemn wave of hand brushing aside all the reasoning of the Pandit as you would a cobweb, said, 'Not so! The real revelation of the Almighty Father that rules this heaven and earth is that which He, our Lord God, stretching his mighty hand out of the burning cloud of fire and flame that surrounded Mount Sinai delivered to Moses on that fateful day. If Vedas were true, Jehova would have at least mentioned them once in that Holy Book. But, on the contrary, he expressly rules out your Molachs and Thors, your Maruts and Varuns. Jehova is a jealous God and bears the presence of no other God before Him. So only obey and reason not. If others contradict his our Holy Testament, they only belie themselves.' 'True! True! what my friend says is even so! But, persuasively puts in my friend, the missionary, so meek, so humble, at this stage, 'but the Law of Moses emanating though it did from the Lord was nevertheless supplemented and fulfilled by a later revelation which even He, our Father in Heaven charged. His son, the Prince of Peace to proclaim, as was even foretold by Moses and the Prophets of old. The Code issued on Mount Sinai was like an angry ordinance of some sullen Sultan meant only for the troublous times, times of emergency when men went astray and sacrificed to Molachs and worshipped the Golden Calves. But the Law of Life, the law as such that brings Peace unto men contained in the sermon on the Mount. The New Testament is the fulfilment of all old revelations. Question not, reason not, nay even fear not, only believe in the Bible, in our Lord Jesus the Christ, and thou art saved. Leave all and follow me, says the Christ! But all of a sudden, an angry voice interrupted him here and throwing back the crowd of many a respectable representative of scores of other prophets and Gospels. each claiming his book as the real God-sent book that had been waiting there to take a chance of finding a new recruit in me to their respective faiths, an excited moulavi darted forth and simply commanded me to believe none else but him. 'Behold', said he, stroking his beard with fiery restlessness 'behold this Holy Koran! Abraham and Musa and Isa and other Prophets were prophets indeed but their works, these old and new testaments are, as men now possess, full of interpolations and absurdities. As to the Vedas, it is sacrilege even to name that mumbo-Jumbo of idolatrous crowd along with the works of prophets that went before. It was to end the reign of these scheming impostors that God ordered the last and the greatest of the line of his prophets, Mohomed the Prophet—be his name ever blest, to reveal the Holy Koran on earth. This and this alone is God's work, all else is the work of Satan. And the only way how man should read it and nothing else! Trust it and reason not. If they do so well and good: if they don't, to eternal perdition they go!' At this outburst of this zealous Moulavi, those representatives of several other Gospels who were waiting with equal earnestness to do me a good turn of saving my soul by recommending to me their respective Gospels as the only authentic ones, gently fell back to avoid any unpleasant development their intrusion seemed likely to cause. But I myself rose up and approaching them requested to oblige me by favouring me with a copy of each of their own Gospels and assuring, said, 'Gentlemen, I revere every one of these God-sent books as deeply as you do though perhaps for reasons other than yours. All these books that claim to be divine revelations are doubtless a precious treasure, which men will do well to guard and preserve and use for their benefit. God-sent or not they are partly Godly indeed. It cannot be for nothing that millions of men have for generations owed allegiance to them and many a soul might have found a solace in them as in no other wordly thing.' Being requested thus, they all presented me with copies of their religious books—the stately looking Parsee who kept watching over conversation but seemed very reluctant to show off his sacred book as the hawkers do their tinsels in the market place, presented me a copy of the ancient and renowned Zendavesta; the yellow-clad Bhikku of his venerated and venerable and Tripitaka but seeming quite indifferent to claim for his Holy books, the gilded title of a God-sent revelation! The followers of the unlucky prophets Museilama and Al-aswad who set themselves up as rivals to Mahomed and claimed the prerogative of Prophethood for themselves, the followers of the Veiled Prophet' and of the 'Moon Maker' and of the Prophet Karmala and of several others offered to me copies of their Gospels. Even the Mormons obliged me by letting me have a copy of the famous golden book the Prophet Mormon received only very recently in America as an up-to-date word of God. Nor did any one of them forget to recommend to me and for reasons similar to those used by the Pandit and the Missionary and the Moulavi, that his Gospel was the only real revelation of God and the best way how man should read it and it alone. Thereupon, I thanked them all and bidding goodbye, bowed low—and as I was doing so, I awoke.

But the impression that the dream had left upon my mind was so vivid that I could hardly avoid believing it, as innumerable saints are reported to have done under similar circumstances—to be an actual visitation and no ephemeral illusion. I decided, therefore, to take it all seriously and pondering deeply over what the pious men had said found to my great relief that although each of them had denied to human reason the right of questioning the truth of whatever be the contents of his sacred books, his God-sent Gospel, when one has accepted it as such, yet they all seemed to sanction or concede the use of reason in the act of making one's choice as to which of the several alleged revelations was the most authentic one. Nay, strangely enough, they had to advance reasons even to prove that men should not reason at all, indulging in the contents of a divine revelation when once your choice is made. In fact, missions as such are but bodies that are out only to reason and argue and persuade men to distinguish the true Gospels from the false ones. Not only that but even the Prophets themselves did not hesitate to argue and reason with men so that they might be able to separate the wheat from the chaff, the imposters from the Prophets and come to believe in the really God-sent books. Does not the Arabian Prophet, for example, thunder from Sura, from paragraph to paragraph, that those who refused to believe in the Holy Koran revealed to him, will be eternally lost and consigned to perdition? And is not this pointing to a rod also a way of reasoning? When asked by the Faithless to produce a sign to prove his divine mission, did he not chide them by reminding them that they had tried to test even the Prophets that went before him, and failed to extract a sign from them too, and later on pointed out to this wide earth and the rising mountains and the bounteous fields as mighty signs and miracles that attested to his being the real and the only messenger of God? Nay, sometimes, as is recorded in the second and some other chapters of the Holy Koran, he challenged the unbelievers to produce a single line in such a polished Arabian style as that, which marked the lines, in which the Koran was being revealed and flourished their inability to do so as a conclusive proof of the Koran's being a really inspired and God-sent work. He taunted every now and then the false Prophets who write a book with their own hand and pass it on as God-written and God-sent. This also proves that the art of issuing counterfeit Gospels was well known to the generation and people amongst which the Prophet flourished. It was also for this reason that he not only permitted but commended men to argue and compare such books with his own in the light of human reason and logic and even diction. In the Holy Bible too, we meet every now and then with arguments advanced by Jesus and Christ to combat those who questioned his inspiration and Prophethood. Those who demanded signs and miracles, were at times rebuked for want of faith and at other times supplied with them. 'Ye build sepulchres unto those whom your fathers stoned to death' he sternly reminded his persecutors and quoted old prophesies to prove that all they had foretold came to pass in his life and corroborated his Prophethood. In the Vedic-fold, too, lengthy and elaborate discussions as to the authenticity of the Vedas as a God-inspired scripture are a common feature in works, not only heterodox but even orthodox, that aid to interpret them. Even Jaimini himself, after mentioning that a school existed even then, which did not attribute the Vedas to any divine and impersonal agency but boldly asserted that they were the work of men, though highly gifted and spiritual, enters into reasoned argumentation to prove otherwise.

All these facts enable us to conclude that on the following four points at any rate, there reigns perfect unanimity amongst the followers of almost all sacred books that are extant today and looked upon as God-sent by the respective creeds. To start with, our friends, the Pandit, the Missionary, the Moulavi, the Rabbi down to the followers of Mormon and Al-swad and the Moonmakers and even of the Aga khan and Kadiani, each and all, not only admit but strongly maintain that all these books that claim to be God-sent cannot altogether be such, as the mutual contradictions and glaring antagonisms, with which they abound, do incontrovertibly prove. The second point that characterises each and all of them equally, is the insistence in which they indulge in citing these very contradictions as an undeniable proof that all the Prophets and books that differ from their own, must be misleading and false for the simple reason that their own Gospel being God-sent and true cannot be false, and therefore the other books, which contradict it cannot be true. The third point that seems common to all, is the latitude which not only their respective followers but even the Prophets to whom these God-sent books were severally revealed, conceded though very confusedly and reluctantly to human reason, the right of distinguishing the false Prophets from the true one and the man-written books, that merely pose as God-written and God-inspired from the truly-inspired revelation in the light of logic and tradition and such other wordly tests of comparative criticism. The fourth point that distinguishes the sectarian propaganda of each and all of these conflicting religious schools is the fact that each Prophet, although he does not hesitate to lay human reason under contribution so long as it is useful to him in exposing the falsity of all other Prophets, excepting himself, to win over recruits to his side with a very laudable desire to save their souls, proceeds straight way to deny the right of human criticism and argument and reasoning to those very recruits, as soon as they get themselves definitely enlisted in the roll of believers in his creed. They are, thenceforth, to obey whatever the Prophet or his God-sent book commands and question naught or argue.

Taking our stand then on these points, which more or less are common to all the Prophets and holy books of the different religious systems that prevail today, not to mention those that flourished in the ancient Babylonians and the people of the Pharaohs and other now extinct races and systems, it seems quite permissible to us mortals even consistently with the Prophetic traditions of yore, to subject these God-sent books and scriptures to human criticism and comparative study, if we but do it for the sake of ascertaining which one of these Gospels satisfies most our human expectation of perfection that a really God-sent book ought to possess. Although as we have seen already, all of them cannot be equally true, if at least one of them comes up to our expectation at the end of this enquiry and reveals all the attributes—which we are justified in associating with a God-sent book, with a work that emanates from the source of wisdom and goodness and knowledge from Providence, at once omniscient and omnipotent—blessed indeed are we! That was the most cherished boon we longed for; but if unfortunately our investigation proves barren in the end and none of these revered works seems likely to establish its claim to the right of being regarded as Divine revelation it is given out to be then we must make ourselves bold to acknowledge and proclaim the truth and expose the superstition that attributing Divine infallibility, to human institutions, opinions and fancies however exalted, admirable and even beneficial they be in themselves relatively to human knowledge and ability, gave rise to so much bloodshed and misery in the past. If comparative criticism led in the light of human reason brings us further on to assess the true value of these revered scriptures, which when looked upon as man-written instead of God-written, will perhaps command greater respect from all reasonable men and could be read, interpreted and followed in a way that will save these precious books from being abused by fanaticism and render them not only quite harmless but even more useful and beneficial to man than now in his search after the True and the Good and the Beautiful.

With this end in view, let us first address ourselves to the task of reviewing the Vedas, the Holy Bible, and the Quran sharif in the searchlight of human reason, before we pledge our allegiance to any one of them as an inspired and infallible scripture, as God-sent Gospel.

Abhinava Hindu Dhwaja (Hindu National Flag)

The National Flag does not only indicate but also establish the National Ideal.

A nation's greatness invariably finds expression through its ideal. The character of a nation depends upon the ideal that the nation sets upon itself. Nations with narrow ideals never achieved lasting greatness in the past. A sublime ideal has been the necessary requisite of a nation's success to greatness and glory.

Nations after nations illumined the pages of the world's history only to disappear after a while, most of them having their downfall even before attaining the pinnacle of prosperity. The Hindu Nation alone traces its unbroken train of civilised existence from beyond the dawn of history and will continue its victorious march so long as its noblest ideal and its imperishable widest outlook on life are not forsaken.

Speaking generally, the ideal of other past and living western nations has been considered to be Abhyudaya (worldly prosperity) for worldly enjoyment, which, being confined to mere material prosperity, cannot solve the knottiest problems for the amelioration of mankind.

But the Hindu nation is the only one that has accepted the ideal of perfect Abhyudaya as based on the foundation of complete Nihshreyas (Spiritual bliss). Hindu philosophers maintain that worldly Abhyudaya is imperatively necessary for mankind in order that by acquiring a happy and easy-going worldly life it may ultimately lead to the highest Nihshreyas (bliss). They know that the culmination of worldly Abhyudaya cannot be any other than Nihshreyas itself. It is Abhyudaya that makes human Nihshreyas possible, and it is Nihshreyas that purifies and controls the highest goal of Abhyudaya. It is because the Hindu race maintained this eternal ideal of harmony of worldly and spiritual aspirations that the Hindu Nation, in spite of successive waves of calamities, which overtook it, came out triumphantly again-and-again and is still a living race holding its ground.

Hindu social lawgivers laid down the foundation of social organisation on the non-competition principle of division of functions and mutual aid in order to realise glorious Abhyudaya on way to Nihshreyas. To enable the smooth development of it, the Hindu society from the Sudra to the Brahmin have been allotted their respective duties. But for the proper fulfilment of all these duties and for the protection of the social life, there is necessity of Kshatra Tej (power). Its symbol is the Kripana (sword). In the absence of this Kshatra power as protector, the modus operandi of the Brahmin, the Vaishya and the sundra, which are conducive to the welfare of society, are almost impossible. The community that does not possess such Kshatra Power is bound to die. If education, agriculture, cattle-production, commerce and all arts and crafts are divorced from society, the community may still continue its lingering existence, but the want of Kshatra Power is likely to endanger the very existence of society. The Kshatra Power, in fact, guides, protects and harmonises the national commonwealth.

All these considerations ought to be borne in mind when we set ourselves to the task of determining the flag of the Hindu Nation. The earth that feeds society, the law that gives nourishment, the book that imparts wisdom, the spinning wheel that symbolises arts and crafts—all these and many others can become symbols and much can be said in respect of each of them. But the crowning representative of all these symbols—the only correct symbol of Abhyudaya—is Kripana (sword). In this one, all other symbols are represented. The main symbol for the Hindu National Flag, therefore, should be the Kripana.

But the ultimate aim of the Hindu Abhyudaya is Nihshreyas and keeping this in view, the Hindus should endeavour to reach the highest goal humanly possible, which is the special characteristic of the Hindu Nation.

Hindus have perfected a science based on experiment, which can be termed the highest blessing on human life. This Shastra is called the Yoga. It is the highest means of the full development of man's internal powers. It is, therefore, very necessary that a clear symbol of Yoga, which indicates the way to the highest bliss should be fixed on the flag of the Hindu Nation.

The symbol is that of the Kundalini. It is not the characteristic of any particular Jati or Varna. It exists in all human beings. On both sides of the Merudanda (spinal cord), there are two *nadis* (rivers), which are named by the Hindu Yogashastris as the Ida and the Pingala. They are intertwined with each other like a garland. Between these two, there is a third *nadi* called the Sushumna. In them, there are centres of nerves, which are designated as lotuses in the Yogic language. There are chiefly six lotuses, known as the Muladhara, the Swadhisthana, the Manipura, the Anahata, the Vishuddha and Sahasrara. In the Muladhara chakra, there is a marvellous power, which is coiled up. By Yogic and meditative practices it gets awakened and passing through every lotus (nerve center) and experiencing wonderful psychic superhuman experiences, reaches the Sahasrara lotus. Then the person practicing Yoga experiences wonderfully super-sensous and intense joy and bliss. This stage is designated by the Yogis as that of Kaivalyananda, by the Vajrayanis as that of Mahasuka, by the Adwaitees as that of Brahmananda, and by the devotees as that of Premananda. To acquire this supreme joy or bliss is the highest ideal of man, be he a Hindu or a non-Hindu (Muslim, Christian or Jew) i.e. believer or non-believer, citizen or forester. This Yogashastra is a science of personal experience. Hence, there is no place for difference of opinions. Therefore, the Kundalini that is the Muladhar Shakti or man's highest progress and eternally blissful state of superconsciousness, which can be personally experienced, can alone be the symbol of the great ideal, at which the Abhyudaya of the Hindu Nation aims.

Thus, the Kundalini represents all the ultimate aspirations, feelings, and powers of mankind and the Kripana, which represents the all-sided Abhyudaya aiming at and leading to the nation's ideal prosperity.

These two alone being depicted on the national flag, will be able to indicate and inspire the ideals of Abhyudaya and Nihshreyas.

Pointing at the flag, every Hindu will say:

This is the Kundalini—this is the Kripana—the one represents the highest bliss, the other worldly prosperity; they combine Shanti and Shakti, Yoga and Bhoga, Nivritti and Pravritti, Dhyeya and Dharana; the one symbolizes Aupanishadic Vidya (Highest spiritual attainment), the other denotes Aupanishadic Avidya (worldly advancement); the former reminds one Yogeshwar Krishna, the latter Dhanuradhara Partha of the Geeta. The Kundalini means Jnana Yoga and the Kripan means Karma Yoga.

'For the protection of the good and the destruction of the wicked.' All this, whatever that moves in the world, does so, because it is indwelt by the Lord. "Enjoy thou what he has allotted to thee." This is the Universal message of the Hindu flag to the world. This is the national declaration.

In order that kingdom, power and glory may not become polluted by the actions of tyranny and in order to keep the central truth of virtuous conduct always before mankind, the background of this Hindu flag is made of Bhagawa (red orchard) colour. This is the colour of renunciation. There is no *Tyaga* without *Yoga* and *Kshema*. Therefore, the Kripana is for the *Yoga Kshema*. We not only want to become free, powerful and liberated ourselves, but we want also to make the world so. Therefore, the colour of the flag of prosperity is Bhagawa. The deeper meaning and the philosophic secret of the Hindu flag is, thus, denoted by this Bhagwa-zenda, which is adorned by the kun*dalini* with *Omkar* and which also holds the Kripana, this has got a very great historical importance. This flag is the final stage in the evolution of the traditional Hindu flag in the past. This is the consummation and perfection. From the very ancient times, the colour of the Hindu flag has been Bhagwa. Even today, the zenda indicating the ideas of victorious Pravritti and Blissful Nivritti is seen always and everywhere on the Hindu temples. When the Moslems were encroaching on the Hindusthan, the Maharashtriya Hindu padpadashahi, which succeeded in overthrowing them by its great forces with Herculean efforts and by organising the Hindu power, had as its flag Bhagwa zenda and everyone knows that the national Guru Samartha Ramdas, who bestowed it on the national hero Shree Shivaji Maharaj, gave it as the flag of Hindu religion for the great national purpose. For the establishment of Abhyudaya and Nihshreyas, Shri Ramdas has defined Dharma as—

'Activity generates power. He who is active possesses it, but it must be based on the highest ideal of Nihshreyas, firstly as expounding the Kshatras of great Avatars, secondly Rajakaran (politics), thirdly watchfulness regarding everything.'

This very meaning is denoted by the Hindu flag. Along with the Royal Bhagwa colour of the Maharashtriya Hindu power, there is also the Kripana of the Sikhs indicative of the memory of Guru Govind Singh, another great protector of Hindu nation. Guru Govind Singh used to keep Kripanas by his sides and used to say: 'The one is of Yoga and the other is of Bhoga, the one is of Shanti (eternal peace) and the other is of Pushti-tushti (prosperity).' Our Hindu flag also gives the same message. This Kundalini means Yoga and the Kripana means Bhoga.

In the same way, Onkar is the sacred name of the great One, with whom the liberated souls become one, is the Highest state of Nihshreyas of Vaidic, Non-Vaidic, Sanatani and modern Hindu. Be there everlasting victory and eternal life to the Hindu flag bearing the symbol of Kundalini with Omkar and of Kripana from this end to that of the world flying with the prowess of millions of warriors accomplishing the highest happiness of all mankind!

Since the time when in the Shradhanada paper, Syt. Savarkar propounded very clearly and appropriately the idea of the Hindu national flag, it is being welcomed everywhere. At the Session of the Akhil-Bharatiya Hindu Mahasabha at Surat, its learned and venerable president hoisted the flag. At that time, the whole Mahasabha got up, saluting the flag hoisted triumphantly. In the year 1928, the Morshi

Taluka Hindu Parishad held its session under the presidentship of Lokanayaka Aney. At that time, the audience, which was more than 5000, stood under the flag and sang the song of the 'Hindus' 'We Hindus are all brothers.'

The C.P. and Berar Hindu Mahasabha met at Akola under the presidentship of Pandit Madan Mohan Malaviya. At the time of entering the mandap (pandal), all the persons assembled saluted the flag.

In the Hindu Youth Conference at Akola under the presidency of Dr. Savarkar, the Hindu National song was sung under the very flag. After the Surat Session in all the sessions of the Hindu Mahasabha, which took place at Bezwada under the presidency of Dr. Moonje, at Akola under Sjt. Vijaya Raghava Achariyar's presidentship, at Delhi under the presidentship of Sj. N. C. Kelkar of Poona, there was a grand salutation of this Abhinava Hindu Dhwaja; the Hindu Flag continued hoisted and flying in every one of the sessions that was held in subsequent years including the last session of Cawnpore under the presidentship of Rev. U. Uttama.

□

Facts without Comment

Many a good-natured Hindu simpleton is heard to ejaculate with a prudish air: 'How can this be? I don't think the Mahomedan proselytising campaign is so bad as your comments suggest. Facts would certainly belie them!' If they would, none would be gladder than we. But friends, don't you see that between us, the comment which is decidedly based on a mere 'I think', a mere silly hope that hopes against hope, is the only comment that you just passed on my comments? For, my comments are avowedly not based on a mere 'I think'. But your remark that want only asserts 'facts would certainly belie them' is certainly belied by facts, for it is confessedly guilty of being based on no more solid a foundation than a hollow 'would'. Is it not your business also, Oh good friend, to leave your cosy corner and gather facts for yourselves, if only to prove my comments false? What right have you to demand facts from me alone? Why don't you bring out your facts which you say would certainly belie my comments?

But, although, you have no right to dub my comments as certain to be belied by facts without citing a single fact to support your own, nevertheless, I have determined to treat you with an unalloyed dose of facts and facts alone for which you so dreadfully thirst but to get at which, you would not stretch out your lazy hand so much as an inch further. I hope your green opium dreams would not be disturbed even by this strong dose.

We cite only those reports that come of the papers published during this current month alone. If all reports that the press had reported of Mahomedan campaign of conversion during the last four years are to be cited, a volume would not suffice. So, we call only a few of them and only out of those which happened within the last month alone.

Mr. Vilas Rai Dal reports from Sambhar: 'Ever since the Hasan Nizami scheme has begun its nefarious activity, several Hindus have been converted to Mohamedanism. Almost every Mohamedan down to the street urchins are ever on the lookout for a helpless or unprotected Hindu that they might hammer upon and entangle him in their net. Only very recently, they caught hold of two Brahmin women and made them Mohamedans. One Hindu preacher opposed them. But as the chief officer as well as lower ones are Moslems, they soon intimidated him into silence. The Moslem shopkeepers, those who visit Hindu ladies for selling glass bangles, Moslem servants in Hindu houses—all try to seduce or kidnap boys and girls and generally force them to accept Mohamedanism. Only the other day, I visited one of these victims and as a sample of what happens in scores of cases at Sambhar, I reproduce our conversation. The name of the victim is Taka. He was a Brahmin. He burst into tears as soon as the subject of this apostasy was touched and said: I was a Kashmiri Brahmin. I was one day suddenly called by a certain survey officer who was a Moslem, notorious for partiality and fanaticism in Hindu circles. He offered me a pan but as I refused to eat it, his servants suddenly fell upon me and belaboured me so mercilessly that I fell senseless on the ground. When I recovered, I found myself a helpless prisoner in the Moslem hands who took me to a mosque, cut off my choti (shikha), paid off my debts to the Hindu shopkeepers, changed my name to Nizamuddin and kept me under a close Moslem surveillance. My wife and uncle came to see me but returned deadly shocked and weeping at my helpless state.' This Brahmin wished to come back to the Hindu fold. He disclosed several cases of Hindu victims in Sambhar alone, whose names were noted down by me. The Christians also are making great progress in this State. If things go on like that, Sambhar would cease to contain a Hindu home."

The *Hindu* reports "The Mohamedans have organised a secret society in the district of Nababshah whose activities are assuming dangerous proportions. In this one district, and in one month, four or five Hindu lads have been kidnapped.

"A Hindu woman has lodged a complaint that some Moslems of Karachi have decamped with her young son and that she could not ascertain his whereabouts.

"In the town of Naushahara, the Hindu papers report the presence of a disciple of Hasan Nizami school who, guised as a Sufi, has been busy seducing young Hindu boys away, making them abjure the Hindu faith. One of his own pet disciples gave out his secret designs."

The *Sindh Kesari* reports that Moslems have kidnapped a young Hindu lad at Karachi aged 16. The *Daily Hindu* of Hyderabad observes: "The campaign of kidnapping, seducing and abducting Hindu boys and girls is being persistently carried on throughout Sindh. The Khilafatists are at the forefront. On the 17th of April, some Mohamedans had secured a Hindu lad—Har Nathoo, eight years old. They had kidnapped the boy at some other place. Evidently a Hindu leader came to know of this wretched affair and succeeded in recovering the boy, who was duly re-initiated into the Hindu fold by restoring his sacred thread and the Shikha. Thereupon, the local Mohamedans made a Mohamedan woman to file a suit against the Hindus for having forcibly converted to Hinduism her lad, namely, Har Nathoo. But the police inquiry resulted in establishing the Hindu contention. But seeing the case had resulted against them, the Moslems stole the lad right from the police custody and were on the point of despatching him to Hyderabad. But fortunately, some Hindu gentlemen detected the poor lad thus being forcibly smuggled by the Moslems and once more, the police secured his possession. None of the Moslems is as yet arrested."

The same paper publishes that a Madrasi Hindu with his wife and daughter got stranded in Hyderabad on account of his money being robbed on the railway station. Moslem propagandists, who are ever on the lookout in Hyderabad for an opportunity to catch any helpless Hindu in their nets, got hold of that Madrasi and took him to Moslem quarters. But fortunately, a Hindu Sikh gentleman got news of the affair and took the duped Madrasi, his wife and daughter to the office of the Hindu Sabha, and thus saved them.

A Hindu girl was abducted and held in illegal custody by some Moslems in Hyderabad. The Hindus on coming to know of this dreadful affair, informed the police and released the poor girl.

Mr. Subhanilal reports that a Hindu woman named Amara Bai was on the point of being abducted by two Moslems, Muhmud and Jumma. They had arranged every thing for the forcible carrying away of that woman. Just then, some Hindu gentleman detected it and informed the police. But the police too seemed inclined to let the Moslems have the possession of the woman. As the Hindu yielded not and threatened further proceedings, they at last succeeded in saving the woman and sent her back to her husband, who is a resident in Delhi.

The scandalous activities of Bengali Moslem gundas and

proselytisers, working hand in hand, have become so persistent and so notorious that one cannot understand how the Hindus in East Bengal have grown so incredibly emasculated. Hundreds of cases have occurred in that part continuously for the last three years and more, monotonously repeating the same story of a Moslem abducting or outraging and then forcing the Hindu girl or wife to Mohamedanism. To choose only one case, let us cite the story of Gubrasani, the daughter of the mukhtyar of Gaivanda. Khijuruddin and other Moslem rowdies rushed in the house of her father and forcibly carried this poor girl away. She was confined and tortured, dishonoured and outraged, but she refused to give her consent to live with them as a Moslem. She once got an opportunity, effected her escape and reaching a railway station, was on the point of leaving the place. But the Daroga there happened to be a Mohamedan, he intervened and handed back that helpless girl into the hands of those Mohamedan miscreants who had abducted her. At last, the whereabouts of the girl being known, the police arrested those Moslem criminals along with that Daroga and the case was tried before the Magistrate of Rangpoor. The miscreants were punished but an important side-issue brought to light in an authoritative way the evil that is corroding Hindu life in Eastern Bengal not only now—now that it is brought to light—but for decades and decades in the past. The accused in this case wanted to get their case transferred from Rangpoor to some other court on the ground that the popular feeling at Rangpoor was so excited against them as to affect the decision of their case. The Magistrate set aside and refused to grant their petition, observing with silent eloquence that cases of Hindu women being similarly abducted and ill-treated have become such a common occurrence in Eastern Bengal, that people have ceased to take any special notice of them and so they could never excite the popular feeling there. These words of a magistrate are so plain and yet so dreadful that the 'Agrasar' is made to observe that no stronger remarks could be passed in condemning the effeminacy that has overtaken the Hindus of East Bengal and the criminal negligence, with which West Bengal passively witnesses all this, without so much as raising a word of protest against this Moslem rowdyism that has such a fanatical method in its monstrous madness. A breath of Lord Lytton has shocked our sense of chivalry, but the rude and indecent clasp of the garlic-smelling Moslem gunda may be silently borne.

From Badan, the sad tale of the oppression of Mohamedan Zamindars informs us that one Devi Bhavani, a Hindu Chambhar, was the latest victim of religious fanaticism. He was all of a sudden attacked by half a dozen Moslems, under the protection of Zamindars, and was forcibly fed with unclean food at the hand of Mohamedans; the whole society of the Chambhars is being intimidated and oppressed with a view to forcing them to embrace Islam. The Zamindars have ordered washermen, barbers and other castes not to render services to the Chambhars unless they leave the Hindu fold. The Mohamedan police too is passively witnessing this dreadful and criminal campaign of religious persecution. The villages of Datagant, Bikhanli, Khiri and several other places in the district of Etava are groaning under similar religious persecution and Hindus in dozens and scores, have been systematically forced to leave the faith of their forefathers. Mr. Devi Dutt Dwivedi declares that some of these Hindu victims to Moslem barbarism have prayed to be readmitted into the Hindu fold through shuddhi.

Before the District Magistrate of Sylhut, a Hindu widow stated that she got widowed at the age of ten. She was aged about fourteen years, at the time of her complaint. Once while she was bathing at a ghat, one rascal Mubarik suddenly fell on her, thrust a piece of cloth in her mouth and decamped with her. He kept her in confinement and committed a series of outrages. He took her then to a rich Mohamedan, threatening her all the while with a pointed dagger to acquiesce in all that he did and said. In the meanwhile, she saw her brother coming down with a constable, at the sight of which, she suddenly cried aloud 'brother! oh my brother! Here, am I, thy sister Tarangin!' The story and its pathos need not be gone into further enough to state that in this case, at least the rascal Mubarik got sentence of four years rigorous imprisonment.

We can multiply similar incidents reported from Kashmir to Kamorin *ad nauseum*. But we refrain from doing so and will end this sad tale with two significant remarks. One is a caution printed prominently in the *Arjun*—the leading Hindi Daily of Delhi. It warns all Hindus that inasmuch as the filthy activity of Moslem gundas has been renewed in Delhi, Hindus should not allow their sisters and wives and mothers and daughters to go unattended, to bath, to the ghats of the Jamanaji nor would they remain outside after dusk. For, several reports have reached us that show that Moslem gundas take most indecent liberty with Hindu ladies and harass them most dreadfully in some quarters of the city. This is the state of the capital of all India! What are we to think of out-of-the-way villages and towns on the frontier or in the Punjab in Sindh and other provinces!

This also must be borne in mind that each of these cases that has come to light conceals behind it dozen that are not known.

Last of all, in the presence of such grave and persistent provocation, there is not a single case of a Hindu being guilty of carrying or trying to kidnap or abduct a Moslem boy or girl under the influence of fanatical barbarism. Fortunately, it is not in their grain.

Here then, are a few facts and no comment. In fact, comment on such facts does only clothe their naked heinousness. Let them see, who have eyes to see!

—*Mahratta, 3-5-1925*

□

The Late Shriyut V.V.S. Aiyer

In Memoriam

Heavy griefs have often embittered our life, but none heavier than what thy sudden death caused, Oh friend, ever taxed our capacity to endure. Memories of those momentous years and trying days rise in a flood and struggling to find a vent, keep knocking at the gates of our heart. How we wish we could have spoken them all and recited our reminiscences; but our lips must remain sealed. How we long to write of thy goodness and gentleness of disposition—how, when betrayed, thou stood'st unshaken, how thou served'st them who owned thee not and how thou suffered'st when unknown and madest not the slightest mention of it when thou gotst known—how we long to write of it all; but our pen is a broken reed. The noble story of thy life must for, the time being, may perhaps for all time to come, remain untold. For while those who can recite it are living, the time to tell it may not come, and when the time comes when all that is worth telling will no longer remain suppressed and will be eagerly listened to, the generation that could have recounted it might have passed away. Thy greatness, therefore, must stand undimmed but unwitnessed by man, like the lofty Himalayan peaks. Thy services and sacrifices must lie buried in oblivion as do the foundations of a mighty castle.

The news of thy sudden death was bitter enough. But bitterer by for, is this our inability to relate to posterity under what heavy obligations thou hast placed them and to express the fulness of our personal and public grief.

For, indeed, he was a pillar of strength, a Hindu of Hindus and in him, our Hindu race has lost one of the most exalted representatives and a perfect flower of our Hindu civilization. Ripe in experience, hallowed by sufferings and devoted to the service of man and God, the cause of

Hindu Sanghatan was sure to find in him, one of its best and foremost champions in Madras.

In 1907 A.D. or somewhere there, one day the maidservant at the famous India House in London handed a visiting card to us as we came downstairs to dine, and told us the gentleman was awaiting in the drawing room. Presently, the door was flung open and a gentleman neatly dressed in European costumes and inclined to be fashionable, warmly shook hands with us. He told us he had been a pleader at Rangoon and he had come over to England to qualify himself as a full-fledged barrister. He was past thirty and seemed a bit agreeably surprised to find us so young. He assured us of his intention to study English music and even assured that he was eager to get a few lessons in dancing as well. We, as usual, entered our first mild protest against thus dissipating the energy of our youth in light-hearted pastime when momentous issues hung in balance. The gentleman, unconvinced but impressed, took our leave promising to continue to call upon us every now and then.

He was Shriyut V.V.S. Aiyer

In 1910 A.D., somewhere in March, we stood as a prisoner then only very recently pent up in Brixton—the formidable prison in London. The warder announced visits. Anxiously, we accompany the file of prisoners to the visiting yard. We stand behind the bars wondering who could have come to call on us and thus invited the unpleasant attentions of the London police. For, to acknowledge our acquaintance from the visitor's box in front of the prison bars, was a sure step to eventually get behind them. The visitors are let in. They crowdedly pass past our window. Presently, one dignified figure enters the box in front of us. It was V.V.S. Aiyer. His beard was loosely waving on his breast. He was unkempt. He was no longer the neatly dressed fashionable gentleman. His whole figure was transformed with some great act of dedication of life. "Oh leader!" he feelingly accosted us, "why you left Paris at all"! Soothingly, I said: "Friend, what is the use now of discussing it here. Rightly or not I am here, pent up in this prison-and the best way now is to see what is to be done next, how to face the present."

While fully occupied in discussing future plans, the bell rang and the warders came rushing and shouting unceremoniously: "Time is up." With a heavy heart, we looked into each others' eyes. We knew it would perhaps be the last time we ever saw each other in this life.

Tears rose, Suppressing them we said: "No! no! We are Hindus. We have read Gita. We must not weep in the presence of these unsympathetic crowds." We spoke in Hindi; curious crowds of English men watched the 'young Indian rebel ' and his friend. We parted, I watched him till he disappeared and said to my mind: "Alas! it is well nigh, impossible to see this loving soul again." For, one of the two fates was certain to fall to my lot, the gallows or the Andamans, and neither could hold any prospect before me of seeing my friends again.

This was in 1910 A.D.; fourteen years rolled by, and the impossible actually happened. Travelling the most dangerous and meandering bypaths and bylanes and subterenean passages of life so formidably bordering the realms of death, I met Shriyut Aiyer a couple of months ago. He had travelled all the distance from Madras to Bombay to enable us to revel a few hours in the wines of romantic joy. We forgot for a while, the bitterness and the deep pangs of the afflicted and tortured past and lightly gossiped as boys fresh from schools meeting back after a long holiday. He took my leave. I watched him disappear and said to my mind, now can call him again, any time I like.

Little I knew that it was then that he was to disappear beyond all human recall. When human wisdom shook its head and snorted out 'impossible', events proved it possible and when it gaily assured itself 'at any time,' Destiny put in a stern never; thus oft, fate seems to act with no nobler intention but to mock and humiliate human calculations!

With Aiyer, the politician, we cannot concern ourselves here. It is the loss of Aiyer, the scholar, the friend, the noblest type of a Hindu gentleman, the author of *Kural,* the saintly soul, whose life has been one continuous sacrifice and worship that we so bitterly bewail to-day and bitterly chafe at our inability to pay a public tribute to his memory in a fashion worthy of the noble Dead. Oh, the times on which our generation has fallen! The noblest sink down and are washed off to the shores of Death, while the unworthy keep gaily swimming on the tides of Life.

But thou hast done thy duty. Friend! It was for Human Love that thou livedst and thou diedst too for Human Love, even as a martyr unto her.

Thou knewst no peace in life, oh, soldier of God. But Peace be with Thee in Death. Oh friend! Peace be with thee and divine rest!'

—*(Mahratta 28-6-1925)*

□

Then Who is Who, Pray?

While cursorily glancing over the papers, our eye caught a heap of capitals, which, scanning a little closer, revealed a list of names of Pratap, Shivaji, Govind singh and others. Out of respect for these heroic representatives of our race, we naturally read a sentence or two of the article wherein those occurred, when to our surprise, we found ourselves face to face with the ghost of that hackneyed lie which had been killed and buried a dozen times over in the past and which asserted that the Hindus could not be said to be a race and could not, therefore, claim to inherit the blood of Pratap and Shivaji and Govind. We were just on the point of sweeping aside this statement as a contemptuous vapouring of foreign malice or ignorance, when somewhere about the sentence, the eye caught another familiar name. It was of Mahatma Gandhi. Without going further in the article, we instinctively felt that he must have been the author of that statement. It was worthy of no one else in India. From what other source can such profound shallowness flow than from the perennial fountain of 'Himalayan mistakes!' To level down to dust at a single non-violent stroke, the cherished love and pride and exalted emotions of a whole race that fondly felt in its vein the blood of a Shivaji and a Shankaracharya or a Pratap or a Chhatrasal or a Chaitanya flow—only a Mahatmaic audacity can accomplish that! Let the silly and unscientific Hindus disown forthwith the superstitious belief that after all, they were the sons of those sires who fought at Haldighat and were martyred at Sarhind and won at Udgir and ruled at Delhi!

Gandhiji tells us we cannot be said to inherit the blood of Pratap and Shivaji and Govind. But then do we inherit any one's blood at all? We are born in Maharashtra—can we claim to inherit the blood of Shivaji at least? The caste system that prevails amongst the Hindus and the consequent absence of the custom of intermarriages amongst them, which seems to be the reason, which prevents a Gujarati from owning the blood of a Rajput Pratap or a Maratha Shivaji in his veins, ought to, if true and sound a reason in the first case, prevent us also from claiming to inherit the blood of Shivaji. For, Brahmins in Maharashtra married not with the Bhonsle and other Kshatriya castes. Taking a step further, not only the Brahmins but also the Vaishyas and Shudras and Atishudras, the Prabhus and Saraswats—almost all of those crores of Hindus who go by the name of Maharashtrians, cannot look upon Shivaji as one of their forefathers any more than a Gujarati can. Even amongst those who are Kshatriyas of Shivaji's caste, all cannot claim him as their ancestor; for many—nay, the majority of their families had no blood connection with the Bhonsles or the Jadhavas. Leaving aside the question of Shivaji, we cannot positively succeed in proving that we possess the blood of even the Peshavas in our veins unless and until our genealogy reveals a marriage connection with the Bhats and other families relating to the Peshavas. All Brahmins also cannot claim common blood, for they all do not intermarry. So, then taking the last case of Maharashtra, not only does a Gujarati or a Bengali or a Madrasi or a Punjabi Hindu fail to establish his superstitious belief that claims Bajirao and Shivaji and Ramdas and Nana and Bhau and the hundred other heroic figures that fought for, died for and won the cause of Hindu-patpadashahi in the past as his glorious forefathers, but even a Maratha, a Maharashtrian, must disown them unless indeed, any one of them can produce a genealogy establishing an individual blood relation through inter-marriage. Nor can all Rajputs claim Pratap for their ancestor, nor the Sikhs Guru Govind for theirs. In such an anomalous situation, all that one can state is that Sambahji alone inherited the blood of Shivaji or following the more unobjectionable style of Satyakama Jabali of old, assert that any given person can claim the blood of his mother alone—and of no one else.

So, then, the poor Hindu is no racial entity at all. Shri Ram and Shri Krishna are mere persons to him, with whom he has nothing more in common either in blood or ancestry than he has with the citizens of Timbuctoo or with the man in the moon! Thus, he who used to live and breathe and had his being in a sublime conviction of his consanguinity and affinity with the seers and heroes and warriors, with Ram and Krishna and Shivaji, find the stream of his lifeblood suddenly choked and dried up, lost in bogs and sands of Mahatma Sahara of absurdity, and stand alone, a unity by himself, no one in the world whom he can call his kith or kin outside the scrap of his family-genealogical chart.

But then, the Hindu suffers not alone. He has to undergo the pangs of bereavement in company with almost all the world. If a Hindu cannot be said to possess the blood of a Pratap or a Shivaji, as Englishman too cannot by the same analogy, be said to be positively entitled to inherit the blood of a Cromwell or a Shakespeare. For, in spite of a general custom of intermarriages amongst the English people, no one can assert that every English individual has affinity with all other English people or has entered through his family in an individual blood relation with every other English family, which he can prove as soon as summoned by M. Gandhiji to do so. How can the cockney in the East London dare to claim to inherit the blood of the house of York or the proud Earls, whose pedigree boasts of pure patrician blood, that for generations and generations admitted none but a patrician within its sacred precincts? If a Hindu cannot be said to possess the blood of a Pratap and Ram or Rohidas Chambhar on account of the absence of the custom of intermarriages amongst castes and consequent absence of individual blood relations with the persons or their families, with whom he claims consanguinity, then an Englishman too cannot necessarily be said to inherit the blood of a Shakespeare, or an American of Washington, or an Italian, of Mazzini, or a German, of Frederick the Great, on account of the absence of any positive proof of his or any of his family being allowed to mix his blood with that of the other, in spite of the custom of intermarriages amongst the European nations that can suggest a mere possibility of consanguinity or affinity, but cannot in itself be a positive proof thereof. The only advantage that a cockney of East London has over the Hindu is that the cockney may be imaginatively looked upon as a blood relation of, say, Henry VIII. Just as he may be imaginably looked upon to be the prospective King of England or, for the matter of that, of all Europe! But just as in spite of this imaginable possibility of being the Emperor of all Europe, he, so far as facts are concerned, remains a cockney amongst cockneys; even so, in spite of a possibility of being otherwise, he, so far as all practical proofs are concerned, cannot be said to inherit the blood of a Shakespeare or Hampden or Pitt or the Black Prince and, most certainly, not of all these put together. And yet the school-children of these every cockneys are made to short till they get hoarse in their school: We are the sons of sires that baffled, crowned and martyred tyranny! They defied the field and scaffold, for their birthright-so will we!"

Foolish rhodomontade! How can all English children be supposed to have entered through their families into blood relation with all those Englishmen, who centuries and centuries ago, 'baffled, crowned and martyred tyranny! We sincerely hope that if ever Mahatma Gandhi comes to wield the power of a Supreme World Censor—God forbid!—which he hypothetically granted to himself on the occasion of opening the offices of the *Hindusthan Times* at Delhi, he would give his second attention to suppress throughout Europe—nay all the world over—these foolish blusterings of intoxicated fancy that sings "We are the sons of sons that baffled." What lies! No man should be allowed to state that he is the son of any other sire, but his individual father and mother and at the most, of those, whom he can prove on written testimony to have entered into blood connection with his family. We were going to claim *his first* attention for this task but that he has already reserved, as he declared in that speech for the still more urgent business of suppressing all other papers but *Young India and Nav-Jivan*! The poor *Mahratta*, of course, being destined to be the first fat kid to be sacrificed to the Goddess of Liberty, as Gandhiji had seen her.

But if a mere chance that the cockney in the East London has, of conceivably being related through blood in the ninetieth generation before him to, say Thomas-a-Backet by virtue of the custom of intermarriages, entitles him to claim him as his sire, then surely, the chance, that the poor Hindu too has, of being somehow, somewhere and somewhen relation through blood to the illustrious names of Hindu history must entitle him, in spite of the caste system and absence of the custom of intermarriages amongst the Hindus, to claim to inherit their blood. For, first of all, the racial stock of the Aryans used to intermarry amongst themselves. Even a casual acquaintance with the Vedic literature can convince—has convinced, every one, of the fact, outside the Sabarmati Ashram. Secondly, even the mere mention of the Aunloma (अनुलोम) and Pratiloma (प्रतिलोम) theory of marriage, which the most ancient Smrities record, and the hundreds of examples that lie scattered throughout the pages and periods of the history and mythology of our race, prove that these systems actually affected the everyday life of the people. The mere mention of these should be enough to prove that the racial blood of our ancestors could never be said to have been absolutely locked in watertight compartments. Mahabharat abounds with precedents—the very heroes of that epic show that even the kingly houses, did at times, admit strains of popular blood. The birth stories of Vyasa, Valmiki, Parashuram or Vashishtha, the origin of the castes of Suta and Magadha down to Chandals, the descriptions of the harems of Krishna and Arjun and Bhima—who married Hedamba—Chandragupta and Ashoka-down to Mahadaji Scindia who descended from a Rajput mother and a Mahratha—all these and hundreds of other illustrations joined with the supreme fact that Nature has and will ever prove stronger than all the caste rules and regulations, prove to the hilt that the caste system has not been and perhaps was never meant to be, an absolute and imperious dam and that the life-current of our mind flowed richly from the Himalayan altitudes of our ancestry to common plains. We, Hindus, own a common life, a common blood pulsed through our veins, and we have as much a right to assert that we inherit the blood of Pratap and Shivaji and Shankaracharya, as the Englishman has to claim that of Shakespeare or the American of Washington. Dravidians or Aryans—we are, Indians even through blood, Hindus first and everything else next.

—Mahratta, 14-6-1925

□

Crushing Reply to Sir Kishan Prasad

The following statement is issued by Br. Savarkar, the President of the Hindu Mahasabha, in reply to the Article published by Maharaja Sir Kishan Prasad of Hyderabad regarding the Hindu Civil Resistance Movement:

In spite of the personal respect, which every Hindu feels for the elderly, noble and highly placed Maharaja Sir Kishan Prasad, we cannot but denounce the statement he has recently issued carrying down the Hindu Mahasabha and Arya Samaj Civil Resistance Movement against the intolerably anti-Hindu policy of the Nizam Government as untrue, timid and treacherous. His charges against the Arya Samaji in particular are not only baseless but base. For, if during the last fifty years or so, any section of Hindudom had really proved itself to be the Defender of the Hindu faith, culture and community, it is the Arya Samaj that has done so.

Neither the Hindu Mahasabha nor the Arya Samaj has launched this civil resistance movement in a light mood. Thousands of Hindus groaning under the Nizam Rule had for years been calling upon the Hindu Mahasabha to come to their rescue. Just on the very eve of the Civil Resistance Movement, the Maharashtra Provincial Hindu Sabha had deputed trusted workers to investigate into the grievances of our co-religionists in the Nizam State and they, after studying the situation on the spot, had published reports full of unimpeachable facts and figures to substantiate that the condition of the Hindus was actually worse than what had come to light. The leaders of the Civil Liberties Union, who hail from the state itself, have borne ample testimony to the same fact. Nay, the Hindu leaders, who now under the spell of the State Congress, are persisting in a guilty silence had only the other day, been loudest in condemning the Nizam Government's policy as most detrimental to Hindu interest and dictated by Moslem fanaticism. Does the Maharaja, Sir Krishan Prasad venture to say that he has any better right to represent the Hindu feeling than these thousands of aggrieved Hindus in the State?

But apart from all that, the very statement of Maharaja carries with it its own refutation. During the course of the statement, he boastfully asserts that he and his ancestors had ever gloried in living contentedly under the subjection of the Moslem rule for generations together. The long subjection of the Hindus in Hyderabad State is a historical fact and one can understand if a Hindu tolerates it as an inevitable evil. But what are we to think of a Hindu of the eminence of the Maharaja, who glories in the fact that his Hindu ancestors had been contented slaves throughout centuries under the political domination of the Moslems? Is it not a fact that it is these contented Hindu slaves who proved traitors to the Hindu cause in the past, fought for their Moslem masters against the emancipating forces of the Maratha Empire and enabled the Moslem rule to survive in Hyderabad? The Nizam was defeated in battles after battles at Bhopal, Udgir, Kharda and the Marathas liberated Hindu Provinces from Nagar to Nagpur and from Nagpur to Orissa from the grip of the Moslem rule. But it is to the treacherous assistance of these contentedly slavish 'Ancestors', that gave the Nizam Government the long lease of life it enjoys. Otherwise, the forces of the Maratha Empire would have freed the Hindus in Hyderabad long ago and spared them their present serfdom, Instead of hanging his head down in shame at the thought of this continuous political and racial subjection of the Hindus to Moslem domination, the Maharaja parades it as if it was an additional feather in his cap. This one fact proves as no detailed Hindu grievance can ever do, the thoroughness with which the anti-Hindu policy of the Nizam Government has succeeded in emasculating the Hindu spirit in the dominions and how not a vestige of self-respect is left even in the best of them by the age-long serfdom to which the Moslem rule had reduced them.

It is this supreme task and not only the removal of local and detailed minor grievances of the Hindus—this task of emancipating the Hindu mind from this slavish mentality—that the Hindu Mahasabha had set before itself. The Mahasabha demands that the Hindus in the Nizam Dominions must be allowed all Civil Liberties in equal measure in common with other non-Hindu citizens, so that they may grow to their full height as self-respecting men, who would not tolerate anything that implies racial inferiority or humiliation to which they are subjected as Hindus.

So far as the right of representing our Sanatani Section which the Maharaja wants to monopolise is concerned, it cannot be better refuted than by pointing out to the one single fact that the President of Warnashram Swaraja Sangha of Maharashtra and the leader of the Sanatanists all over India—Dharmaveer Vishwasrao Davre—is rotting even at this moment in the Nizam's jail under the very nose of the Maharaja, for championing the cause of the Hindu Mahasabha and Arya Samaj Civil Resistance Movement. The spirit of the real Sanatan Dharma is represented by Dharmaveer Davre. What Maharaja Kishan Prasad represents in his article is not the spirit of Sanatan Dharma but of Sanatan slavery. He is playing that part today, which Raja Man Singh played so ignobly in days gone by when he posed as the leader of the Rajputs in lieu of Rana Pratap.

It is not even now too late for the Maharaja to repent, to go in sackcloth and ashes and as a gentleman bold enough to make amends for this untrue and treacherous article by boldly confessing the truth.

—*Mahratta 12-5-1939*

□

Freedom and Democracy

The following Cablegram was sent by Br. Savarkar, the President of the Hindu Mahasabha, to President Roosevelt of U.S.A. on 23rd April, 1939:

"If your note to Hitler is actuated by disinterested human anxiety for safeguarding Freedom and Democracy from Military Aggression, pray ask Britain too to withdraw her armed domination over Hindusthan and let her have free and self-determined Constitution. A Great Nation like Hindusthan can surely claim at least as much international justice as small nations in your opinion do."

Britain's Policy towards India

The statement issued by the Viceroy regarding Britain's policy towards India with reference to the present war situation is disappointing to a degree. The four or five columns of the verbose statement could have well been compressed into four or five sentences, so far as substance is concerned. The rest is full of platitudes.

The Viceroy refers to the old and often discarded declaration that India's ultimate goal is Dominion Status, made somewhere in 1919 A. D. It has not materialised since during the last twenty years and was almost forgotten till this war broke out. The present repetition of those same vague phrases may share the same fate, if things are allowed to drift in this manner by the Indians, till another war breaks out some twenty years hence.

H.E. the Viceroy should realise that India is sick of running after this wordy mirage. She refuses to look upon the Dominion Status as an ultimate goal. But instead, insists upon it as an immediate step to be taken. A constitution based on that Status must be conceded by Britain to India, just at the end of this war, at the latest. A definite and the shortest time limit to the actual introduction of this constitution was the essential thing, which was expected by the Indian political world and it is precisely this very point that has studiously been omitted in the statement issued by His Excellency.

Even now, it is not too late to mend. The British Government must bear in mind that India can never extend a willing co-operation unless she feels that the cause of her own freedom is likely to be served in a substantial measure by offering responsive co-operation to Britain.

The Advisory Board contemplated in the statement is welcomed. But then, it has not its functions and powers defined. If it is going to be a mere appendage to serve as a camouflage to conceal autocratic high-handedness, then it can only mean an insult added to injury. But if it is made to serve as a tentative measure with powers, more or less equal to a Federal Board of Ministers, is entrusted without reservation with matters concerning Indian defence during the war time and if its advice carried into effect as that of a responsible Council of Ministers, it may prove a step in advance on the line of political progress. But much will still depend on its composition. The Hindu Mahasabha must secure such a representation on it as is in keeping with the proportion to population of the Hindus!

□

Moslem Chinaman: Hidden Motive of Chinese Moslem Mission to India

The following statement is issued by Barrister V. D. Savarkar, the President of the Hindu Mahasabha, in connection with the Chinese Moslem Mission to India:

We had no mind to give expression to the details, which point beyond doubt to well-concerted activities on the part of the Indian Moslems to inject the Chinese Moslems too with the Pakistani virus, while the Chinese Moslem Mission led by Mr. Woo was in India on behalf of our friendly neighbour China. But the Moslem Mission is grievously transgressing its national and friendly task and has, in its message recently sent to the Moslems at Nellore, been guilty of betraying anti-Hindu tendency. It has, consequently, forfeited the right of a national hospitality on the part of the Hindus and I feel myself quite justified in exposing the real nature of the movement, so that Hindudom may be warned of the dire consequences, which must result, if it is not watched, opposed and checked in time.

Burma Lesson

A couple of years ago, I had issued a statement warning the Burmese that there was growing rapidly a hybrid Moslem population in Burma, which would in near future constitute a similar danger to the homogeneity of the Burmese people, as it did in the case of India. The Moslems used to marry Burmese girls in large numbers for at least a century in the past and were very particular in bringing up their progeny as Moslems, while no Moslem would, as a rule, give his girl in marriage to a Burmese. The easy-go-lucky Burmese hardly suspected political danger out of such designed social relations. But soon after that, the Burmo-Moslem riots, miscalled the Indo-Burmese riots, started. The Moslems paid a heavy price for their mischief and the eyes of the

Burmese got opened. Just then, the Japanese invasion took place and held all such questions in suspension.

China Follows Suit

Next to Burma comes China. The Moslem population there is to be counted in crores. China was once ruled by the Tartars, and when the Tartars embraced Islam, these Moslems made China their home and for a short period, even looked upon themselves as a ruling class. But the great Buddhistic Empire, which rose on the ashes of the Tartars, showed the Moslems their right place and they were more or less thoroughly reduced to unquestioning subjection. But the fall of the Chinese Empire, the Japanese conquest of the large portions of the Chinese territories and the simultaneous rise and spread of the pan-Islamic movement about the time of the last great European war stirred up the Moslems in China too, with the consciousness which was latent in all Moslems through the Koranic teaching itself of being a separate entity unallied with and even antagonistic to, anyone else, who did not believe Koran and especially the Hindus, including Buddhists. We know how the Moslems bore a special hatred to and massacred the Buddhists on their way to India and how the word Buddha prashasti, which means, in fact, the worship of the Lord Buddha, had come to mean the greatest sin man can commit in the Moslem eyes. The Chinese Moslem Federation was formed and a large section of the Chinese Moslems refused to merge themselves with the Chinese, but maintained that they should keep up their separate entity and even a political brotherhood.

The Marshal's Fable

We have great respect for Marshal Chiang Kai Sheik as a doughty warrior and a farsighted statesman. But that is the very reason why he could not but tell us the fairy tale that in China they were all Chinese first and last and in politics there was no clash between the Buddhists and the Moslems. But in face of facts we cannot but take this statement of the Great Marshal with a pinch of salt. Was it not only a couple of years ago that a batch of young Chinese Moslems was sent to Turkasthan and Egypt to get themselves initiated into pan-Islamic mysteries and who, on reaching Bombay, sought the interviews of Mr. Jinnah and other Leaguers, discarded their National Chinese dress and paraded their newly-bought fez caps as an insignia of a new order? This present mission, led by Mr.

Woo, is a far more significant step on the part of the Chinese Moslems and is primarily meant and was perhaps invited by the Indian Moslem Leaguers themselves to establish a closer pan-Islamic contact. They have chosen to interview the leading lights of the Pakistani movement including the Nizam, and they are already emboldened to talk such trash as that they would not fail to help their Islamic brothers in India after the war is over. But are they sure whether they themselves would be in a helping or a helpless position at the end of this war? A covenant between the sparrows and the rabbits to defeat the eagle has no sense so long as the eagle dominates the field. Again, what kind of help and against whom are these Chinese Moslems going to render to the Islamic brothers in India after the war? Against the Hindus and to prop up Pakistan?

The appointment of Sir Mohomed Zaffarulla Khan as Indian Agent General in China under such circumstances bodes nothing but evil. He may represent the pan-Islamic or Pakistani principles there as every dutiful Moslem is expected to do.

A Mere Dream!

The Indian Moslems, who want to carve out a Western Pakistan from Delhi to the Tribal regions, have openly declared more than once that they would depend upon their co-religionists outside India from Afganistan to Turkey. But they could not indulge in any such airy nothings, regarding the support for their Eastern Pakistan to be constituted out of Bengal and Assam. That is why they are trying desperately to forge a pan-Islamic line between the Burmese and the Chinese Moslem groups and now that the Chinese Moslems have promised them help after the war on the Eastern side, they may very well build castles in the air hoping thereby to frighten the Hindus in the East, too.

If that be so, I can only remind them that the Hindus have also some trump cards in their hand. If it is feasible for the Indian Moslems to have a united Chinese Moslem front on the East, whether cultural or political, then it is at least as feasible, if not more, for the Hindus to have a united Hindu-Buddhist front from Jammu to Japan. Just as the frog cannot but remain a frog even if she jumps into the sea, so also the hopeless Indian Moslem minority can never grow into a dominating majority, even if Mr. Woo woos them with all the Chinese Moslems.

—Mahratta, 29-5-42

□

Gandhi-Jinnah Negotiations (September 29, 1944)

Emphasising that the proposal to vivisect India had assumed 'a far more dangerous aspect today when the Gandhi-Jinnah talks are adjourned than it had on the day when the talks began', Mr. V.D. Savarkar, President of the Hindu Mahasabha, in a statement, appeals to all those opposed to the partitioning of the country to support the Akhand Hindusthan Leaders' Conference to be held at Delhi on October 7 and 8.

Mr. Savarkar says: Mr. Jinnah demands vivisection of India even more relentlessly than before. Gandhiji wants to placate that intolerable demand even more relentlessly than before. The Moslems are openly claiming that they have nothing to do with the so-called Indian nation, that they are a different nation by themselves and that they want to cut off as many provinces of India as possible, utilise them as a territorial base to rear up an anti-Hindu Moslem state quite independent of any central Indian Government. Gandhiji, who confidently asserts in getting the Congress to support him, is ready to hand over, at any rate, four frontier provinces, which form the natural and invulnerable Himalayan borderline of our Motherland, to the Moslems for the above treacherous objective, for the mere asking of it without firing a shot.

The tragedy of it all is that the 'Indian National Congress', which was ushered into existence to consolidate the Indian nation, has itself betrayed its sole mission. The very justification of its existence and falling a victim to the pseudo-nationalistic malady, had dealt the unkindest cut of all at the 'Indian national integrity. The Indian National Congress itself is indulging in treacherous conspiracies to vivisect the oneness of that Indian nation so as to wipe out the very name of India from the map of the world.

When Gandhiji started from Wardha by 'the Pakistani train' almost in a triumphal mood, he left orders behind to the country or to the Congress at any rate to keep peace, to have complete confidence in him and not to criticise the Gandhi-Rajaji proposal while his talks with Jinnah continued to find out a way to Hindu-Moslem unity on the basis of handing over to them some of the holiest and cherished parts of India and acknowledging their right to form a separate and sovereign state there.

This trick, in fact, was so transparent that it was not likely to dupe any sensible politician. What reliance could there be on the assurance of a leader like Gandhiji, who only the other day, asserted that vivisection was a sin and is today supporting Rajaji's Pakistani proposals. Only those Congressites and some other leaders among the Hindus, who had grown in the habit of accepting any Gandhist 'mumbo-jumbo' as a gospel truth, obeyed those orders and tried their best to stand tongue-tied. Not only that, but they wanted to hush-hush even the Hindu Sanghatanists and other far-sighted politicians, who refused to be duped by that flimsy political trick and refused to acquiesce in such a guilty silence.

Whirlwind of protest

The whirlwind of protest raised by the indignant people, the forest of black flags and picketings, through which that triumphal Pakistani train had to pass crestfallen from Poona to Panchagani, Panchagani to Wardha and Wardha to Bombay, the trenchant statements issued by some of our foremost leaders in the country condemning the treacherous proposal, those thousands of meetings and signed protests wherein millions of Indian citizens led by the Hindu Sanghatanists pledged themselves to stand by the integrity of their Motherland and to resist the Pakistani proposals, defeated the design of the Gandhist group to lull the whole country into a false sense of security, and by demonstrating the fact that there was a country-wide challenge thrown to them, made it impossible for Gandhiji and others of his pursuasions to claim the leadership of the whole country in general and of the Hindus in particular.

It was to organise this whirlwind of protest against these sinful designs to break up the integrity of Hindusthan, as a nation and a state, and to consolidate all those leaders and citizens who had thus protested publicly against the Pakistani proposal that the Akhand Hindusthan

Leaders' Conference was convened to meet at Delhi on October 7 and 8.

It was supported by hundreds of prominent leaders from all parts of India including the accredited representatives of the Sanghatanists, Sikhs, Arya Samajists and other Hindu Sanghatanist organisations, as well as by several leaders of note in their personal capacity. This conference had, from its very inception, almost nothing to do, to the beginning or ending of the Gandhi-Jinnah talks. It is an independent effort to consolidate those who stand by the integrity of India into a common front. Many of those Congressites and others who had secret sympathy with Gandhiji's unholy mission either through conviction or want of foresight, tried their best to frustrate the efforts of holding such an Akhand Hindusthan Leaders' Conference.

Gandhi-Jinnah talks were over simply because Gandhiji said: "Let no one speak against the Gandhi-Rajaji proposal till we are trying to arrive at a compromise with brother Jinnah!" But the organisers of the Akhand Hindusthan Leaders' Conference did not yield to these efforts simply because the very starting point of those Gandhi-Jinnah talks was the acceptance in this or that form of the treacherous concession of Pakistan. It was impossible, as the Rt. Hon. Shreenivasa Shastriji said, for a genuine Indian nationalist to remain tongue-tied while the integrity of our Motherland and hoty land was being openly sold at auction.

Political Matricide

Even now that the Gandhi-Jinnah talks are over for the time being, none should overlook the point that Gandhiji had made it quite clear that they are only adjourned 'sine die.' Are we also going to remain tongue-tied without raising a finger in defence of the integrity of our nation or without uttering a single word of protest against the political matricide and keep looking on it unconcerned 'sine die'?

I earnestly request those Congressites and other leaders who wanted to wait till the Gandhi-Jinnah talks were over but were in their heart of hearts against the Pakistani proposal, to take courage in both hands to conquer their own inferiority complex and come forward to condemn all further efforts to vivisect India and attend the Akhand Hindusthan Leaders' Conference to consolidate the anti-Pakistan front. They would doubtlessly be welcomed in the conference by each and every one who had consented to attend it.

But even if some of those do not find themselves to do so, the

Akhand Hindusthan Leader's Conference will meet at Delhi irrevocably on 7th and 8th of October.

The prominent leaders of our Sikh brotherhood, the Mahantas of different Mathas and Ashramas, His Holiness Shankaracharya of Puri, the Sanatani, the Arya Sanghatanist leaders and their personalities occupying prominent position in the social and political life of the country, have already consented to attend the conference.

A hope that specially in view of the adjournment of the Gandhi-Jinnah talks and the consequent commitment, which Gandhiji and almost all the Congressite press, and the fact that the Congressite following has now made to accept this or that proposal to vivisect India, it is all the more urgent to consolidate the anti-vivisection party. As a first step towards it, the genuine national leaders all over India will not fail to join the Akhand Hindusthan Leaders' Conference at Delhi.

□

Problems before Hindudom After Bloodless (!) Vivisection

RETALIATION

The vital interests of Hindudom demand that some maxims and arguments emphasized in chorus by the Congressite Ministers, leaders and the press should be promptly refuted. For example, Pandit Nehru has been reiterating, of late, that the right of retaliation or punishment belongs to the state alone and in no case, the people (meaning in this case Hindu-Sikhs) could be justified in exercising it on their own initiation and responsibility. In laying down this maxim, Panditji has happily refused to indulge in the mischievous mumbo-jumbo of Gandhistic morals. He stated clearly that he was not talking about the morals of this question but the practical aspects of it only. So far so good. But he conveniently forgot to touch the most crucial and practical aspect of the question—what were the people to do, when the state proved either so unwilling or so pusillanimous as to fail miserably even to defend its own people, not to speak of retaliating to avenge the wrongs perpetrated on their hearths and homes and honour?

Even an individual has a legal right of self-protection and of retaliation in so far, at any rate, as it forms an inevitable weapon of self-defence against a violent aggressor, when the police is nowhere in evidence or is unable, or the worst of it all, is unwilling to face the aggressor for fear of displeasing him. Verily a people must have this fundamental right that every citizen possesses.

What were the thousands of Hindu-Sikhs to do when faced by an imminent danger of being massacred in cold blood, looted, 'burnt alive,' forcibly converted, in short, of being exterminated as a racial and national being by the most barbarous attacks of an organised, dangerously armed and fanatically hostile foe, and especially when the state as such was nowhere in evidence so efficiently as to render any the least protection to them? While the state of Pakistan allowed firearms and explosive to be distributed to the Moslem population throughout Western Punjab, the League leaders were openly inciting their people that Pakistan was but a springboard to pounce upon Hindusthan and the Moslems in their thousands were parading in the streets, in towns and in cities, dangerously armed and raising terror-striking slogans 'Haske liya Pakistan, marke lenge Hindusthan.' While the Moslem state was planning in this wise definite campaign of invading Eastern Punjab and capturing Delhi in order to celebrate the inauguration of Pakistan, what were the Government of Indian state doing in their capital at Delhi to counteract these dangerous developments on the part of our enemies? The first step the Congressite Ministers took was to deny emphatically that there existed any enmity at all between the two states, that they had won a triumph in bringing about a bloodless revolution by vivisecting our Motherland to avoid bloodshed and the only thing that their immediate duty demanded was to order a day for general rejoicings to celebrate the inauguration of their Indian State. In Delhi itself, they allowed some fifty thousand Meos and several Khaksars to concentrate with secret stores of firearms and explosive and with an ill-conceived design to capture the capital wherein fifty per cent of the police were allowed to be Moslems under the command of Moslem Commissioner. The Hindu Sanghatanists kept shouting from housetops throughout India 'Danger Ahead'! This is no time for rejoicing, while you are stranded on the top of a volcano already in erruption! But they were declared as traitors and communalists, and were hunted out and imprisoned from provinces to province. The Frontiers of East Punjab were left to rally undefended. The consequence was that two days before the 15th of August rose, a general massacre of the Hindu-Sikh population accompanied with indescribable horrors became the order of the day. But while that Moslem Province was resounding with shrieks of thousands and thousands of Hindu-Sikh women, men and children being outraged, murdered, thrown into flames alive, and was having a bloodbath in rivers of Hindu-Sikh blood there, here in Delhi, the Ministers of the Indian State were literally feasting and fiddling to celebrate their bloodless revolution!

Nehru Nero

Under these circumstances, what wonder is there that millions of

Hindu-Sikhs prompted by the instinct of self-preservation and animated by the spirit of pan-Hindu consolidation, rose in arms in East Punjab, in Bharatpur, in Alwar, in Patiala and in Delhi itself and responded to the best of their might and means so furiously and effectively as to checkmate the Moslem hoards from attempting an invasion of East Punjab, threw them on their defensive and saved Delhi itself from being captured by the Moslems concentrated there. If Panditji and his Congressite comrades are still safe and secure in their seats, they owe it to this brave fight which the Hindu Sanghatanist and Sikh forces gave in the nick of time. And still, it is he, who unblushingly comes forward to deliver to them a sermon on the exclusive right of the State to retaliate!

Had a Shivaji or a Ranjit Singh been at the head of the State, they could have demanded with propriety that the people should leave the right of retaliation in their hands alone. But when the puny Pandit tries to demand it in the accents of Shivaji, it strikes as funny as it would do, if a pigmy standing on his tiptoes tried to rival a giant in height.

Nevertheless, in all sincerity, I exhort once more my Hindu brethren in the Congress and the cabinet to take a lesson, at least now, from past errors, cease to be ideologues and join hands with Hindu Sanghatanists, to face realities as revealed by the recent happenings. The stark realities in the main are these:

(1) That the Moslems have tacitly declared a war on Hindusthan with a view to transforming it altogether politically, religiously and culturally into a Moslem-Sthan

(2) That intense preparations to invade Hindusthan with up-to-date arms and air force are already afoot and with the help of the Pathans and Baluchis across the Frontiers and perhaps under the lead of the Amir of Afghanistan, they mean to open two extensive fronts in the main, one from Kashmir to Junagad, both included, and the other in the South under the command of the Nizam threatening the territory from Macchallipatam to Goa on one side and C.P. and Berar on the other.

(3) That the Moslem, in India are bound to rise in revolt simultaneously with this invasion from outside to sabotage and stab our state from within.

(4) That to forestall and counteract this Islamite peril, our State must raise a mighty force exclusively constituted of Hindus alone, must open arms and ammunition factories exclusively manned by the Hindus alone, and mobilize everything on a war scale.

(5) That we should make it quite clear that the Moslem minority in Hindusthan shall receive the same treatment for better or worse, in kind and in scale, which the Hindu-Sikh minority receives at the hands of the Moslem Government, in all respects such as representation, services and even rights of citizenship.

(6) As in the very nature of things and on their own confessions neither the Gandhistic ideology nor the pseudo-nationalistic ideology of the Congress can ever cope with this Islamite offensive and as the Hindu Sanghatanist ideology alone can and will be able to fight out this danger successfully, the Government should consist of such Ministers alone, who are pledged to the Hindu Sanghatanist ideology alone. If the Congressite Ministers are unwilling to accept this indispensable programme, they should at least be patriotic enough to resign and hand over Government to the Hindu Sanghatanists and Sikhs.

It is a self-conceited plea that questions the ability of the Hindu Nation to replace the present Congressite Ministers by leaders as able or even by better ones. If the Government is handed over to a Sikh-Hindu Sanghatanist coalition, a cabinet could be formed within a week, which will be not only more efficient but what is chiefly important, shall also be far more willing to accept and carry out undoubtedly the above programme, which as we have proved, is absolutely indispensable to face the stark realities as noted above.

—*Mahratta, 25-9-47*

□

Nehru's Nightmare—Hindu Raj?

Carpet Knights

The Gandhist ministers, leaders and newspapers have recently trotted out a new stunt to cover their dismal and disastrous failure to protect the life, property and honour of our nation and perhaps with a crafty design to capture Moslem votes in the joint electorates to come. Pandit Nehru, their megaphone, has recently been addressing a number of meetings, wherein instead of assuring and enlightening the people as to how his government is going to forestall and frustrate the covert machinations and overt challenges of the Moslems to conquer and convert the whole of Hindusthan into a Pakistan, he has been indulging into furious denunciations against the demand for a Hindu State! As if the mere demand for a Hindu Raj constitutes a danger to his Government, so much more imminent, impending, incalculably disastrous as to call for his immediate attention than the already established Moslem Raj in Pakistan, where fanatical atrocities, arson, bloodshed and butchery have been the order of the day and millions of Moslems keep parading the streets with such war cries as 'Haske liya Pakistan! marke lenge Hindusthan!' Pusillanimous enough to tolerate these diabolical actions and threats on the part of the Moslems against his 'Indian Union,' Pandit Nehru and his pseudo-nationalistic section in the Congress are delivering mock heroics against the Hindus and swearing that they will fight tooth and nail against those who demand a Hindu Raj!

Pandit Nehru swaggers on, that if the Hindu Sanghatanists persist on in their efforts to establish a Hindu Raj, they would meet with the fate of Hitler and Mussolini. He forgets that the Hindu Sanghatanists are led by hundreds of those seasoned veterans, who had fought in the vanguard of Indian Revolutionist forces against Britain when Gandhiji, speaking politically, was still in his clothes and the Pandit was not yet born. So many of them defied the sword and the scaffold, and the sacrifices and the sufferings undergone by each of them in the fight for Indian Independence outweigh the sacrifices of all the Gandhist ministers totalled together. They cannot be terrorised by the threat of such Carpet Knights as the Pandit and his clan. In case they fail in aiming so high, they are prepared to face any fate in the defence of the honour, greatness and glory of Hindudom. But what in case they succeed in establishing a Hindu Raj? What fate should the Pandit and such other traitors to the Hindu Raj deserve?

The demand for a Hindu Raj, these pseudo-nationalists say, is communal, stupid, mediaeval, theocratical, a menace to the progress of mankind itself! But they conveniently refuse to tell us what they precisely mean by Hindu Raj, before they characterise it in the above-mentioned vilifying terms. Nevertheless, assuming for the sake of argument that the demand for a Hindu State deserves this condemnation on all these counts, may we ask them, was not the demand for a Moslem State at least equally condemnable on these very counts? Did the Moslems not base their claim to own the Pakistani Provinces on the ground that the Moslems constituted the major community predominating there? How then that communal claim was respected by you as so fundamentally national as to vivisect our Motherland to make room for an Independent Moslem State? Why did you not refuse to listen to that 'Communal' claim as 'stupid'? Did the Direct Action the Moslems resorted to, not prove it to the hilt that the Moslem State they demanded was avowedly theoretical, setting the hands of the clock of Human Progress back not only to the 'Mediaeval' but to the beastial age? But instead of fighting against that demand for a Moslem Raj, you actually abetted the crime of cutting integrated India right into two pieces directly on communal lines, which the Anglo-Moslem conspirators perpetrated and handed over Pakistan to the Moslems so ceremoniously, with such ease and grace as you would hand over a cup of tea to a welcome guest! With what face now can you vilify the demand for a Hindu Raj on these very counts, even if it could be said to possess all the above traits?

Perverse Gandhism

Had not Gandhiji himself conspired with the Ali Brothers to invite an invasion by the Pathans and to enthrone the Amir of Afghanistan as the Emperor of India? Had he not declared again in the year 1940 in writing and repeated it now and then that if the Nizam, subduing the

Hindu Princes and with the support of Frontier tribes, took Delhi and became the ruler of India that would be a perfect Home rule, a cent per cent Swaraj? Thus, a Pathani or a Nizami Moslem Raj is to Gandhiji a cent per cent Swaraj. But a Hindu Raj! Oh no! It would be communal, fascist, anti-national and an anathema!!!

You contend further on that our country and our state can not be called Hindusthan and a Hindu State as some non-Hindu minorities too are citizens thereof. But how is it that in spite of the presence of Hindus, Christians, Parsees and other non-Moslem minorities in its territory, all of you and Gandhiji in particular, keep 'salaming' saluting the newly, carved out Moslem Raj as 'Pakistan', which avowedly and literally means a Holy Moslem Land, a Moslem State? Is it not a fact that almost all states and nations are called after the names of what the League of Nations termed 'National Majority' predominating in each? Nor have you yourselves ever felt any qualm of conscience in recognising Baluchistan, Vaziristan, Afghanistan, Turkastan or the Turkish State as such, in spite of the presence of non-Moslem minorities there? How is it then that the very mention of the name of Hindusthan or the Hindu State alone takes your breath out, as if you were smitten by a snake bite?

Bloodshed or?

The only reason you have been so emphatically reiterating to defend your recognition of Pakistan as an Independent Moslem Raj in spite of all these objections to it, is to the effect that you were faced with the only alternative 'bloodshed or Pakistan' and so to avoid bloodshed, you were persuaded to accept Pakistan. Leaving aside, the fact that such a cowardly reason condemns your action more than defend it, we only ask, do you not thereby insinuate unwillingly enough that if but the Hindus too face you with a similar alternative bloodshed or Hindusthan, you will be persuaded to accept Hindusthan too with equal readiness?

I warn the Hindu electorate categorically for the thousandth time that unless they remove these pseudo-nationalist leaders from the helm of our state, the Gandhistic Indianism will allow Moslems inside India to capture key posts in the army, the police, the state. These Moslems will rise from within as soon as the Pakistani forces invade India from North, East, West, South, as they are sure to do in near future, and taken 'unawares' as usual, this Gandhist Government of today will go down in no time and India will be converted by the Moslem conquest into an Akhand Pakistan.

Warring Ideologies

The choice, therefore, is not between two sets of personalities but between two ideologies, not Indian Raj or Hindu Raj but Moslem Raj or Hindu Raj, Akhand Hindusthan or Akhand Pakistan.

The Hindu Sanghatanist ideology alone can, therefore, save our nation and re-establish an Akhand Hindusthan from Indus to the Seas.

—*Mahratta 25-9-47*

□

Before they vivisect India, let us vivisect their Pakistan first (23rd May, 1947)

"Let Bengal Hindus beware of the scheming platitudes and pro-Muslim designs of Gandhiji, who started for Bengal straight after his interviews with Mr. Jinnah, avowing open hostility towards the demand for framing a Hindu majority province in Bengal. No compromise should dupe us into abandoning that demand as Moslems are sure to repudiate their part as soon as we are trapped. Pakistan or no Pakistan, we must have now a Hindu province in Bengal, Punjab and Sindh in the interest of Akhand Bharat itself. For, even if the impossible happens and Britain concedes integrity of India under a strong Central Government, then new Hindu majority province in Bengal can openly serve as a faithful sentry checkmating any further treacherous attempt on the part of Moslem majority there. On the other hand, in case Pakistan is thrust on us by Britain, the creation of these provinces shall form an unbroken link of Hindu majority provinces from East Punjab to West Bengal and with the Hindu kingdom of Nepal and Kashmir in the North and Hindu Assam in the east, would consolidate and enable Hindus to reannex the revolting Pakistani areas, provided of course we 'Hinduise all politics and militarise Hindudom."

—V. D. Savarkar.

□

Bengal—A Hindu Majority Province

The following Telegram was sent to Dr. Shyamaprasad Mukherjee by Veer Savarkar on March 21, 1947:

"I support emphatically your demand for separate Hindu Majority Bengal province owing loyal allegiance to a consolidated strong and sovereign central Hindusthani state.

We shall be better equipped to protect Hindu minority in eastern Bengal than we are at present."

—V. D. Savarkar

□

Independent Jewish State

The following statement was issued to the Press by Veer Savarkarji on 19-12-1947:

"I am glad to note that the overwhelming majority of the leading nations in the world should have recognised the claim of the Jewish people to establish an Independent Jewish state in Palestine and should have promised armed assistance to get it realised. After centuries of sufferings, sacrifices and struggle, the Jews will soon recover their national Home in Palestine, which has undoubtedly been their Fatherland and Holyland. Well may they, compare this event to that glorious day in their history when Moses led them out of the Egyptian bondage and wilderness and the promised land flowing with milk and honey came well within sight.

Judging from the Indian Press in general, our public seems to be misinformed by a sinister pro-Moslem propaganda regarding this Palestine issue. It must be emphasized, therefore, that speaking historically, the whole of Palestine has been, from at least two thousand years before the birth of the Moslem Prophet, the National Home of the Jewish people. A long line of their great prophets and kings, of Abraham and Moses, of David and Soloman, has endeared that country to them as their Fatherland and Holyland. The Arabian Moslems invaded Palestine only a few decades before they invaded our Sindh and just as their fanatical fury exterminated the ancient Egyptians or Persians, they attempted to wipe out with fire and sword the Jewish people too. But they failed in this unholy ambition. The Fatherland and the Holyland of the Arabian Moslems lies in Arabia and not in the Palestine.

In justice, therefore, the whole of Palestine ought to have been restored to the Jews. But taking into consideration the conflict of self-interests of the powerful nations in the UNO, their support to the resuscitation of the Jewish State in a part of Palestine at any rate, wherein they still happen to be in majority and which includes some of their prominent Holy Places constitutes an event of historical justice and importance.

It is consequently to be regretted that the delegation that represented our Hindusthani Government in the UNO should have voted against the creation of the Jewish State. The speeches of Shrimati Vijayalaxmi in particular were justly ridiculed when she declaimed melodramatically that the Indian Government refused to stab the unity and integrity of the Palestine State in the back by carving out a separate Jewish State—forgetting for the while that the very Indian Government had stabbed the unity and integrity of their own nation only the other day and gloated over it as an event for public jubilations! Pandit Nehru made his case more untenable by stating that the creation of the Jewish State was opposed by his Government to secure the goodwill of the group of the petty Moslem States in Asia. But what about the loss of the goodwill of the Jews in India and outside and of the powerful nations which voted in support of the Jewish State? As a policy, it is as absurd to sacrifice the goodwill of an army of giants as to secure the unjustifiable goodwill of a handful of pigmies. Moreover, can Hindudom, at any rate, forget that these petty Moslem States and even the Chinese-Moslems, who are conspiring to create a Chinese-Moslem State, are always enemically disposed to Hindusthan as a State?"

□

Do not allow Non-Hindus in Hindu Mahasabha

The following telegram was sent to Dr. Shyamaprasad Mukherjee by Veer Savarkar on 27 July, 1947 after partition:

"In as much as the proposal of throwing open full or associated membership of Hindu Mahasabha to nationalist non-Hindus has been publicly discussed in press, I must express my view in time against it. If non-Hindus are admitted as members in the Hindu Mahasabha, whether on political or economical point, it is bound to be detrimental to the Hindu solidarity because every political question is in India, either religious or cultural and every religious and cultural question is political. Shuddhi, though religious, is political and Pakistan, though camouflaged as political, is religious. The Hindu Mahasabha is a mandir for Hindu worship where Hindus alone can go to worship their nationalist Shiv. Let us not turn that mandir into a masjid or bazar. By such an error, the Hindus will lose their self by those very steps by which the Congress degenerated into a chaos. We may join any nationalist association on a separate platform, where we Hindus as an undivided entity join hands in special matters like the election campaigns, so far as it is not detrimental to Hindu interests, with our non-Hindu nationalists. But the Hindus must have an organisation of their own, where they can think, plan, consolidate and act as Hindus without check, from any non-Hindu, who enters by right. Otherwise, one day, a Moslem may come to preside over the Hindu Mahasabha too. As long as there are purely Muslim, Christian and Parsee bodies in India, so long at least, the Hindus must have an exclusive organisation of their own. On this spirit, the Hindu Mahasabha was found and rose to be the center of Hindu solidarity and power. Let us not undo this monumental work for the vicious temptation of a few seats of offices. Let us leave to the next generation, true ambition of rendering the Hindu Mahasabha itself, the National Parliament of Hindusthan."—*V. D. Savarkar*

□

Oppose the united front of the Christian, the Congress and the Muslim League

The following statement had been issued to the press by Swatantrya Veer V. D. Savarkar on 6-7-1959:

"I exhort the Hindu Sanghatanists in Kerala to render all possible support to the Communist Government led by Shri E. M. S. Nambudripad in their struggle, which they are bravely carrying against the united front of Christian, the Congress and the Muslim League, all of whom are sworn enemies of Hindu cause.

"The Hindu Sanghatanists cannot forget the religious and political persecution to which the Congress Government led by the Christians had subjected them and from which they got liberated by the advent of the present Communist Government alone.

"Even when and if elections come, specially on the issue of the Education Bill, the Hindu Sanghatanists should vote, in their own interest, for the Communist candidate as long as there is no Hindusabhaite candidate, just as the Hindu Sanghatanists are doing in Maharashtra on the issue of United Maharashtra.

"I also exhort the Communist Government never to resign under the pressure even of the central government to intervene and to take over the administration or never to compromise especially on the leading issue of Education Bill."

—*V. D. Savarkar*

□

On Immediate Problems

To

Shri N. C. Chatterji, Bar-at-Law

Dear Mahashaya,

Though I have since long been confined to sick-bed due to age debility and protracted illness and had consequently been forced to retire from all public activities, still I feel it my duty to congratulate you publicly on your thumping electoral success, defeating the rival Congress candidate for the Lok Sabha.

I strongly hope that now at any rate, our Bengali Hindus and Hindudom in general, will find an able and indomitable advocate in you to defend the Hindu cause in the Lok Sabha. Three demands above all and immediately must be emphasised. First, all Hindus in East Bengal should be allowed to come over to Western Bengal and at least an equal number of Moslems from West Bengal should be sent to Eastern Bengal, if necessary, per force. Second, for every aggressive step taken by Pakistan, whether military or otherwise must be met by prompt reprisals, military or otherwise by the Hindusthan Government kind for kind, measure for measure. Third, not an inch of our land should be surrendered to Pakistan without the consent of the Hindu Public either on the Eastern frontier or the Western.

Bombay,
28th December 1947

Yours Sincerely,
V. D. Savarkar

□

Co-operation with Other Parties

It is imperative that in the interest of Hindudom, it is absolutely necessary that there should be an organisation manned by Hindus only to represent Hindudom as a whole and to protect the interests political, social, cultural, economical, etc., of the Hindu people as a whole. It was with this particular mission that the Hindu Mahasabha was started by such eminent patriots like Lala Lajapat Rai, Madan Mohan Malviya and others and led by Dr. Moonje, Bhai Paramanandji and other great champions of the Hindu cause. Ever since its start, the Hindu Mahasabha has been recognised by other political organisations and even by the British Government also as the foremost, if not the only, political representative of Hindudom.

Consequently, any question of a merger or a compromise for a common front for elections or any other object, which demands first of all the liquidation of the Hindu Mahasabha as a political body representing Hindudom and seeks to reduce it to a social and cultural organisation only, cannot but prove most detrimental to the Hindu cause and should never be countenanced at all.

Inasmuch as the proposals made recently for such a compromise to one and all seek to deprive the Hindu Mahasabha of this, its main mission of representing and defending the political interests of the Hindus and inasmuch as seek to compel it to merge as a Hindu political body into any old or new organisations, which are open to non-Hindus as well, the acceptance of any such proposal cannot but constitute the betrayal of the two most fundamental bedrocks, on which the Hindu Mahasabha was founded and has been solidly and devotedly taking its stand, namely its mission of representing Hindudom alone and being manned by Hindus alone. Consequently, none of these proposals or any new one of the same nature should ever be even entertained, much less accepted.

Nevertheless, a common front for elections or for any issues commonly accepted can be formed with the Hindutwanishtha bodies in particular, and with any political body in general, if that co-operation with those bodies does, in no way, affect the existence and freedom of the Hindu Mahasabha as a Hindu organisation representing Hindudom politically and in all other spheres of national life.

In short, co-operation and no amalgamation or merger is the formula that should guide all activities of the Hindu Mahasabha.

□□□